LEAPS

OF

FAITH

LEAPS

OF

FAITH

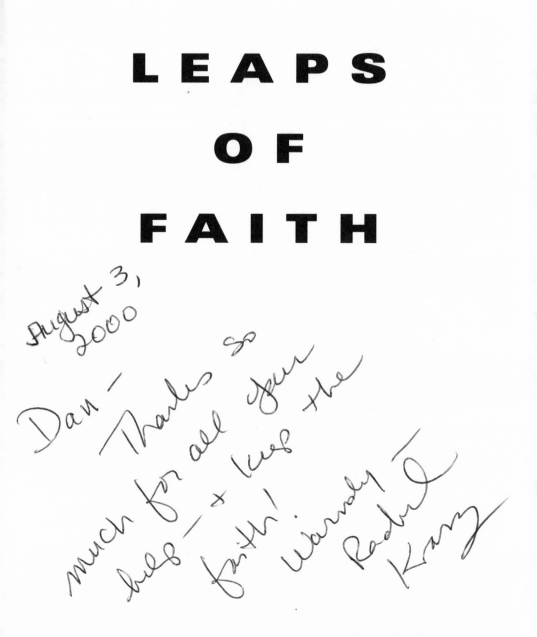

August 3, 2000

Dan —
Thanks so
much for all your
help — + keep the
faith! Warmly
Rachel Kranz

RACHEL KRANZ

FARRAR · STRAUS · GIROUX / NEW YORK

Farrar, Straus and Giroux
19 Union Square West, New York 10003

Copyright © 2000 by Rachel Kranz
All rights reserved
Distributed in Canada by Douglas & McIntyre Ltd.
Printed in the United States of America
Designed by Jonathan D. Lippincott
First edition, 2000

Library of Congress Cataloging-in-Publication Data
Kranz, Rachel.
    Leaps of faith / Rachel Kranz.—1st ed.
        p.   cm.
    ISBN 0-374-18444-5 (alk. paper)
    1. Gay actors—New York (State)—New York—Fiction.   2. Gay men—New York
(State)—New York—Fiction.   3. New York (N.Y.)—Fiction.   I. Title.

PS3561.R268 L42 2000
813'.54—dc21

                                                                99-058517

Every effort has been made to secure the right to reprint previously published material in the book. Grateful acknowledgment is made for permission to reprint excerpts from:

"Big Yellow Taxi" by Joni Mitchell © (renewed) Crazy Crow Music. All rights reserved. Used by permission. WARNER BROS. PUBLICATIONS U.S. INC., Miami, FL 33014

"Solidarity Forever" © Alpha Music Inc. All rights reserved. Used by permission.

"A Room in Bloomsbury," by Sandy Wilson © Chappell & Co. (ASCAP). All rights reserved. Used by permission. WARNER BROS. PUBLICATIONS U.S. INC., Miami, FL 33014

"Freedom Is a Constant Struggle" by Roberta Slavit © 1965 (renewed) by STORMKING MUSIC INC. All rights reserved. Used by permission.

"Chapel of Love" written by Phil Spector, Jeff Barry, & Ellie Greenwich © 1964 (renewed 1992) Trio Music Company, Inc., Universal-Song of Polygram, Inc., Mother Bertha Music, Inc. & ABKCO Music Inc. All rights reserved. Used by permission.

Grateful acknowledgment is made for permission to reprint "The Acrobat of Xanadu" by Dan Georgakas. Reprinted by permission of the author.

CONTENTS

You never know what spark is going to really result in a conflagration. . . . You have to do things, do things, do things; you have to light that match, light that match, light that match, not knowing how often it's going to sputter and go out and at what point it's going to take hold.

—HOWARD ZINN

You better be careful what you believe, 'cause you might believe in anything. You better be careful what you *don't* believe, 'cause you might believe in *nothing*.

—ROCHEL HERBERT

This novel is dedicated to Ellie Siegel and Sally Heckel, comrades in art.

ONE

LOVE AND

AMBITION

S T U N T   M A N

The acrobat from Xanadu disdained all nets,
And when we saw him make the central twirl
Of his triple forward somersault through space,
We understood his purity went beyond mere pride:
That certain flights require total risk.

—DAN GEORGAKAS

I've always wanted to be Peter O'Toole. My sister says that really means I want to sleep with Peter O'Toole, and she may be right, not that I think Peter O'Toole would ever actually sleep with me. Still. It started when I saw that movie, *The Stunt Man,* you may have seen it. Peter O'Toole plays this *très* flamboyant director, whom we're actually supposed to believe is having sex with Barbara Hershey, but really, the interest is all between him and the stunt man, an actor whose name I can't remember (and isn't *that* my worst nightmare. I'll *be* the lead in a major motion picture and no one will even remember my name.).

Anyway, the stunt man isn't even an actor, but in the course of working with Peter O'Toole, whose dedication knows no bounds, he becomes an artist. And his artistry lies where Peter O'Toole's does—in his complete and absolute willingness to do anything. I want to add "anything for the truth," or maybe even "anything for art," but I would be lying. It's simply his willingness to do anything. (Steve Railsback. The actor's name. Thank God. Maybe now I'll be remembered. If only as an afterthought.)

"Sure he'll do anything—anything the director wants," my sister says dryly. And although she'd be the first to agree that I am a *fabulous* actor, still she wonders, "Why take orders when you can give them? Why walk when you can fly?" She doesn't understand that acting *is* flying.

Though sometimes, I must admit, crawling seems more like it. The movie I'm making now, for instance, on location in Connecticut. OK, so it isn't exactly "on location"—Davis is shooting his first feature in some friend of the family's back yard. But he's at least somewhat talented, and *very* rich, so I really think he might be going places and maybe I can go there with him.

Except that the project is crap. OK, not crap but—well, yes, it's crap. The script is really awful—and not even awful in an interesting way, but the kind of awful that every new filmmaker is guilty of. Every straight male filmmaker, anyway: the hero loves a woman, who leaves him for another guy, so he suffers to a truly extraordinary extent, mostly by having to eat alone in restaurants. Finally his rival is rude to our heroine at a party, and there she is, looking all hurt and bewildered, which is apparently a terrific turn-on to our hero, who tries to punch out the new guy and of course gets beaten up himself, which is apparently a terrific turn-on to our heroine, and—I'll leave the rest to your imagination. Though what you probably *can't* imagine is the actual look on the heroine's face, because even the actress (a decent actress, I've worked with her before) can't imagine it. Try as she might, she just isn't giving Davis— who also plays the hero, did I mention that?—what he wants. He keeps going in for her close-up, as the other guy says, "Jesus, Letitia, just get off me, will ya?" and shoves the bewildered heroine away. The actress's eyes fill up with tears, her lip trembles, her breath flutters—and Davis yells, "Cut!" and makes her do it again.

"Don't you think he's enjoying this just a bit too much?" That's my friend Tanya whispering in my ear. We're both hungry and tired, and we've got a 6 a.m. call tomorrow, but we're all staying in Davis's parents' country house, so we can't go home until he does.

I'm playing the hero's best friend, and despite my previously established talent, I can't help wondering why. Am I the token white included to give the movie some weird crossover appeal? Or am I there to keep Davis from looking too angry, too anti-white, let's face it, too *Black?* Does he just want to prove that he *can* direct white people? Or, though my character is relentlessly straight, does Davis think that the contrast between us makes him look more butch?

Tanya is playing the hero's faithful woman pal, the one who's secretly in love with him herself, so that we see what an ungrateful little bitch the heroine is for not taking the guy when she has the chance. That at least is Tanya's analysis, but since she used to sleep with Davis and the actress playing the heroine is his current girlfriend, she might be just a tiny bit biased.

"I don't think he's *enjoying* it," I whisper back diplomatically, although obviously, he *is*. "I think he's just a perfectionist."

"Child, please," says Tanya. "He wouldn't know perfect if it bit him with a stick." She's always splicing together sayings like that, apparently without realizing it, since she gets offended if you notice or God forbid, laugh. Rosie—my sister—once asked me if I didn't think it was racist *not* to notice, but I don't think even Rosie is that earnest. I think she was just being provocative.

So now Tanya tosses her head and makes her braids swing, a gesture she's perfected for casting directors who call her in for sassy-girlfriend and wise-best-friend roles—what she calls "Sapphire and Mammy parts." "Mmm-*mmm*!" she says, in this accent she puts on for my benefit. "When it comes to climbing up on the backs of they women, Black mens is almost as bad as massa hisself."

"Ex-cuse *me*, miss," I whine, making my voice lisping and faggy for *her*. "But *as* a white man—"

"Child, please." She rolls her eyes like Hattie McDaniel. "We both know you ain't *no* man!"

Davis sighs loudly and says "Cut." The actress sniffs, and I wonder when she's going to start crying for real. Cruelty, incompetence, or a pardonable directorial technique?—You be the judge. I'm too busy trying to remember why I ever wanted to do this in the first place.

"Besides," Tanya goes on. "Letitia won't take much more of this. That girl wants to worship the ground he walks on, but her mama didn't raise no doormats." I snort, and the assistant director glares at us. Letitia looks into Davis's eyes and goes on nodding, in perfect time to the rhythm of his words. "Oooh, baby," Tanya murmurs. "When Sleeping Beauty wakes up, is she going to be *pisssssssed*."

All right, so this doesn't exactly qualify as *model* set behavior, and I figure I'd better take myself out of harm's way before I lose my last shred of professional credibility. I go get a cup of coffee from craft services—I wouldn't mind some actual *food* at this point, but by 6 p.m., picked-over Cheetohs are the best you get on *this* set—and I wave goodbye to Tanya, who *is* laughing—silently—and I go off to sit under a tree somewhere. Trying *not* to think about Warren.

You know. Warren. We'd had a huge fight last week, right before I came up here for this shoot, and while I thought it was pretty clear to all concerned that I had won, I couldn't resist having it again and again and again—in my mind, I mean. Just to be sure I *had* won.

The thing about Warren is that he's a psychic, which makes him *extremely* arrogant, because he really *doesn't* know *everything*, despite what he tells his clients. Though I'll be the first to admit that he certainly knows a lot. I keep telling him it's a golden rule of psychic phenomena that the more important a person is to you personally, the less you can see into their life.

"Well, in *that* case"—oh, you can imagine the line I keep setting him up for. Wouldn't you think I'd learn?

We met last year, at one of those East Village parties, crowded together into the corner of somebody's cramped little kitchen. You know, dingy white cabinets and that awful white fluorescent light that *nobody* looks good under, and the counters all crammed full of liquor bottles and those little plastic bowls of hummus and guacamole. And the air was so full of smoke, it *was* smoke.

I caught Warren's eye and was interested and didn't want to be, though I have to admit he looked good for his age, which at that point was forty-four, a full thirteen years older than me. He was looking straight at me, but it was the blankest look. Well, no, not blank, and not neutral—it was full of *something,* but I couldn't say what. He didn't smile, and he wasn't friendly, and it wasn't a sexual look, exactly, or a meaningful one, meaningful sexually, I mean, but—how can I say this? It was solid. You could feel its weight. I asked myself, if I had to play that look, what direction would I give myself, and usually that's a question I can answer, but this time I was baffled.

So I felt totally awkward, and like I usually do in such situations, I started to talk.

"Do you know *Chapter Two,* by Neil Simon?"

Warren shook his head.

"Oh, good for you. I'm *glad* you don't know Neil Simon's work—he's such a hack. *Anyway,* it's a play, and a movie, about this Neil Simon–like play-wright who loves his dead wife, and someone tries to set him up on a blind date with Marsha Mason—who in real life actually *was* Neil Simon's second wife—and the playwright keeps resisting and resisting, but finally he says to her, 'You know, maybe we should meet. Have you noticed that we both talk in the same rhythms?' Which I thought was so lovely and romantic, only I also wanted to scream, 'Of *course* you both have the same rhythms, asshole! You both talk exactly like Neil Simon!' "

Warren looked at me blankly. "You know," I continue, "how like in Woody Allen movies, all the main characters sound just like Woody Allen, even the women?" More blankness. At least I thought it was blankness, and now I was looking for a way to get out of this horrible fiasco, since obviously we *didn't* have the same rhythms or even speak the same language, when Warren said, "You know, I imagine that's quite a common habit of yours."

"What? Dissing the most successful figures of the American cinema?"

Completely without warning, Warren grins. Also without warning, my heart turns over.

"Well, that, too," he says. Then he gets that blank look again, which I later found out was his "psychic" look. "But I was thinking of the way you tell your story through other people's stories. But you aren't a writer, are you? No, let me see. You're an actor. Oh, of course. So you don't invent stories, you just refer to them."

I was flabbergasted. I didn't know whether to be flattered that he saw I was an actor (I certainly was *not* impressed—come on. This is New York. You don't have to be psychic to recognize an actor.), or insulted that he thought he could analyze me, or well, to tell you the truth, I was actually touched, along with being a bit freaked out. I mean, he hadn't shared my rhythm. But he had smiled at my joke. And he had seen me, even if not in a particularly flattering light.

"But enough about me," I said. "Why do *you* think I have this terrible compulsion to live through other people's words?"

Amazingly, he grinned again. "I'm a psychic, not a shrink," he said, and I could see how often he'd used that line before. So maybe he hadn't seen me, maybe he *was* just a prick. A smart, perceptive prick.

Then suddenly he looked—beyond blank, almost frozen. "Oh, you have a sister, don't you. An older sister? She's—something to do with long meetings. She gives speeches now. And she did all the talking before. She had all the words." He had this sharp little sideways smile, *very* Mona Lisa, only more smug. "She sucked all the air out of the room. So you quote."

My jaw dropped. "She's a union organizer," I said.

He looks upset. "I'm not very good with details," he says in that angry, self-deprecating way that even then made me want to throw my arms around him. Now I'm breathless—but I rally.

"Oh, well, who needs details when you can go straight for the heart?"

Score one for me, because he looks completely startled. Off-balance. "I think you're the one who has the talent for going to the heart," he said softly.

OK, OK, he saw me. I was hooked.

So that night we slept together, and then we started living together, and then we had this fight. If I was going to be charitable—or rather, if I was going to take the view of the fight that was most flattering to both Warren and myself, I'd say that we had the fight—excuse me, that *he* started the fight—because I was going out of town and he was going to miss me. I realize it's a cliché, but for a psychic, Warren had remarkably little insight into himself. He told me I was incredibly self-absorbed, and I told him *he* was. He said why was

I in a field where I was never going to make any money, and I said why was he. He said at least he paid his share of the rent out of his earnings as a psychic, whereas I paid my share of the rent out of my earnings as a bicycle messenger, which besides being a dead-end job was not even a lifelong dead-end job, unless I planned on getting hit by a bus before I turned thirty-five. I said—OK, I was momentarily stumped because I had been working off of him. So I walked into the bedroom, where I started packing. I thought, I am packing up this fight with me and I am taking it out to the country, which I certainly did not want to do, but since I kept on packing, maybe I did. Maybe Warren was giving me his most vivid self to take away with me, and I was taking it.

Suddenly I surprised myself by saying, "Warren, I'm only going away for two weeks. I'll *be* back."

He looked—insulted? Furious? Mortified? Was I *not* supposed to know that he loved me so much?

"Oh, that is so typical of you," I am sorry to report that he said next. (Because it makes him—us—sound like such a cliché. But the first thing you learn as an actor is how hard it is to be original, not because clichés don't exist in real life, but because they do. They are the air that *is* smoke.) ". . . so typical, to think that everything is always about *you.*"

"But we were fighting about me. We weren't exactly fighting about world peace."

"Not you, but how I feel about you. To think I'm saying—to dismiss what I'm saying because you think it's how I feel. But it's the truth, Flip. You want to be an actor, but you're *not* an actor."

The worst insults you ignore, or you'd never stay together. So I just said, "Oh, right," and kept on packing.

God knows, Warren won't disclose one *syllable* about his feelings 98 percent of the time, but once you get him started, you can't get him to stop. So then he said, "I don't care how talented you are. All right, so you are. But you don't *live* as an actor. You run around from one audition to the next trying to make yourself believe it's going to make a difference to how your life finally comes out, but you know it's not, and I know it's not, and every moment that you spend deluding yourself is a moment that's lost forever and you'll never get it back." He turns his back on me and my suitcase. "Actually, *we'll* never get it back, so all right, this is how I feel about you, but that doesn't make it not the truth." He takes a deep, coarse breath. "You don't really listen to me, and I wish you would."

There are times when Warren can just draw me to him like a magnet. I go over to him, and I put my hands on his shoulders and I just stand there, looking at the hair on the back of his head—he has this very short, dark hair. I can smell the bleach from his T-shirt. And his smell. "OK, OK, I'm listening," I say finally. "What do you think I should do?"

And through the palms of my hands, I can feel that psychic look come into his body, and I know that whatever I hear next is going to be exactly the truth he sees. "You have to kill something in yourself," he says slowly. "I don't know what, but you do."

"Oh, what does *that* mean?" I say scornfully, but my palms are cooling off. This enormous coldness, which moves right through me.

"I'm going to bed," Warren says abruptly. He gives me a look—his own, not partaking of any psychic information or support. If I had to play that look, what direction would I give myself? I would say I had been betrayed.

So Warren went off to sleep on the couch and I left at five the next morning to make this movie, and we haven't spoken since.

Well, of *course* I'm haunted by what he said! Wouldn't you be? Please.

So I'm thinking maybe it's about time to leave *this* tree and go find one *without* so many painful memories when suddenly I look up, and there are Davis, his cameraman, and six other guys from the crew playing touch football. Who are they, the Kennedys?

Eventually I walk over to Davis, who has just caught the ball and is holding it high over his head, cheering for himself. "Hey, Flip," he says cheerfully, pulling the ball down to his chest and tossing it from hand to hand. "Want to play?"

I didn't even want to play in junior high, and it was a *requirement* then. "Uh, no, no thanks. I was just wondering, are you guys going to be very much longer?"

Davis considers me as though I've just asked him a pithy question about my character. "Well," he says seriously, "it stays light until about eight-thirty."

"But Davis. We haven't had dinner yet."

"My parents won't mind if we get in late."

"And we've got a 6 a.m. call tomorrow morning."

"Yeah? So?"

"Davis, I'm cold, and tired, and hungry, and I want to do my best for you tomorrow. I think we should go home now."

Five minutes later, I am heading for the train station. Davis has accused me of conspiring with as-yet-unnamed others to undermine his authority and sabotage the picture. He has fired me and is sending me home.

I mean, he wasn't paying me *that* much money to begin with. But five minutes ago, I *was* a working actor. What am I now?

I trudge the last few steps to the station. And there, sitting way down on the open platform, at the end of one of those long, wooden, pseudo-rustic benches, is Tanya.

"So you're my co-conspirator," I say, sitting down beside her. She leans against me, which is nice, because among other things, it's warm. And I'm sure she's going to come out with some nasty little joke or some nice sarcastic remark about Davis, and I'm just getting *my* incredibly clever answer ready, when she turns around to face me, and she just looks *ravaged*.

"That son-of-a-bitch, not that it's his mama's fault how *he* turned out."

"Tanya, what the hell happened?"

She's so angry, her whole body is shaking. There are actually tears in her eyes.

"He thinks I'm jealous of him and Letitia. Please! And then, to rub salt in the insult, he says I'm trying to sabotage him. Why would I drag my ass all the way out here to the pale people's world unless (a) I needed a job, or (b) I was trying to help him out? Would I give up two weeks of my life and a whole *lot* of my sleep just to make him look bad? Is he *that* important to me?"

She gets up, and her back is trembling. I'm *sure* she's going to start crying. So I say, "You know, Tanya, none of this would have happened if we'd been staying at a Motel 6. I didn't even know Black people *had* country houses."

And her back just goes rigid. "Well, we try to keep it quiet," she says finally. "No use pissing people off." Then she walks all the way down to the other end of the platform, and when the train comes, she gets in the back car, and I get in the front car, and we ride back to the city like that.

When I finally get home, it's almost 2 a.m. Warren wakes with a gasp as I come in. "My God, you really frightened me," he says. Some psychic.

Now, at this point, the only thing I want in life is just to sink down onto our bed and feel him holding me. I want it so much I *can* feel it. But he's really angry. "What are you doing here?" he growls.

"I got fired." He switches on the lamp, the one with the square white Japanese screen, and pulls the covers tighter around himself. They're my favorite sheets, too, those ice-blue ones, which of course *he* brought with him when we moved in together. His stuff is so much nicer than mine.

"You got fired?" he says now. "What did you do?"

"Jesus, Warren. I didn't *do* anything." I move away from the bed, since obviously I *can't* sink down into it. Or him. "The director is a crazy person, that's all."

He's staring at me, this haunted, angry look. "So is this it for you, then? Or are you . . ."

"Am I *what*, Warren?" Well, I certainly can't get into bed *now*. "Am I ever going out of town again? Am I ever going to do another movie? Am I still determined to be an actor, even though it's so obviously not working out? What, Warren, what?"

And the temperature in the room shifts. Suddenly I *can* go over to him, and I *do* sink down onto the bed, and Warren *does* put his arms around me. It feels exactly how I thought it would.

"It isn't that you leave," he says so softly I can barely hear him. "I could get used to that. You're just so unhappy, and I can't stand to watch."

"Then don't look," I say into his chest. Above me, I feel him shaking his head.

"I see you, Flip," he says softly. "I always see you. That's just how it is."

Afterward, after we've finished making love and we're lying there in the dark, I ask him.

"Warren?"

"Hmm?"

"That thing you said before I left, the thing you said I had to kill?"

"Hmm."

"What was it?"

I don't even think he's awake. But he says distinctly, "I said I didn't know. But you do."

"Oh. But I don't."

"Yes," he says maddeningly, "you do," and then he *is* asleep. Well, I'm glad one of us is.

The next day is Sunday, so I couldn't earn money even if I wanted to. I call my sister and since one of the few things we have in common is our love for old movies, we arrange to meet at the 1930s fest at Film Forum without even checking the schedule. Warren *might* have wanted to come—he likes old movies, too, though he doesn't seem to have heard of any film made *after* 1959. But Sundays are always a big client day for him. "I'm not saying I *wouldn't* have rescheduled," he says, as I am going out the door. "If only I'd *known* you were coming back." So I guess that tells *me*. Anyway, not checking the schedule turns out to be my *second* big mistake, since the only film in today's festival is *Gone With the Wind*.

I would never have told Tanya (every time she came back from a casting call, if you asked her how it went, she would roll her eyes and say, "I don't know nuthin' 'bout birthin' no babies, Miz Scarlett!"), but I just love that movie. All through high school, I would watch it every time it came on TV, and I still rent the tape about once a year. I love how much Rhett loves Scarlett and how he can't tell her. I love how desperately she loves him back and doesn't even know it. And OK, OK, so I am the cliché that *is* smoke, but I love the goddamn clothes. I wouldn't tell Tanya that either.

Rosie isn't exactly my ideal companion here, since for some reason she considers *Gone With the Wind* an actual political statement about the Civil War—a statement that offends her, needless to say. But she seems to be absolutely *desperate* to see a movie, and God knows, I am, too, so *Gone With the Wind* it is.

Besides us, there are only two other people in the theater: in the front row, an old man wearing a fedora and a raincoat and slouched so low in the seat that I'm afraid he's going to start masturbating (Butterfly McQueen! *Vivian Leigh!!* OLIVIA DE HAVILLAND!!!), and, a few rows behind us, one of those people that look a little borderline—this woman in her fifties, with intense, scary eyes, and a tiara.

Rosie *does* try to restrain herself, but I can feel her blood boiling all the way over in my seat. She would never, ever talk during a movie, but when the carpetbagger offers all the freed slaves forty acres and a mule and we hear this "Negro" voice say, "And a *mule?*", Rosie's silence is so deafening that the woman behind us says "Shhhhhhh!"

"I didn't *say* anything," Rosie mutters, but you don't have to be Warren to hear her when she's quiet. (Warren says that he's a receiver, but she's what they call a sender. I say that in that case, they should be very happy together.)

Meanwhile, this white-trash redneck and this big black buck are about to rape Scarlett, though luckily her loyal slave—well, ex-slave, but you can tell *he* misses the plantation—rescues her. So naturally, the noble white men have to organize a Ku Klux Klan raid to clean out the bad element. Besides being ruthless, the Black men are really stupid, and you know what? I'm thinking of Davis, and I'm enjoying myself. Having this particular kind of pleasure next to my sister feels more daring—and more titillating—than if I were sucking off the guy in the front row. My sister will say *fuck, suck, cock, prick,* but she always calls *that* word "the n-word," even when she's quoting someone else who used it. So I sit there thinking "n-word, n-word, n-word" at Davis, and I'm getting such extraordinary pornographic pleasure, I have to keep focusing on Olivia de Havilland to calm myself down.

And now Vivian Leigh is moaning, "Where's Rhett? I want Rhett," and as God is my witness, my eyes fill up. And Rhett is standing at Scarlett's sick-room door, and he's in *so much pain,* I just love it, I mean, Clark Gable, and suddenly the old man in the front row is saying hoarsely, "Come on, you motherfuckers! Just say it! Tell her you love her, and then fuck her and be done with it!"

And the woman behind us screams at the top of her voice, "Oh, shut up, you wino!"

So he croaks back, "You shut up, you—you feminist!"

"Right," says Rosie under her breath. "With that tiara. What is she, queen of the feminists?"

Rosie and I burst out laughing—and they both glare at *us*. But we can't stop laughing, so we grab our bags and stumble out of the theater.

"I don't know," says Rosie, as we head for the restaurant. "Let's not even talk about the racism, but the sexism! No, not just the sexism. The romance. It's like a prison, the way everything has to always end with a man and a woman in love."

"*Gone With the Wind* doesn't end with a couple in love. In the end, Rhett leaves Scarlett's selfish little ass and goes off to greener pastures."

My sister looks frantic, as though I've let her down in a way she never could have imagined. I don't know why—we have the exact same argument every time we go to the movies.

"And you of all people should object," she says. "You're gay."

"Honey, it's a sexual preference, not a religious vow."

She holds the restaurant door for me. We always go to Veselka's, this once-authentic, now-gentrified Polish dive that we both still love. "Fine," she says. "But you're an artist. You're supposed to care about art."

"I do care about art."

"No, you don't. If you had any artistic integrity at all, you might *go* to racist, sexist, heterosexist movies, but you certainly wouldn't defend them. And you'd find a way to *make* some art, instead of those ridiculous little projects that you always actually do."

I am speechless. I pointedly study the menu, even though we always get the same thing: a BLT on white to split, and French fries with brown gravy. "Fine," says Rosie after the waiter leaves. Typically, *she's* offended. "You tell me, Flip. If you could do anything in the world that you wanted—as an artist, I mean—what would it be? What do you really want?"

"I want to be a working actor," I say promptly. "I want to make a living at my craft."

"Oh, give me a break," she says impatiently. "Come on. What do you *want*?"

I can't *believe* how she always drags an answer out of me. "What I want," I hear myself say, "is to be in a movie—or a play, I don't care which—where I get to use everything I have. I mean everything. What my body can do. My voice, my mind, my feelings. Something where I get to use everything I am."

"Fine," she says again. "But to what end?"

Well, I *certainly* don't have an answer for this. But then I say, "Because everybody's life is just so goddamn *small*. And everything around us is just to make us be smaller and smaller. Just get up and go to work and buy things. But if people can see something—I don't know, big. If I'm using all of my-self—if I'm using *more* than myself. I don't know. Maybe it will be inspiring."

To my total shock and amazement, my sister actually looks impressed. Then she says, "So what's going on with your latest project?"

Great.

Of course, she *is* a union organizer. So for once in my life, she takes *my* side, urging me to tell her what happened in minute detail, right up to the moment where Tanya walks away down the platform. And then, of course, the honeymoon is over.

"Flip, how could you?" she says.

"How could I what?"

"That racist remark about country houses."

"It wasn't a racist remark," I say. "Davis fired *me,* as a matter of fact. As my boss, he was oppressing me."

"Well, *that* was wrong. But—"

"Come on, Rosie, he fired Tanya, too. He's just an asshole."

"A Black asshole."

"Assholes come in only one color. Pink," I say rather smugly.

"Fine, but you can't use the n-word about someone who's pink."

"For the five millionth time, I *wasn't* using it!"

Rosie gives me a sly look. "Not with Tanya, maybe, although how could she know that?—"

"Because I'm her friend, that's how!"

"But during that—that racist movie. You were, Flip. I could hear you thinking it."

Oh, so now she's a receiver too? Between her and Warren, I obviously don't have any privacy at all.

"You spoil everything," I tell her. "First of all, that just happens to be my fa-vorite movie, as you well know. And second, what I think doesn't hurt any-one. It's an entirely private matter."

"Flip. You're an *artist*. Don't you think art should make people think more—more complicated, questioning thoughts? Or is it all right if a movie just reinforces everything that's narrow and romantic and childish about them—"

"Excuse me, we're talking about *me*."

"For a change." This stings. But as usual, she barrels on. "I'm just saying that as an artist, I would think you'd want to be responsible for your art."

No one is more surprised than I am when tears come to my eyes. Rosie doesn't notice, perhaps because at the same time, I burst out laughing.

"Oh, I'm responsible," I say. "That's probably why I got fired. I was too *responsible* for the project. That's probably why Tanya isn't even speaking to me. She knows better than to blame Davis—*I'm* responsible. The only one who thinks I'm *not* responsible is fucking Warren. And you, apparently."

OK, so now she notices. She stares at me for the longest time. Then she says quietly, "Flip. I'm sorry you got fired. I'm sorry, all right?"

I shrug.

"I didn't realize," she says slowly, "how much it mattered. I was wrong, and I hope you'll forgive me."

I open my mouth to announce that I'll never forgive her, never, not unless she grovels a while longer. "So," I say instead in this tiny little voice, "you really think I'm an artist?"

Monday morning I get up at six and call my messenger service, and by seven-thirty, I am bent over a bike that should have gone to ten-speed heaven long, long ago, my nose stuck up some bus's ass as we fight our way down Seventh Avenue. When I first came to New York, before I ever thought of *being* a bike messenger, I used to think of them as flying. Now it's the most earthbound job I can imagine, where every turn of the pedals is a physically painful reminder of the gap between what my body could do and what it actually does. I would never, ever tell this to Rosie, but on hot, muggy days (which this is), I can actually see the boss's profits come pouring out of my body. The more I work, the richer he gets, and what do I get? I get to destroy my instrument, the only thing of value I have to sell. I mean, to use. To make art, to make art, to make fucking art.

After work, I have this feeling that Warren might be waiting for me. But I've been out of town for over a week, and my dance teacher hates it when you miss a class. We line up at the back of the room, and he shows us a leap we've never done before, a way of scissoring out your legs and throwing back your head to make it look like you're flying. My knees and thighs are screaming from my day on the bike—why can't I have *another* body? That one for the boss, this one for me.

When I finally get home, Warren is eating dinner at a table set for one. He's gone the whole way—one ivory candle flickering on the table, a single glass of Sauvignon blanc, a little plate of crudites and aioli, quail and mushroom fettuccini in an individual casserole. And on the kitchen counter, one chocolate mousse in a fluted glass. He must have been cooking for hours. Oh, and a sprig of lily of the valley in the Lalique bud vase that the host of that East Village party gave us when we moved in together. Nice touch, Warren, especially since lily of the valley is *my* favorite flower. He always says he can't stand the smell.

"Someone named Pietro called," Warren says between bites. "He said to tell you that Davis put you back on the film and your call is tomorrow at 6 a.m."

Up to this moment, I had just been totally hungry. Now I am totally floored.

"I know you hate this, Warren, but I really think I have to go."

Warren dips the last piece of endive in the aioli and finishes it off. He takes the cover off the casserole. Steam fogs his glasses.

"He has so much *money,* Warren. I just know he's going to make another film."

A bite of foccacia. A sip of wine.

"OK, so it isn't—practical."

"You mean it isn't *sane,*" Warren says, but then right away he's sorry he said anything.

"Warren," I say. God, I'm *starving.* "I can't not finish it." He doesn't exactly look at me, but I feel his glare. "All right, fine," I say. "I don't *want* to not finish it, all right, Warren? I don't do *that* many films. I want to finish this one."

But I had told the truth the first time. I can't not do this. I don't understand it, but I can't.

"Let me get this straight," says Warren, setting down his fork—it was the *good* silver, this romantic little dinner for one. "Davis screws you. Shut up, Flip, you know what I mean. Davis screws you *and* your best friend Tanya—"

"Well, she's not my *best* friend—"

"—on a project which you say is crap anyway. He insults you, humiliates you, humiliates *her,* and sends you both crawling home at your own expense. Now he wants you, and you're just going to go crawling back out there? At your own expense?"

"Well, I assume he'll pay."

"Oh, well, then," Warren says, "I suppose that makes it all all right." He gets up, walks into the kitchen, and dumps all his food into the sink—the half-finished glass of wine, the hunk of foccacia, the barely touched fettuccini and quail, even the mousse, which he scrapes clumsily out of its narrow glass. With two rough twists he turns on the faucets. "Yours is in the oven and the fridge," he says. Then he stalks into the bedroom and slams the door.

I can't help it, I look inside the stove. One individual casserole, the exact mate of Warren's. And in the refrigerator, a tiny plate of crudites with its own little ramekin of aioli, a matching mousse, even a chilling wine glass.

Warren comes out of the bedroom, carrying an enormous suitcase. "I'll get the rest tomorrow when you're gone," he says.

"Oh, right," I say as he heads down the hall. "Now I remember. I'm the actor, you're the drama queen. Come off it, Warren."

He keeps going. "You do know this is blackmail, don't you?" No reaction. "Fuck, Warren, stop it. Just *stop*."

Warren stops but he doesn't turn around. "I told you, Flip," he says quietly. "I won't—I won't watch you waste—Flip. You *said* it was crap."

"I know, Warren," I say gently. "It *is* crap."

"Then, Flip. Why do you want to do it? Just tell me why."

"Because it's what I do."

"Crap is what you do?"

I don't know how to answer him. Crap is what I'm doing tomorrow, I guess. Just like trying to make that leap was what I did today. I don't know. Sometimes taking one step after another is all you have.

"Or in your case, one leap after another," Warren says. Oh fine, Warren. Be psychic *now*.

Warren's back trembles. But he doesn't turn around. "I already told you," he says evenly. "I can't stand to watch."

Eventually, I call the train station. I pack a bag. I take the 2 a.m. train out to Connecticut and catch a few hours sleep on the chilly bench until Davis's assistant Pietro comes to take me to the set. And there, to my total shock and amazement, is Tanya. Playing a love scene with Davis. I mean, a real love scene, with lights and a camera and cleavage. Apparently Davis the character has realized his mistake and chosen Tanya, the patient, loyal pal. Tanya is positively glowing. She's not *that* good an actress.

"Where's Letitia?" I mouth to Sheila, the wardrobe mistress. She gives me an evil grin and draws one finger slowly along her throat.

"Cut!" yells Davis. There is a reverent murmur in the shooting area as they rush to reset a light. Davis takes Tanya's face in his hands and stares deep into her eyes. Well, she'll make someone a beautiful bride, won't she? Maybe she and Davis will move out to Connecticut, where their firstborn child can integrate a private school. Shut up, Rosie. She was supposed to be my friend.

Davis gives me a big wave and a smile as he heads in my direction. Behind his back, Tanya stares right through me, until I finally have to look away. *God* knows why, since *she's* the one entirely in the wrong.

Davis throws his arm around my shoulder. He waves his free arm behind my back, and Pietro magically appears with some new pages from the script.

Davis is staring into *my* eyes now. "We have a new ending here, Flip," he says solemnly. "Of course, it's a physically demanding concept, but I know you're up to it. In the best of all possible worlds, we'd take a day or two just to get this shot. But in this actual world, we've got—an hour. Can we count on you, Flip? Because we're really up against it."

I restrain myself from shrugging out from under his arm and look down at the pages. Jesus Christ. For plot reasons too complicated to go into, my character has to make a running leap from a jeep into a moving truck, while Davis and Tanya drive off into the "sunset."

"We've got to be done by eleven," Davis is saying, "because my parents need the jeep to go to an auction. But that still gives us time for three or four takes. What do you say?"

God knows, I have enough emotional material at my disposal to control my urge to burst out laughing. So I just say, "I think we're talking one take here, Davis. If that."

Davis is grinning at me like I'm his new best friend. "I'll need to see the trucks," I hear myself saying. "And I want to talk to the drivers."

"Anything you need, Flip," Davis says. "Anything at all. Pietro is yours for the morning." He looks deep into my eyes again. All right, if you quote me, I'll deny it. But for a minute, I can actually see what Tanya sees in this routine.

It doesn't matter. I'm not doing this for Davis. I don't exactly know why I *am* doing it, but it's certainly not for *him.*

So Pietro finds me the drivers, and we have some surreal conversations about speed and terrain and trajectory, and eventually the D.P. joins us, and we figure out the slowest possible speed that will still *look* fast, which turns out to be twenty-five miles an hour. Enough to break a leg, or a neck. Enough to get caught beneath the wheels of a moving truck. Enough to give Rosie, and Warren, and probably anyone who's ever known me, a lifetime's worth of "I told you so's."

Though I do tell Davis, "No rehearsals. And no second takes. This is strictly a one-time deal."

Davis beams with pride. "Go for it, dude," he says. Tanya shudders. At least she doesn't want to see me dead.

The drivers start their engines. The trucks take off. I feel the road bumping along beneath my feet. It feels as if we are going incredibly fast.

You don't have to do this, Warren would say if he were here. Maybe he's saying it anyway, who knows? *Now can you tell me why?* he's asking me. *Or do you have to break your neck first?*

Warren. I *said* it's what I do. Or do I mean, it's who I am?

It's time. I gather as much of myself as I have access to, hoping it's enough. Then suddenly I'm doing it, propelling my body from one moving car to the next, my legs out, my head back, to give the illusion of flying.

And as I take that leap, I feel something within me die. No, Warren, I *don't* know what it is. Why can't I stop *here,* in mid-air, where everything is still possible? *I am my leap, I am my art.* What is the name of that dead thing, Warren? I couldn't possibly care less.

And then I land, both feet smacking hard against the floor of the moving truck. The shock of the landing moves up through my ankles, my knees, my neck, and I have to swallow to hide the pain. But I did it. Trembling with triumph and exhaustion. Wondering what I've killed.

I am my leap, I am my art, my body sings. *And what you killed was hope.* Anything could happen now.

PSYCHIC IN EXILE

It only takes a little courage to fulfill wishes which until then have
been regarded as unattainable.

—SIGMUND FREUD

SUNDAY

I'll tell you the truth: The worst thing about being a psychic is having to know
so much.

No one ever believes me when I tell them I don't like it. Or they think of
it in much too simple a way. They think the problem is seeing disasters for
people. In fact, that's the easy part. You tell them, or you don't. I don't mind
that. It's what I have to know about them.

I haven't done a very good job of explaining this, have I? Let me give you
an example.

A woman came to me about some trouble in her marriage: she wanted to
know if her husband was having an affair. I suppose it's silly to say this makes
me feel like an intruder, as though I've already found out more than I'm supposed to know. In any case, I made the same arrangement with her that I always do: twenty-five dollars up front for the time and effort, and another fifty
if I actually get a vision. I have to tell you, I really hate calling it that. It makes
me sound like something out of *Song of Bernadette*. But anything else I could
call it—a sending, a message—sounds even more pretentious. And if I simply
say "information," which is how I often think of it, then what the hell are they
paying for?

The reason I make that arrangement is not because I usually don't get anything, or even because I often don't—for a client. It's only for me and the people in my life that the process is so damnably unreliable. No, the reason I make that arrangement is because I'm compelled to remind myself, each and every time: it chooses you. You ask, nicely, to be told something, to be shown something, which you have to hope is something that you actually want to know. And then you learn something, or you don't. It really isn't up to you.

Fortunately, as I said, the process usually does work for me, though when it actually takes hold—a flurry of information or a full-blown vision—it really hurts. I may ask for it, but I don't exactly want it.

Anyway, this woman. She had come to me in serious distress about her marriage, and I'm sorry to have to tell you that I had my own insight before I even started asking whatever it is that gives me the other kind of information. I thought, "Oh, her husband is gay." All right, that's not so surprising, but what made this particular insight unfortunate—for me, I mean—is that along with the knowledge, I felt how she would feel if I told her the news. Believe me, I'm not a very sympathetic person, and I don't really feel for other people. I wish I did. But feeling *with* them, that's how I know things.

Anyway, this woman. She sat down at the little white table in my office, setting her purse in her lap with her leather gloves on top of it. She shrugged out of her black sealskin coat—oh, yes, she had money. Not that it made any difference to me. I grew up around money, it doesn't affect me one way or the other. She was probably about thirty, maybe a little younger, but somehow the money made her look older. "Do you think you can help me?" she said.

"Usually I can," I said. "As I told you on the phone, it isn't really up to me." She handed me a check made out for seventy-five dollars.

"Because I really want to know," she said.

I did not want this to affect me, but it did. But I wouldn't take the check. I made her tear it up and write out two others, even though it was eminently clear to me by now that of course I was going to get information about her— I was already getting it. I put the check in the gray metal money box I keep in my desk and came back to sit with her at the table again. She held out her hand. I shook my head.

"That isn't necessary. Just let me concentrate a minute."

The information came slowly at first, and, as usual, in a not terribly reliable fashion. At first, I simply know things, the way I know anything. Eventually, if I need to know more, I might have a vision, which is more intense, and, frankly, more painful. And not necessarily more accurate. What's the difference? With information, I am more or less on the outside. With a vision, I am in it. That hurts.

So I knew that her husband was having an affair with—now here, trying to get the information was like, say, trying to remember the names of three people who sat near your desk in fifth grade. You know, but it probably isn't information that's right there at your fingertips. So you search and search for the information, but can you find it? And when it finally comes, will it be accurate? Will you remember Mary as "Darla," or think that Joey had thick, curly red hair when he actually had fuzzy white-blond hair and looked practically bald? But when you see a yearbook or an old class picture or maybe receive the correction from a friend, then you *know.* And then you realize that those two kinds of knowing, accurate and inaccurate, often feel exactly the same.

So I knew that her husband was having some kind of sex with some kind of man. But I thought for seventy-five dollars and what would probably be the end or at least the transformation of her marriage, I should try to do a little better.

I had two vastly different images—and this is still on the level of information, I haven't even gotten to the vision yet. One image was that her husband was cruising Central Park and picking up men—boys?—at the fountain, every time he told her he was going for a walk to stretch his legs. (I had seen from the address on the check that they lived on Central Park West, so you can imagine before I even tell you that the power of suggestion, unfortunately, plays a large part in this process. Which, also unfortunately, doesn't necessarily make it wrong.)

The other image I had was that her husband was passionately in love with a man in his office, a younger man who was interested but couldn't believe that the husband was, too, partly because he really did care for him and it was too much like a dream come true, partly because the husband, as you've seen, was pretty goddamn rich, which was also too much like a dream. That story began to intrigue me, actually, and I started to hear the name of the younger man—Jerry, how boring—and to see the color of the husband's eyes—deep, fascinating green, all right, that's better—and to hear the conversation they had had that Friday as the husband was leaving for lunch with a client. Something about how *they* should have lunch sometime, which was boring, but the younger man looked so strained and hopeful and disbelieving and triumphant all at once that I became somewhat interested.

As you can probably tell, I use my interest as a guide to what may be true. This sounds incredibly cold, but I can only tell you that it's fairly accurate. I don't think you can do this work if you're not somewhat cold. There's simply too much to know.

I looked around the image to see how I might test it. I probably would have done this for anyone, but I especially didn't want to hurt this woman any more than I had to. I don't know why it mattered—the torpedo in her life certainly wasn't going to come from me.

"Is your husband named Stanley?" I asked her suddenly, out of the blue. Impulses seize me, and I've trained myself to be open to them.

"Yes," she said, worried.

"And he works in a—" I've never been very good with details. So was it law, or insurance, or accounting, or what kind of office was it? This is why psychics tend to give you lots of stupid little bits of physical information—they are *much* easier. "—in an office with a green door? And the elevator is stainless steel? And he gets to work each morning about 8:10, 8:15? And he always starts the day with a cheese danish, and if they're out, he doesn't ever have the strawberry, he just has coffee, but then he puts sugar in his coffee, because he says he likes to have *something* sweet to get him through the morning and the caffeine just isn't enough?"

Well! Where did that come from? But she's nodding through every strung-together clause, looking more and more dejected. She knows the axe is about to fall. She probably knew it before I did. After all, it's her husband.

"And there's someone named Jerry in your husband's office?"

She nods again. "Well, it's Jimmy, does that count? Not his assistant, but his partner's. He's often said he wishes he could steal him for himself."

So now I see that I am probably not giving her such new news anyway, and I say as gently as I can, "Well, Mrs. Mallory, I doubt that anything has happened yet, but if your husband were to have an affair with anyone, Jimmy would probably be the one."

I've overestimated her. She looks at me as though I have maggots crawling out of my nose and says in a low, controlled voice, "You *faggot*. That's a disgusting thing to say."

I shrug.

"And now that you've started, you're just going to have to tell me the rest, aren't you? Whether I want to hear it or not. You're just going to force your disgusting little fantasies on me, aren't you?"

I stifle a sigh. People often do this. They want what you have, but they want you to be responsible for it. I suppose I shouldn't care, as long as they pay. But something about this is worse, I don't know why. No, it's *not* that she called me a faggot. Please. I grew up in America, didn't I? I went to junior high. I doubt there are any more surprises in *that* department.

Maybe it was because I could feel everything she was feeling, including her terrible fear. How much she hated me for making her feel it. How much she needed me to tell her the truth. How angry she was that I was the one she needed. My God, I thought, what *is* the matter with me? Usually I am much better at staying out of clients' feelings than this. If I had broken up with my boyfriend recently, instead of three months ago, I might have understood it, but obviously it wasn't that.

"I *am* paying you, you don't have to worry," she says as nastily as she can manage, but her anger is running out. Something inside me rips, shreds. I'd better finish her off fast and get her out of here.

So I try to repair the disturbance to my concentration—because I'll tell you, if you don't *want* to know what you've asked to find out, it's much, much harder. That's why it's so hard to get any psychic information about yourself or the people you love—who could bear to know any more? It's bad enough feeling what they feel. Or what you do.

Anyway, I see her eyes, intense and determined, and somehow that steadies me. Though the vision, when it comes, is like a blow to the stomach. So then, of course, it's almost a relief to put it into words, because that makes it so much less. Only I can have the vision, and that hurts. Anybody could say the words.

"You. And your husband. You were at the beach. You saw him looking. Oh, God, at that man, at that boy, at that other man. Red hair, boy's shoulders, knees. You saw it again and again, whichever way you looked. Oh, I see. So you've known about this for a long time. You simply thought you were wrong. And you picked a gay psychic so that when I told you the truth, you could say I was lying. *How* long have you known? Two years? I wonder why you want to know now, then?"

I think I'm going to regain control, turn to her, apologize. I don't usually get so personal. And I certainly don't *have* to say anything. But if I do speak, it must be exactly the truth I see.

Then the second wave of vision hits me, with even more force than the first.

"Oh. He's so happy. Oh, my God. He's so in love. He's never felt like this before—which is a shame, if you want to know the truth, because this Jimmy is totally going to break his heart. I think he's fairly shallow—Jimmy. You're much deeper." Now I'm out of the vision, but I have to look at her and finish the report. "You see," I say as gently as I know how, which probably isn't very gentle. Flip would be much better at this than I am. "You see, Mrs. Mallory, he needs to be with someone shallow so that the in-love is all about him. About his feelings, I mean." My clumsy words. I hate this part, too. "If he loves another human being right now, he won't know whether what he's feeling is about that person or about himself. And he needs to know it's about himself. He needs to be in love with his own love. Is this making any sense to you at all?"

She stares at me, hurt and trapped. I try one last time. "You're too real. Plus he wants a man. But not a real man, not yet. So he isn't really *in love* with Jimmy, he wouldn't want to be. Or rather, he is in love but he doesn't *love* him. And he probably does love you, but it isn't going to do you any good, Mrs. Mallory, which is probably what you came to ask me, so I hope this is the answer that makes sense to you, because it *is* your answer."

She still doesn't speak, just hands me the second check and walks out. "And don't forget to recommend me to your friends!" Flip would say if he were here. Well, he would never be *here*. But when I told him at home. Which is not where he is now, either, because we've broken up, as I may have mentioned. Though even if we hadn't broken up, he probably wouldn't be home, because—all right. Enough. I lock up the office and *I* head for home. The end of another perfect day.

When I get home, there's a message on my answering machine from Loulou, my parents'—what would you call her? Manager, I am tempted to say. Secretary doesn't sound quite right, and social secretary sounds far too pretentious. Although true. My parents ought to have produced another John Cheever, but instead they got me.

There's also a message from Flip. In the three months since we broke up, he's done an incredible job of never once actually talking to me. When for some reason he's had to get in touch, he's left messages.

"Hi, Warren, hope everything is fine for you. No, I don't, I hope you're absolutely miserable, which is no more than you deserve. *Anyway,* you asked me to tell you the next time I was going to be out of town, and for some strange reason, *God* knows why, I agreed, so here it is. You know, Warren, considering that a huge part of why we broke up—excuse me, why *you* broke up with me—was because you hated how much I was out of town, you've done a fantastic job of keeping track of my schedule since then, don't you agree? I would have thought *not* knowing was one of the perks. *Anyway,* we start shooting tomorrow, Monday, and I won't be back till the following Monday, so you've got all that time to *finally* get the rest of your stuff out of [and here is the one slight pause] *the* apartment. Although I *really* don't know why I'm telling you this, because your stuff is much nicer than mine and I'm not in any particular hurry to get rid of it. Still, someone might wonder why *you* aren't in any particular hurry to get it back, don't you think? Bye!"

Flip is an actor, and that's a performance if I ever heard one. (Yes, he's a *good* actor, though I can't help thinking that *something* must be at fault for him not to be further along in his career.) I stand fascinated while the message plays, listening to the words and the silence after them. *It wasn't that you went out of town,* I can't help thinking. *I told you. It was that you were so unhappy and I couldn't stand to watch.* Well, he certainly doesn't sound unhappy now. Maybe he's seeing someone. Or several people. Probably someone *and* several people. I flip back the tape to hear Loulou's message again.

"Warren, honey, it's me, Loulou. Your parents want you to call them tonight if you possibly can. Nothing's wrong, but it's truly urgent, so do please call. They have a thing at five-thirty, but they'll be home after eight. By the way, I know it's just November, but I do have their Christmas list, if you want a confidential conversation some time in the next week or so. But do please call tonight, if you possibly possibly can, because it truly is urgent. Thanks, darling!"

Flip loved Loulou. He couldn't decide whether she should be played by Claudette Colbert or Carole Lombard, but he was fascinated by a real live person who actually called you "darling," like something out of a Philip Barry comedy. I glance at the clock. Still too early to call.

By the way, this is an excellent example of what I've been trying to tell you. I'm a psychic, so I'm supposed to know why Loulou called. Not a clue. And believe me, I wouldn't even try, because to put that kind of energy in the direction of my parents' house. . . . Still, the non-psychic part of me has to wonder what is so terribly urgent, because my parents, while attentive in their way, aren't exactly—well, you saw how they had Loulou make the call.

When I actually reach them, they still won't tell me what it is. "Just come on out here," my mother says, "and we can talk about it then. But how soon can you come, Warren, because really, the sooner, the better." A pause. "And of course, we'd love to see you." Another pause. "And, Warren, much as we *like* your friend, it might be best if you didn't bring him this time. Family business. I think we'd all be more comfortable."

I think about sharing the news that Flip and I broke up three months ago, but finding the words seems way too daunting. The only reason they even know about Flip was because he had the truly insane idea that we should be a part of each other's families. "My God, Flip, *I* don't want to be a part of my family," I had said to him. "Why should you want to?"

He had stared at me in surprise. "But you're always talking about them. How wonderful they are. Those childhood memories— Sledding down your own private hill? Snowmen all over your enormous back yard? Cook making hot chocolate for you and your sister—one and a half marshmallows for you, rainbow sprinkles for her?"

"A lot of good those sprinkles did her," I say. If I ever want to worry about how my life has turned out, it's enough to remember that at least it isn't Madeleine's.

"Skiing in Vermont," Flip goes on. "Big family Thanksgivings, with fireplaces and chestnuts roasting on an open fire—or did you save that for Christmas? Those wonderful reunions after your term ended at boarding school?"

"All right, so you *are* joking."

"Not entirely," Flip says with a grin. "I have to admit, since you were the exact people I envied growing up in glorious *Pittsburgh,* I can't help enjoying this look at the dark side."

"God help the working classes," I say, in my best Connecticut lockjaw, "if they grew up envying *us.*"

"Well, we did," Flip says, coming over to me, "and now that I *am* all grown up, I want to see what I missed." He puts his arms around me from behind. "Seriously, Warren," he says, resting his chin on my shoulder. "It's where you grew up. I want to see it." He nibbles at my earlobe. "Don't you want me to? I would let you see where *I* grew up."

"Oh, right," I say, turning around to face him. "Like we would *ever* go to fucking Pittsburgh."

This is apparently one of those things he is allowed to say but I am not, as I see by the shimmer of expressions that pass across his face. I'm not sure if apologizing will simply make things worse—but I *am* sorry. So it was Thanksgiving in Connecticut for us, and I have to admit, I liked having him there. I liked him seeing what my life had been. I liked having him as a witness to my family, so that when my mother said, "I feel so sorry for you boys having to live in the City, where everyone is so pushy and rude," I wasn't the only one who heard it. I mean, *heard* it.

The worst part is knowing how much of that life is still in me. I'm totally unfit to live there: no family, no recognizable job, and way too far out of the closet ever to get an acceptable distance back in. (Because, let's face it, simply *being* gay is hardly enough to make someone unfit to live in Connecticut. Not that part of it, anyway.) But I am continually haunted by the feeling that *there* is where I truly belong.

"Goodbye, then, dear," my mother says now. "We'll see you tomorrow."

"Can't you at least tell me what it's about? Or *who* it's about."

I hear her catch her breath and sigh. "Your sister," she says finally. "It's about Madeleine." Then she laughs. "And now you *will* have to come out if you want to know the rest!" This shift, from quiet, restrained suffering to cocktail-party flirtation, is so typical of my mother that it really shouldn't surprise me. But it does, every time.

MONDAY

Going out on the train today, it's as though the fates have conspired to show Connecticut in its best possible light. It's what the natives would call a glorious November morning, clear golden bars of sunlight slashing through the thick foliage, which still clings to the trees with lingering traces of red and gold and slivers of green. Madeleine and I really did go to boarding school, but nearby, each of us less than half an hour's drive from home. On a weekend like this, my mother might drive out and pick us up—and then, later, only me, sitting in the front seat of the station wagon as my mother shook her head and said brightly to some imaginary guest, "Oh, that Madeleine! Until she settles down!"

"What?" I was still foolish enough to ask when I was, say, ten, and Madeleine was fifteen. "What is she doing?"

"Oh, Warren, it doesn't matter," my mother would say, as though she had just that moment remembered I was there. "She's young. She deserves to have a good time while she still can." My mother turns her beautiful face to me and smiles one of her heartbreaking smiles. "Madeleine has what is known as *joie de vivre,*" she says, lingering over the furry French words. "She finds the most unlikely things to give her pleasure—she's really quite gifted that way."

She looks back at the road. "Well, *I'm* young," I say. "I deserve to have a good time, too."

My mother laughs, that cocktail-party ripple. "Oh, Warren, you will break my heart if you're not careful! I swear you will absolutely break my heart. I suppose *we're* not going to have fun, you and I. I miss you while you're away, you know. But I don't like to think of you suffering. Shall I drive you back to school so you can have a nice weekend with your friends?"

"I like coming home," I offer. "I don't really want to go back." (Not that I had any friends at that age. It's a bit disconcerting to recall that I had boyfriends before I had friends. If you want to call them boyfriends.)

"Now don't you say that just to be polite!" she goes on in that bright, cheerful tone. ("Your mother is such a *flirt,*" Flip whispered to me as we all moved from the dining room into the sitting room. "She needs a whole *roomful* of gay men to satisfy her!" "What did you mean by that?" I asked him later, when we were, amazingly, alone in one of the guest rooms. "Why not straight men?" Flip looked at me in surprise. "I realize she's your mother, *darling*," he said. "But even you can see that she doesn't actually want to have sex.")

"I'm not being polite, Mama," I say, wondering where Madeleine is. If she'd been there, she'd have been sitting in the back seat, fighting with one of us or telling some long, drawn-out story about people we'd never heard of. My parents hated how much Madeleine talked and they were always trying to get her to stop, but it was only my grandmother who chose to be explicit. "For heaven's sake, Madeleine, stop talking!" she used to say. "People will think you're Jewish."

So where *was* Madeleine, do you suppose, while I sat in the front seat of the station wagon conversing with my mother? Probably off with *her* boyfriends. Or girlfriends. There was a period, just after I started to have my first sexual encounters ("experiences" is far too gentle a word), when I admired Madeleine—madly. I thought she was a free spirit, because she slept with anyone and it didn't seem to carry any consequences. I thought she was an artist, because she was always making something—paintings, sketches, fabric art, elaborate hand-printed cards for her latest love interest.

Eventually I got older, and I knew better. I understood that what Madeleine had was a series of sordid one-night stands and some boxes of pretentious junk.

Then the last time I was out at the house—for Thanksgiving, in fact, with Flip—I went to take a look at Madeleine's room, which my parents had preserved more or less intact, her art all over the walls. I was astonished.

"Well, well, so the slut had talent," said Flip as our gaze passed from one miraculous piece to the next. There was something so prodigious about this display, the sheer quantity of Madeleine's work, its—what is the word I'm looking for? Its *integrity*. As if each piece, with all its clumsiness and youth, still strove for exactly the truth she saw. This should have saved her.

"At least your sister has an interesting past," Flip says, touching a sculpture with one careful finger. Metal and stones, a barren landscape. "All my sister did in high school was read and pray."

"As long as she never had shock treatment," I say, and Flip stares. "I told you Madeleine was crazy. I wasn't speaking metaphorically. Doesn't Rosie seem normal now?"

"I'm not sure," Flip says, looking around the room. "Rosie drives *me* crazy, so maybe it all evens out." I can see how shaken he is. "What happened?"

"Well, the first time was after high school. Just about six months after she first left home. She went away to college—Smith, of course—"

"Of course."

"And she became obsessed with some woman on her floor, a dorm resident. One day they found her sleeping on the floor in the hallway, curled up against the woman's door. She went back to college six months later, she finished four years in three, with honors in her major—French, as it happens—and a lot of D's in art history, and an A in math, and many, many incompletes in studio art—*very* weird grades—and then she went to Europe, and the same thing happened, some kind of obsessive following a person around, not stalking, exactly, I suppose it was more pathetic than that—only with a man this time. I was away at school then myself—"

"Dartmouth, of course."

"Of course. Actually, she had gone to college to study art. And she went to Europe to study art. But when she came home after the second breakdown, that was it. She said that obviously she wasn't cut out to be an artist, that she was completely done with that part of her life, that she had learned her lesson. And apparently, it worked. She spent some time in the hospital and some time here, and then she went back to Europe, and she's been there ever since, except for those interludes of varying lengths when she comes back here and lives at home again."

"No."

"Oh, yes. In the past thirty years, she's lived here in our house for a total of, oh, maybe six years? No, because once she was here for two years running. So more like eight years. Maybe ten. No hospitals, though." I look at one of her fabric pieces, velvet and satin and corduroy. One half of the piece is blue and black and silver, while the other half is pink and orange, red and gold—rich, jewel-like colors that glow.

"That one's really amazing," Flip says. He reaches out to touch the velvet, then pulls back his hand. "Look at the black lines on that half. Trees at twilight."

I look at the piece more closely. Something about it bothers me, though I couldn't say why. "I would have thought she would have packed all this stuff away, but maybe our parents wouldn't let her. Their own special form of torture. Or maybe she—" The image of Madeleine in this room year after year catches up with me, and I stop talking.

"How long since she was last here?" Flip says, carefully not looking at me.

"Oh, it's been ten years at least. That's why I haven't been in here—God knows why we came in tonight."

"One artist calling to another," Flip says dramatically.

"What an excellent role model for you. My crazy sister who also never earned a living and ended up living with her parents half her adult life."

"Mmmm," Flip says with a sigh. "I can just imagine how she felt."

"Oh, please."

"You never went to Paris to see her?"

"None of us did," I say as we walk out of the room. "I don't think she wanted us to. If she wanted to see us, she came back here."

Flip turns to me as I shut the door. "You could go now," he says brightly. "*We* could. I bet she has a great place."

"She's probably a heroin addict," I say. "Frankly, I don't think I want to see what her life is like. I think if she had anything to be proud of, she would have invited us."

"Us?" Flip raises his eyebrows.

"Well, one of us, yes. Someone from our family. You know what I mean."

"Mmmm," Flip says. He gives me a sly, sidelong glance, which I really resent, because I feel he learned it from me. "So I'm just wondering," he says. "Has she ever seen where *you* live?" He looks around my parents' house. "Other than *here*."

Well, I suppose to someone like Flip, it does look like the set for a Philip Barry movie. To me, it's simply my home. "For someone who complains about *your* sister all the time, you're getting very family oriented," I say as we go down the long, curving stairway.

"Mmmm," Flip says again. "Like we would *ever* go to fucking Pittsburgh."

I think of all the things I've had to teach myself since leaving home. How to cook. How to make a bed. (Yes, we had a housekeeper, Vernice, to do it for us.) How to earn money. How to make friends. How to make love. (Though not, God knows, how to have sex.) As I said, I could have stayed here. I was unfit for this life in every possible way, but I could have made myself fit. Plenty of other people do.

Flip is watching me as though he can read every one of my thoughts, whereas at the moment, I can't even read his expression. "We could go to Pittsburgh," I say. "Only let's not go there on the bus, all right?" Which is how Flip travels the one or two times a year that he goes to visit his family. His mouth twists, and he looks away. "Because I think my constitution is rather too *delicate* for any type of public transportation," I continue. "I don't know how you people stand it, really, I don't."

He can't help it, he has to laugh. "All right, all right," he says, bumping shoulders with me, and I stifle a sigh of relief.

Although we only came out here once, almost a year ago, it seems incredibly strange to be stepping out onto the train platform without him. My mother has sent Loulou to pick me up—when needed, she works on Saturdays and even Sundays—and Loulou has brought her own car, a sporty little

Saab, which my parents must have bought for her. I suppose I had been imagining my mother in the latest version of the station wagon, but if you want to
know the truth, I'm grateful that it's Loulou in the Saab.

"Warren! Darling! Don't you dare not give me a kiss!" She throws her
arms around me exuberantly and makes those little air kisses on either side of
my face. I can't help smiling. She *is* like some madcap heroine, impulsive and
conventional in a single gesture. I'm more glad to see her than I would ever
have imagined, and I give her a real hug, feeling her body meet mine for an instant and then pull away.

"Come on, Warren, they're all waiting for you," she says briskly, bustling
me into the car.

"Madeleine too?"

Loulou's expression is unreadable. "No, not Madeleine."

"Loulou. What is all this about?"

She starts the car and backs out of the station in a rush. She never looks
where she's going. "Now, Warren, tell me how you are." The houses in this
part of Connecticut are more like estates, set so far back into the woods that
all you see is the occasional discreet fencepost with a mailbox attached. "And
your friend, what was his name, Flip? He was delightful. How is he?"

"He thought you were delightful, too," I say. "Unfortunately, we broke up."

"Oh, dear, I'm so sorry, that's such a shame," Loulou says, catapulting us
onto yet another country road. "But perhaps it's all for the best. I'm sure
you'll find somebody else."

"I don't know, Loulou." This road is so familiar. It welcomes me, envelops
me, as though I could never imagine being anywhere else. "My track record in
that department is not too good."

She looks at me intently, although the car doesn't slacken its speed. "You
mustn't give up," she says emphatically. "Promise me, Warren, that you will
not give up. You have to find someone to love in this world, and I don't want
to hear that you've stopped trying."

Someone to love? What about her, for God's sake? Surely she doesn't love
my parents—not in that way.

Suddenly I have a flash of vision, although at first I think it's just nausea
from Loulou's driving. "Oh, my God," I say without thinking. "You and Sossie.
You and Sossie Anne."

Loulou looks astounded, and I am very sorry. If I hadn't been caught off
guard, I could have stayed silent.

"I have a friend named Sossie, yes," she says slowly. "But I don't believe
you've ever met her. Nor has anyone else in your family."

"No, Loulou, no one has said anything, I simply—It was only a feeling."

"Not everyone is like you, Warren," she says, her eyes firmly on the road. "Not everyone—lives where you live. Not everyone lives the *way* you live."

"I know, Loulou. I'm sorry. Really." Though even without benefit of vision, I can well imagine it. Either they're roommates, and everyone simply assumes they're two lonely spinsters, saving money, or perhaps keeping each other company. Or else they're "girlfriends"—they go shopping, go out to dinner together, have a few drinks at the local inn . . . Loulou probably could have told my parents about her roommate, mentioned her good friend, and known it wouldn't have made any difference. Maybe that's why she didn't want to tell.

Loulou opens her mouth to speak, and then shuts it. If I apologize again, it will make more of this, and she wants to make less. So neither of us says anything, and we ride in silence for the next twenty minutes, until Loulou finally pulls up onto the driveway disguised as a country road that leads to my parents' house. "Did you bring a bag?" she asks, a sure sign of how flustered she still is. The Loulou I know would be unpacking it by now.

"It's in the back," I say. "Loulou, I can take it in—it's only an overnight bag."

"Don't you be silly," she says, still not looking at me. "I'll take care of everything." Then she does look at me. "Even though you came without your friend, I thought you'd like to have the same room you had before, so I put you in there. Is that all right?"

"Oh, Loulou." It's like with that woman in my office yesterday—I feel thoroughly overcome, and there's no earthly reason why I should. "That was a nice thought," I say as formally as I can manage. "That will be fine, thank you."

I think she might be about to speak or at least to smile, but she simply goes to get my bag out of the back seat. There's nothing left but to go on in, through the glassed-in porch that Flip insisted on calling the conservatory. I told him he made my house sound like a game of *Clue*. He said he was sure there were dead bodies to be found in every room, ha, ha.

From the porch, there's a view out back, a rolling hill that rises to the woods beyond. In the clear afternoon sunlight, I see a little girl running furiously up the hill, her legs pumping, her arms flailing, as she pushes herself to go faster, faster, as she pushes herself to fly. When she reaches the top, she whirls herself around, spinning as fast as she can until she collapses onto the ground. She rests for a moment, then flings herself down the hill, rolling over and over, until she finally arrives at the bottom. Another moment of rest, then she throws herself up onto her feet and starts the upward run again, pushing herself forward. When she reaches the hill the second time, I realize she's a

Black child. Vernice's daughter? No employee's children ever played here before, but maybe my parents think it's safe, now that Madeleine and I aren't here.

"Warren, dear, thank you again for coming," says my mother, rising from her chair in the living room. She takes me by the shoulders, holding me at arm's length while she kisses me, pressing her cheek to mine. My cheek burns where she touches me. "So kind of you to take the trouble."

"Really, it's no trouble at all," I say. "Only I wonder what—"

My mother hushes me with one raised palm. "Let's catch up a little first, shall we?" she says. "There's time enough for business later." She looks at her watch. "Your father should be joining us soon. I think he's just catching up on some paperwork."

Oh, please. My father is getting quietly drunk in his study, which at least is an improvement over his getting noisily drunk with us. On the other hand, would I really want my mother to have a "frank, honest" talk with me about this? Would I really want my parents to get openly drunk, fight out loud, insult each other? "They're such fucking hypocrites!" Madeleine used to say, a sixteen-year-old hippie. (Being at boarding school, it had taken her a while to find out about hippies, but she was always a quick study.) "Why can't they be more honest? Why can't they let their feelings *out*? It's just such *shit!*"

"But Madeleine," I would say, a shocked eleven-year-old. "They really love each other."

"Oh, Warren, get real. They hate each other, but they're too fucked up to realize it." I suppose I had heard the word "fuck" by then, but never in my house.

"They hate each other? You mean like divorce?"

"More like a long, slow murder," Madeleine said dramatically. Then she saw my face. "Oh, get over it, Warren. I'm speaking metaphorically."

"No. They still love each other."

"Like that's my idea of love," Madeleine said scornfully. "Like that's *any-body's* idea of love. Warren, that can't even be *your* idea of love."

But they do love each other. It isn't my idea, but it's theirs.

My mother pours me tea, offers me cake and cucumber sandwiches. (You can imagine Flip after *that*—he was doing Oscar Wilde for a week.) Normal social conversation doesn't work with me: she can't ask about my wife, my children, or things at the office. So she has evolved a series of Warren-specific party questions: "Have you been to any good concerts lately?" "What kind of weather are you having in the City?" and "What did you think of that fascinating article in last week's *Times*?" Well, all right, at least she tries.

Still, the conversation gets fairly thin. "Who was that child I saw on the lawn?" I ask rather desperately. "I never saw any of Vernice's children here before. Or would she be a grandchild?"

"No, dear," my mother says with admirable calm. "That's your sister Madeleine's daughter. If you've already seen her, then you understand. We have to decide where to keep her until Madeleine gets well."

Gradually the story comes out. While Madeleine was in Paris she had some child none of us had ever heard about. Apparently, her name is Juliet and she's eight. Eight! I don't know why her age upsets me so much, but it does. This *child* has been in the world for eight entire years, and I never knew till now.

"Well, it's not as though you were the *father,* Warren," my mother says, and bursts into her festive laugh. "I suppose if Madeleine didn't *want* to tell us, she was under no real obligation."

"I think she had an obligation!" I say rather frantically. "I think she owed us that!"

"Well, be that as it may, dear, she *didn't* tell us. And now that she's indisposed—"

I walk over to the window. I am so angry with Madeleine that I want to put my fist through it. I feel my mother watching me, amused. "I really don't understand why you're so upset," she says. "Poor Madeleine, of course, but she *is* being taken care of. It's an excellent hospital. They speak English there. The grounds are supposed to be beautiful—they faxed us a picture. It was color, which didn't reproduce too well, but you could see it was a lovely place. She'll have a good rest, and then she'll come back here." And do what? Live in the room upstairs with an eight-year-old girl? "And now we simply have to decide what to *do* with the child."

"Why can't she stay here?"

"Oh, Warren. You said you saw her. Obviously she can't stay here."

I promise you that I didn't understand. At that point, I really did not understand.

"The schools we know of," my mother was saying, "won't take anyone under the age of ten, and she's eight. And I'm not sure she would be happy in any of our places anyway, Warren, which is why we wanted your help. We thought you might know of somewhere in the City. She has her father's last name, you know, Bidjane, though I really can't imagine that Madeleine got married without telling us, can you, dear? But perhaps they thought the child would stand out less with a name like that. Though why they named her Juliet . . . 'Juliet Bidjane'—*I* can't see it."

Against my will, I hear Madeleine's voice. *"Juliette,"* she says, pronouncing the name in French. "Zhoo-lyet Bee-DZHAHN." Slowly I say the name aloud.

"Well, yes, dear," my mother says. "That's how *she* says it. But I don't think that makes it any better, do you? It's still more or less a case of the canary and the crow."

"I'll take her," I hear myself saying, and no one could possibly have been more surprised than I was.

"So you *do* know a school," my mother says brightly. "Marvelous! I hoped you would."

I can't help remembering all those drives back from school, the ones after Madeleine stopped coming home with us and I was finally alone with my mother. I remember how quickly those drives always ended. It didn't matter how much time I got with her, it was never enough.

"No, I mean, I'll *take* her," I say. "She can live with me."

"Oh, for heaven's sake, Warren, don't be ridiculous," my mother says, truly annoyed. I was so happy to be alone with her, that was the terrible thing. Particularly since I could never make *her* understand that. "I wouldn't have asked you out here if I thought you were going to make a joke out of the whole thing." Her good mood is gone, probably for the rest of the night.

"I'm not joking," I say. "I'll take her." Just then my father comes into the room and we have to go through the whole business all over again.

I don't suppose I would ever have won this argument, except for one odd thing. Madeleine, although anyone's last choice for a mother, had at least *tried* to be responsible. Before abandoning her daughter altogether, she had gotten herself to a lawyer, where she had named me as Juliet's guardian, arranged for someone to take her to America—and, for some strange reason known only to Madeleine, specified that Juliet should come here first.

"So, legally, of course, it is your decision, Warren," my mother says after she, my father, and I have all sat down to dinner. Sometimes Loulou ate with us, but I suppose she had gone home this time. "We certainly won't contest it. We won't fight it in court."

"If we did, you'd lose," says my father bluntly. "What kind of a judge would find *you* a fit parent?" He helps himself to glazed carrots and looks at me. "I hope you're not taking offense, Warren, because I'm not speaking personally. I'm simply stating a fact."

What kind of judge would find *you* a fit parent, Dad? But I say calmly, "On the contrary, I doubt you would win." When he gets annoyed, calmness drives him absolutely wild. "After all," I say, serving myself a portion of buttery, glistening *haricots verts,* "I have the mother's express wishes in writing. That's usually decisive, don't you think?"

My father doesn't even bother to look at me as he rattles off his counter-arguments. "Incompetent mother. Guardian with no visible means of support—"

"I support myself! *And* I have money."

"—*and* with an unconventional lifestyle, no experience of children, no fit domicile, no visible means of support—"

"You said that already."

"—as opposed to a stable couple, also related to the child, custodial history with the parent," he looks at me and my mother significantly, punctuating this point with his fork, "previous experience of children, eminently fit home, a stable relationship—"

"You said that, too."

"By the way, dear," says my mother, pouring herself a second glass of wine, "how *is* your friend? I hope you told him we were sorry not to invite him this time. I expect you'll be bringing him for Thanksgiving."

Checkmate. It has often occurred to me that I inherited my psychic abilities from my mother. God knows what she did with them, married to my father.

"We aren't seeing each other any more," I say. Then I wonder why I told them. My father shrugs, having already lost all interest in our argument. My mother actually looks distressed. "Oh. I'm sorry." Her voice is desolate. "I'm so sorry, Warren."

I shrug. "It's all right," I say. "It happened in August, so—"

"Three months ago!" says my mother. "All that time." She pushes her plate away, and her glass. "I'm sorry you couldn't confide in us," she says. "You must miss each other terribly."

Does she think we're the only two faggots *in* New York? "That's nice of you to say, Mama, but really, it's all right."

"But you were living together," she says. "That's why you brought him out here. Doesn't that mean anything? Is that just a casual thing with you all?"

"No, it—Yes, of course it *meant* something—I only meant that—"

"Don't you think we should save the personal conversation for after dinner?" my father says.

My mother rallies. "Well, there won't be time for it then," she says. "We still have to figure out what to do with Madeleine's child."

"Where is she, by the way?" I ask.

"Oh, she's eating dinner with Vernice, in the kitchen," my mother says. "We thought she'd be more comfortable there."

"Well, I think after dinner, I should at least meet Juliet," I say.

My parents look uncertain for the first time. "Of course, dear. She's a charming child," my mother says. "She speaks English beautifully—well, of course, she would, living with Madeleine."

"Being Madeleine's daughter," I say.

"I know," my mother says, and sighs. "It's just so hard to believe." She pulls her wine glass back to her and takes another sip. "Of course, there's no doubt at all once you see her. Not in the least. She looks *just* like Madeleine, don't you think so, Frank? I mean, except for being black."

My father shakes his head helplessly.

"About your friend, dear, is it really final?" says my mother, with one more concerned look. I shrug and look away. "Well, I just liked thinking of you settled and happy," she says. "And he seemed quite nice. It's so sad when nothing works out."

"Please," says my father, "can we keep the conversation on topics of general interest?"

As dinner goes on, I watch my mother become sadder and sadder, a thick cloud of sorrow that she ignores. After dinner, my father says simply, "Well, you don't need me for this," and withdraws back into his den. My mother calls Vernice on the house phone, and Juliet comes out to meet us.

She is exquisite, is my first thought. Small, precise features, delicate and sculpted. Café-au-lait skin. Rich, wavy black hair, pulled back now, but you can see how it would cascade to her shoulders, how it would shine as it stood out from her face. She stands before my mother and me in her robe and slippers, letting us look at her, as though she were quite used to being—not on display. But *shown*. I imagine Madeleine, enormously proud of her creation, presenting her child to every stranger that came into her home.

Then I think that perhaps I am being unfair. Maybe it never occurred to Madeleine that anyone could *not* be interested in this miraculous child. Obviously, Juliet knows better, but she lets us look.

"You see, dear," murmurs my mother, just softly enough that Juliet can't hear her words. "Doesn't she look exactly like Madeleine when *she* was eight? Only much prettier, of course. Isn't it extraordinary?"

How should I know? I want to answer. When Madeleine was eight, I was three. And then I see it—catapulted back to a sight that I knew only as a child, my amazing big sister whose presence was almost as precious a prize as my mother's.

Unlike Madeleine, though, Juliet is quiet. Or is that only the effect of being among strangers? Perhaps she's quite different at home. Which is where, now?

As usual, my mother takes the initiative. "Juliet, this is Warren. He's your uncle. You're going to go and live with him. In New York City."

Juliet studies me. "Should I call you Uncle Warren?" she asks. Her English is almost without accent, but there's some flavor to it—the vowels are shorter, brighter, the consonants roll.

"Just Warren," I say without thinking, and from the corner of my eye, I catch my mother's disapproving shake of the head. Children need to know their place, she would say if Juliet weren't there. They need parents, not friends.

"New York City," Juliet repeats. "Do you live in Greenwich Village?" The place name, for some reason, she says in French, "Gre-niche Vi-lage," so that it takes a minute for me to translate.

"No," I say. "I live in another neighborhood, Chelsea." When Flip and I lived together, we had to have an apartment where he could afford to pay half the rent, so we lived in Hell's Kitchen. Now that he's gone, I can live where I want. "How do you know about Greenwich Village?" I say the name in English, and I can see her memorizing the pronunciation.

"Mama told me," she says, saying the word *Mama* with exactly Madeleine's and my accent. "She thought maybe you lived there."

Did Madeleine never even have my address?

"No," I say. "I never lived in the Village. Too expensive." Juliet looks around the house, and if she were older, I would swear she was thinking, "Oh, right. Like there's anything that *you* can't afford." I have the bizarre wish to explain it all to her: Yes, I have money from my family, something I never told Flip about, actually, because I *don't* use it, it's simply there. And not nearly as much as you might think, either, since in our family, you're supposed to live on what you earn. Only when I moved out from Flip, I couldn't bear to go back to the kind of apartment I could afford by myself, so all right, I bought a co-op. But in Chelsea, not the Village, and I do earn the maintenance. Other people get help from their families, don't they? Why shouldn't I?

"It's a nice apartment," I say now. "There's a room we can fix up for you—"

"Thank you, I'm sure it will be very nice," she says politely. Then she looks at me more closely and pats my hand. "Don't worry, Warren, I'm sure I'll like it," she says, and I can hear her reassuring Madeleine. Oh, Madeleine, I think, touched and horrified, you should have done better than this. No one told you to go have a child.

"It's time for bed," my mother says. "Juliet, tell Vernice to help you pack so that you and Warren can leave in the morning." My mother looks at me. "Unless you'd like some more time, Warren. You could stay another day or two. You might want to make some arrangements from here."

That would make sense, but I shake my head. "No, she's right, Juliet. We'll go in the morning—if that's all right with you."

Juliet looks panicked. She wants to say what I want to hear, but I haven't let her know what that is. "If you want to stay longer, Juliet, you can say so," I say as gently as I know how.

"I think if you're going, you should go soon," my mother says firmly, and I see how relieved Juliet looks. She says goodnight to both of us and goes back to Vernice in the kitchen. "Honestly, Warren, you can't give a child so many choices," my mother says. "Children don't know what they want. You have to tell them." She gets up from the couch. "And now, let's have some Benedictine, or cognac if you'd rather," she says, "and you can tell me all about the rest of your life."

Eventually, it's time for bed, and I make my way to the guest room. When I finished college and moved to New York, my parents redecorated my room, turning it into a kind of study for my mother, though I've never known what she does in there or even whether she goes in there at all.

When Flip and I were here, this room was freezing. Each room in this house has its own separate thermostat, and whoever had gotten this room ready for us had forgotten to turn ours up. We climbed into bed, trying to burn the icy edge off the sheets with the heat from our two bodies. We made love vigorously, fiercely, trying not to laugh, trying to make no noise at all, even though the other occupied bedrooms in the house were far, far away from this one. At that moment, his body was the most precious object in the world to me, and I wondered how to make him know that.

Afterward, Flip pulled away and rolled to the farthest edge of the bed, burrowing into the chilly bedclothes. When we had first gotten together, I couldn't fall asleep unless our bodies were touching, snuggled up against him or my hand on his stomach, his cock, his thigh. But by this point, it was the other way around—I needed space to sleep—so that night, he pulled away first.

Suddenly, I am rolling after him, pressing my body against his. Then that's not enough; I have to throw my leg over his, stretch my arm across his back. His hand feels heavy with meaning when it reaches to take hold of mine. He pulls our clasped hands in against his chest. "Is this all right?" I whisper.

"Yes, love," he murmurs back, and then he is asleep in that instant, total way that I envy so much. I lie against him, my nose pressed into the back of his neck, my forehead covered by his silky hair. I would press in closer if I could,

I would envelop him, I would crawl inside him. As I lie there, warm inside the icy sheets, my skin full of his touch, my senses full of his particular smell, his taste still in my mouth, it seems to me that no greater happiness in the world exists than to lie here with this man inside my arms, here in this place that I call home.

Tonight, Loulou has not only set the thermostat, she has turned on the electric blanket, so that the temperature in the room, and in the bed, is neutral. I roll over to find that exact spot on the far side so I can wrap my body around his phantom limbs, breathe in the memory of his warmth, his smell. *Is this all right?* I send out. Flip isn't even home tonight, he's on a shoot, God knows where, with God knows whom. *Is this all right?* I fall asleep imagining his answer.

TUESDAY

I oversleep the next morning and awaken to the incomprehensible realization that somehow I have agreed to take on the care of an eight-year-old child. A girl, no less. A Black girl. I am so full of absolute panic that I feel as if the parts of my body will simply detach. If there were ever a time when I would welcome a vision of my own future, some sign or image of what to expect, this would be it. But nothing could possibly come to me in this state. The moments between getting out of bed and arriving at the train station are at least imaginable, so I concentrate on getting through those.

Juliet has breakfast with Vernice, of course, so I don't even see her until my mother is ready to drive us to the station. I head for the front seat, Juliet for the back. Her lovely miniature-Madeleine face is blank and silent as Madeleine's never was, but I recognize the look all the same, though I don't know why. Then I realize. It is mine.

The expression "heart-rending" literally means to tear the heart in two, doesn't it, or perhaps it means to render the heart into fat and blood and gravy, cooking it down over a slow fire? Take your choice, and then imagine that instant as heart-rending for me. Am I dreading the moment of being alone with her or looking forward to it?

"Goodbye, Warren, dear," says my mother at the platform as I unload my overnight bag and Juliet's two small suitcases from the back of the station wagon. "I won't wait, if you don't mind. You know I can't bear to say goodbye to you." She laughs. "That was the worst of sending you away to school so early—you were always leaving me." She presses her cheek to mine once more, her hands like iron upon my shoulders. "Miss you, dear," she says as our faces touch. "Don't stay away so long next time, please." She pushes me away. "You know you can always bring out any of your friends that you want us to meet," she says. "Please don't let *that* stop you from coming home."

"No, Mama. I won't."

"All right, then," she says. "Bye-bye, Juliet!" She waves at Juliet, who is standing beside her suitcases just behind me. "Mind your Uncle Warren."

"Bye-bye, Madame," Juliet says, a quick study. *Grand-mère,* I want to say, grandmother, not *Madame.* Surely my mother knows the difference. But she just waves at us both, a twinkling of her fingers, and then she is gone.

I expect the next moment to be absolutely blank, and I prepare to panic. But I haven't counted on Juliet. She turns to me and smiles as though she is the hostess. "Uncle Warren, I mean, Warren," she says, "I'm curious. Do you speak French?"

"Would you rather call me Uncle Warren?" I say. "You can." She shrugs. "Yes," I say, "I do speak French. But probably not as well as your mother."

"Well, that's because she lived in France," Juliet says. "She says you were better at languages than she was, but she was more interested. She says that if she hadn't moved to France, she never would have spoken French. But I was born in France, so I speak both languages, French and English. Didn't you ever want to go to France?"

"I've been there," I say. "But not since—" Not since you were born? Since your mother never told any of us about you? "Not since your mother lived there."

Juliet nods. "She says that you always got better grades than she did, but she was the one who remembered everything. Everything that really mattered."

"Well, I don't know about that," I say. "I remembered a few things."

Juliet shakes her head, and her pony tail flaps back and forth. "She says you were the one who *knew* things, things it would be very unusual for a child to know. You told her. And she remembered them."

The train comes while I am still digesting this. I prepare to help Juliet on, but she grabs my overnight bag and bounds up the steps, leaving me to pick up her two suitcases and follow. She dashes into the car on our left, scanning the seats intently as she walks down the aisle. I see her reject several places until she finds the exact seat she wants. Even then, she doesn't sit down right away but stands in the aisle, looking over possible alternatives, as the train strains to leave the station and then tosses us forward.

"Juliet, sit down," I want to say, but I stop myself. But she seems to have heard it anyway, because she looks completely abashed and sits down instantly, my overnight bag at her feet. Gently I reach down and remove it, placing it in the baggage rack next to her two suitcases. She is staring hard out the window as I sit down beside her.

"What else did Madeleine tell you?"

She turns to me instantly, the words pouring out of her as the immense relief shimmers on her face. "She said that she was always getting into fights, but you knew how to get along with everybody." She laughs. "She told me that she and *Grand-mère* used to fight *all* the time. *All* the time!" This idea seems to delight her, and she looks at me to see if I share it. "She told me if I ever *met* *Grand-mère,* which she said probably wouldn't even *happen* until I was all grown up, but she said if I ever met her, I should call her 'Madame.' She said *Grand-mère* wouldn't even know enough French to know that was the wrong name!"

I've got to hand it to Madeleine. She saw that one coming. Juliet looks at me again. "She told me that *Grand-mère* likes very quiet children—like you, Uncle—*Warren.* So I told her that *Grand-mère* would probably like me, because I can be quiet sometimes, especially if the person wants me to be quiet, and she said that was probably a good thing."

"It's certainly a good thing around your grandmother," I say, taking my own illicit pleasure in saying the word. Juliet nods.

"*Warren,*" she says carefully, proud of getting it right this time. "She said to give you a message. She taught it to me. She said to tell you, *Peut-être bien que c'était pas sa conception d'amour, mais qu'elle espère bien que c'est pas la tienne, non plus, au moins pas maintenant.*"

Maybe it wasn't her *idea of love, but she hopes it isn't mine either, at least not any-more.* I can't believe she remembered that argument. Of all the messages Madeleine could have sent me through Juliet, why the hell would she choose that one?

Juliet must think she has upset me, and she immediately begins to ask a flurry of questions about the places we're passing. "*Warren,*" she says, so that I hear the absence of the word "Uncle" every time, "what town is this? How far is it from New York City? Is it a big city, or just a little town? What do people do there? What kinds of industry do they have? We studied that in geography: industry, imports, exports, farm products, animals, livestock, and main types of employment. Of course some places are cities, they don't have farms and animals—except cats and dogs, of course. And pigeons. You have pigeons in New York, don't you? We had pigeons all the time in Paris. They were so loud! Are they loud in New York? Do they wake you up? One morning, we were sleeping, we were sleeping late—you know, really late, past ten o'clock, because we had been up so late the night before, and, imagine, *Warren,* the *pigeons* woke us up! Did that ever happen to you?"

I am very careful not to even think, "For heaven's sake, Juliet, stop talking!" Actually, I like listening to her, although I also find it wearing. When Madeleine was this age, I worshiped her. But surely Madeleine was never so frightened and small.

Suddenly I remember the time I first met Flip. We were at some party in the East Village, and he came over to me, and I thought, "Who *is* this boring little man and why is he talking so much?" I felt I saw him so clearly then. Then I *kept* seeing him—with his sister, as a child—and I *never* do that, I don't do readings for perfect strangers that way, like some kind of party trick. And then he said something to me—I don't even remember what it was—and then I fell for him, I simply fell. And that was the moment when I stopped seeing him clearly. Then I was in it blind.

("Oh, bullshit, Warren," Flip said once when I tried explaining this to him. "You were out to get me from the moment you laid eyes on me, and you know it. You gave me that look, you know, that *look.* You made me come over to you, you and your magnetic powers. Then you told me all these *things* about myself so I couldn't leave." This was at a rocky point in our relationship—I think I was trying to explain why he shouldn't expect too much from me because I had never truly intended to get involved with him. So I don't really give too much weight to what he said next, which was, "Actually, you're always making me come to you. And then you say I want too much.")

Juliet has seen that I'm not paying attention to her, and she's stopped talking. Her back turned emphatically away from me, she stares out the window. I can't help it, I feel her tremendous fear. It's so much bigger than she is, like a wave crashing over her head, burying her under three stories of water, so deep that she'll never reach the top. I feel what she feels, so the wave is bigger than me, too, and it takes everything I have to fight it off.

"Juliet!" I say, as forcefully as I can. She turns around. "Juliet, can you do me a favor? Can you call me Uncle Warren? I think I'd like that better."

She shrugs and nods. But underneath her blank, indifferent look, I feel the fear subside, not all the way, but a little. Enough to let her breathe.

We both lean back in our seats, turn our heads idly toward the window. I realize too late that I should have spoken to her in French. But I pull away from the idea—it seems too intimate. That we would have a private language. That we would be—the word comes to me completely without warning. That we would be family.

The morning after Flip and I spent the night at my house—I mean the one in Connecticut—we woke up slowly, drowsily, the bed finally warm. I remember being barely awake, I could have gone either way, when I feel Flip stroking my hair, my cheeks, my forehead, his tenderness flowing over me like silk. "Warren," he whispers, "Warren," over and over, his voice and his hands. "Oh, my God," I think suddenly, "I am his precious object. He thinks I'm the prize."

I don't remember what happened next. I promise you I don't remember. But is there anyone who doesn't feel that monstrous wave, swamped by so much feeling from another person? Is there anyone who doesn't remember the desert, at least for a minute, with nostalgia?

Juliet says suddenly, "Excuse me, please," and stumbles awkwardly across my feet to escape into the aisle. In a minute, she is out of sight. I assume she's just gone to the bathroom, but when she doesn't come back after five, ten, fifteen minutes, I begin to worry, all the more because I feel so foolish. How long is too long? What if she's in mortal danger and I haven't done anything? What if I do something—Look for her? Call the conductor? Scream for her at the top of my lungs?—and she turns out to be all right? Whatever I do or don't do, everyone will know how little I know.

Then suddenly, just like that, I do know where she is. I see her quite clearly, sitting in the café car, her face pressed against the window. Is she crying? Trying to keep from crying? Did she find it so upsetting to be with me that she simply had to get away?

Here is something else I don't want to remember, though I suppose I will: I don't go after her. She's not in any physical danger, I'm sure of that, so all right. She can come back when she's ready. Because if I go after her—I've already explained this. I don't want to feel what she feels.

In a few moments, she does come back and I'm reading the book I brought in my overnight bag. I see her start to ask me what it is (it's Proust, which I swear is pure coincidence), and then I see her make herself stop. She climbs up to pull her own book out of her suitcase, then scrambles across me into her seat. Have I made her be this way? Has Madeleine? Or is this simply how she is? I'd love to know what she's reading, but she's turned as far away from me as she can get, and I really *don't* want to talk to her, so we ride back to the City like that.

Then we are at Grand Central Station, and all of Juliet's fascination goes outward. She stares and stares at everything.

"Uncle Warren," she says, unable to contain herself, "is this a train station? A real, regular train station?"

"Yes. It's called Grand Central Station." She is positively starry-eyed, but I don't see why—it's just Grand Central, in that weird transition from elegant landmark of old New York to fast-food mart and way station for the homeless. At night, they are there in droves, but now it's only noon, so we see mainly suburbanites, Sarah Lawrence students, business people, and that New York City cast of thousands, all those people simply *there,* everywhere you go.

"Mama said sometime I would see a train station, because I always wanted to, she promised me, she promised me I would see one sometime, but—" She sighs, overcome. "I just never thought I would."

I try not to smile. "But you have train stations in Paris," I say.

"Oh, yes," Juliet says, never taking her eyes off Grand Central. I see her look at the signs for the platforms, a woman in a blue plaid coat and bright green shoes, the gold bars at the ticket window, a blind man with a black dog. "Oh, yes, in Paris we have four. The Gare du Nord goes north to Normandy and la Bretagne; the Gare de Lyon goes south to la Cathédrale de Chartres—" She looks up at me a moment. "Do you have cathedrals in New York?"

"Well, not like Chartres, but yes, I suppose so. St. Patrick's Cathedral." She doesn't say anything but just looks up at me, pleading. "We could go there if you want," I say finally.

"Oh, Uncle Warren, that would be great!" She can't help herself, she has to ask. "Could we go today? Could we go *right now?*"

"We can't go now," I refuse instinctively. Although why not? What do we have to do today that's more important than going to St. Patrick's Cathedral? If I had come back to the city alone, as I'd planned, what would I have done? Gone to a museum in the afternoon, maybe, or a concert in the evening. Had lunch at a new restaurant. Read my book. Not one single one of these activities is thinkable with Juliet, partly because the whole point of them is that they are things I like to do alone. I have no idea what we can possibly do now, I realize. No fucking idea.

"But Juliet," I say quickly, before she can sense the panic, "didn't you ever go to Chartres with Madeleine? With your mother?"

Juliet shrugs. "Mama doesn't like train stations," she says matter-of-factly. "And she doesn't like going places. Not places on the train. She likes going places she can walk. She likes walking around our neighborhood, saying hello to the *boulanger,* and the *épicier,* and the *confisieur,* and the *laitière.* Everybody knows her, and she knows everybody—me, too, they all know me, too. And she likes buying a little something at every single store, and saying hello, and then she and I have a snack at a café."

"Hot chocolate," I say without thinking.

"No, she has coffee, and I have *limonade,*" Juliet says seriously. "We don't like hot chocolate. We think it's too sweet. And then we go home and she cooks the food. And then we have dinner, just her and me, just the two of us, she says we're the best company for each other. Except sometimes, she says, it's nice to have other company. But in our apartment. That's what she likes."

"But you like going places on the train."

Juliet shakes her head impatiently. "No. I like train *stations*." She pauses in the interest of accuracy. "I mean, I like going places on the train. But that's not what I *like*. What I *like* is train stations."

"I understand," I say, and actually, I do. "But what about cathedrals?"

For the first time since we got off the train, Juliet looks sad. She doesn't answer me. She looks around Grand Central and catches sight of someone eating a frozen yogurt. "Uncle Warren," she says, "can I have one of those?"

"What about the cathedrals?" I say again, and then I feel this awful sense of recognition, because she looks even sadder. *This is what I do to people,* I think, no matter how hard I try to push the thought away. *This is what I do.*

"It wasn't cathedrals," Juliet says in a low voice, looking down at the floor.

"What?"

"It wasn't *cathedrals*," she says in a frustrated whine. Then she sounds ashamed. "It was just Chartres." Then her voice gathers strength as she whines again, "Uncle *Warren*. I *said,* can I have one of those?"

I look down at her and I can't pretend I don't have the right words in my mouth. "Hey, Juliet," I say, "let's go see St. Patrick's Cathedral *right now*. We can take a taxi."

"No, Uncle Warren," she says, in Madeleine's bossy, impatient tone. "We have to go there on the *subway*."

"Juliet, the subway doesn't go from Grand Central to St. Patrick's. And anyway, with the suitcases—"

"No, Uncle Warren," she repeats firmly, trying to lead me out of the station even though she has no idea where we're going. "We have to take the subway."

"Why?"

She looks at me, surprised. "Because it's New York." When she sees I don't understand, she explains impatiently, "Mama doesn't like to take the Metro. But she said when we go to New York, we can take the subway. She says in New York, everything is so far, you *have* to ride the subway."

Thanks a lot, Madeleine, I can't help thinking. You're in Paris living off your trust fund, and now you've got me taking the subway.

From here, the day gets worse and worse. We go to St. Patrick's, but Juliet is extremely disappointed, though she can't say why. I have this wild idea that if only I knew, if only I understood, I *could* satisfy her somehow—but either she can't say, or she simply won't tell me. What made it so special, in her eyes. What she was counting on. What she knows she'll never have, now.

Then she insists on taking the subway home, and it's rush hour, and I keep worrying about losing her in the crowd, so I yell at her. I can't help it, it simply comes out. Comes out of where, I want to know. Of course, my father never spoke to us, so he didn't really need to yell. But my mother would never do more than look either disappointed or extremely disappointed.

Juliet looks devastated when I raise my voice to her, and that makes me feel even worse. I suppose Madeleine never loses her temper. (When she and my mother fought, my mother never even raised her voice, but Madeleine's screams could be heard all over the house.) Of course, Juliet is her child. That must make a difference.

Then we get to my apartment, and I can see how disappointed Juliet is once again. Only this time it's worse—for me, I mean—because we don't have to go back to St. Patrick's Cathedral, but I live here. I watch her study the ochre walls, the burnt-orange leather couch, the Bauhaus chairs. She looks at me for permission to walk into the kitchen, my bedroom, the spare room off the hall. This room isn't really decorated yet, though there is a foldout couch in one corner which I had bought with some vague idea of out-of-town guests. I have no idea who—no one has used it since I moved in.

"We can get you a real bed," I offer, trying not to sound too desperate. "We can pick things out . . ." She is using everything she has to keep from crying.

"Juliet," I say without thinking, "what about your things from Paris?"

"NO!" she says immediately. "I need those for when I go BACK."

I am so taken aback, I have to lean against the doorway. "Juliet," I say carefully, "you might be here for a while."

"No!" she says more quietly. "Mama told me. She said that she needed to rest for just a little while, and this would be a chance for me to take a trip, so I could visit you in New York City, and *Grand-mère* and *Grand-père* in Connecticut. But I'm not *living* here. I live in Paris, with Mama."

But I can see she knows better. Now she lives *here,* in this disappointing house.

"Look, Juliet," I begin, "we can find out how long—" And then I see her whole body trembling with the effort not to hear anything more. I sit down on the couch. After a moment, she sits down too, not beside me, exactly, but not at the other end, either.

"Juliet," I say finally. "Can we take it one step at a time? I would like to fix up this room for you, so that it's the way you like it. But it can be with things that we get in New York. And that way, whether it's a long visit or a short one, it will be nice for you here."

"Uncle Warren," she says sternly, giving me a piercing look. "Why do you have two bedrooms in your apartment if you are the only one who lives here? Mama and I have two, a big one for her and a little one for me. She says nobody needs more than that."

"Um, well, Juliet, lots of people *do* have more rooms than that. *Grand-mère* and *Grand-père,* for example—"

"Oh, them," Juliet says. "They're rich. Mama says rich people have more than they need of everything. She says it's better to have just enough. But you're not even using this room." She points to the bare walls, the empty shelves. "It looks so lonely."

"Maybe I thought someone else would live here someday," I said. "Maybe all this time, I've been waiting for him—or her—to come fill up this room."

Juliet shakes her head. "I'm sorry," she says politely. "I told you. I live in Paris, with Mama. You could visit us there. She'd like that, probably."

"I'd like that, too," I say. "First you visit me. And then I'll visit you."

Amazingly, this makes her smile. And so again I feel relieved.

WEDNESDAY

Suddenly, even the simplest things require enormous amounts of effort. At breakfast, for example, Juliet is used to hot milk and fresh bread with chocolate spread, none of which I have in the house. (Obviously, she can't drink coffee, but I didn't realize that she wouldn't be used to orange juice, either.) I'm willing to go out and buy whatever she wants, but the neighborhood bakery I know about doesn't sell French bread, I don't have the right kind of bowls for the milk, and I have no idea where to get the chocolate. I can see how she tries to hide her disappointment, but I feel it all the same.

Money is another concern. Each time I've set myself up in an apartment, I've dipped into the family money (well, why *shouldn't* I start off with nice things?), but is that how I'm supposed to furnish Juliet's room? Typically, although Madeleine had drawn up papers telling me to take care of Juliet, there were no documents about who should pay for it.

I call Connecticut for more information, but Loulou tells me that my parents, exhausted by this whole experience, have gone to the Islands for a few days. "You know the kind of thing," she says, in her old confidential, breezy way, except now there's an unmistakable sting of coolness beneath. "They're hidden away in some secluded spot and someone would have to sail over and give them the message."

I find this hard to believe. It doesn't sound like the kind of vacation my parents would want. But I agree with Loulou that there's nothing to do but wait till they get back.

Luckily, I don't have any clients today, but I have a few tomorrow, and several more over the weekend. And obviously, Juliet should be in school, and I'm sure there are a million and one other things that I haven't even thought about yet. The feeling of absolute panic returns. It's not a new feeling, though I haven't had it lately. It's the feeling of knowing absolutely nothing.

And that, if you want to know the truth, is why I'm willing to be a psychic. Because nauseating though it is to have those visions—I'm not being metaphoric, they make me want to vomit, which actually happens sometimes, and I always get at least somewhat dizzy, and if I don't watch the energy very carefully, I get terrible sick headaches. But dreadful as the *knowing* might be, it is not one ten-thousandth so awful as the sensation of *not knowing*.

So this morning, while Juliet eats my best imitation of her French breakfast in the kitchen, I shut myself in my bedroom and pace. Amazing to think that Madeleine, of all people, could do *this*.

And then somehow the thought comes to me: Rosie. Flip's sister. She's always dealing with other people's problems, though Flip has a nastier way of putting it.

It's still only about eight o'clock (Juliet gets up *much* earlier than I usually do), but apparently Rosie has already been at work for a while. She sounds far gladder to hear from me than I ever would have expected and I explain the situation as best I can, against the phones ringing in the background, and the people calling to her from across the room, and the people trying to get her to take other calls. I must sound terrible, because she fends everybody off until I'm done. Then she says, "OK. So mainly what you need is a sitter and a school."

Is that all?

"I can't deal with the school today," Rosie says brusquely. "All *right,* Tito, I *said* in a minute. Well, I'm sorry too, but Jesus Christ! Excuse me. You hear how it is today, Warren, we're trying to get people over to Schwartz & O'Malley by noon, actually it was supposed to be by nine, so there would be a picket line by the strike deadline, but someone screwed up with the buses, so we moved the deadline, which is really *not good,* it isn't good." She pauses, considering the situation. "It just isn't good. Anyway, where are you living now? You're in the Village, aren't you?"

Why does everyone always think that? "Chelsea," I say.

"OK, there's one of our members, ex-members, actually, well, technically, she's still a member, but she's been out of work for six months. Anyway, *she* lives near the park, Washington Square, which isn't too far from you, is it? She does home day care. You might have to make some kind of overall commitment, but I'm pretty sure she'd help you out. I mean, you'd be paying her, but that isn't a problem for you, is it?"

"No," I say. "That isn't a problem."

"Mmmm," Rosie says, and I can just imagine what she's thinking. But she says, "OK, good, so when you call her, explain that you're still not settled, and you don't have a regular schedule yet, and also you want to see how Juliet likes it. No, don't tell her that, she'll be offended. If Juliet *doesn't* like it there, you can always tell Marta—that's her name—that there was a scheduling problem. But I think, OK, Lucy, OK, thank you, sweetheart, yes, this is perfect, thanks. Can you give a copy to Tito? And Isabel. Thanks, love. All right, Warren, here's the number. Marta Rodriguez." She starts to spell the name for me. Flip would say that this whole conversation is just so typical of Rosie, the way she can't believe you could figure the simplest thing out for yourself. But at the moment, I'm grateful that that's what she thinks.

"I'm sorry it isn't more," Rosie says, sounding genuinely regretful. "I just—OK, Lucy. They're over there. Under the—no, the *gray* box. Never mind, I'll get them. Look, Warren, my advice would be, try Juliet at Marta's for a couple of hours this afternoon, and you stay, too, at least part of the time. Then if you like it, leave her there longer tomorrow, and come on up here. If you can meet me at—" a sigh and a long pause, in which I imagine she's checking her book, "Oh, shit. Come at ten. No, nine-thirty. Can you do that, Warren? And I'll try to get some numbers together, schools or—Lucy, I said I'd get them! Warren, I really have to go."

Rosie was wrong about Marta's address—she's in Chelsea, too, less than five minutes away from me. Apparently she takes the children down to Washington Square Park when the weather is nice, which is why Rosie got mixed up. Anyway, I don't suppose any of that matters, except that it was very odd finding this other apartment a block and a half away from mine that was in such a different world. It would have been easier, somehow, if she had lived farther away. She lives in one of those old, un-gentrified buildings near Ninth Avenue, with a fresh white coat of paint in the hallway that has already been marked with red and black graffiti, that weird, crammed-together writing that you can't even read. And the steps in the stairway—of course, there's no elevator, but she only lives on the third floor—the steps are chipped and splintering, although they've also been recently repaired. What am I trying to say?

That everything is dingy and unkempt, and also, well cared for—but it simply doesn't make any difference. Well, I suppose if you were concerned about falling through an unrepaired step, it would make a difference that the steps were *repaired*. But having acknowledged that you *could* walk up the stairs, then you had to notice the graffiti, and the wobbly handrail, and the fusty smell (I don't even want to think what it is), and the weird yellow-gold light from the bright, unshaded bulbs.

Obviously, I've come here with Juliet—that was the whole point, wasn't it?—so I am already feeling more or less guilty for exposing her to all this. And, if you want to know the truth, I am also wondering if she actually does feel at home here, because who the hell knows where Madeleine has been living, or how. I mean, Chelsea is almost completely gentrified now, thank God, but this particular half-block is still full of dark-skinned people speaking Spanish. But then maybe Juliet's block was full of dark-skinned people speaking Arabic or Swahili or whatever. After all, look who her father was. I give her a sidelong glance, and she looks blank, terrified and self-contained, the way she did the morning we left Connecticut. But of course, this is all just one more new place for her.

Marta is nothing like what I imagined. Rosie had said "unemployed," which I suppose made me think slippers and bathrobe, although would I really leave Juliet with someone like that? On the other hand, what choice did I have? And on the phone, Marta had said practically nothing, so I thought of a timid little woman, maybe someone who didn't speak much English, which I wasn't ex- actly thrilled about. (Although of course, that *is* who most New Yorkers leave their children with, I do that much.) And then you know about the hall- way, and I don't even want to say what I imagined from that.

But when I see her, Marta just looks like a secretary. She's even wearing a straight skirt and a blouse, which I think is a bit odd for someone who's taking care of children, but maybe she had a job interview or an errand or some- thing. Only later did I think, maybe she wanted to make a good impression on me.

The apartment behind her is much nicer than the hallway, which I have to admit is an enormous relief. Of course, it's totally messy, with children's toys all over the place, but that's to be expected. But I can see that it's clean. And I know this sounds silly, but it mattered to me that it was light. The door opens into the front room, with tall, sunny windows overlooking the street. Off to the right is a dark hallway that I suppose leads to the rest of the apartment.

"Hello," Marta says uncertainly. Well, I have some manners. I hold out my hand to her, and after another uncertain moment, she takes it.

"Hi, I'm Warren. We spoke on the phone earlier today . . ."

"Yes, I remember," she says formally.

"And this is Juliet." Juliet, watching me, also holds out her hand. For the first time, Marta looks amused.

"Juliet," she says, as she shakes Juliet's hand. "That's a pretty name."

"It's French," says Juliet. "My mother and I live in Paris."

"Oh, really? I thought maybe Romeo and Juliet."

"By William Shakespeare," says Juliet. "But my mother says he got the name from France. She says it's really a French name. *Juliette.*"

"Oh, really?" says Marta again, clearly trying not to smile.

"Do you speak French?" Juliet asks. She's not being a snob, I want to say. She's only looking for someone who speaks her language. But Marta takes the question at face value.

"No, not French. I studied it in high school, but I never really learned it. Spanish, though. Do you speak Spanish, Juliet?"

"No," says Juliet, proudly. "I don't speak Spanish. I speak French." And again I want to explain, not because there's anything wrong with Spanish. But Marta still looks amused.

"Well, come on in, Warren and Juliet," she says. "Come in and meet the other children."

I am impressed by how quickly Juliet fits herself into this new space. Marta has a daughter who is nine, one year older than Juliet, who got home from school about half an hour ago (which is why Marta suggested we come when we did). Sara's skin is much darker than Marta's, who is a pale olive. Sara is that dirty—well, I'm sorry, but that's what it looks like to me—that dirty, wood-stained color, redwood I might call it. She leans against her mother and stares at Juliet, who stands very straight, as close to me as she can get without touching, and stares back.

"Sara, why don't you show Juliet your My Little Pony?" Marta suggests.

Juliet looks eager but restrained. Sara shrugs and goes off down the hall-way. Without looking at Marta or me, Juliet follows. Marta offers me coffee and leads me down the hallway, too, toward the kitchen, which is all the way at the back end of the building. I catch a glimpse of Juliet and Sara, sitting on the floor of Sara's bedroom, each with her hand on a toy horse. The horses are approaching each other, but the two girls aren't saying a word.

Marta laughs. "Sara, she's usually talking a mile a minute," she says. "And I can see your little girl is the same. But now they're both so shy!" She looks at me searchingly, and I wonder how much to tell her. All I had said on the phone was that I needed a place for an eight-year-old girl to stay, maybe per-manent, maybe temporary. Marta hands me a cup of coffee, espresso in the bottom of a blue mug.

"She's my niece, actually," I say. Then I think, well, if Juliet is going to be staying here any length of time, it would probably be helpful for the person taking care of her to know the situation. Even though I really don't like telling family business to strangers. It seems unfair to Madeleine.

I can almost hear Madeleine's barbed laughter. "Honestly, Warren," I imagine her saying, "Juliet didn't grow up in a hothouse like we did. At least I managed that. And I'm still her mother. Do you think she'll just forget about me?" *Like you did,* she thinks but does not say. Or maybe I'm the only one thinking that.

Anyway, I try to explain some of the story to Marta. "Juliet's mother, my sister, Madeleine—she had sort of a, a breakdown, I suppose. She's in a hospital in Paris. Well, just outside Paris. Paris is where they live."

Marta nods. "Juliet just said," she reminds me.

"Oh, right." Suddenly I want to give Marta a complete detailed report of every single thing that has happened since I first laid eyes on Juliet. I want to tell her exactly what I know, and then I want her to take over. I smile apologetically.

"Sara goes to St. Francis Xavier," Marta offers. "If you're looking to put Juliet in school. It's right in the neighborhood. It's a pretty good school. But maybe you're not Catholic."

I am about to say, no, of course not, when I realize that actually, I don't know what Juliet is. Who knows what Madeleine did when she was living in France, which is after all a Catholic country. Maybe she converted. Maybe that's why Juliet is so fascinated by cathedrals. That would be like Madeleine, taking up some new religious devotion. Or who knows, maybe she's a Muslim. Maybe that explains Juliet's last name.

"We weren't raised Catholic," I say, which seems safe. I don't have to confess that my sister and I haven't spoken in over eight years, do I? I don't have to tell that much family business.

Marta looks concerned and starts to ask another question when we hear the sound of a baby crying. "Oh, that's the end of nap time!" she says and sets her coffee cup down on the counter. The sink is crammed full of dirty dishes, but the counter and the stove are clean.

"Let me go get them up," Marta is saying. "And then I thought we would go to the park today. It's so sunny. You could come with us if you want."

"Maybe I could walk you there," I say. "I thought I should leave Juliet with you for a little while at least."

Marta gives me another searching look over her shoulder as she heads toward what is now the sound of two crying children. "Leave her tomorrow," she suggests. "Come play with us today."

So there we are walking down Eighth Avenue, Marta pushing a double stroller with her youngest, Rogelio, whom she tells me is eighteen months, a more bronze version of Sara's wood-stained skin, and a three-year-old whom she takes care of, Oscar, who is just black. Sara and Juliet actually have made friends, and they walk together, deep in conversation. I walk beside Marta, thinking how odd this would look to anyone who saw us, that Juliet and I would be with these people. Then I look at Juliet and Sara, side by side. Well, no, in fact, Juliet would not stand out. Except perhaps that she's so much more beautiful than the other children. And of course, better dressed. But otherwise, no, it's only I who must look out of place. Though I can't quite understand why Juliet, who looks so exactly like my sister, should appear more to belong with Marta's family than with me.

Because we're getting a late start today, we're not going to Washington Square Park after all, but to a smaller playground farther down Eighth Avenue. In Abingdon Square, actually, across the street from the Paris Commune, a restaurant where I've often had brunch. As if the general mortification of this day were not enough, now I am embarrassed to realize that I never even noticed the playground before. Further evidence of my general unfitness for things.

Juliet, having heard about Washington Square Park from me and I suppose from Sara, wants to know if that's what this is. "No way," says Sara. "This isn't anything *like* Washington Square." She glares at her mother. "We *never* go to Washington Square."

Marta is unconcerned. "We'll go tomorrow, if it's a nice enough day."

"But it *won't* be," says Sara. "It's *never* a nice day when we want to go."

"That's enough, Sara," says Marta. "Go show Juliet the jungle gym."

Juliet has been watching them, fascinated—as am I, actually—her eyes first on Sara, then on her mother. "No!" she says daringly now. "We don't want to go to the jungle gym. We want to go to Washington Square Park!" She doesn't quite have the name right; it comes out sounding like "Squarepark" is one word. "Right, Sara? That's what *we* want!"

Sara is shocked, then delighted to have an ally. "YES!" she says. "Yes! That's what *we* want!"

"And if we have to stay here at this park, we'll—"

"We'll run away!" says Sara.

"No," says Juliet, thrilled with herself. "We'll build a bomb, a huge, colossal, gargantuan bomb, and we'll put it *under* the jungle gym, and it will blow everybody up! Except Oscar and Rogelio. Because it's not *their* fault we have to stay at this park—"

"Which we *hate,*" adds Sara, fascinated by Juliet and the whole conversation. "And *then* we'll run away, right, Juliet?"

"Yes, and we'll take Oscar and Rogelio with us, so you'll never never never find them again—"

"Well, they wouldn't anyway," Sara points out. "They'll be all blown up."

I can't help it, I have to laugh.

"Stop *laughing* at us," says Juliet, really angry. "We *will,* that's what we'll do, so stop laughing!"

"Juliet," I say through my amusement, "you're being very rude. Apologize."

Juliet looks at me defiantly. Hasn't Madeleine taught her any manners at all? I can see Juliet weighing the situation like a diplomat: how important is it to her to stay on my good side versus how much she doesn't want to back down. The decision is all the harder because she can see I'm still amused and she's also angry about that. Apparently, she decides that my good will is worth more to her than any of the other considerations involved, and for one moment, I see what it costs her to decide this. Then she decides to make the apology her idea. "We're sorry, aren't we, Sara?" she says brightly. "Forgive us, please! Actually, this park is *just fine.* It's an exceptional, matchless, sublime park, isn't it, Sara? Thank you *so much* for bringing us here!" Then she runs off toward the jungle gym and Sara has to follow.

"I'm afraid she needs to learn better manners," I say apologetically as Marta settles the younger children in the sandbox. "I'll talk to her later. I suppose my sister—well, it can't have been easy, bringing up a child by herself. Though of course, you . . ."

"What?" says Marta, more or less politely.

"I only meant, I realize that you're bringing up two children by yourself—"

"Oh, no," says Marta. "What gave you that idea? I'm married." She shows me her wedding ring. I wonder if there are any more embarrassing things I could possibly do or say. Surely there must be a few more ways I could humiliate myself, if I really put my mind to it.

"Anyway, I'm sorry about Juliet," I say again.

Marta laughs. "She really knows a lot of words, doesn't she? A sublime park! She's quite a little poet."

I don't even know what to say at this point. Marta looks at me closely as I stare fixedly at the two girls, playing on the jungle gym. "Cheer up, Warren," I hear her say. "You've only had her for two days."

"Three days, actually."

"Oh, well, three days," says Marta. "In that case, never mind. You should be an expert by now."

Suddenly, I give in and just feel grateful. "In that as in all things," I say rue-fully, and surprisingly, Marta laughs.

After we leave Marta and the others at their corner of Eighth Avenue, I make another mistake. We need to get some things for dinner, so we stop at the store—actually, three stores, the bakery, the grocery store, and then the deli, because given what Juliet has for breakfast, we now need to buy more milk—and by the time we get home, Juliet is exhausted. And hungry. I seem to be accumulating little bits of information at an incredibly slow rate: Chil-dren are hungry by five, tired by six, exhausted by seven.

Juliet's exhaustion makes her sad and withdrawn, which I suppose is better than a tantrum. Maybe not. When I go into her room, she's sitting on the cor-ner of the bed, staring at the floor. Her room is still very much in transition. The foldout couch is crammed into the other corner of the room, along with some leftover boxes and the metal rack of shelves. We have managed to find her a child-sized bed, maple, with four spindly, shiny posters. Over the bed hangs a poster that Juliet chose, from the children's book *Madeline,* which seems to have been a special book for her and Madeleine. We haven't had time to get it framed, so I've just taped it up to the wall, which will have to be re-painted anyway. One corner of the poster is already curling down.

"Dinner's ready," I say. When she doesn't move, I sit down.

"Uncle Warren," she says finally, "after dinner, can I have a bubble bath?"

I can't believe she's been here three days and I haven't even thought about her needing to bathe. "Of course you can," I say. I wonder if I have any bubble bath.

"And will you sit with me while I have it?" she says, still not looking at me. "Sometimes I get lonely in the bathtub."

"Did Madeleine sit with you?" I say, to cover the fact that I don't know how to answer.

"Sometimes," she says in a very small voice. Then she looks at me. "If you don't want to, Uncle Warren, it's all right. I don't mind."

"No, I want to," I say. "After dinner, all right?"

She nods, still looking down at the floor. I stand up and take her hand. "Come on," I say. "Let's have dinner." I realize it's the first time I've touched her, I mean, when I didn't have to help her get her jacket on or something. Her hand is warm and uncertain inside mine.

I do find some bubble bath—I think it used to belong to Flip, but some-how I ended up packing it when I moved out. It's lily of the valley, a smell I don't even like, but maybe Juliet does. I am monitoring the rapidly filling tub from my place on the closed toilet seat when Juliet comes in, eager but sub-dued. "Is it ready yet?" she asks.

"Just about." Then it occurs to me I've probably made it too hot for a child, so I run some more cold into it. "Just let me make sure it's cool enough."

"No, Uncle Warren," she corrects me, "baths are supposed to be hot, not cool. I'll show you." She reaches out to put her hand under the faucet and I quickly grab her wrist.

"Juliet, no. It might be hot."

She gives me a scornful look. "I know all about hot water," she informs me. "Mama always used to let me test the bath water. For my bath *and* her bath."

"Really."

"Well, she didn't let me do it last year," Juliet says. "I mean, not last *month,* even. But this month, she said I was old enough."

I feel I should be taking charge, somehow, perhaps helping Juliet to get undressed. But she matter-of-factly steps out of her clothes and stands there with her back to me. Her bare, smooth back, her bottom, her legs, are all that same café-au-lait color, luminous in the reflection of the bathwater. Well, what did I expect? That she would be white inside her clothes?

I see one dark, thin, glowing leg go over the side of the tub. Then she steps all the way in and sinks down into the bubbles. I would never have expected the look on her face as she enters the bath—it's as though she's come home.

How curious am I about her body? How curious am I allowed to be? Once I had a boyfriend, the last serious boyfriend before Flip, actually, although we never lived together, who had a sister only a year or so younger than he. He used to take baths with her—when they were little, I mean. Why do I even know that? Because he used to want to take baths with me, which I found extremely uncomfortable. I mean, the lack of privacy. I suppose to him it was some way of going back to a time when he was completely un-self-conscious about his body. But it only made me think of taking showers in the locker room after gym class in junior high, which was not exactly a time in my sexual history that I wanted to repeat.

I watch Juliet slide all the way down under the sparkling white bubbles. Then her face—so much like my big sister's, *that* is the view from *my* childhood—rises up through the foam, her eyes closed tight, her head shaking, her pony tail flapping back and forth. She sighs with satisfaction and says matter-of-factly, "You know, I really needed to do that."

Remembering the scene in the park earlier, I manage not to laugh. Still, her expression changes. "What is it?" I ask.

"Nothing," she says quickly.

"No, Juliet, what is it? Tell me."

"I don't suppose you have any bath toys," she says in that hoping-against-hope tone she used to ask about cathedrals.

Suppose? Is she using my words already? Or has she said that before? I will think anything to keep from noticing that here is yet another disappointment. "I think I have something," I say finally. "Will you be all right if I leave you for just a minute?" She nods, a serious answer. I come back with some old plastic takeout containers and her face lights up.

"Oh, Uncle Warren," she says. "These are *perfect*. Thank you!" Then she looks at me sternly. "But I'm not allowed to play with them until you wash my hair."

"All right," I say. She turns the back of her head to me, and I pull at the elastic holding her hair in place. I haven't seen it down yet. Is this like the bath, something I've left undone? Or has she been brushing her hair, at night or in the morning, without my knowing?

She shakes out her hair, and it does stand out in dark, dramatic waves. Not at all like Madeleine, who has—or had—fine, wispy, pale brown hair, very nondescript. Juliet's hair is more like something out of Gauguin.

She turns to face me, and she isn't exotic anymore, she's just Juliet. I don't know how to see her. Madeleine's face, Gauguin hair, dark skin—and then sometimes, a facial expression that I recognize as mine. Which she's either picked up from me in the past three days, or which somehow Madeleine transmitted to her—how? Madeleine never looked anything like me. And then sometimes, she simply looks *familiar,* this person I simply—well, I don't *know* her, I suppose. Recognize, maybe. This person I recognize.

"Uncle Warren," Juliet says impatiently. "You're supposed to be washing my hair. Don't you care if I get clean or not?"

This person who makes me laugh. "Of course I care," I say. "I couldn't care more, actually. It's the most important thing on my mind, if you want to know the truth."

"Oh, right," says Juliet. "You shouldn't tease me, Uncle Warren. It's very rude."

"I'll try to remember that," I say, reaching for the shampoo.

Juliet has to talk me through the shampooing process, but we manage pretty well. Then she starts to play with the plastic bowls. As best as I can follow, it's some elaborate game where one of them is a boat and it has to rescue people on one of the other bowls, except that there are monsters floating under one, and a pirate ship with space invaders on another one that also doubles as a mermaid. She is completely absorbed, talking and answering in many different voices, but the moment I even shift my weight on the closed toilet seat, she looks up at me in alarm.

"I'm not leaving," I say.

"Uncle Warren!" she says impatiently. "This is my play time. You're supposed to be quiet now."

"Oh, right," I say. So I suppose she does want me to be here. But apparently that's all she wants. Apparently that's enough.

"Now we have to sing the magic song," one of her characters announces. And Juliet starts to sing:

> *A la claire fontaine, m'en allant promener,*
> *J'ai trouvé l'eau si belle, que je m'y suis baignée;*
> *Il y a longtemps que je t'aime, jamais je ne t'oublierai.*
>
> *Sous les feuilles d'un chêne, je m'y suis fait sechée,*
> *De la plus haute branche, un rossignol chantait;*
> *Il y a longtemps que je t'aime, jamais je ne t'oublierai.*
>
> *Chante, rossignol, chante, toi qui a le coeur gai,*
> *Tu as le coeur à rire; moi, j'en ai à pleurer;*
> *Il y a longtemps que je t'aime, jamais je ne t'oublierai.*

I don't say anything, but I must have made some sound, or maybe Juliet can feel my expression change, because she looks at me again, worried and impatient.

"Did your mother teach you that song?" I say, although of course I know the answer. She nods, still uncertain, and I have a flash of what life is like for her these days, never knowing what ordinary thing now signals danger. Like today at the playground—even if Madeleine did teach Juliet some kind of discipline, she would obviously never have said what I did. And of course, Madeleine would know to give Juliet a bath, and brush her hair, and have bath toys, and God knows what else that I don't even know I'm not doing until Juliet finds the courage to tell me.

"It's only that I always really liked that song," I explain. "I always liked that song *a lot*. I thought it was so sad, and so beautiful, it always made me think there was some other place, some other beautiful place, that your mother knew about and I didn't. Your mother used to sing it when I was little. Not as little as you. But when she was in high school, and learning French, and I was still, well, pretty little. I wanted her to teach it to me, and she tried, but I didn't know French yet, so I could never remember it."

"You could have just sung the music," says Juliet, trying to be helpful.

"Maybe," I say, "but I couldn't remember that very well either."

"But when you heard me, then you did."

"Exactly. And then later, when I did learn French—" How can I explain this part? "She couldn't— She was away at school by then. And the times she came home—she was too—busy to teach me." Against my will, I see Madeleine's room. That stony landscape, that glowing piece of fabric art. "So I never learned that song, and then your mother went away to live in Paris, and for years and years I never even heard that song, until you sang it here. That's why I was so surprised."

"You could have come visited us in Paris," Juliet says. "Even if my mother was still too busy, I could have sung it for you there."

"Well, that's clearly what I should have done," I say. "Did she tell you what the words mean?"

"Uncle Warren!" Juliet says in her new favorite phrase. I suppose now she knows she can get away with that, at least. "I speak French. And English. Do you want *me* to tell *you?*"

I also speak French and English, I want to tell her. But I say, "Yes, please."

" 'A la claire fontaine': An English translation," Juliet announces. She stares straight ahead as she recites:

> *By the clear fountain, when I was going out for a walk,*
> *I found the water so beautiful, I took a bath there.*
> *I have loved you for a long time, I'll never forget you.*
>
> *Under the leaves of a—a* chêne,

she falters. *An oak,* I almost say, but I stop myself in time.

> *Under the leaves of a* chêne ["That's a tree," she says.]*, I dried myself.*
> *From the highest branch, a—*

She stumbles, but this word she retrieves, triumphantly,

> *—a* nightingale *sang.*
> *I have loved you for a long time. I'll never forget you.*
>
> *Sing, nightingale, sing, you who have a heart that's gay.*
> *You have a heart to laugh; I have one to cry.*
> *I have loved you for a long time. I'll never forget you.*

She breathes a sigh of relief.

"Thank you, Juliet," I say. "I'm glad Madeleine taught you that song."

Juliet shakes her head. "Mama didn't teach me. I learned by myself. Because she always sang that song, so I heard it, and I have a very good memory, Uncle Warren. I have an excellent memory, if you want to know the truth. She always sang that song when she was in love. So I heard it, and I learned it, and then when I wanted to, I could sing it by myself."

I smile. "That's when she sang the song in high school, too, actually. Whenever she was in love."

Juliet smiles with me. And I wonder what that smile means. Does she like remembering when Madeleine was in love? Were things better then, lighter, happier? Because what I remember is, "Oh, Madeleine, you were *always* in love, always rising into hope, always falling into heartbreak. But either way, you always sang the same song." Which I now find incredibly sad. Not least because that seems to be my history, too, now, however many years I spent believing that Madeleine's life was totally different from mine. *I have loved you a long time.* Well, it seemed long then. Now it seems way too short. *I'll never forget you*—a blessing or a curse? Here I sit before a tub perfumed with lily of the valley, a scent I don't even like, and I find myself smiling.

Well, obviously Juliet isn't thinking any of that. Or is she? Is there a point where anything that reminds you of the beloved simply makes you smile, no matter what the circumstances? We are talking about Madeleine, and it makes Juliet smile. We are talking about love, and it makes me smile. I remember Madeleine coming home from some date in high school—was it Christmas break? Summer? I'm sure the man or woman in question was a terrible person who eventually broke her heart in some apparently new and shocking way, but it didn't matter: she was glowing with happiness, shining with the glamour of a dream finally coming true, against all odds, against all hope. I wanted *that*—what she had. At the very least, I wanted to know the magic song.

I blink away the threatening tears, I get Madeleine's child out of the bath, and I ask her to teach me the song. And as I dry Juliet's strange, familiar body, I finally learn it.

Juliet goes to bed easily enough, but later that night, she has a nightmare. The force of it is so strong that it wakes me up, all the way over in my room, where I was sleeping, dreaming of Flip, if you must know, though I would certainly not have remembered anything about the dream if I hadn't been shaken out of the middle of it by the shock waves from Juliet's room. In my dream, Flip was laughing at me, not the affectionate, teasing laughter I actually do remember, but exactly the way somebody would laugh when he finally discovered your worst secret. "Nobody would consider *you* a fit parent," he said, which I was embarrassed to realize in my befuddled waking state was of course exactly what my father had said to me the other day, and since two men more unlike in every possible way than Flip and my father could hardly be imagined—and of course, I realize that's no accident. I haven't done *everything* wrong. But since they *are* so different, I wasn't sure what I was trying to tell myself by conflating them. The obvious meaning seemed far *too* obvious.

So I lie there in my tangled bedclothes, trying to pull myself up out of that horrible image, when I feel a huge, crashing wave knocking me sideways. The mate to the one that had woken me up. And then another, and another. My whole body vibrates with the shock. I can feel the contours of Juliet's dream—I can't avoid feeling them—and when I shut my eyes, I see it through her eyes. I *am* her, buried under a monstrous mountain of ice-green water, clear and tinted like glass, a pressing weight, a massive suffocating sea, cold and full of bubbles, and when she—and I—try to swim up, up, to where we hope the sunlight is, to where the water is light and friendly, it turns out to be hopeless, there's far too much water. We can't give in and drown, but we can't save ourselves, either. I feel the terror, but worse than that is the shame: However hard we swim, it will never be enough. There is nothing to expect but this.

Then I am outside the dream, watching Juliet in it. I see her frightened eyes, her determined mouth, her lips trembling with the first faint wish to surrender. *Give in,* the ocean would say if it were interested enough to communicate. *Give in and save yourself the trouble.* And she wants to. Or maybe she doesn't want to, but she thinks she should.

So here is a new worst secret: once again, I don't go after her. I know it's only a dream. And she isn't crying or screaming or doing any other physical thing to verify that she really *is* having a nightmare. There might even be people who would say, Well, it is *her* nightmare, and she has the right to have it by herself.

But I know that isn't true. I know that what she really has the right to is someone who'll come in and tell her that she doesn't have to drown. Only it won't be me.

FRIDAY
Today we have to be at Marta's by eight-thirty if I'm going to get to Rosie's office by nine-thirty. I was raised to be punctual anyway, and given how kind it was of Rosie to make this time for me, I would especially like to be punctual

for her. So Juliet and I have to rush, which we've never had to do before, and now I find out exactly how bossy and impatient I can be, too. There's a moment where she's telling me, "I don't *have* to tie my shoes, you know. Mama lets me leave the laces open." And I am saying, "Well, I don't *care* what your mother says. *I* say you have to tie your laces, and you have to do it *right now!*" And suddenly I want to sit down and laugh at this ridiculous shouting match. I don't know why it seems so funny, but it's too bad that it does, because Juliet thinks I am laughing at her, which makes her even angrier, and she storms out of the room, and we lose another five minutes.

Remembering how Marta managed Sara yesterday, I am sure she never has fights like this. But when we get to Marta's at five minutes to nine, the house is full of yelling that is far louder than anything I've ever heard, in my home or anywhere else. Which of course makes me wonder again about leaving Juliet here.

Marta opens the door, looking harried. She's wearing jeans and a man's shirt that doesn't even look like hers, more like something of her husband's that she quickly threw on—I hope not just to answer the door. I hope she wasn't running around half-dressed, with all those children. I can hear both Oscar and Rogelio crying in the background, and Sara fighting with somebody—her father? Or is she yelling at Marta?

"Hello, Warren, hello, Juliet," Marta says, trying to smile at us. "Today is very hectic around here." Her accent seems stronger than I remember it.

"MOM!" says Sara, running in. "Oscar *still* won't give me back my homework, and he's *drooling* on it. It's going to be totally messy. And I'll get in trouble, and it will be all *your* fault, because you didn't make him stop. And Rogelio needs to be changed, I can smell him all the way over in my room." Then she sees Juliet. "Hi, Juliet," she says. "Are you coming to my school?"

"Not today," Marta says. "Sara, for heaven's sake, if Rogelio needs to be changed, go change him. Juliet, you go too."

"But MOM," says Sara. "My HOMEWORK."

"If you give him a toy, he'll give it back to you," says Marta. The whole time she has been moving around the living room, frantically leafing through the papers spread out on every available surface.

"He *won't* give it to me," Sara whines. "I tried."

"Sara," says Marta sharply. "I already told you once today, I don't have time for this. Go work it out, and take Juliet with you. *Ahora mismo*—right now!"

Sara explodes in a big, dramatic sigh, and stalks out of the room. Juliet is transfixed, which Marta actually finds a moment to notice in the midst of her feverish paper-sorting. "Go with Sara, Juliet," she says, gently but firmly. "Go on, she's in Rogelio's room. You know where that is." Juliet throws me a help-less glance, but she goes.

"I'm sorry it's so crazy around here," Marta says to me, throwing a folder down onto the couch in disgust. "The city sent us a letter yesterday, they're screwing around with our lease—excuse my language, but—Sara!" she yells suddenly. "Bring me in the blue folder from the shelf in the bedroom. The top shelf!"

"I can't," Sara's voice comes back. "I'm changing Rogelio."

"Then let Juliet do it!" Marta calls.

"No," Sara calls back. "She doesn't know where it *is*!"

"Then *tell* her, *ay bendito*!" Marta yells. "Right now, right now, we're in a hurry!" She looks at me apologetically. "We have to go to Housing Court this morning," she explains. "Not Housing Court really, but the one for people with buildings from the city. They sent us a certified letter, and somehow it got delivered to Iraida, and then she just tells me about it today? Her name is still on their list from ten years ago? What is going on in this city? Anyway, I'm very sorry, but I'm the only one who can go—it won't take long. But I have to be there by ten, and I have to find the—" She breaks off as Juliet comes in, shy but important, carrying a blue folder. Maria ruffles through it and breathes an enormous sigh of relief. "Yes! Thank God! Thank you, Juliet! Not in this house five minutes and you find this thing I've been looking for all morning. . . ."

Juliet looks incredibly pleased. She waits a moment to see if there's an-other errand, then she heads back down the hall. "Sara!" we can hear her call-ing. "I found it! It *was* in the blue folder."

Marta sighs again. "OK," she says. "Now maybe we can get out of here." She looks down at herself. "As soon as I get changed." She takes a step toward the hallway, then stops. "We won't be there long," she tells me. "Someone just has to hand this in in person, and I'm the only one who can do it. Once we're down by City Hall, I'll take the kids to Chinatown or something. It will be an adventure."

Sara slams by us, backpack over her shoulder. "And now I'm going to be LATE," she says. "And I'll tell them it was all your fault!"

"Sara!" Marta says in a dangerous tone that stops Sara mid-step out the door. "Excuse us, Warren," Marta says, and she takes Sara a few steps down the hall.

"When there's an emergency," Marta says grimly, "I expect cooperation from you. Do you understand? And I expect you to treat me with respect. Do you understand *that*?"

"But, Mom, I hate being late. You have to stand in front of the class for ten minutes, and everybody laughs at you. And—"

"Sara, did I make myself clear?"

Silence from Sara.

"So what do you do now?"

"I'm *sorry* I was rude to you," Sara says defiantly. "Except I'm really not. Why do you want me to apologize when I don't really feel sorry? Do you want me to *lie?*"

Even from the living room, I can feel Marta's annoyed surrender. "This isn't over," she says as Sara dashes past me out the door. "We're going to talk about this tonight."

Marta comes back out into the living room. Clearly, she's annoyed that I'm still here, but she's trying to be polite.

"Um, how are you going to get everyone down to City Hall?" I say.

She seems surprised that I would ask. "Oh, we'll take the A train down to Canal and walk over," she says. "It's not too far."

"You could take a taxi."

She laughs. "Right, a taxi."

"No, really, I could—Let me—" I reach into my pocket.

"Oh, no, Warren, don't be silly," Marta is saying, but there is this embarrassed frozen moment, because clearly, she would much rather take a taxi at this point than struggle up and down the subway steps with three children and a double stroller. And I have my own mixed feelings, because obviously, I've got the money, I mean, fifteen dollars for two taxi rides won't break me, but also this isn't actually my problem, and I am already paying Marta to take care of Juliet, which really shouldn't include trips down to Housing Court. So reluctantly, I hold out the money, and after a moment, reluctantly, she takes it, and then there is this embarrassed pause that obviously neither of us can afford—it's already nine-fifteen, which means I'll have to take a taxi up to Rosie's, too—and then Juliet comes in, carrying Rogelio.

"Could I change him next time?" she says to Marta. Then she realizes something is going on and she pulls back. Well, Madeleine probably never had to rush anywhere—she didn't work. She didn't even have other children, only Juliet. They could afford to take the whole afternoon, strolling around to the baker's and the grocer's and the dairy, sipping coffee and lemonade in a neighborhood café. Why does that make me so angry? It's not as though I have to get up and go to an office every day. It's not even as though Marta does.

For the first time, I find myself wanting something for Juliet: that she should be able to walk into a home like this and be comfortable here. Something I will obviously never be able to do. So it's actually a good thing that we never got to Pittsburgh. He would probably have seen me in a whole new light.

"Good luck," I say to Marta. "Have fun in Chinatown. Bye, Juliet."

"Uncle Warren," she says, "Sara changed Rogelio, but do you know what I did? I found his favorite toy, which I noticed from when I was here yesterday, because I'm very, very good at noticing things, and I *noticed* that he really liked this blue monkey, not the plastic one, the one made out of—well, it's like a beanbag toy. You know, the Beanie Babies? Sara showed me. They're so cute. And I was the one who knew he liked that toy, and I gave it to him, and *that's* when he stopped crying."

Marta tucks the money into her jeans pocket. "Thank you, Juliet," she says. "Thank you, Warren." I wave goodbye and dash out the door.

Rosie's office is on the Upper West Side, up near Ninety-sixth Street. By some miracle, I find a taxi, we *don't* run into traffic, and I'm only ten minutes late. Which is bad enough, I think, bracing myself for the onslaught of noise that I heard yesterday. But when I get to the office, it's deserted. There's only Rosie, sitting at a desk by the window.

She's so absorbed in her paperwork that she doesn't even notice me. "Hi, Rosie," I say, rather awkwardly.

At first she looks completely startled, and totally annoyed as well. I'm surprised how hurt I feel. Then she recognizes me and her face lights up in welcome. "Warren!" she says, leaping up to hug me. "You made it! Wow—you have a whole new person to take care of. These are amazing days, aren't they? Sit down, sit down—can I get you something? Oh, I don't think there is anything. Except tap water, which I'm sure you don't want, because who wants that, right? Everybody's gone to a staff meeting downtown, but I'm excused because I'm not even supposed to be here, I'm supposed to be up at Olympia. I was going to have to cancel you, and then they canceled me. Well, put me off, till eleven. Which gives us until ten-thirty. So, we were lucky, huh?"

I think Flip used to get jealous of Rosie and me sometimes, because I liked her so much. (He complained about Rosie continually, but you could see that he wanted her all to himself.) But when he asked me what I of all people could possibly see in her, all I could do was shrug. I don't even like her physical style. Sometimes she's fat and sometimes she's almost fat, and she has this big, frizzy wild hair, which is always getting in her eyes. She almost always needs a haircut.

I have no idea why she likes me so much, either, because I disagree with her on virtually everything, and disagreeing with Rosie is no minor detail—

she lives to argue. Plus she's pretty generally biased against people with money, and she knows how little I think of unions. (I mean, at least the employers are *doing* something—making something, or providing a service. What do the unions do?) And yet here I am, in the middle of her tacky little office, grinning with pleasure to see her. It drove Flip crazy.

"I'm sorry I'm late," I begin, and she interrupts me.

"Oh, please. Who can be on time in New York City? And with a child? I'm surprised you got here at all. So tell me about—Juliet, right? Or is it *Juliette?*"

I'm touched that the French pronunciation for Juliet's name would even occur to Rosie. "Well, I've been calling her Juliet, because—I don't know why exactly. Because she calls herself, or Madeleine called her *Juliette,* you know, the French pronunciation—oh, right, you just said it."

It's possible that a flicker of annoyance crosses Rosie's face again, but she brushes it away and comes back with another rush of questions. "Do you think that maybe you wanted to have a special name for her, I mean, one that was yours and not your sister's? Or did you want to think of her as more American—or maybe to help *her* feel more American? Because you know, Warren, children are terrible about strange names, and it's kind of a drag to never have anyone pronounce your name correctly, so really, if you've been using the American pronunciation, I think you've actually done her a favor. Or wasn't that what you had in mind?"

"I don't know," I say slowly. I am torn, because I would like to follow her down this intriguing path—I haven't gotten to talk to *anyone* about Juliet, and more or less any part of that experience would be a relief to share. But also, we have only—well, forty-five minutes now (even if she didn't have to go, I have four clients starting at eleven o'clock), and I'm worried about all the things I *have* to know. With Rosie, it's always hard not to feel that the conversation has slipped completely out from under your control.

But I find myself saying, "You know, I think she would like it if I spoke to her in French, and I certainly could. I mean, my French isn't great, but it's probably good enough for an eight-year-old child."

Rosie laughs and says, "Well, if she's a native speaker—" I stop and she looks puzzled. And then ashamed. "Go on, go on," she says. "I forget, when I interrupt, you think you have to let *me* finish."

"I'm not even sure what I'm trying to say."

"You think she wants to hear you speak French to her—the language her mother uses, right?"

"Well, I'm not sure, because if Madeleine only spoke to her in French, her English wouldn't be so good."

"Oh, I see," Rosie says. "So if you and she spoke French, then the two of you would have this special French secret, the way she and Madeleine have this special American secret. And then you'd really be her family. And you think she might want this, but for some reason *you* don't."

Maybe this is why I like Rosie, even while finding her totally disconcerting. Nobody else I know would even think that, let alone say it to my face. "I suppose so," I say. "I don't know *why* I don't, though."

"Oh, for heaven's sake, Warren," Rosie says, "of *course* you feel overwhelmed. A whole child, my God. I mean, she's your niece. She's family. But you've never seen her before. That must be strange."

"You know what's the strangest?" I say, finally sinking into this conversation with relief. "The oddest thing is that she looks just like Madeleine, but because she's Black, she doesn't. I mean, she's part of my family, and I can see that in her. But she also looks like nobody else in our family, like nobody else ever *will* look in our family. She looks much more like part of Marta's family, for example, although not really that either, of course, because she has these kind of exquisite features, and this really beautiful skin, that classic café-au-lait color, not exactly like Lena Horne, but that kind of wash of color, and incredible hair, which again is so odd for me, because there's Madeleine's face and then there's this dramatic dark wavy hair—"

"Well," says Rosie coldly. "You're certainly lucky she isn't fat, black, and shiny, with nappy hair and big lips. Then it might be *really* hard to see her as part of your family."

I am so taken aback, I don't know what to say. Rosie and I have disagreed lots of times, but she never sounded so angry. So personal.

"I mean, Jesus Christ, Warren, who the fuck do you think you are? Listen to yourself, talking about how exquisite she is. She's going to be facing the worst kind of racism here, Warren, the absolutely worst kind. Do you have any idea what's even going on in this city? It isn't going to protect her, having white family—in fact, that will probably make it harder for her. Do you have any idea the kind of assault that African Americans and Latinos are facing every day? One of our lawyers, Elena, she got picked up in Washington Heights by some cop, not even for a busted taillight, because by this point, she knows better than to have *anything* wrong with her car, but just for who knows why, and all of a sudden, she's guilty of a minor violation, and it's Friday night, so she's going to have to spend the weekend in jail. A lawyer, Warren, a nice, middle-class lawyer who graduated from Columbia Law School, so you can't even say she doesn't know her way around the city. And when she told the cop she was a lawyer and she wanted to know why she was being arrested, he charged her with resisting arrest, and they handcuffed her, Warren, and believe me, if she hadn't've been a woman, they would have beaten her up for sure, and as it was, they shoved her around plenty—I mean, she was a lawyer, but she had dark skin, although I don't know if it was exactly café-au-lait, but you can't talk about people like that, come on, Warren, if you're going to be raising an African-American child, you've got to do better than that."

"I'm not sure that I am going to be raising her, actually," I say. "That depends on Madeleine, doesn't it?"

"Yes, and look at how you talk about Madeleine," Rosie goes on, as though I had personally insulted her. "You're a man, and a gay man, so you get to have all the sex you want, you people aren't even monogamous, not even now, when it's so dangerous, everyone is dying from AIDS, and you *still* go out and do whatever you want—and then you have the nerve to blame *Madeleine?* You don't even know if she *wanted* Juliet—you talk about it like she's just this slut who runs around having miscellaneous sex, I mean anonymous sex, but even if Juliet was an accident, so what? So Madeleine raised her for eight years, while the rest of you are still running around having all the sex you want, no consequences, nothing to take care of afterward. Even Flip—he gets to be an artist, and OK, so it isn't easy for him, but he can do it. Madeleine tries that and it drives her crazy—I mean, doesn't that tell you anything, Warren, about what she was up against, a woman who wanted to be an artist and have sex . . ."

She stops when she sees the expression on my face. Which I imagine is complicated, because of course, while I think that everything she's saying is complete nonsense, I am sorry to say that there's something in it that I recognize. That tone of being betrayed. That's mine, too.

Suddenly she shifts, totally and completely. "Oh, God, Warren," she says, "I'm sorry. You didn't—" She stops to pick her words carefully. "I can see how it wouldn't be helpful to hear all that in just that way," she says finally. "And I can just imagine how much you must be going through—I mean, I can *only* imagine it, because I don't even have children, let alone an eight-year-old to take care of out of the blue. I just—I hear this stuff so much, it's hard to hear it from you, Warren. Help me out. What am I trying to say here?"

Help *you* out? I want to say. In God's name, why—so you can insult me some more?

But it's really hard not to answer Rosie. So I find myself saying, "I think you're trying to say that I should have more sympathy for Madeleine, and for your lawyer, and for everybody else who is having such a hard time these days. But Rosie. It really isn't my fault."

Now she looks more distressed than ever, but at least she doesn't look possessed. She thinks for a moment. "OK, Warren," she says. "Try this one. You're on some ship—I don't know, like the *Titanic*. You have this life, you're going along, and suddenly, bam, this huge iceberg rams your ship, and all of a sudden, you're in mortal danger. Even if you do know how to swim, it's the North Atlantic—the cold alone will kill you. Your only hope is to get yourself into a lifeboat. Only now, you've got to get yourself *and* Juliet into a lifeboat, right? Isn't that why you called in such a state?"

"More or less," I say cautiously.

"OK, but Warren," she says. "And bearing in mind that of *course* you want to save this innocent eight-year-old child from drowning."

Well, that's an unfortunate image, under the circumstances.

"But come *on,* Warren. At least you're up there on deck. What about all the eight-year-old girls whose parents *don't* have money? And all the rest of them down there in steerage? Beaten down with clubs before they can even *get* to the lifeboats."

"What do you expect?" I ask her. "Should the people with money have stepped aside and let the other ones have all the room? Would that have made it any better?"

Rosie bites her lip. "I just want them to be real to you," she says.

"You don't think Madeleine is real to me? She was my big sister. My *older* sister, Rosie. I was in junior high the first time she went crazy. There wasn't a whole lot I could have done."

"Oh, Warren." Suddenly, she takes a small bottle of something—oil? lotion?—out of her desk and pours a blob of it into her palm and rubs her hands together. Then she grabs *my* hands, pressing them between her palms. "Stop a minute," she says softly.

I try to pull my hands away. "Come on, Rosie . . ."

"No, Warren, seriously, this will help you relax." She looks at me sternly. "It's not going to kill you."

It seems easier to give in than to argue, or maybe there actually is something soothing about her hands massaging mine, her skin against my empty skin, her thumbs pressed into my palms. . . . Slowly, very slowly, something in me loosens and lets go. The lotion—sandalwood? musk?—has a faint, spicy smell that grows stronger as Rosie's hands grow warmer, and then my hands are warmer, too. And then she lets me go.

"Did it work?" she says. "You look much better."

"I do feel better," I say, flexing my hands. "What was it?"

She shrugs. "Oh, I think you're supposed to do it to feet, actually. But *that's* not very practical, is it? All the little things you learn to keep yourself going when you're working at ninety miles an hour." She starts to push herself to her feet. "Come on, Warren, we still have about thirty-five minutes, don't we? Let's get *out* of this office and go get something to eat, because I have back-to-back meetings from eleven to five, and then I have to—anyway, come on."

She starts loading herself down with bag after bag: a briefcase, a carpetbag stuffed full of leaflets, one of those African woven straw bags that she has packed with folders, a bulging travel bag with the union logo on it, and her purse, a huge shoulder-strap affair. I would offer to help carry something, but by the time I realize what she's doing, she's already wearing all of them. "My God, Rosie, what have you got in there? Do you really need all that?"

The flicker of annoyance returns. "Well, obviously, or I wouldn't be taking them, would I? I have a very long day coming up, Warren, and—" She stops herself in mid-sentence. "I don't think I should say another word until I've eaten something," she says grimly. "You talk. Tell me how Marta is working out."

"Actually, Juliet really seems to like it there," I say, as we get into the elevator, "although it seems too soon to tell. Both because it's only been a couple of days, and because—well, I keep wondering what's going to happen when Juliet actually realizes that she's not going back to Paris any time soon. She keeps talking about Madeleine in the present tense."

Rosie nods. "Whereas you think of her in the past tense."

"I didn't say that."

I'm starting to have more sympathy with Flip's view of Rosie, if you want to know the truth. Which makes it doubly disconcerting to hear her say, "I wondered how you'd feel leaving Juliet with Marta, because I know that building has had a lot of problems."

"Yes, actually, Marta had to go to Housing Court or some city office this morning, some emergency."

Rosie sighs. "I *thought* the situation was OK, finally, or believe me, Warren, I would never have recommended her to you. And I figured you could figure it out for yourself, once you got there. I mean, Marta isn't the problem. People are just— We're all being terrifically assaulted, and it's hard to know what's safe, or what's, I don't know, possible."

"What *is* the problem, Rosie? I still don't know what you're talking about."

Rosie steers us into one of those typical New York Greek diners, deserted at this hour of the morning. We settle into a back booth, and Rosie orders an omelette. I really hate the food, and the coffee, in places like this, but it seems rude to sit and not eat, so I get a bran muffin and juice. They can't screw that up too badly.

"That was one of the buildings that the squatters got from the city," Rosie explains. "The cases for all the other buildings like that are pretty much settled, I think. But for some reason, there's still some odd tax problem with Marta's building, and the city keeps acting like they owe huge amounts of money in back taxes, and they have to keep going down there and explaining that no, they don't. So the case gets settled, and then somehow, someone decides that no, they do, and they have to go down there all over again. It doesn't ever seem to go any further than that, but of course, it's pretty nerve-wracking."

I've managed to follow about half of this, which I suppose is evident to Rosie, because she says, "You know, in the late seventies, the landlords were abandoning all those buildings, and the tenants just took them over, not really squatters, because they had come in paying rent, but then the landlords left, plus they hadn't paid their taxes in about a million years, the landlords, I mean, and the *tenants* certainly couldn't afford to pay what the landlords owed—not that they should have anyway, obviously—and so the city had to work something out. And at first they figured, OK, fine, let the tenants have these rotten old buildings that nobody wanted anyway. But then of course, there was that terrific real-estate boom in Chelsea, and suddenly every landlord in the city wanted to own a potential co-op building there, and then it got really ugly."

"No," I say, "that's when the neighborhood really improved."

"Oh, Warren," Rosie says. The waiter brings our food, and she starts to eat. "Maybe we shouldn't talk about this," she says. "I did get you some information about schools." Her mouth still full, she bends down under the table and searches in one of her bags, somehow managing to come up with a few sheets of paper in time to take the next bite. "It isn't all that helpful," she says, her mouth full, "because most of the information numbers have been eliminated—with all the cutbacks, I don't know what you'll find. Maybe I can think about it more next week."

I suddenly realize Rosie is talking about public school. "Rosie, this is so kind of you, really, but it's all right. I can take it from here."

Rosie gives me a piercing look. "Look, Warren, there are magnet schools, and special programs and—"

"Rosie, I can't believe even you would think I would ever put Juliet in the New York City public schools." She purses her lips, in and out. It almost looks as if she's going to cry. "Rosie, if you had a child, would you put her there?"

She looks completely discouraged. "I know, I know, even Marta sends her kids to parochial school." Then, suddenly, she laughs. "Well, *I* couldn't afford private school anyway," she says. "And *I* went to Catholic school, so I certainly wouldn't send any child of mine *there.* So I would have to fight for our public education, Warren."

"I can't believe you think I should make a child fight that battle."

"Warren, that's kind of the point—all the children who *are* in public school are already fighting it."

"I don't see how it helps them to put one more child in danger."

"I don't know, Warren," Rosie says. "You have this huge, overwhelming, I would have to say inordinate. Inappropriate, even—sense of responsibility for every emotional pimple, every emotional ingrown toenail of about four people. Some of whom I also care for, so I'm not saying you shouldn't care about them. But it's like there's no limit. And yet the idea that you're part of a system that puts people like Marta out on the street, a system that used to send goons to beat people up to get them to move out of Chelsea so that their apartments could be sold to—well, excuse me, Warren, but to rich gay men—I mean the idea that you have any connection to *those* people, that leaves you completely cold."

"I feel responsible for the people I know," I say with as much dignity as I can manage. I'm not going to touch *inordinate,* let alone *inappropriate.* I know we both have to leave in ten minutes, so I suppose it seems easier simply to wait this out than to make some kind of statement by leaving now. It's not as though I ever have to see her again.

Rosie shakes her head. "You're a psychic," she says. "Your specialty is what's invisible to the rest of us." Unexpectedly, she laughs. "Do you know what Flip said about us once? You and me, I mean. He said, 'Warren knows everything and you,'" she points to herself, "'can do everything, so there aren't any jobs left for me.'"

Well, if she's going to talk about *Flip* . . . "And what did you say?"

"I told him it was his job to create something new," Rosie says ruefully, "and you can just imagine what a big hit *that* made. I was then subjected to the fifteen-minute condensed version of the 'You just don't understand how hard it is to be an actor' speech, and I tell you, it was only condensed because we were in a movie theater and the first feature was *Holiday,* and Flip is as bad as I am about missing even one second of a movie."

"*Holiday,*" I repeat. "By Philip Barry."

"Mmmm," Rosie says, and looks dreamy. "Isn't Cary Grant the perfect man? In that, anyway. Except that you can't understand how he could prefer that rich sister to Katharine Hepburn for even a moment. Well, Hepburn was rich, too, granted. But she didn't *like* being rich. She was just waiting for Cary

Grant to take her out of that huge mansion so she could be poor and bohemian like him."

"I wouldn't know," I say rather wistfully. "I always identified with Neddy."

"The alcoholic brother? The one who has the great intellectual affinity with Grant and Hepburn and all their bohemian friends but he's afraid to leave the house?"

"More or less."

"Oh, Warren." She's as distressed as if I'd actually told her something important. "But she's going to come back for him, you know. Once she and Cary Grant are secure. She says—" and here Rosie does her best version of a Hepburn accent, but it comes out sounding like Brooklyn Irish, in my opinion—"I'll come back for you, Neddy, you see if I don't!"

"I'll be here," I say.

"What?"

"That's what Neddy says. He toasts her with his martini glass and says, 'I'll be here.' "

"Oh, Warren," Rosie says again. Then she looks stern and starts to say something, but I quickly head her off.

"So help me, Rosie, if you start to tell me how many people were unemployed during the Depression while Philip Barry was writing that play, I'll—"

"Oh, yeah? What will you do?" Rosie says, getting up. "Anyway, he wrote the play in 1927. They just made the *movie* during the Depression." She starts draping herself with her collection of bags. Then she gives me that piercing look again. "*Not* that I approve for one second of you blithely going off and putting Juliet into a classroom with a lot of *other* rich heirs to a family fortune. But if you absolutely insist on private school, you might try Parkston. At least they *say* they believe in social responsibility, though at their prices, they obviously think social responsibility is a privilege reserved for the ruling class." I must be staring at her blankly, because she sighs impatiently and says, "One of my co-workers sends her kids there. Here, I'll write it down for you."

I am slowly folding the paper up and putting it away when I hear her say, in a completely different tone of voice, "So, Warren, you're still doing readings?"

"Yes."

"Maybe I'll make an appointment sometime. If you'd be willing. If it wouldn't be too awkward." She looks completely at a loss. And do you know what's really odd? After all the insulting things she's said and done, my heart goes out to her. I actually do wish I could help her. Which is not a feeling I have very often, about anybody.

"I'd be happy to—"

"If I could afford you," she says, and laughs nervously.

"My God, Rosie, how can you even say that? I couldn't possibly charge you."

"Oh, well, then, I wouldn't feel right about coming," she says, still looking down. "After all, it's your work. It's what you do for a living."

"After all the trouble you've gone to for me——"

"Oh, it wasn't *trouble*," Rosie says. "That's just what people do. Besides, you're my brother-in-law."

I'm surprised how much it means to me, to hear her say that. "Ex–brother-in-law," I say.

"Mmmm," says Rosie. They both do that. It's very annoying.

"Well, come and see me any time you want to," I say. "Consider it the family rate."

Rosie smiles, still embarrassed, but I can see she's touched, too. "All right." Then she looks stern again. "You know, Warren, I know better than anyone what a total pain in the ass my little brother can be, but you really might think about giving him a second chance. It would be very Philip Barry of you."

"What?"

"Oh, you know," says Rosie airily, saddling herself with the last of her bags. "*The Philadelphia Story.* And all those other screwball comedies that *weren't* by Philip Barry—*The Awful Truth, His Girl Friday.*" She looks sad for a minute, and I do wonder what is going on with her. "Maybe they weren't screwball comedies so much as romantic comedies. Anyway, love was always better the second time around. You know, the couple that splits, and they think they've found somebody else, and then it turns out that they really belong with the first person." She pauses. "Come to think of it, they all starred Cary Grant. Who we now know was gay. So why do you think they——"

"Are you trying to tell me that Flip has found somebody else?"

Interrupted in her analysis of old movies, Rosie looks momentarily startled. Then she grins—that sidelong smile that I saw Flip take from me. "See?" she says. "Do yourself a favor. Be your own romantic hero! Act today."

I shrug. "I'm sure Flip *has* found somebody else by now. Besides, he wasn't really happy with me."

"You left him," Rosie points out. "At least, that's the way I heard it." She shakes her head as I stand up, too. "I can't fathom a relationship in which there are two people of your gender," she says. "How do you manage it? Sometimes even *one* of you is too much." She gives me a thoughtful look. "You know, Warren, in another life, you and I would probably have made a good match. Even though you have such lousy politics, and I'm so not your type." She grins at me again. "But then, in another life, you would have better politics. And I would probably be thin."

I find myself taking hold of her hand and kissing her on the cheek. "Thank you," I say, almost in a whisper. "For everything."

Through all the bags she is carrying, she somehow manages to give me a real hug. "Fight the good fight," she says and pulls away. "Remember the *Maine*. And the *Titanic*."

"Oh, shut up, Rosie," I tell her. But affectionately.

I have to take a cab back down to my office, too, which actually is in Greenwich Village, but only because that's a good neighborhood for people who want to visit psychics. Somehow I manage to be a whole five minutes ahead of my first client, so at least that disaster has been averted. I settle myself behind my desk and try to get myself into some kind of state where I might actually be able to know something.

I don't know what's going on with me today, but for every single client— and I have four in a row—I have a full-blown vision, I mean a really thorough, exhausting one, as though everything were happening to me. With the first woman, I'm following her through an apparently endless twilight region, and since her issue is vision anyway—seeing for herself—the whole experience is about not being able to keep my eyes open—and then I have to feel *her* anger, *her* despair. How can I avoid feeling those things, when it's through feeling that the information comes?

And of course, she doesn't even want to know what I've found out—she wants to know when she's going to fall in love, and what's going to happen with her career, and when she's going to have more money, and all those other things that everybody always asks. I try to answer the questions people actually have, or they won't come back, and they certainly won't recommend me to their friends, but if you want to know the truth, I find it depressing, what people want to know. The information that somebody—some force, the universe, their own higher power, however you want to interpret it—the messages that some *something* bothered to send, *that* they don't want. The date they're going to meet their one true love, that interests them. As if knowing that would make the least little bit of difference in their lives, and that's exactly the kind of information that's least reliable anyway. Any psychic will tell you that, if they're being honest.

And then, if they don't like your answers, people want you to twist the truth and reassure them that you *didn't* know, you *didn't* see, something that was right there, something that they could have seen, too, if they'd been willing. But I can't afford to lie about this, not ever, because somehow I am absolutely sure that the day I start lying about these visions will be the day I stop having them, and what will I do then?

When I was a child, I simply didn't tell anybody about what I saw. Anybody except Madeleine, of course, who actually did believe me, though she pretended not to. At first I didn't even know what they were. How did I know that Vernice's daughter was in the hospital, for example? Vernice was shocked when I asked her when her daughter was coming home—even my parents hadn't known she was sick. I don't know what reasons Vernice had been giving them for all the work she'd been missing—all this happened when I was about three—but I suppose she thought that telling them the truth would suggest that she'd be less than totally available for a while, whereas if she took it excuse by excuse, she might be able to preclude their getting upset.

I don't even remember what finally happened. Did Vernice swear me to secrecy? Did I take that vow and tell Madeleine anyway? And then did she or I tell my mother, or let the truth slip accidentally? Or perhaps Vernice simply went straight to my parents to try to clear things up—and then found out that she needn't have, because in fact they *didn't* know?

But of course, after Vernice or I or Madeleine told them, then my parents *were* upset. As they saw it, they were paying for a full-time housekeeper, not for someone who was going to be missing one or two days a week at unexpected intervals—I can only imagine that the missed work coincided with some sort of treatments, or maybe it had to do with the days that nobody else was available to sit with the girl in the hospital. In any case, Vernice was told she could come back whenever she wanted, because my parents wanted to be fair to her, and also they felt that she knew the household really well. But they thought—again, I'm only now piecing this together—that while the crisis was going on, Vernice should concentrate on taking care of her daughter and let them find someone who could devote full time to our house.

I don't remember Vernice actually leaving. But I do remember her coming back two years later, when I was five (she was there when I got home from school, that's how I remember). *Did* she feel betrayed? How could she possibly have felt otherwise? But again, I don't remember. And if she was in any way different toward me when she came back—less loving, less trusting, less, I don't know, *familial*—how would I know that, either, after all these years?

Anyway, my second client is a man who just got divorced because his wife fell in love with another woman. He thinks he wants to know when he's going to fall in love again himself, and he's also concerned about money for the child support, or maybe it was alimony—he wasn't exactly clear about the details. Anyway, it doesn't matter, because clearly, what he really wants to know is why he wasn't enough of a man to prevent his wife from leaving him. Like the woman the other day, he's obviously chosen a gay psychic on purpose, whether he knows it or not. I suppose in his case, he thinks *I'm* not much of a man, so it will be less threatening to hear the truth from me. ("Aren't you Miss Lonelyhearts today," Flip would say. If he were here.)

So I find myself wandering in this man's private nightmare sexual gallery, half of which is luscious, mocking lesbians, who perfectly fit *his* sexual fantasies, but who, of course, wouldn't give him the time of day, which is more or less the point, isn't it? It's no accident whom *he* ended up marrying. Well, it never is. (Yet another thing that nobody ever wants to know.)

And the other half of his vision—and may I say, I really resent having to go there with him—is this dim, cloudy region with weird gray and yellow light, an overcast world full of sticky pits, like monstrous mud baths. I suppose it's lucky for me the man *hasn't* read Freud, or he'd think I was making it up. If I had told him what I saw, which of course, I didn't. He was there with me, he should have been able to see it for himself.

I can easily imagine that he will fall in love again, even remarry. It wouldn't necessarily make him happy, but it would be what he wants. So I try to tell him both what he wants to know and what might actually help him. "Before, you looked for women who weren't going to give you the love you deserve," is how I put the taunting lesbians to rest. "Now you must find someone who loves you for who you are." I would have told a better truth if I thought he had been willing to hear it.

The third client is a mother who wants to know what's going to happen to her children. She thinks her eldest son, a high school sophomore of fifteen, is doing drugs. And her second child, an asthmatic girl of twelve, simply has no friends, and she wonders if it's the asthma. "You know how children ostracize anyone who's different," she says. Well, of course, I can see that her son is gay (again, no accident that they come to me), although he is also doing drugs. This session is triply hard—I've been nauseous after each of them, but I actually throw up after this one—because I can't be in her vision only, I have to go after the children, too, in a kind of sickening montage: the woman on the phone, trying to find out where her son is; the daughter in her room, using a razor blade to make small, evenly spaced cuts on the inside of her arm; the son getting silently fucked in the gym shower by some older kid at school, not knowing if he likes it or even if he's supposed to like it (that one is particularly painful for me); the family playing miniature golf together on some vacation while the son sulks and the mother yells at him and the father tries to pacify everyone and the daughter is there being the good girl. I honestly don't know what to tell her. Your love didn't cause the problem; your love can't fix it, is what I would like to say. But no one wants to hear that, either.

Luckily, the fourth client is late, so I can be sick in private. And then she arrives—an actress, and of *course* she wants to know when she's going to be successful. Actually, in her case, I do get a very specific vision of the future, although visions of the future, however specific, are virtually worthless (another thing that any honest psychic knows). Let me revise that: visions of the future that you couldn't see just as well without psychic support are virtually worthless. Because things can change. And the things that can't change, you don't need psychic information to see.

So I actually do see her future very clearly: she'll get one national commercial in a year and four months from now, she'll make enough money from it to live on for the following year, and then she'll never work again. The hitch being that I can't tell her about the commercial without also telling her about the not working. Bearing in mind that either, or both, might be a chimera, or something that she could somehow refuse, or transform. Whereas telling her will make them both seem fixed, and then they will happen, and she would at least have the comfort of knowing that she had seen it coming, but I don't particularly want to give her that. Cold comfort, I believe it's called.

So in her case, I make a special effort to find out what *she* thinks about her career. What does she want?

Her face lights up. "I want to be so famous, that nobody can ever dismiss me. It wouldn't have to be *famous*. But at that certain level. Where whenever you want to do something, you can."

"And what would you do?"

She shrugs. "Oh, Shakespeare. I've always wanted to play Portia—I've worked on her monologue, but I've never gotten to do all of her. And *Long Day's Journey,* but of course, I'd have to be older for that. And I know this sounds silly, but I'd like to do both Laura and Amanda in *Menagerie.* I really identify with both of them."

"Well," I say as carefully as I know how, "I see something coming up in about a year and—let's say three to five months. That might bring you some kinds of financial success. And then I see hardship after that. So I would say—"

"What kind of hardship?" she says quickly. Just as I feared, she looks completely upset, every word I'm saying is gospel. Well, I *am* telling her the truth. But I'm not writing her future. I don't know how to explain the difference to her, though.

So instead I say, "Actually, Felicia, could you not interrupt? I mean, you can certainly ask questions afterward, anything you like. I'm here to—to share anything I can with you that might be helpful. But when you interrupt, it more or less breaks the flow. The information comes as part of a package."

She nods seriously. I don't like this. It's the wrong kind of power for me to have. But that is why people come to me. Out of the blue, I think of Juliet, who at eight years old doesn't look at me with the kind of perfect trust that I see in twenty-eight-year-old Felicia. It's because Felicia wants to believe in me so much. Whereas Juliet—I suppose she wants to save that trust for Madeleine.

Felicia is still waiting. "I see success for you in the next fifteen to eighteen months," I repeat. "And then hardship after that. I suppose—you asked about the kind of hardship—I suppose it's the hardship of not being recognized. Not having people recognize your gifts. So what you have to do, Felicia," and I look into her eyes as far as she'll let me, because suddenly I want very much for her to understand. Wouldn't you know, as soon as I make that choice, she looks away. But now I can't not tell her. "What you have to do, Felicia, is recognize yourself. Do you have any idea what I mean?"

By accident, I've actually found the answer, because of course, this is sufficiently intriguing and mysterious and "psychic" for her, and also disguised enough—though I hadn't meant it to be—that she doesn't have to face it. Or do I mean, that she can face it in her own time? "You have to recognize, as specifically as possible, who you are as an actress, why you want to act, exactly how acting is your gift to the world. I'm trying to tell you that no one else is going to recognize you during the period I'm talking about—so you have to. And then you can use that recognition to be seen."

"You mean, if I believe in myself, other people will believe in me, too?"

"No. I mean, that's good, too. But I'm not talking about believing. I'm talking about knowing. You have to know who you are as an actress. Like those projects. You have to—"

"I have to know what projects I want to do."

"No." My clumsy words. "There is something about you that no one else in the world has," I say finally. "I don't know what that is, but you do. But you're keeping it secret from yourself. Do you understand? That's what you have to find out."

She still looks puzzled, but I really can't try anymore. She'd keep me here all day if I let her. As she's going out the door, she says, "But you did see something good coming up in the next year? Year and a half?"

"Something very good," I say. "Something you've wanted for a long, long time. That part will be exactly what you want."

After she goes, I sink down behind my desk and rest my head on my palms. My hands tingle and tremble, and I can still smell the musky oil from Rosie's hands. My God, I think, and she wants me to connect to people I don't even know. There would be absolutely nothing left of me.

Suddenly I get this powerful urge to go back to the apartment I shared with Flip. He won't be home until Monday. And I have Juliet now, I could use the things I left behind. There was great light in the old apartment. The thought of standing in those sunny rooms seems an almost unbearable relief.

The taxi drops me off, and I pause for a moment in our old vestibule. I am surprised at how much seeing his single name on the buzzer hurts my feelings. Not that I thought he *should* have left mine there after all this time. It's just the thought of him coming down and scraping it off.

I climb the two flights, turn the key, and pause again. Well, it's probably easiest to start in the bedroom. And there, asleep in the bed—his head sprawled back, his mouth open, his limbs entangled in one of *my* ice-blue sheets—is Flip.

I stop short, and as if on cue, he begins to stir. I could still get out. It always takes him forever to wake up. In fact, when he sees me, he isn't quite awake, and at first, he smiles.

Then suddenly he is awake, and he stops smiling. "What the hell are you doing here?" he says, but not unkindly, really. He simply wants to know.

"I'm sorry," I say, as casually as I can manage. Is he naked within those sheets? I see only bare arms and one bare leg—his long, narrow foot and muscled dancer's calf sticking out beneath a corner of the sheet. "I thought you were going to be shooting through the weekend."

He stares at me. "We were. *Two hours ago* they decided to cut my last three shots and let me go home. I just got in. I've been up since five, so I decided to take a nap. And so—" he glances at the clock, "*five minutes ago,* I lay down and went to sleep. You walked in at the first possible moment you could possibly have woken me up, Warren. What's going on?"

"Clearly, it's a coincidence. I said I was sorry."

Flip bursts out laughing. "Oh, right, the great psychic. Perhaps the most impressive moment of your parapsychological career, and you don't want to claim it. I believe *that.*"

I feel myself starting to smile, but it seems very important that I stop. Flip watches me—he is still smiling. I should simply leave. Instead, I sit down on the corner of the bed.

I can feel him watching me. As I've said, I'm far more of a receiver than a sender, but on this particular occasion, I am sending as hard as I can. All the while receiving, of course. I can feel Flip's puzzled look, I can hear how he stops smiling, I can almost taste the intent look at the back of my head that takes the place of the smile. "You always do this, Warren," he says quietly, or did he only think it? Slowly, he moves toward me, and the waiting is unbearable, but I sit there and bear it, every single granule of time until I feel his arms around me, his hands gripping my chest, his chest hard against my back. I could not possibly describe the relief.

Slowly, deeply, he presses his mouth into my neck, slowly he unbuttons my shirt and rubs the heels of his hands over my nipples, hard. My eyes are closed, I'm alone in the dark. *Thank you,* I am thinking as hard as I know how. *Thank you, Flip. I love you. I need you. Go on.* But he stops.

"I need to hear you say it, Warren," he whispers. "I need to know that this is what you want. I need to know that *you* know."

It's like pushing away a boulder when all you have is a puff of breath. But I grasp his hand, hard, and manage to breathe the word "Yes." Still he waits. "Yes, Flip. *Yes.* It's what I want." I wait for the boulder to roll back and crush the breath out of me. But all that happens is that Flip turns my face around to meet his, and I feel him close his eyes, too, and we're alone together in the dark.

Afterwards, as we lie tangled together in the sheet, I even manage to open my eyes. He is sleeping, one arm thrown over me, as though he would wake in an instant, if he had to, to keep me there. Because he is asleep, there are no words to send or receive, only our two bodies, dumb and warm and peaceful in the bed. I am grateful for his restraining arm, but this is something I could never tell him, with or without words. And by the time he wakes, I may feel differently.

I must have fallen asleep myself, because when I wake up, I am wrapped so far around him that I have pushed him over to the far edge of the bed. As we awaken, slowly, together, I pull away, out from under his two arms, away from his reaching hands. I see his hurt look, quick, and then something slower. Shame. And then that look is gone, too, covered with his waking face, and I can't help it, I have to put my hand on his head, to feel his silky hair, the curve of his skull pressed into my palm. I don't want to see how relieved he looks. I can't help seeing it.

When we first got together, I had to touch him all the time. My body against his hands, his limbs, his skin. My skin was sand in the desert, soaking up his touch. It didn't matter how much I got, it was never enough.

And the words, whispered and interchangeable. *There. Yes, there.*

Don't stop. Don't stop. Don't let go.

I won't let go.

Now he rolls away from me and stands up. "Don't worry, Warren," he says. "I won't misunderstand. I know this doesn't really change anything." He walks away into the bathroom and I hear the shower running.

After a moment, I follow him. "Flip—"

"Don't come in, Warren," he says from behind the black and white shower curtain. What *will* he do if I take back all my things? Still naked myself, I reach out to push the curtain aside. "Warren!" His voice is furious. "Go away!"

But I do push the curtain aside, and although it's hard to be sure, since he *is* in the shower, it seems to me that tears are streaming down his face. He gives me a look of pure fury and shoves me aside, grabbing a towel and rushing into the other room, leaving me to turn off the water. Angry myself, I follow him back into the bedroom.

"Oh, this is so typical of you," I say. But he won't look at me.

"Don't talk to me, Warren. Don't even fucking talk to me."

"What the hell just happened? Why are you so upset?"

"Oh, please," Flip says, flinging himself down onto the bed as he puts his socks on. "You're the psychic. Figure it out."

"And *that* routine is getting rather tired, don't you think?"

"I'm warning you, Warren," Flip says, putting on his shoes. "Don't say another word. Or, I'm warning you, I'll—"

"You'll what? Run outside with half your clothes on?"

Incredibly, I see this get to him, and he almost starts to smile. Then he starts to shake.

Without thinking, I rush to him, kneel in front of him on the floor, try to pull him down into my arms. "Flip, I'm sorry," I say. "Whatever it is, I'm sorry."

Even through his tears, he has to laugh. "Jesus, Warren, give me a break," he says. "You *know* what it is." He grips my shoulders, holding me at arm's length as he forces himself to take deep, even breaths, to stop laughing, to stop crying. I reach up to touch his face, but he pushes my arm away. "Don't," he says. "Please don't." He stands up and continues getting dressed. "See?" he says. "You really don't have anything to say."

"I thought—you were in the middle of something," I say. "I was waiting until you were done."

"*Warren.* Jesus Christ." Then he stops himself. "You know, Warren," he says, in a voice so final, I feel my chest fill up with stones, "I used to think you *did* need an explanation. Or *something*. But let me give us both a break, because honestly, Warren, you know *everything*, right, so anything you don't understand, it's because you just don't want to." He looks at me, and I really wonder what he sees. Does he see this stonelike feeling of doom, this barren world, this ice-bitten desert? Does it look like I like it? Does it look like I'm at home there? "Warren," he says gently. "You *know* I love you. I just can't stand that it doesn't make any difference."

He actually comes over and puts his arms around me. "You know I love *you,*" I say. It comes out angry. "Why do you have to hear it all the time?"

Flip sighs. "I don't know," he says in an empty voice. "Maybe I don't."

Is this supposed to give me hope? Because as the energy flows out of him, it flows into me. "I miss you," I manage. "I miss being with you." But inside my arms, his body still feels defeated. *This* is what I can't bear, I want to tell him, and also, "Fuck it, Flip, stop being so unhappy! Just stop it!"

Eventually Flip and I let go of each other and finish getting dressed. We leave the apartment together without either of us mentioning when I am supposed to come back and gather up my things. "So, where are you going now?" Flip asks, able to play the question casually, even cheerfully, once we are a block or two away from home. (Former home.)

"Actually," I say, "I have to pick up my niece."

"Your niece?! You never told me you had a niece."

"I didn't know myself. Apparently Madeleine had a child eight years ago, and we only just found out about it because she's back in the hospital again, and the child—Juliet—came here."

"And you've got her? Not your parents?"

"Well," I say, feeling something beyond relief at being able to talk to him again, and about this, and on this day, after everything. "Actually, she's Black."

"Your niece is Black? Oh, that Madeleine. Her freedom of spirit knows no bounds."

"Well, that's one way of putting it." I find myself savoring each exchange, each thing that goes without saying. I hadn't remembered that we talked so well together. "And of course, the product of such a union could hardly be raised in Connecticut."

"You mean, your parents wouldn't do it?" I can see that he is genuinely shocked.

"Would yours?"

"Family is family," Flip says flatly. "Which doesn't mean that any child who brought home a Black grandchild wouldn't have to hear about how the races were never meant to mix, from now unto the seventh generation. Or matricide, whichever came first. But to let the child be raised out of the family— no, hardly."

"Well, she's not exactly being raised out of the family," I remind him. "I've got her."

"Jesus, Warren, since when?"

"Since Monday, actually."

"My God, Warren. So now you're raising a child."

"Well, nobody knows how sick Madeleine is. I mean, how long she'll be indisposed."

Flip laughs. "Listen to you—indisposed! You could be talking about some survivor of the greatest natural disaster known to man, someone who's lost both arms and both legs and is blind, deaf, and totally traumatized, and you'd be saying, 'Well, we expect he'll be *indisposed* for the next twenty or thirty years.'"

"Not that bad, surely."

"*Surely,* there's another one," Flip says. "I must say, Warren, I had forgotten how you people talk."

I haven't forgotten how you talk. Maybe he hears that thought, because there's a short, uncomfortable pause, which Flip, of course, finally breaks by saying, "So until Madeleine gets better, you're living with an eight-year-old girl?" He starts to laugh. "I'm sorry, Warren, really. It's just—it's like some weird movie of the week, except if it were on television, you would be the father. You're not, are you?"

"Well, apart from anything else," I say, trying to be offended instead of amused, "I haven't seen Madeleine for at least twelve years. I haven't even spoken to her on the phone."

"Oh, and of course, *you're* not Black," Flip says. "For a minute, I almost forgot. So where is this mysterious niece now?"

He has been walking with me down Eighth Avenue. Neither of us has mentioned a destination.

"She's in Washington Square Park."

"By herself?"

"Obviously not. Actually, she's with a woman Rosie found me."

This really throws Flip, as I should have known it would. Or was I simply trying to pay him back? For being so much better at this than I, as I measure every inch of space between us, as I weigh each word he says. "Oh," says Flip, and somehow the fun goes out of his voice. "You called Rosie?"

"Well, I more or less had to." So. Yet another injury. "I mean, Rosie was literally the only person I could think of who—I mean, I simply had no idea what to do."

"I'm sure Rosie had several ideas about what you should do."

"Actually, she did. I must say, although I know we've disagreed about Rosie in the past——"

"Oh, we haven't *disagreed*," Flip says acidly. "You've just been *wrong*."

"Well, be that as it may, I feel I more or less owe you an apology. She really is——"

I stop, because on the word *apology,* I hear Flip catch his breath, sharply. "Don't fucking apologize to me about *Rosie,*" I imagine him saying. "She's hardly the worst sin on *your* list." And then he sees that I get this and he lets it go.

"I really am sorry," I say.

"Yeah, I know," Flip says. "What did Rosie do this time?"

So I tell him. Apparently, we're going to walk all forty-five blocks down to Washington Square Park—fifty-four blocks if you add in the crosstown.

"Well, that certainly sounds like Rosie," Flip says when I finish telling him about this morning. "No quarter asked and none given."

"I know."

"And she's so weird on gay stuff. Half the time she talks about it like it's *her* issue, and then she comes out with these incredibly—I mean, you know, Warren, when they start rounding us up and making us wear badges saying, 'I'm not allowed to be in the army and don't fuck me because I might give you AIDS,' you *know* Rosie will be there like it was happening to her. And not just because of me."

"I believe you."

"And then she can say, 'You go around having anonymous sex and there aren't any consequences.' " Flip shakes his head. "It makes me absolutely crazy."

"I know," I say again. "Although I also have to say, it was extremely kind of her to take all that time, and to find me Marta, which was a godsend. That's the only reason I called her, Flip, because I really did need help."

"Well," says Flip. "I suppose if I had to take care of an eight-year-old child out of the blue, she wouldn't necessarily be the *last* person I'd call."

He still looks so forlorn, beneath the anger, but I don't know how to apologize anymore. "So, why were you out of town?" I say instead. "You told me *when*——"

"Apparently not."

"—but not for what."

"Oh, it's *très* bizarre," Flip says, and gives me a sidelong look. "See, your niece isn't the only one who speaks French. But this was so one of those flukes. Davis's assistant, Pietro—oh, you never heard of him."

"No, I did. He was the one who called."

"Oh, right." Another uncomfortable silence. We turn east toward Fifth Avenue. Well, we've certainly managed to avoid my new apartment. Or does Flip even know where that is?

"Anyway," Flip says quickly, "it turns out that Pietro's lover was also making a movie. He's in his fifties, so imagine, because Pietro is only about ten years old, well, all right, eleven, but he *looks* younger—anyway, Pietro's lover, who actually is called Massimo, I'm not making this up, *was* working in Italy, but some Italian TV–German TV–Canal Plus–Miramax deal came through and he got the money to make a movie in America. And Pietro brought him to the screening of Davis's movie, and he saw me, on film, I mean, although also in person, but it was the screen presence that really did it for him, and then, of course, he had eyes for no one else. Of course, he *wasn't* casting any Black actors, but I'd like to think I'd've been his top choice anyway. So now I'm in *his* movie. Which is actually going to play in theaters."

I am stunned. "My God, Flip," I finally manage to say. "That's wonderful. Congratulations."

"Yes, well—" He actually seems embarrassed.

"I mean, when you said you were on a shoot out of town, I didn't think— you didn't say—"

"You mean, why didn't I tell you, Warren? Why didn't I come running to you right away with the fabulous news? Or at least take the chance to say, 'I told you so'?"

"Something like that."

"Well, apart from the reasons too obvious to go into here," Flip says, "I have very mixed feelings about it, actually."

"Really."

"Of course, it's a great opportunity. And I'm doing a fabulous job for them, *obviously*. But . . ."

"What?"

"If I tell you, Warren, will you promise not to lecture me?"

I can't help laughing. "You mean, you want me to simply listen and not tell you what I think? And the last time that happened was when, exactly?"

"Oh, all right," Flip says to cover *that* unfortunate choice of words. We turn left on Fifth Avenue and start heading downtown. "It's nothing all that specific. It isn't even a very big part, although that *doesn't* bother me, that's not it."

"I believe you."

"It's not a bad movie, either," Flip says. "It just isn't an especially good movie. I mean, so what, finally. Is how I feel about it. And my part—I'm a newspaper reporter, I have this kind of quirky relationship with the hero, who is on a quest to find out who's going to blow up the Statue of Liberty or the Brooklyn Bridge or something equally stupid. I mean, not *stupid,* it's just a thriller, and I have this nice little comic bit, and there's also this one serious moment . . ." His voice trails off again.

"So it's this great opportunity," I prompt.

"Yes, but—OK, Warren, I know this sounds completely stupid, but it doesn't *mean* anything. It's nothing anyone is going to remember by this time next year."

"But you like lots of movies that aren't—I don't know, that are just—you know what I mean."

"Romantic comedies," Flip agrees. "Thrillers, musicals, film noir, all the classics. I know. But there was something really big and great about them. They were—I don't know. They could be a part of my life."

"And this couldn't."

"God, I don't know why anyone would want it to be. It's just a nice, inoffensive little movie." We stop for a red light at Thirty-fourth Street. Our bodies move one inch closer, and my whole skin seems to pull in his direction. "I just thought I was capable of more," he's saying.

"But all that time, with Davis's movie and all those other projects, you never—"

"No, because they were supposed to be on the way to something else," Flip says. "But if this is my big chance, it's supposed to *be* something else." He looks away. "I told you it was stupid."

"I don't think it's stupid."

"Well, what *do* you think?"

"So now you do want me to lecture you."

"Or you could just give me your notes after class."

"Ha, ha. All right, let me see." I feel a rush of warmth from Flip. Which, frankly, makes me nervous. But I say, "I think *you* think you'll be safe as long as you don't know what you really want. So when you're not making a living— from acting, I mean—you can say that's what you want. And then when it looks like you *are* making a living, you can say, 'No, no, that's not what I meant.' But you never say what you *do* mean."

"But I thought—" Flip begins.

"What?"

"I thought I did know."

"What?"

"Nothing. Never mind." *No, wait,* I want to say. *Tell me what you want, then, if you know what it is.* But once again, he's on the verge of misery.

"And those other two times you were out of town," I say, trying not to sound desperate, "you were working on this movie, by what's his name? Maximilian?"

"Massimo," Flip says absently. "No, those were industrials." Then he looks at me with the trace of a grin. "Oh, right, you don't know this, do you, Warren? I've been making money. I mean, not *money* money. But yes, this month *all* of my share of the rent—and now, of course, it's a much bigger share—all of it came from my earnings as an actor. As it happens."

"So there," I say, feeling completely at a loss. I know I should be happy for him. But all I can think is, *Now he has everything. I'll really lose him now.*

Suddenly he takes my hand without even looking at me. Of course, some of that is simply that we're out in public. Even though now we're below Fourteenth Street, where two men holding hands is not usually that big a deal. But he takes my hand as though it were a secret from both of us. In the very center of my palm—or is it his?—I feel a tiny pulse, trembling and insistent.

We drop hands when we get to the park, and I realize I have no idea where to look for Juliet. Flip nudges me and points to the playground near the Arch. And yes, there are Juliet and Sara, scrambling over the nearest of the three jungle gyms. It occurs to me that at some point, I'll have to do a laundry of Juliet's clothes. "That's her," I tell Flip.

"The one in the red jacket?"

"No, that's Sara, Marta's daughter. Juliet's the one at the top."

"She *is* beautiful."

"And that's Marta," I say, pointing to the bench near the sandbox where she's watching Oscar and Rogelio. "I must say, she's been extremely helpful. I mean, yesterday I was feeling at the end of my rope, and she said—though I'm not sure I should tell this to *you,* actually. But—"

Flip is staring at me. "What?" I say.

"Sorry, Warren," he says, shaking his head. "I'm trying to imagine you and that woman having a conversation about *anything,* other than you telling her to be sure and scour the toilet extra hard today—"

"Flip!"

"I just can't see it, Warren, that's all. What *has* been going on since I last saw you? You have this whole different life."

"Only since Tuesday," I say. I don't know whether I'm more offended on Marta's behalf or my own. And I have *never* had a cleaning woman. Not since I left home.

This is the point at which Juliet notices that I'm here, and she starts to wave excitedly. "Uncle Warren!" she calls as she comes running. I can't imagine what Flip is making of all this. He has that unreadable expression again.

"Uncle Warren!" She runs right up to me and stops. "Sara is having a birthday party Sunday night, this Sunday night, the day after tomorrow, and she invited me. Can I go?"

"I don't see why not," I say. "If it's all right with Marta."

"Uncle Warren! Of *course* it's all right with Marta. She was *there* when Sara asked me."

"Well, then, good," I say. Having Flip watch all this is extremely disconcerting.

"*And,*" Juliet goes on, "it's a *slumber* party, so if I go, I'm supposed to bring a sleeping bag and stay the whole night. On the floor. In Sara's room. But I don't have a sleeping bag."

"We could probably get you one," I say, which seems to be *my* new favorite phrase. "But are you sure you want to do that? Spend the whole night there?" Have you ever done that before? I want to ask. Eight seems so young. Of course, these days, Juliet's whole life is sleeping away from home. I just wouldn't have thought she'd want to go someplace *else* so soon.

"Of *course* I want to go," she is saying. "Sara said we're going to make somemores. We don't have them in France, but people eat them here. Sara told me. You have to toast them, like over a campfire, but we can't have a campfire at Sara's house. So Sara says we'll just have to toast them on the stove. They have a gas stove, not like yours, Uncle Warren. Their stove has real flames."

"It was nice of Sara to ask you," I say, as Flip murmurs in my ear, "They grow up so fast, don't they? Don't worry, Pa, she won't forget you."

"Juliet," I say, "this is my friend, Flip."

"Hello, Juliet," says Flip, squatting down so that he's eye level with her. She looks at him intently, as if trying to recognize him. And then apparently, she does, because she throws her arms around him.

"Flip," she says, when they stop hugging. "That's a very unusual name."

"Well, it's a nickname," he explains. "Short for Philip."

She studies him. "No, Flip is better," she says seriously. "It fits you more precisely."

"Really?" he says. "Why do you think so?" Oh, come on, Flip, she's only eight. You don't have to get *her* to talk about you, too.

But Juliet is eager to answer. "It sounds like you. *Flip,*" she repeats, and in her slight accent, the *i* is colored *ee,* the *p* lands lightly. "It's . . . a good name for an actor."

Flip looks at me. "Did you tell her I was an actor?"

I shake my head. "It seems to be something that's apparent to everybody."

Flip seems to be inordinately pleased about all this, and he offers to push Juliet on the swings. She goes with him without a backward glance, and I go sit next to Marta. I can see the two of them, laughing, then deep in conversation. Then he pushes her and she screams with pleasure. Well, of course actors *are* charming. That's their stock in trade.

I am asking Marta if she knows where I could buy Juliet a winter coat while wondering whether I really want to shop for Juliet at the same place Marta shops for Sara, when Flip and Juliet come back, holding hands. They stop talking very suddenly, and Juliet starts giggling. "And we *weren't* talking about *you!*" she says delightedly. "That's *not* why we stopped talking."

"Oh, I see," I say. "That was very polite of you."

"In fact," Flip says, "that's just what we were talking about, Warren, on our way over here—manners. Right, Juliet?"

Juliet giggles. "Marta, this is my extremely polite friend, Flip," I say.

Marta is amused by all of this. She and Flip shake hands.

"Well, people," Flip says. "This has been delightful, but it's gone on long enough. I'm afraid I must be going."

"No, Uncle Flip!" Juliet says. Flip carefully avoids catching my eye. "You should stay longer!" she says.

Flip squats down again to say goodbye to her. "You see, Juliet," he says solemnly, "if I don't go now, I'll be late. And the person I'm supposed to meet will be waiting, and waiting, and waiting, and maybe they'll think I don't like them anymore."

"But you *do* like them," says Juliet.

"Yes. So that's why I have to go. That's why I have to go *right now.*"

I notice he doesn't say he'll come back. I notice Juliet doesn't ask.

"Bye, Uncle Flip," she says sadly, and gives him another hug.

"Bye, Uncle Warren," Flip says to me. "Bye, Juliet, Marta." He waves at all of us and then he's gone.

I am about to ask Juliet what she and Flip were talking about, when I realize that if I do, my voice will probably fail. "Come on, Juliet," I say, getting up from the bench. "We should go, too."

"Uncle Warren," Juliet says as we leave the park, "is Flip your very good friend?"

"I suppose so."

She sighs. "I wish he was *my* very good friend."

There doesn't seem to be much to say to that, so I say, "You know what I was thinking, Juliet? I was thinking we should go to the store and buy some lemonade."

"Uncle Warren!" she says. And I think, it's all right. If she has to correct me a million times a day, at least she knows she can. "Uncle Warren, I don't drink lemonade. I drink *limonade*." She looks at me sternly. "*Limonade* is French for lemon *soda*. Lemonade in French is *citron pressé*—lemon juice. Which is *too sour*."

"Thank you for explaining that, Juliet."

"Now when you go to Paris, you won't get mixed up," she says.

"And it will be all thanks to you." She actually smiles at this. "But I'm still wondering," I say. "Should we go and buy some lemon soda, then? I thought that was your favorite drink."

"That was in Paris," she says. "My favorite drink in New York is chocolate milk. I had it at Sara's house."

"Then let's go get that," I say. "You can have some at dinner."

She shakes her head. "No, Uncle Warren. Chocolate milk is a lunch drink. You can't have it at dinner."

Throughout dinner and Juliet's bath, I try to focus on her. But as soon as she's gone to bed, I start thinking about Flip and I can't stop. First I have to re-live our love-making this afternoon, although that's difficult, because I can't get the images to stop at any of the places where we actually connected. They keep skipping over to that awful moment of waking up. I do get one or two good minutes out of the walk downtown. But the more I watch those scenes rerun, the clearer it becomes that he's over me. All right, so the sex was good—that was never the problem between us. But obviously, he can take it or leave it; obviously, he's gone on to other people where the sex is equally good. Or maybe it *wasn't* so good between us; maybe I have no idea what good sex is; maybe I had Flip fooled, too, but—

It doesn't matter. Whatever I might feel now, it's still quite clear that I had to leave then. And I do mean *had* to. I can still feel the frenzy that took hold of me that night, the unbearable relief that came with leaving. How can I still feel that longing—the desperate desire to be out of that house—when now I *am* out and it's no relief at all?

It's at this point that I start thinking about calling him. Which is obviously an extremely foolish idea—it's now one in the morning, and either he's sleeping, out on a date, or home *with* a date.

It doesn't matter. I have to call, though of course I get the machine. I can't help that either: I have to listen to his voice for as long as he's speaking. I try to hang up exactly as he finishes, so the machine won't have anything to record.

At one-thirty I find myself calling again, and then again at two, and at two-fifteen, and again at two-eighteen. I pace around the living room, my whole self concentrated on the moment when he picks up the phone, because I am sure that if only I can make that moment happen, everything else will work out. Whatever *that* means.

Then I start to get an image of Flip and some man named Michael. I don't really get a physical image—I'm sure that's because I so don't want one—but I do get that other kind of knowing. He's much younger than Flip, which I assume makes him even more attractive, and unlike me, he's—well, the words "a sunny personality" come to mind. "Strong" is another word I hear, and "great body." "Handsome," of course, and "loving." All the things Flip has been missing when he was with me.

By four, I am truly desperate—he certainly isn't coming home this late, and if the phone were going to wake him and Michael, it surely would have done so by now. But the idea that it's out of my power to reach him is absolutely unendurable. How will I live through even the next moment?

Then a light comes on in the hall, and Juliet stands in the doorway, holding out a washcloth.

"Juliet! What are you doing up? Are you all right?"

She takes one shy step into the room. "I heard you," she says in a very small voice.

"Oh, Juliet, did I wake you? I'm sorry. I thought I was being quiet."

"No," she says. "I *heard* you." She holds out the washcloth. "At home, they're in the freezer," she says. "But you don't have them here. So I just put cold water on this. I think it will still make your head feel better, though."

Is she sleepwalking? I hold out my hand to her, and she finally comes in. "Maybe you should sit on the couch," she says. "That way, when you start to feel better, you can just lie down and go to sleep." I let her show me where to sit. "Do you want the light on?" she says. "Sometimes it's too lonely sitting up in the dark." I let her turn on the lamp. I don't have a headache, I want to tell her. But I let her arrange the cool washcloth across my forehead. "Now your head will feel better," she says. "Very soon. I promise. You have to close your eyes, though." I do what she says. "Do you feel better yet?" she asks after a minute. "I think it's better when they come out of the freezer. We could put some there for next time."

I open my eyes and put the washcloth on the floor. "Juliet, it's all right," I say. "I do feel better. Much better. Thank you." She is still watching me, and now I can see how worried she is.

"Uncle Warren," she says, "you were worried about your boyfriend, weren't you?"

I nod and she nods back. "But, Uncle Warren. He likes you best. I can tell."

Does she actually know something? Or is this just the conversation she has learned for Madeleine over the years? The awful thing is, I do feel better.

"Juliet," I say, "come here." She shakes her head.

"I can get you something else," she offers.

"Juliet," I say, "listen to me. I don't have a headache. I'm not sick. I was only upset. And now I feel better." She looks at me soberly but she doesn't move. "Juliet," I try again, "I know your mother got very sick. Did she used to have headaches? Is that what happened?" I can see how torn she is. She doesn't want to talk about it, but she's afraid not to give me what I want. "Did she get—very upset? Is that what happened, Juliet? Did she get so upset that she couldn't take care of you anymore? And you tried to help her, you tried so hard, but nothing you did made her feel any better? Or maybe she did feel better, but then she didn't again?" She keeps staring at me. "Juliet," I say, "I'm not going to get sick. Whatever happens, I can still take care of you. You don't have to take care of me."

"Didn't the washcloth help?" she says.

"Juliet," I say. "Please come here." I put all the authority I have into my voice, and after a moment, she climbs up onto the couch beside me. "No," I say, "come *here*," and after another pause, she climbs slowly into my lap. I put my arms around her, and she starts to shiver.

She's wearing a flannel nightgown, pink and blue like the colors she picked out for her room, but she's barefoot. I help her tuck each foot into the leather cushions behind me, feeling the narrow bones of her feet, her sharp ankles. She puts her forehead against my chest, pressing hard in that one round spot, and I can smell the shampoo from her hair. I try to make a place that will help her to stop shivering, and after a few minutes, she does.

"Uncle Warren," she says in the smallest possible voice. "Is my mother sick in the head?"

"Well, Juliet," I say, "that's one way of putting it. We could also say she's sick in the heart."

"What does that mean?"

"I don't know exactly. But that's why she can't take care of you right now, even though she wants to, Juliet." She shakes her head, against my chest. "I know you wish you could make her feel better," I tell her. "I do, too. But we can't."

"Why not? I want to. I did before." She looks up at me. "You said I made *you* feel better."

I reach down and smooth the hair off her forehead. "I know you wish it could have been her," I say, and I am surprised how much it hurts to say this. "But that's because right now, she's sick, and I'm not. It's not so hard to make me feel better."

Juliet shakes her head vigorously, and I take back my hand. "I could try harder," she says.

And what can I tell her now? Because yes, she could, but it still won't make any difference. But no one ever wants to hear that.

So I put my arms around her more securely and I try to think what I *could* give her. She has already shown she is a receiver, so I summon up my best resources and try to send to her. Not words, because God knows, she has already had enough of those. A sense of safety? Well, yes, that would be nice. But it's hardly going to come from me.

So I keep it simple. I try to send her warmth—just warmth, no big deal. Except to do it, I have to find the heat in my own body, the movement of my blood, the coiling of my muscles. I don't want to go into my body that way. I don't like being in there. But for Juliet, I do it. Her hand drifts down to rest on the rough, dark hairs of my arm, her cheek falls against my chest, against the cushion of flesh there on one side. Her thin bottom sinks down into my lap, and slowly, slowly, her body grows warmer and heavier within my arms, until finally she relaxes into sleep.

Eventually I carry her back into her half-finished bedroom and put her into bed, turning the pillow for her so she'll get the cool side against her warm cheek, pulling the covers up around her to keep her warm. I wish I could get into that warm, peaceful bed with her. I wish it could all end here. But I go back into my own room and get into my own bed, and surprisingly, I also fall asleep.

SATURDAY

This morning, I am awakened by the ringing of the phone beside my bed. "It's me," says Flip on the other end of the line.

"Oh, hi." I struggle to sit up in bed.

"Listen, I thought, since it's another warm day, if you and Marta were going to take Juliet to the park again, I thought maybe I could come, too."

"Oh," I say, completely surprised.

"I don't want to intrude," Flip says quickly—and very uncharacteristically, I might add. When did he *ever* worry about intruding?

"No, no, it would be great to have you," I say. "It's only, let me think a minute—"

"Did I wake you?" Flip says. "I'm sorry. I assumed with a child in the house . . ."

I look at the clock. It's past nine. "Well, we had kind of a late night last night," I say. "I don't think Juliet is even up yet. But it's a good thing you did wake me, because I have clients at, oh, shit, ten. We don't have Marta today. I gather that weekends are the time for her to spend with her own family."

"Except for the occasional sleepover," Flip says.

"Right." Part of my mind is completely absorbed in his voice—every breath, every pause, every hesitation. And the other part is running over the litany: if I get Juliet up in two minutes, and if I can convince her to get dressed *very fast* and *right away,* we can be done with breakfast by nine-thirty-five, and if we take a taxi, if we can *get* a taxi—we can be at my office by—

"So what are you going to do with Juliet during your clients?" Flip asks.

"I don't exactly know. I more or less hoped I could set her up in the waiting room with a book and some things to do." What do eight-year-olds do? Color? Draw pictures? There's no television there.

"Well," says Flip in this completely unrecognizable voice. I mean, he didn't sound this uncertain when he first asked me to spend the night. Not that he exactly asked. "Well," Flip is saying, "if you want, I could take her. To the park, I mean, while you have clients. Then you could meet us there."

It's probably a good thing that I don't have time to take in all the various implications of this conversation. Thanks to the pressure of time, I can simply say, "Flip, that would be fabulous," and mean it wholeheartedly.

"OK, good," Flip says. And for once it's me barreling on with the conversation, telling him to meet us at my office and reminding him of the address.

It's probably also a good thing that I don't have time to talk to Juliet about last night. I'm not even sure whether I should, but in any case, the next several minutes are all about waking her up and getting her ready to leave the house. It occurs to me that when Marta was working, she did this with two children, five days a week. How on earth did she manage?

Nor is there time to say much to Flip when he meets us at the office, except "Thank you so much," and "I'll meet you at the playground at two."

Juliet, of course, lights up when she sees Flip. She can't believe she gets to spend the entire morning with him. "We might do some things in the city before we go to the park, right, Juliet?" Flip says. "And if Uncle Warren isn't going to meet us until two, I think we should have lunch." Well, where did *he* learn so much about taking care of children? But for the moment, I don't have the energy to be anything but grateful.

I don't seem to have much energy with my clients, either. Which for some reason seems to make everything go remarkably easily. How can I put it? For once, I know exactly what they need and I give it to them. For once I don't care whether they want it or not.

When I get to the park, Juliet and Flip are playing on the swings. But to my surprise, when Juliet sees me, she comes running right over. "Uncle Warren, Uncle Warren!" she says. "Uncle Flip took me to see a puppet show, and it was in *French!*" She lowers her voice as she reaches me, looking over her shoulder to make sure Flip can't hear. "And he doesn't speak French, but I told him what they were saying." She raises her voice again. "And then he took me to have lunch in a restaurant, and it was a *French* restaurant, and I got to eat *snails,* which are my favorite food in the whole world, and they were absolutely delicious. And the waiter didn't speak French, but the owner was there, and he did, and I got to talk to him. He was very surprised to hear someone my age speak French, but I told him it was because I had lived in France. He said it made him homesick for France, to talk to me, and I said it made me homesick, too, except it also was a good thing, because I haven't really spoken French for a whole week, and I don't want to forget it, and he said I probably wouldn't forget it, especially if I kept practicing. But he said I could come back and talk to *him* anytime, so can we go back there, Uncle Warren, sometime? We wouldn't have to order anything expensive, we could just have something to drink."

"We went to Florent," Flip explains in an undertone. "You know, the *cheap* French restaurant."

"Juliet, that sounds wonderful. Yes, we could go back there. Tell me about the puppet show—what happened?" I am looking at her, but I am so aware of Flip standing behind her. I am incredibly moved that he did this for her. And of course, it makes me wonder why I haven't.

Flip must have some idea of how I am feeling, because when Juliet finishes her report, he says, "Juliet, how about if you go play on the jungle gym for a while? I haven't seen your Uncle Warren all morning, and I want to talk to him, too."

Juliet looks at both of us. "I'll give you *some* time to talk," she offers, "and then I'll come back, and we'll all do something together."

"Sounds great," says Flip, watching her run off.

"Flip," I say, "that was really—thank you. How did you—"

"Oh, I just thought there would be something at the Alliance Française," he says, not looking at me. "I did a show there once, remember? When they were doing those dual shows in French and English. Oh, maybe that was before I knew you. Anyway, I just thought— You know, that's the kind of thing you *can* think when you're the one who just shows up for one morning." He grins at me, finally. "What is usually the uncle's role."

What is this *modest* side to him all of a sudden? "I didn't even think about money for lunch," I say, reaching for my wallet. "Let me pay you back."

He waves me away. "It's on me," he says.

"Right," I say. "Now that you're doing so well."

He looks at me sharply to see if I'm making fun of him. And I was, a little. He says evenly, "You know, Warren, for someone who talks all the time about being a receiver, you sure do a lousy job of receiving, if I may say so."

Suddenly I am so sorry, I can't stand it. "Flip, I apologize," I say. "Really, Flip, I'm sorry. It was incredibly nice what you did. I think I just—I just wished that I had thought of it first. Which is incredibly stupid. I'm just— Forgive me, all right?"

He keeps looking at me, his expression undecipherable. "It's a whole new world, isn't it, Warren," he says drily. "Me with money."

"Oh brave new world," I say, "that has such people in it."

Flip laughs. "Well, I never thought I'd hear you quoting Shakespeare."

"I remember *some* things," I say. "I held book for you when you were working on that play, don't you remember? That all-male production of *The Tempest* where you played Miranda—*I'll* never forget it. And for some reason you kept saying 'creatures' instead of 'people,' God knows why, because 'creatures' doesn't even make any sense. It's the idea that the world is full of *people* that surprises her, not just her and her father and this one other man she's fallen in love with, and not the weird creatures on the island, either, but all these other *people* all of a sudden, human beings like her. But trust you to take a simple idea and make it complicated."

Flip looks at me sharply again. "You're right," he says. "I am surprised you remembered that."

So are we even yet, I want to ask? Maybe not, because Flip says, "So Juliet told me you gave her a bubble bath with *my* bath stuff. She said lily of the valley is now her favorite kind of bubble bath."

"My God," I say. "I didn't tell her it was yours. I wasn't even sure it was." Flip maintains a skeptical silence. "I must have packed it up by mistake—"

"When you left."

"Well, yes." More silence. "I mean, I don't take baths, and—"

"And the smell makes you sick. I know."

"It doesn't make me *sick*," I say. "I just don't like it."

"Funny," Flip says. "Juliet said you did. She said it made you smile because it reminded you of me."

All of a sudden I hear myself saying, "So where were you last night? I called, but you didn't seem to be home." The minute the words are out of my mouth, I wish I could take them back.

"Really?" says Flip. "I was at Rosie's. You know, it's an hour and a half from my place to hers, and I ended up staying so late, I just stayed over. She's in a state about this new boyfriend, Michael, whom she's *finally* told me about, and since he's *so* much younger than she is, and so much handsomer than the guys she usually goes out with, and so much nicer than the guys she usually goes out with, she just doesn't know how to handle it."

"And since you've had so much experience in that department, she naturally came to you." Well, I seem to be making this worse and worse.

"Don't change the subject," Flip says, and I am sure he can see how relieved I am. "I must say, Warren, I certainly like this image of you calling all hours into the night, worrying about me." It's no use, I can't help smiling. Finally, he smiles at me, too, a real smile. "Look," he says, "one of those guys that sells honey-roasted whatever. Let's go get some."

The vendor is only a few steps away from the playground. I look back to make sure that Juliet can see where we are, and she waves to us from the top of the jungle gym.

But as soon as Flip has paid the man for his little sack of peanuts, he starts in again. "You know the fantasy I always used to have?" he says in a daring whisper as we go to lean against the playground fence. "I used to imagine coming home from a shoot or a rehearsal—some long day of work—and by the time I'd get home it would be late, and you'd already be asleep, but you'd wake up a little, just for me. And I'd get into bed in the dark and you'd put your arms around me without saying a word, just envelop me in your arms and hold me. And then we'd make love. Which would have been—perfect. And of course, I did come home late, lots of times, and you would be in bed, Warren. But it never happened that way, never—you were always angry with me, at least at first. When I first got home, I mean, when I first got into bed. You would loosen up later, maybe, because the sex was always so good, but you always started out angry. It was a cold house you kept, John Proctor."

"What?"

"Oh, that's from *The Crucible*," Flip says. "Haven't you read *anything*? John Proctor has been having an affair with Abigail, the little teenage vixen who accuses everyone in the village of being a witch, and he's trying to apologize to his wife, Elizabeth, now that Abigail's accusations are going to get them both killed, which is a bit of an unfair punishment for one little affair, but all right, they're Puritans, and Elizabeth says that actually, the affair was probably *her* fault, because *she* was always such a withholding bitch. 'It was a cold house I kept, John Proctor'—that's what she says."

"Are you trying to tell me that while we were together, you were having an affair?"

"Oh, fuck you, Warren!" Flip explodes, so loudly that heads turn, though not, luckily, Juliet's, because we both check. Flip takes a few steps away from the fence, dropping his voice to a furious whisper. "Do you know what my life was like after you walked out on me?" He is stuffing peanuts rapidly into his mouth. "Do you have any fucking idea? I was in agony, all right, Warren, in complete and total agony." He is practically whispering in my ear. "I was the walking wounded, all right, Warren? I couldn't look at another man, I couldn't even think about touching another man, I was like on fucking Antabuse with men, even thinking about anybody who wasn't you just made me nauseous." He keeps viciously eating peanuts. "I was a fucking zombie, all right, for six weeks I was the night of the living dead. Waiting for you to call, if you want to know the truth. *Praying,* actually, that you would call, that you would change your mind, that you would come to your senses. And then when you didn't, when you didn't make one fucking phone call, not *one move* in my direction, not even to get your goddam *stuff*—then yes, Warren, I went out and fucked everything in sight. Which is what I'm still doing, if you want to know the truth, so yes, I *am* seeing other people, but no, *no,* I wasn't when we were together. I know you always thought I was, Warren, but no—I was just too goddamn fucking in love with you, which was obviously my first mistake."

"See, Flip, I remember things a little differently," I say shakily. "Those nights you came home late? You didn't come back home to *me.* You just had to find some hole to crawl into, someplace to get away. I was like your pillow. You *didn't* get into bed and crawl into my arms. I would have been—it would have been—" I can't believe my voice is failing me now. "That would have been *fine.* But you were *never* happy to see me. I *did* put my arms around you, I *did* make love to you, but whatever I did, however glad I was to see you, it didn't make you happy. It didn't satisfy you."

"It did," whispers Flip. "I *told* you it did."

"No. It didn't. You weren't getting the parts you wanted, you weren't doing the work you wanted, and *that's* what you brought into bed. *That's* what I was supposed to make love to." My voice rises, and I force it down again. "In your fantasy," I whisper fiercely, "I don't wake up?—"

"Barely wake up."

"In your fantasy, I don't say anything? We don't talk? All you wanted to *do* was talk, why you weren't getting cast, or why it wasn't the right part, or why it *was* the right part but you *still* weren't getting paid. I wanted to fix it for you, I did, so much, but I couldn't. And don't say you didn't want that from me, Flip, because you goddamn well did."

There is a long pause.

"You always say you didn't make me happy," Flip says in a small voice. He has finally stopped eating. "But, Warren. You did." He puts his hand on my wrist, not holding, not pressing, just there. "How come you know so much and you don't know that?"

"It didn't feel like happiness to me, Flip. It felt like I was always failing."

"No," says Flip. "*I* was the one who was always failing."

"That's what I mean."

"But *you* made me happy." Then he finally looks ashamed, the look I always remember. "If anyone could."

Aha, I want to say, there it is. How can you feel that way and then think that you never, never blamed me for it? You just said so. If I had been happy to see you instead of angry, if I had been there with my arms ready for you . . . But what about all the times I did that and it didn't work? How you remember it, even now, is that I didn't do it.

And also, I just want to put my arms around him. I just want to put my arms around him and go home.

But we can't do any of that, because here comes Juliet, finished with the playground. She takes one of his hands and one of mine, and pulls us toward the center of the park. Maybe she simply wants to get us away from this place where she must know we've been arguing.

Flip gets it, too. "Oh," he says to me over her head. "Another receiver. Apparently it runs in the family."

"Yes," I say, mindful of her down there, but I can't help it, I have to talk to him. "It's rather disconcerting being on the other end of it for a change."

Right on cue, Juliet says, "Uncle Warren, what does disconcerting mean?"

"Something that throws you off balance," I say. Flip snickers.

"See, Juliet," he says, "your Uncle Warren is used to being the one who knows everything—"

"Yes," says Juliet. She just gets this *look* whenever Flip pays attention to her, like she's holding a bowl full of something delicious and one wrong move might make it spill.

"And then you come along," Flip says, "and you know quite a lot, as I'm sure you're aware. You know things—"

"That would be very unusual for a child to know," Juliet says helpfully.

"Exactly," Flip says. "Things your Uncle Warren thinks that only he knows, so when he finds out that other people know them too—"

"It's disconcerting," says Juliet.

"Exactly," Flip says again. And I can't help it, I too taste something delicious, and I also have to smile. And then I see it, whether I want to or not, the quick pleasure on Flip's face. He sent something. I received it. And now he's happy.

At the south end of the park, we pass a young woman with a guitar and an open case, singing some pop song from the radio in a loud, sweet, nasal voice. Juliet hears the music and lights up. "I know this song, I know this song," she says. And she starts to sing along.

> *I'm lonely and can't understand,*
> *Why you don't want to be my man*
> *I have no scheme, I have no plan,*
> *I just want you to be my man.*

She actually has more of a French accent when she sings. "I *love* this song," she says to me excitedly when the singer pauses to play a few chords. "We *always* sang it."

"You and Madeleine?"

"No, she doesn't like music from America. Me and my girlfriends."

> *When you walked out, my heart was lost,*
> *Too much pain, can't count the cost,*
> *But I will never understand,*
> *Why you don't want to be my man.*

Flip looks at me over Juliet's head, and it's all either of us can do not to burst out laughing. So instead, Flip also throws himself into the song:

> *If you knew*
> *How much I love you*
> *If you only knew-ew-ew-ew*
> *How much I love you.*

Juliet turns to Flip indignantly. "Uncle Flip, how do you know that song?"

"They play it here, too, you know. I like it too."

Then the last verse comes along, and Juliet joins in, singing every fervent syllable. Flip joins in, too, looking at me meaningfully, mockingly.

Some kind of man, without a doubt,
Some kind of man, who just walks out
But I will never understand
Why you don't want to be my man.

The guitarist picks out the last few, circular chords, and we applaud. I give Juliet a dollar to put in the guitar case. "We should go home *right now*," she tells us. "Before anything happens to spoil it." She sighs blissfully. "I can't wait to tell Mama that I heard that song."

Flip walks us up as far as our corner, but he doesn't come home with us. As soon as he leaves, Juliet asks, "Is Flip your boyfriend, or your very good friend?"

She knew this last night. "Boyfriend," I say. "Well, he was."

Juliet nods. "So who is your boyfriend now?"

"I don't have one."

"Mama said you did," Juliet says. "She said *pédé* is the bad word, and I shouldn't use that one. But *gai* is the good word, that's the one to use. Right?"

"I think so," I say, trying not to sound surprised. "Juliet, when did your mother tell you all this?"

"Oh, a long time ago," Juliet says airily. "She said that someday, you'd probably come to visit us. And then these were things that I should know."

I'm sorry, I want to tell Madeleine. I'm sorry I never visited. I'm sorry I never saw you with your daughter.

Then I think, Damn it, Madeleine. You should have invited me. I would have kept your secret from our parents if you'd asked me to.

I'm not exactly sure that's true. But it might be. I would like to think so, now.

Later that night, the phone rings. Juliet is just finishing her bath, but she waves me away impatiently. "I'm a big girl, Uncle Warren," she says reproachfully. "I can *certainly* take a bath by myself."

"Did I interrupt something?" Flip says when I somewhat breathlessly pick up the phone in the bedroom. "I was trying to time it for just after bedtime. Juliet's, I mean."

"Oh, hi," I say, lowering my voice for some reason. "No, she's just having her bath. We got a late start because we stayed so late at the park."

"Yes, well," Flip says. "I was thinking about that, actually, what you said."

"Yes?" I turn on a lamp. It gives off a tiny golden light inside the dark room.

"And I decided," Flip says, "that you were right."

"Really?" I say, sitting down on the edge of the bed. "That must have been a refreshing change."

"Yes, well, don't get too excited," Flip says. "What you were right about—I was unhappy, Warren. I guess. And it wasn't all because of you, even though I know you like to think that every single blip on my emotional radar screen is somehow intimately related to you."

"Look who's talking," I say. "I think the word *self-absorbed* comes to mind."

"Yes, but in my case, it's a simple matter of fact," Flip says. "Every blip on *your* emotional screen *is* intimately related to me. But be that as it may—"

I miss him so much at this moment that the longing itself fills me up. Maybe this longing is all I need.

"Be that as it may," Flip goes on, "I think you were right—I *did* think you could make it all go away. I thought that because I loved you, all right? And also because you *did* make me happy, when you wanted to."

"I always wanted to."

"Well, anyway," says Flip, "I figured, if this much, *this much,* why not more?" His voice grows hoarse. "If this much, why not everything?"

Maybe it isn't longing. Maybe it's just love.

"Some of it was because of you, I guess," Flip is saying. "How you always pulled away."

"Not always."

"Eventually always," Flip says. "Eventually always, yes, I think so. But that isn't what I called you up to say." There is a huge, long pause, a pause you could drive a truck through, Flip the actor would say, if he weren't having so much trouble with his own end of the conversation.

"I guess I wanted to say two things," Flip says finally, and way in the distance I hear the water run out of the tub.

"So one," says Flip, catching his breath, "is that I'm sorry, Warren. I really am. I'm sorry—for refusing to be happy sometimes. I guess I thought if I was miserable enough, you would—I don't know. Take pity on me. And then you would have to—make it better. So I guess you're not the only one in this relationship that knows something about emotional blackmail. Though I do think, compared to you, I'm a mere novice. Unless I'm biased."

"Which of course you are," I manage to say.

"Of course," Flip says. For once, his voice sounds as stilted as mine. "Well, that's the good news—as far as you're concerned. I mean, I don't *know* if thoughts of a reconciliation were on your mind—"

He pauses again, but I'm certainly not going to take *that* bait. But maybe he is a novice, because he says, "I know they were on mine, *obviously*. But I don't think so, Warren. That's the other thing I realized. Because—" He stops.

"What?" I say, trying not to sound impatient.

"It wasn't just when things were unhappy," Flip says. "That you—that you didn't—I mean, it was in our best times, too. You know what I mean. Like in Connecticut."

"You're talking about one incident, just one time out of a whole year—"

"You can't say I was unhappy then, Warren. In fact, the opposite." His voice falters. "About as opposite as it's possible to be, as a matter of fact."

"I remember," I say, to stop him from saying any more.

"And then when you walked in yesterday," Flip goes on, inexorably. "It was the same thing. I was so happy to see you, and you—"

"I know," I say quickly.

Flip laughs. "Of course you know. Good heavens, what was I thinking? Well, then, you must know what I'm going to say next, don't you, Warren? I mean, I don't *know* if you were having any thoughts of getting back together, I'm so *self-absorbed,* I probably wouldn't even notice if you were, but I just thought I ought to say, you know. Don't."

"And that's what you got from seeing me in the park today?"

Even over the phone I can feel Flip smile. What's weird is that even under the circumstances, I have to smile with him.

"No, Warren," he says, very gently. "I liked seeing you in the park, that's my point. I liked seeing you yesterday, too, remember? And a lot of good that did me, finally."

"But this morning you called me."

"I know," he says, in a very small voice. "I know, Warren, and I'm glad I did, but really, I think, you know, enough. I think you should come over here—soon, Warren—and get whatever you want to take with you, and let's just—" His voice breaks off.

"All right," I say. I just want this conversation to be over. Though I'm terrified of what will happen as soon as I hang up.

"So when can you come over?" Flip is saying. "To get your stuff, I mean."

"Juliet is going to be at Sara's tomorrow night. Since Monday isn't a school day, for some reason. Which means I'm free after about six."

"Well, then, come for dinner," Flip says. "We can pack up afterward."

I must admit, if I didn't feel as though my body were slowly turning to stone, I might actually be suspicious. Wait a minute, I might say. Haven't I seen this scene already? Lombard or Colbert or maybe even Katharine Hepburn telling the hero, "Don't even *think* about getting back together," just before that last scene where she finally reels him in?

No, it's the end of *His Girl Friday.* Cary Grant again. He acts as if he's totally ready to let Rosalind Russell leave, he even offers to help her go. And when she finally realizes he has tricked her again, she bursts into tears of re-lief.

That night, Juliet has another nightmare. And how I know is because I am in it with her.

We are wandering through a rocky desert, surrounded by huge buttes and towering stone structures, ochre and burnt orange, under a yellow sky. There's no heat and no cold—the temperature is neutral. And although the ground is barren, it's rough—endless rocks to clamber over, endless inclines to negotiate, up and down. At least the dream of drowning had a point—to save ourselves. What is the point of this?

When I wake, I know Juliet is still wandering in that dream. And this time I know that I have to go after her. There's nobody but me to do it.

I pull myself out of bed and go to Juliet's door. All I can hear is her deep, even breathing. Still, this much closer to her, I can feel the strength of the nightmare, its weight, its despair. I force myself to go into her room and sit down beside her on the edge of the bed. Even that doesn't wake her. After a minute, I put my hand on her shoulder.

"Juliet," I say quietly. "Wake up."

It takes her a few minutes, but when she looks at me, I see that she is fully awake, the way she was last night, although she is still so tired. On her face is the same despair I saw in the dream.

"You were having a bad dream," I say. I hope that what she sees in this wak-ing room offers her more than the barren landscape of the dream. I hope that without much hope.

She studies me in the darkness. I reach out and turn on the light beside her bed. She hides her eyes. Then, very slowly, she crawls into my lap. I put my arms around her.

"I miss her," she says. "I miss her all the time."

"I know," I say. "It hurts, doesn't it?"

"Sometimes it hurts," she says. "And sometimes I like it. Sometimes miss-ing her . . ."

". . . is like you're with her," I suggest when her voice trails off.

"But I forget things every day. I don't remember *anything*." She starts to cry. "I want to remember *everything*," she says. "But I can't."

So now I know what my knowing is good for. "I don't know about every-thing," I say, and I can feel her listening to me through her sobs. "But I can help you remember some things. If you want me to." Finally, she nods.

"But Juliet," I say. "Sometimes it hurts to remember. You know. Sometimes we remember things that—weren't so good."

She shakes her head. "But if I don't remember," she says. "Then it's like—like I made her go away."

"You didn't make her go away," I say, but this is yet another thing that no one ever believes.

"All right, Juliet," I say. "You remember her. And I'll help. All right? You think about her. And I'll try to say what you remember."

She looks up at me. "You might remember something, too," she says. "You could tell me, too."

Exactly what I don't want. But I say, "Yes, I could."

She snuggles more closely against me. I feel her fear, pulsing with her blood beneath her skin. I pull the covers up around her as best I can, and she sighs and sinks down into me a little deeper.

"Just let your mind go, all right, Juliet?" I say softly. This is harder than anything I've ever done, partly because nothing has ever mattered so much. But I can't do it *through* my body, either, like last night. This time, I have to use everything.

The first memory, when it comes, is simple. Madeleine and Juliet sitting at their sidewalk café, Madeleine drinking coffee, Juliet drinking *limonade*. Juliet raises her head to look at me, interrupting us both. "But Uncle Warren," she says. "I remembered this already."

"Juliet," I say, "it's really hard to talk and remember at the same time. Most people can't do it."

She studies me, and I can see how tired she is. "When you want to stop remembering," I say, "that's when you should start talking." She nods and puts her head back against my chest. Then she looks up at me again. "You don't have to talk, either, Uncle Warren," she offers "You can just help me remember."

"No, Juliet," I say. "Somebody has to say the words. Otherwise, you'll forget again."

So there are Madeleine and Juliet at their café. At first, the memories are very physical. Tiny bubbles popping out of the *limonade*. The sharp smell of Madeleine's coffee. Then I get a look at Madeleine's face, so much like Juliet's, but so much older. She's still a beautiful woman, which takes me aback, because I am not used to thinking of my sister in that way. But she looks so old. It's like seeing an old movie star in the present. "What are you talking about?" I say aloud. "Oh, you're telling her about something that happened in school—one of your girlfriends got in trouble for talking back to the teacher. And you're saying, 'It wasn't fair! It wasn't fair, Mama!' And she's saying,

'You're right, Minou. What do you think we should do about it?' And you're saying, 'What *can* we do?' And she's saying, 'Oh, there's always something to do—it's just hard to know what, sometimes.' And you're thinking, and she's watching you think—and she has this look on her face, Juliet, and you look up and see her looking at you, and you can see—" That she's in love with you, I want to say. "She thinks you're a wonderful girl," I say. "She's so proud of you. You can see she's so happy just to sit and talk with you—" Nothing could ever make her this happy, I want to say. My voice falters.

I feel Juliet's tears against my chest, and the memory shifts. "Now you're a baby," I say, "you're remembering back when you were such a little baby, this isn't even a memory in your mind, it's still a memory in your body. She has you on the changing table. I think she just changed your diaper. You're by a window, and sun—warm light—pours through the window. And I think you're hearing pigeons, though of course, you don't know what they are. But just the noise, that cooing sound. It's loud, and it makes you laugh. And your mother puts her face down and rubs her cheek against yours, and you laugh some more. You feel her cheek, it's soft. And the way her cheekbone presses . . . It's hard, but it doesn't hurt you. And she rubs her face back and forth against yours, and that feels good—fuzzy, kind of tickly—and you laugh even more. And you can't see her very well—her face is so close, and your eyes aren't very good yet, but you feed her smiling and smiling at you . . ."

The image hovers, suspended in my mind. Juliet is so still, I can feel the beating of my heart against her cheek. I force myself to take deep, slow breaths and I feel her breathing grow deeper, and she sighs. Maybe this is enough.

Then the image darkens, turns cloudy, and I see Madeleine lying on the couch, with two washcloths—crimson and royal blue—arranged across her forehead. Juliet is standing in the doorway—no, that's my memory. Here, she's sitting on the couch. Madeleine's legs are pulled up, and Juliet is sitting on Madeleine's feet, to keep them warm. "You're leaning against her legs," I say, "and she has one hand on your head. Her fingers are playing with your hair. And you're so scared, because she's so sick. And she wants to tell you not to be scared, Juliet, it's only a headache, it hurts but it's not serious—" and now we're in trouble, because I can't tell which of this is Juliet, and which is Madeleine, and which is me. "—Well, it *feels* serious when you have a headache like that, that's what your mother wants to say to me, Juliet, it *feels* like you're going to be in terrible pain for the rest of your life—all right, Madeleine, not just pain—agony. Hell, torture, torment. All right? But it only feels that way, right, Madeleine? There's nothing for Juliet to worry about.

Having a migraine is awful, and you really *can't* get up and act as though everything were normal, but when it's over, it's over, and life goes on, so don't worry, Juliet." I pause for breath. I'm going to have to do better than this, or we'll have to stop, and this would be a terrible place to stop. But I don't have any idea how to talk to Madeleine, how to imagine her. *Well, whose fault is that, Warren?* All right, Madeleine, let it be my fault. But you left first—you left so many times. You could have done anything. What happened?

But I can't keep thinking these questions because obviously she doesn't know. In fact, she must be asking them herself, because if she weren't— *That's right, Warren. If I weren't, maybe I wouldn't have gotten sick again. That's when I get sick, Warren, when I wonder how my life could still be different.*

The force of what she's saying fills me like a gust of wind, and I have to fight for my own breath. Now I want to be back in my body, alone with Juliet in her dark bedroom. I'm here, I think. I'm *here*. It's so easy to be somewhere else. But my body is only here.

I can feel Madeleine hovering—somewhere. All right, Madeleine, fine. You can come in now. What is it you want?

"So, Juliet," I say. "This is something I remember about your mother. From when she was a little girl. But still bigger than me, of course. I suppose she was your age, Juliet, just eight years old. And I was about Oscar's age, about three." Against my chest, I can feel Juliet smile.

"We're playing in the back yard of our house, you know, the house in Connecticut, the one where *Grand-mère* and *Grand-père* live." I have no memory of any of this, I have no idea what's coming. Madeleine doesn't care. She remembers. So I remember with her.

"It's wintertime. There is deep, deep snow. It's incredibly cold. We both have thick, warm coats—we're so bundled up, it's hard to move. And we have big, heavy boots—mine are blue, Madeleine's are red—so it's hard to move our feet. And still, we are just *so cold*. Maybe we've been playing outside for too long. The snow is that kind that has a crust on top, so if you stand in one place, or jump, or run, your foot breaks through the crust, and the snow is all powdery, and it's hard to get your foot out again.

"Now Madeleine—your mother—wants to go exploring. Which we *weren't* supposed to do. You remember that hill behind our house, Juliet—you don't know this, but I saw you running up it the first day I met you. You were running up to the top and twirling around and rolling down to the bottom, remember?" Against my chest, Juliet nods.

"All right, so now we're climbing up that hill—that's as far as we're supposed to go. I'm not even supposed to go that far. Madeleine is helping me.

Usually, she doesn't want me to come with her—oh, no, right, that was later, maybe when she was ten? Now she likes taking care of me. All right, not taking care of me, no, I remember this, too. We were—a team, I guess. She had girlfriends, but—oh. No, she didn't, not *real* friends. Not until she went away to school. She didn't have any friends when she lived at home. Well, I thought she was wonderful. I would have followed her anywhere. I would have—" My voice falters as this starts to become my memory, too. I still can't remember the ending, but I can imagine how painful it's going to be.

Coward, whispers Madeleine in my ear. *You want me to face my whole life, and you can't even bear to remember this?*

I try to imagine where Madeleine is now. It's almost ten in the morning, Paris time. What is she doing? Lining up for medication, sitting alone in her room, talking to a therapist, a nurse, a fellow patient? Suddenly, I miss her so much, I can hardly stand it. Just like Juliet, I want to be with her. Only, do I want to be with her as she is now, do I really want that? Or do I want to be with her when she was eight and I was three?

Both, probably. All right, Madeleine. I'm ready now. "The snow is getting in my boots," I say. "But I pretend it isn't, because I think if Madeleine finds out I have wet feet she'll take me back. And she's so happy to have me along. 'Come on, Warren,' she says. 'When we get to the top of the hill, we can roll down.' Only we can't, because it's all woods on that side. So we have to walk down, which is harder, going downhill, and more snow gets in my boots. I don't care—it's an adventure. Madeleine's special times.

"It's getting later. The snow is blue. Like ink. The sky is lower and lower. The trees are black. I think I'll never forget the way it looks, black trees and blue snow, and silver light, the last light reflecting off the snow. 'Look,' Madeleine says, and turns me around. When we face the other way, the sun is setting. And on that side, the snow is pink, and orange, and red, and gold, and also bluish, and also glowing." That piece of art on Madeleine's wall . . .

"Oh, Juliet. It's like magic. 'It *is* magic,' Madeleine says. She's whispering in my ear. 'Warren, this is a magic place. We could make a wish *right now,* and if we knew the magic words, it would come true.'

"I think she knows those words. No, she says, she doesn't. 'But you'll learn them, right, Madeleine?' She thinks she will. I think she will, too, and I think I'm so lucky, because then she can teach them to me."

I don't want to tell the rest of the story. How we couldn't get back up the hill because I was too tired to climb that far, and too cold. How they came and found us, finally, angry and worried—my mother was so furious with Madeleine, it was the one time I ever did hear her raise her voice, saying terrible things that I suppose I'm lucky not to be able to remember.

But that isn't the part of the story that matters. There were plenty of times that Madeleine fought with my mother, then and later. Madeleine and I were as close as ever afterwards—that didn't change until she went away to school.

It was just that moment when the world seemed magic. Though I still don't understand why Juliet needed to hear it.

Juliet is looking up at me, her eyes wide. "I saw it, Uncle Warren," she says in almost a whisper. "I saw it. It *was* a magic place. She *was* magic."

"Oh, Juliet. No, she wasn't. I mean—Juliet—" I don't know how to do this. Madeleine, you've left me the hardest job, and I don't know how to do it.

"Juliet," I say finally, "I know that if your mother was magic, she would make a wish. And that wish would be that she would be all better and you would be with her again. And she would be so happy to be with you. But she can't do that, Juliet. I mean, not now." I stop and take a breath.

"I mean, Juliet, she isn't really magic. We only think so because we love her. Someday she'll come back. But until then—we can't do anything, Juliet. We simply have to wait."

"I hate waiting," she says.

"I know," I say. "I don't like it much either."

"No, Uncle Warren. I really *hate* it."

"You know what?" I say. "Madeleine hated it, too. Because she didn't even want to wait until the next day to go exploring. She could have waited for a warmer day. She could have waited—" until she was older. Until she could really leave. Until she could really leave and not come back.

"And then you wouldn't have seen the magic part," Juliet says.

"No," I say. I am completely confused. I don't know what I learned from any of this.

Then Juliet says, "Will you tell me that story again tomorrow?"

"Yes, if you want," I say, surprised.

"And the day after that? And the day after that?"

"Yes," I say again.

"You can tell it to me *every* day," Juliet says. "And I can tell *you* a story every day. And that way, we won't forget."

"All right," I say, brushing her hair off her damp forehead. She climbs back into her bed, and I tuck her in.

I want nothing more than to sink into my solitary bed and fall into a sleep as blank as I can make it. But of course, it doesn't work that way. An open door is an open door. And what I have to remember is that morning in Connecticut, the one where Flip and I woke up together. His hands on my face, my neck, his miraculous skin against my skin, so that my whole body opens to absorb him. "Warren. *Warren*," he's whispering, but I am saying, "Don't. Please don't." As I soak up as much of him as I can get, as I push him away as hard as I can. As I say, "I *told* you no," my own fierce whisper. As I say, "You always *want* something. Stop *crowding* me."

I hear a knock on my closed door. "Uncle Warren," Juliet is saying, with her precise, pointed little accent, "I want to come in."

"All right," I say, too surprised to consider my reply.

The door opens, and Juliet comes right up to the edge of my bed. "Uncle Warren," she says, "can I get into bed with you?"

"All right," I say again, still surprised, still confused.

She might be making the bed, she turns down the covers so precisely. Then she pulls them back up—sheet, quilt, coverlet—and arranges herself against me, her back curled into my stomach as I hover over her, lying on my side.

"Mama used to let me do this if I had a bad dream," she explains. "Then when I was already asleep, she would take me back to my own bed. But sometimes, if it was a *very* bad dream, she would let me sleep with her the whole night. And Uncle Warren, I had a *very* bad dream tonight. So can I stay here all night?"

"All right," I say. "Sleep well, Juliet. *Fais de beaux rêves.*"

"*Toi aussi,* Uncle Warren. Sweet dreams to you too."

SUNDAY

This morning, Juliet and I are rushing yet again so I can be on time for my clients. I set her up in the waiting room with her books and the few toys that somehow got packed for her in Paris, and I can't help imagining how nice it would be if, say, Flip, were available today as well. But even if he were in the picture, he was supposed to be out of town this weekend. The two of us being together would hardly solve the child care problem.

Just when I think the last client has left and Juliet and I can do something together before the sleepover (we still have to find her a sleeping bag, for one thing), Mrs. Mallory, my client from last Sunday, walks through the door. "I know I don't have an appointment," she says, glancing at Juliet, who is talking under her breath with a collection of two dolls, one of Sara's beanbag animals, and some ceramic figurines from my living room. "But something has come up, and I wondered if you could see me."

I want so much to say no. But then I look at her face. Now that she's facing a future she never imagined, she wants some idea of what will happen to her. I'm sorry to say I can understand that. I'm also sorry to say I can use the money.

"Go on in," I say, motioning her to the office. "I can give you half an hour." Her face falls.

"I can pay you extra," she says, "if that's your point. Because I think the situation is really quite complicated—"

A woman in distress *and* someone who's used to paying for what she wants. I don't particularly like feeling compassion for her. But I don't seem to be able to help it.

"I can imagine how difficult everything is right now," I say firmly. "Believe me, I can. But half an hour really will be enough." She wants to argue, but she's more desperate than stubborn, so she goes in. With yet another glance at Juliet.

Suddenly—well, all right, I'm slow today—I realize how out of place Juliet must look to her in this office. Is she wondering if Juliet is the cleaning woman's child? Did Juliet notice? And if so, what did she think?

"Juliet," I say, "that woman who just came in—she didn't have an appointment. But I need to see her anyway. So it's going to be another half hour before we can go."

She shrugs, reminding me of that day on the train when I asked if she would rather call me Uncle Warren.

"But as soon as I'm done with her, then we'll go get you a sleeping bag for tonight," I say. "And I suppose we should go pick out a birthday present for Sara." Shit, I had forgotten about that. Now we really will be pressed for time. And the present will have to be wrapped. And a card . . .

Juliet is looking off into the corner of the room. "Uncle Warren," she is saying, "do I have to go to the sleepover?"

"No, of course you don't have to go," I say, mindful of the client waiting through what I'd expected to be a two-sentence conversation. "I thought you wanted to go. Is this your first time to spend the night—" *away from home?* Obviously not.

But Juliet is saying, "No, no, in Paris I went on lots of sleepovers—they were great. But I lived there. I don't live here. So when I go to sleep at Sara's house, where do I go *back* to?"

"You come back to our house," I say, swallowing hard.

"See, Uncle Warren," Juliet explains. "I want to go to the sleepover. And I want to stay in your house, with you. But if I go there, I won't be at your house. And if I stay at your house, I won't be there."

"I'm afraid that's more or less the way it works."

"But I don't *like* that."

"Nobody does," I say as drily as I can manage.

"Why can't everyone stay in the same place, then?"

"Because then your mother would have stayed in Connecticut," I say. "And you would never have been born."

She considers this. "Well, why can't everyone stay in the same place starting *now?*"

"Starting when?" I wait for her to figure it out.

"So, then I would stay in Paris with Mama, and you would stay in New York, and Sara, and Flip, and we still wouldn't all be in the same place."

"Probably not," I say.

"Well, I guess people will just have to visit," Juliet says. "But if you want to know the truth, it isn't a very good solution."

"No argument here," I say. "So, are you going to stay at Sara's tonight?"

"If I don't like it, can I come back?" she says. Now *there's* one of the few advantages of childhood.

"Of course you can," I say. "I'll give you my number, and Flip's number—remember, I'll be there tonight. But you can always call me either place, and I'll come and get you as soon as you call."

"Well, not as *soon* as I call," Juliet points out. "It will take you *some* time to come over, especially if you're at Uncle Flip's. That's farther away from Sara's house than your house is, in case you didn't know."

"Juliet, how on earth do you know that?"

She shrugs. "You better hurry up, Uncle Warren. You said *half an hour,* and you've already used up *ten minutes.*"

When Flip answers the door of what used to be our apartment, I feel a push from him like the negative force of a magnet. If I had thought our bodies would solve this problem by themselves, I seem to have been wrong. About Flip's body, anyway.

Flip offers me a glass of wine, says dinner will be ready soon, invites me to sit down. Nice touch, Flip, considering that we bought most of this furniture together. He tells me that Davis has called him again—apparently he doesn't yet have a distributor for his movie, but he's already on to a new one. "That script isn't even *done* yet," Flip says, "but of course, he must have *me* for the best friend again, at some unspecified point in the future. And this time—oh, you don't know any of this, but he got back together with Tanya, for just as long as the shoot lasted, because he rewrote it so that *she* played his girlfriend—"

"Life imitating art."

"Life imitating ambition is more like it," says Flip, "considering that their romance only lasted until the rough cut, or maybe all the way through the mix, I'm not sure. But now he's dating another actress, so this new screenplay is written around her—"

"Oh, let me guess. He wants you to be in love with this other actress while he's in love with Tanya. And then the two of you can switch."

Flip laughs, although something happens in his face when I mention Tanya. "I won't even bother being impressed by that," he says. "It's more of a commentary on Davis than on you, don't you think?"

"Are you going to do it?"

He sighs. "I don't know. It's complicated with Tanya, because—" Then he looks at me. "I'm sure you have an opinion on this, too."

"No," I say truthfully. "Actually, I don't."

"Why not?"

"Well, Flip. You aren't telling me anything."

"Like that matters," Flip says. "I'm sure you even knew what the end of that sentence was going to be."

I don't expect this to hurt my feelings. If pressed—all right, if pressed really hard—by someone who wasn't Flip—I might even admit that I deserved it. But still, it does hurt, and I suppose Flip can see that. "Who *are* you?" he says. "I turn my back for five minutes, and you turn into this totally different person."

"You don't approve?"

"Well, it's certainly an improvement. I'm just not sure I like it."

I can't believe this is the last time we'll talk like this. If Flip were here, he'd burst into Joni Mitchell: "Don't it always seem to go, that you don't know what you got till it's gone?" But Flip *is* here, and he's *not* doing that. Well, soon I'll have the pleasure of imagining him all I want, unimpeded by his actual presence.

"Can I ask you something?" I say abruptly. "Why do you think things took off for you all of a sudden? Professionally, I mean."

Flip looks at me with the hint of a smile. "You mean, was all I needed to be a success just to get rid of you?"

"Well, you know," I say in a low voice. "Was *that* what you had to kill?"

I must say, he looks completely startled. "God, that never even occurred to me," he says. "And," he adds, watching me, "I can't believe you don't know this. But since you apparently don't, no, Warren. Of course not. It didn't have anything to do with that."

Once again, I am sure he can see how relieved I am. But he just goes on to tell me about finishing Davis's movie. "And then Massimo said he saw something 'abandoned' in that fucking leap," he says ruefully, "even though there's nothing at all *abandoned* about the part I'm playing for *him*. In fact, there's nothing *abandoned* anywhere in his whole movie."

"Still. That was why he hired you."

"Yes, but that isn't the reason. That things took off, I mean." Flip is twisting in his chair, struggling for words. "I don't know, Warren. Taking that leap—somehow, that was mine." He bites his lip. "But the industrials I got after that, and Massimo's movie, and all the rest of my good fortune—I mean, I thought they were what I wanted but—"

"But they weren't *yours.*"

Was even that too much for me to say? Apparently not, because Flip is saying, "Right, and what *would* be mine, at this point? What *would* be the—I don't know." He shrugs. "Rosie says, well, you're still not being an artist. But it's easy for her to talk—she *has* a job. Doing what she loves, apparently, although it will probably finish her off before she's forty at the rate she's going. But at least she'll die happy."

"Whereas you'll die healthy, rich, and miserable. If not under the wheels of a truck."

Flip laughs. "Something like that," he says. Then his mouth twists. "See?" He gestures with each hand. "Still unhappy. Not your fault."

"Oh, I don't know," I say. "I'd like to think that I'm still making you at least a little unhappy. Especially tonight."

We look at each other until the timer rings in the kitchen. "So you probably have all sorts of insight about what I just said," Flip says as he heads for the other room.

"No, actually, I don't."

"You mean now that I want to listen, you don't want to tell me."

"Well," I say, "I'm a psychic, not a shrink."

From all the way off in the kitchen, I feel his double-take. And then I hear him laugh.

"I don't know," I say, following him into the kitchen. "I could probably tell you something."

"Maybe later," he says, bustling around with the food.

"I mean, I *do* think that—"

"Warren. I said no."

I press my lips together as Flip watches me with that sideways smile. "So," he says. "Apparently the old Warren is not entirely gone."

"Nor the old Flip."

"Well, they weren't so bad," Flip says. "In their way." He motions me to sit down. It's so odd to be sitting here, having him serve me food. Usually, I cooked. It's almost too much, to look at the salad—in *my* huge farmhouse bowl, the beige one with the pink and blue stripes—but not my salad. I would have had arugula, endive, mushrooms, cilantro. He has iceberg, cucumbers, green peppers, tomato. And pasta, some kind of ziti with red sauce, sausage. There are mushrooms in that. "It's good," I say. "Thank you."

"Well," he says breezily, setting down the basket of French bread, "it isn't fettuccini and quail, but—"

"Don't," I say. "Please don't."

Suddenly everything stops.

We stare at each other across the crowded table, eyes locked. And out of that frozen landscape, I hear myself say, "I don't think I can be here without touching you."

"I have no objection to that," he says. But blank.

It takes everything I have to stand up. But I do it. I walk over there, and turn him to face me, and he lets me do it, but he doesn't move. I put my arms around him, feeling the exact curve of his shoulder blades, the way they fit into his back, like wings. I feel every ridge along his spine, the dip and curve at his waist, the way my palms fit over his ass, his muscles hard, then soft. Still, he doesn't move. I reach under his T-shirt, feeling the smooth skin just above his waist, and he shivers, he can't help it. But he's still so far away.

I feel I've come to the end of my knowing, like a road that simply runs out. It took you here. What takes you on?

"Flip," I say. "Please. Let me come back."

"I don't know, Warren." He shakes his head. "I just don't have any hope that it would ever be any different."

"But it *is* different. Can't you feel that it is?"

He starts to cry, a jagged river that swirls around me, full of ice and broken glass. I want so much to let go. But whatever I caused or didn't cause, all I can do now is hold on.

Finally, he moves. He puts his cheek against mine. It burns where it touches me. Still, I don't pull back. All the information I have is here, at this moment, just this warm, blind, wordless zone where our two bodies touch.

It doesn't seem like much.

It's all I have.

So I stand here with him in what used to be our kitchen, wondering what is possible now.

TWO

SOLIDARITY

FOREVER

To Gerrie Casey

THREE

PYRRHIC VICTORIES, GLORIOUS DEFEATS

Those to whom I had entrusted the letter
Threw it away. But those I paid no attention to
Brought it back to me.
Thereby I learned.

What I ordered was not carried out.
When I arrived I saw
It was wrong. The right thing
Had been done.
From that I learned.

—Bertolt Brecht, "The Learner"

COMMUNITY

ROSIE: Oh, God, another surge—I'm sure that particular gush of menstrual blood has soaked through both the tampon *and* the pad, and it's only a matter of time before it makes its way through my underwear, pantyhose, and pants. Charles Marsden, the president of the university workers' local, is in mid-sentence, but I have to find a bathroom *now*.

What is wrong with me? With my body, I mean. I know, I know, "my body, my self." But now that my body is in such distress, I feel totally controlled by it and totally alienated from it. I'm only thirty-five, this can't be the flooding that brings on early menopause. Which leaves one other obvious possibility, but it can't be that either; calm down, Rosie, it's *just* a heavy period. Just your third unusually heavy period in a row.

I sidle out the door, picking up a disapproving glance from Isabel and a surprised one from Tito. The fact that all three of us have to be here says something about how important this meeting is, how essential it is to demonstrate to Charles—to the members, of *course,* but particularly to Charles—that he has the full support of the union, so that he doesn't go off half-cocked (don't you love that phrase? How do you imagine someone going off fully cocked? Well, picture that, and you've got Charles), and here I am, actually leaving in the middle of one of Charles's long, convoluted sentences (not that I have the right to say anything about *that,* God knows, but I like to think that mine are at least *interesting*). And the worst of it is, I can't explain. Even if I said, "I had to pee," or something like that, I'd be expected, and I think, rightly, to have more self-control. One of my first inklings of what the life of a union organizer would be like was during the first negotiations here at Olympia University, when I was still a secretary. I was on the negotiating committee, of course, and I watched Connie Chapman, our staff organizer, suffer through three smoky hours (in those days, people still smoked at negotiations) of agonizingly dry contact lenses because it would have been a sign of weakness to go and take them out. And everything I knew about how things *should* be, said, "Well, that's ridiculous," and "Why should we play the men's game?" but it was crystal clear, watching Connie flirt and charm and bulldoze her way through that particular midnight to 3 a.m. session, that if she had broken the rhythm and gone to make herself more comfortable, she *would* have lost face (no pun intended) and we *would* have lost valuable items on our list. ("But darling," said Flip when I told him this story, "it's *much* easier to flirt in contact lenses," but what does *he* know?)

Where was I? Oh, yes, I was watching my fellow organizer Isabel glare at me, though I'm sure Isabel wouldn't take it at all well if I left a huge red puddle on my chair. But obviously I can't tell her that.

Getting out the door is tricky, because I feel a second surge coming on. Of course Charles gives me that hurt, puzzled look—how did he *ever* get elected? Well, that look is probably part of the answer: he brooks no opposition from anybody, but that includes the boss. And the members probably like his adversarial relationship with the union, which at least some of them see as "just like the boss." No, no, we're *family,* I always want to say. Of course we make mistakes, of course we act badly—but when things get bad, we're the ones you can count on. Whereas the boss is the enemy. He—or OK, these days, she—really does want to take your time and energy and precious spirit and turn it into profit, or at least into power, making himself bigger and you smaller, every single day you go to work.

God, these pants are tight. My bloated stomach presses hard against my waistband as my womb contracts. I scuttle frantically to the end of the hall and fling myself into the bathroom, just in time for another surge to gush out into the toilet.

I suppose I'll have to see a doctor. I pull out the tampon and drop it into the toilet, then examine the stuff that's made it onto the menstrual pad. Big red chunks, besides the bright red blood that has soaked in, a cheerful, vital color. The chunky stuff is like—what? Something clotted—liquid and solid at the same time. Let's face it, I'm fascinated. I've always liked my periods, the things my body does on its own. All the fluids—first that cloudy jelly, then something clear and flowing, and then that milky moisture. And then those last three days: first tired and miserable, then a surge up (about twenty-four hours before the period actually came), then a real crash (twelve hours later), and then an amazing sense of relief. And out of that relief, that newfound calm, the blood would start to flow.

Now that old familiar cycle is gone. I could make friends with this one—but it's not making that easy. Finally, I'm clean, dry, protected—at least for the moment. I slide back into the meeting as Charles reluctantly wraps up his remarks. Isabel and Tito turn to look at me. And now it's my turn to speak.

TANYA: Child, I came to this meeting all in good faith, but I was *not ready* for this. My old friend Malik, whom I've known since before high school, got his social service agency to come out with some money to do a play—something for the community, which I'm all for, and Malik wants to start a theater company with it, Tiger's Eye, which I'm also all for, but look. Not fifteen minutes into the meeting and it's all ego, ego, ego. Though you'd think after umpteen years doing theater I would be used to that.

"The problem with your play, Idris," Bernard is saying, "is that one of the main characters is a white man. Which means that if we do it, we have to bring somebody else in from outside."

"Luis could play that part," Idris says.

"Idris, *mi amor,* I really don't think I could pass for white," Luis says. "If I could, believe me, I would be working all the time, baby, *all the time.*"

"Is casting really the issue?" says Janie, who is white, so you know *she's* got an ax to grind. "Shouldn't we just pick the best project and cast whoever's right for the part?" I don't know. Maybe I'm just ready to jump all over Janie because of all that leftover bad feeling about Flip. I do *not* like to be let down.

"Well, we can't plan around particular people, anyway," says Elinor. "Because you know whoever we cast, we're going to lose two-thirds of them by opening night."

"We're not going to lose anybody," Malik says. "People are getting paid here, remember?"

Elinor laughs. "Getting paid? Right, Malik, all of one hundred dollars a week. Somebody's going to get film work, or an industrial, or a road show of

The Lion King, and they'll be out of here before you can say, 'No money for un-derstudies.' "

Malik makes a face at me, hoping I'll find a way to turn the tide. So I say, "Child, please. Go back two steps. Why are we doing this in the first place? Because we're *tired* of that old paying work. Lord knows, *I* am. Mammy and Sapphire parts for the girls, gangstas and best friends for the guys—and lucky to get it, right?" Elinor twists her mouth but has the grace not to interrupt. Just *like* Flip, I can't help thinking, feeling all lonely and left out with his job on Davis's film, and then he has to take it out on *me.* But come on, Tanya, be-cause maybe *this* group could *be* something. Maybe.

"Well," I say, "you *know* I'd kill to get any one of those jobs, so long as they paid me, but still. Here's our chance to do something really *fine.* Something that people really *need* to see."

Malik applauds. Bernard frowns. Elinor shakes her head.

"That's not why I'm here," Luis says.

"Me neither," says Bernard.

"OK, why?" I say.

"Frankly?" says Luis. "I want to do something different. That I wouldn't get a chance to do otherwise." Luis makes a living in three ways: he does Spanish-language voice-overs for radio and TV; he does the Hispanic businessman type in industrials that want to reach out to the multiculti world; and he some-times gets the Latin lover in those TV movies. You know, the kind of guy that walks up to the heroine when she's depressed and says, "Ah, a beautiful woman like you should never be sad, señora."

"What do you want, Luis, to play a villain?" Elinor says drily.

"Richard the Third," Luis says promptly. "Now is the winter of our discon-tent—"

"Hold it," says Idris. "Not on my dime you don't start quoting Shakespeare, thank you very much."

"My point being," Luis says, unfazed as usual, "that I could give a fuck what 'needs' to be done, excuse my French. We're actors. It's not our job to think about the audience."

"Can we get back to the main point here?" Bernard says. "Whose play are we going to do?"

"Bernard, honey," I say, "you wrote a lovely play. Really. I would love to play Edesha, in fact, so please keep me in mind, but for this project—child, you wrote a love story."

"Right," says Elinor. "And I agree, it's a good piece of writing, so Bernard, congratulations, but it isn't—it isn't part of our *mission.*" Well. Aren't too many white people would say *our mission* at this particular meeting.

"Hey, baby, you *can* get cast—" Luis begins.

"As Richard the Third?" Elinor says hotly. "Don't talk to me about type-casting, all right, Luis? Just don't even start. Till some casting director tells *you* that if you're not ten pounds *under*weight, you're a character actress who won't work until you're forty-five, and we all *know* how many great women's parts there are then. So please don't come crying to me, Luis, because I'm here for the exact same reason you are, which is that I'd also like to do something that no one else will let me do, and that's not anything in Bernard's play. No offense, Bernard, you certainly don't have to write plays with me in mind—"

"Oh, thank you *so* much," Bernard says. "What a relief."

"Fine," says Elinor. "But it's self-interest that keeps a group like this together—it is, Tanya, so let's just all be honest and find something that *is* in all our interests, and then maybe we'll have a fighting chance of getting halfway to opening night." She glares at Bernard, Malik, Luis, and me in turn.

"Maybe we should just take a vote," Malik says.

Janie shakes her head. "I don't think we should do it that way." She stops and blushes. "I think we should—"

"Spit it out, baby," says Luis. "Don't be shy." With this very *fond* look. My gaze meets Idris's, and we roll our eyes. Privately, since it might *not* be Janie's fault.

"Consensus," Janie says finally. "A decision that works for all of us. So maybe we shouldn't do either play." She hesitates again.

"Hey, Janie," Bernard says, giving her his special melting look. "Just tell us." Oh, rub salt in the insult, Bernard. Not that I have a particle of interest in him, or Luis either, but that doesn't mean I want to watch them fall all over themselves.

"All right," says Janie. "I think we should create our own material. And Malik should direct, because it's his project—"

"No," says Malik.

"And either Idris or Bernard could create a play—a script, I mean—with parts for the rest of us, but we could help, you know, input—improvisation, or brainstorming . . ."

Bernard is *so* torn, because he hates this idea for about a million reasons, but now he's got this Janie thing going, though honestly? It's more of a Luis thing. Bernard is *definitely* a leading man in *his* own mind, even if the world gives him mainly voiceovers. And all that regional theater that they *have* to cast Black—you know, August Wilson and Othello and the local color in Tennessee Williams. I don't think he's much of an actor myself, but lots of people *do* like that big-voiced thing. And Malik has always enjoyed his company, but

Malik always *does* see the best in everyone. And *that* is why I miss Flip, to tell you the honest truth. Because I could just look at him and know that he saw what I was seeing, and that's harder to replace than you might think.

"First of all," Malik says quickly, trying to head off the big fight he sees coming, "I'm not a director, Janie."

"I'll direct," Elinor says unexpectedly.

"You?" says Bernard.

"Why not?" Elinor says. "I've always wanted to."

"We never even thought about who would direct," Idris says thoughtfully. "But if you do, Elinor, I'll write something. You're someone I could work with."

"Thank you," says Elinor, surprised and genuine.

Bernard shrugs. "If you're not going to do the play I wrote, I'd rather act anyway."

Luis gives Janie a significant look. "Then do we need another actor?" he says. "Or an actress? You know." He pauses to give the line full mileage. "To keep Janie company."

"I know someone," I say, surprising myself. "A man."

"A white man," Idris says.

I nod. "But he won't try to take over—"

"No such animal," Luis says with conviction, and Elinor nods.

"Oh, Luis, like you're such a wilting flower," I say, and Luis grins. "Seriously," I say, "he wouldn't. Not that it matters, but he's gay. So we'd have *that* perspective, too, if we're talking about us participating and all." Honestly. Watch how Bernard and Luis both relax when they hear *that* news. Elinor, too, if it comes to that.

"Why is everybody so concerned with representing the gay male perspective, particularly the white gay male perspective, but no one ever even mentions the lesbian viewpoint, particularly the Black womanist point of view?" Idris says.

"Cause dykes is nasty," says Luis, and grins again.

"Hello! The seventies are over!" Bernard says at the same time.

"But, Idris, you *are* a part of this group," I say seriously, before I see her grinning. So the meeting breaks up—Malik, Idris, and Elinor talking business; Luis, Bernard, and Janie talking whatever. And I sit here by my lonesome and wonder why I've just put myself in a position where I have to call Flip.

ROSIE: So now it's my turn to speak. We're having this meeting in a large classroom—it's in our contract that the University has to give us meeting space, but they don't have to give us *good* space. And this is only a meeting of the local union officers, the stewards, and the negotiating committee—about sixty people, all told. Plus the three of us from downtown, which is what the workers always call us since union headquarters is downtown, even though *our* office is uptown. ("How do you feel about being a tub?" my best friend Marcy asked me when I got this job. I thought she was making some crack about my weight, although that seemed so unlike her, I knew it couldn't be that. "You know, a TUB," Marcy said, grinning. "A trade union bureaucrat.") So here we are, crowded into this classroom that was never meant to hold more than about thirty-five—an insult they would never wreak on their own elite students.

I briefly consider saying something like that, then decide it will make me sound petty. After Charles, I need to get them thinking *big*. I look at all the glazed-over faces he's left behind. Still, they're devoted to him. They'll zone out while he talks, then vote the way he's asked them to. If I don't do *my* job.

"So, here we are again," I say ruefully, surveying each individual face. I get the same feeling I always get—this amazing love for every single person in this room. I never feel it so fully anywhere else, except at a demonstration, of course—so buoyed up, so moved that we're all here together. If I'd gotten this feeling more often in church, I would have stayed un-lapsed. "Here we all are, and the University is acting in bad faith *again,* and negotiations have been dragging on since April, and now it's halfway through November. So we're all saying the same thing, right: 'How long can this go on?' " A murmur of response. I've been here forever, so most of these people know me, some as a fellow secretary from the old days, but most, admittedly, as a tub. Albeit a tub they like. This hasn't been my permanent assignment for about four years, though, so a lot of them don't know me very well.

"And just to make things that little bit more interesting, just to add that little bit of spice to the stew, Amy picks *this* month to have her baby." Two months early, granted, but the negotiations were supposed to have been over months ago. Why downtown took such a long time to see the writing on the wall and replace her is beyond me. If Charles wants to hint that we're short-changing them, he's not exactly short of material. I don't believe it *was* that. But calling it plain old incompetence hardly makes us sound any better.

"Look," I say, "I know this is one of the toughest times in any negotiation, OK? I was on the organizing committee here before we even *had* a union, I was on our first negotiating committee, and then when I came on staff, I handled our next two contracts after that. It's only the last four years that I haven't been around—obviously, I missed the best part . . ." This gets a little laugh, about what I could hope for.

"What I'm trying to say is that I don't have any illusions about what we're up against. They're a monster, OK, they're a giant. They're the third largest landlord in the city of New York. Their budget is in the millions. Their trustees run the city. We all know that, but OK, we can remind ourselves once in a while." I laugh, and a couple of people laugh with me, the way that some women do, just to stay in sympathy. "I remember," I say, "writing those facts over and over and over again, one newsletter after another, when we were still trying to *get* the union. Because in those days, if you don't mind my saying so, it seemed *really* hopeless—only about three other private universities were even organized, and who were we to think we could organize this— leviathan? This behemoth?" OK, *that* was a bit much.

I lean forward on the podium, focus again on their faces. "The point being," I say, "that we won. The point being, they only *look* unbeatable. The point being, we beat them. For the past eight years, every single contract we've gotten has been better than the one before. Every single contract, we've won something that they didn't want us to have. Every single contract has made our lives better—OK, not as much as we'd like, not as much as we deserve— but *better,* definitely better. Am I right?" A few nods. Some people muttering to neighbors, which I welcome, actually. Let them disagree. If they wake up, they can think about what I'm saying, and then they *will* agree. Or at least we'll be talking on different terrain. Charles's "we can't trust the union" routine is so damn deadly.

"Now we're at a very difficult point in the process," I say. "Those of you who have been through it before know what I mean. There's always this point, this space of time, when winning just looks impossible. When it looks like they're so big and we're so small. And this particular time around, we have the added complication of Amy going out and me coming in, which, to be perfectly honest, is not exactly terrific timing. We all know that, OK? I'm not pretending any different."

Isabel's mouth tightens. She's from the old school, although she's younger than I am—she never wants to hear us admit mistakes, because in her view, the union is infallible. Now she's going to go right back downtown and tell them I was bad-mouthing the leadership. Of course, she could say that any- way—some of my colleagues would. But Isabel's not malicious, just rigid. She would be much happier if I scolded the local, from Charles on down, which of course would be *so* effective, Isabel, thank you very much.

Come on, Rosie. Focus. I fix my gaze on Tony, sitting in the front row. Patrice, next to him. Elena, next to her. "Look at you!" I say suddenly. "I have to say it, people, you are amazing! You're working eight hours a day, sometimes ten, night shifts, weekends—and month after month after month, you've kept this going. You go to negotiations at night, and meet with your buildings on your lunch hour, and make phone calls to get people out for rallies, and answer all those *questions* everyone's always asking, right? 'Why isn't the union *doing* anything?' 'Why is it *taking* so long?' 'Why don't we have a *contract* yet?' Am I right?" This does get a laugh, because yes, this is exactly what they've been going through, and they didn't think we knew.

"And you're starting to wonder yourselves, why it's taking so long, and why we're not making more progress. And you look at their negotiators, who are paid full-time to be at these meetings, who get to go home and sleep late the day after an all-night session, when *you* have to be back at your desks at 9 a.m. sharp; you look at their negotiators, who have MBAs and law degrees and really expensive suits—what do you think those suits cost, actually? Two hundred dollars?"

"Two hundred?" someone yells out. "Try five!"

"More like a thousand!"

"Nothing wrong with wearing nice clothes," someone else comments.

"Nothing at all," I say. "And if they give us the raise we've been asking for, we can maybe afford some too, right? The point being, people, that if we let them psych us out, we're going to act from a position of weakness. And I want us to come from strength. I want us to look around this room and see the incredible strength we represent, the way we're all here together, all different types of jobs, all different races and backgrounds, male and female, gay and straight—when do people *ever* come together like this? This is what freaks them out. This is what blows their minds, because they can't believe that here we all are, together, on our own time, these stupid little secretaries and file clerks and xerox operators, from their point of view, because—until we don't show up Monday morning—they have no idea of the work we do, am I right?" This gets nods, agreement. "And they can't understand how we can be holding out so long, how we don't just cave."

I take a deep breath. This is it. Here's where I have to win them over without bad-mouthing Charles. Or alienating him. The pompous fool.

"OK, so let's get down to it. Charles is proposing that we either get the contract we want, or go on strike January 4th, the day the students come back from Christmas vacation. And, in order to put pressure on the University, Charles wants us to announce that deadline now." I take another breath.

"I really struggled over this one, people." Well, I struggled over how to explain what a truly horrible idea it was. "There's always this point where we have to ask ourselves, have we been too nice for too long? Is this the time to get tough? And Charles—we've been in this together a long time, so I can say this to you, right, Charles?—" What's he going to say—no?

"Charles is always the first one to stand up and say, 'We're not going to take this any more!' Which is why he's your president, right, which is why you elected him, because you know you can trust him to stand up and tell you when it's time to be militant. And when you do, people, remember, we're behind you all the way." I gesture to Isabel, who looks stern, and Tito, who smiles and shakes clasped hands over his head.

"But I'd like to respectfully suggest, people, that what Charles is proposing is—not wrong, it's not wrong at all, it's classic union tactics, it's our strength. But maybe, I think *maybe,* it's premature."

Charles glares. Well, come *on,* Charles. Did you really think the union was going to let you call a strike at *this* stage? My God, if we *have* to talk strike, at least let's wait till the goddamn holidays are over. Till people have bought their Christmas presents and paid their January bills. Not to mention that nobody wants to picket in the goddamn cold—have you been living in Florida for the past eight years? Spring term starts April 12th, so if there *is* going to be a strike, which God forbid, isn't *that* the day to shoot for?

So I lay this out, a bit more tactfully, along with some standard-issue optimism about what we might achieve in negotiations between now and then. That part is hard for me, because I *don't* actually believe it. Charles is right about one thing: the University isn't going to budge. But OK, Amy or somebody should have caught on over the summer and called a strike for fall. Now it's too goddamn late, and if we have to shuffle and backpedal and make up stories until April 12th, well, then we do.

So I lay out my mixture of half-truth and whole-truth, pep talk and analysis, optimism and realism. I lay out my sincerity, my faith, my love. And now—and this part is always thrilling, and somehow reassuring, like a roller-coaster that you really *don't* expect to crash—now it's their turn.

FLIP: I am just getting out of rehearsal—if you could even call it that. I mean, this director! Her idea of direction is telling you to talk faster. I don't know why I even bother doing showcases anymore. The pay is literally token, meaning subway fare, and half the time they find some reason why you don't get even that. And the play always reeks, unless it *is* Shakespeare or some classical thing, and then there's never enough time to actually do anything with it, only you always think, well, I'm a fabulous actor and I've always wanted to play that part, so why not?—and then you do it, and you find out why not.

And they're always in some dingy little space that no one can even *find,* and if you have six people in the audience, it's a good night. So why *do* I keep doing them? Because—I don't know. I actually don't know why.

Anyway, I am just getting out of rehearsal, which was in some cheap space at the Lesbian and Gay Community Services Center, though it isn't a gay project, far from it, it's Moliere's *Tartuffe.* And I am in it because I have always loved that play, even though I'm *not* playing Tartuffe, I'm Damis, the dumb son, the dullest part in the world. So is it just being *around* the play that I wanted? Just to be somewhere in the vicinity of where it's being done?

Anyway, I'm just getting out of rehearsal when I run into my friend Mario. "Flip!"

"Mario? My God, is that you? How long *have* you been working out?"

Mario's face falls. "My boyfriend and I just broke up, so I've had lots of time to go to the gym."

"Well, at least you look fabulous," I say. "My boyfriend and I just got back together, so now my body will probably go completely to hell. Leaving me with absolutely no resources in reserve for the next time we break up."

"No kidding?" says Mario. "You and Warren are back together?"

"More or less." And may I add that I am perfectly well aware that "more or less" is *Warren's* phrase, not mine? Am I going to turn into one of those awful halves of a couple that dress alike and do everything together and have these little pet phrases in common? We already finish each other's sentences.

"Not that I wouldn't prefer you to elaborate on 'more or less,' " says Mario. "But I'm on my way to a meeting—were you, too?"

I shake my head. "I don't do meetings, remember? I had a rehearsal."

Mario shakes *his* head. "You don't *do* meetings—listen to you."

"Well, I don't," I say. "I'm an artist, not an activist." This sounds a bit pretentious, even to me. But in my experience, you have to be really firm with Mario. His whole life is meetings: Adult Children of Alcoholics, the gay chapter; Overeaters Anonymous, also the gay chapter; some ACT UP affinity group called "Not us, Not anymore" (something like that); the Gay Pride committee, which apparently meets year-round even though all they do is plan the events in June; some gay Italian pride group, which does something around Columbus Day; a support group for people who are HIV-positive (well, I suppose I can see why he would want to go to *that*); and probably six or seven other groups that I've either forgotten or that he's added since the last time I saw him. I've often thought that he's the kind of gay person Rosie wishes I was, except for the HIV-positive part, of course.

"Look," Mario is saying, "why don't you come with me, and then after-

wards we can go get coffee and you *can* tell me what's up with you and Warren." Well, that's tempting. It's typical of Mario that he wouldn't even mention
talking about him and *his* boyfriend, even though in my opinion, a breakup
takes precedence over a reunion.

"It's not the Adult Child of Alcoholics meeting, is it?" I say. "Because you
know I'm *not* an adult child of alcoholics. In fact, to hear some people tell it,
I'm not even an adult."

Mario laughs. "No. I don't invite people to twelve-step meetings unless it's
clear they really want to be asked."

He starts to explain what the meeting is, but in the twisting and turning
through the maze of corridors and stairways you always have to go through to
get anywhere at the Center, I don't follow all the details. It doesn't matter. I
shouldn't even be doing this—I didn't exactly give Warren a definite time that
I would come over, but it shouldn't be too late. And if I left right now, I could
get there before Juliet's bedtime, which might be nice. But I find myself following Mario.

The meeting is in the so-called "People of Color" room—like I said, Rosie
would fit in well over here—although the vast majority of the people at this
meeting are white. The room is crammed full of folding chairs—oh, come *on*.
Nine o'clock on a Thursday night, and these people have nowhere better to go?

Of course, *I'm* here. But I *have* somewhere better to go. I'm just not going
there.

If I have to sit through this, I would love a little running commentary from
Mario—the kind that Tanya, say, used to be so good at providing. Well, she
probably still *is* good at it, but since she's still not speaking to me, I couldn't
say for sure.

Mario, on the other hand, is hardly the kind of person to whisper during a
meeting, or to tolerate being whispered *to*, by the looks of it. He's turned his
folding chair around so he can rest his folded arms on the back—his incredibly well-developed, muscular folded arms, with his white T-shirt nicely setting off his deep winter tan (either he's been hitting the tanning salons or else
his job at Paradise Holidays gets *him* free weekends in South Beach)—and it
occurs to me that his presence at this meeting may not be purely selfless. Although if that were the case, why would he have dragged me along?

The first speaker is a thin, intense woman in a lavender vest and purple
harem pants—oh, please, honey, you're *at* the Center, we *know* you're a dyke.
She seems to be giving some kind of summary of their last meeting, which I
can't follow, not that it matters, because, as is usually true in the theater, too,
it's a lot more interesting to watch the audience.

The chairs are set up in a circle, and the two guys across from us look totally bored, in their leather jackets and white T-shirts. Surely there are better places to show off *their* assets. A whole row of dykes beside them, for example, hardly *their* target market, offering us a virtual Benetton layout of the latest lesbian styles: one shaved head and long earrings, one plaid shirt and jeans, one silver tank top and dark-red lipstick, one Wall Street power suit, and one set of multiple piercings set off by a few well-placed tattoos.

The argument starts to get more heated, as I can tell more from the audience reaction than from the speakers, all of whom sound equally earnest and intense to me. But as often happens, when the rest of the audience listens more intently, I start to hear more of the dialogue, too.

". . . an army of lovers, in reaction *against* compulsory heterosexuality, so that the bourgeois institution of marriage is hardly a model for *our* community. And need I remind *anyone* of the specific source of oppression that marriage has *always* been for women, even straight women, but of course, lesbians in particular . . ."

". . . these really tired old seventies attitudes, I mean, come *on!* Straight people are allowed to get married, we should have the same right. It's as simple as that."

"I didn't join this movement to get married!"

"So, don't do it."

"Where else am I supposed to go? I thought this was supposed to be *my* movement."

"Well, honey, it isn't. Deal with it."

"If anybody *wondered* why lesbians don't want to work with gay men—"

"—it's because dykes have no sense of humor, but we already knew that."

"*Some* lesbians *want* to get married, so please don't generalize about *my* position. I can speak for myself."

"Actually, I really resent your coming to this meeting and bashing gay men. I thought the whole point of this group was that we were supposed to work together. And *as* a gay man, may I also say that I have serious reservations about an institution that is supposed to promote monogamy and assimilation into straight culture. Not to mention the way it virtually annihilates the sexual minorities within our own movement. I mean, where is there room for our leather queens and our S&M brothers and sisters and our transvestites and transgendered people and even our bisexuals in a paradigm that channels us into these rigid, heterosexist roles?"

"Oh, please. Get *over* yourself."

The first speaker stands up again and announces that the group is supposed to be based on mutual self-respect—well, *that* can't be right—and so would people please (a) not interrupt, and (b) not insult, and (c)—at this point, my mind starts to wander again. Actually, I am thinking that maybe I should call Warren.

It's very odd being at this point with him. I mean, it's not like we're dating, exactly. But we aren't really living together either. Except I think we have been together every single one of the last eleven nights since we got back together. Mostly at his place, because of Juliet, although once he brought Juliet over and we fixed up a bed for her in the back room.

My God, that first speaker is *still* talking. Apparently she's taken advantage of her intervention to make her own point about gay marriage. "Certainly we in the lesbian and gay community can celebrate our couples with commitment ceremonies," she's saying. "The question is, why we feel the need to call it marriage."

"Because," says one of the leather-jacketed guys in the front row, "marriage is what it's *called*." Well, I certainly can't imagine *him* getting married. Not unless your concept of marriage includes being out at a club every morning of your life.

"It's just like going into the army," says the clone next to him, a remark that immediately evokes such a chorus of boos and hisses that I almost don't hear the first speaker say, "We agreed to keep off that topic, remember, Brad." Well, if his name hadn't been Brad before, he would have had to have it changed, right?

The storm of disapproval goes on for so long that Mario actually takes his eyes off the center of the circle and leans toward me. "Feel free to jump in any time," he says in a low voice. I suppose talking during booing doesn't count as poor meeting behavior.

"Thanks, Mario, but I really don't have anything to say."

He looks genuinely shocked. "But you're back with Warren," he says. "How can you *not* have some position on gay marriage?"

Because I really do like Mario, and because he just broke up with *his* boyfriend—and who knows, maybe they *were* talking about getting married, although I think they were only together for about six weeks, so probably not. Mario is so hunky, he seems to be able to get any guy he wants, but I've noticed that his relationships never last very long, which, considering how nice he is, is also surprising. Anyway, out of respect for Mario, I don't burst out laughing at the idea of Warren and me talking about marriage. Instead I say, "I think we're having enough trouble just figuring out whether we're really even back together."

"But for the future. I mean, with him or someone else. Don't you care?"

"No, actually. I don't see the point."

"The point?" says Mario, his voice rising. "The point is to have some kind of

stability in your life! The point is to have some kind of faith that your relationship is going to last! That it's not just—you know, what they're always saying about us. That it's not just sex. That it's not just—hedonism."

Well, there's a word. But I say, although admittedly, my respect might be
wearing a bit thin, "Yeah, but Mario. You can have those things without being
married. I mean, even most straight people don't get married. Well, OK, actually most of them do get married. But most of *them* get divorced."

"But when it does work for them, they're together for years and years,"
Mario says. "And why? Because the society supports them, it supports their
relationship. Not just economically, but you know. Emotionally."

"How does it support them?" I say. "By turning them into nice little husbands and wives with their lives all mapped out for them? By giving them
some rules about not fooling around and earning a living that have nothing to
do with the actual people involved? By making them feel like failures if they
don't get married?"

To my enormous embarrassment, the rest of the talking has died down by
this time and everybody is listening to *me.* To my further mortification, I actually get a round of applause, mainly from the lesbians, but also from the guy
who talked about sexual minorities. Oh, please.

"OK, point taken," Brad says, leaning toward me across the circle, "but
don't you think—what's your name?"

"Flip," I say, forcing myself to speak loudly and clearly, because at this
point, the only thing worse than being asked to say my name would be being
asked to repeat my name because they didn't hear it the first time. Luckily, all
those years of vocal training pay off. The price being that Brad is now calling
me by name.

"So, Flip," he's saying, "two things. First, don't you think that the economic
part *is* important. You know, health insurance, Social Security, property
rights, inheritance."

"Not to mention child custody," says the bald lesbian.

"And what about hospital rights, next of kin," says Brad's matching leather
jacket.

"Right," says Brad. "That stuff. And two, Flip, what about the civil rights
aspect? I mean—OK, OK, *not* to mention the military, OK, I won't do it. But
the principle. That what they can do, we should be able to."

Everyone in the whole fucking room is actually waiting for me to answer
these questions. So I can't actually kill Mario right this minute, but I'll put it
on my to-do list. And the most annoying part is that these are just the kind of
questions that Rosie could answer without thinking twice. So how come she
would do a better job at my meeting than I would?

All right, let's consider this an acting exercise. If I were Rosie, how would I instruct Flip to answer these questions? And if I were Flip, well, obviously, I *am* Flip. *As* Flip, how would I tell Rosie she was wrong?

"Actually, Brad," I say, with that feeling of walking out into empty air that I always get when I start improvising. "Actually, I think those are the wrong questions. Because if we want those things, there are other ways to get them. Or there should be. So the question isn't why can't we get married so we can have those things. The question is, why do you have to get married to have them?"

I don't fucking believe it—more applause. Well, thanks, Rosie. I guess. Actually, I think I even agree myself with what I said. I just resent being asked to come up with an opinion on demand. On a topic that doesn't really interest me. Though I suppose I can't say that it doesn't really affect me.

With the final applause for me, the meeting breaks up, although nobody actually seems to leave. They all form little arguing clusters and go on saying exactly what they were saying before. Mario looks at me strangely. "I thought you weren't going to participate," he says.

"Well, Mario. You didn't exactly give me much choice." Which is about all we have time for before Brad and the bald lesbian come over to argue with me some more, and since they and Mario actually do agree—apparently they want this group to take up defense of gay marriage as its next big issue—I leave the three of them to their caucusing and go call Warren. Who, since it's now past ten o'clock, is not exactly pleased, though he does try to control his annoyance.

"I really am sorry," I say. Thinking, well, at least I'm calling. When we lived together, I didn't do that. I mean, it was my right to come and go as I pleased, right? One of the big advantages of *not* being married, as a matter of fact.

But maybe Warren has changed more than I've given him credit for. Because he says, "No, it's all right. I'm glad you called. I just miss you, Flip, when I'm waiting for you. Especially when I don't know when you're coming."

Which I have to admit, more or less hits me in the pit of my stomach. A flood of—well, love. "I'll be there soon," I say softly. "I'm just at the Center. I could take a taxi."

"No, save your money," Warren says. "A cab would only save you about five minutes at this point. What are you doing at the Center, anyway?"

"Mmmm," I say. "Wait till I tell you."

ROSIE: So we open the meeting for discussion, with Charles simmering in the background. There is that simmer-y moment among the workers, too, where you can feel the group building up to speak. "I was not ready for this," I hear one woman mutter to the man standing next to her. "Not ready *at all*."

But Elena was with me, wasn't she? So when she timidly raises her hand from her seat in the front row, I call on her.

"I am very surprise to hear what Rosie say," Elena begins in her Russian accent. She works as a xerox operator, which used to be a job reserved for African-American and Latino men, or I want to say boys, because it's one of the lowest-paid, hardest jobs at the school, and they could never find anyone over the age of twenty-one to do it. (Young, unskilled women could usually be receptionists.) Then we got hit with a flood of Russian emigrants, and the ones with poor English—or at least what the University considered poor English—got some of the xerox and mailroom jobs, which naturally raised all sorts of problems since Olympia's percentage of minority workers was already way too low. That went triple for minority men, in such a female workforce. To say they couldn't have even the worst jobs seemed the ultimate insult, particularly since many of the Russians weren't exactly, shall we say, enlightened, when it came to people of color. I like Elena, though the few times we've talked, I've disagreed with just about every word that came out of her mouth. But she is a staunch union supporter, I'll say that for her.

"I am surprise," Elena continues, "because from the first, Union is telling me, strike is our power. Strike is our weapon. So now, Rosie, you saying, no, not now. But why not? They make us wait, since June we wait for contract—and now is November. If we wait longer, they know we are weak. So I say, now is time to be strong. And strong means strike." She gets a decent round of applause, which surprises me. Charles, too, by the look on his face. The buzz increases.

I call on a round-faced man in the back row, whom I know only by sight. I think he got Pavel's job in the B-School, though I might have him confused with somebody else. He stands up, genial and relaxed. Maybe he'll chill things out.

"Jack Kim," he introduces himself with a smile, and you can see the people around him smile in response. One of those people whom everybody trusts instantly, because they seem to have absolutely no axe to grind.

"I'm actually pretty confused," he says with a truly innocent air—my God, he's charming. "Because we've been hearing nothing for months except how the negotiations are proceeding as well as can be expected—that's the phrase, isn't it?" *He* gets laughs. "But now we hear that, no, the process is at an impasse. So then, it's *not* going as well as can be expected? But I always thought, when that happened, you know. What a union was supposed to do was start organizing for a strike. And Rosie agrees that we *should* do that. But not now. At some later, unspecified date. Something to do with Christmas presents and credit cards.

"But see, this is why I'm so confused. Because if negotiations *aren't* going well, what would make them go better? Well, the only thing I've ever heard that the University—or any other employer—responded to is brute strength. Not that we're brutes, of course." Another laugh. Oh, God, he's probably with one of those ultra-left groups, Maoist, Trotskyist, something like that. "So like I said, I'm confused. Why *wouldn't* we want to start showing our strength as soon as possible?"

Isabel is about jumping out of her seat. But I've just been talking for fifteen minutes, Isabel. Wrong as they may be, we have to let the members talk.

"I just don't believe this!" says a tall, heavy-set woman, Odessa, I think her name is, from the Comptroller's office. In the old days, before we had a union, the entire Comptroller's office was staffed with African-American women, virtually all of whom had children. They worked at Olympia from nine to five at laughable wages for the health insurance, then took the train downtown and did nighttime temp work on Wall Street for the money. Now our contract includes a minority salary fund that has closed some—but not all—of the minority-white wage gap. Plus the eighties are over, so the temp work comes and goes.

"Rosie, this is nothing personal against you," Odessa is saying. "But I do *not* believe this. The University keeps pushing us around, and we're just supposed to take it? What do we have a union *for?*" Big applause. Odessa is usually extremely cautious, so this outburst makes a big impression—on me, too, if it comes to that.

"I really don't see," says the young white woman I call on next—Anna? Annette? Nancy? Nina?—anyway, she's a faculty secretary for either History or Econ, putting her in Olympia's own little labor aristocracy. When I was a secretary, *all* of the faculty secretaries were white—can you believe it? Every single one. Now only about three-quarters of them are, though most of the additions are Asian. Which, although obviously they face enormous amounts of prejudice, seem to engender a very different response from the white faculty than either African Americans or Latinos.

"I really don't see," Anna/Nina is saying, "how I can possibly go back to my department with this. I've been telling everyone—the students, the faculty, the other secretaries in my building—that if the University doesn't treat us with respect, well, then, we'll have to strike. So what do I tell them now?"

Charles is looking extremely smug, and I am, frankly, confused. *Nobody* starts organizing for a strike right before the Christmas holidays, especially at a university, which is going to be deserted for most of December. But the feeling in the room is unmistakable. So again, I have to ask myself, what do the members know that I don't?

"OK, time out," I say. "Let's take a step back. No, Charles, hang on. I see you want to speak, and you'll get your turn again, believe me, but I have to get clear on something first." I take a deep breath. I have absolutely no idea what I'm going to say next.

"So the sense I'm getting from everyone is that we're all fed up with how slowly negotiations are going, and we want to show the University our strength, am I right?" Puzzled nods. The members aren't used to seeing an organizer so uncertain.

"So my question is, can we think of any way of showing our strength short of actually setting a strike deadline? Is there maybe some more—what's the word I want?—more *creative* way of being strong?"

One look at Isabel and you can see she is preparing a mental transcript of my heresy to relay downtown as soon as possible. Because of course, the rule for a union organizer is pretty much the same as for a trial lawyer: never ask a question for which you don't already know the answer. Well, maybe I'll *find* an answer.

Oh, God. Another menstrual surge. Now I have two impossible alternatives: stay here and bleed all over the floor, or leave.

Fortunately or unfortunately, there is a puzzled hum among the members. They just can't figure out where I'm trying to take them.

"Look, it's after ten o'clock," I say quickly. "Let's take a break. And then let's come back and see if we can come at this in a new way." This is a *very* dangerous move, because it's so late—people may just leave. As I dash for the bathroom, I'm wondering just how many supporters we'll lose.

"Rosie Zombrowski," Isabel hisses at me through the stall door. "What in the world do you think you're doing?"

"At the moment, Isabel, I'm changing my tampon, if you must know."

"Couldn't you do that before?"

"I did do it before. I needed to do it again."

"Ay, Rosie, are you all right?"

"I don't know," I say, emerging from the stall. "It's pretty weird, as a matter of fact."

"You should see a doctor," Isabel says. She looks completely concerned, which is touching. "My mother had bleeding down there, it was terrible, she wouldn't see a doctor, wouldn't see a doctor, next thing you know, she was flat on her back on the operating table. We thought she was going to die."

"Well, there's a cheerful story," I say, splashing water onto my face. This last gush has left me weaker than I'm comfortable with, but if Isabel would leave me alone, I could probably rally.

"No, Rosie, really, see a doctor."

"What did your mother have?" I can't help asking. I know the answer to *this* question, obviously, much as I don't want to hear it.

But Isabel says, "Oh, that's what's so stupid, Rosie. She only had fibroids, only she let them go so long because she was too scared to have them checked out. She's very old-fashioned, very Puerto Rico—you know. You don't see a doctor unless you're dying. But it was so stupid, because fibroids, no big deal, right? If she had only just gone to the doctor, so you go, too, Rosie, you have to take care of yourself."

As a matter of fact, just hearing some other possible diagnosis than the one I've been dreading makes me feel a million times better already. "All right, Isabel," I say gratefully. "Thank you. I will."

"But Rosie," she says, shaking her finger at me, "what in the world are you doing? You're going to end up with a strike vote, which is completely ridiculous. You've completely lost control of the meeting. Do you want me to step in? Or Tito?"

"Isabel, I don't think we ever *had* control of the meeting. They blew it when they waited so long to replace Amy."

Isabel looks stern, but I also see how frightened she is, which I didn't expect, and which somehow I find touching. The more so when I realize that she isn't frightened for herself, but for the members. "But you can't let them go on strike, Rosie," she says. "We aren't prepared, and December is coming, and the strike fund will run out, and they'll just lose everything."

I sigh and lean against the sink. "What do you suggest, Isabel?"

Isabel is shaking her head and starting to say something sorrowful when to my complete surprise, Charles bursts into the ladies room. "What's going on?" he says irritably. "We're all waiting for you."

"I'm sorry, Charles," I say, but he barrels on.

"Were you caucusing in here?" he says. "Because it's really not appropriate to—"

"Charles, we weren't discussing union business, honestly. I was just—Isabel was helping me out with a medical problem, if you must know. A women's problem."

I'm hoping this will embarrass him enough to shut him up, but apparently I've underestimated him. Because he just brushes that aside and says, "What the hell *are* you doing out there, Rosie? Obviously, the members want to strike. How can you justify—"

"Charles, be serious." Usually I try to curb my tendency to interrupt, but with Charles, it gets free rein. "You know as well as I do that it's ridiculous to start talking strike before the Christmas holidays, and that we can't possibly organize anything by January 4th, so what's the deal? Obviously, the time to strike is before the spring semester starts—"

"That's not till April!" Charles says. "Do you expect us to just sit on our thumbs until then?"

"No, Charles, which is why I brought up the idea of an alternate plan."

A night of surprises, because this actually gets through to him. "OK," he says warily, "what is it?"

Isabel shakes her head in warning, but I've about had it. So I say, "I don't *have* a plan, Charles. That's why I asked the members to come up with ideas."

"You mean you really don't have one?"

Isabel jumps in.

"No, Charles, she really doesn't. I was just asking her." And since admitting an apparent failure is so uncharacteristic of Isabel, he pretty much has to believe her.

"Look," I say, trying to capitalize on this unexpected moment of communication, "clearly we're in a bind, all right, Charles? You've got them all pumped up to strike, and I take my hat off to you, but we both know it's premature— the time to start that talk is in February. But you're right, we can't just do nothing. You want my personal opinion, we should have struck before fall semester, but nobody asked me, and it's too late now. And obviously, none of the three of us has a ghost of an idea what to do, because we haven't been thinking along those lines, which is all of our mistake, OK? So let's go back in there, and perhaps not be *quite* this honest about the situation, but let's open it up, and see what we come up with. What other choice do we have?"

"I didn't pump them up," Charles says, rather stuffily, under the circumstances. "It's the will of the members."

"Fine," I say. "Then I admire you for being so attuned to their political moment, OK? We're supposed to be on the same side, here, Charles, even though I know you don't believe it."

Isabel is shocked, but Charles does look a bit ashamed.

"If we all go back together," he says, "they'll think we've been planning something."

I burst out laughing. "Well, under the circumstances," I say, "is that a good thing or a bad thing?" And in fact, as the three of us walk out of the ladies room together, Jack Kim is coming down the hall.

"We wondered where you all were," he says. "We're ready to start."

"We were caucusing," I say, thinking, well, what's one *more* lie? "Actually, we've come up with a proposal."

Jack looks skeptical, but in that charming way, like he wishes he didn't have to. "I hope so," he says. "Because, I'll be honest with you, some of us are pretty concerned."

"There's nothing to be concerned about, Jack," Charles says. "Rosie is going to present our proposal, and then we'll discuss it." Apparently he has decided that distancing himself from us would look worse than the alternative, especially now that he's been seen coming out of the ladies room.

The three of us walk back into the meeting and even the easy-going Tito looks concerned.

Odessa raises her hand. "You want something on the way to a strike? All the work-study students have to come into our office on January 5th."

"No, Odessa, it's the 4th," whispers her neighbor.

"The 4th? The 5th? Which day is Tuesday? I'm all mixed up," Odessa says.

"The 5th is Wednesday," says the man on the other side of her.

"OK. The 4th, then. All the work-study students come to see us on the 4th, because that's payday. So why don't we have a petition, something for them to sign, saying that if there's a strike, they won't work, either."

"What *is* our position on the work-study students?" Jack says.

"We don't want them to lose their paychecks," I say. "Because after all, they're workers too, but since they're not allowed to join our union, they're not eligible for strike benefits."

"How much are strike benefits again?" someone else calls out.

"Hang on a minute, people. One thing at a time. So our position on work-study students is that they should try to call in sick, work something out with their supervisors, reschedule their hours for after the strike is over, like that. And if they can't, then we don't ask them *not* to cross the picket line, because most of them would get thrown out of school—they're working for tuition, not just paychecks."

"But *we* can't afford tuition for our kids!" someone shouts from the back of the room. "Why should they get to—"

I hold up my hand. "And we ask them to agree to do only their work, not ours."

"Not exactly solidarity," drawls Jack.

"On the contrary," I say, "if we asked them to drop out of school while we're on strike, frankly, they wouldn't do it. Not most of them, anyway. If we ask them to do something they *can* do, we have a chance to win their support."

Jack laughs. "Doesn't sound like much to me."

"Odessa has a proposal on the floor," I say, trying to suggest reproach without actually sounding reproachful. "Can we focus discussion on that, please?"

"I like it," Charles says, which I totally and completely don't expect.

"I like it," he repeats, "because it is a way of showing our strength, of demonstrating our support, while building support at the same time. It is a way of sending a thoroughly clear message to the administration, and to the trustees, and to the community as a whole, that we have a broad base of support and that we intend to stop at nothing short of victory. It is a way—"

I stifle a sigh. On my side or not, Charles is a pain.

"Other discussion?" I say when Charles finally finishes.

Nina/Nancy/Annette raises her hand. "Those of us who have work-study students can start discussing this with them now," she says. "Can't we?"

"If we agree on this approach, which I think is excellent, by the way," I say, "then yes. The more preparation the work-studies have, the better, because if we *do* go ahead with Odessa's idea for a petition, we really have to make sure that at least—what would you say, Charles?" No harm in being a *little* diplomatic. "At least one-third of the students would have to sign it, or we look really bad, wouldn't you agree?"

Charles considers this question with the utmost seriousness. "From one-fourth to forty percent would be our minimum," he says finally, "but I see no reason why we can't achieve an even higher level of support. Particularly if every single worker makes a commitment now to—"

"What if there are no work-study students in our office?" a worker in the back calls out.

"There are plenty of ways that everyone can support this effort," I say, "which, if we agree, should be the focus of a work-study committee, that we should form tonight. Only for stewards, I think, right, people? The negotiating committee has enough to do."

We vote, the motion passes unanimously, and we form a five-person committee. I arrange to meet with them after work on Monday.

"What about the strike, then?" says the charming Jack Kim, giving it one more try.

"Obviously, we need to keep it right in the front of our minds," I say quickly. I certainly don't want to get one-upped by *him*. One of the few Asian-American members here, too, so my duty is clear: I have to get him more involved, even though right now, believe me, I'd like to ice him. "But I think we also need to be—what's the word I want?" As if I didn't know. "Circumspect. Because let's be honest, people, we're walking a fine line here. If we show our hand too soon, that gives the University lots of time to come up with ammunition against us. We don't want *them* reminding the members that Christmas is coming. Let's remember who the real enemy is here, all right?" He actually has the grace to smile apologetically. Well, I'll give those ultra-leftists this much—they certainly attract good-looking men. I prefer the politics of the Old Left, myself, but most of *their* men are over sixty. Except for some tired, depressed husbands in their thirties and forties who do more housework and childcare than any other men I ever saw, which is probably why they're so tired and depressed.

The meeting breaks up, finally, and Tito, Isabel, Charles, and I gather in a little cluster as the members hurry out to their late-night trains.

"Charles, I really think that went well, finally," I say before he can start complaining. "Between your pushing strike and Odessa pushing petition, I think we ended up with the best of all possible worlds. Because now we *have* started preparing them for a strike—or I guess I should say, *you* have."

Charles looks enormously pleased. I wish I'd known it was *this* easy to flatter him.

"I'm still concerned," says Isabel. "I don't think the members realize what's involved in a strike. I think we have to prepare them *more*." To my surprise, Tito agrees.

"I bow to experience," I say to all three of them. "I've been in strikes before, of course, but I haven't actually led one. As you all know."

Charles frowns. "I didn't know that. Why did Harris put you here, then, Rosie? Is this his way of saying he doesn't want us to go out?"

So the honeymoon is over. And so soon. "No, Charles," I say, trying fairly unsuccessfully to keep the annoyance out of my voice. "He put me here because I've *been* here for six years. I practically still know everybody's name, as you may have noticed."

"But you *haven't* been here for four years."

I shrug. "Who would you prefer, honestly, Charles? Let's go ahead and have this out, why not? If you'd rather have Tito or Isabel, I'm sure Harris would agree." Not in a million years—*he* makes the assignments, based on whatever combination of personal whim, internal politicking, and brilliant organizing instinct has brought him to his present position. And it's incredibly stupid to have said that to Charles just now, and in front of Tito and Isabel, too.

But Charles actually smiles. "OK, Rosie, I can respect what you're saying," he says. "It's so unfortunate about Amy. But if we can't have her, then you're right. Logically, it should be you." He glances at Tito and Isabel. "No offense."

They were shocked by me and surprised by Charles. But they rally quickly. Tito smiles and shakes his head. "No offense at all," says Isabel.

Charles actually turns to me and holds out his hand. "Welcome to Olympia, Rosie," he says. "We're very happy to have you."

"How can you welcome me, you idiot?" I want to shout. "I was here before you were!"

But it *is* the members' union. Charles is right to act like he outranks me, however grating I find it. So I take his hand, and say as warmly as I can, "Thank you, Charles. It's good to be here." I even accept his invitation to go out for a beer, as lucky Tito and Isabel prepare to escape to their homes and families.

I feel so weak, suddenly, that I have to clutch the table to hold myself up. But the rule about physical self-control is still in full force, so I smile at Charles as I get my coat. His face is still serious, though a trifle less sullen, as he holds the door for me.

So was tonight one of my greatest triumphs, or the dumbest luck I've ever had? And tomorrow it could happen all over again, and I'd *still* have to come up with a new response. It's when you stop making it up as you go along that you really get into trouble.

TANYA: I am not at all sure about what Elinor considers directing. She's been taking some kind of theater workshop since our first meeting, and it's gotten her all fired up about a kind of theater that I have been trying to avoid since college—people doing improvisations and feeling the energy in the room and all that other nonsense that to my mind is just a way to avoid doing *real* work. My training is about actually having some craft, using your mind and your body and your voice to create a character. To show people something that they couldn't see otherwise. I didn't go into theater to play *myself.*

On the other hand, we don't have a script, so at the moment, there *are* no characters to create. And when Elinor said, "Look, bear with me, I've always hated this stuff, too, but this workshop is different, and I'd like to try it out"— well, honestly? That was the most enthusiasm I'd ever heard Elinor express about *anything.*

Plus I *have* invited Flip into the group, and this *is* our first rehearsal, and I think it would look bad to all concerned if I start in expressing doubts. (Though it turns out Flip already knows Luis from some industrial, and he and Janie were in some showcase together before *I* even knew him. It's always that way.)

But I can see how doubtful Flip looks, too. Not like there aren't other reasons for him to be nervous. Credit where it's kept—not too many white men, gay or straight, would walk into a group like this one and not go right into showing that they owned the place, or else into showing that they didn't and then wanting credit for *that.* Whereas Flip acts as normal as any new actor *could* act. Only thing I miss is him grinning at me or catching my eye or doing *something* to show he sees me seeing him. Which, under the circumstances, is probably too much to expect.

"OK, then," Elinor says. "Let's begin. Please form a circle. Now start to run, keeping the person ahead of you and the person behind you always in sight. Pay attention. What does it mean to run like this? As if you'd never done it before. What new thing can you find out about each step?"

Oh, please. When I saw people doing this kind of shit in college, I ran the *other* way. Plus it hurts my knees. I glance across the circle to where Flip is trotting along between Luis and Janie. His face is dead serious. Of course, he *is* a dancer.

"Now," says Elinor, "at the same moment, no leaders, no followers, the whole group should just change direction. Keep running, same speed please, but in the opposite direction." Luis starts to say something. "No talking, please. And no cuing. Just decide together."

How? I run along for about a million years, trying to stay focused on Malik ahead of me and Bernard behind, but my calves are aching, and nothing is happening. So I switch directions as forcefully as I know how, sweeping Bernard, Malik, and Luis right along with me, and then Flip and Janie catch up. OK, that's done.

"No leaders, Tanya," Elinor says. "Decide *together*. Try again."

The next time, it is Bernard who starts the turnaround, and I'm paying close enough attention to him to match his movement, and Malik is doing ditto to me, and Janie to Malik, and on down the line. A ripple effect.

"No leaders, Bernard, Tanya," Elinor says. "Decide *together*." Maybe she senses the mutiny building in my lower back, because she says sternly, "How can you decide together? Figure it out."

"Without talking, how can we?" says Luis. "Come on, baby—"

"Figure it out, Luis," Elinor says curtly. "No talking. Change directions again, please. As a group."

I glance at Flip again, who still has that same look of total concentration, and this time he does catch my eye, and then, I don't know how to explain it, something happens. I mean, there's something *there,* and Luis sees it next, and then of all people, Bernard, and then Malik, and finally Janie, and suddenly, we *know.* Now. And we switch.

"Yes!" Elinor says, and I'm sorry to say, I can hear the relief in her voice. Didn't *she* think this was going to work? "Again, please," she says quietly, and though our next reversal isn't near as clean, even I have to admit we know something. It's as if the temperature shifts, we feel *that,* and that's when we switch. What changes the temperature, though?

So Elinor keeps us running for about a million years, sometimes changing directions, sometimes stopping and starting, sometimes leaping up into the air and coming down, but always together. And I will say this: we can repeat it. She says, "Reverse," or "Leap," and we can. If you can repeat it, you've learned it, as every actor knows. But why this is knowledge that I'll *ever* need to have, that I do *not* see.

Finally, Elinor says, "All right, very good. Cool down, please—keep moving in a circle, only walk. Try to keep your breathing at the same level."

"Why did—" Luis begins, and Elinor says again, "Still no talking, please, Luis. Pay attention." Idris puts her head close to Elinor and whispers, and Elinor adds quickly, "As if you're taking each step for the first time. No automatic pilot, please. Discover *everything*."

Another murmur between her and Idris. You know what I think of, suddenly? Playing *Star Trek* with my girlfriend Jolene, both of us ten years old and taking it totally to heart. She always wanted to make up her own adventures, but I took it even more seriously than that. I would sit watching the reruns on TV, memorizing every word, every move, every turn of the head. The way the real actors did it.

"OK," says Elinor, "keep walking, but instead of a circle, walk on a grid, please. Pretend there's a big sheet of graph paper on the floor, and you can only walk on the lines. Explore the restrictions. As if every single step were brand new."

Flip is taking *this* shit totally seriously, I can see *that* from the corner of my eye. That solemn glow that dancers get, like they're listening to some instruction the rest of us can't hear. "And explore your partners," Elinor is saying. "Bodies together in space." No, Elinor, thank you very much. I *know* these people—I'm here to *work*.

"All right," says Elinor. "Now, besides walking on the grid, you can run on it." Going on to add leaping, stopping, and falling down.

Now it gets more playful, though still embarrassing. Luis comes running right up into Janie's face, stops short, falls down. Without missing a beat, she steps over him, keeps walking, slow and measured. Bernard walks straight up to her, same pace, they do this sort of half-tango, him forward, her back, then at the same exact moment, they switch—her forward, him back. Then Flip joins in, behind Janie, and Malik, behind Bernard—tango tango, back and forth, with Luis stretched out on the ground. And then, at the exact same moment, all the tango people break apart in different directions as Luis rises straight up, jumping into the rhythm as though there really were a beat to follow.

Fine. I can see I have some catching up to do. And much as I don't want to, I can see it's the goddamn circle all over again, because *choosing* what to do doesn't work, it makes my body separate and awkward, like being the one dancer in the group without a sense of rhythm, which, child, is *never* going to be me. So I understand there is some door inside me to open up, to let that *thing* take over—which is what, exactly? Maybe if I call it temperature. Or rhythm. Or spirit. Which is way, *way* too much like church to leave me comfortable, but what *is* the word for something you feel and cannot see, something you *touch* but cannot see? Because when it touches me, this *whatever,* then yes, I hear the rhythm, I feel the beat, I find myself standing stock still in the corner of the room, and then, as if some dance coach tapped me on the shoulder, I leap straight up into the air the exact same moment that Flip collapses to the ground. And if we'd tried to rehearse it that way? Never would have happened.

"All right, everybody, take a break," says Elinor, who seems awfully pleased with herself. Just *like* a director, because what did *she* do? "Ten minutes," she adds, then hangs with Idris, which I'm sorry to say gets to me more than I would have thought. Elinor and I have been sort-of friends for about ten years now, ever since I played lady-in-waiting to her queen in *The Winter's Tale,* a downtown production that I managed to get into even though I was just eighteen at the time and still a freshman at NYU. Now I'd see it as just one more showcase—no money except subway fare, which I didn't even get, not being in the union. But it was Shakespeare, which in those days was a magic word to me.

Flip is hanging back with Janie—what *is* it with that girl? Obviously he's not going for the same prize as Luis or Bernard, nor do I think it's because the two of them are both white. Flip was extremely surprised when I called him for this group—as well he should have been, but still. He asked a lot of reluctant questions, such as, "How long did you say we'd be rehearsing?" and "Who's going to see it?", and he didn't seem any too pleased with the answers—"Rehearsals from December through April, performances in May and June. We'll be touring for people in the community—schools, churches, youth centers, maybe a prison or two." And when he heard there was no script for him to read? You know that was the *end.* Still, you could tell he didn't want to say *no* to me, either.

"Well, Tanya," he said finally. "It's an awfully long time, is the problem. I mean, if it were a showcase, you know, with only three weeks rehearsal and a week of shows—"

"If it was some goddamn showcase, you wouldn't do it, and neither would I," I say bluntly. "The *point* is that it's different."

"Oh, I don't know," he says. I can hear him acting casual, and he can hear me hearing him. "I'm doing a showcase now, actually," he says. I roll my eyes, and maybe he hears that, too, because he laughs. "And don't say another word, Tanya, because it's just as awful as you are thinking, so I'm sure whatever your group is doing can only be an improvement." Then he sounds uncomfortable again. "But if I got a film or something—"

"We've got nothing *but* working actors in this group," I say, as crisply as I can. Just because Pietro's boyfriend was all over *him* at the screening.

"No, I just meant, I didn't want to say I was going to do something and then let you all down," Flip says. "But if everybody else is there with the idea that they might have to leave—"

"Don't put words in my mouth," I say. "The *idea* is to stay. But we're all working actors. Shit happens."

"Yes," says Flip, his voice all of a sudden very dry. "Shit certainly does happen." So we sit there on the phone, thinking of all the shit that has happened lately, until Flip finally says, "OK, Tanya, if it's understood that something might—come up, then OK, yes, why not? It sounds interesting."

"All right, good," I say. We both sit there a while longer. "So what *are* you doing?" I say finally.

"Oh." He sounds embarrassed. "Well, it's *Tartuffe*. Not that I even get to play Tartuffe."

"Who are you, Orgon?"

"Not even. Damis." Should I have offered to come? Usually, if somebody wants you to see their work, they ask you. I kept thinking about *The Winter's Tale,* how I wrote my folks that I was finally doing Shakespeare. I thought they'd be impressed, but they weren't, really. My father builds houses, my mother's a nurse. *Real* jobs.

Now Flip looks up from whatever he and Janie are talking about to see me watching him. He looks like he's about to say something, when Elinor says, "Break's over." She indicates that we're all supposed to sit together, like an audience. "All right," she says, doing her damnedest to sound certain. "Think of a situation, one you were in or one you observed, but something that actually happened. A situation that reveals something about—" She looks at Idris, who nods. "Something about power. The situation must have at least two characters, and you have to play all of them. You can talk directly to us if you want, but you also have to show us."

"About *what,* again?" says Bernard.

"A story about power," Elinor says sharply.

"Power in what sense?" Bernard asks. "Do you mean—"

"Figure it out," Elinor says. "Whatever it means to you." She glances at Idris again. "Just do it, Bernard. We'll talk about it later."

Bernard shrugs. Malik, ever helpful, says, "I have one."

Elinor is trying *really* hard not to look grateful. "Can we use props?" Malik wants to know.

For the third time, Elinor looks at Idris. "Anything you want," Idris says.

Malik gets his backpack and gym bag from the back of the room and drapes them around his shoulders. "May I?" he says to Luis, and takes *his* backpack, too. "And——?"

"Go ahead," Flip says.

Loaded down, Malik places himself in front of us. "It's Saturday night, about six o'clock," he says. "It's freezing." He begins to shiver. "My feet are frozen. I'm tired, I'm hungry, Laila is waiting for me, she's probably got dinner ready. I want to go home." As he talks, his body droops, his face falls, the bags get heavier and heavier. I've watched Malik work for years, and he always starts out clumsy. This time, I must admit, he makes me see it all—how the wind is blowing, how his coat's too thin. "The hell with it," he says. "Taxi!"

Groans of recognition—from most of us, anyway. We see him gesture for a taxi. Then he shows us how a cab sweeps by him. OK, it's a little hokey—his head turns way too far and he loses the sense of the wind, but then he finds it again. "I can't even afford to *take* a taxi," he mutters to himself. *"Taxi!"* Another cab passes by. Another. And another.

"Yeah, right," mutters Luis.

"Take the subway!" calls out Bernard.

Finally, a cab pulls over—I don't exactly see it, but Malik is headed *somewhere.* He walks up to the door, grateful, exhausted, and reaches for the handle.

Suddenly, he throws off all the bags, takes the driver's place, turns around and sees "Malik." "Oh, sorry, sorry, man," the driver says in a heavy Indian accent (not Malik's strong suit, either, but OK, we get it). "I thought you were Pakistani."

Back to being Malik, stunned and loaded down, as the cab speeds off. We applaud.

I look at Flip and Janie. They are laughing, too, along with the rest of us. Including Elinor, who had to hail a cab for me once when I was late for an audition. I stood on the curb while she stuck her arm out.

Idris is also laughing—and taking notes. And I feel two ways. Of *course* I'd love to walk into a theater and see that. But I want a *part,* a real live character to play. Malik was just playing himself.

Janie does one about flirting with her boss to get a job, that high little voice she has sounding even more babyish and breathy. That's always been my big objection to her stuff—it all comes out sounding the same. Some of it's a vocal problem, but some of it's definitely her acting. (Malik has more range than that—he just will not use his body. But these days, he seems more interested in being a social worker, anyway. One *more* companion lost along the road.)

Janie playing herself may be boring, but she does a good job of showing us her boss. He sits back in his chair, sneering at her, legs spread wide—I can almost see the penis. Then he leans forward, inspecting her—face, breast, crotch.

When it's Bernard's turn, he makes this enormous deal out of setting up an empty chair in the center of the room. He grabs up Idris's big square plaid scarf and pulls it over his head. "This is my grandmother," he says. He takes off the shawl, kneels on the floor, and hugs the chair. "And this is Bernard, age six. A story about power."

If it was six months ago and I was sitting next to Flip, I would be whispering, "Talking about himself in the third person? Child, please. The man must think he's James Earl Jones."

"Mmmm," Flip would whisper back. "This is Flip, age thirty-two, being bored."

I toss a glance Flip's way, and his lips twitch, but he's still got that good-boy rehearsal face on. Bernard sits down on the chair and puts the shawl over his head. "Well, child," he says in his grandmother's voice. "Well." He leans way back in the folding chair, making us think *rocking chair,* making us see it. So far he's the best in the group at this physical environment stuff, which I suppose makes sense when you think of how his acting *is* just one trick after another.

He squints up his eyes and contrives to wrinkle up his face, so that he truly does look old. "I have something real important to tell you now, Bernard. Real important."

He slips off the shawl, kneels on the floor, looks up at his grandmother. And you *know* it's a shock to see the grandmother go—though I see her again when Bernard does. *Damn.* He is *good* at this.

"What is it, Granma?" says the child Bernard. The grandmother reaches down with a wrinkled old hand—yes, he even makes us see her *skin*—and takes hold of the child's chin. "You got to remember, Bernard," she says as the child looks up at her, "you are someone *special* in this world." Well, wouldn't you know she'd be telling him *that.* "So when people try to tear you down, when they try to hurt you or make you feel small, you got to remember how special you are."

Bernard shows us the six-year-old child, eyes big, hanging on every word his grandma says. "Not like *this* isn't some special Hallmark moment," I am thinking. Only at the same time, yes, it's touching.

"All right then," says the grandmother. "Don't forget now. I won't be here much longer to tell you myself." He stands up and becomes his old self again, and I find myself missing the other two. Which is not anything I've *ever* thought about Bernard's work. Why is he all of a sudden so good?

No. So real. Yeah, sure, he had a trick or two. But there was also—something else.

We clap for Bernard, very forceful, but, you know. Unsettled. "When *did* she die?" Janie asks respectfully.

"Oh, she's still alive," Bernard says as he hands Idris back her scarf. "We're all driving down to see her this Christmas."

I start wondering what I'll do. I don't want to play myself—ever. But Elinor hasn't left me much choice.

"My turn!" says Luis, leaping to his feet. He gestures around the empty space. "So," he says, "the setting for this is a very fancy cocktail party, right? My agent had invited me. He said—" and Luis starts doing his agent, Jewish accent, real fast talker—"Nu, Luis, this is a big deal, a very big deal, right? Right? Right? You can meet lots of important people here, big movers, big *machers,* producers, directors, casting agents, you name it, you got it, they'll be here, you be there, look good, talk nice, make nice, schmooze, booze, who knows? Maybe we'll both get rich." Luis grins at us. "Manny is *very* optimistic," he says. "He thinks *very* positive. So, OK, I go to this party, I get myself a drink—" he mimes holding a drink, "I have a couple of chips and some dip, no caviar, sorry to say, but some very nice guacamole—not as good as what *I* make, but OK, my catering days are long over, thanks be to God, so now I start working the room, right?" He saunters over toward the far left end of the room, elbowing crowds of people as he goes. He doesn't really make us *see* the scene, like Bernard did—it's more indicating. "Oops, sorry, was that your drink? *Sorry.*" Finally he arrives at an empty space. "And there is this very beautiful lady, excuse me, *woman,* all right, people? Before you all bite my head off. So this very beautiful woman—I don't mean anything by it, I'm just stating a fact—gives me the once-over. 'Well, *hello* there. What's *your* name?'

" 'Luis Mendoza.' "

" 'Loo-eess?' " Luis has the woman speak very loudly and distinctly. "Um, do—you—speak—English—Loo-eess?"

Luis grins at us again, then gives the woman a very serious look. "Certainly I speak English," he says in his best Shakespearean tones. "I was born in New York City, and I have ten years of vocal training, including a summer at the Royal Academy of Dramatic Art in London."

" 'Oh, well, I'm sure we don't have anything for you, dear,' " the woman says. " 'We only use *real* Hispanics.' "

Luis rolls his eyes at us, and we laugh and applaud. OK, so it's not the greatest work in the world, but I must admit, I feel a thrill. Why? Not like we haven't all done improvs one time or another.

At this point, the only ones left are Flip and me. Both of us used to being top of the class and not wanting to find out otherwise. So I just sit there and sit there and sit there. Till finally Flip pushes himself up to the front of the room. Then, of course, he makes the space his *own*.

"OK," he says, making that nice eye contact with every one of us. "This is something that happened—let's see. Last week—the Monday after Thanksgiving. In Chelsea, which, for those of you who just got to New York this morning is more or less—*mainly*—a gay neighborhood."

"No!" says Luis, who would not shut up to defend his life. Flip widens his eyes.

"I didn't mean to shock you," he says politely. We laugh.

"Anyway," says Flip, "so here we are in Chelsea." He walks up to the far right corner of the room. "Where my boyfriend has lived for the past, oh, three, three-and-a-half months, which I guess makes it *his* neighborhood by now. So here I am—" and he shows us Flip sauntering down the street. Showing us he's a man in love, and therefore not paying attention.

"And here is Warren, my boyfriend." Flip moves over to show us the man walking beside him. I've heard plenty about Warren, but I never actually met him, which I guess tells you something about *that* relationship. So Flip shows us him and Warren, walking along, eyes only for each other. And first one of them reaches out his hand and pulls it back, and then the other one does the same. Flip turns out to us. "Now this is Chelsea, and we've both seen guys necking on the street corners here, so I start to think, oh, come on, we're being just a little bit too cautious. I mean, it's *Chelsea*." Flip shows himself reaching out to put his arm around Warren's waist, going to, going to, going to . . . and then he freezes. He looks out at us again.

"OK," he says. "So we're *there*—" He points to the center of the room. Then he goes back to the right and shows us three guys, walking together. Yes, I'm impressed—he makes us see each one, their shape, their face. The first has this way of swinging his arms. The second one snaps his fingers. The third one pounds his fist into his palm, which should have looked corny, but didn't. So we see three guys watching Flip and Warren, looking at each other, moving forward.

"OK," says Flip, moving back to his and Warren's position. "So now we hear them behind us, and of *course* we want to see what they look like. So we're like, 'Oh, yes, here we are, out for a nice evening stroll in our own neighborhood, under streetlights so bright you could fucking *read* by them, plus there are only like one million people on each side of the street, all right, half a million—it's a weeknight—but we're not exactly talking about some burned-out block in the South Bronx, this is *Chelsea*. So of course, *we're* not scared, *we're* not the least little bit nervous . . ."

Back inside the story, Flip looks over his shoulder like he's trying to pretend he's not—a pretty piss-poor job of pretending. Then Warren looks. His pretending is even worse. They whisper to each other. Look again. Make themselves not look. More scared than *I* would ever admit to being in this group, and I'm not even Flip. But he's totally into it now—I see him on that street, scared and ashamed of being so. And when he and Warren suddenly turn into an all-night deli, and wait and wait and wait, I see that, too. Somehow that part is even more shameful.

Flip looks at us again, signaling that the story is over. There's a moment of silence, then big applause. Flip tries to look blank, but to my mind, he looks relieved.

"I have just one question," Janie says softly. Halfway back to his seat, Flip turns to look at her.

"When you said, 'This is Chelsea, not the South Bronx,' " she says, "what exactly did you mean by that? Because it sounded like you were saying that it *was* OK for someone in the South Bronx to get beat up—just that it shouldn't happen in *your* neighborhood."

"No," says Flip, still blank. Impossible to tell if he's mad or what he is. "That *isn't* what I meant. I meant that if I had been in the South Bronx, I would have expected to have to pay attention. Me especially, because it's *not* my neighborhood. Or a neighborhood that I think of as particularly okay for two gay men to hold hands in. As opposed to Chelsea. *That's* what I meant."

Janie nods. Nobody could be as innocent as that.

"We're asking people to share something from their lives," Idris says quietly from the back of the room. "I think if this exercise is going to work, we need to respect that, and not put people on the spot." Elinor nods.

Well, now it's my turn. And I am *not* going to say I won't do one, not after every single other person has leapt from the frying pan into the flames.

On the other hand, I have no idea. Well, all right, I have *some* idea. One little glimmer of an idea, not big enough to fill *that* stage. But I feel it pulling me, making me rise to my feet and get on up there. I'm going to have to be led.

"Something I observed about power." See, now, in real theater, you don't look at the audience. And eventually, you have lights, costume, a character. It's not just you up there, naked and alone.

"This was about ten–twelve years ago, in church—not the one I go to now. The church where I grew up, in Cleveland. Home from college on vacation, going with my family to church. Only for some reason, they weren't there and I was."

I start setting up the folding chairs, making three pews that face the audience. "So here I am," I say, and I try to show them college Tanya, sitting all the way in the back pew, trying so hard to be cool and above it all. Little bits of laughter as I toss my braids and look down my nose. Is this a *real* character though, or just me playing myself?

"And there was this woman. I didn't even know who she was." I move to the front row, try to sit like the woman I remember. Now she *is* a character. Spreading hips, churchy hat, elbows sticking right *out* of her lap—you're not getting any of *her* space, honey. Face enraptured, nodding to the rhythm of the sermon. Foot tapping, shoulders shaking. And then suddenly, she stands right up. As if called. I start to sing with her voice:

Wo-oke up this morning, and my mind, it was stayed on Jesus,
I woke up this morning, and my mind, it was stayed on Jesus—

Eyes uplifted, and closed. Body not swaying, not rocking, but not still either. Trembling. Full of more power than it could hold.

Woke up this morning, and my mind, it was stayed on Je-e-sus—

Foot tapping, hips swaying just a little extra, saying *yes* to the rhythm, *yes* to whatever was flowing right through her.

Hallelu-, hallelu-, hallelu-u-u-jah.

I open my eyes, look at *my* audience. Who are transfixed. "And I've never seen anything like this," I say, working my way back to the third pew. "Not during the sermon, just bursting out into song. And I—well, in those days, you know, I was nothing like the way I am today. I was *shy*." They are watching so hard, nobody even laughs.

So I hum on through the second verse of the song, all the while showing my silent college self staring at the woman. First I'm like, Oh, please, wait for the choir. And then I'm interested. And then, I'm pulled. And my college self is standing, singing in my pitiful little voice, nothing like that woman's power, you can bet on *that*. But still singing the bridge:

I met my brother on the street. He had a smile on his face, and his mind on
freedom.

I look at my audience again. "See, she sang *Jesus,* but I had actually learned that song, not in church, but at some folk-song group back in high school. And we sang *freedom.* So I sang it that way, because you *know* I had no idea what I was doing by that point. I was just *going.*"

I met my sister on the street. She had a smile on her face, and her mind on freedom.

I dash for the front row, show the woman turning around, singing full out, straight at that college me:

I met my brother on the street. He had a smile on his face, and his mind on Jesus. *Hallelu-, hallelu-, hallelu—u—u—u—jah.*

The woman starts to clap at me, trying to get me to clap along with her.

I woke up this morning with my mind, it was stayed on Jesus.

I dash back to my place, start to clap uncertainly, then more certainly, then full of conviction. But still singing in that pitiful little voice.

I woke up this morning, with my mind, it was stayed on freedom.

And then, for those last three hallelujahs, my voice builds. It soars. It goes right up into the rafters. And nobody is more surprised at that voice than me, then *or* now.

"*Hallelu—*" clapping and singing. Soaring and shaking.

"*Hallelu—*" *my* eyes closed. *My* face twisted up to the ceiling.

"*Hallelu—u—u—u—jah.*" A moment of quiet, face uplifted. Feeling the power rising right up through my closed eyes. A beat of silence—my theatrical instincts are not completely gone. Then I open my eyes and look at the group. Who burst into big, excited cheers. Like I have just done something for *them.*

Whatever in the world got me to do *that?* And how do *I* feel, standing up here in my own body, those two characters gone? Like I said, naked and alone.

ELINOR: It's probably a mistake to feel so excited, but I do.

Of course, it would be hard *not* to be excited at what Tanya has done. And everybody else. But I can't help but feel astonished at what *I* have done.

"That was great, Tanya," I tell her, even though, honestly, she doesn't look much like she *wants* to hear a compliment at this point. Still, I have to smile at her, even tease her a little. "And now that we know you can sing . . ."

"I can't."

"Yeah, right," says Luis, scornfully. "Sure. If I could not-sing like that—"

"You'd be in *West Side Story,*" Tanya says. "Small loss."

But Luis won't laugh.

"Let's take another break," I say.

"Whoa!" says Luis. "What about you two? Aren't you going to do one?"

"Yeah, come on, Elinor," says Bernard. "It's your turn."

"Or Idris," says Janie diplomatically.

Idris shakes her head. "I'm not a performer."

"Well, Elinor is," Bernard says.

So. The moment I've been dreading. "I'm not performing," I say as confidently as I can manage. "I'm directing."

"That's not fair," says Luis.

"I thought we were all members of the group in equal standing," says Bernard. "I thought that was the point, wasn't it, Malik?"

"Look, guys," I say, jumping in before Malik can answer. Because if I don't establish this *now* . . . "If you want me to direct—" I try not to swallow, "then you have to let me have that power. Or I can't do it." I force myself to look at each of them, calmly, serenely. I *am* a good performer. Just not a successful one.

"Well, I *definitely* think you should direct," says Janie. "That was an amazing first rehearsal. I mean, I *have* done exercises that were not so far away from what you did—but, I don't know. You got us to do *more.*"

Luis has gone from staring at Tanya to staring at me. "For my money, you just keep on going," he says. "If it doesn't work for me, I'll say so."

"Well, I definitely want to hear more about *where* you think it's going," says Malik. "But of course you should direct."

"I didn't mean to ask for a vote of confidence," I say. "I was just—"

"We got it, baby," says Luis. "Now, do we get a pee break or not?"

"Ten minutes," I say, drily, gratefully.

Idris grins at me as we look over the remaining notes on her legal pad. "See?" she says softly. "I told you. You're a natural."

When the break is over, I ask them all to close their eyes and call out what they remember about the evening. Because that's all theater *is,* isn't it? Those one or two moments you sometimes can recall? God knows there's nothing *else* of it that lasts.

"A room full of amazing bodies, amazing stories," Janie says breathlessly.

"Luis—saying, 'Right? Right? Right?' " says Malik. "You could *play* that agent, Luis."

"If they'd ever let him play a Jew," Tanya mutters.

"Being really *with* each other," says Janie.

"Tanya singing," says Flip, and there is a chorus of *"Yes."*

"Feeling stupid and 'I don't know what the fuck I'm going to do,' and then just doing it," says Luis.

"My aching back," Tanya says, and there is another chorus of "Yes."

"Jumping out of the frying pan into the flames," Flip says softly, and there is a quiet, charged moment. Then Tanya says, "I thought that, too, actually. This is some *scary* shit, Elinor."

"All right," I say. I'm scared, too, but somehow I didn't expect them to be. "Open your eyes and keep going. What worked for you about tonight?"

"The way we were in the stories and out of them at the same time," Janie says. "They were us. But also, not us. More *me* than I usually am when I'm acting. But more—not-me, too."

Tanya starts to say something, stops.

"What?" I say.

"Is that your intention?" she says, looking from Idris to me. "To write scenes about *us*? I didn't spend umpteen years learning my craft so I could play *myself*."

"What do the rest of you think about this issue?" Idris says quickly.

"Hey," says Luis, "it's always you anyway, baby. You can't get away from yourself." For a minute, he actually looks shy. "Man, the audience was really *with* us when we did that shit," he says. "That's what you *pray* for."

"Yes, but that was only because we all knew each other," says Bernard.

"Not really," says Malik. "I didn't know Flip, for example. But I was completely with him."

"I felt that way, too," Flip says. "On both sides, performer and audience."

"Felt *what* way?" Bernard says scornfully.

"Like I was a part of something," Flip says, sounding troubled. "Like there was something there to *be* a part of. I have felt that way, once or twice, in some shows I've done. But never so much so soon."

"*Maybe* you get to this point by opening night," agrees Luis. "*Maybe* you carry the audience with you."

Flip is shaking his head. "Yes," he says, "but I agree with Tanya. I mean, I share her concern. This is all fine for an improv. But I don't exactly want to play myself for an audience, either."

So now they are all nodding and looking concerned, and since Idris *isn't* saying anything, it would seem to be up to me.

"Neither of us is planning on *you* being the characters," I say slowly, and Idris nods. "But we do think the material should come from you. We thought we'd do these kinds of exercises for a few weeks on various themes—money, power, violence . . ."

"Sex!" Luis calls out. Idris laughs and writes it down.

"Spirituality," says Bernard.

"Family," says Malik.

"In that vein," I say. "So Idris and I will come up with various exercises, and out of them, Idris will create a script. Just thirty or forty minutes, so there's time for audience discussion afterwards. But what I've realized from the workshop I've been taking, is that for this kind of material to work, you have to be *behind* it. Not literally playing yourself, *that's* not very interesting. Even if you *can* sing." Some people laugh, including Tanya. "But you have to *mean* what you're showing us. You have to *care* about it. Even if you're playing a villain, *you,* the actor, have to want us to see what's so awful about him. Like—I don't know. Malik's cab driver."

"He wasn't a *villain,*" Malik says quickly. "He was tired, scared—"

"Right," says Tanya. "Like he *wasn't* too tired to pick up somebody who *wasn't* a few shades lighter."

"Well, whatever he was," I say, "he wasn't Malik. But he did represent Malik's point of view. Do you see what I mean?"

"So it's all going to be just our *opinions?*" says Flip.

"This doesn't sound very interesting," says Bernard. "Frankly. Something on the level of sketch comedy."

"Is that what you saw tonight?" I say. "Is that what you *did* tonight? Playing your grandmother—was that sketch comedy?"

"No," Bernard says slowly, "it *was* acting."

Tanya rolls her eyes. But she says, "You're right, though, Elinor," and I am surprised by how much that means to me. "When I was watching—it meant something different. It wasn't that usual *acting* shit, you know. *Tricks.*"

"All right," says Idris diplomatically. "Do we like this idea enough to go ahead?"

Slowly the yes-votes come in. "This could really be something," Luis says, and the rest of them nod.

"For us *and* the community," Malik says, and they nod again. The actors look thrilled and terrified, and I wonder if I look that way, too.

TANYA: In the middle of the usual mad dash for coats and bags, Flip comes over to me. "So," he says, with that same blank look he had for Janie, "you want to go get some coffee?"

Not like I've got *nothing* to do tomorrow. A 7 a.m. call for a nonspeaking part on a soap, but I don't need hours of beauty sleep for *that*.

Around us people are running out like it's their last chance before the flood, dashing for the train that's going to get them home by eleven, or even later if they live in Brooklyn or Queens. And then we can all get up in the morning and go to work.

"Yeah, OK, why not?" I say. We're all the way over on the Lower East Side, where rehearsal space is cheap, but both my train out to Brooklyn and Warren's apartment are on the West Side, so we head across town to an all-night coffee shop.

All the way over, I am so mad at him, I can hardly hold a decent conversation, though Flip is certainly trying. "So, Bernard, what's his story?" he says as we walk into the restaurant.

"What do you mean?"

"Well, he's such a closet case." The waiter comes over and we order. I just have coffee. But Flip is always hungry. He orders a hamburger and a chocolate shake.

"Bernard?" I say. "He's always got some woman hanging around."

"So?" says Flip.

"Ofttimes two or three women." Flip shrugs. "Are you sure you don't mean Malik?" Because he's the one who, so he tells me, keeps getting mistaken for gay, although to my knowledge, he has been hot and heavy for the past fifteen years with Laila, his high school sweetheart. Not my type, and out of bounds anyway.

"No, Bernard," Flip insists. "The tall one, with the bald head. Do you think I can't tell them apart?" Is he teasing me or actually taking offense?

"Look, Tanya," he says, finally. "You're going to have to help me out here, because *I* don't think I've done anything wrong. But obviously you do. So come on. You tell me, and we'll both know."

I should not have to explain this. I should not have to explain this to *him*.

"Let's just forget it," I say, reaching for my bag. Now he *is* offended.

"So I'm not worth five minutes of your time to tell me why you're so pissed?" he says. "You're just going to write me off?"

I cannot *believe* he's still acting like he doesn't know what he did. I look at him closely to see which part of this lie *he* believes. He looks away.

"I know what *you* think I did," he says. "But you're wrong. We were friends. We said things to each other. We always said those things, you just as much as me. I thought it would make you laugh, what I said."

I keep studying him.

"*I* never took offense," he says. "At anything *you* ever said."

This actually does make me laugh. "Because *I* never crossed that line."

He shakes his head. "You were my friend. You could have said anything."

"Oh, really? Does that go for now, too?"

"Of course it does."

"Really?" I say again. "So if I find some truly disgusting way of calling you a cocksucking faggot, or saying, Gee, you and Warren are back together? I didn't even know you people could *have* relationships. I thought all you could do was screw around and give each other AIDS. Or maybe if I said——"

"All right," says Flip quickly. "That's enough."

"Not like I haven't said worse."

"Oh, I don't think you ever said anything worse," Flip says. "I certainly don't think *I* did." This is what always happens. You say anything about anything, and they get mad at *you*.

The food comes, but Flip still doesn't give up. "I would still really like to say, I didn't mean anything by it," he says stubbornly. "It wasn't even about you. It was about Davis, who, as I'm sure you recall, had just fired both of us. And you were so upset, Tanya. You were mad at him, too, at that point."

"I know," I say, "the dog. I should have stayed mad."

"Well," Flip says, "you're mad at him now, aren't you? That's something."

I have to smile. "Yeah," I say, "counting up my small favors." If Flip had been around a bit later, I *would* have told him about Davis. Would have asked him how I could have let myself get fooled so bad. Not that I didn't go over it, chapter and verse, with Verity and all my other girlfriends. Still. Flip's a man. Sometimes they know things.

"I don't know," he says after a few more bites. "I still don't like it."

"What?"

"If I'm going to piss you off so much, I would at least like to know I did it. It just doesn't feel like anything. I can't find any—bad intention toward you."

"I don't think you did have any bad intention," I say. "To my mind, that makes it worse."

Flip makes a face like the meat went bad. "What?" I say.

"Oh, that's just way too much like my sister to make me happy," he says. "She never has any bad intentions that I can see, and she always drives me absolutely crazy. And she *always* crosses that line, Tanya, including the time she told me I should never have made that remark to you and you were right to get pissed off."

"Well, that wasn't any of *her* damn business," I say.

Flip laughs. "All right," he says. "Thank you." He turns his hands palm up on the table. "And, I'm sorry. Even though I didn't— Anyway. I'm sorry."

"OK," I say finally, wishing we were—I don't know. In some *other* restaurant. Having some *other* conversation. "Apology accepted."

"I mean, you could have said something," Flip says. "I'm not saying it would make any difference, anything *you* said, but I wouldn't *not* listen. Probably."

He is just too damn good at making people laugh. "Is that how you got Warren to take you back?" I say. "By telling him some shit like this?"

Flip makes a face, but he keeps his voice light. "I think you've got that backwards," he says. "Warren was the one who had to come crawling back to me."

We stare at each other for a minute.

"OK," I say after a minute. "So now tell me why you think Bernard is such a closet case."

"God," Flip says, picking up his sandwich again, "how can you even ask? It's too, too obvious."

I laugh. We keep talking. Not like it *won't* ever come up again—he's surely right about that. Still. We might as well enjoy the intermissions.

FAMILY

FLIP: It seems like a long time since Warren and I have done anything normal, if you know what I mean, and so when Mario called to invite us—now, *there's* a word—to a dinner party at his boyfriend's place out in Brooklyn, I was happy to say yes. Warren was too, as it turns out. Maybe he feels the same way. At least he won't be home alone, waiting up for me, I can't help thinking, and then I shiver, because I could swear, I hear Warren thinking the same thing.

So Warren arranges for Juliet to stay at Marta's that night, with the understanding—carefully worked out with both Juliet *and* Marta—that we will pick Juliet up at Marta's on our way home (that was Juliet's bargaining point) and that we won't be back any later than midnight (Marta's). I do my best not to have any feelings about this, except possibly gratitude that it worked out so easily and *I* didn't have to be involved in any of the arrangements, but what I'm really thinking is, "Why do *I* have to be home by midnight? What am I, Cinderella?" Which, if I were sharing these thoughts with Warren, would probably lead to a whole riff on foot fetishes, but I'm not, so they don't.

"God, I'm glad *we* don't live out here," I say as we walk the long, *long* three blocks from the F train to Mario's boyfriend's apartment in Carroll Gardens. The edge of Carroll Gardens, really, not the long-time Italian part, but the gentrified section, which seems to be half upwardly mobile Italians (you can tell by the stone Madonnas in their front yards) and half gay men (you can tell by the exquisitely renovated facades).

Warren raises his eyebrows at me, but has the sense not to point out that *we* don't actually live anywhere, in the sense of living there together. A discussion that we've managed not to have so far, although clearly Warren would like to.

Instead, Warren says, "I don't know. I kind of like it out here. It's so green. Or it would be, if it wasn't December. Look, the brownstones actually have lawns."

"See, Warren," I say, "the whole reason I moved to New York City is because I don't *want* a lawn. It's practically the last remaining place in America where you don't have to have one."

Warren laughs. "And what about trees?" he says. "Does your objection to greenery extend to them, or are they somehow exempt?"

"No, trees are OK," I say, "as long as they're on the sidewalk. But way too many of *these* trees are actually on someone's *lawn*."

Warren laughs at this with so much obvious enjoyment that my heart turns over. Again. I bump my shoulder against his as we ring the buzzer, and although he usually won't do anything remotely affectionate in public, even in as non-public a public place as the hallway of Mario's boyfriend's brownstone, he presses back against me, warm and unmistakable. "Oh, fine," I whisper as some garbled voice over the intercom buzzes us in. "Start something *now*." So we are both smiling as we walk in.

I've never actually met Mario's boyfriend, since they've only been going out for about two weeks. Mario obviously adores him, though—everywhere Joshua goes, Mario follows him with his eyes, if not with his actual body, as when Joshua goes into the kitchen, for example, which he does almost as soon as he lets us in. We've been in his house all of three minutes and I don't think he's smiled once, let alone *said* anything. When Mario told him our names, I think he nodded.

Luckily, I do know some of the other people here, and so does Warren, except not the same people. (We really *didn't* do much as a couple.) Though we both do know Chris, the one who invited us to that party in the East Village, where we met. Chris is really, really young, and incredibly sweet. Normally, I find that particular combination incredibly annoying, but in Chris, I don't, which I suppose is a testament to just how sweet he is. Chris no longer lives in the East Village because he now lives with Paco, who is neither young nor sweet (salty, maybe), whom I know from dance class when he used to be a dancer. Now Paco does something on Wall Street—I've never gotten straight exactly what—and Chris is starting graduate school—I've never gotten straight exactly what there either, although that really isn't my fault, because Chris has changed his mind about what field to go into about forty-seven times. As a result, it's already December and Chris isn't actually enrolled anywhere yet.

The other couple here are Simon and Ian. Simon actually *is* enrolled in graduate school, at Olympia, where he's been for about three million years, though he keeps insisting that it's not that much longer till he actually gets a degree. Ian I've never met before, so of course, he's the one Warren knows. Actually, they also met at Chris's party, I discover in the midst of the introductions, which I have to admit, I find slightly disconcerting. As though fate could just have turned its dial a few degrees to the left and our whole lives would have been different.

"Well, Flip," says Ian, "I'm sorry I didn't meet *you* at that party. Where were *you?*" Or, that's another way of looking at it.

"Oh, I was in the kitchen most of the evening," I say. "I always meet the most interesting people in the kitchen." There. Warren should appreciate *that.*

"The kitchen," says Ian, in that incredibly wonderful Oxford/BBC/Royal Shakespeare Company accent that *every* American actor totally and completely envies and don't ever let any of them tell you any different. "Well, next time, I'll be sure to start there."

All right, I've had my fun for the evening. Now we can go home. Luckily for all of us, Joshua and Mario finally come out of *their* kitchen, bringing wine glasses and a choice of wine (three couples—three bottles) for Warren and me. Poor Warren—I can tell he wouldn't mind a look at the labels, but even he knows he can't really do that at a dinner party.

"So, Flip," says Simon, who I suppose is used to Ian's little ways, since *he* doesn't seem to bear me any ill-will (or Ian either—are you taking notes, Warren?), "I hear that you were the hit of the Lesbians and Gay Men Together meeting last month."

I expect Mario to be annoyed at this—this seems to be an unusually fraught evening, and we only just got here—but Mario is so preoccupied with Joshua that he just motions for Warren and me to sit down. There's still room for one person on the couch, so Warren sits there, and I perch on the flat wooden arm beside him. Which for any other boyfriend in the known universe might be an occasion to put his arm around me, or at least to somehow invite me to lean against him, but evidently a living room populated with three other male couples still counts as a public place to Warren. Well, I can always live vicariously through Simon and Ian, who are in the parallel positions at the other end of the couch—Simon beside Warren on the cushions, Ian perched on the arm with his fingers rather absent-mindedly ruffling Simon's hair.

"I wish I had seen it," Simon is saying. "Flip making a political speech."

"It wasn't a *speech,*" I say. "Although if my casual observations are going to galvanize such incredible response, maybe I *should* go into politics."

"The gay Ronald Reagan," says Paco.

"Oh, please," I say. "The gay Jimmy Stewart. The gay Ronald Reagan can be my best friend."

Of course, Ian, being British, doesn't get this, and Simon has to explain it to him. "The American movie executive Samuel Goldwyn once heard that Ronald Reagan was running for governor of California."

"No, no," Paco corrects him. "He had already been elected."

"Well, whatever," Simon says. "So Goldwyn supposedly said, 'No, no, Jimmy *Stewart* for governor.' "

"Wasn't it Gary Cooper?" says Paco.

"Or Gregory Peck?" says Chris helpfully.

"God, it wouldn't have been Gregory Peck," says Paco. "He was *much* too young." None of us wants to say—and perhaps some of us don't even want to think—that for someone Chris's age, these distinctions tend to fade.

"*Anyway,*" says Simon, "Goldwyn supposedly said, 'No, no, Jimmy *Stewart*— or some other leading man—for governor, Ronald *Reagan* for his best friend."

"Oh, *I* see," says Ian, in one of those mock-innocent, really nasty line readings that you really do need a British accent to pull off. "It's a *movie* joke."

"Well, go on, Flip," says Paco. "Don't keep us in suspense. Which of your words of wisdom brought the masses to their feet?"

"They didn't actually *stand,*" I say. "But it was all Mario's fault. He was actually talking to me *during* the meeting. Of course, I was shocked, because I would *never* say a word while anyone *else* was talking, particularly at a public gathering."

Mario laughs. Then, would you believe it, he looks at Joshua, who is still maintaining that same stony silence, and he stops laughing. Oh, please.

"*So?*" says Simon. "What did you say?"

"Oh, just that I didn't think marriage worked particularly well even for straight people, so why should we saddle ourselves with yet another set of expectations that we can once again fail to live up to?"

Warren surprises me by speaking up. Since he's more or less—all right, I give up, that phrase is now officially part of my vocabulary—sitting behind me, I have to twist around to look at him. Which would be easier if, say, I could put my hand on his shoulder. But that might look too much like a public display of affection.

"I don't know," Warren says. "Marriage works for some straight people."

"Oh, right," I say. "Who? Your parents? My parents? Please."

"Well, *my* parents are happily married," says Chris. Wouldn't you know? *His* parents are probably still teenagers. "And I think my brother is, but I only see him once a year, so it's hard to say."

"My parents aren't happily anything," says Simon, "but I suppose if anything *could* make them happy, being married to each other probably would. Certainly *not* being married to each other would make them even more not-happy than they already are, if such a thing is possible."

"I'm with Flip," says Ian, giving me such a—well, *significant* look, that I can't possibly believe Warren doesn't see it, too. "They invented marriage. Let them suffer the consequences."

"What about those gay marriages in the Middle Ages?" says Chris. "The ones John something wrote about?"

"John Boswell," Warren says, surprising me again.

"Right, John Boswell," says Chris. "He said straight people's marriages involved property, so they got married in court, but gay people's marriages involved only love, so they got married in the church."

"Oh, honey," says Paco, "that's so romantic." Typically, he's sitting in the one comfortable chair in the room—a huge armchair across from the couch—with Chris sitting on the floor in front of him—at his feet, actually, though it sounds worse if you put it that way. (Paco is only thirteen years older than Chris—the same age difference as between Warren and me, but for some reason, 22 and 35 seem *much* further apart than 32 and 45.) Paco is so delighted with Chris's little historical observation that he leans down and kisses Chris on the forehead. Which might have been all right, but then Chris puts one arm up and strokes Paco's cheek, and the kiss turns into a more lingering moment, and I'm thinking, well, all right, *some* public displays of affection probably *don't* belong in public. Or am I just envious?

"I don't think you're telling the whole story, Chris," Mario says earnestly, oblivious to the fact that Chris is otherwise engaged. "First of all, it wasn't all gay people who got to have those ceremonies, it was just men. Lesbians didn't marry."

"Can you imagine a world in which gay men marry and lesbians don't?" says Simon.

"A world gone mad," agrees Ian.

"Are you sure?" Chris asks Mario as he and Paco disengage.

"Well, at the very least, most of them didn't," says Mario. "Secondly, property *was* involved. Gay serfs couldn't marry—"

"Gay surfs," murmurs Ian, looking over at me again. "Sounds like the name of some nude beach in Mykonos."

"—because they *didn't* have property," Mario continues. "Only gay aristocrats."

"Lord and lord of the manor?" says Paco.

"And finally," says Mario, oblivious to all interruption in a way I have to kind of admire, "gay Jews, and gay Muslims, and other lesbians and gay men of non-Christian faiths couldn't get married, only gay Catholics."

"Now there's a heartwarming family scene," says Simon. "Mom, Dad, the good news is, I'm finally getting married. The bad news is, it's to a man, and I'm converting."

"You know," says Joshua, and since these are the first words he's spoken all evening, we all lean forward to listen, "you all are making it really difficult to carry on any kind of serious conversation. Mario was trying to make a point, but you won't let him talk."

There is a brief, shocked silence, which threatens to become a long, embarrassed silence.

"Actually, Joshua, I think I was done," Mario finally says. "With my point."

"And what a lovely little point it was," says Ian.

"I was just trying to say that the gay marriages in the Middle Ages didn't go far enough," Mario says. "Wonderful as it is to know they existed." Then he turns to Joshua. "But thank you for speaking up for me, Joshua," he says. With a perfectly straight face, so apparently, he means it. He turns to the rest of us. "Even though, you know. It was fine."

I suppose it's a tribute to how much we all like Mario that we rush to continue the conversation just as though nothing weird has actually happened. "Actually, I do have fantasies about getting married sometimes," Simon admits. "What's interesting is that in these fantasies, the person I'm marrying is completely vague. I mean, it could even be a woman."

"Well, that's tremendously flattering, thank you *very* much," Ian says.

"Oh, shut up, Ian," says Simon good-naturedly. "I mean that what I fantasize about is all the *stuff*, you know, how happy it *would* make my parents, however temporarily. How every relative I have in the world would show up, which isn't going to happen even at my funeral, so my one chance to be the center of attention for the Isenberg clan is if I get married. I mean, I'm the oldest son in a Jewish family, I have the *right* to be the center of attention at least once before I die."

"I thought firstborn Jewish sons got nothing *but* attention," I say.

Simon shakes his head mournfully as Ian says, "Apparently, all the attention goes to the mothers. Or so I'm given to understand."

"You know," says Simon. "The chance to feel normal, for once. An insider."

"You know when I think it would be convenient to be married?" says Paco. "Is when everybody else at work is talking about their wife this, or their husband that. If I were married, then I could say 'my husband' too."

"But honey," says Chris. "You're not *out* at work."

"No, but if I was," says Paco.

"I hope no one is forgetting that people who are married are supposed to be monogamous," Ian says, with yet another lupine glance at me.

"Is it still considered monogamy if your partner is present *while* you're dallying with someone else?" Simon says. "I'm not sure I *could* restrict myself to that, but I'd be willing to try." He and Ian share a brief, evil smile.

"Really, though," Paco says, "the only reason I can see for *anyone* to get married is for the sake of the children. And since none of us have children . . ."

"I do," says Warren.

"Warren," I say, "you don't *have children*. You're taking care of one child. Temporarily, right?" I deliver most of this speech facing out for the benefit of the group, but by the end, I've managed to twist around to face Warren, and I'm surprised at how upset he looks.

Of course, he doesn't say anything, he just shrugs, and I think that's going to be the end of it, at least until we get home—I mean, back to Warren's apartment—when Ian surprises me by leaning toward Warren and saying, "How old is your child?"

"Eight," Warren says. "Almost eight-and-a-half." He smiles. "She says, 'eight-and-three-eighths.' I got her this calendar, and we marked off in red when she was eight-and-a-quarter, and in blue when she was eight-and-three-eighths, and in green when she would be eight-and-a-half, and so on. We thought about shaving it down to the sixteenths, but she said that would be just *too* fussy."

"When did all this go on?" I say.

Warren shrugs again. "You're usually not home before she goes to bed," he says with what I'm sure *he* feels is admirable restraint. "The calendar is right there in her room."

Ian clears his throat, and I'm sure he's going to make yet another sarcastic comment in that delicious voice. "My daughter talks about it in terms of months," he says instead. "Ten and five months, ten and seven months, that sort of thing." He clears his throat again. "At least, she did when she *was* ten and seven months. Now she's nearly twelve, so perhaps she's outgrown that particular habit."

"Is she still in England?" Chris asks sympathetically.

"No, in Vermont," Ian says. "My cunt of an ex-wife is an American, actually. So believe me, children, when I talk about the disastrous consequences of the institution of marriage, I know whereof I speak."

"At least you got a green card out of it," Simon says, and you'd think it would be apparent to everyone that we should just change the subject now. But instead, Chris says, even more sympathetically, "And she won't let you see your daughter?" at the same time that Joshua says, "I realize this must be a difficult topic for you, Ian, but I don't think there's any excuse for using that word."

Ian surprises me yet again, because he sighs and says to Joshua, "You know, Joshua, much as I'd like to call *you* a cunt, I actually happen to think you're right. It's just that the word seems to fit my ex-wife so perfectly, the temptation to use it is well-nigh unavoidable. And no, she won't let me see my daughter. Not because she has any particular concerns about homosexuality, in case any of you were wondering, but because she remarried, and she and her husband decided that since it would be too confusing for Rosemary to have two fathers, they would do better to eliminate the one who didn't actually have the privilege of living with her."

"But don't you have visitation rights or custody rights or some legal something that would—" Chris starts to say, as Paco whispers, "Honey. Honey. He doesn't want to talk about it."

Ian shrugs. "My wife may not have had any concerns about homosexuality, but the judge certainly did."

"I'm sorry," Warren says. "I can only imagine. I'm really sorry."

"Look," says Ian, "who do you have to fuck to change the subject around here?"

Now, wait a minute. It's one thing to flirt with me in front of Warren, but it's another thing to insult him outright. Especially when he was just trying to be nice. I am just about to say something, when Warren actually puts his hand on my arm. I am so surprised, I twist around to look at him. Warren shakes his head. Slowly I turn back, more disconcerted than I would have expected. Who am I, Joshua?

Meanwhile, Mario is talking. "I don't think we *should* change the subject," he says passionately. "We're supposed to be a community. We're supposed to be there for each other. Ian, tell us. How can we support you around this?"

Ian purses his lips. He looks alternately furious, amused, offended, and then, finally, touched. "Only in America," he says with a sigh. "Does the distinction between public and private really mean nothing to you people?"

"I don't think it doesn't mean anything," Warren says slowly. "I think it's more a question of figuring out which is which." His fingers tighten on my arm. I get the message. I put my hand over his.

"Well, I have a question for you, Mario," says Simon. "Which is this: What's the difference between community and family?"

"I don't get it," says Mario.

"Well, family is supposed to be private, right?" says Simon. "And community is supposed to be public. Or do you just not make any distinction?"

"I still don't know what you mean," says Mario. I notice Ian gradually relaxing on the wooden arm of the couch. I notice Simon noticing Ian, even as he keeps Mario talking. Behind me, I can feel Warren also noticing Ian. Now it's my hand that tightens over his, though I have no idea why.

"Doesn't *everything* affect all of us?" Mario is saying. "Even the most private stuff, isn't it all public? I mean, we might *do* it in private. But it's outlawed in public. That's *why* we need each other."

"You mean the sodomy laws?" says Chris. "Weren't they repealed?"

"In New York," Mario says. "But they're on the books in a bunch of other states—you can get twenty years for sodomy in Massachusetts. Plus all the other things—housing rights, child custody—"

"OK," Simon says quickly, "so you think the community *is* our family."

"Excuse me," says Paco, "but I don't have any idea what the fuck you're all talking about. The community, the family, what difference does it make? We're all individuals. I don't know about the rest of you, but I live my life the way I want to. The 'community' doesn't have anything to do with it. And my family doesn't either."

"What about Chris?" says Mario. "Isn't he your family?"

Paco leans down and wraps his arms around Chris, so that his cheek is resting on Chris's head. "Chris is my boyfriend, and I love him dearly, as everybody knows," he says, "and I would do anything in the world for him, of course. But that's because I want to, not because he's my family."

Mario is about to argue with that, but Joshua, of all people, saves the day. "I think dinner is probably ready," he says.

"Thank God," says Ian. And when we all turn to look at him, he says, "Well, after all. This is a *dinner* party. Is it really so unreasonable to expect actual *food*?"

Joshua goes out to the kitchen, and Mario restrains himself from following long enough to seat us around the table, which is set up in the middle of the living room. Conversation stays fairly general during the first course—which I must admit is fabulous, a wild mushroom soup that apparently Joshua made, so at least he has *one* redeeming quality. But during the second course—some kind of spectacular baked fish and braised winter vegetables—we break off into little groups. Down at the far end, Mario, Paco, and Simon are talking about Mario's HIV support group, which wouldn't be *my* idea of dinner-party conversation, but they all seem interested. And at the other end, Chris is telling Joshua about his latest grad school decision, which I suppose is an excellent topic, as it doesn't require much if any participation from Joshua. Warren and Ian, sitting side by side, are deep in a conversation which they are conducting in such low voices, I can't really make out more than a few words, though I *think* they're talking about their respective children. Which leaves me temporarily alone with the fish, though granted, I *could* join in just about anywhere *except* with Warren and Ian. So naturally, that's the conversation that interests me.

I am sitting directly across from Warren, but he's turned so far toward Ian that he doesn't even notice me watching them. And suddenly—and believe me, I've never done anything like this before—I find myself slipping off my right shoe—luckily, it's a loafer—and putting my foot into Warren's lap. With fairly decent aim, I might add, and what I don't achieve in the first moment of contact I make up for fairly soon thereafter.

Lucky for Warren, he has a lifetime of concealing his feelings to come to his aid. He barely blinks, although I'm sure he must be surprised. Ian goes on murmuring with no change of expression on *his* face, and the rest of the group are all busy with their conversations. My foot is busy, too, and for a moment, we go on like that.

Then, not taking his eyes off Ian for a moment, with not the slightest change in expression, Warren reaches under the table and takes my foot in both hands. He pulls off my sock and begins to massage my foot, except *massage* is not exactly the right word. I had no idea you could arouse such reactions just from touching somebody's *foot*. Oh, God, Warren, what *are* you doing? I try to pull my foot back, but Warren won't let go. And all this time, would you believe it, he goes on talking to Ian.

Just when I'm sure that I *won't* be able to control my breathing any longer, Warren lets go. Though how he knew, since he *still* hasn't taken his eyes off Ian, I *don't* know. And, at this point, don't particularly care. I'm far more concerned with getting my bare foot back into my shoe—as if *that's* going to help much. Across the table, I see the corners of Warren's mouth twitch in a tiny smile. Oh, all right, Warren. You win.

Just before dessert, Warren excuses himself to go to the bathroom, and when he comes back, I follow suit. In what I suppose I have to consider a more or less generous gesture, he's left my sock curled around the doorknob. And when we settle back into our old places in the living room for coffee, Warren on the couch, me perched on the arm beside him, he actually does put his arm around me, and I do lean back against him. Will wonders never cease.

Perhaps it's because dinner was so delicious (Joshua actually made chocolate crème brûlée for dessert, which must have taken him hours), or perhaps it's because this new position is so comfortable, that I can afford to be generous, too. Because when I look over at Mario and Joshua, who as the hosts have taken the least comfortable places, two gray metal folding chairs set side by side, and when I see Joshua sitting in his usual stony silence as Mario tells us about how much fun he's having in the Gay Men's Chorus, I find myself thinking about Joshua, "Oh. He's scared." I imagine his relief when all of us leave and he and Mario are finally alone. Or maybe he's scared then, too. Maybe that's when he's most scared.

"I sang in a choir at school," Ian is saying. "I was actually considered quite a promising soloist until my voice changed."

"Oh, I'll never be a soloist," Mario says. "I'll never be that good. You sing, though, don't you, Flip?"

"Not really," I say. "I take voice lessons, when I can afford them, but it's more for training purposes. Breath control, for example." Behind me, I can feel Warren smile.

"I played violin," Chris says.

"I never knew that," says Paco.

"Oh, for years," Chris says. He laughs. "I played in a community orchestra all through high school, and I actually got paid for it."

"Why did you stop?" Paco wants to know.

"Because I was at the point where I couldn't stand how I sounded if I didn't practice at least two hours a day, and I just wasn't that committed. But I did love being in the middle of the orchestra. Inside all that sound. I still miss that."

"So do I, actually," says Ian. "Lucky you, Mario."

Mario shrugs. "The chorus is pretty much open to anybody," he says. "You could all join."

I look around the room. Well, not that I need *another* family. But if I *did* want one, I suppose these people wouldn't be so bad. Except for Joshua, and he could be an in-law. They're supposed to get on your nerves.

When it's finally time to go, we say goodbye to Chris and Paco, who are getting into Paco's car and driving back to Paco's co-op in Brooklyn Heights. We walk to the subway with Simon and Ian, who are taking the F train in the opposite direction, out to Simon's apartment in Park Slope. The four of us talk about getting together some time. Apparently, Warren has already invited Ian to meet Juliet, and now they're talking about doing something afterward, maybe dinner at our house. Once again, I have the uneasy feeling that Warren has become a completely different person from the man I first knew.

We get on the train, and I discover that the down side of having sat with Warren's arm around me for the whole last part of the evening is that now I'd like to do it again. But even I am not brave enough to sit like that on the subway, especially not coming home at this hour from this part of Brooklyn. So we don't even sit next to each other, but at right angles, which means I am staring dreamily at Warren and thinking about what I'd like to be doing, until Warren finally says, "This isn't working, Flip. Think about something else."

"Three million gay men in New York City, and I have to get involved with a psychic," I say. "Should we talk about how weird Joshua was? What was with him, anyway?"

"Oh, he was just scared," Warren says. "He's terrified that Mario will leave him, among other things, but I don't think he will."

So now I stare at Warren for a different reason. "That's just what I was thinking," I say. "How terrified Joshua was."

"Well, it's kind of an all-purpose comment, in my experience," Warren says. "My clients always love it when I tell them that they're scared. It makes them feel so brave."

"And here I thought I was the manipulative one."

"Live and learn," Warren says. "I did think they were awful, though. Mario and Joshua."

"The way Mario kept following Joshua into the kitchen—I mean, I know they were cooking, but still. What were they, joined at the hip?"

"What about Paco and Chris?" Warren says.

"Oh, I know. I mean, on the one hand, it's sweet. But on the other hand . . ."

"I did like Simon and Ian, though," Warren says, suddenly sounding uncertain. "You did too, didn't you?"

This is so not the conversation I thought we'd be having about Simon and Ian that I have the sudden impulse to burst out laughing. I don't, though, because it would either hurt Warren's feelings or I'd have to explain, and at the moment, I don't particularly want to do either. "Yes," I say instead. "It would be fun to see them again."

Warren grins at me. "Then I'm glad things worked out so that we can," he says. "Because I could certainly imagine scenarios that might have been, oh, *awkward*."

"Mmmm," I say. "Scenarios to be avoided at all costs, apparently."

"Flip," Warren says suddenly. "Are we ever going to talk about living together again?"

"Oh, why not?" I say.

"Why not talk about it, or why not do it?"

"Well, since we actually *are* talking about it, in case you hadn't noticed, I suppose I meant why not do it. You said before you wanted to go back to the apartment in Hell's Kitchen."

"Yes, well, I was thinking about that, actually," Warren says uncomfortably. The train pulls into Fourteenth Street, and we start walking over to Marta's apartment. "Because of Marta," Warren is saying. "I mean, because of Juliet, it's so convenient to be so close. And Chelsea is so much better a neighborhood for her than Hell's Kitchen."

I find myself wondering how Warren could all of a sudden afford a two-bedroom apartment in Chelsea. After all, none of the other people at tonight's party could. Even Paco, who works on Wall Street, had to settle for Brooklyn Heights, where a lot of stockbrokers seem to live. Of course, in some cases, that's because they actually prefer Brooklyn, hard as *that* is to believe.

I yawn. "Can we talk about that part another time?" I say. "I don't think I have the energy for it tonight."

Warren looks at me uneasily, and I wonder how many of my questions he's picked up. He goes up by himself to get Juliet, and comes down carrying her on his shoulder, already sound asleep. I see his point—it's only about a block and a half from Marta's place to his. I see his point about the neighborhood, too—there aren't even any playgrounds in Hell's Kitchen.

As we wake up the next morning, Warren is lying on his side and I am pressed up against his back. I can feel him reaching for me, which really moves me, I have to tell you, because this kind of snuggling used to make him so uncomfortable, especially if we hadn't had sex yet. Somehow that made it better, though not always even then. But now I put my arm over him, and he takes my hand and kisses it and pulls it in close to his chest, which actually makes me want to cry. Instead, I throw my leg over his hip, and with his other hand, he begins to stroke the inside of my thigh. I don't know if it's because Warren is a psychic, or because he knows me so well, or if he just *is* that way, but as we established last night, there are these places on my body he can find that even I don't know about, and he finds one now. (Although, my God, if he could do this with anyone, you would think he would have men lined up around the block. I should have to fight my way into his apartment every night, instead of him worrying about what *I'm* doing every time I come home late.) Oh, God, Warren, what *are* you doing? I push up harder against him, my crotch against his ass, and then suddenly, we hear Juliet calling, "Uncle Warren! I'm up and I don't have anything to *do.*"

After the moment it takes me to catch my breath, I mutter, "When *we* were little, we weren't allowed to wake our parents until at least ten o'clock on a Saturday morning." Another breath. "Of course, they probably *were* sleeping."

Warren is already up, pulling on his bathrobe. "They did have three of you," he points out.

"Not those parents." He is tying the sash. "It was my stepfather by then."

"Oh, right." He looks at my face. "Give her a break, Flip," he says. "She hasn't even been here a month. And there's only one of her." Oh, so now I'm frustrated *and* selfish.

Warren pauses at the bedroom door. "I'll be right back," he says. "Don't go anywhere."

"I think you have a few minutes before you have to worry about that." I hear some muffled conversation in the next room and then the sound of the television. Which is another thing that freaks me out—Warren with a television set. When we lived together, he couldn't stand having mine on—I practically had to lock myself away in the bathroom if I wanted to watch something. But he bought one for Juliet the day after she got here, apparently, and now he's even got one in his office waiting room, with a VCR, for the times he has to have her there.

Warren comes back into the bedroom. "We have exactly forty-eight minutes and thirty seconds," he says, taking off his robe. "Which, if you're interested, is the running time of *The Little Mermaid, Part II.*"

"Well, I never thought I'd see you making love to the sound of a television set," I say as he gets back into bed.

He turns onto his other side, so he can face me. "Does it really bother you so much?"

"I don't know. I don't want it to, but it does."

Warren puts his hand on my shoulder and just waits. Another thing he never used to do.

"I don't think it's mainly Juliet," I say after a minute. He waits some more. "I don't know," I say again.

"Yes, you do," he says. "Come on, Flip. Know. Tell me."

"It's just so much," I say. "Not Juliet, especially. You. I'm not used to it."

"And you don't like it."

"I didn't say that. I just wonder sometimes—it's more that *I* feel so different."

The television gets louder, which Warren doesn't seem to notice, but which I find extremely distracting. Then it goes back to its somewhat less annoying background hum. Juliet must have turned it down.

"None of this bothers you?" I say.

"Actually," says Warren, "my thoughts were running in the opposite direction." Suddenly, he looks a lot more uncomfortable. "I've been thinking about getting married."

"To *me?*"

"No, Flip, I was thinking that Juliet needs a mother. Of course, to you. Who the fuck else would I be thinking about marrying?"

"Well, that's a romantic proposal," I say more or less automatically. "My God, Warren, I go to one little meeting, and look what happens."

"It has nothing to do with that meeting," Warren says. "I mean, I do live in America, Flip. I have *heard* of the institution of marriage."

"Then you must also have heard that—now, how can I put this?—oh, yes. We're not allowed to do it."

"Well, so what?" Warren says. "We do all sorts of other things that we're not allowed to do."

"I meant what I said at that meeting, actually," I say. "The whole idea of it—I don't think it even works for straight people."

"Well, we don't have to *call* it marriage," Warren says. "We can call it something else. A commitment ceremony."

"God, that's worse. It's so, 'Oh, we're gay and we're not allowed to get married, so let's make up some really *cute* name to disguise the fact.' "

"Well, so then we *could* call it marriage," Warren says. "Which I prefer, actually. But I don't care what we call it. I just—" He takes a deep breath. "I just like the idea that you'll always be here." He forces himself to look at me. "I really missed you those three months, Flip. I don't want to go through that again."

Then don't leave, I am tempted to say, but he is obviously working so hard not even to look away that I really don't have the heart. The television gets louder, and this time I can hear Juliet jump up and run to turn it down. "Well, she's very considerate," I say.

"Is she really not the reason?" Warren says. He turns onto his back. "Because . . ."

"What?"

"Well, I finally found out how to get hold of Madeleine's doctors. I'm still not allowed to talk to *her,* of course. But they think, maybe by June."

"That she'll be out."

He nods. Well, that explains why he got so upset last night. "Is that why you want to marry me?" I say. "So we don't both go?"

Warren turns his face to me again. "I don't know," he says. "But I *don't* want you to both go. I don't want either one of you to go."

"Come here," I say, and he almost throws himself on top of me. I can feel him shaking. "I don't know, Warren," I say. "Let me think about it, OK? I missed you, too, those three months. You know that." He nods. I'm sorry, I can't stand how important this is to him. Except, lying pressed against him like this, my body has ideas of its own. Ideas which apparently Warren divines, even in this unhappy state, because he reaches down and finds one of those places again.

"Oh," I say, rather breathlessly. "Now you're just trying to get me to marry you."

"Is it working?"

"I don't know. I'll let you know. How much is left of *The Little Mermaid?*"

ROSIE: Look, do *you* think I did the right thing? I don't think Michael would be happy at my family's house for Christmas, honestly, I don't. But I'm not sure that's why I didn't let him come. Since bringing home a twenty-four-year-old Black boyfriend sounds like my idea of hell. The staring, the questions, the naked horror. And then the naked relief when we eventually split up. I'd have to actually *be* planning to marry Michael to put both of us through that.

I don't even know why I'm *going* home this year, to tell you the truth. I mean, Flip didn't, last year. Which caused something of a scandal, given that it was the very last year his godparents (Poppy's old union brother, Mitch, and his wife, Susan) were going to be in Pittsburgh, before Mitch retired and they moved to Florida. No one could understand why Flip wasn't coming home—Mitch and Susan even offered to pay for his ticket. Only I knew that it was because he wanted to spend Christmas with Warren—the rest of the family barely even knew Warren's name at that point, even though he and Flip had been living together practically since August. So you'd think *I* could miss this year, wouldn't you, to spend Christmas with Michael?

Only I can't. Don't ask me why.

The plane sinks into the Pittsburgh airport like a stone dropping into a well, and I scramble for my bags—overnight case, briefcase, carryall, shopping bag full of presents. There's always that pang when there's no one at the gate, even though I know Danny is waiting for me out front, double-parked by the entrance. He thinks that makes it easier. No, Danny, what would make it *easier* would be if you met me at the gate and helped me *carry* my bags, and then I wouldn't care if we had to walk five miles. But he's always so pleased at being able to do something for me, it seems mean to make him do it my way.

The person I'd *really* like to be bringing home is my best friend, Marcy. She's Jewish, so her family doesn't even care about Christmas. All through college, she came home with me, and even for the first few years afterward. Then she married Joe, and although he's also Jewish, they go out to his family's on Long Island for Christmas, which they even celebrate, with a Christmas tree and stockings and all the rest, which I personally think is weird, though obviously, it's not for me to judge. And now Marcy's pregnant, so I'll probably never spend Christmas with her again.

Michael didn't even believe me when I tried to tell him how my family would be. He thought that since they love me, they'd be glad to meet the man who makes me happy. (And he does, he does, he definitely does.) But when I tried to explain that my happiness wasn't exactly their first priority, he didn't believe that either.

"Hi, Rosie!" It's 6 p.m. on Christmas Eve, the airport is packed, but Danny has managed to get his car into the prime spot beside the sidewalk. I toss my bags in the back of his station wagon and climb into the front seat. "That's all you've got?" he says in that boyish voice—he always sounds just like when we were little. But he looks so grown up. Maybe it's the wife and three kids, or the real job (as opposed to Flip's and mine)—he manages a local chain of bakeries that seems to be constantly expanding, but he never seems busy or overwhelmed, just—settled.

"Hi, Danny. Yup, that's it." I lean over to kiss him on the cheek. He smiles shyly. "So," I say, "how's Betsy? And the kids?"

Danny just lights up, as he does whenever anyone mentions Betsy. He really is too good to be true. So is Betsy, if it comes to that. It's a good thing they married each other, because they'd make any other conceivable spouse feel just too totally inadequate.

"Oh, Betsy is fine. She's just glad it's Christmas, because she's been working so hard lately. She even has to work this afternoon." Now he looks concerned. "Actually, Rosie," he says, continuing to maneuver around the Christmas Eve traffic. It's still only about six-thirty, but because it's so dark, it *feels* late. "Actually," he says, "I am kind of worried about her. They're treating her so badly at the nursing home, giving her all the worst shifts. Maybe you could give her some pointers."

Pointers on what, Danny? How to organize a union? How to get the good shifts *without* a union? As usual, part of me is touched that he thinks I can do anything. And part of me is so frustrated, because look—he has no idea what I actually *do*.

"I'd be happy to talk to her," I say. "If you think she'd like it."

"Oh, she'd be flattered," Danny says immediately.

"Danny. It's just me."

"Well, she thinks very highly of you," Danny says. "I'm sure your opinion would mean a lot."

For one deluded minute, I consider trying to tell him about my work. Explaining how it really *doesn't* apply to Betsy. But instead I ask him about each of his kids, a conversation that lasts until he pulls into our driveway. "Welcome home!" he says brightly. Home, but not where I live.

I load myself up to go into the house—*now* Danny offers to take something, but now there's no point, right? He opens the front door for me, and I brace myself against all the noise and heat I always forget with my mind but remember with my body, every time I enter this house. "Look who I brought!" Danny says as we walk into the living room, making barely a dent in the billowing noise. It's always such a shock, the solid *groupness* of them all.

Naturally, Flip is sitting between Ma and Dad in the center of the couch. I can't *believe* he's left Warren and Juliet all by themselves, all the way over on the other side of the room. (At least I assume that's Juliet. I haven't actually met her yet. Flip wants me to know all the least little details about every single person in his life, but he doesn't like it if I actually spend time with anybody.) I can't believe Flip got to bring Warren, either. Of course, as someone whose status is completely indefinable, Warren doesn't have to actually *stay* in our house. Apparently Flip has arranged for him to rent a car and stay with Juliet in a nearby motel. Where Flip, of course, will stay, too, even though officially, he's sleeping upstairs, in his and Danny's old room. No one will ever notice that *his* bed hasn't been slept in. Whereas if Michael had been staying in the guest room and I'd met him there for even five minutes, all hell would have broken loose.

Ma's attention is divided between Flip beside her on the couch and four-year-old Lily, the apple of her eye (after Flip), at her feet. Of course, Ma likes—loves—eight-year-old Shannon (who is currently leaning against the empty wing chair, eyeing Juliet), but Shannon is too moody to be the apple of anyone's eye. And Peter is this very *boy* boy, not exactly Ma's type. At the moment, he's sitting by the fireplace, playing a very loud game involving sirens and gunfire. So that leaves Lily, cute, self-confident, and still young enough to adore Nana without reservation. Today she's wearing a furry white sweater and a white ballet tutu that sticks out so stiffly, it's a wonder she can move at all.

"Lily, don't roll around on the floor like that—you'll ruin your pretty dress," Ma says. "But they are hiring you these days, aren't they, Flip? A lot, it sounds like. No, love," she stage-whispers into Lily's ear, "don't sit with your legs open—sit like a lady."

"But, Nana," whines Lily. "But Nana, I have *tights* on!"

"So do they pay overtime, then?" Dad is asking Flip, who typically manages to be in every conversation at once—except any conversation involving Warren, who is obviously not going to get one single chance to open his mouth this whole three days, since in *his* family, apparently, no one talks when someone else is talking. "What would happen if you *didn't* have tights on?" Flip says to Lily, at the same time that he's telling Dad, "Not overtime, exactly, but if they bring you in from out of town, you get expenses."

"Then they would look at my underpants!" says Lily. "And then I'd have to *kill* them!"

Ma laughs, her head thrown back. She has this way of completely abandoning her whole body to laughing, even though she doesn't actually move much.

"So it's a seller's market," Dad says.

"*God,* no," Flip says. "There are only about eight hundred *million* actors who would take any acting job in the known universe at the drop of a hat. Before the hat even *started* to drop. Before it had even left—well, where *do* hats leave, when they start to drop?"

"The head, wouldn't you think?" says Ma. "Lily, darlin', why don't you go get your coloring book? Although I guess it would more be *falling* if it was off the head."

"At the *fall* of a hat," Flip says. "Sounds like something Tanya would say."

"Who's Tanya?" says Ma, sounding hopeful. Oh, Ma. With Warren sitting right *there*.

"Uncle Flip," says Lily, pulling on his knee, "do you want to see me do a back *flip?*"

This is the point where Flip looks up and sees me standing in the doorway. "Hi, Rosie," he says. "Are you planning on sitting down, or are you just going to stand in the doorway until it's time to go to Mass?"

"Well, since *you've* got the most comfortable seat in the room," I say. Warren looks even more uncomfortable, if that's possible.

"Rosie, don't talk to your brother that way," Ma says automatically. "He was only trying to be nice. Lily, you can't do a back flip in the living room, love, it isn't big enough."

"Yes, Rosie," says Flip with a smirk. "I was only trying to be nice."

"That's enough, Flip," Ma says. So I smirk at *him* and go sit in the empty wing chair near Warren. Pausing only for Dad's kiss on the cheek and Ma's tight, preoccupied hug as she whispers, "Hello, darlin'. Welcome home."

As I sit down, Shannon wraps her arms around me and puts her head in my lap. "Aunt *Rosie*," she says wistfully.

"Niece *Shannon*," I say as I hug her, and she lifts her head and gives me a mournful, dreamy smile. "Did you meet Juliet yet? Hi, Warren. God, didn't anybody get you any eggnog? Do you want some, love? Shannon! How would you like to go out to the kitchen—"

"It's all right, Rosie," Warren says quickly. Well, he *must* be at his wit's end—he actually interrupted me. "I had some before." And God help me, before the words are even out of his mouth, I'm thinking. "What's the matter, Warren, isn't our eggnog good enough for you?"

"*Yes*, I met her," Shannon is saying, tugging impatiently on my arm. "I know her *name*."

"Actually, *I* haven't met Juliet yet. Juliet, I'm Rosie. I'm Flip's sister."

"*And* Warren's friend," Juliet says.

I laugh, and Warren looks slightly less uncomfortable. "Yes, definitely, *and* Warren's friend," I say.

"Uncle Flip is Uncle Warren's *boyfriend*," Juliet explains to me, "and you're his *friend*."

"No, he *can't* be his *boyfriend*," Shannon says. "Warren is a *man*, so he can't have a *boy*friend. And Flip isn't your parents' brother, and he isn't married to your mother, so he can't be your uncle, only *my* uncle."

Juliet gives Shannon this very Warren-like look of disdain, which when Warren does it means he's feeling completely at bay. Warren and I both start to say something—*not* Flip, I notice, still patiently explaining to Dad that sometimes he gets a flat per diem and sometimes he gets reimbursed for receipts (which, by the way, is also true for me, not that I've ever been asked *one question* about that or any other aspect of my job). But before either Warren or I can say anything, Danny calls over from the other side of the room. "Shannon!" he says firmly. "Come here for a second, honey."

Shannon starts to protest. "Shannon!" he says again. "Now, please, honey."

Glowering at all three of us, Shannon goes over to Danny, who pulls her up onto his lap. She promptly flings her head down onto his chest.

"Rosie!" Juliet is saying to me. Not *Aunt Rosie,* apparently. "Rosie, do you speak French?"

"*Un tout petit peu,*" I say. "I wish I spoke more."

"That's all right," says Juliet. "If you practiced, you'd learn more. And your accent would get better, too."

"Juliet!" says Warren, completely mortified. "What have we said about correcting people?"

"But Uncle Warren," Juliet says. "I wasn't *correcting* her. I was telling her how she could get better."

"It's OK, Warren," I say, though I am not exactly scot-free of embarrassment myself.

"No, it's not all right," Warren says. "She has to learn—Juliet, you have to learn to think about people's feelings."

Shannon comes back, her head held high. "I'm sorry I said Flip couldn't be your uncle," she says defiantly to Juliet. "My Daddy explained it to me. He said if you loved Flip very much and he was a very important person in your life and *especially* if you lived in the same house, then you *could* call him uncle."

"But that's not the reason—" Juliet says, and Warren and I both start to interrupt her again. Though part of me has to wonder, why? Just because nobody *else* in our family seems to want to acknowledge Warren's status—including Flip, apparently, still holding court over there on the couch. Honestly, can you *imagine* me bringing Michael into this house?

All the same, I stand up quickly, before Juliet has time to enlighten Shannon any further. "Juliet and Shannon!" I say in hushed, conspiratorial tones. "I have a project for you."

They look at me suspiciously. "What project?" Shannon says skeptically.

Juliet thinks even faster. "I want to stay down here with everybody else."

"Well, that's too bad," I say. "Because this is a very exciting, secret project, but it can only be done upstairs."

"Why?" Juliet wants to know.

"Yes, why?" says Shannon, not to be outdone.

"Because that's where the materials are."

"What materials?" they both say.

"Ma," I say, probably interrupting about three conversations, but this involves children, so I have priority. "Are those things—you remember—the ones you and Poppy used to, you know—are they still in the attic?"

"No, they're in your closet now," Ma says. "The attic has mildew. What do you want with those old things?" I indicate Juliet and Shannon and somehow,

in that one gesture, Ma understands my entire plan, including the need for secrecy. She nods and turns back quickly to the multiple conversations on the
couch, which is her way of helping to keep the secret. But in the moment before she turns, I see—what? How much she approves of me.

I can't stand how much that means to me. I feel my whole spirit lighten.
"You know," I say, kneeling down to face the girls, "if we went upstairs, I could
show you the materials."

Juliet and Shannon look at each other, almost allies. Shannon cracks first.
"All right, Aunt Rosie. But if we *don't* like it, we're coming *right down*." Juliet
nods. Honestly, if it were up to Danny and Warren, they'd just be hanging
around downstairs, left out, miserable, probably fighting.

It's always a shock seeing my old room again—that tiny single bed, the
white acrylic bedspread with its very '70s-looking flowers, hot pink and electric blue, that seemed so daring at the time. And the white dressing table covered with a matching skirt. I remember the day I painted that table, so
impatient that I didn't even stir the paint. I had this vision of what my room
would look like, and I couldn't believe that all that stood between me and my
dream was painting that stupid piece of furniture. Flip stood in the doorway—I had to leave the door open because of the fumes—saying over and
over how ugly it looked, and pointing out every single time I got paint on my
hands or my jeans or my hair. Finally, when I was near tears, he said, "Rosie!
You have to *stir* the paint first. With a *stick*. I'll show you, stupid." God, what
was he? Eleven, I guess, because I was fourteen—the paint, bedspread, and
matching skirt were partly my fourteenth birthday present, partly paid for
with the babysitting money I had been saving for months. (We never got al-
lowances, so we had to earn our own money—partly on principle, partly out
of necessity—and I was pretty much equally proud of both reasons.)

So Flip actually went down to the garage and came back with a paint stick,
saying, "*God.* Don't you know *anything?*" He stirred up the paint and said,
"OK, now try it," and I was desperate enough that I did, and OK, yes, it *did* go
on better. And Flip said, "White is a dumb color for furniture. If it was my
dresser, I'd paint it black." And then he started *singing* "Paint It Black," which
was a double insult, because he knew how much I hated the Rolling Stones.
Then he came back about fifteen minutes later with a smaller brush, saying,
"You're supposed to use a different brush for the wavy parts, but I bet *you*
didn't know that."

"How do you know so much about it?" I said, rather desperately, since by
this point, I had paint all over myself, and the dark wood *still* showed through.
(Though not through the parts I'd done after Flip had stirred the paint.)

"I know lots of things you don't think I know," Flip said. "Now you have paint on your *eyebrows*."

"Aunt Rosie," says Shannon, completely uninterested in my room, or my memories. "Where are the materials?"

"I think they're back here," I say, opening the closet. "Can you two help me?" The three of us drag the trunk out, and I fiddle with the latch until we manage to open it. And there, in my opinion, are the most glamorous, mysterious clothes in the world: Ma and Poppy's old costumes from when they went ballroom dancing. They actually used to enter contests. The most wonderful treat in the world was when I got to wear them to play dress-up, which Ma let me do even after Poppy died. (I still think that's pretty amazing.) I'm a little worried that Juliet and Shannon won't see how special these clothes are. But no, they're thrilled.

"So," I say, as they stare into the trunk, mesmerized by the shiny satins and sequins. "Your job is to try on every single thing in this trunk, *very* carefully, because these are *very* old clothes—and then tell me and Nana which ones we should keep and which ones we should give to the Good Will."

"What if we want to keep all of them?" says Shannon.

"We could do that," I say. "But before you can decide, somebody has to try on every single one. Can you do that?"

"Yes!" says Juliet, and Shannon nods. Allies at last.

"Mind if I join you?" Warren says, suddenly appearing in the doorway.

"Oh, Warren, no, of course not, come in, love, sit down. The mob scene is finally getting to you, huh? Or maybe *finally* isn't exactly the right word."

To his credit, Warren laughs. "Let's just say that I can see why you and Flip are both so good with large groups." He sits down beside me on the bed.

"Aunt Rosie!" Shannon is tugging on my arm. "I have to talk to you in *private*." She pulls me off the bed. "Aunt Rosie," she says, in a stage whisper. "We can't get undressed if there's a *man* in the room."

"But Shannon," says Juliet, "we're going to put these clothes on *over* our clothes. We're not going to be *naked*."

Shannon considers this, then shrugs. "OK, stay, then," she says. "I guess we don't *need* privacy."

I go back to sit by Warren. "I suppose this kind of thing is going to come up more and more often," he says in a low voice. "Which I suppose makes it a good thing that Madeleine . . . I mean, that it won't be—it won't be *so* long . . ."

"You mean before Madeleine takes her back?" I say, in an equally low, almost equally distressed voice. We both look over at Juliet and Shannon, who are devising some kind of elaborate system of turn-taking and voting. "Oh, Warren," I say. "When?"

"Well, not until June," he says. "Maybe later. That's the latest news, any-way."

"Oh, Warren."

"Actually," he says, "if you don't mind, we probably shouldn't talk about it now."

"Because of—" I gesture toward Juliet.

"Not only that," he says. "I just get completely—I mean, I'm glad I told you, I wanted to tell you. But—"

"It's OK," I say. "I understand. So on what I assume is a happier note, how are things going with my little brother? If you don't mind my asking."

"No, it's nice that you asked," Warren says, looking pleased and embar-rassed and, I guess, triumphant. "Well. I'm here. So that says something."

"It certainly does. I mean, God, Warren, what a price to pay. But yes, it says a lot." I giggle. "I would tell you you're the first boy he's ever brought home, but that makes me sound like his mother, doesn't it?"

"Am I?" says Warren. "He never actually said, but I suppose I assumed—but it's nice to actually know."

"God," I say, "the only way he could take things any further—well, I sup-pose you guys *could* start living together again—officially, I mean. But the only *other* step left for him to take would be to actually marry you."

Warren stares at me.

"Oh, God, Warren," I say, "don't tell me. You aren't actually going to get married? Oh, my God. Congratulations. Really, that's wonderful. Or should I say, I'm sorry I guessed?"

"Well, don't tell Flip I told you," Warren says. "He'll kill me, because he hasn't actually said yes yet, so—well, I don't know. We haven't really talked about it since the subject first came up at the beginning of this month."

"Well, he's totally crazy if he *doesn't* do it," I say. Trying not to think, but I've seen Flip at least three times since then.

"And how are *you?*" Warren is saying uncertainly. "And—Michael."

"God, Michael. *There's* a sore point. I mean, I suppose I can see why he might be hurt, but honestly, Warren, you're here, and you see—I mean, would you honestly think that a twenty-four-year-old African-American man would be *happy* coming here for Christmas? Of course, *he* thinks I can just—"

"Rosie," Warren says, actually interrupting me for the second time today, "is that really why you didn't ask him? To spare his feelings?"

"Well, mine, too, obviously. I mean, not my *feelings,* but come on, Warren. My parents don't even know about Michael."

"You're joking," says Warren, truly shocked.

"No. I mean, if we were getting married or even living together—not that there's a chance in hell of *that*—but till it actually *is* official, why should I put up with them asking me all sorts of questions, and—" I can feel myself getting close to tears, which completely surprises me, but Warren is listening very sympathetically. So I take a deep breath and say, "I really can't stand to think about it, Warren, how much they would hate me being involved with him. I don't want to see them that way. So until I absolutely have to, I would just rather not look."

Warren is looking at me searchingly. "I do know what you mean," he says.

"But?" I say. "I can hear the 'but' in your voice. But what?"

He doesn't say anything.

"Really, Warren, it's OK. Tell me."

"Well," he says slowly. "I'm hardly the expert on any of this. But in my experience, I mean, my *personal* experience. The things I don't want to look at usually have more to do with *me* than that."

"Are you saying *I'm* the racist?"

"I'm not saying that's *true*," says Warren. "It's certainly not how *I* see you. I'm just saying, that's what *you* don't want to look at. Whether it's there or not."

I am absolutely floored. I stare at him, and he just waits, not even trying to make it better. Well, maybe from his point of view, it's not so bad. After all, *I'm* the racist. Even if he doesn't think so.

"I *don't* think so," Warren says quietly. Oh, right, he's psychic, too.

"Well, all I can say is, poor Flip," I say. "Between you and me, he really *doesn't* have a prayer."

Warren sighs. "Maybe that's why he doesn't want to marry me."

Just then, Shannon calls out, "Aunt Rosie!" at the same time that Juliet says, "Uncle Warren!"

"Look at us!" they both say.

We look. Shannon is wearing a low-cut red satin evening gown with a full red net skirt—and a black tuxedo jacket. Juliet is wearing a bright orange tango dress with a slit up the side—and the black tuxedo pants. Both of them have wrapped the matching cummerbunds around their heads, like turbans. Each of them is wearing one high heel and one man's dance shoe.

Warren and I burst into applause. "You girls look *beautiful*," I say.

"And *handsome*," Shannon says.

"OK, you look handsome."

"No, no," Shannon says. "We look beautiful *and* handsome. We're wearing girls' clothes *and* boys' clothes. So we're beautiful *and* handsome."

Looking very full of themselves, Shannon and Juliet make their way slowly down the stairs in their too-long clothes and too-big shoes. Warren and I follow.

"Thank you, Rosie," Warren says. "I'm not at all good at helping her make friends, and she's always in so many new situations, sometimes she needs help. At school, for instance, I don't think she—anyway. Thank you."

"She's a great kid," I say. "What *about* school?" Shannon and Juliet take the last few steps into the living room, and are greeted by a chorus of oohs and ahs, among which I hear Betsy's voice. I have the feeling Warren both wants to say more and is afraid to, given that he *did* enroll Juliet in the private school I recommended (either a place opened up in the middle of the term, or else he just bought her way in). And I *would* like to hear what's going on—I'd like to spend more time with Juliet herself. But now we're in the living room.

"Look at these beautiful girls!" Betsy is saying, as Shannon is saying, "Beautiful *and handsome*, Mom!" Betsy is sitting in what was formerly my chair, looking exhausted. As soon as she sees me come down the stairs, she somehow divines that it *was* my chair and starts to get up.

"Don't be ridiculous. Sit," I tell her. I go to kiss her hello, and as usual, I just have to marvel. Ash-blond hair, big blue eyes, beautifully dressed—and she makes it all look so effortless. She kisses my cheek, warmly, her hand on my shoulder, and for just a second, her arm seems to weigh a million pounds. She must be really exhausted.

"How are you?" I say, perching on the edge of the wing chair. Behind me, Warren pauses. Betsy immediately turns to him and holds out her hand.

"I'm Betsy Zombrowski," she says. "I don't believe we've met."

"Warren Huddleston," he says, shaking her hand, and then Peter launches himself across the room and into Betsy's lap at the same moment that Shannon, having made the circuit of the living room, comes to stand insistently in front of Betsy, saying, "Mom! I have something important to *tell* you!"

"Excuse me, Warren," Betsy says. "I have two very rude, interrupting children here whom I am *very* glad to see, and who I *hope* can remember their manners *very* soon."

Flip glances at me. "Are those Poppy's old tuxedos?"

I nod. Thinking that maybe he too is going to thank me for helping Juliet.

"I'm not sure that was such a great idea," he says. "They're practically the only things of Poppy's we have left. What if they rip them or something?"

"Oh, shut up, Flip," I say. "Till you have a better idea about what to do with the girls."

"Well, it's not like I *need* any kind of an idea at all, do I?" says Flip. "Given that *you're* here, and you *always* know what to do."

"Rosie, leave your brother alone," Ma says automatically.

"Oh, Rosie doesn't have to leave me alone, Ma," Flip is saying. "I never pay any attention to her anyway." And of course, I *know* it's a joke—but the meanness in it isn't a joke.

"Oh, shut up, Flip! Just shut the hell up!" I say, which of course shocks and embarrasses both Betsy and Warren, which in turns mortifies me. Particularly since Shannon is now saying plaintively, "Aunt Rosie said *hell,* Mom."

God, do I need a witness to *this.* Though to be perfectly honest, I'm just as glad Michael wasn't privy to *that* little encounter.

Meanwhile, of course, I have to leave the room, preferably before Warren and Betsy start explaining my bad behavior to their respective children. Thank God Ma missed *that*—she's gone off into the kitchen, to assemble our Christmas Eve dinner. I follow her there.

"Doris Anne Kearney Zombrowski Hanson," I say, leaning against the kitchen door. As always, Ma is making pierogi, kielbasa, cabbage soup, and blintzes—what she calls "the Polish Christmas," even though without Poppy, there really isn't anybody Polish here to eat it. Plus she makes lutefisk and lefse and krumkakke for Dad, and, would you believe it, Irish soda bread, as if there weren't enough starch on the table already. "You're a regular United Nations," I say, trying not to listen to what's going on in the living room.

"Oh, shut up, Rosie," Ma says, opening the oven door. A cloud of steam rolls out of the oven.

"You know, Ma, I wish you wouldn't say that. I hate being told to shut up. I always have."

"Well, darlin', you do run on."

"Mmmm," I say. "What can I do?"

"Nothing, love. Just sit down and keep me company."

"I'd rather help."

"Well, I'd rather you sit. I have a system. You'll just mess it up."

"So, Ma," I say, sitting down. "What do you think of Juliet?"

"She's a beautiful child," Ma says. She opens the lid of a huge, boiling pot. "Of course, all children are beautiful, as far as I'm concerned. It's God's way of keeping us from killing our young." I laugh, and she turns her head to smile at me. Her face is damp with steam, her hair curling in tiny ringlets around her face.

"OK, so she's beautiful," I say. "What else?"

"What else do you want, Rosie? Don't make trouble."

"I just wanted to know what you thought of Juliet," I say. "My God, she's this *child* who lives with Flip. That's fairly significant, don't you think?"

"As long as your brother is happy, it's not for me to interfere," Ma says. "I just wish he'd go to church more often."

"*More* often? He *never* goes to church!"

"He goes on Christmas," Ma points out. "And he told me he goes on Easter."

"Oh. Well, he might do that. Aren't you going to ask how often *I* go to church?"

"I don't have to. I'm sure you go when you can." Gee, maybe I *should* have brought Michael home. The level of transgression I would have to commit to get some attention around here.

"Hand me that potholder, will you, love?" my mother says. "And tell me how you are."

This would be the perfect opening to tell her about Michael, and God help me, I am actually considering it, when Betsy walks through the door. She *must* have been tired, not to have been in here before. "What can I do, Mom?" she says, and so help me, my mother says, "Why don't you start by getting the good serving dishes down?"

"Ma!" I say. "You wouldn't let *me* help!"

My mother gives me an innocent look. "Well, Betsy knows where everything is."

"So do I."

"No, your father painted the kitchen after Thanksgiving, and everything's all moved around. Even *I* don't know where anything is any more."

"Rosie," says Betsy diplomatically, already up on the kitchen stepladder, getting the good serving dishes from the far cabinet—where of course, they've been for over thirty years, ever since *Poppy* last painted the kitchen— "how is your health? The last time we talked, you were still having problems."

"Oh, my God, Rosie, is that business still going on?" Ma says. "Haven't you been to a doctor yet?"

"Yes, Ma, I've been. Last week, actually."

"Why did you wait so long?"

"Do you want to yell at me, or do you want to hear what she said?"

"Excuse me for being interested," Ma says. "I won't say another word. Even if you fall down dead of cancer and female problems combined."

"Thanks, Ma. I appreciate that."

"Well, Rosie, what did she say?" says Betsy, not the least embarrassed by *this* kind of family bickering.

"She said I had fibroids," I say, and both Ma and Betsy cluck sympathetically. Betsy climbs down the stepladder, carefully balancing a stack of serving bowls.

"Now the good silver," Ma says. "And the napkins." Betsy goes over to the linen drawer while I open one of the cabinets. "And don't forget the butter knives," Ma says to me. "You always forget the butter knives."

"It's a conspiracy, Ma. I'm trying to shame you in front of the family."

"So what are you supposed to do about fibroids, then?" Ma says.

"Actually, Betsy, whatever *you* know, I'd love to hear," I say. "Because the gynecologist really knew almost nothing, short of an operation, and I can't believe *that's* my only alternative. And I don't have time to do it anyway, at least not until the Olympia negotiations are over—"

"Of course you have time to do it!" Ma says. She opens another huge pot, boiling on the stove, and holds out a spoonful to me. "Here, taste."

"More lemon," I say. She puts in more vinegar and offers me another taste.

"Of course, you have time," she says while my mouth is full. "Your health is your most important possession."

"*More* vinegar," I say, and Ma puts in some lemon. Then she offers a taste to Betsy. "No, Ma," I say. "The last organizer they had at Olympia just left to have a baby."

"Well, *that's* certainly more important than any job."

"Maybe. Anyway, I can't be the second one who leaves."

"I can't believe your job is all that important," Ma says. "There must be somebody else who can do it, isn't there?"

"Oh, probably just about anyone off the street," I say. "But who would work for *my* salary? So, Betsy, do you know anything? About fibroids, I mean."

"I didn't mean it that way, Rose Ellen Joan Frances Zombrowski, and you know it," says Ma.

"I don't know much," Betsy says quickly. "Most of my patients are past that point."

"You say you can't afford to take care of your health," Ma says. "But I say, you can't afford not to." She starts to ease the pierogi out of the other pot— you'd think her arms would be covered with steam burns by now. "After all, if you're bleeding so bad each month, you're not much good to anyone, are you?" How can she always be so right about everything, in a way that does me no good at all?

"What else, Mom?" says Betsy.

"Nothing, love, nothing at all," Ma says. "Go set the table." Betsy takes an armful of linens and backs out the door. I pause uncertainly.

"Did *you* ever have fibroids?" I ask finally. "Or anything like that?"

Ma hooks the ladle on the edge of the soup pot and wipes her hands on her apron.

"Ma. Tell me." It's extremely weird to see her standing so still. "Ma. If there's any family history—you know. I should tell the doctor."

"I had an operation last year," Ma says finally, her back completely to me. She bends down to get something from the cabinet by the stove. "Because the bleeding wouldn't stop."

"What? You had what—a hysterectomy? You're kidding. I don't believe it."

"Well, believe it or not, I don't care," Ma says, standing up. Now she looks at me. "I had my children," she says. "But you're still young. You do what the doctor tells you."

"How could you not tell me? Especially when you knew *I* was—"

"You don't tell *me* everything, Rose Ellen Zombrowski," says my mother. "I certainly don't have to tell *you* everything."

I sink back down onto one of the kitchen chairs. "I don't fucking believe it."

"And if you're going to use language like that, you can leave this kitchen," Ma says. "There's *no* excuse for that."

"So was it fibroids?" I say. "Or some other reason? You have to tell me, Ma." I honestly don't know if I'm more upset for her or for myself.

"No, just fibroids," Ma says. "They did a biopsy and all. It's not *that* unusual, even at my age. There was no reason to worry you. And I hope you won't say anything to Betsy or your brothers."

Suddenly my whole face is full of crying. Tears in my eyes, my nose about to start running, sobs caught in my throat. I swear, the only noise I make is to breathe in, and Ma says, still facing the stove, "Don't cry, Rosie, or I'll start, too, and there's no reason for it. I'm fine. And you're going to be fine."

I might be taking a step toward her. Or I might only be thinking about it, imagining what it would feel like to put my arms around her as she stands at the stove, to rest my head on her shoulder. But just then Betsy comes in, and the two of us go finish setting the table.

Then when dinner actually starts, I just can't face it. "Excuse me," I say to no one in particular, and retreat up the stairs to the bathroom.

I open the window and a sharp blast of air slices through the overheated room. It's an odd form of luxury, overheating. I remember how cold it always was in this house, pressed up against that necessity every single day of our lives. I lean my elbows on the sink and look into the mirror. If Poppy were here, I'm sure I'd be fighting with him, too. But since he isn't here, I miss him.

You know what I miss most? He's the one who looked like me. Ma is thin, wiry—you can see how Flip and Danny take after her. But Poppy was big. Meaty. He had broad shoulders and a heavy face, and I thought *he* was handsome. Plus he was a union man. He might not be asking me about my per diem, but I bet he'd be asking me about the strike. I always thought he made his union sound like the sky itself—you could find a place for *everything* underneath. You could be talking about why there was no traffic light by the school crossing, or why property taxes were up so high, or why we were sending troops to Viet Nam, and it was still a union issue as far as Poppy was concerned.

I splash cold water on my face and head downstairs. Ma has left me a seat at Dad's end of the table—she herself is down at the other end, where Flip seems to be in the middle of a long, involved story about that movie shoot that he was on last August, the one where for some odd reason, he felt compelled to risk his life. He's telling it like one of those comic action stories, with each new level of danger getting funnier and funnier.

Warren is sitting across from me—as far away from Flip as Ma could put him. He's looking down at his plate, pushing a piece of pierogi around with his fork, and I can see at a glance that this is just the kind of food he hates, and that whatever else Ma doesn't like him for, this disdain for her food is just the icing on the cake. Actually, it doesn't do much for me, either.

Then suddenly I remember that this shoot was the incident he and Flip broke up over. Oh, come on. What kind of weird, elaborate torture is this? Compared to Warren, I'm obviously getting off easy.

"So apparently, the slowest speed we could actually get away with was twenty-five miles an hour," Flip is saying. "Which of course was still fast enough for me to break a leg. Or a neck." Across the table, Warren shudders. Does Flip really not notice, or does he just not care? Suddenly Warren looks up, and our eyes meet. God, I would look away faster than Flip, if I could— he's so unhappy. In that dumb, suffering way, as though of course he deserves it. Is that how *I* look?

"So finally we take off," Flip is saying. "And I'm really not sure whether I can do it or not, but I know I have to try." And suddenly, I hear what Flip wants that he's never going to get. Because if Flip really wanted Warren and me to understand why for him, that leap was cold air, it was earning your own allowance, it was the only thing he *could* do—if Flip *really* wanted Warren to understand all that, or me, he could have that wish. Or at least part of it.

But Ma and Dad won't ever see what he means. That leap won't ever be anything more than an interesting story to them, if not outright proof that Flip should quit acting altogether. So what *I* want to know is, why does telling that story to Ma and Dad mean so much to Flip that he's willing to have Warren look like this? And why does *something*—and at the moment, I can't exactly remember what—mean so much to *me* that I'm willing to—I can't catch hold of this sentence either. Oh, Warren. It's not that he doesn't love you. He just wants them to *see* him.

Dinner goes on, with seconds and thirds and desserts and coffee, all of which Warren has the sense to accept and even ask for. It's not just that you're gay, I want to tell him. It's that you're rich. What *would* it be like if Flip had brought home a guy who was—I don't know, more like us? I smile suddenly, tasting something bittersweet, because I can see how well Michael would fit in here if he *weren't* Black. I can just imagine how he would adore my mother and respect my father. How happily he would sit down and stuff as much food into himself as he could, both because he truly thought it was delicious and because he was brought up right and he understands about accepting food. How honored he would be when my mother finally started to tease him, to scold him and insult him, because he would understand that now he actually was part of the family. Whereas Warren—my God. Even if by some miracle my mother did decide to insult him, you can just see how mortified he'd be. He doesn't understand that my mother considers politeness—giving *or* receiving it—the worst insult of all.

After dinner, Ma organizes the ride to church. Even she wouldn't try to separate Juliet and Shannon at this point, so the girls are riding with Danny and Betsy. You'd think that Flip and Warren could at least drive to church in their rented car and have ten minutes to themselves. But no, Ma arranges for me to ride with them, and for us to pick up Auntie Mavis and Uncle Patrick on the way. "Why can't you and Dad pick them up?" I say.

"Because we're giving a ride to Orrin and RoseAnne." Danny's godparents, and my parents' best friends.

"Well. Why can't I ride with you, and then Danny and Betsy could—"

"Rosie," says Flip, and I can't tell *what* he's feeling. "It's all right. I don't mind picking them up."

Flip is quiet on the drive over, too. I'm sitting in the back, of course—at least Warren gets to sit next to Flip in the *car*—and I slide over as Auntie Mavis and Uncle Patrick come gingerly out of their house, clutching each other so as not to slip on the icy walk. Flip jumps out to open the back door for them. But Uncle Patrick says, "Would it be all right if your Auntie Mavis sat in the front seat? She tends to get carsick."

"Oh, Patty, I do not," says Auntie Mavis. She's Ma's younger sister, and she looks like a softer, more timid, and somehow less glamorous version of Ma. "I haven't been carsick for two years."

Warren is already climbing out of the front seat and helping Mavis in.

She's charmed, but Patrick glares at him as though he should have done it before.

"Thank you, darlin'," Mavis says. "Flip, aren't you going to introduce us to your friend?"

"Sorry," says Flip. "Uncle Patrick, Auntie Mavis, this is Warren Huddleston." Warren shakes hands with first Patrick, then Mavis, still settling herself into the front seat.

"We'd best get in the car," Patrick is saying, looking at Warren with distaste. "We're letting all the heat out."

I lean forward to kiss Auntie Mavis on the cheek. "Rosie, darlin'," she says. "Are you having a good time out there in the city, or are you planning to come home soon?"

"No, I'm pretty much there for the duration."

"And do you have any good news for us yet?"

"Well, we might be on strike at Olympia in April."

"That's not what I meant, and you know it," says Mavis.

"Make the bastards pay," says Patrick, fastening his seatbelt as Flip eases the car onto the icy street. "You know, Rosie, I kept my union card as long as I could, even after I became a boss. I paid my dues as long as they'd let me. Nobody understands how the working man needs a union."

"Well, I organize mainly working women," I say. "But I suppose the principle is the same."

"Don't tease me, young lady," says Patrick. "You know very well what I meant. People make all this fuss about language, and what's the result? Squabble, squabble, squabble, and only 11 percent of the workforce organized."

"Don't look at me," I say. "I personally helped raise that number up from 10.999 percent."

Patrick laughs. "I bet the bosses run when they see you coming, Rosie," he says. "I know I would."

"And what about you, Flip?" says Auntie Mavis. "Your ma says you're in a movie?"

"A couple of movies, actually," Flip says. "But only one that's likely to play out here. It opens in March, I think. *Tower of Fear*."

"We don't get to the movies much any more," says Auntie Mavis. "I don't like Patrick driving at night, and if you go during the day, people *talk!* You can't hardly hear the movie. Are you doing anything on television?"

"Not at the moment," Flip says. "I've come close a few times, this past month—"

"Really?" I say. "You never told me."

"Well, it was mainly under-fives," Flip says. "I'm not sure how much they count. And a callback for a featured part, which I didn't get."

"Flip is being way too modest," I say. "Callbacks are when they like you so much, they call you back to have you audition again."

"Right," says Flip. "And under-fives are when you have less than five lines."

"Well, at least it's a foot in the door," says Uncle Patrick.

Auntie Mavis turns her head back to us. "And what do *you* do, Warren?"

Without missing a beat, Warren says, "I counsel people." Oh, good save, Warren. Though it seems to me that Flip stiffens slightly. Well, come on, Flip. Do you want him to come out about that, too?

Of course, I should talk. If Mavis asks me whether I'm seeing anybody special, I have the choice of saying no, mentioning Michael's name ("Is he Irish?" they'd say hopefully), or making this whole big point of telling them his race, as though I, too, thought that were the most important thing about him.

Luckily, at this point, we arrive at church. Danny and Betsy are already here, standing with the children in the entryway, and Juliet comes running over to Warren as though she hasn't seen him in months. Then she runs right back to Shannon, and the two of them start whispering.

"Oh, is that your little girl?" says Mavis. "Doris told us about her. She's beautiful."

"My niece, actually," says Warren. "But thank you." He smiles for the first time. "I think she's beautiful, too," he says. "But I don't get too many chances to say so when she can't hear me."

"Oh, that's very wise," says Mavis. "You don't want them growing up vain of their looks."

Patrick looks simply too shocked to respond. "I had lots of colored men in my shop," he says finally. "Both when I was working and when I owned. But I always thought they didn't like mixing either. We're proud of being Irish. They're proud of being colored. You can't be proud if you mix."

"But Ma married Poppy, and Dad," I say. "First Polish, then Norwegian. She mixed."

"That was before I came into the family," Patrick says. "I had nothing to say about that."

"Well, it's over and done with now, Patrick," says Mavis. "It's not the child's fault, anyway. It's just lucky she turned out so well."

Warren clearly wants to say something, but he doesn't seem to be able to get the words out. Luckily, at that point, Ma and Dad and Orrin and RoseAnne walk in, and Uncle Patrick and Auntie Mavis go over to say hello.

There is a moment when I see the six of them looking at Flip and Warren and me, and I really wonder what they see. I can imagine RoseAnne comforting Ma in the car, saying, "Well, Doris, at least you've got your youngest." But I can also imagine her scolding, saying, "Oh, Doris, you have three beautiful children who come home to see you every Christmas. As long as they're happy and healthy . . ." I suppose the only thing I can't imagine is them having any idea of what our lives are actually like.

I used to think that that was what family was supposed to be. Real family, like Uncle Patrick and Auntie Mavis, Ma and Dad. Honorary family, like Orrin and RoseAnne. People whose love was based on knowing who you were. But that's not them, that's Marcy. And, OK, possibly, Michael. Neither of whom is here. So who are these people? And what would you call Marcy and Michael?

I watch Flip go over to greet Orrin and RoseAnne, still with that quiet, preoccupied look he's had since dinner, though they light up with pleasure to see him. I notice he doesn't bring Warren, or go fetch Juliet. "Go ahead," Warren whispers in my ear. "I'll be all right."

I shake my head. "Let's go sit down. I can say hello to them after the service."

I never go to church any more, except when I'm home for Christmas. Which, when you think what a big part of my life it was in high school . . . Until I discovered politics, I guess. Whenever Flip feels like being nasty, he'll tell me that my union activity is just a substitute for the Church. When he's being *really* nasty, he'll say that no matter how many boyfriends are in the picture, I still live like a nun.

I think he's right, though I'd never in a million years admit it to him. Devotion, discipline, community—what's wrong with that? Frankly, my personal life doesn't interest me all that much. What I want is a whole new world. I can have a personal life inside *that*.

I watch Flip dip his knee and genuflect as he comes down the aisle. How can he *do* that? I may not be religious, but I still believe in sacrilege.

The rest of my family has filed in around me—Ma, Flip, and Dad in the pew ahead of us, and in our pew, me, Warren, and Juliet, with Shannon on her other side. Flip turns around to look at Warren. "You know," he starts to say, but Ma interrupts to ask him what he thinks of the flowers they have this year. Then, the bell starts to ring.

"Five thousand years after the Creation," intones a voice from the balcony, and I feel the familiar thrill. I love this funneling of time, all of history being poured into a single miraculous moment. And then the smell of incense, tiny pungent clouds inside the enormous volume of the cathedral, and the sound of singing, and the choir marching in, shining in their white and gold robes.

We sing "*Adeste Fideles*," and I can hear Flip's voice soaring beyond everyone else's. I don't understand why he thinks he can't sing.

Warren beside me is singing, too, in a low, buzzing voice. Something about it makes him so vulnerable, I can't even bear to look at him.

O Lamb of God, chants the reader, *You take away the sins of the world.* When I was eight, and nine, and maybe even ten, I used to think Poppy was the Lamb of God. Well, obviously, I didn't think he actually *was* that—I understood the theological point that the Lamb was Jesus. *You are seated at the right hand of the Father; receive our prayer.* I suppose I liked picturing Poppy there at the dinner table, listening to me.

The Liturgy of the Word begins, with its reading of the Old Testament. "Great," Marcy always used to say. "We get the book that *your* book refutes." That was freshman and sophomore years in college, when I still *was* religious. Whereas Marcy was totally secular and always had been. I used to join her family for Passover, which they celebrated in what her father called a "completely historical sense." Later, when I went to more political seders, we'd sing "The Internationale" and "Solidarity Forever" and nothing specifically Jewish at all. Which also struck me as weird, but again, it's not for me to judge.

I help Warren find the place in the program for the responsive reading of the psalm. There's just something about hearing a thousand voices, all saying the same thing. *In our hands is placed a power greater than their hoarded gold; Greater than the might of armies magnified a thousandfold . . .* No, that's *my* hymn, isn't it? "Solidarity Forever," the union anthem. What we're actually supposed to say is, *They who do justice will live in the presence of God,* which still isn't bad, though of course, Ma is shaking her head. "This new priest," she stage-whispers to Flip, "you never know *what* he's going to come out with." I can't help smiling. I guess I learned my arguing from *somewhere.*

Flip asked me once whether, if I was going to criticize the church, I didn't have to admit that *my* movements were also guilty of terrible sins. I suppose they are. I know one officer in our union who actually raped another officer when they were both away at a convention—what can you say about that? And out of loyalty to the union, she didn't even report it. What can you say about *that?* I'm not even sure she was wrong to keep it quiet—we were right in the middle of some organizing drive, and it probably *would* have hurt us among the members. I was outraged, of course. But I didn't lose faith in the whole—just in one or two of its parts.

The priest clears his throat for the Homily, and static bounces at us over the sound system. (I didn't mind it when we were little, but it seems so intrusive now.) He's a fairly young man, shockingly blond, with narrow shoulders that pull together as he leans forward, gripping the lectern. My mind wanders through most of the sermon—but my attention is caught when he says, "And remember the question asked by Our Lord: 'What shall it profit a man if he gain the whole world but lose his soul?'" Well, *that's* an odd thing to say on Christmas morning.

Apparently, Ma thinks so, too, because she leans over to Flip again and says, "They weren't going to *let* Father Casper take the service, but Father James had a sore throat." Dad tries to shush her, but Ma whispers back loudly, "I'm only telling Flip what happened."

"And what we have to understand from this," the priest is saying, "is where Our Lord is telling us to *make* our home. With the families we were born into? No, because Christ says, 'I come bringing not peace but a sword.' He says, 'I come to divide brothers and sisters from each other, to divide children from their parents.'" If I were sitting next to Flip at this point, I would elbow him and feel him smile.

"Neither is Christ telling us to make our homes in this world," says the priest. "Of course, we have to *care* for this world, for its people. 'As you have done unto the least of these, so have you done unto Me.' But is this, finally, where we are to make our home?"

Yes, oh yes, I want to shout. This earth is what I want. This earth and all its people. *Would* I be willing to lose the whole world so long as I saved my soul? No, no. It's the other way around. The world is where my soul *is.*

I see Flip in his place between Ma and Dad, filing out to take communion, and again I wonder, how can he? Marcy once said she would go to services when she had children, though she never goes now. When I asked her why, she said, "I get to be the kind of Jew I am because someone else is holding the fort. If there weren't religious Jews, pretty soon there wouldn't *be* secular Jews." God knows, that certainly applies to Catholics, too. But I don't care. I'll come on Christmas as long as the Church is here, but I won't lift a finger to keep it alive, because I think something else *should* take its place. *We can bring to birth a new world from the ashes of the old.* My hymn again. Even here, I feel it, that holy thing that happens when a room is full of people. "Joy to the world, the Lord has come," we sing. As if anything was possible now.

WARREN: As we're leaving the church after Midnight Mass, Flip's mother turns her head and says over her shoulder, "Well, Flip, didn't you think that was the nicest service ever?" She's walking ahead of us, arm in arm with her husband. Flip and I, of course, are *not* walking arm in arm, and somehow Flip floats up to walk next to her. Beside me, Rosie rolls her eyes. "Typical," she mutters. I have to admit, it's—what's the word? Instructive, to see the two of them with their parents. That alone was probably worth the trip, even if the price is that I—well, that doesn't matter.

"Uncle Warren," Juliet says, "Dan and Betsy want to talk to you." Is it foolish of me to wish she could call them Uncle Dan and Aunt Betsy? I fall back to walk with them.

"Since Shannon and Juliet are getting on so well," Betsy begins, and Juliet jumps right in.

"Can I stay at Shannon's tomorrow night too?" She's so excited, I don't have the heart to correct her for interrupting Betsy.

"Is that how long you were invited for?" I say instead.

"Oh, the more, the merrier," Betsy says, and Dan nods. "I mean, staying in a motel room with a child," Betsy says. "There's no privacy."

Two steps ahead of us, Rosie sizzles so hard I can imagine her melting the snow. Now, Rosie. They didn't exactly *say* that Flip and I are these depraved perverts who shouldn't be left alone with a minor. They might only have meant that, like any couple, we'd rather have our own room.

I have to admit, I don't really believe this myself. But it would be so much nicer to be able to believe it, that I'm not sure if the reason I don't is because it actually isn't true, or if Rosie is simply so committed to thinking the worst about everyone in her family that she's starting to affect me, too.

Meanwhile, Flip is telling his parents that he's going to drive me back to the motel, giving them some long, convoluted explanation of why I can't simply drive myself. An explanation that seems all the more ludicrous when you recall that Flip is thirty-two and I'm forty-five—by anybody's estimate, grown men. As opposed to naughty teenagers, which is how all this open fiction makes me feel.

On the other hand, if we actually were teenagers, we would have to come up with a cover story that someone might actually believe. In a way, this is worse.

Finally, Flip and I are settled in the car, alone together for the first time in hours. But he still doesn't say anything. The motel room is freezing, for some reason, though it's actually a nice contrast to all the overheated rooms we've been in all day. We get undressed and get ready for bed, with Flip saying barely two words to me. But the minute we get into bed, he practically throws himself on me and we start making love.

He is incredibly tender and attentive. When he's lying on top of me, when he's inside me, I feel—surrounded by him. By his love. Actually, I feel—and I don't think I've ever felt this with him before. Or with anybody, so maybe it's something different in me. I feel protected. As though I could just abandon myself to him—as though I *am* doing that—and it's all right.

Afterwards, his whole body still covering mine, he slides forward a little, so he can rest his cheek against mine, so he can stroke my hair. And then when he slides off me and prepares to go to sleep, cuddled up against me with my arm over him, I am so lonely, I can't stand it.

"Flip?"

"What?" he says, almost asleep.

"Don't go to sleep. Stay up and talk to me." This startles both of us, since it's obviously not the kind of thing I ever say.

"All right," he says, and I hear how tired he is. "You say something, OK? While I wake up."

"What should I call your mother?"

He laughs. "Well, *that* certainly got my attention. What do you mean, what should you call her?"

"You know. Doris or Mrs. Hanson or what?" I have to say, I feel incredibly stupid calling her Mrs. Hanson. As though I really were a teenager.

"I don't know. What does Betsy call her?"

I can't believe he's asking me that. "Betsy calls her 'Mom.' " I can't help adding, "And *her* children call your mother 'Nana.' "

Flip sighs. "Didn't *she* tell you what to call her?"

"Flip. She barely said anything to me." I can't stop myself from adding, "I don't think she likes me, if you want to know the truth."

Flip laughs again. "Well, Warren. Of *course* she doesn't like you. You're my boyfriend—what do you *think* she's going to feel about you?"

"My mother liked you," I say wistfully, although of course I regret that, too, the minute the words are out of my mouth.

"Well, *I* can't help it if your mother has such a thing for gay men," Flip says. Then he tries to soften this by taking hold of my hand. "If it's any comfort, my mother wouldn't like you any better—really, not *any* better—if you were my girlfriend. That's just—you know. That's just how she is."

"She likes Betsy."

"That's different."

"Why?"

"Because she just has this whole different relationship with Dan than with either Rosie or me. Besides, for years and years, she *didn't* like Betsy. Hard as that is to believe, considering that Betsy is just about the perfect daughter-in-law of the universe. But she really didn't like Betsy until Shannon, no, Peter was born." He thinks about this for a moment. "Maybe not even until Lily, really. Then she kind of adopted Lily, so she more or less had to adopt Betsy, too."

"Well, if that's the case, then why was it so important to—why were you so eager to bring me back here?"

Flip shrugs. "They're my family," he says. "That's what you do."

"What?"

"I don't know," says Flip. "You visit them and you put up with them."

"But we're *not* visiting them. I mean, we're not staying in their house."

"God, would you *rather* be staying there?" Flip says. "In the guest room?" He shudders. "You know," he says, "if Rosie brought someone home—well, that's why she didn't bring Michael home. One of the *many* reasons. Although she *could* have had him stay in a motel. She says she couldn't get away with that. But I think she's exaggerating." He considers this. "Maybe not."

"You mean, because they can believe we're just friends, even though they obviously know we aren't, it's all right for me to stay in a motel, but if Rosie is bringing home an official boyfriend, he has to stay in the house? But not in the same room?"

"You got it."

"What if they were married?"

"Rosie and Michael? I don't know, I suppose then they would stay *somewhere* together. Probably in the house, but that might be negotiable in Michael's case. They might be so glad he *wasn't* staying under their roof that they would decide not to feel insulted."

"Well, what if we get married? Or whatever we decide to call it?"

"Why are we talking about this?" Flip says in exasperation. He turns over, and at first I think it's to get further away from me—which would be a feat, in this tiny, freezing bed—but no, he's pulling even closer, nuzzling my neck, stroking my hair, and I sigh and sink against him. "Why are we talking about this?" he says again, more softly. "Aren't you having a good time?"

"I didn't say that."

"Mmmm," Flip says skeptically. "You and Rosie certainly seemed to be finding a lot to talk about, anyway."

"I was grateful she *felt* like spending so much of her time with me," I say. "Let alone the way she organized that whole activity for Juliet and Shannon."

"Oh, that's just so typical of Rosie," Flip says with disgust. "It's always *her* party. You think she's difficult now—well, obviously you don't right *now,* Warren, you're so in love with her at the moment, but if you just think back to more frustrating days—"

"I remember," I say.

"Well, imagine that *plus* being three years younger than her. I mean, it was actually true, she really could do—not *anything,* of course. But it always *seemed* like anything. And then she always had to rub it in. I remember one time—this is so stupid, I can't believe I'm telling you this."

I brush a stray hair off his face. "Yes, but you are telling me, so please don't leave me in suspense."

"Well," says Flip, "it's not *that* interesting a story. Not up to my usual level. But OK, I remember she was fixing up her room. This is so stupid. But at the time, that seemed like the most amazing thing in the world to me. I mean, she had this plan, she had figured out all these things she wanted to do, she was even painting some of her own furniture, which just seemed—I mean, I thought furniture had to be the way it was. It never occurred to me you could *paint* it."

"How old were you?" I say.

"I don't know. Nine? Ten? And she was so—I don't know. Like *of course* she could do this and I couldn't. I remember, she even said to me, 'Flip, you don't know anything about anything, so why don't you just go away.' Which I realize is a completely and totally ridiculous thing to remember after all these years, and I can't believe that I *do* remember it, and I certainly can't believe that I'm telling *you* about it."

"I'm your boyfriend," I say. "You're supposed to tell me these things."

Suddenly Flip just curls into me, his head against my chest, his whole body curled up against me, so that I have to curve myself around him. "I love you, Warren," he says in a very small voice. Speaking right into my chest. "I love you the best."

"Oh," I say, caught completely by surprise. "Well." But I manage to say, "I love you the best, too."

"Good," he says, and we both sigh. And then he turns over, still curled tightly against me, and goes to sleep. You know, sometimes he can be right here and I still miss him.

Amazingly, given how late we went to bed, Flip wakes up early, well before the alarm, even though at home, even with the alarm, it's usually an enormous production to get him to wake up at all. But this time he wakes me up, quiet and insistent in the dark-blue light, and we make that silent, personal love again. Only this time Flip crawls under me, and I try, I really do, to give him that same sense I got from him, of being surrounded, protected by my love. And afterwards, he curls up against me as he did last night and says in that same small voice, "Merry Christmas, Warren."

"I love you best," I think again, though I don't dare say it. Thinking of Madeleine and Loulou, Juliet and Vernice. Thinking, well, I *have* to love him best. He's the only one who isn't going to leave.

Later, when we're driving over to Flip's house, Flip says, "You know, we could go somewhere tonight. Rosie and I usually do. Nowhere very glamorous, because what's open on Christmas night, but there's a House of Pies that's open either all night or till 1 a.m., it changes from year to year. Everyone is usually winding down about nine or ten o'clock, and we go then." The morning is very cold and white—all the snow on the street makes everything seem incredibly quiet. "We don't absolutely have to take Rosie," Flip is saying. "But you're the one who seems to want to spend every minute with her anyway."

"Only for lack of a better alternative," I say, not because this is strictly true, but because it seems like the easiest way to take care of several problems at once.

"Mmmm," says Flip. He brakes for a red light and the rented car skids a little on the ice. It's still so early—early enough to make it plausible that no one saw Flip around the house this morning, before he woke up and "picked me up." Which probably *is* why he woke up so early this morning. As opposed to—

It doesn't matter. Going out with Flip and Rosie tonight sounds incredibly nice. As though I get to share in *that* part of their family, at least. I am just about to say some version of that to Flip, when he says, "You don't exactly lack for other alternatives, Warren. There are lots of people there you could talk to."

I consider several different replies, but there's something so obviously wrong with each of them that it's more or less impossible to say anything at all. Flip glances over at me and God knows what he sees, because suddenly, he's pulling over to the curb and stopping the car. And right there on the street—although we're still several blocks from his family's house and there's nobody out at this hour anyway. But still, right there on the street he slides across the seat and puts his arms around me.

"Is it really so bad?" Flip says, with me still, well, I suppose clinging to him would be the expression. He sounds so disappointed.

"Oh, Flip, no. Really, it's not bad at all. It's just that Rosie is the only one I know."

"But you don't like my family," Flip says in a forlorn, wistful tone of voice that's meant to sound like a joke. "I liked *your* family."

"Well, my mother has a thing for gay men, remember. She's easier to like."

At least that catches him off guard enough to make him laugh. He slides back into the driver's seat and we ride in silence for a few blocks.

"Going out tonight sounds very nice," I say. "Actually, what I was thinking was that it was nice of you and Rosie to include *me*."

Flip gives me another sidelong glance as he pulls into his driveway behind his father's car. "Yeah, right," he says.

"I'm only trying to say . . ." My voice trails off.

"Oh, I know what you're trying to say," Flip says. "It's just my luck that she's the one member of my family you like. So you get to be in the middle of me and her, and you get to like her, too."

"Yes," I say, surprised. "That's it exactly."

"Nobody ever gives me any credit for knowing *anything*." Flip says, opening his car door, which means I have to open mine and get out too. "If I may say so." Then he looks at me across the top of the car. "Except you, Warren. You also give me too *much* credit for knowing things. Not that I'm not flattered, but. It can be wearing. Once in a while, you should just *tell* me."

"Sorry," I say. "I'll try to get it right."

"Mmmm," says Flip. "See that you do."

ROSIE: As I walk from the church to the parking lot after Midnight Mass has ended, the day suddenly catches up with me. Suddenly I am so exhausted, I can barely make it to the car. Through my tired fog, I hear Betsy inviting Juliet to spend the next two nights with them. Isn't that just like Betsy? She's totally exhausted, anyone can see that, but she just keeps on giving, giving, giving all the time. At least *somebody* in our family is being nice to Warren.

Finally, I'm sitting drowsily in Ma and Dad's car, letting them drive me home. "Nice service," Dad comments.

"Well, you'll like anything," Ma says. "Who can go by *you?*"

When I was little, this would be the occasion for an enormous fight, one that might go on for hours and hours. Hearing this in the back seat would be particularly terrifying, given that there was no place to escape to. Now, however, Dad just laughs. "You go give the priest hell, Dorie," he says. "See where that gets you." Ma laughs too, and I sink back down into my seat. Why should I care if they fight? But I couldn't help jolting awake, that perpetual alertness that I remember from all the years I lived at home.

"What did you think, Rosie?" Ma says now. "How did this year compare?"

"I don't know, Ma," I say. "I liked the carols, of course. And the psalm."

"Well, you would," says Ma. "That 'justice' thing. Who can go by you?"

"OK, so now you've eliminated both me and Dad," I say. "What did Flip think? Given that his opinion is the one that *really* counts."

"Leave your brother alone," Ma says automatically.

"Ma. He isn't even here."

"Don't make trouble for your mother," Dad says.

Then Ma says, as Dad pulls into our driveway, "Three days isn't really enough, Rosie. It isn't even three full days. I wish you were staying longer."

I sigh. Maybe I *would* rather have her scolding me. "I've got to get back, though," I say as we all climb out of the car. "If we really do set a strike deadline for April 12th—"

"Oh, I can't follow all your scheduling," Ma says. "Just tell me when you actually know."

"Fine," I say, annoyed again. "I'd hate to burden you with *too* many details about my life."

I am so tired, I don't feel anything as I climb the stairs to my room. But when I'm finally in bed, of course, I'm totally restless. The heat is still puffing up in huge invisible clouds through the baseboard heater. I wouldn't dare fiddle with the thermostat, so I get up and open my window a crack. A knife blade of cold air slides in. And then something is pushing me out of my room, down the stairs, and into the guest room—as the room farthest from my parents' bedroom, it's the most private, and thank God, it's equipped with a phone. I wish with all my heart that I could call Marcy. But she's at Joe's parents' house. I'll just have to wait for our phone date tomorrow.

So there I am, dialing Michael's number in the dark. If he could have afforded it, he might have gone to spend Christmas with *his* family, who just moved back to Jamaica last spring. I might even have gone there with him.

The phone rings and rings and rings. I don't even want to think that he might not be there. But finally, on the twelfth ring (which, I swear, *would* have been the last), I hear his sleepy voice say, "Hello?"

"Hi, Michael. It's me."

"Rosie!" he says slowly, drowsily, drawing out the word. "Hey."

"I'm sorry I woke you."

"It's OK."

"It's just that this was literally the first time I had to call since I got in— there's been something going on every single minute, I swear, and you wouldn't *believe* the—"

Michael laughs. "If I wasn't awake before, I would be now, right?"

"I don't know," I say. It's such an incredible relief to hear his voice. "You still sound pretty much asleep." Not just his voice. His pleasure. His pleasure in me.

I can hear him moving around in bed, pulling the pillows up behind him, turning on the bedside light. He has a very student-y apartment—of course, I should talk, because so do I, and as I guess we've already established, I'm eleven years older than he is. ("If he was twenty-two I'd be worried," Marcy said when he was first asking me out, "but you know, Rosie, twenty-four. That's a whole other world." And I clung to that joke like it was gospel.) "Hey, keep talking," Michael says. "I'll wake up pretty soon."

Now I laugh, somewhat bitterly, I admit. "You know," I say, tucking my bare feet under me, "that's the first time today someone has actually *asked* me to talk. Most of the time around here, they're telling me to shut up."

"I don't believe you," he says, in that drawn-out, teasing way that both delights me and drives me crazy. "Why would anyone tell you to shut up?"

"Yeah, right," I say. "I can't imagine." I turn on my lamp, too.

"See, Rosarita?" he whispers. "You should have brought me. I could have protected you."

"Well, that's what I was thinking, actually."

There is a big space of silence on both sides of the phone. Then he says—sounding *much* more awake—"Yeah, right? I'm sorry I'm not there, then."

I sigh. "I'm sorry you're not here, too, Michael. Which is why I called, obviously, so—I mean, sorry both in the sense of, I miss you. And in the sense of, I'm sorry it was such an awful discussion about your coming, really, I am. Really. I am."

"OK," he says. "I hear you."

"But I have to say, Michael, and I'm sorry about this, too, but I guess I also have to say that—" Suddenly, I don't just run out of words, I run out of—I don't know. Spirit. In a minute, I'll start crying.

I can hear Michael listening to me very hard as he sits up in bed. "What are you trying to tell me, Rosie?"

"Are you mad?"

"I'm just trying to figure out what you're saying."

"Because I wouldn't blame you if you *were* mad. But . . ."

He laughs softly. I have to say, at the moment, it's an extremely comforting sound. "I don't know what they did to you out there," he says. "You don't usually have this much trouble finishing a sentence. Two or three sentences, even."

I bite my lip. "Hey, Michael? You tell me, OK? How was *your* Christmas?"

"Oh, I didn't do much. I had to work all evening anyway." Michael works at an all-night drugstore where he used to be a clerk, but they like him so much, they've made him some kind of assistant manager while he finishes getting his degree at City College, which, I am ashamed to say, is where I met him. One of his political science professors—this is too embarrassing—was an old friend who had arranged for me to teach part of a course on labor unions, which Michael, planning to be a labor lawyer, faithfully attended. As part of the course, I told the students about various union events—educational and cultural evenings, rallies—where I might be speaking or, more often, just attending. By the time the class was over—though I swear this wasn't my intention—Michael had been informed of plenty of places to pursue me.

OK, I liked him, of course I liked him. But isn't it obvious what the problems were? I wasn't his teacher when we started going out—I didn't *have* that power. But I *had* had it.

"Then tonight," Michael continues, "I thought about going to a movie, but you know. Christmas Eve—not quite the right time for that. I just came home."

"What are you doing tomorrow?" I say as his voice trails off. Let's see if I can feel a little *more* guilty before this call is over.

"Oh, Doug is coming over." Doug is a friend of his, a hospital orderly, divorced, already with three children. At least I'm not the *only* person in Michael's life who's over twenty-five. "We're going to walk through Central Park."

"What?"

"Didn't I tell you about this?" Michael says. "I've always wanted to do it. I've lived in New York all my life, and I'm like, I just don't know Central Park. Doug neither. So we got a guidebook—well, I got a guidebook, because you know Doug."

"You'll be lucky if he finds your house tomorrow morning."

"Yeah, right?" says Michael. "Doug. So I'm like, OK, I'll get the guidebook, you bring the coffee and the sweet rolls and the egg sandwiches, and we'll start uptown—we'll start in that corner up near Harlem, you know—"

"Harlem Meer," I say.

"Is that what it's called?" Michael says. "We're going to take a map, and we'll see like every single part of the park. Wait, I've got the map." I hear him fooling with the pile of books that is always on his bedside table—if you can call it a table. It's actually two plastic crates stacked on top of each other, covered with a piece of cloth.

"Here it is," says Michael. "Yeah, right, we're starting at the Harlem Meer. What does that mean, do you know?"

"Something Dutch, obviously. Meadow? I don't know."

"Listen to these names," Michael says. "The Harlem Meer, the Conservatory Garden, the Bridle Path, Great Lawn, Cleopatra's Needle . . ." He pronounces each name with relish. "Cleopatra's Needle—I don't even know what that *is*."

"It's an obelisk—" I start to say, and Michael interrupts me.

"No, don't tell me. I want to be surprised. I want it to be like this discovery. I want to have the map in my hand, and I'll come over the hill, or around the corner, and I'll like discover it. And then it won't be this thing that everybody knows about but me. It will be this special thing that I discovered. Well, that Doug and I discovered. We were going to do it at sunrise, but Doug had the late shift. So I'll go to church in the morning and we'll go in the afternoon. If we time it right, the sun will be setting by the time we get to the south end of the park. Sunset on the snow—that should be pretty."

"Oh, Michael."

"What?"

"No, it just sounds so— It sounds really nice."

"Well, if you were here, you could come, Rosarita. Doug wouldn't mind."

"Ha, ha." We're both quiet for a minute.

"You don't have to say if you don't want, Rosie," he says finally. "But you still haven't said . . ."

"I want to," I say. "It's just hard for me to talk about."

"Why?" he says. "They're your family."

"You always say that like it means something, Michael. All it means is that they know all the things that make me crazy. You know, when you said they'd come around as soon as they saw how happy you made me—"

"I didn't say *as soon*," Michael says. His anger is very quiet, but it's sudden. "I didn't say *as soon*, Rosie. You make me sound so stupid. I said *sooner or later*. I said, if we were really happy together, then, like, *sooner or later*, like, *someday*, like, *eventually*, then, maybe—I said *maybe*—maybe they'd come around. At least they would have an incentive."

"I don't think you're stupid, Michael, I think you're very smart, actually."

"You don't have to like *grade* me, Rosie. I'm just saying, if you're going to quote my argument, get it straight."

I gather my last remnants of energy, because to hang up now would be so much worse than never having called at all. "I'm sorry if I misrepresented you, Michael," I say. "Add it to the list, OK? It doesn't really matter, though, because either way, it isn't true. Seeing me happy *isn't* an incentive for them."

"I just think if you gave them a chance."

"Michael, look. Flip is here with Warren, his boyfriend, right?"

"I know who Warren is," Michael says. "I haven't, like, *met* any of these people, but I know who they are."

"It's not my fault that you haven't met them," I say. "Actually, no, that's my fault, too, OK? I hate introducing my boyfriends to Flip—he's always so critical in this way that's totally— Look, do you want to hear about why I don't want you to meet Flip and Warren, or do you want to hear the point I was trying to make?"

Michael surprises me by laughing.

"So now you want me to choose?" he says. "Well, let me think a minute, because that's like a tough choice, right? Why you don't want me to meet your brother—or the point you want to make. Hmmm. What's behind door number one again?"

"Ha, ha," I say again. Suddenly my voice drops. "I miss you, you know that, Michael? Right now, I really miss you a lot."

"I miss you, too, Rosarita. I'm glad you called. Even if it is the middle of the night."

"Oh, God, it's almost four. You must be dead."

"I'm OK. Talking to you is very . . . stimulating. I'm good for a while longer."

"If I was there, I'd have worn you out by now."

"You don't think I can keep up with you?" Michael says. "That's not how I remember it."

"No, me neither, actually," I say. "I wouldn't say stamina was necessarily your *best* quality. But it's certainly right up there near the top of the list."

"Not just stamina," he says in that slippery voice. "Skill."

"Mmmm." If he had come home with me, he'd be here, in this guest room, right this minute. But probably I wouldn't be. I don't know. Maybe it would be worth the explosion from Dad.

Maybe Michael hears what I'm thinking. Or maybe his thoughts are running along the same lines. Because he says, "I didn't even say they'd get over it in one visit, Rosie. I just said, you know. Eventually."

"You might be right," I say. "It's a high price to pay, though, Michael. You should see how they treat Warren. And Flip just ignores it, that's how *he* handles it."

"Well, you wouldn't do that. Would you?"

"God, how can you even ask?"

"I knew you wouldn't," he says. "I just wanted to hear you say it."

Is he still teasing me, or did he really need to hear that? But this is the whole problem, isn't it? I mean, if I knew I was going to be with him for even five years, OK, maybe it would be worth starting the whole weird process with my family. But look at us. Who could possibly believe we'll still be together in six months?

"It's not just Warren," I say suddenly. "It's also Juliet. They ignore her, too.

Well, not Danny and Betsy, granted. But my parents. It's very ugly, Michael."

"I know," he says after a long silence. And now his voice sounds different.

"What?" I say.

"Families are funny about children."

It takes me a minute to figure out what he means. "You mean yours would be, too. You mean, if you brought home a child who was—" I don't even know what words to use. Any name I can think of seems to leave something out.

Anyway, Michael obviously knows what I mean, because he says stubbornly, "I just think you have to give people a chance."

"You know what's really weird, Michael? I don't even *believe* in any of this. I mean, my racist family isn't supposed to make *me* a racist. And your family—" But I can't finish that thought, because I don't feel the same way about them not wanting Michael to bring home a white woman. I've wondered, too, what it means that Michael chose me—I mean, he's young and beautiful, and he's eventually going to law school, which makes him a terrific catch for *someone*. Certainly any African-American woman who sees me with Michael is just as apt to glare: Oh, great, another brother who values white skin so much that he'll even be with someone who looks like *her*. I know what I *am* to Michael, or at least, I sort of know. But I have no idea what I *represent* to him.

"Does it always have to be winning and losing?" Michael says slowly. "You're always, like, 'who wins?' Can't we get outside all that?"

"I don't know," I say. "I mean, you and I, just us, I'd like to think so. But it never *is* just us." I hear Michael yawning and trying to hide it. "Oh, Michael. You must be completely exhausted."

"I'm getting there," he admits. He swallows another yawn. "I have to work Sunday, too," he says. "I just found out. Another double. So I can't come meet you at the airport, and I won't even get to see you Sunday night."

"Oh."

"Are you disappointed?" he whispers.

"Yes, actually."

"Well, that's good."

I laugh. "Oh, you like that? Thinking about seeing you Sunday was all that was getting me through this horrible weekend and now I don't even have that—is that what you wanted to hear?"

"Yes, actually," he says, imitating me. "That's like exactly what I was going for."

"Well, you heard it," I say. "You heard it here first."

"Merry Christmas, Rosie," he says sleepily.

"Merry Christmas, Michael," I say softly into the phone. I turn out the light in the guest room, so I can't see where I am. "Sleep well."

"You too." I wait to hang up until I hear the phone click on his end. What I'm used to, obviously, is fighting for what I want. A strong union. A united working class. A new world. So things would be much, much easier with Michael if only I knew what to fight for.

WARREN: There seem to be two different ways they open presents in this house, and I must admit, I find both of them somewhat disconcerting. The children plow through a huge pile of gifts in about ten minutes, frantically ripping the wrapping paper from each package in their single-minded drive to get on to the next one. (I know this is silly, but it makes me feel sorry for the *present*.) Juliet is done far earlier than everybody else, even though she unwraps each gift far more carefully, at least at first. But everybody gave her only one present, whereas they gave all the other children several.

The adults, on the other hand, sit quietly in a big circle, opening one package at a time, under intense scrutiny. Since Flip has made sure to seat me in the center of the couch, between him and Dan, I find all the attention rather nerve-wracking.

I realize I'm biased, as Flip would say, but it seems to me that of all of them, Flip is the best at finding just the right present for each person. Rosie, for example, gets an incredibly gorgeous briefcase from him, this lovely reddish-brown satchel—with a shoulder strap, of course—that is somehow so beautifully designed, it will look slender and elegant even when it's overstuffed. It's full of little pockets and compartments and intricate little holders, every one of which Flip has filled with something special—an assortment of fancy pens and markers, a rainbow of colored file folders, a tiny pocket calculator. It must have cost the earth. I wouldn't have guessed that Rosie would love it so much—but Flip knew. By the time she looks up from discovering all the bag's little secrets, there are tears in her eyes.

"Oh, Flip," she says. "It's wonderful. It's perfect. Thank you *so much*."

"Flip always gives the best presents," says Dan from the other end of the couch. "Remember, Flip, when you were eleven and I was eight and Rosie had just fixed up her room, and of course, in those days, we really *didn't* have any money—"

"We never got an allowance," Flip explains to me, with a certain amount of effort. "So any money we got, we had to earn."

"Anyway," says Dan, "I was eight, and you were eleven, remember, Flip?

And I think I had like fifty cents, but only because Dad had taken pity on me and hired me to help him shovel the walk."

"You were a hard worker," says Flip's father. "You did your best."

Dan laughs. "I think I maybe transported three shovelfuls of snow in an hour and a half," he says. "But I stayed out there as long as you did, anyway. And Flip, you had a whole dollar-fifty from—what was it?"

"Raking leaves," Flip says rather grimly. As always with him, it's hard to tell just how much of this is a performance. "I went up and down the entire block and knocked at every single door. And every single person said the same thing: 'Why, you're such a little fellow! That rake is bigger than you are.' " Everybody laughs. "I shot up in high school," Flip explains to me again, "but all through elementary school and junior high, I had to struggle with being inordinately *short*. I'm sure it warped me for life, in some subtle yet unmistakable way."

"Not so subtle," says Dan.

"But *very* unmistakable," says Rosie.

"Anyway, with all that, I got exactly three customers," says Flip. "I suppose my particular market niche was limited to those neighbors who were less interested in having their leaves raked *well* than in having such a cute little fellow rake them."

Even I have to join in the laughter at that. "A market niche you're still filling, apparently," says Rosie. She pats his cheek. "Poor Flip. Just another pretty face."

Flip pushes her hand away, but anyone could tell he's pleased.

"And then," Dan takes up the story, "Flip came to me all the way in the beginning of December, and he explained that we could *make* gifts for Ma and Dad, because they already loved us, but for Rosie, we had to buy an actual present. So he convinced me that we should put our money together, and we went downtown to the Woolworth's, and Flip picked out a lampshade for Rosie's room."

"Oh, my God," Rosie says, "that ruffly white lampshade that matched the bedspread and the dressing table. I *loved* that lampshade."

"It was kind of a seed present," Flip says, "you know, like seed money? Because, as I recall, you didn't actually have a lamp."

"All right, enough reminiscing," Flip's mother says on her way to the kitchen. "Flip, what's your next present?"

Mine, apparently. Flip hands me a flat, narrow box, wrapped in discreet gold paper. (Rosie's wrapping paper had big, splashy flowers all over it, so evidently the entire package constitutes a statement, which I find both touching and embarrassing.) I try to unwrap the package as gently as possible. Inside the box is a heavy brass keychain with the interlocking masks of comedy and tragedy.

"Read the card," Flip says, again with a certain amount of effort, and for the first time in the present-giving ritual, the rest of them all start talking to each other, even Rosie.

The card is a folded piece of thick ivory paper. Inside, in Flip's compact, graceful writing, is a miniature message, laid out like a haiku:

> *I have the mate to this.*
> *And since, as we all know, acting is the key to my heart,*
> *Now you have, etcetera, etcetera.*
>
> *Flip*

I don't dare look at him. What did he think he was doing, giving me a present like this in front of his family?

"It's perfect," I say softly, my eyes fixed firmly on the thick, curved masks. I feel his body next to mine with incredible specificity—shoulder, elbow, hip, thigh. "It couldn't be more perfect."

"Good," says Flip, equally softly. And I hear how much it means to him to give me this gift here in public, even though at the moment, everyone's looking away.

My gift to him was actually chosen with that in mind, a present that would mean something to him, but not to anyone who saw him get it—the new biography of Peter O'Toole, whom I know Flip has always liked, and that famous biography of Cary Grant. I watch him tear open the anonymous wrapping paper, courtesy of the bookstore. I see him take in the two titles. He starts to open the Cary Grant, and I say quickly—his family has all started talking again—"I didn't inscribe them yet. I . . . wanted to be sure you wanted them. I can always take them back."

"No, don't do that," Flip says. I wonder if he understands that I also didn't inscribe them because I could imagine his family passing them around—people do that with presents sometimes—and I didn't want to write something with them in mind, too. Maybe he does understand, because he says, "You can write in them when we get home."

"Yes," I say. "That's what I thought."

And then he musters up *something* and looks straight at me. "Thank you, Warren," he says, still with that effort.

I can't even put my hand on his arm. But I can imagine doing it—his soft,

scratchy shirt, his warm, solid arm, the sudden rush of blood as our bodies finally touch. I think he receives *that,* at least. "Thank you, Warren," he repeats,
more naturally.

"You're welcome," I say, and then we look away.

Juliet picks this moment to come show me her present from Flip, still in
its nest of wrapping paper—deep blue tissue paper covered with tiny silver
stars. When did he have time to find all these things? He's gotten her two used
hardcovers: a beautifully illustrated collection of fairy tales, in French, and a
children's book called *Half Magic.* And then Juliet shows Flip *my* present—the
paperback version of *Half Magic,* along with the other six books in the series.
(Rosie told me that when she was Juliet's age, she read them one after the
other, as fast as she could get them from the library.)

By this point, everyone but Rosie has drifted over to the children's side of
the living room. "Don't you two ever *talk?*" Rosie says.

"Not to each other, apparently," says Flip.

"Well, I wouldn't have told Warren to get *Half Magic* if I'd known you were
going to get it, too," says Rosie.

Juliet is watching this whole conversation with growing distress. "It's all
right, Uncle Warren," she says urgently. "I can take your books back to Paris
with me. And I can leave Uncle Flip's book at your house so it will always be
there when I visit."

I am torn between being pleased that it's *my* copy of the book she wants to
take, and feeling sick at the thought of her leaving so soon. But I manage to
say, "Juliet, what do you do when someone gives you a present?"

Juliet goes over to Flip and throws her arms around him. Which completely surprises Flip, who, by the look on his face, has also been digesting the
reminder that Juliet will be gone in less than six months. "Thank you, Uncle
Flip," she says as he hugs her.

"You're welcome, Niece Juliet," says Flip. I can feel the stir this causes over
on the other side of the room.

Then something completely surprising happens. Flip's father actually
waves me over to where he's sitting, in the corner wing chair I had yesterday.
"How old is your little girl?" he says as I stand beside him, looking down at
him rather awkwardly.

"She's my niece, actually," I say, for the umpteenth time. "She's eight."

Flip's father nods. "That's how old Rosie was when I married her mother,"
he says. "It's not an easy age."

I am so taken aback, it's all I can do to nod in return. "Of course, I was a
younger man than you are now," he goes on. "I was probably more flexible.
Still."

Behind me, I hear Juliet explaining the plot of *Half Magic* to Rosie, based on what, I don't know, because she can't have had time to read it yet, can she? Flip's father and I turn to look at them. "And it's a magic charm, but it only grants *half* your wish," Juliet is saying.

"So what if you wished for—a best friend?" says Rosie. "What would happen then?"

Juliet considers this. "Well, I haven't actually *read* the book yet," she admits. "But maybe you would get the *ghost* of a best friend. Or a best friend who lived in your neighborhood only *half* the time."

Flip's father shakes his head. "She seems like a handful," he says.

"Well, Rosie must have been a handful, too," I say. Feeling somewhat disloyal, I say, "She's *still* a handful."

Flip's father chuckles. Then he says, more seriously, "Of course, you've only got the one to worry about. I had three. Danny was always a quiet kid, but regardless. You move into a house with three children, you know you're not a bachelor any more."

"I can only imagine," I say, with a certain amount of awe. "If you don't mind my asking, how did you manage?"

"Oh, it wasn't so bad," he says. "You think it's going to be, but it isn't, really. Of course, *you're* on your own. Lucky you don't have diapers and baby food and that."

"Thank God," I say. "I don't know how I would have managed if I had."

"You know what the hardest part was?" He looks carefully away from me, toward the Christmas tree, where his grandchildren are now playing with Juliet. "It's a very tight family," he says. "And you know what those Irish are—they don't like outsiders. Of course, we was all Catholics, so we had that. And Dorie's first husband was Polish, so you might say he came along and broke the ground. Still. Wasn't easy, being the only Norwegian in the bunch."

"No," I say, surprised by how grateful I feel. "I can imagine that it wasn't."

I feel Flip watching us from over on the couch. What is he upset about *now?* Then Flip's father gestures that I should pull up a chair, and as I turn to get it, I see Flip's face. Oh. He's getting *half* his wish. Because the other half would be for him to come over and sit *with* me, to—I don't know. *Present* me to his father. Maybe, although I feel odd thinking this, maybe even to have his father be proud of him for having me. But for Flip to sit here with his arm around me, the two of us chatting with his father—that's the half of his wish he simply won't get.

Instead Juliet is the one who comes over again, to show me the inscription Flip wrote in her book. "Dear Niece Juliet," he has printed in large, purple letters. "Once I made a wish for two incredibly wonderful girls to come and live in my house and be my nieces. And guess what? You came along! Do you think that was half magic? I love you. xxoo Uncle Flip."

As I am taking this in, Flip's mother calls for help from the kitchen and Flip's father slowly lumbers to his feet. Juliet dashes back to Shannon, and Flip finally comes over, squatting on the floor beside my chair.

"That was lovely, what you wrote in Juliet's book," I say softly. "What you wrote in my present, too, actually."

"Well, I have my moments," Flip says. "You know, I realized, you haven't even seen my old room yet. Come on up now, while everyone else is setting up dinner."

"Shouldn't we help too?" I say.

"We're the men," Flip says. "We don't have to help."

"Your father does."

"Well, obviously, *he* doesn't count—he's married to my mother. Haven't you been paying attention?"

"So did you bring all your boyfriends up to your room?" I say when we're safely up the stairs and in the second-floor hallway.

"No, darling, you're the first," Flip says, opening the door next to Rosie's room. "Believe me, when I lived at home, I kept *all* my boyfriends as far away from here as possible."

Flip's room, which evidently he shared with Dan, has two small single beds, covered with matching bedspreads—the kind with the logos of various sports teams—and two small wooden desks, each with its chair and its row of books. The white wallpaper has a pattern of red rocket ships and blue planets, which the high-school-aged Flip and Danny evidently tried to cover up as much as possible, because the walls are plastered with posters, mainly athletes, which must have been Dan's choice, unless this is a whole other side of Flip that I've simply never known about. Maybe he liked looking at those basketball players, in their tank tops and shorts. There are also two theater posters, which clearly *were* Flip's—*Evita* and *A Chorus Line*—and a poster from some tour of the Rolling Stones. I can't imagine whose idea that was.

I am just about to go over to the desks and see if I can tell which one was Flip's, when Flip backs me up against the wooden closet doors and kisses me. For a moment I hesitate, partly out of surprise, partly out of a very deep feeling that I am violating his family's hospitality. Then I think, "Well, they're *his* family," and I kiss him back.

The kiss goes on for a while and leaves us both a little breathless. "OK," says Flip finally, still gripping my arms, "I guess that's enough of that. Can I trust you to sit with me on the bed?"

"*I* didn't do anything."

"Oh, when do you ever do anything? You just stand there looking incredibly attractive, and then *I* have to come over and do all the work." We sit down, and he puts his head on my shoulder. I put my arm around him.

"All right," I say, "at this point, we can either start talking about something else, or go downstairs."

"OK," says Flip, taking my hand. Our fingers tighten. "Start talking."

"All right. Why are there all those pictures of saints in Rosie's room and none in here?"

Flip laughs. "What do you think, there's a rule, there have to be saints' pictures in every Catholic bedroom? She was extremely religious in high school, as you can easily imagine, whereas I wasn't, as you can also easily imagine."

"You *had* saints though, right?"

"You mean patron saints? Yes, you get those at age thirteen, when you're confirmed. How do you know about all that?"

"Well, I'm not entirely ignorant. I have seen *Song of Bernadette*."

He sits up and stares at me. "What?" I say finally.

He puts his head back on my shoulder. "You have to promise you won't laugh."

"With you, that's always a dangerous promise."

"All right," he says. "She was one of my patron saints."

"*The* Bernadette? The one with the song?"

"Ha, ha," says Flip. "She meant a lot to me at that age. But they always told us the Protestants wouldn't understand."

"Well, take pity on a poor, ignorant Protestant and explain it to me."

"Oh, it was just the idea that nobody listened to her," Flip says. "Even though Our Blessed Virgin Mother thought enough of her to appear and create an entire *shrine*."

"Hmmm," I say. "So was she your only—what is it called again?"

"Patron saint," says Flip. "No, I had two. Bernadette, and Theresa, the Little Flower."

"And why her?"

"Because nobody appreciated *her* either," Flip says. "But then when she died, the whole sky opened and rained down rose petals. And now that you know all this, Warren, if you ever leave me, I'll have to hunt you down and kill you."

"Well, I'm not the one who wants to leave," I point out. "I'm the one who wants to get married, remember? Or whatever we decide to call it. And speaking of which—"

"You know, Warren," says Flip. "I don't mean to be critical, but the next time you make a proposal, you might give just a *little* more thought to the timing. I mean, we can't exactly go downstairs and announce the blessed event, can we?"

We're both quiet for a moment. "This isn't my subtle way of saying no, Warren," he says finally. "I really don't know. And this isn't exactly the place to decide."

"Do you think they'd come? Your family, I mean, if we did get married."

"Oh, I'm sure they would eventually," Flip says. "I would just rather not be in the same actual house with them while they get used to the idea. Would yours?"

"You know, I have no idea," I say slowly. "I wasn't thinking of them when I asked you." Suddenly, Flip kisses me again.

"Are you having a better time?" he whispers when we finally stop. "I mean, under the circumstances?"

"Under the circumstances, I'm having a fabulous time," I say. "It's actually pretty nice even *not* under the circumstances." He smiles at me. "Thank you," I whisper.

He shakes his head. "You don't have to thank me. It's all included in the service."

After dinner, Dan and Betsy finally gather up the children, and Flip, Rosie, and I prepare to go out. "Don't stay out too late," says Flip's mother. "Who's driving?"

"I am," says Flip.

"Well, be careful on those icy roads, darlin'." She looks at Rosie. "Don't let him do anything foolish."

"Oh, right," says Rosie. "After thirty-two years, like I could stop him now."

Rosie generously insists that I take the front seat, and Flip drives us to a diner that actually is called House of Pies, a sprawling coffee shop with red vinyl booths and lots of colorful Christmas lights and Christmas muzak, in an endless loop. It's not the sort of place that I would ever normally choose to eat in, but Flip and Rosie are both delighted with it. Rosie turns to me as Flip pushes open the heavy glass doors. "We *never* went out to eat the whole time we were growing up," she says. "But when we *did* go, for a really, really, really special treat, this is where we went."

The exhausted waitress behind the counter nods as we come in. Only two other tables are occupied, one by a group of teenagers, the other by an elderly man just finishing a full-course Christmas dinner. Rosie sighs. "There but for the grace of God," she says.

Flip shakes his head. "I can't imagine you without seven million friends, each of whom would be perfectly happy to invite you over for Christmas," he says. "If you hadn't come home, *how* many invitations would you have had?"

"Well, *now,* sure," Rosie says. "What about thirty years from now?"

"Mmmm," Flip says skeptically. "Isn't that one of the advantages of having a boyfriend who's so much younger than you? You're far less likely to outlive him, and when you're too old to function, he'll still be able to cook you dinner. A point that *you* should keep in mind, Warren."

"You're not *that* much younger than me," I say.

We choose a corner booth, one of those curving banquettes with its back to the window. Flip motions me to slide in, so that I'm sitting between him and Rosie as they more or less face each other. Suddenly, I am incredibly happy.

"So," says Rosie, as the waitress brings our order (just coffee for me, French fries and a BLT for her and Flip to split). "I still haven't heard about that theater group. The one with Tanya."

"Really?" says Flip with his mouth full. "I thought I told you all about it in excruciating detail."

"No, that was *Tartuffe,*" says Rosie. "Which I didn't think was nearly as bad as you did, by the way. Did you, Warren?"

"Warren hated it," Flip says, "though he's too polite to say so. I always have to drag it out of him, what he really thinks."

"I didn't *hate* it," I say, although it's true, I was bored, except for when Flip was on stage.

"Oh, come on," Flip says with a grimace. "The guy playing Tartuffe couldn't even *talk,* for God's sake. If you hadn't been sitting in the front row, Rosie, you wouldn't have heard a word he said. Let alone any of the rhymes, any of the poetry—"

"Well, no, *he* was awful," agrees Rosie. "But the Madame Elmire wasn't bad."

"No, she was OK," Flip says grudgingly. "She was a real pain to work with, though. I mean, come on, Cynthia. There is a reason they tell you that rehearsal starts at seven. And that reason is not so you can show up at eight-fifteen."

"How do people get away with that?" Rosie says. "Can't the director make them come on time?"

Flip shrugs. "If she were actually *paying* them, I suppose she could threaten to fire them. But under the circumstances . . ."

"But you're always—I mean, you— You always seem very concerned about getting to rehearsal on time," I say.

Flip shrugs. "Well, I am. But I'm alone in that concern, apparently. At least with regard to showcases."

"It sounds so demoralizing," Rosie says.

"It *is* demoralizing," says Flip. "And the worst part is, *I* start feeling like it doesn't matter whether I get there on time or not."

"Why is that the worst part?" I say. I'm fascinated by this image of Flip impatiently waiting for all the others. I always assumed he was punctual because he was afraid of losing the role.

Flip sighs. "It shouldn't be *more* important to me than to anybody else." He searches for the words as he chews. "What keeps you going is the standards you set for yourself," he says finally. "The marks you try to hit. So if nobody *cares* about hitting those marks, why are you even doing it? Certainly not for the money."

"But you don't get paid for being in Tanya's group," Rosie says.

"Actually, I do. But that's different anyway."

"OK. Why?" Rosie says impatiently.

The waitress arrives with their pie. Flip orders coffee, too, and Rosie orders tea. Flip laughs. "There's a real gender division in our family when it comes to hot drinks," he says to me. "Rosie and Ma drink tea. The men all have coffee. And the women all take milk and sugar. But the men, being real men, drink everything black."

Rosie looks wistful. "Poppy drank his coffee with milk and sugar. Sometimes he let me put the sugar in for him."

"Right, I remember," Flip says quickly. "I did that, too."

Rosie looks skeptical, but she doesn't say anything. Instead she says, "So what *about* that group with Tanya?"

"It's called Tiger's Eye, actually. Now *there's* a catchy name." Then his face softens. "Actually, I like it." He looks puzzled. "It's very different. I mean, I'm used to having a script, and going home, and learning my lines, and figuring out every little thing about my character that I can. And then I come into rehearsal, and I just *do* it. And if my scene partner is any good, or if the director is, then, OK, they have some influence. But either way, you know, I'm just doing my part."

"But in that group . . . I don't know." He shakes his head. "Nothing is ever *mine*." He swallows a bite of pie—he got the coconut, which happens to be my favorite—and he pushes the plate in my direction.

"Just leave me *some*, all right, Warren?" he says. And though normally I would never eat off someone else's plate, I take a bite. It's not so bad.

"So what's wrong with it not being *yours*?" says Rosie. "Or not only yours?"

"It makes me feel like I don't matter," Flip says. "If I'm just doing *my part*, I could rise above the others. But this way, I'm more or less stuck with them."

Rosie is smiling. She starts to say something and then stops.

"You know what it is?" Flip says in that troubled voice. "It's like—really, there are six of us, right? But when we're really *on,* it's like there's an extra actor there, this seventh actor, and *he's* doing all the work." He looks at Rosie and makes a face. "Or she. But this *us.* This thing that's *more* than us. The work belongs to him."

Rosie leans forward eagerly and I feel like warning someone. But what could I say?

"OK," she says, "so in Tiger's Eye, do people come on time?"

Flip thinks about it. "Yes, I suppose they do."

"And if people are late, in those other situations, even if you *can* rise above it, it still affects you, right? It demoralizes you."

"I just said it did."

"Well, OK, so then you *always* need everybody you're working with. It's just that in Tiger's Eye, you have them."

"I always need everybody else?" Flip says. "Even in that awful *Tartuffe?*"

"Well, you don't need them to work *per se,*" Rosie says. "Obviously, you can always do *something.* And since you *are* talented, you can usually do something good. But the quality of your work in *Tartuffe* and the quality of your work in Tiger's Eye—how do they compare?"

"You know," says Flip, "you might actually be right about this, but if you are, I don't want to know it."

"Why not?" Rosie says, practically bouncing out of her seat.

"Because this is a very unusual situation," Flip says, "one that I probably won't be in ever again. And if something better comes along, I'll have to leave this time, too."

"Why?" says Rosie. "Why can't you just commit to Tiger's Eye?"

"Yeah, right," Flip says. "I should *plan* to never make a living for the rest of my life. I should *plan* to stay with a group where I'll never be seen."

"Some people will see you," says Rosie. "You said the show is going to community centers, prisons . . ."

"Well, *there's* the career I had in mind."

"Oh, really?" says Rosie. "What career *were* you planning on? *Television?*"

"Rosie," says Flip, and I hear how much he wants from her. "Even Tanya auditions for TV, all the time. That's how you earn a living." Almost absentmindedly, he pushes the last bite of pie in my direction. Then he waits to make sure I take it. "She doesn't want to be temping for the rest of *her* life, either."

"Well," says Rosie, "I don't know about her. But if you want to be an artist—"

The waitress comes with the check. Rosie and I both reach for money but Flip says, "I've got it," and waves us away. The waitress leaves, and there's a long silence.

"What?" Flip says finally, looking at Rosie. "What were you going to say?"

"Look," says Rosie, "maybe we shouldn't talk about this."

"Rosie," says Flip, grinding out the word, "I hate when you do this. You started something. Now finish it."

Already he's looking cornered. Which should make me want to help him, shouldn't it? But what I really think is that he should know better. He asked Rosie what she thinks. Now she's going to tell him.

"OK, look," she says. "I look at you, and I see my brother, Flip Zombrowski, this very interesting person, this gay man, all right? With all this incredible talent, all these *things* to say to the world. That's how I see you—I mean, the real you."

Now her voice has that desperate, pleading quality. "So then I look at your eight by ten," she is saying, "that picture you use to try to get one of those *jobs* you're always talking about, and it's this whole other person. What's the name you're using now, Philip Bernard? This guy who we're supposed to think is straight? Who wants to use his talent on some racist cop show? *That's* your career? *That's* your life's work? *That's* what you'll look back on from your deathbed and say, 'That's how I spent my time on earth?' "

"God, Rosie, you're such a snob."

"*I'm* a snob?" Rosie says. "You're the one who's always saying this actor's no good, that actor's no good. You get three of those jobs, you'll be just like them."

"No, I won't. First of all, if you're really committed—"

"Fine. So you'll do a *good* job selling soap instead of a bad one. Even *you* can't set your sights *that* low."

"Those aren't the *only* paying jobs," says Flip. "There are movies. There are—"

"Movies?" says Rosie. "Listen to yourself. When was the last time you had anything good to say about any movie made after 1972? Even *you* don't consider that stuff art, Flip, so why do you want that kind of success? It's never going to make you happy."

"How the fuck do you know what's going to make me happy?"

"Not only won't it make you happy," Rosie says, even more desperately, "but since you don't really want it, not really, you won't even be successful. The part of you that really *does* want to be an artist is going to hold you back. So you won't have success, and you won't have art either. You'll just have nothing."

Flip stares at her for the longest time, trying to speak. Then he turns to me with such a look of betrayal that it takes my breath away. Suddenly he throws down his napkin and walks out. A moment later, we hear the car drive off.

Rosie and I sit there, more or less in shock. Rosie looks absolutely shattered. I remember the day I went to see her about Juliet, how at the end of everything, I felt bad for *her*. Despite everything, I can't help feeling that way now.

"He *asked* me," she says. She picks up her fork and puts it down again. "He *kept* asking me."

"I know," I say.

"Does he do this with you, too? Storm out of the conversation like this?"

"Well, no," I say, and she looks even more ashamed. "But only because I'm more the one—I mean, he's had reason to be afraid that—I would be the one to leave."

She bites her lip.

"It's all right," I say after a minute. "You know how much he cares about you."

She sits there stiffly. "Not really."

"Oh, Rosie, come on. He talks about you all the time. Every move he makes, even with me, he tells you right away."

"He didn't tell me you were thinking about getting married," she says. "Or whatever you decide to call it." I must admit, I can't help being pleased about that. "Anyway," she says helplessly, "I know I'm important to him. But he wishes I wasn't. I'm like this *monster* who's ruining his life."

I take a breath. "Well," I say, "he would kill me if he knew I said this to you. But Rosie. That's what he does. He asks for help. Or advice, or whatever. And then—"

"And then he gets mad when you give it to him. I know."

I sigh. "Not just help. Attention? Or—"

"Or love?" she says bitterly. "I *know*. The difference is, he feels guilty about that with *you*."

"Really?" I didn't think Flip ever felt guilty about anything.

"Maybe guilty is the wrong word," says Rosie. "Maybe it's more that he feels inferior. You know. He wishes he could be on your level."

"In *what*?"

"Oh, come on, Warren." She sits up a little straighter. "I mean, you're ready to live together again, and he still isn't sure. And I didn't know you had proposed marriage to him. Or whatever. But you did kind of one-up him."

"That's hardly why I did it."

"Of course not. That makes it worse."

"Jesus Christ." Now I have a new reason to be in shock.

Rosie shakes her head. "I shouldn't be saying this to you, Warren," she says, "so please forgive me, but I hope he does stop speaking to me. I don't want to talk to him, either."

I wouldn't have believed how much this frightens me. "Does that mean you'll stop speaking to me, too?"

"Oh, Warren." She takes my hand, and I let her. "He's your boyfriend. What are we going to do, call each other when he's not home?"

"Well, since he's never home, that shouldn't be hard."

"Oh, Warren." She starts to laugh, helplessly. "I don't know," she says when she's finally done. She clasps my hand, hard, then pushes me aside. "Come on," she says, "I guess there's one all-night taxi left out here."

When the cab pulls up to Rosie's parents' house, she leans over and kisses me on the cheek. "Thank you, Warren," she says. "For everything, OK? Thank you." I watch her let herself into the dark house. I see the little lamp go on, the one with the ruffly shade.

When I get back to our room at the motel, Flip is already in bed. I still can't get over what Rosie said, that now he's upset about—I can't repeat it, even in my thoughts. I thought that was what he *wanted*.

"Well," he says the minute I come through the door. "You certainly took your sweet time about coming back."

"You took the car," I point out. "We couldn't exactly pick up and go."

"I'll bet." He rearranges himself on his little strip of bed, pulling all the blankets over to his side. "How is she?" he says suddenly.

"Jesus, Flip, how do you think she is? She's fucking upset."

"If you're going to take her side, I don't want to hear it."

"If you don't want me to take her side, don't leave me alone with her in a restaurant in the middle of fucking nowhere."

"It isn't the middle of fucking *nowhere*," he says. "It's the middle of fucking *Pittsburgh*. It's where I grew up. It's a very important place in my life."

"And now I'll never forget it, either," I say. "You've made it completely memorable for me, too, thank you."

"You *are* taking her side."

"This whole conversation is ridiculous," I say as I try to get under *some* of the covers. "She's your sister. You two figure it out and leave me out of it."

"*Fine*," Flip says, all the way over on the other edge of the bed. "And don't even *try* telling me what *you* think about what she said."

"Methinks the lady doth protest too much," I take great satisfaction in saying, but it's a rather limited satisfaction, because after that he's absolutely quiet, though I don't see how even he could fall asleep that fast.

The next day, he barely speaks to me. Even Juliet seems awed by how angry he is—of course, *she* can tell right away—and she avoids him for virtually the whole day at his parents' and the flight and the taxi back to our house. He sits stormily in the living room, while I put Juliet to bed, and he's still there when I come out of her bedroom, twisted around sideways with his leg hanging over the side of the chair.

"That looks very uncomfortable," I say. "Are you *ever* going to speak to me again, or are we going to our graves like this?"

He looks up at me. "All right," he says. "I'll marry you. Or whatever we decide to call it."

"What?"

"Well," he says, "I really hate you right now. I'm furious with you, as a matter of fact. You *always* take Rosie's side. What's worse, you never take my side, with Rosie or anybody else. With me." He swings his leg. "But mad as I am, I don't actually feel like leaving. I mean, I could have gone to my place. There's absolutely no reason for me to be here. But here I am. Presumably, this is the worst that it gets. So, OK. I'll marry you. Or whatever we decide to call it."

I am still staring at him. "Only you could say something like that," I say finally.

"Is that a problem for you?"

"Look, why don't you let me know when you're through being mad," I say. "Because otherwise, I'm going to get so mad at you, I don't know what I'll do, and why should we both be furious?"

"That is so typical of you, Warren. Why won't you fight?"

"What are we even fighting about?" I say. "I've lost track." I look at him, sullen and miserable. I sit down on the couch. "Only you could accept a proposal in just that way," I say after a silence.

"Do you withdraw your proposal?"

"Jesus, Flip. No."

"Well, so, that's what I mean. This is the worst that it gets, and we're both still here."

"I'm not at all sure that this *is* the worst that it gets," I say. "But I'm glad you want to stick around and find out."

He bites his lip. "Why didn't you stick up for me with Rosie?"

"Because she's your sister," I say, "and I didn't want to get in the middle. And—"

"And you did agree with her."

"Somewhat, yes," I say. "But somewhat, no. But I think *you* agreed with her, and that's why you're so mad."

"I didn't ask you that."

Suddenly I've had it. "Well, then, fuck you, too, Flip. If you don't want to hear what I have to say, then don't start the goddamn conversation. Advice that might stand you in good stead with Rosie, by the way."

"In good stead?" he says, but I am already walking out of the room.

After a minute, he comes into the bedroom. "Is it too late?" he says. "Or are you already so mad that now I've missed my chance to make up?"

I sigh. "I'm fairly mad. But I don't think you've missed your chance. You might have to work at it, though."

He comes over and puts his arms around me. It's amazing how much that means to me, at this moment. There's something so—terrifying, I suppose, is the word—about us being mad at each other. The way I felt scared when Rosie said she wouldn't speak to Flip for a while. It's like death.

"You're really not very good at fighting, are you?" he says softly. "It just happens, Warren. It's no big deal."

I swallow hard. "Maybe not for you. But for the people you're fighting with—"

"You think I don't fight fair?"

I consider this. "I think you don't fight safe. Something really dangerous can happen when you're mad, Flip. Or at least it seems that way."

"Look who's talking. At least I never walked out on *you*."

"Now you have."

"I didn't *leave* you, I just went home. You knew that."

"Rosie didn't."

"Well, she was right," Flip says. "I *don't* want to speak to her for a while. But I didn't leave *you*."

Loyalty to Rosie versus Flip here in my arms. It's not much of a contest. Sorry, Rosie. Though I can see why you'd want to stop speaking to me, too, in that case.

"The first night there was nice, wasn't it?" he says, pulling me down onto the bed. We sit there with our arms around each other, his face buried in my shoulder. "I'm sorry we didn't get to enjoy the second one."

"Well. I suppose there will be other nights."

"I'm falling asleep," he almost whispers. "Now that we're not fighting, I'm just falling out here. Given that I got like two hours sleep."

I am truly astonished. "I thought you were sleeping that whole time."

He laughs. "Darling, I'm an actor. I was *acting* sleep."

I feel my body go rigid. "Flip," I say, "do me a favor. Please, please, never do that again."

"What?"

"Pretend that you're asleep if you're not." Well, that sounds stupid. "Pretend that you're *all right* if you're not. I thought I was the only one who—"

"Who minded sleeping so far apart," Flip says.

"Well, yes."

"OK, point taken," Flip says. "Because I thought you didn't mind, either. The whole way you were—I don't know. You just didn't seem like you minded."

"It's like death," I say. "I can't stand it."

He is quiet for a moment, taking this in.

"Also," I say, "please don't walk out that way. I mean, I won't if you won't."

"OK," Flip says. "No pretending to be asleep and no walking out of a restaurant. Or an apartment. Got it." Then he pulls back his head and looks at me. "Do you feel better now?" he asks gently.

"Yes, as a matter of fact, I do." But as soon as I say this, I feel a chill. As though I've given up something very important, something I should have kept. Maybe this *is* the worst that it gets. To feel in so much danger and to want him so much anyway.

ROSIE: The whole day after Christmas, no one even notices that Flip and I aren't speaking to each other—except Warren, of course, and he already knew. I don't know how he would have handled the situation if left to his own devices. But I don't want to *watch* him choose Flip over me, so I just avoid him until it's finally time for Danny to detach himself from Shannon and take me to the airport.

"Another happy family Christmas," I say as he pulls out of the driveway. Danny gives me a quick look.

"Not a good one for you this year, huh?"

"Oh, Danny. I don't know. I always think I'm going to know better, and I never actually do." I look at him there beside me, his long fingers wrapped around the steering wheel. "Three children," I say suddenly. "How do you do it, Danny? Plus Betsy, of course, and your job, and aren't you teaching Sunday school this year or something?"

"Substitute teaching."

"Well, so, that's still a huge commitment, isn't it? I can't imagine having even one child." I make a face. "Or even one adult, actually."

"Well, it does change your whole life," Danny says matter-of-factly. "But that's why you do it. For a while, at least, you don't do other things. Your family becomes more important."

"More important than the whole rest of the world?"

Danny shrugs again. "You and I are different that way, Rosie. I like my job. But it's just a job. Yours is more of a calling."

I sigh. "Like a nun."

Danny laughs in an embarrassed way. "You know, Rosie, I never told you this, but it made a huge impression on me, when you took your patron saints."

"You're kidding. Why?"

"Well, not Saint Francis so much. But Saint Joan."

I laugh. "I can't believe they let me do it."

"Well, it didn't affect me so much at the time," says Danny. "But later on, when I found out who she was, you know, all the plays that had been written about her . . ."

"She was more famous," I offer.

"She was more real," Danny says. "No one but us ever cared about the rest of them. But *everyone* had heard of her. And I thought, Wow, my sister picked that one. My sister is going to do something important someday, just like Joan of Arc."

"God, Danny. That's incredibly sweet."

"And now you're still—crusading."

"Oh, well, obviously, you're biased. But thank you." Marcy is a crusader, too, isn't she? She teaches feminist studies at a small college in Boston, and she's on the editorial board of a women's literary magazine, and she writes articles analyzing slave narratives and pioneer women's diaries and the stories by workers in old union magazines. And she's politically active, mainly on welfare rights, but also in that general way, where if there's an important demonstration on any topic, she'll try to go. How will she do *any* of that with a child? Not something Saint Joan had to worry about.

"I wish you and Betsy had had more of a chance to talk," Danny says. "She's really torn up about this work thing. And I'm sorry you didn't get to spend more time with Peter and Lily."

But Betsy didn't want to talk to me, not about anything serious. And Peter and Lily were much more interested in Ma. And Flip.

Suddenly I remember my lampshade. Flip got all the credit for giving it to me. But one-fourth of the money was Danny's. "Oh, Danny." I don't even know *what* to say. "Why don't you guys come visit me in New York sometime?"

Danny laughs. "Let me tell you, Rosie," he says. "You haven't lived till you've taken a trip with three children."

"No, I guess not. Not that my place is big enough for you anyway."

"Well, you could always come for a longer visit," Danny says. "You don't have to spend every night at Ma and Dad's. You could spend part of the time with us."

"God, can you imagine how Ma would react if I did?" I say. "She would just be over at your house every single minute. Or she'd, I don't know, kidnap the children."

Danny laughs. *He* never tells me to shut up. "We could probably fend her off for a few hours," he says. "Think about it."

"I will." Though the next time I *do* manage some time off, I can't really see using it for Pittsburgh. So then what have I been asking for all weekend?

We pull up to the departures terminal. "Danny," I say impulsively, as I reach for the last bag. "Would you—I don't suppose you'd want to park in the long-term and come and wait with me?"

He looks worried. "Won't you be OK by yourself? By the time your plane takes off, it will be rush hour and the traffic will be murder. And Betsy's alone with the kids." Well, technically, she's not *alone*—she's still back at our house. But I suppose it's admirable that he thinks of it that way.

"No, it's OK," I say, wishing I hadn't asked.

It takes forever to drag all my bags into the airport, and then again onto the plane. Finally, though, I'm in my seat. I get out my Olympia files, which I've packed in Flip's new briefcase—yes, of course I'm going to use it. I love it—and I don't feel much of anything (except, possibly, concern for Olympia) until the plane touches down.

Suddenly I'm swamped by regret that once again, there's no one to meet me at the gate. I know my life isn't really desolate. It certainly isn't empty. But I have the awful feeling that I could disappear, right now, and no one would even know I was gone.

Then I walk into the airport. And there, my God, are Michael and a very pregnant Marcy, arms outstretched behind the railing.

"I don't believe it," I say as they both hug me. "I really don't."

"Well, you may not see me the whole rest of the week," Michael says, smiling, "but I negotiated some time off today. I was like, this is stupid. I should be here."

"And I worked out this incredibly complicated deal with Joe that involves spending the next three major holidays with his family, don't ask," Marcy says. "But it means I get to spend tonight in New York with you."

Without even asking, they reach for my bags. "Jesus, Rosie," Marcy says, "have you ever heard of this invention, it's called a *suitcase?* You open it up and put all your stuff in it and then you have only *one* thing to carry."

"Welcome home, Rosarita," Michael says.

"Happy non-denominational holidays," Marcy says. "Now, tell us every single thing that happened. Don't leave out even one deadly insult."

Michael laughs. I guess from *her,* he thinks it's funny. But I start to tell them the story of the weekend as we fight our way through the post-Christmas crowds. Feeling an unbearable relief to be back with my people, here at home in New York.

FOUR

PLEASURE

Time passes. . . . we must wait for the future to show.
—Virginia Woolf, *To the Lighthouse*

TELEVISION

Tanya: Child, you take one look at the TV, seems like we be all *over* the place.

So why are we still invisible? That's what I want to know. I see myself everywhere I look. But never anywhere it looks like me.

Flip: Behind me, I hear Warren come into the room. Oh, Warren, not *now*. "*Previously on Hell Street* . . ." Clips from earlier episodes flash by. I can't *believe* they've added a gay character to this show. He's only the clerk who takes phone messages for the real cops, granted, and maybe he doesn't exactly flap his wrist and bat his eyes at all the butch detectives, but picture one inch short of that, and you've got it. So, OK, not *exactly* the reason I became an actor, but honey, let's face it: on this show, that's the part for me.

"If you've got a minute, Lieutenant," the guy is saying, and I lean forward to catch every not-quite-lisping word.

"Flip," Warren is saying, "where did you put the—"

"Wait, wait, wait, wait, *wait!*"

"It's about my friend, Mary—" Oh, right, *Mary.* No, that's not his boyfriend—I don't think he even *has* a boyfriend. His entire emotional life seems to be bound up with this straight female drug addict he somehow ended up taking care of.

"I think Mary's in trouble, Lieutenant. Big trouble." The clips switch to Charice, the other squad room secretary, whom I don't care so much about (although Tanya does, understandably, I suppose). "OK, Warren, what is it?" But he's already left the room.

TANYA: "It's my son," Charice is saying to the Lieutenant, and I try to see myself in *that* part—respectable, distressed, lip always on the verge of trembling. But that's not who I'm auditioning for tomorrow—I'm the welfare queen on crack. I've been studying this show all season long, watching every Black woman they put up there. Now it's my turn.

ROSIE: God, sometimes I think the credits are my favorite part. The music—drumming, ominous, thrilling. The people—that turn of the head, the special gesture, that moment when you just *know* them. You're saying their words, you're living their lives. And sooner or later, their lives will happen to you.

My character in this show is Lieutenant Trish Hunter, head of the squad room. OK, so she's got long perfect ringlets and a size two figure and I would never look anything like her in a million, billion years. But she *is* single, and she *is* in charge. (And she's white. Sorry, but Charice just *can't* be my character. None of her troubles would *ever* happen to me.)

"Can I see you in my office, please?" Trish says crisply to Perez and Galliano, the second banana cops who get all the truly bizarre cases. And the pitiful personal lives.

"Well, Lieutenant," says Perez, in that sexy, drawling voice. "We interviewed that skell you sent us out to see. But I got to tell you—"

Don't you think Trish and Perez should get together? Every time they fight—which is practically *all* the time—the sparks fly. And you think, "God, he wants her *so much.*"

"Sorry, Detective, but you seem to have misunderstood," Trish says coolly. "This time, *I'm* telling *you.*" I can't take my eyes off her. Don't even ask me why, because in real life, someone like her would make me sick—she's a cop, for God's sake. And so fucking fragile.

TANYA: Thin, white, spoiled. I sure don't want to be *her*. I didn't even want to *be* on television, when I first became an actress. I wanted to do Shakespeare. I don't know why. Just, that *was* theater for me. Going to shows at the Cleveland Playhouse with my class at school. Something about the *occasion* of it—velvet seats, lights out, everybody quiet and excited. It was *special,* but it was work, too—even then, I could see that. Learning all those lines. Saying all those words. Making us see those *other* people. I went to Black shows, too, at Karamu, but that was more—ordinary. You really had to *know* something to do Shakespeare.

I wouldn't mind having Trish's suit, though. She always wears those short skirts with the long jackets, tailored but sexy. Child, you *know* my legs are as good as hers. But it doesn't matter, because the Black women who have *power* on TV—bosses, judges, doctors—are all *much* older and, let's face it, less sexy than I am. Mammy smartened up and with a college degree. Only white women get to be that young and thin and sexy and still in charge of a room full of men.

ROSIE: I just don't think that suit would look good on me. It's cut so narrow.

FLIP: *That's* who I'd like to play—Detective Marcus Clegg. All right, he's Black. But he *did* do Shakespeare at the Public, and he's the one with the movie career. I can't *believe* Rosie has a crush on his white partner, Trask— Clegg is much sexier. Of course, *I* always have a crush on the best actors.

Warren is once again waiting—I might even say patiently—a few feet behind where I am lying, stretched out on the couch. I make the supreme sacrifice and twist my head away from the screen.

"You don't have to stand there, Warren. You could come over here and watch with me."

"No, I don't want to watch—"

"You're such a snob."

"Well, *that* seems to be your favorite insult these days." He still thinks he can get me to be the one to call Rosie. Yeah, right. I can't exactly imagine never speaking to her again—I mean, if Warren and I *are* getting married, I suppose I'll have to invite her to the matrimonial event. Meanwhile, though, she can fucking well be the one to apologize.

"Oh, Flip, I was supposed to tell you. Tanya called."

"I know. She wanted to remind me to watch *Hell Street*."

"Wouldn't you have watched it anyway? I mean, why does she care?"

"So she can talk to me about her audition, I suppose." Clegg and Trask are interviewing suspects. Clegg is totally intimidating, and sexy at the same time. He just radiates power. In that suit. Is it Armani?

"What exactly—I mean, you've seen the show before. Several times. And so has she, I would assume."

"Warren. I'm trying to watch." Trask comes discreetly up behind Clegg, pointing out Lucas Rider, Trish's ex-boyfriend and a cop from the 16th Precinct who's just been picked up in a drug-related brawl. Well, clearly *he's* high as a kite.

Behind me, I hear Warren sigh and leave the room, as Clegg gives Trask another *significant* look. *I* think there's something cooking between Trask and Trish Hunter, even though Rosie says no, the next guy who falls for Trish is going to be Ralph Perez. But maybe she just wants Trask all to herself.

MARIO: Sometimes Joshua and I kiss and make out during the commercials, and sometimes, like tonight, he sits next to me and watches the commercials with exactly the same intense, concentrated expression that he uses to watch the rest of the program. He's so amazing—everything he does is intense like that.

I can't imagine what he *does* see in these particular commercials. The beer commercial we're watching now, for instance, has these two out-of-shape guys—I don't like to judge them, but the whole point is how completely unattractive they are—watching the half-time football game, and some button on their remote control makes all these blond cheerleaders come dancing out of the tube. And then the guys' ugly girlfriends—again, this isn't me judging, this is the point of the commercial—their ugly girlfriends come into the room, and the guys hit another button, and the cheerleaders *swoosh* back into the tube, taking the guys with them.

Now, here's what's weird. Because I certainly don't admire or envy or have any positive feeling that *I* can identify about those two overweight straight guys—I mean, they're really *not* very attractive. But there I am, watching their every move. And all I want in the world is just to get inside that TV, so I can be with them.

ROSIE: Only Marcy could get me to turn away from this show and call her. Still. Her message said, "Call by eleven if you *possibly* can." She doesn't say that very often.

"Just when *Hell Street* is starting—I *am* honored," she says when she hears my voice.

"It's the commercials."

"Oh, God, well, I'll try to talk fast then, and what we don't do now we can do on Sunday. So I already told you about this crazy woman—"

"Monica."

"Right. So today she gets up at the Gender Studies meeting—"

"Oh, damn, wait a minute, Marcy, someone on the other line." I hit the flash button and it's Michael. He *knows* this is my time.

"Like I'm sorry, Rosie," he says when he hears the TV noise in the background. "I forgot."

I sigh. "It's OK, Michael. Bad enough that *I* have *TV Guide* imprinted on my brain. Can I call you back at eleven? Or is it important?"

"I should probably be in bed by then," he says. "I have an eight o'clock class tomorrow. It's OK, Rosarita. I just wanted to hear your voice."

"Oh, God, yes, my beautiful voice."

I had this boyfriend, Ira, just before Michael—*he* had a very, I suppose you would call it sardonic wit, and *he* used to laugh when I said things like that, if not actually say them himself. But Michael, far from making any jokes like that, doesn't even like to hear *me* make them.

"OK," he says after a second. "What about tomorrow?" Shit, now the bowl of ice cream I was saving for the program has started to melt.

"I don't know. I'm going to see that acupuncturist—you know, the one Isabel found for me." Isabel, of all people—she made some joke about Santeria, but she said this woman, Cassandra, had helped lots of people with "female problems." At this point, I'll try anything.

I can hear how much Michael wants to say, "Call me after that, then," but he doesn't. Sometimes, I have to tell you, I hate what he wants. Even if it's me.

TANYA: Black folks in the commercials, too. Ever since they figured out that we buy things. Or make white people *want* to buy things.

I know I'm supposed to be happy about this. All the opportunity. I keep a picture of Dorothy Dandridge over my bed. To remind me—all the things I can have that she couldn't. You know, Dorothy Dandridge? The Black movie star who wasn't one? She only ever got to make but four movies after she made *Carmen Jones,* and in all of them she played a slut. You can't even tell, really, how good an actress she was—only that she had potential.

Of course, she did get nominated for Best Actress—first Black person to do *that*. But where did it get her? At the end of the road, there she was, broke, drunk, and all alone. Just this bright and shining exception hung out there to make the rest of us think we had a chance.

The phone rings, and because it's still the commercials, I pick up. It's my best girlfriend, Verity, wanting to complain to me about her boyfriend.

I listen with half an ear, watching for that moment when the show comes back on. Then she says, "And what about you, Tanya? When are you going to get back out there?"

"Child, please. I got an audition tomorrow. Don't be telling *me* to think about men."

"Oh, like you can't do both. An audition for what?"

"*Hell Street*," I say, watching some mother trying to feed her kids yoghurt. That's a part they cast Black, but she's about six shades lighter than I am.

"Is that a cop show or a soap opera or what?"

"Cop show." Verity doesn't even watch television, but I can hear she is impressed.

"Still and all," she says, "you can do both. No reason why some man couldn't *help* you get rich and famous."

I think about going in there tomorrow, getting in that long line of Black actresses all up for *my* part. All of them just as sexy, just as good-looking, just as much the right type as I am. We might as well be the coffee the producers find in their cup.

"Think I'll just wait till I *get* to the top," I say. "Maybe then I'll have more to choose from."

MARIO: One of the nice things about watching with Joshua is the way he keeps himself so—separate. Not from me, of course. But from the whole television experience. He *likes* watching, of course—*Hell Street* is *his* show, not mine. But it doesn't swallow him up.

Of course, *he* says I tend to give him too much credit for having some kind of special perception, and he might be right. It's because both his parents are Holocaust survivors. They were both in Auschwitz, actually, though they didn't meet there, they met in the United States, after. And he says I tend to romanticize all that, which of course I shouldn't do. It's just that I've always wanted to know. And now more than ever. What it would take to survive *that*.

Anyway, the commercials. It's awful to admit that I like them so much, but I do. Why, exactly? Maybe I *like* being outside, longing to get in. Or being inside, all swallowed up. And either way, always wanting *more*.

ROSIE: Clegg and Trask start interrogating Lucas Rider, who of course is not cooperating at *all,* and then next thing you know, Clegg is beating him up. And I hate to tell you how much I am cheering him on, because come *on.* These are the *cops.* But OK. I do want Lucas to get beat up—to watch this show, I have to want that, and I do.

Then Trish comes by, and you can see her miserable face through the grille. She's still in love with him, isn't she? And you want her to get what she wants, but also, you don't want it. Because what she wants is *always* bad for her. Come *on,* Trish! How can you be so stupid?

No, not stupid. Wrong. Her whole *self* is wrong. And you watch and watch, wondering if she'll ever get broken down *enough.* Wondering who's going to come along and break her, so that finally, what she wants is *right.*

God, I *really* love her hair. That perfect golden red. Nobody is *born* with hair like that.

I take another spoonful of chocolate ice cream and watch Clegg smash Lucas into the filing cabinet. "No Civilian Complaint Review Board for *you,* Marcus," I say, waving my spoon. "Give him hell."

MARIO: When the policeman slams that guy up against the wall, I feel this shiver go right through Joshua, again, and then again. Of course, I don't know exactly what that shiver means. If it means that he's upset. Or if really, it's a thrill going through him.

The two policemen leave that guy slumped over the table, panting, exhausted. With a broken arm and a bleeding nose.

Then it's the other two policemen, Perez and Galliano. "Man, I hate these welfare hotels," says Perez. "Even the roaches have their paws out."

Galliano gives him a reproachful look. "You got to give people a chance, Ralph," he says. "You can't go pre-judging everybody like that."

"It ain't *pre*-judging," says Perez. "It's just plain old *judging.*"

He bangs with one fist, sideways, on the first door he comes to. It's painted this weird mustard color, poor and scummy-looking. "You want the rats to come scurrying out of their holes, you have to shake things up a little," he says to Galliano.

"All *right,* honey! Don't get your knickers in a twist. I'm coming," says a high feminine voice with what I guess they want us to think is an inner-city accent. And there is this tall, bedraggled drag queen in a robe and a torn black teddy, and of course, fishnet stockings.

"Well, well, well," says Perez. "Look what the cat forgot to drag out."

I know I shouldn't feel this way, because I *know* our community has to include everybody, and I even know people who do drag—well, nobody who does it all the time, or professionally, or anything like *that,* but people who like doing it more than I do, and certainly people who like *watching* it more than I do. But honestly? It makes me *extremely* uncomfortable.

"Mmmm, Detective," says the drag queen, giving Perez a long, sexy look. "I assume you're not here for the policeman's discount."

"We're here about all those bodies been turnin' up in your dumpster—" says Perez.

"Not *my* dumpster, Detective," says the drag queen.

"—and while you probably don't get too good a view of the alley on your *back*—"

"—hardly my favorite position," the drag queen says. "But then your poor wife probably hasn't seen a position other than the *missionary* since 1984 . . ."

Perez explodes, grabs her by the throat. "You leave my wife out of this, you pervert!"

"His wife left him two episodes ago," says Joshua, his eyes still on the screen. Perez slams the drag queen up against the door. I don't want it to be thrilling, but it is.

FLIP: "My God, Flip, how can you *watch* this?" says Warren, making yet another foray into the living room.

"Calm down, Warren, you've seen drag queens before."

"You know what I mean."

The camera closes in on the drag queen's face as Perez puts his face right up next to hers. Meaning to be threatening, of course. But then there is a very, shall we say, *significant* moment between the two of them. Perez breaks the moment by looking totally freaked out, but she looks absolutely triumphant. You go, girl. I'm with *you.*

"Just answer the question, bitch," Perez says. I burst out laughing.

"Come on, Warren," I say. "At least he got the gender right."

"That's how they see us? I think it's disgusting."

"It was probably some gay writer who slipped it in," I say. "But how do you suppose they got away with that *look?* My God."

"Is that the kind of part you want to get?"

"Honey, for union scale, I'd play that part in blackface," I say. "Puerto Rican accent and all."

Behind me, Warren is completely at a loss for words. Oh, shut up, Warren. You *have* a job in your field. Such as it is.

MARIO: Perez is still shaken up by what happened with the drag queen, so it's Galliano who bangs on the next door.

"Do you ever worry about getting beat up?" I want to ask Joshua. I always worry about it, not for real, not like I think it's actually going to happen. It's just always there.

The guy who answers the next door is clearly a junkie. He shuffles backwards into the room as the cops come in, shaking his head with that blissed-out look. Trembling. Emaciated.

"They don't absorb nutrition when they're at that point," Joshua says.

Well, at least they're not going to beat *him* up. Though I suppose they might shove him around a little.

"I *told* you," says the junkie, in this thin, reedy voice. "I ain't seen nothin'."

"You go out to make your connection, though, don't you?" says Galliano.

"No, man," the junkie says. He looks really old. "Ever since I got the AIDS, I cleaned up *my* act. I goes to a clinic!"

"Great," says Perez. "Keep him alive so's he can spread it around."

Joshua puts his arm around me, his fingers pressing into my arm. He is so scared I'll leave, no matter how much I promise him I won't.

"So when you do go out," Galliano is saying, "did you ever see this guy?" He shows the junkie a photograph, and the junkie looks absolutely terrified.

"You got to go now, man," he says, shaking wildly. "You got to go."

Perez shoves Galliano out of the way and grabs the old man by the collar. Joshua puts his hand on my thigh.

"What's the matter, scumbag, afraid you'll miss your next appointment at the *clinic?*" says Perez. "Or are you just concerned that we'll make a lot of noise taking you outta here, and all your neighbors can tell Mr. Psycho there in the photograph who they saw you leaving with, so that when you come back—"

"All right, all right," says the junkie. He starts talking, but he's trembling so hard, he can barely get the words out. Joshua's hand is moving up my leg. I catch my breath.

"Uh, thank you sir," says Galliano as Perez finally goes out into the hall. "We appreciate your cooperation."

The junkie gives Galliano a long look, sizing him up. Then he spits. We're both shaking, Joshua and I. I really want to promise him I won't leave. But to him, people leave when they die, too, and of course, I *can't* promise him about that.

"Better clean that up, sir," Galliano says. "On account of the germs." He's always polite—that's his trademark. He goes out, and the camera stays on the old man's face. Bitter, defeated. Joshua yanks me by the shoulders, almost banging my body into his, and we start kissing. Commercial.

ROSIE: "So what did happen last night?" I ask.

"When'd you stop watching?" Margarita wants to know. She's a secretary in Dowling, the Engineering building, one of our weakest areas, and when no one from that building showed up at today's noon meeting, I volunteered to take the newsletters over there myself. It's a key area if we strike.

Of course, if I *want* to know what's going on, I should ask Charles, or else the negotiating committee member who represents the building. That's why people are *on* that committee—because they're the real leaders. You go into an office and you look for the person who everybody listens to, everybody re-spects. Not necessarily the person that folks want to have lunch with, or even the person that they *like*. But the one who, whenever something comes down, people are always saying, "What does so-and-so think?"

But the committee member from Dowling is out sick today. And I just don't trust Charles. So of course I have to—

All right. I admit it. I am also here because I know Margarita watches *Hell Street*. I'm certainly not going to call *Flip*.

"I stopped watching about ten-thirty," I tell Margarita. "Let's see—Clegg and Trask had just beaten up Lucas Rider. And there was some big problem with Vernice's son." Then Patrice called, all upset, because her husband had fi-nally convinced her that she *should* get off the negotiating committee, and I had to spend the next half hour convincing her that she *shouldn't*. Then I had to throw out the ice cream, which had melted. And run to the bathroom, luckily in time to prevent an accident.

"Oooh, you missed the best part, Rosie," says Margarita. She's a stalwart supporter, but there's no one in her office to cover for her, so she can't get to lunchtime meetings. And she takes care of her daughter's little boy while her daughter goes to nursing school, so she can't get to after-work meetings, either.

"OK, so then Lucas just sits there in the cage, very upset, and Trish comes in—"

"No! To a suspect, alone?"

"I'm telling you. It's foolish, no? Because she's in love."

"Oh, well, love."

"Well?" says Margarita. "What am I saying? And she gives him this look, you know——" She shows me—bitter, disappointed, defiant. I nod. "Mmm-hmm," Margarita says. "And she says, 'We really could have been something, Lucas.' "

"Oh, please. He's only lied to her about a million times."

"Right? And he's looking away, like ashamed, you know, but then he looks right back, straight into her eyes, and he says, 'No, baby. That was all you. *You* could have been something. *I'm* no good.' "

"Oh," I say. "Well, at least he knows it."

"Right?" Margarita says again. "And she looks like she's going to cry, and she turns around and leaves on out of there, right? And he just sits there and does like this." She bangs her hand down onto her desk, hard.

"Wow. So what happened next?"

"So *then*," Margarita begins, but then her boss comes back from lunch, and you can tell she wants me out of there right away. God, how will she *ever* be ready to go on strike by April 12th? And who's going to tell me the rest of *Hell Street*?

TANYA: As soon as I walk in the door, the phone rings. I get it before the service can.

"So, how'd it go?" It's Flip.

"Oh, shit, it's you."

"Oh, Jesus, you thought it was them. I'm sorry, Tanya."

"No, it's OK. Not like they're going to call all this soon. I mean, I literally just walked in."

"So how *did* it go? *And,* I'm really sorry I didn't call you back last night. Warren and I got into this horrible fight right in the middle of the program, and by the time I looked at the clock, it was midnight."

"That's OK," I say. "I thought about calling you, but you know. If I can't play a welfare queen by *now* . . ."

"I don't know," Flip says, "did you remember to roll your eyes?"

"And snap my gum?"

"And neglect your kids?"

"And sit there with my blouse half open and my bosoms hanging out?"

"Well, I certainly wouldn't have told you to do *that*," Flip says. "I was more going to go for the eyes filling up with tears turning into hysterical sobs kind of thing."

"No, that's for the ones who are clean and sober. This was a junkie, re-member? I just had to say stuff like, 'Darnell!'—my son—"

"So I imagined."

" 'Darnell! Bring Momma back some twinkies from the store.' Excuse me, 'sto'. 'And don't you be eatin' none on the way like you did the *last* time.' "

"I realize I'm no expert," Flip says, "but shouldn't that be '*lass* time'?"

"I decided to play her like she *had* finished high school," I say, "but that when she graduated, she just couldn't get a job. And then when she got preg-nant—cause you know we *all* sleeps around—she figured she'd make more money having babies for the welfare than she'd *ever* get working in some Burger King. And with all that cash rolling in, child, you *know* she became a junkie. Of course, I only had three lines. But that *t* in *last*—that made it *all* come across."

Flip laughs. "Sounds like it went well."

I sit down on the couch and tug at my high-heeled boots. "Actually? It was pretty awful. There were like a million of us. Two of them even had my boots."

"Those purple suede ones?"

"Yeah. What are the odds, right? And you could hear everybody practicing. You'd say *hi* to someone, and they'd say *hi* in this normal tone, and then they'd be reading to themselves, and it'd be like, 'Dar-*nell!!!* Brang Mawmaw back some—' Well, you get the idea."

"I can imagine."

"Not even loud," I say. "All that practicing, under their breath. *I* couldn't tell us apart."

There is a tiny pause, like maybe he's wondering how much more comfort there is to give. Not like *he's* had a TV audition this whole past month.

"So how did you do," he says instead. "Finally?"

"Child, please," I say. "You know I was *good*. I just . . . I don't know."

"Well, take a guess," he says, which I appreciate.

"Like I was helping them far too much," I finally say. "Like they weren't paying me near enough to help them all *that* much."

"Mmmm," says Flip. "But you'd still rather play a maid than be one."

"I'd rather be Dorothy Dandridge."

"Who?"

"*Carmen Jones? Porgy and Bess? Island in the Sun?*" Well, shit, Flip, not like you haven't seen every *white* movie ever made before 1972.

"Dorothy Dandridge is your heroine?" says Flip.

"Child, no one who drinks and drugs herself to death is *my* heroine," I say. "But she's—I don't know."

"Your Peter O'Toole," Flip suggests.

"Are you going to tell me about your fight with Warren or not?" Flip takes a breath, and suddenly I say, "Wait, can you hold on just *one* minute? I'm wearing this leather skirt, and it's cutting into my waist something fierce."

Flip laughs and puts on his "gay" voice. "Ex*cuse* me, miss, but you *are* supposed to be on welfare. Do you expect the government to subsidize your suede?"

I laugh, too. "Well, you know. When Darnell is at the store, I does a little private business. You *know* I gots to look good for that."

"Go change," Flip says. "I'll hold on. Unless you want me to hang up. You know—so you can hear if they call you back."

"No, I don't care," I say. "There were still like a million girls waiting their turn when I left. They won't even see them all till this afternoon."

ROSIE: I always get lost in Dowling—it's a huge building with long confusing corridors, and all of the offices are so *isolated*. No wonder the workers here don't get the idea of a union—they might as well be stranded on a desert island with their boss.

Lissa and Vanessa—cute, huh?—are in the Mines Minerals Project, which for some odd reason doesn't have a faculty secretary, grade 8. So both Lissa and Vanessa are something called a staff secretary, grade 6. Actually, they both used to be grade 5s, but right after the last contract negotiation, we fought to get them upgraded. So I'm kind of annoyed that at least one of them didn't make it over today.

Of course, they do have the boss from hell. He used to be in a much nicer office, in the ivy-covered Admissions division. Then there was some kind of scandal—he's an alcoholic, *and* he sexually harassed one of the secretaries in his office, and that's just the kind of thing that before the union, she would have had no recourse for whatsoever. *With* the union, though, she could file a grievance, which for once they settled fast, because another contract was coming up, and in those days, that made them nervous. So instead of just giving her the next available job, they let *her* stay and moved *him*. Which was nice for the woman who grieved, but not so nice for Lissa and Vanessa.

Luckily, today, their boss is taking one of his longer lunches—a long *liquid* lunch, no doubt—and in his absence they're always very friendly. "Rosie!" says Lissa in her flat, perky Wisconsin accent. "Oh, you've got newsletters. That's nice."

"So, how was the meeting?" says Vanessa, in her brassy Bronx accent. "We're like, starving, here. We never hear nothin' about nothin'."

"Forget about it," I say, which is kind of a standing joke among the three of us. "It was a fabulous meeting, simply fabulous. But where were *you?*"

Vanessa gestures to a huge stack of papers on her desk. "Budget time," she says. "Plus BH——" the boss from hell "——is writing a grant."

"More like six grants," Lissa says.

"I'm telling you," agrees Vanessa. "If BH gets any one of these grants, he can give himself a raise. But *who's* reading his crappy handwriting? *Who's* making all his pidding little changes?"

"I don't like to complain," Lissa says. "But he's kind of, you know. Fussy."

"Fussy?" says Vanessa. "He's like, obsessed. He's like, 'Should I say *a* million dollars? Or *one* million dollars? Gee, I don't know, Vanessa. Like, why don't you do it one way, and then the other way, and then the first way, and just keep on doing it over and over and over and over, until I, like, make up my mind?' "

I laugh. Then I have a thought. "Hey, did either of you see *Hell Street* last night?" Not that I should take union time for *this*. Well, consider it a coffee break.

"I don't really like that show," says Lissa. "Too violent."

"Girl, you been in New York for seven years now, and you think *television* is violent?" says Vanessa. She turns to me. "What'd you miss?"

"I missed the whole part about Vernice's son," I say. "And the part after the methadone junkie."

"Oh, that was good," Vanessa says. "They go through the rest of the hotel, you know, showing that photograph around. Nobody wants to talk. Finally, they find a woman, she must've had, what? Eight kids. You know, they should have like a limit. They should say, OK, we'll pay for the first kid, maybe the second, even the third. Because OK, that's a family. But *eight* kids? Man, that's a *tribe.*"

Well, here's a nice ethical question. Argue with Vanessa about welfare? Or let her tell me about the rest of *Hell Street*?

Well, I'm on my coffee break, aren't I? "So what happened?"

"So Perez says he'll tell her social worker she's neglecting her kids," Vanessa says. "Which she should lose anyway, you ask me, because you *know* she shouldn't have all eight of them in that one little room. Plus she has a boyfriend—so the kids are *right there* when they're getting it on. But of course she *doesn't* want to lose her kids——"

"Well, she's a mom," says Lissa.

"Honey, she's getting *paid* by the child," says Vanessa. "So she tells Perez that Felipe has been dealing drugs out of the hotel, using people's kids to make deliveries—I didn't really buy that part. But you know. It's television. Sometimes they put stuff in just to make it exciting."

I really should explain that people on welfare *don't* have more babies for the money—that the average welfare family has 2.4 children, just like everybody else. But instead I say, "So why were all the bodies turning up in the dumpster?"

"Because Felipe was meeting his connections at the hotel. So when he had to knock people off, he left their bodies there. Which is why I wouldn't want one of those hotels in *my* neighborhood."

"Vanessa," I say, tentatively. "It doesn't actually happen that way. Like you said—it's television."

"Don't tell *me*," she says. "I *got* one of those homeless shelters across the street from me as it is. You want to explain to my kids why all those men are hanging out there? I don't even like them sitting on our front steps anymore."

I am trying to think what to say to this when the boss from hell returns and Lissa's and Vanessa's faces just *freeze*. So of course, I have to leave, just as though we *hadn't* won the right for workers to get union literature on the job. Anyway, it's about time to find another bathroom.

FLIP: "OK, I'm back," says Tanya.

I laugh. "What are you wearing?"

"Child, please," says Tanya. "If I *told* you, you couldn't handle it. What about Warren?" I try to think how to explain, and her voice changes. "Not like I want to push."

"Oh, push," I say. "We all know how hard it is to get me to talk about *my* life." I take another breath. "OK. So *Hell Street* was on, and Warren was hanging around like he always does, like he wants to watch but he doesn't want to watch."

"Like he wants to be with you, but he doesn't want to watch."

"What did *I* say?" I sit down on the couch. "Anyway, so he's basically hovering in the background, and the part with the drag queen came on, remember?"

" 'Just answer the question, bitch.' "

"Exactly. And Warren was offended, and then he was offended that I *wasn't* offended, and he asked me whether I would play that part."

"Not like you could play *that* part," Tanya says.

"I don't think the racial aspect was exactly Warren's concern," I say. "But, yeah, I told him I'd take any part I could get. Not that I have the clothes for a drag queen. But I suppose I could borrow your boots."

"The skirt, maybe," Tanya says. "You'd stretch the boots all out of shape."

"I'd buy you another pair with the residuals," I say. "Anyway, so *you* understand." OK, so she might not understand my little remark about blackface, but I'm hardly going to tell her about *that*. "But Warren was shocked and appalled. And OK, I admit it, I'm a whore, but I *would* take that part at this point, in order to get the chance to eventually do something better, and—"

"I know this part," Tanya says. "Remember? So what did *he* say?"

It makes me mad just to think of it. "He said, 'Methinks the lady doth protest too much.' Which apparently is *his* new favorite line."

"What?"

"Oh, well, it's a long story, but trust me. It was a very underhanded thing to say, especially in *that* argument. So of course, I got even madder, plus I was *supposed* to be watching so I could call you at eleven—"

"Don't blame this on me, white boy," says Tanya. "I don't need Warren mad at *me*."

"Well, anyway, I said, 'Warren, I'm trying to watch. Can we please talk about this after the program is over?' Or words to that effect."

Tanya laughs. "I'll *bet* to that effect," she says. "Like you would say *please* at that point."

Now here's a question. Just how much of the rest of this should I tell her? Because normally, trust me, I would simply *tell all*. Confession being good for the soul, etcetera. But this particular thing—well, it does feel more or less *private*.

"What?" says Tanya when the silence goes on too long. On the other hand, I *would* like her opinion, because I'm not exactly getting very far on this by myself. And God knows, *Warren's* no help.

"All right," I say, "he said, 'Normally, this is the place where I would simply walk out of the room, Flip, but we both agreed we weren't going to do that anymore, so I think you should stop watching and finish this out with me.' Which *was* kind of an agreement we had made, that neither of us would just— walk out. But I thought in this case, it was cheating. Because it meant he got to make me stop watching television. Which he had been trying, one way or another, to make me do all evening."

"You had been watching all evening?" Tanya says.

"You say that like it's a *bad* thing. Why can't he watch *with* me? Anyway, I thought that invoking this agreement was hitting below the belt. Which I told him. And *he* said my watching television instead of talking to him was just another form of walking out. And *I* said, 'God, Warren, you don't even *like* to fight, so why are you all of a sudden so eager to do it that you can't even wait until eleven o'clock?' It kind of went on like that for a couple of hours."

"Wow," Tanya says. "Then what happened?"

"Finally I said, 'Warren. Fuck. Just come over here and watch with me.' "

Tanya bursts out laughing. "No!"

"Yes," I say, feeling embarrassed, actually. "Well, anyway, so, he *did* come over. And he watched with me. For a few minutes anyway." Sitting with me on the couch where I am sitting now. His arms around me, finally. I don't suppose either of us was watching anything at that point. I felt like crying. Like I had already lost something by that point, something I would never get back.

"If you wanted me to watch with you, why didn't you just *ask* me?" he said finally.

"I did ask you."

"I don't remember it that way."

I don't know, maybe I didn't. This is the point where I always feel so defeated.

"So it all worked out," Tanya says.

"I suppose," I say. "More or less."

Later, after she and I hang up, I remember that I didn't even ask her what happened on the rest of *Hell Street*. I try to think who I know besides Rosie who watches this show, and finally I think of Mario.

"Paradise Holidays," he says when he picks up the phone.

"Hey, Mario, did you watch *Hell Street* last night? I missed the part after the drag queen."

"Us, too, actually," Mario says. "She was great, though, huh?"

"Well, *I* thought so," I say. "Apparently that's a minority opinion in *some* circles."

Mario considers this. "Maybe I wouldn't have liked it so much if I had *been* a drag queen," he admits. "Which of course is no excuse for not being sensitive to that point of view. Maybe I should rethink the entire show from that perspective."

"That's OK," I say. "Because then you'd also have to consider the actor who played that part. And you know *he* was grateful."

"But he's just one person," Mario says earnestly. "Millions of people watch the show. Shouldn't their needs take priority?"

"Not till they can afford to sponsor a show of their own," I say. "And even then, only if they're good to their actors."

ROSIE: "Breathe," Cassandra says. "Breathe deep."

I take a deep breath and try to feel it penetrating all the way down into the soles of my feet, as Cassandra is suggesting. "Again," she says. My eyes are closed and her voice seems very far away. I have to tell you, it's a little hard to have confidence in an acupuncturist who is actually named *Cassandra*. It isn't even her real name—she chose it when she decided to become a healer, or when she was *chosen* to become a healer, as she explained. Of course, Cassandra *was* always right—the one in the Greek myth, I mean. It was just that no one ever believed her.

"Is that why you picked *that* name?" I asked when she explained all this to me. "You know, like a warning? So that people *would* believe you?"

Cassandra widened her eyes and shrugged. "It was the name that was right for me." I don't know. I do like her, I guess. She gave me a big questionnaire to fill out, which seemed like a fairly standard medical history, and then she looked at my tongue, which was weird, and felt my pulse for a long time, listening to *something,* and then she said, "All right. I can work with you. Can you work with me?"

"I don't know," I said, completely taken aback. "What exactly is involved?"

Once again, she shrugged. She's extremely dramatic-looking—a huge mass of dark, wavy hair, pulled back off her face with a leather clip; olive skin. (I assume, from Isabel's reference to Santeria, that she's Afro-Caribbean, otherwise, I might have thought Greek, from the "Cassandra," I guess.) And her office is completely nondescript: some Chinese music playing over the sound system and a couple of acupuncture charts on the walls are the only indication that I'm not at a regular doctor's or dentist's or somewhere normal.

To her credit, she does try to answer all my questions, even the ones she clearly doesn't see why I—or anybody—would want to ask. "What's involved," she says slowly, in her thick, husky voice, "is being open to my suggestions while being honest about your own reactions. Do you think you can do that?"

I think she can't possibly *want* me to do that. But I nod.

She continues to study me closely. "Then let's start with some breathing," she says. "I think that would help you."

"I thought you did acupuncture."

"We'll get to that. Are you in a rush? I'm not in a rush."

Now it's my turn to shrug.

"This is precisely the problem," she says. "You want to fix things. But you have to let your body fix itself."

"But it *can* be fixed?" I say. Well, don't I sound desperate all of a sudden.

"Everything can be fixed," she says. "Don't you think your body would rather be healthy?"

"I don't know," I hear myself saying. "If it wants to be healthy, then why am I so sick?"

She narrows her eyes at me. "*Would* you rather be sick, Rosie? I'm sure your body *does* have the energy to heal itself. But maybe being sick is just what you need right now. What do you really want?"

I am completely at a loss. I don't know why. It seems like a fairly simple question.

"You mean, in my life?" I say finally. "Or from you? Or—"

Neither her face nor her voice changes. "What do you really want?" she says again.

"Well, I *do* want to get well. I mean, I don't want to be bleeding all the time. It's up to ten days, now, instead of five, and a couple of those days are *really* heavy. And I've been getting dizzy from the loss of blood, although I wonder if—"

"What do you really want?" she says for the third time.

And all of a sudden I say, "I want to know what happened on *Hell Street*. I missed the last half of the program because people just couldn't stop calling me, and I *did* find out some of it but not all of it, and I can't tell you, Cassandra, it's this horrible feeling, missing that show. Like something is lost and I'll never get it back. Why do you think that is?"

"Which story line?" she says.

"What? Oh. The one with Vernice."

"I believe the problem was that the teachers had found her son smoking a joint with two of his classmates," Cassandra says. "And he assures his mother that he didn't enjoy the marijuana anyway, and he understands that it won't help him to confront his life. And his mother is extremely relieved, and then they cry together."

I cannot tell you the extraordinary relief I feel when she gives me this. I don't even remember to say thank you, but maybe that doesn't mean so much to her, because she just says, "All right, now, close your eyes. Take a deep breath. Again."

BODIES

FLIP: Look, it's not like I don't think things with Warren have gotten better. They're like, *enormously* better. It's just that sometimes—

The other night, for example—the night *before* our infamous television fight—I was deep asleep, and I felt him shaking my shoulder. I wake up slowly, struggling. Peering through the darkness, I see his face, frightened and ashamed. Now that I'm awake, his urgency loses its edge, but it's still there.

"I had a bad dream," he says in a low voice. "And I didn't—I didn't—"

Now, you figure it out, because I promise you that this is just the kind of thing I would have prayed for all those months he couldn't fall asleep if even our fingertips were touching. And of *course* I felt for him, and, you know, for *Warren* to do this—it kind of took my breath away. So I brush the damp hair off his forehead, pull the sheets smooth as he crawls on top of me, rub the back of his neck. He sort of burrows into me, still frantic, still escaping something, and I hold him as hard as I can, and it's even arousing, a little, his weight on me, the force of what he wants, but—how can I explain this? It's as if he's going *past* me. And what I don't want to admit is that this is what he said *I* used to do, all those months. Treating him like a pillow.

And then the next morning, I wake up to him kissing my face, and this clearly *is* him and me, this is the best of us together. His tongue is in the hollow of my neck, rough and delicate, and I can feel him *calling* me— "Oh, Warren, yes. *There*. Yes, *there*. Don't let go." His tongue over my nipples, his mouth running down the dip in the center of my chest, my skin buzzing beneath his hands— "Yes. *Yes*. Don't let go." And finally he takes my cock in his mouth, warm and wet, and he's pulling his tongue along the bottom, he's drawing me on, he's sucking me into him, and I am going with him, I am inside him, I am . . . I am . . . I am . . . I'm dissolving, I'm melting, and he's covering me with his body, and our bodies know each other so well by this point. And my body just *sings*.

It's not that I *don't* want this. I do. It's just that he wants so much.

ROSIE: "Keep breathing," Cassandra is saying. Her voice is like velvet. "Feel your breath feeding every single cell in your body. Your separate body in its separate skin."

My eyes fly open. "No," I say, before I even know I am talking. "No, no, no, no, no. Not separate, *not* separate—that's what makes people sick!"

Cassandra looks just as bored—or just as interested—as before. "Here you are," she says. "Alone in my office. Who else is here?"

"Everybody. My parents—I mean, it's their body, too, isn't it? They made it. And—I don't know. The men I've made love to. Or maybe it's just their body, *our* body, when we *are* making love, I don't know, but I'm not separate *then*. And—" I don't know how to explain it, the way I feel a part of things. At a demonstration, at a meeting, even at Midnight Mass—that sense of sharing a body. "When I'm on the subway," I say desperately. "And I'm feeling miserable or sick or in love with the wrong person. And I know that in the car ahead of me and the car behind me and the car two cars down everybody else is having exactly the same problem, or their version of it—" I look at her calm, blank face, and I can't *believe* she doesn't understand me.

Finally, she shakes her head. "You're born into your own body," she says. "You die in that body, too. And in between, if you don't take care of that body, you get sick."

I look back at her, helpless, defeated. "You *are* sick, aren't you?" she says. "Why do you think that is?"

You know what I remember? The first morning I spent with Michael. We had spent the night at my place, a hot August night. Months and months he'd been pursuing me, and finally, he had me. Our bodies inside one body. The two of us making something new. Something *else*.

And then the next morning we went to this little coffee shop down the block. Dingy tin plating up all around the counter, and these *narrow* little booths with ripped brown vinyl, and the most delicious food in the world, diner omelettes and watery coffee and those crusty hash browns, which you never get anywhere *except* a diner. We were both ravenous. And satisfied.

"So, Rosarita," Michael said, and I was so full of delight that every sound of his voice, every breath of air on my bare arms, every smell of burnt toast and bacon only thrilled me more. "So, Rosarita, what do you want to do today?" And I had to stop myself from saying, "You mean there's *more?*"

"God, Michael, I'm sorry," I say instead. "I'm afraid this is it—I've got a noon meeting downtown."

"But it's Saturday."

"You don't have to tell *me*. If I had a nickel for every weekend meeting I've had to go to, I'd be rich enough to *quit* my job."

"No rest for the class-conscious," Michael says, and I laugh in astonishment. "You shouldn't sound so surprised, Rosie," he says, surprising me more. "I like learned *some* things, listening to you."

"Oh, well, if I taught you class-consciousness, then all has not been in vain."

"Not in vain, no," Michael says, in that soft, slippery voice, which catches me in the pit of the stomach.

"Say something fast, Michael," I hear myself saying, as he reaches under the table and puts his hand on my knee. I expect it to be sweet and seductive, like his voice, but it's just—gentle. Tender. "Start talking *now*," I say. "Because otherwise I'm going to—I mean, it's not a meeting I can miss."

"You talk, Rosarita," he says, reaching across the table to brush the hair back from my face. He leaves that other hand there on my knee, and I can't take my eyes off him. "Tell me about this meeting. What's it about?"

"The paralegals at Schwartz O'Malley—" I take a deep breath.

"Keep going," he says.

"It's that classic thing," I say, "where they want them to take a two-tier contract, you know, a fairly decent raise for the ones that are there now, but a much, *much* lower starting salary for everyone that comes in after September 1st. Or whenever we actually ratify the contract. Not that we're going to, not *that* contract. I mean, my God, do they actually think we're *that* stupid?"

"Oh, you know," Michael says. "People always underestimate you."

"Mmmm," I say ruefully. "I suppose they do."

And then he surprises me once more. Because he says, "No, Rosie, I didn't mean *you* underestimating *me*. I meant, people who like have power. I mean, that's the big advantage you have on the other side, right? That they think— they always think—you're less than you really are?"

I can't help it. I sighed then, and I sighed now, sitting here in Cassandra's nondescript office. Both times amazed, both times wondering, *Is this mine, is this really mine?* Me and my separate body—it didn't seem possible.

ELINOR: Idris is coming over to work on the script. There's music playing, and I'm making brownies—an extremely complicated recipe requiring five different kinds of chocolate, along with an enormous amount of concentration and precision, which I welcome. The way I welcome the work that Idris and I are about to do together—a thick, delicious piece of work.

Whenever she comes over, it's like music. That way that music flows right through you, making you feel—something else. Confusing and delicious.

It's so odd. I keep wondering, *is* it really possible? Because honestly, I always thought my body belonged up there on stage. Whereas now, I sit in rehearsal hall while the actors work in front of me, and I watch their bodies move and grow and change because of what *I* say, and I just marvel. I don't recognize myself, but I don't mind.

So I'm smelling the chocolate, soaking in the music, waiting for Idris, and I never thought I could be this happy. *You can, though,* my body says, and maybe I should believe it.

WARREN: A few weeks after Flip and I got back together, I woke as he was getting into bed. "No, I'm up," I say, as he slips under the covers very, very quietly. "How was rehearsal?"

"Have you been lying here awake all this time?"

I turn over to face him. We'd been back together less than a month, at that point, and he'd spent every single night in this bed, except for the few nights we went to our old place. But the bed was never full of him. It was full of all those nights without him.

"No, I was asleep. Tell me how it was." He is studying me in the dark. "If you want to," I add.

He reaches for the bedside lamp. "No," I say helplessly. "Come here." And when he is filling up my arms again, I say, "I'm sorry, Flip. For . . ." My voice trails off. We haven't even talked about why we broke up or how things will be different now. But Flip shakes his head.

"Well, I'm sorry, too," he says. "But really, Warren, so what?" He pushes himself up on one elbow so that he's looking at me. "I mean, do you even care about—you know. All the things that happened. Does it still matter?"

"No," I say slowly, as the bed fills with his warmth, his heat, his smell. "No, I suppose not."

"Well?" says Flip. "Me, too. Or do I mean, me neither? Anyway, so what?"

But that can't be right. Everything he did to me, everything I did to him— is it all just simply *gone?*

I see him suddenly with such a shock of recognition—*Flip,* here before me in the dark. I never thought I'd have that view, *this* view, ever again. I reach for him, and then he reaches for me, and I feel his skin against my skin, his wiry hair against my chest, his two hands gripping my ass. Where *did* everything go? So much of it I didn't like, but that doesn't mean I want to lose it.

And then I feel the weight of it, inside him, inside me, so that when our tongues meet, our thighs, our chests, finally it is our histories that touch. We'll never get away from it, I think. Whenever we touch—all that weight. I'd have to erase my body to get rid of it. And even then, his body would still be here.

ROSIE: Cassandra comes in to take the needles out, then leaves me alone to get dressed. She comes back in with some plastic bottles of pills, which turn out to be herbs, and a xeroxed sheet of paper that includes information on diet.

"Basically," she says, "you want to avoid fat, sugar, alcohol, and caffeine. Take these—the instructions are on the bottles. Make a weekly appointment with the receptionist. Then we'll see." She's about to leave when I stop her.

"What about chocolate?"

She turns back, unsmiling as usual. "Fat, sugar, caffeine. Not a good idea."

I don't exactly want to tell her that chocolate ice cream sometimes seems like the one reliable pleasure in my life, because I'm perfectly well aware of how that makes me sound. But it's true.

"Don't you think," I say finally, "that if you enjoy something, then it's good for you? I mean, that *something* about it does you good?"

"*Good* is a slippery word," she says. "All I know is what might stop your bleeding and address your tumors." I shiver. I'm not used to calling them *that*. "In fact," she continues, "often when people are healing, they do feel worse. Your cells have grown used to absorbing toxins. Then, in a healing environment, your body tries to release them. Which can initially make you feel—not so good."

"So getting better makes you sick." *There's* a cheerful thought.

"If you want to look at it that way. After all, at this point, the disease *is* you. I might say, for example, that toxins are stored in the cell. But I might equally well say that they are now *part* of the cell. So for the cell to lose a part of itself—for you to lose a part of *yourself* . . . That's always painful."

But you think I *will* get well? I want to ask her. Stop the bleeding, eliminate the fibroids—OK, the *tumors*? So I can go back to eating ice cream and to—well, to whatever else there is to go back to.

WARREN: The day after Flip and I have that fight about television he actually does come home early enough to eat dinner with Juliet and me. And after dinner he plays with her, some made-up game they invent together. I hear them whispering and laughing in her room while I wash the dishes.

"Uncle Warren," says Juliet, when I come in to tell her it's time for bed, "you know what I want? I want one of those Tamagochi cats, you know, like Shannon had?"

"Those virtual pets?"

"They're just like a *real* cat, Uncle Warren. And I want one, I want one a *lot*. Did you know, if you don't take care of them right, then they *die*? But Uncle Flip said he'd help me take care of it."

"Really?" I say. "But what Uncle Flip probably doesn't know, because he didn't talk to Dan and Betsy about those cats when we were in Pittsburgh and I did, is that they really are a *lot* of work, Juliet."

"Oh, come on, Warren," says Flip, from the corner of the room where he and Juliet have constructed some kind of village with her dolls and beanbag animals, along with some magazines and vases—fairly fragile vases, actually—from the living room. "It's an electronic cat—how much trouble could it be?"

"According to Dan and Betsy—" I say, and then I stop myself. "You know what, Juliet? Let's talk about this when it's not so close to bedtime."

Juliet looks stubbornly from Flip to me. "Uncle Flip *said* he'd help me take care of it," she says, lifting her chin. "Do you think he's a *liar?*"

"Yes, Warren," Flip says, teasingly. "Do you think I'm a liar?"

"I think Uncle Flip probably would help you on the nights he's here," I say. "But remember, he's gone almost every single night. So we would still have to figure out what to do on the nights he's *not* here."

Flip stands up. "Well, I guess that tells *me,*" he says. "Goodnight, Juliet. I'll see you in the morning, OK?" He kisses Juliet goodnight, and she glares at me as he goes out. A minute later, I hear the television go on.

When I've finished putting Juliet to bed, I stand for a minute in the living room doorway, waiting until the commercials start. "What was all that about?" I say finally.

Flip twists his head around. "So do I still have to give you a formal invitation to come in here and actually *talk* to me?"

Slowly I start to go over to where he is lying stretched out on the couch. My body knows what to do—or at least, it knows what it wants. Is that a look of triumph making his lips twitch?

Just then, the phone rings. Flip holds out the receiver.

"It's for you," he says. "Ian."

The commercials have come to an end, and he's already watching again. "I'll take it in the kitchen," I say.

"So, Warren, how's life treating you and that beautiful niece of yours?" Ian says. Although we had talked at Mario's dinner party about him spending time with Juliet and me, what actually happened was that he and Simon came over for dinner one night in December, and although Ian did *meet* Juliet, it was really more an evening for the four of us than anything else.

"My main concern is making sure that everything is set for school next week," I say.

"Juliet's at Parkston, isn't she?" Ian says, and I'm touched that he remembers. "I've heard that's a good place."

"They pride themselves on being very individualized," I say. "A special learning plan for every child." I must admit, Juliet seems less than thrilled about going back there, though that's probably normal—don't most children feel that way about school? And I suppose it's also normal that she would keep telling me how much she wants to go to school with Sara, who is after all her best friend.

"Ah, the joys of school," Ian says. "Which was *your* favorite part when you were a boy? Mine was games, I think. So character-building, being the last chosen for every team. Such *good* preparation for later life."

I laugh. "Well, you're hardly the last chosen for *anything* these days, are you? My impression is that you're quite in demand."

"That sounds like an extremely biased impression."

You know, I haven't heard Flip hang up the phone. Although I can't believe he'd actually listen in on a conversation.

"No, I'm never biased, actually," I say, lowering my voice all the same. Which of course makes the whole call so much more—well, *private*.

"Ah," says Ian again. "So when you say I'm in demand, you're . . ."

". . . simply stating a fact."

"Well, this is fascinating," Ian says.

To me, too, actually. I must admit, it's an enormous relief to know I can still do this. Particularly with someone as—well. With someone like Ian.

"And how are *you?*" I say. "And Simon, of course."

"Of course," says Ian. "I am the same as always. And Simon—well, Simon is rather worried, actually."

"Oh? Why?"

Ian laughs. "Not what you might think. He's been hearing rumors about a strike at Olympia. More than simply rumors, in that they've asked him to cir- culate a petition among the other work-study students, promising to support the toiling masses if they finally do take up arms against the University, which in principle, of course, Simon is all for. In practice, however, he's afraid of los- ing his grant. Or his fellowship, or whatever it's called here. I'm surprised you *haven't* heard about it, Warren, considering that Flip's sister seems to be in charge of said toiling masses."

"No. I didn't know she had anything to do with Olympia."

"Really?" Ian says. "I had the impression that she and her brother were practically joined at the hip. And of course, that he told *you* everything."

I laugh. "We don't exactly tell each other *everything*."

"Really?" says Ian again. "I must have got the wrong impression."

"Somewhat wrong, perhaps." I must simply not have noticed when Flip hung up. "Although I do seem to hear everything there *is* to hear about Flip and his sister. But they had a huge falling out over Christmas, so neither one of us has heard much from her lately."

"I see," says Ian. "But enough about Simon. And Flip. When shall *we* see each other again?"

"You mean with Juliet?" I say. Then I wish I could take back those words, because whether he did or didn't mean with Juliet, it's still an incredibly awk- ward thing for me to have said, isn't it? Or do I mean, incredibly revealing?

But either Ian doesn't notice any awkwardness, or else he's more tactful than I tend to give him credit for. "Of course, with Juliet," he says easily. "I must say, Warren, it's extremely nice of you to share her with me."

"Not at all," I say. "While *I* still have her, anyway." I would love to go on and tell him all about what happened tonight. I'd love to ask him, What *do* you do about the toys they want that you don't want them to have? How do you ever make up for all the things they miss?

However, if I were to have this conversation with Ian, it wouldn't be here on the phone with Flip in the other room. Bad enough that I said what I did about him and Rosie.

"Flip has rehearsal all Saturday afternoon," I say instead. "Why don't we do something then? If it's nice, what Juliet likes is to go to Washington Square Park." I don't know if she's always liked to do the same thing over and over, or if that's simply a reaction to everything she's been through.

"Saturday would be perfect," Ian says. "What time shall I come by?"

Flip's rehearsal is at one, which means he'll have to leave by twelve, twelve-fifteen at the latest. "Come at twelve-thirty," I say. "We can have an early lunch and then go do something."

"*Something*," Ian repeats. "I'll be looking forward to it."

"So will I." After a pause, I say, "So will Juliet."

Ian laughs. "Well, I'm glad it's unanimous." I stand there in the kitchen, my hand still on the phone, and slowly, a kind of glow creeps over me. That lovely feeling of being overcome.

And then do you know what's really interesting? What I really want to do, with all this feeling, is to go into the living room and be with Flip. I mean— now, I can.

Of course, he's still stretched out on the couch, watching television. So this time, I do sit down beside him. He leans back against me, the way he did the other night, and starts to stroke my arm, a gesture that for some reason I have always found incredibly comforting. "OK," he says softly, when the commercials start again. "We can talk now."

I'm not sure what to say. "Juliet said I hurt your feelings."

Flip laughs. "Gee, Warren," he says, "and I thought by now there wouldn't be any—what should I call it?—any *mystery* left in our relationship. Thank heavens I still baffle you to the point where you need *Juliet* to explain me to you."

"So I *did* hurt your feelings."

He sighs. "I don't know. Whatever I do with her, you want to say I'm doing it wrong."

"Not *wrong*. It's that you're never here."

"I'm here now."

"Only until rehearsals start. Then you really will be gone."

"Oh, I might come back *once* in a while," Flip says. "Just to make sure you're sufficiently miserable without me." He turns around and kisses me—a very sweet kiss. "Let's go to bed," he whispers. "Since we *don't* actually want Juliet to find us *in flagrante* on the couch. Which I hope proves to you, Warren, that I can be just as *responsible* a parent as you can."

ELINOR: Idris and I are sitting in the kitchen, finishing our work. The air is warm and chocolatey, with little gusts of snowy air sneaking through the drafty windows. We've planned rehearsals for the next few weeks, we've written an outline for the script that Idris will create. And once again I have the feeling of wandering out into completely unmarked territory.

"Are we done?" Idris says, bouncing up out of her chair. "Because I want some more of those brownies. And wait, wait, wait—" She goes running off into the hallway, where she left her backpack. Around us, the music rises— Van Morrison singing "Bright Side of the Road." His voice overflows with yearning and—sweetness.

"All right," says Idris, coming back in. "Here." She hands me a package.

"No. You shouldn't have. Why?" I love the wrapping—deep, shiny red, with a cluster of dark green leaves and red holly berries in the corner.

She grins at me. "Just because." Her smile gets sweeter. "I *could* say, because you made me brownies. Or because I am *so* glad to be here and not spending the rest of the evening with Pauli." Her ex-girlfriend, with whom she had dinner tonight. "But maybe we should stick to, just because."

"Brownies first," I say quickly. "So you have something to eat while you *watch* me open it."

"Well, aren't you the one who thinks of everything?" says Idris. "This time, I want mine with milk." I hold the knife over the pan to show her the size brownie I intend to cut. She gestures, *bigger, bigger, bigger,* until finally I push the pan and knife in her direction. Then she cuts herself a tiny little sliver and eats it, licking her fingers. This is one of those times I can't take my eyes off her.

"Do you really think it's all going to be all right?" I say abruptly. "With the group, I mean. Because it's so wonderful whenever things just—"

"Take off."

"Yes. There is *something* going on, isn't there? It's not just my imagination?"

"But?"

"Oh, *but* everything else," I say. "When it *doesn't* take off, isn't it just too dreadful for words? Theater games, and self-indulgence, and long pointless improvisations that don't *go* anywhere. I don't want to put my name on *that*."

"Well, the final performance won't be that way," Idris points out, cutting herself another sliver of brownie. "You seem to forget that I *am* writing us a script."

"All right, you tell me. Why does it happen that I'm so worried about this and *you're* not at all concerned?"

"Well, if you ask *me*," Idris says, "this is all just your fancy way of avoiding the moment when you finally get to open my present."

I can actually feel myself blushing. Which to my surprise makes me feel triumphant. Because she has me cornered? Because she *wants* me cornered?

I open the flimsy cardboard box and pull out—a robe. A brilliant red robe of some shiny, patterned material, with a long, fringed sash to tie around the middle.

"Oh, my God," I say, completely overcome. "Oh, Idris. It's beautiful. It's too much."

"So," says Idris, not taking her eyes off *me*, "do I get to see you try it on?"

She takes one of my hands, and I let her. She leans forward across the table to kiss me, and I lean forward to kiss her, too. Thinking that I won't know how. Finding that I do.

I could be anything, I think. I *could*. You think your body just *is* a certain way, and that's the way it will always be. But why couldn't I be—something else?

WARREN: After we've finished making love, Flip says drowsily, "Warren?"

"Hmmm?"

"Don't go to sleep yet. Stay up and talk to me."

No, I'm exhausted, I want to say. Even if six-thirty weren't Juliet's usual waking time, she and I both have to be up by then to get her to school by eight. But I manage to say, "About what?"

"Well, let's see," Flip says. "We could talk about, oh, say, where we're going to live. I mean, *I* always thought that was included in the idea of getting married, but maybe I was wrong." He bends down and sings insistently into my ear. *"All I want is a room, in Bloom-sbury . . . Just a dear little room, for two, or three . . .* That's from a musical called *The Boyfriend*, Warren, in case you haven't gotten the hint."

I sigh. "All right, Flip. I'm really torn. I do prefer the other apartment, except for Juliet. And if she *is* leaving in June . . . But then I keep thinking. Maybe after Madeleine gets better. Maybe there would be some way Juliet could still live here, part of the time. I don't know. I don't even know if she'd want to."

"Oh, I think she'd want to," Flip says, and I'm surprised at the conviction in his voice. "She adores you, Warren, anyone can see that."

"Really? I don't see it."

"Well, you never see when anyone adores you," Flip says. "Who can go by *you?*"

I can't help remembering that *overcome* moment after the phone call from Ian. But this is hardly the moment to think of that.

"It's not just that, though," Flip is saying. "She *counts* on you. In this very deep way. You're like her root."

"At least until Madeleine gets better."

Flip is quiet for longer than I would have expected. Then he says, "Look, Warren, I realize she's your sister, and I know you're trying really hard to—to respect her relationship to Juliet, all right? But from Juliet's point of view—I mean, Madeleine's the one who got sick. She's the one who *kept* getting sick. She's the one who left."

"But Juliet is dying to go back to her."

"Oh, sure," Flip says. "I know that. But you're the one who *didn't* leave."

I am so taken aback by this view of me that I have no idea what to say. After a moment, Flip says uncertainly, "Are you upset?"

"Just—surprised."

"Well, anyway," Flip is saying, in a shaky voice, "that's *why* it's so important to me, Warren, to . . ." His voice trails off.

"What?"

"Well, I can't exactly stop going to rehearsals, can I?" he says. "And if I *do* get work out of town, not that *that's* happened in a while, or any kind of work at all, really. I mean, if it keeps up like this, I'll be riding a bicycle again by next month. But I *am* in Tiger's Eye, and that *does* meet evenings and weekends, and I do have—you know. A life. I can't just stop having it."

He sounds so distressed, I can't bear it. I pull him roughly down on top of me. I know I'm being unfair, but I don't care. I just want this to stop.

Flip lies there, his head on my chest, for what seems like a long time. Even I have to see that this isn't *just* like all those other times, when he came home so unhappy. For one thing, he isn't saying anything.

"Sing something else," I say impulsively. "I love hearing you sing."

"Oh, right," Flip says. "Me and my beautiful voice."

"Don't say that," I say. "It *is* beautiful."

He is quiet for a long moment. "All right," he says finally. "I had to learn this song once, when I was in *Spoon River Anthology*. Though why they had *me* sing it . . ." He takes a breath and starts to sing, this haunting wistful melody, full of longing, and—I don't know. Sweetness.

> *There is a ship, and she sails the sea,*
> *She's loaded deep as deep can be,*
> *But not as deep as the love I'm in,*
> *I know not if I sink or swim.*
>
> *The water is wide, I cannot get over,*
> *Neither have I the wings to fly.*
> *Give me a boat that can carry two,*
> *And both shall row, my love and I.*

He stops singing and looks at me. "My God, Warren," he says. "Are you *crying*? You never cry."

I pull him down to where I can whisper in his ear. "If I weren't already completely, totally, madly in love with you, Flip, hearing you sing that song would do it." And since I've never said anything even remotely like that to him before, maybe it does make him feel better.

TANYA: Ever since I did that piece for Tiger's Eye—you know, the one with the singing—I keep remembering all that time before college. When I *did* sing in the choir.

I got solos, too. Filling my lungs with air. Letting my voice fly *out*. All those voices, and the organ, and everybody's hands clapping so loud you couldn't even think. And my voice, lifted up on top of all that sound.

It's funny to remember it now. Because what I *liked* was being invisible. I didn't *want* anybody looking at me. I just wanted them to hear my voice.

ROSIE: "Tell me something I don't know about you," Michael is whispering in my ear. We are lying in his double bed with the ugly yellow headboard, with the clean, cool white sheets and ordinary blue blanket. Of *course* I came here straight from Cassandra's. Where else would I go? As soon as I walk in the door, we get into bed together, thirsty for being naked, for that feeling of our skin, open and whole together.

"Tell me something that nobody else knows, only me."

"Oh, Michael," I say without thinking. "I'm really scared. She called them *tumors.* How could I have these tumors that are *part* of me? What did I do?"

"You didn't do anything, Rosarita," he says, softly, sweetly, even. "Some things just happen. You'll go to this person, and she'll do her thing, and then they'll be gone."

"No, Michael. She said they wouldn't. She said, if I didn't eat differently, and work differently, and think differently—" I press my face against his shoulder.

He brushes back my hair. "You think these—whatever you want to call them—"

"Fibroids," I say firmly.

"Fibroids. You think these fibroids are, like, your *fault,* Rosie?"

"I don't know," I say. "I don't know what I think anymore. You want to know something no one else knows, Michael? I don't recognize myself."

"You don't seem so different to me."

"I have to keep *stopping.* Wondering if I'm going to have an *accident,* for God's sake. And I'm so tired all the time, and I keep—"

"Maybe you just need to rest more."

"I don't *want* to rest more. That's what I mean. *I* don't have to rest."

"And now you do." He pulls my face away from his shoulder and kisses me very gently on the lips. *Yes,* I think fiercely, *this,* and I try to kiss him back.

He's climbing on top of me, which usually I like—which usually I *love,* his warmth, his weight. But tonight, it's too much. I slide out from under him. "I'm sorry, Michael," I say. "This is what I mean. Nothing feels the same." I start to cry.

ELINOR: Idris runs her fingertips over my body, so lightly she's barely touching me. The hairs on my skin rise to meet her, the blood under my skin leaps to meet her hand. My whole body reaches for her, not moving, but shivering.

It's amazing to want somebody this much. She draws it out, longer and longer, brushing me with her fingertips, running her lips over my skin—and then suddenly her hands and her mouth and her body are all over me, full, hard, complete. And when she puts her mouth between my legs—her lips warm against me, her tongue hard inside me—I feel as if my body will burst and burst and *burst,* until we both drown in this delicious flood.

ROSIE: I don't actually mind crying—in fact, I kind of like it. But I can tell it bothers Michael—well, who can blame him?—so I make an effort.

"Michael? Do you think I could have a Kleenex or something?"

He gets out of bed and I watch his naked body going into the bathroom. He's so beautiful. I really like to look at him—is that wrong? Most of the men I've been with, honestly, it's the last thing I'd notice. But I feel like I just stare at Michael all the time.

He stands by the bed, holding out some toilet paper. "Do you want to eat now?" he says while I blow my nose. "I made dinner."

Am I hungry? I haven't eaten yet, and it's almost ten o'clock. But I don't seem to want anything there, either.

"No," I say. "Get back into bed." He looks so disappointed. "Tell me something about *you,* Michael," I say suddenly. "That nobody knows but me."

He looks surprised. And—angry? But it can't be that.

Still standing naked by the bed, he reaches out a hand to stroke my hair. I do have nice hair, don't I? Not when I'm dressed—then it's just a mess and nothing I can do with it, but when I'm naked or in a nightgown, then I like it, big and springy, wild, bright.

"It doesn't have to be a *secret,*" I say. "Just—something. How was work today? What do you hear from your family? How are things going at school?"

He shakes his head, his fingers still combing through my hair. "Just tell me—" he says, and then stops.

"What?" I say nervously. "Just tell you what?"

"Is there some *other* way things are supposed to be?"

"What do you mean, some other way?"

"You know," he says, his voice low, ashamed. "Like when we first got together."

"You mean, you made me happy then? And now I'm such a mess?"

"Rosie. I didn't say that."

And then suddenly, I understand. I feel so excited to actually have the answer. "Oh, Michael. You're thinking, the one thing we could always count on was making each other happy in bed. And now I'm not letting you do that, and you think that's *your* fault."

"Rosie. I didn't say that, either."

"Well, then, what *is* it, Michael? Tell me. Are you still mad because I wouldn't take you home for Christmas? Is that what this is all about?"

His fingers hit a tangled place, and he tugs gently. "I'm not *mad,*" he says in a low voice.

"Hurt, then? Mistrustful? Frustrated? Not sure where you stand?" He shrugs. "Was it that you expected more from me?" He looks at me with his beautiful face. "You know," I say urgently. "Like you expected me to—to *claim* you or something. In front of my family. As if you thought—I mean, you *do* make me happy, Michael. And considering that they *don't*—I mean, you have a right to expect that I'd put you first. Or at least, up there. Well, I *do* put you up there. But—"

"Rosie," he says finally. "I'm not saying any of this."

"Well, what *are* you saying, Michael? *Tell me.*"

He shakes his head. "I'm sorry, Rosarita," he says. "You're sick. Let me go heat up dinner. Don't you want me to? It's pretty late."

No, Michael, I don't want food. I want you to stay in here and talk to me.

But I've asked for that twice already, and both times he's said *no.* So I nod and watch him smile as he goes off into the kitchen, while I pull the covers up to my chin. I feel all my flesh settle deep into the bed, so heavy I'll never lift it up again. And deep inside me, something throbbing—God, for twenty-two years I've never even gotten *cramps.*

WARREN: Flip is gone again on Wednesday—some playwright that he and Tanya know is giving a reading.

It's not as though I have *nothing* to do with Flip gone. Now especially, with Juliet, I'm even busier. (Even though she wears uniforms to that school, there always seems to be something missing. Yesterday morning we spent twenty minutes looking for her school shoes, and we only found one of them. She had to go to school in sneakers.) Still, through the whole evening routine and the free time afterward (I could listen to music; I could go through that new cookbook I started *before* Juliet came; I could look over the concert listings in the *Times,* so I'll have something to say to my mother next time she calls)— but all evening, whatever else I'm doing, I find myself thinking of Ian. Well, not exactly thinking. More—playing. Playing with the thought of him in my mind.

When Flip finally does come home, I wake as he gets into bed. "Oh, good, you *are* up," he says cheerfully. "So how did things go around here in my absence?"

As opposed to what? I'd like to say. But instead I ask him, "Do you remember that part of *Half Magic,* the chapter about Jane?" Juliet and I have been working our way through that book since we got back from Pittsburgh.

Flip stretches and sighs. "Is that the part where she misses her real father? And then she says, 'I wish I didn't even *belong* to this family,' and the magic makes her belong to that really awful family, the one where everyone is so weird?"

"The one where everyone is so *neat,*" I say. "And no one laughs or plays or has a good time. And as soon as her real family come to save her, she goes back with them."

Flip sits up. "And when you got done reading her this chapter tonight, Juliet said, 'Gee, Uncle Warren, don't you think there are some eerie similarities between *your* overly neat house and the really *creepy* family in *this* book? And doesn't it make you realize that I just can't *wait* to get back to my *real* family so that I never have to see *you* again?' "

I sigh. "Well, actually, what she said was, 'When Jane was in her second family, why didn't she remember her first family?' "

"And what did you tell her?"

"I said, 'What do *you* think, Juliet? Why do *you* think she can't?' And she thought about it for a while, and then she said, 'Because then she would just go home.' "

Flip is quiet for a moment. Then he says, "Come here, Warren," and sort of tugs at me until I put my head in his lap.

"So now you think everything I said to you last night doesn't count," he says.

"Well?"

"When Poppy died, I was only four," Flip says finally. "So I don't exactly remember what I thought or didn't think. But I know I felt—*bad*. I mean, like I had been bad. I mean, everybody else had a father. Why didn't I? Anyway. I just don't think it has anything to do with you, Warren, all right?"

"How can it not?" I pull my head away.

Flip sighs. "I know you don't believe me," he says. "You never do, if I'm saying anything you might possibly *want* to hear."

The next night, Flip is gone again. This time, he and Mario have theater tickets.

"Hm," I say. "So is tonight business or social?"

"Why?" he says. "Am I allowed to leave the house on business, but not if it's *just* to spend time with a friend?"

Tonight, Juliet tells me several times that all the people at Sara's school are much, *much* nicer than the people at her school, both the children *and* the teachers, although since she admits she hasn't met any of them, I'm not sure what she's basing this on. "Why *can't* I go there?" she asks me throughout the evening. "You keep saying no, Uncle Warren, but you won't ever tell me *why*."

"Well," I say when I am finally sitting in the rocking chair beside her bed, "you know that Sara goes to Catholic school. And you're not Catholic."

"I could just not pay attention during the Catholic part," Juliet says. "That wouldn't bother me."

"And besides, Sara is older than you, so you'd be in a different grade. I'm not sure you'd see all that much of her anyway."

"We could see each other at *lunchtime*," Juliet insists. "And we could walk there together, and we could walk home together, instead of going there in a taxi with *you*, Uncle Warren. And that way, I'd meet other people, too, who live in our neighborhood, so I could play with them, too. They might be in my grade."

"Juliet," I say finally, "I don't think Sara's school is as good as your school, if you want to know the truth. I want you to go to the best school."

She gives me a look of such betrayal that it takes my breath away. I can't help remembering *my* good school, which was on a lake (an artificial lake, I realize now, but even so it was lovely), my excellent school, with its enormous wood-paneled library and its spectacular faculty. (The dormitory rooms were old and crowded, but I spent as little time *there* as I could manage.) It's hard to imagine what *would* have been a good school for me, though, given who I was.

When I don't say anything, Juliet flings herself all the way over to the other side of the bed, burying herself under the blankets. "Good night, Juliet," I say softly, but she refuses to answer me.

On Friday, Flip is invited out to some kind of club with Chris and Paco, which is so not the kind of thing that interests me, and also, I couldn't get a sitter. Since Flip has a dance class that afternoon and a make-up voice lesson that evening, he doesn't have any time to come home, but he does call me from a pay phone between lessons. "So what's happening with *Half Magic?*" he asks.

"We read the next-to-last chapter last night," I say. "The one where the mother marries her new boyfriend, and they're all about to live happily ever after. But Jane still has the magic charm, so I imagine there's one more adventure still to come."

"Yes, well, I was thinking about that, actually." Suddenly Flip sounds very uncertain. "Do you want to hear this?" he says.

"Go ahead."

"Well, just that what Juliet said, what *you* told me she said, was, 'Why can't she *belong* to her second family and *remember* her first family?' Right?"

"It always amazes me, how you remember every single word anyone says. Yes, I suppose it was something like that."

"Well, Warren. *She* didn't say how awful the second family was. *You* were the only one saying that."

The phone clicks. "Anyway, I'm out of change," Flip says. "I'll see you tonight when—" and then the phone cuts him off. I stand there with my hand on the receiver, trying to think of something, anything, to make this moment pass.

Tonight what happens in *Half Magic* is that Jane feels terribly guilty about being so happy with her new stepfather. And the magic sends her a dream in which her real father appears, assuring her that he is happy for her and it's all right.

After we finish the book, Juliet is very thoughtful. Then, to my surprise, she climbs out of bed and into my lap. Automatically, I put my arms around her. It makes me realize how little of this we've done—hug or cuddle or even hold hands—since the first week she was here.

But tonight, we sit and rock together, her head buried in my chest. "Uncle Warren," she says finally, not looking up, "I'm *older* than eight and three-eighths now. I'm almost eight and a half. I'm probably too old to sleep in your bed."

"Probably," I say. "Although maybe not. But I do have another idea."

"What?" she says, defiantly. She tightens her grip around me.

"I could rock you like this until you fall asleep," I say. "And then I could put you to bed right here. Should we do that?"

"Yes," she says in that same defiant tone. But her fingers don't loosen.

"You know what I liked about that story?" I say finally.

"What?"

"I liked the way Jane was happy *and* sad. She didn't forget her father—"

"Because she *missed* him," says Juliet. "She missed him *a lot*."

"Do you think her new father minded that?"

"He wasn't her *new* father," Juliet says. "He was her *stepfather*. She called him *Uncle*. Uncle Hugo."

"That's right, I forgot," I say. "Do you think her uncle minded if she was sad?"

"No," says Juliet eventually. Finally, her hands relax. "She was just sad about somebody else."

"Do you want to talk about your mother?" I say. "Do you want to tell me something you remember about her?"

Juliet shakes her head without raising it from my chest. "Not tonight," she says. "Maybe another time. Now I just want to think about her by myself."

So I sit and rock with her until she falls asleep. I keep thinking I know what my body is good for. I keep having to learn it all over again.

MARIO: When Joshua and I get into The Deep End, it's so dark and noisy, it's like walking into a secret place. I feel unsettled—it's *very* crowded, and I don't know anybody.

There are just so many chances for going too far. Eating too much, for example. Getting so ugly and out of control. Or drinking—not that *I* like drinking so much, but Joshua does. Though that clearly isn't something he worries about. The opposite, in fact. Coming to a place like this is his *chance* to go too far.

We're sitting at a patio table way over in the corner—I guess the idea is that there would be patio furniture around the deep end of the pool. Suddenly I see Paco and Chris coming off the dance floor. And Flip. I stand and wave to them, and they come over.

It's impossible to actually talk, of course. But they all kiss me hello. The three of them are clearly high on *something,* and Joshua is finishing his fifth drink by now. I've had two drinks, which is a lot for me, but I'm nowhere near where the rest of them are.

Somehow Flip figures out what everybody wants, and he waves away our offers of money and goes off to the bar. And immediately Chris throws his arms around Paco's neck and they start kissing. Well, not just kissing. Chris climbs up onto Paco's lap, and Paco has his hand way up under Chris's shirt. There's something about the way they're so *hungry* for each other. Of course, you always see them being affectionate, but this is more—out of control. But on purpose.

Joshua is usually very restrained around other people, but maybe this is why he likes this whole scene. Because when he puts his arm around my waist, it's so *charged* it makes me dizzy. I can feel it all pulling on me, the kiss, and the darkness, and the smell of people's bodies, and I want to melt into it, just go under, sink into this secret place with him. Why not? But I'm not— well, it doesn't make *me* feel safe.

"I like you, Mario," Joshua is saying, and somehow, noisy as it is, I understand him. "You're so—good. You're good." I hear his voice wobbling, I feel his hot breath in my ear. He throws his arms around my neck just as Flip comes back with our drinks. Flip stands there for a moment, watching the four of us, and you can't tell *what* he's thinking.

I lean forward, and Flip offers me his ear. *"Where's Warren?"*

He shrugs. *"He doesn't like clubs."*

Joshua is holding his new drink with one hand, but he's put the other one right on my crotch. Very gently, which surprises me, because this isn't how he touches me when he's sober. When he's sober, he's more—insistent. We can't do this here, can we, in front of all these people? Paco and Chris are still going at it, over in their chair, and Flip is watching the dancers. Joshua is pressing harder now, as the music changes to another song, but it's still that loud, pounding beat, with the hot white lights sweeping slowly over the dancers, and Joshua's hand presses even harder, and it feels so good, and I want it to, and I don't want to be the one who makes him stop, and if we don't stop soon, I won't be able to stop. My eyes are half shut, I'm leaning into him, that fuzzy feeling, growing, growing—and then suddenly, he does stop.

So is he now so drunk that he really isn't paying attention to me? I'm not complaining, of course, I'm just asking. Or did I do something? I want his hand back there, and also I don't, but also—I didn't want him to just stop.

ROSIE: He just really knew how to wait. Michael, I mean. That whole spring and summer, he kept showing up at those union events. Waiting for me to ask him out for coffee. Or to come back to my place. Waiting for me to ask for whatever I wanted.

At the time, I thought it was a gift. I still think so, mostly. Because clearly, he wanted me, but that way, I got to want *him*. And then after all my weeks of holding out, there I finally was, letting him into my narrow front hallway, where he stood, politely, waiting. Until I had to squeeze past him to get into my living room, my thigh rubbing softly against his leg, and then, all right, I *did* want him. I mean, then I knew it.

"Well," he says, smiling at me, because I have turned around and am just staring at him. I remember, he was wearing an amber-colored T-shirt that was damp against his chest—it was a very hot, muggy night, and I had planned to go right over and turn on the air-conditioner. But I had to turn around and see what had just happened. My stomach suddenly tight with wanting him so much.

He was like a statue. I just stood there, looking and wanting. And he smiled.

Of course, sometimes that's a wonderful feeling. Wanting something so much that you don't care what it costs. What it costs you or *anybody*.

MARIO: Paco and Chris have gone off somewhere, and Flip motions to me—do I want to dance? Joshua can't possibly mind, the state he's in, so I follow Flip to the dance floor. He's a fabulous dancer, of course. I love watching him.

I love my dancing, too—leaving everything behind but the dance floor, while the music and the bodies and the beat move right up inside me. *Yes.* Until finally the music slows down and the lights go dim, and there are Paco and Chris over by the video screen, kissing passionately as they dance.

Flip catches my eye, and we both know we're not going to do *that*. Though there is this *look* that goes between us—no, not sexual, nothing sexual. He smiles at me, and almost winks, and heads off toward the bathrooms. And of course, I follow him.

ELINOR: Idris and I are lying together in my bed, where we have just made love, and she has just said that she has to go. Why? Because she has to meet Pauli. Apparently there are some things they still have to talk about.

"At twelve o'clock on a Friday night?" I say. "Is *that* why you haven't called me all week?"

Idris thinks this is funny. "Jealous?" she says in that furry, teasing voice.

With a man, I would know how to do this. The knives would come *out*.

"Why don't you tell me what's going on?" I hear myself saying instead.

"Look at you," Idris says in that delighted tone she used when she learned I'd made brownies for her. "You *are* jealous." She runs her hand along my leg. "Oh, look," she says, pausing over a stubbly place. "You missed a spot." A spot she then starts to kiss. "I suppose I can keep Pauli waiting another hour or so," she murmurs. "Since you're so *jealous*."

I thought everything would be different. New. Uncharted. But it isn't any different, really. Although I suppose that *I* am different.

I put my hand on Idris's head—the beautiful shape of her head, under her short, *short* hair—and gently push her away. "Go on," I say. "Since you're going."

She comes after me into the hallway. "Don't be that way," she says pleadingly. "I said I'd stay."

I cross my arms and lean against the wall. I thought everything would be new. But this is all so familiar.

Idris puts her hands on her hips, one hip cocked forward. "So what *do* you want?" she says. I stand my ground. Finally, she says, "Have it your way," and goes back into the bedroom. I have the odd feeling that when she comes out again, she'll make me give her back the robe. But all she says is, "Now I've got to get all the way back from *Queens*."

"You would have anyway," I say finally. And then I can't stop talking. "Whatever did you think was going to happen? At twelve o'clock on a Friday night? What other reaction could you possibly have expected?"

"Have a safe trip?" She lifts her chin. "You didn't call me either. I don't see why it was *my* responsibility. I'm not the man here."

"If you had been the man, I *would* have called," I say. "If only to ask why *you* weren't calling." Which makes her laugh, though it's only the unfortunate truth.

"So now you're disappointed," she says, in that mischievous voice. "Your feelings are hurt."

She moves toward me again, and I can smell the snow in her coat. "Girl, you are *hard*," she says when I don't move one inch. "I pity the person who crosses *you*."

So maybe I'm not any different.

She turns away and reaches for her backpack. "How about if I call you to-morrow?" she says. *Why* was I so happy before? She shrugs her pack over her shoulders. "How about if tonight, you kiss me goodbye?"

"Why not?" I say. Kissing her sounds so nice, at the moment. Though I still wish I could say *no.*

Maybe not. Because when she puts her strange, familiar tongue into my mouth, when she presses her leg between my legs and I press back, then I know: Oh. It's going to be all right.

She slips out, smiling, and I lean against the door, my bare feet cold on the wooden floor. Go on, I think, go back to bed. Go on to sleep, right this minute. And when you wake up, she'll call.

MARIO: The bathroom is huge, and we're the only ones in here. It's silly to be embarrassed about peeing next to *Flip*, of all people. We've peed together lots of times—nothing's any different now.

I go wash my hands, which, though it doesn't make any real difference, is something I always do these days. All those little things that probably don't matter—washing my hands, putting food right into the refrigerator—what difference could any of it make? But I do it anyway.

It's such a shock to be somewhere quiet. And this lounge is really bright—white fluorescent lights, and lots of mirrors, and the shiny white tile from the bathroom. It makes me dizzy, all of a sudden, and I lean against the wall. Immediately Flip looks at me with concern.

"No, Flip," I say, "this is nothing. Just—you know. Two drinks."

"The original cheap date," says Flip.

"That's me," I say, relieved that he believes me. Usually people look away or change the subject or—well, in my experience, what people usually want at this point is to escape. But Flip can't take his eyes off me. He stands right beside me, his face just inches away from mine. "Really, Flip," I say softly. "I *am* fine."

"OK, good," Flip says. He reaches out one hand and runs it slowly down my hair, my face, my shoulder, my chest. "I'm glad you're OK." He leaves his hand there on my chest, and we just look at each other, until finally he leans forward and kisses me slowly on the lips. "Come on," he says, looking happy again. "Let's go dance some more."

"Yes," I say, following him out into the darkness and noise and smoke. I feel like someone has just given me a birthday present. *Yes,* I love this. *Yes,* I do. Inside my body. Leaving everything behind.

TANYA: The walls in my apartment are way too thin for my taste, especially in the bedroom. Because pretty nearly every night, I hear the neighbors' television. I can't help but wonder—what can *they* hear?

So tonight, I try to keep it quiet. As I lie there, my hand between my legs, thinking of an image that haunts me these days—a woman in silver lamé, blue spotlight, smoky nightclub air, and there's something in the air that's like a drug, something in the smoke, sweet, too sweet, it makes you dizzy.

Makes me dizzy but gives me power. So that when I sing, that smell, that power, is in my voice. You can't *not* listen. The smoke makes me high, but I make them high, those men—they start out just ordinary, and then slowly, my voice creeps into them like smoke. *Yes, I'll do anything, yes, I'll be your slave,* only let me just keep breathing this sweet, funny smoke, *yes, I want more. And more. And MORE.*

I focus on this one man's eyes, how they look straight into mine, he *can't* look away. I make him *want* to look, and he's hard and moaning and ready to do anything for me. He's moaning, I'm moaning, and that outside part of me is saying, "Be quiet, you don't want the neighbors to hear." But now *I want, I want,* and if I don't make noise—

Not yet. So I focus harder on the man's eyes, how they make him walk closer and closer, his whole body saying, *Yes. Yes. Anything you want, Tanya—take it all. It's all—for—you.*

The waves are bigger, thicker, swallowing me up, and I focus on his eyes, how much he wants me, how he'll do anything I want. *Yes,* he must—a deep, wide wave—*yes,* he must, *yes,* he must, more, and *more,* and *MORE.* All of him. All of me. Hear my voice cry, make my voice *sing.* My *voice,* my voice, my own . . . voice.

WARREN: When Flip gets into bed at about 2 a.m. I can't stop myself from saying, "Well, *you* must have had a nice time."

"Yes, I did," he says. "But why *didn't* you come, Warren? It would have been much nicer."

"You know perfectly well why I didn't come," I say. "I couldn't get a sitter, for one thing."

"Oh, right," he says, shaking his head with that exaggerated, drunken slowness. "You've had Juliet for, what? Two months? I think if you had really wanted to find a nighttime sitter, you could have done so by now."

"If I had really wanted to? Why *wouldn't* I want to?"

He is about to answer me when he suddenly collapses backward onto the pillow. "My God," I say. "You really *are* out of it."

"Mmmm," he says. "Yet despite my advanced state of inebriation, or maybe intoxication is the word I want—although neither of those is quite the right word when drugs as well as alcohol are involved—so I suppose I should say, despite my advanced state of altered consciousness, but in any case, I think my point *was* a point well taken. Which is why *you* are trying to change the subject as usual, Warren."

It's amazing to see that, drunk and high as he is, he can *still* perform. Or do I mean, amazing to see how much he *wants* to perform? How much he wants to perform for *me?*

He flops over onto his stomach, as close as he can get to me without actually touching. With what looks like an enormous effort, he opens his eyes and for a long moment, we simply stare at each other. Finally, I can't help it. I simply have to grab his hand and wrap it around my penis, holding his fingers there with mine.

"I *wouldn't* have gotten high if you'd been there, Warren," he whispers fiercely. "Because I know how much you hate it. I would just have had a couple of drinks. We could have danced together. Oh, right, you say you don't dance. Yet another thing you won't do with me."

I'm guiding his hand with mine and he's not stopping me, but he isn't doing anything else, either, staring at me through those half-closed eyes. "I hate places like that," I whisper back. "I don't mind if you go. But it's not what *I* like."

"That's not what I'm saying," he says. "You know that's not what I'm saying." He's half on top of me now, moving his tongue into my ear, which he *knows* makes me crazy, and I don't even think he's excited. "You never want to go anywhere with me," he whispers, and I wish so much that I could just push him away. Does he think I don't *know* how he felt about my waking him up the other night? He's pushed up against me, too, now, and yes, of course, he's excited—triumph or surrender?—and I can hear myself moaning and sighing as my fingers tighten around his, as I press back against him as hard as I can, as I try so hard to make his body do what mine wants.

DESIRE

TANYA: I wake up this morning hungry for everything. Work, love, a place in the world. I can't stop thinking about Davis—not him (the long smooth muscles in his arms and his back, that shiny dark skin), but me with him. Getting fooled so bad. How did *that* happen?

I remember using *my* muscles, back when I was thirteen, fourteen, helping my Daddy fix houses. In and among the times he got regular construction work, he'd go out and fix houses on his own, and since my brothers *wouldn't* go with him after they got older, he took me. Teaching me pretty much everything a fourteen-year-old *could* learn about using tools. Even if he never seemed all that happy about having me along. But that was just his way—he was strict.

Anyway, the memory that sticks with me is this one August day when it was *hot*. Sweat dripping down my back, drops gathering in the backs of my knees. My muscles stretching up *high* to hand him up a hammer, there on his ladder. My shirt all wet and sticky, stuck against my skin.

It was something *useful,* that's what I'm trying to get at. If I was hungry for work, there it was. He put himself *into* those houses, even when he was just sweeping up the trash at the end of the day. He wanted you to put yourself there, too.

I thought my work would be useful, too, when I first started doing it. Maybe my family didn't understand that, but I did. I thought that doing my work would be as good as being a nurse, good as giving somebody a fixed-up house to live in. Giving my audience—something *else.*

I look up at that picture of Dorothy Dandridge—cool, beautiful, looking like nothing in the world could ever touch her. *Did* she know something I don't know?

WARREN: I must say, it's torture waking up when Juliet knocks on the bedroom door at six-thirty in the morning. "Uncle Warren," she's saying insistently, "I'm really really, *really* hungry." As soon as she sees me come out into the hall, she comes over and leans against me. I put one arm around her. After a minute, I put the other arm around her, too. Her chin just reaches my waist.

"Did you have bad dreams?" I say softly. "Or did you just wake up feeling sad?"

She shrugs.

"Should we go and rock some more?" I say. "And then I'll make you breakfast?" She nods.

By the time Juliet and I make it to the kitchen, Flip is sitting at the kitchen table, looking absolutely exhausted. Usually, he goes back to sleep after Juliet wakes us, but today he's clearly done his best to wake up, taken a shower, even made coffee.

Even in this state, Flip can tell what I'm thinking about *that,* and he grins at me. "Don't worry, Warren," he says. "I *can* make coffee." He looks at Juliet, still leaning against me. "Come on, Juliet," he says, "come and keep me company while Uncle Warren goes to take *his* shower."

When I come back, Juliet is sitting on Flip's lap and he's telling her something about his father, not the one I met in Pittsburgh but the other one, the one who died. Flip looks up as I head toward the refrigerator. "I would have made breakfast," he says, "which I also *can* do, in case you were wondering, Warren. But, actually, I couldn't even stand up, because Madame Juliet here started asking me questions that had *very* long answers, and—"

"*Not* 'Madame,' " Juliet says. "I *told* you. Mademoiselle."

"Oh, right," Flip says. "I do keep making that mistake, don't I?" He winks at me as I walk slowly over to the stove and start scrambling eggs. "And if I forget another time, what will you do then?" he says to her playfully. "Will you make me stand in the corner? Or don't they do that at your school?"

"It isn't the *corner,*" Juliet says. "It's time out. But I'm never bad, so I never have it."

"Really?" says Flip. "You're *never* bad? Your teachers must love you, Juliet."

Juliet shrugs, and I suddenly have an image of her sitting in her desk at the end of the second row—is that where she sits? We've never discussed it. But I see her pretending to look at the bulletin board—there's some kind of elaborate winter art project involving white wax and glitter, and science projects on snow and ice, and social studies papers on Inuits and the Arctic. And it's one of those times when the teacher has had the children break up into groups, and everyone is moving their desks around, except Juliet, who just stays there in her desk at the end of the row, trying not to watch.

But that can't possibly be right. That might have happened to me, when I was in third grade (though I honestly don't remember much of anything from back then). But there's no reason for it to happen to Juliet.

After breakfast, Juliet wants to watch a video, but she says she really, really, *really* wants us to watch it with her. Flip shrugs—he's ready to oblige. But the whole point of the videos is that they're something she's willing to do when I'm doing something else. So I say, "Juliet, you have a choice. You can watch a video—*one* video—by yourself. Or you can stay in here and talk to us and maybe also help me clean up the kitchen."

Juliet looks at us thoughtfully. "Well, *I* want to watch the video—"

"Good choice," says Flip. "That's what I'd pick."

"But I want you to talk *loud,* so I'll hear you in the other room."

As soon as she goes into the other room, Flip comes over to where I am standing by the sink and hangs on me. "I'm so tired, I think I am going to *die,*" he whispers in my ear.

"I don't hear any *talking!*" shouts Juliet from the other room.

Flip starts to say something three times and then stops.

"What?" I say.

"Look, Warren, I get that you want her to watch videos by herself—I mean, I get that it's in *my* interest that she's willing to, all right? But maybe to-day—I mean, I'd be happy to go in and watch with her." I stare at him. "Well," he says uncomfortably, "I just have the impression that this is kind of a bad day for her. I mean, some days, you just *do* want someone there every minute."

I am this close to saying, "Oh, really? And how would *you* know?" I look for something, anything, to keep me from saying it. "Is that something you re-member doing with your parents? Watching television, I mean? Or simply . . ."

To my surprise, I can't finish the sentence. I start to wipe off the stove.

Flip is at least pretending to treat this as a normal conversation. "Are you kidding?" he says. "You saw my mother—she would never sit down long enough to eat three bites of food in succession, let alone watch an actual tele-vision program with us."

I never would have thought I'd feel any sympathy whatsoever for Flip's mother, but yes, I can imagine the amount of work there must have been in that two-story house, and with *three* children. I toss the washrag into the sink. "Well, actually," I say, "Juliet *is* having a bad day. I think you sitting on the couch watching videos with her would be her idea of heaven on earth."

Flip looks at me with that skeptical half smile. "You mean as opposed to *you* watching with her?"

I wonder suddenly what Ian would think of all this. After all, he *has* a daughter. He must have some idea what to do with a child who misses her mother.

ROSIE: The coffee in the blue and white cardboard cup is sweet and milky, and I love the heat against my palm, making it glow in the cold morning air. My God. To get so incredibly much pleasure out of *coffee.* But I do. So much so that I don't even remember I'm not supposed to have it until I've already drunk half of it, at which point it seems silly to throw the rest away.

Up on the elevated subway platform, I feel exhilarated all over again.

Wind, sun, the sound of a train. The memory of sex this morning with Michael, which I was *finally* able to have, so thank you, Cassandra, with your herbs and needles. And the caffeine getting right up inside my happiness, pushing it higher and higher.

The train comes, and I settle blissfully into a seat. Nobody can believe I love the subway, but I do, I do, I honestly do. The train itself is fairly low-energy—some exhausted guys on their way home from the night shift; a bored young mother and her fussing baby; two teenage boys horsing around *very* quietly; a large, weary, middle-aged woman, probably a housekeeper on her way into Manhattan. (Michael has shown me the corner in the Bronx where those housekeepers used to stand, waiting for day work. The Slave Market, they called it.) Still. When I close my eyes, I feel the world I am part of. Right now, all I want is this.

WARREN: Flip and Juliet watch videos for a while. Then Flip convinces Juliet to go play with whatever it is they're building in her room. While I get started on the dusting, and the vacuuming, and yet more loads of laundry. Flip keeps glancing at me, as if to say, "Warren! Stop doing all that *housework* and play with us."

But then, of course, at eleven-thirty, Flip leaves Juliet playing by herself and comes into the bedroom, where I am folding laundry. He needs *this* half hour to get ready for rehearsal, he says, and stretches out on the bed, opening his script.

"I thought you didn't have a script yet."

"No," says Flip, "the no-script extravaganza is our infamous Tiger's Eye production—*those* rehearsals start *next* week. Today is just Tanya and me working on that scene from *Measure for Measure* to audition for that lab—you know, that extremely snotty and pretentious and yet somehow terrifically prestigious workshop run by The Players Group. I *told* you, Warren—there's no money involved, and they don't do actual productions, and yet, since the term 'working actor' is such an oxymoron, there *are* a fair number of working actors in it, working, in this case euphemistically, for free, and you practically have to hand over your firstborn child or give someone a blow job even to be considered for membership. I just wish I could figure out who was supposed to *get* the blow job, because then I wouldn't have to bother with the audition. I told you this, Warren, I know I did."

"I don't think so," I say. "I would have remembered the part about the blow job. But why do you—"

"Warren," he says patiently, "I really would like to talk about all of this with you. But now I have only twenty-five minutes to get ready—I'm kind of push-ing it as it is."

"All right," I say, putting the last few pairs of socks into our respective sock drawers. "Just tell me when you're going to be back so I have some idea about dinner."

He doesn't even look up from his script. "I won't *be* home for dinner, I don't think. After rehearsal, I have to go to the gym."

"You won't be home for dinner because you're going to the *gym?*"

He's clearly trying to keep his temper. "You always say that, Warren, and I always say, yes, I have to go—"

"Well, everybody has to go, but not for—"

"*Yes,* for three hours at a time, because not that anyone is *going* to audition me for a nude scene, or even for a commercial with my shirt off. But it has been known to happen to *some* actors who actually *have* careers, and God for-bid if the reason I didn't get a part was because some producer thought I looked flabby."

I have to admit, there's a certain amount of justice in what he says. But I say, "And of course, the *only* reason you do it is for your career."

"No, Warren," Flip says patiently. "Even if I weren't an actor, I would still want to look fabulous. I just wouldn't be quite so disciplined about it."

"Well, sorry to interrupt. I shouldn't be talking to you, either—I have to make lunch. Ian's coming over at twelve-thirty and it's almost twelve now."

"You didn't tell me Ian was coming over," Flip says, still not looking up. "I wish you'd picked a time when I was going to be here, too."

Well, he certainly made *that* easy. "I did think of that," I say, heading for the door, "but since it's so hard to find a time when you *are* here—"

"Oh, right," says Flip. "Because I was just gone all morning, wasn't I? Good point."

"And besides," I say, "if you were here, well, that would more or less defeat the purpose, wouldn't it?" *Now* he looks up.

"Defeat the purpose?" he says. "What are you telling me, that it's a date?"

"Flip. It's not a date."

He sits up on the bed, staring at me. "You are. You're *telling* me you have a date with Ian."

"I *don't* have a date with Ian. Obviously. He's just coming for lunch and to spend time with Juliet."

His script is in a three-ring binder, and he closes it sharply with a snap. "Not enough that you actually *have* a date," he says, "you have to make this whole big point of *telling* me about it. Five minutes before I have to leave for rehearsal, no less."

I lean against the bedroom door, balancing the laundry basket against my stomach. "Evidently you're allowed to spend any amount of time with *your* friends, but if I spend just one afternoon with mine—"

Flip is shaking his head as he throws his script into his backpack. "So that's why you were being so nice to me Tuesday night. You had just made a date with Ian."

Well, I certainly didn't expect *that*. "First of all," I say, "I wasn't 'being nice' to you Tuesday night—"

"Apparently not."

"And secondly, whatever I *was* doing, it had nothing to do with him."

"Well, Warren," Flip says, lifting his gym bag and his backpack onto his shoulder, "I would love to stay and play out this little Noel Coward–out-of–Henry James scene with you, but unfortunately, *I* have, not a date, but a rehearsal, and while it *is* considered acceptable, even intriguing, to be late to a date, I'm afraid that the same can't be said for an actual professional commitment. So if you'll excuse me—" He pushes past me toward the door, and he is so angry, I actually step back a few feet. Then he pauses.

"Just to make things *quite* clear as per our earlier agreement," he says, "this is not me storming out of the house and refusing to talk to you. This is *you* telling me you have a fucking *date* five minutes before *I* have to leave for fucking rehearsal. And because Juliet is here, I'm not going to slam the door, but fuck you, anyway, Warren. Consider the door slammed." I hear him say goodbye to Juliet in a surprisingly normal tone of voice.

Juliet comes right into the bedroom and leans against me. "Why is Uncle Flip so mad?" she says in a worried voice.

I feel such a bizarre mix of emotions that I'm almost dizzy. Elated, as though I might float right up to the ceiling.

"Flip is mad because he just found out that a friend of ours, Ian—you remember him, Juliet, he came over in December—Ian is going to be here soon to spend the afternoon with us."

"And Uncle Flip's mad because he doesn't get to see Ian, only we do?"

"Something like that."

"So we're the lucky ones," Juliet says. "The fortunate, happy, *felicitous* ones."

"Yes," I say. "I think we are."

TANYA: Well, *this* scene isn't working.

"OK, stop," says Elinor. "Wait. Somebody tell the story of the scene."

Child, please. I *know* what the scene is about. But Flip says, in his good-boy voice, "I'm in jail, expecting to be put to death. And my sister, who's about to become a nun—" gesturing to me "—has just gone to Angelo, the man in charge, to get me pardoned. And Angelo, who has a reputation for being a total Puritan, has the hots for my sister, as who can blame him—"

"Oh, please," I say.

"Well?" says Flip. "He gets turned on by your brilliant grasp of theology, doesn't he? It's not exactly *my* idea of a sexual attraction, but apparently it's Shakespeare's."

"Fine," I say. Why should he get to do all the talking? "And I come back to tell my brother Claudio, here, that if I have sex with Angelo, he'll save my sorry brother's life. And of course, his life—what's that? Not worth having sex with Angelo for, not if I have to spend the rest of eternity in hell."

"OK, fine," Elinor says. "Now tell me what you want."

"I want to save my life," Flip says promptly. They both look at me.

"Not like I *don't* want to save your life," I say slowly. "But I want to do it some other way. I don't want to—to *degrade* myself, I guess."

"That's what you *don't* want," says Elinor. "But we all know you can't play a negative. So what *do* you want, Tanya?"

And when I don't answer—which pisses me off, because I am supposed to have *done* this homework—then they try to help me out. "To save your honor," Elinor suggests.

"To save *my* life," says Flip.

"To triumph over Angelo."

"To get me to forgive you."

"Forgive *me?*" I say. "It's *your* fault I'm in this mess to begin with." You know, I *got* Flip that part in Davis's movie. And then Pietro's boyfriend goes and hires *him*.

I must have spoken with more energy than I realized, given the way Flip and Elinor are both now looking at me. "You still haven't said," Elinor says quietly. "What is it you want?"

I am remembering going home for Christmas this year, talking to my Daddy after my brothers had all packed up and left with their families. Somehow he and I ended up at the breakfast table together—not like *him* to be hanging around so late in the morning, but he *did* seem extra tired. He asked me how work was going, and I tried to tell him the good news—how for most of this year, I'd made it through on acting work alone (with some temping in the slow times, I'll admit). But somehow he could tell that I wasn't as proud as I was trying to sound. "You're never going to get the parts they give to other folks," he told me, swirling the coffee around in his mug. "They're just not going to give you that."

"You must want something," Flip is saying now, and I can hear how patient he is trying to sound. "I'm in jail, on my own road to hell. What do you think *I* can do for you?"

Just then Idris walks in the door and Elinor turns about three different shades of green. "Can I have a minute?" says Idris, waving hello to us. "It won't take long."

Elinor looks so purely trapped that Flip and I both nod. As they head out to the hallway, Flip raises his eyebrows at me. "Well, is *this* a totally fascinating development, or am I the last to know, *as usual?*"

"If you are, then we're *both* last," I say. "Not like I'm happy about it."

"Oh? Which one did *you* want?"

"Child, please. When the writer and director are involved, I am *never* happy. A point *you* might have thought of, if your mind wasn't all on *your* romantic problems."

Flip gives me another funny look. "And here I thought there was only one psychic in my life."

"Child, I don't even *believe* that shit. I just pay attention."

Flip sighs. "Well, since I'm *not* a psychic," he says, "are you going to *tell* me what's bothering you? Or do I have to wait yet another three months to find out what I did wrong?"

Well. Not like I expected *that.*

"You didn't do anything," I say finally. "Though I've got to tell you, it pisses me off that you never heard of Dorothy Dandridge. Or ever saw any of her movies."

"Well, I could *rent* one. If it means that much to you."

"No, no. Not that *you* never heard of her. That you never *heard* of her. Like she was just this stone that sank into a puddle."

"I think you mean a pond," Flip says. "If she sank into a puddle, you could still see her." He flashes me this very *sympathetic* look all of a sudden. "You never heard anything from *Hell Street,* huh?"

I twist my mouth. "My agent said they were very impressed. Only they don't think I'm hooker material. He says they're saving me for something more classy."

Suddenly we're both laughing. "Too classy to be a hooker on *Hell Street,*" Flip says. "Talk about your back-handed compliments."

"Flip," I say out of the blue, "do you even *like* doing this scene?"

He looks about as surprised as I have ever seen him. "God, I always like doing Shakespeare," he says finally. "Even for a fucking audition." He's playing with this loose thread on the corner of his notebook. "I don't even mind doing it with *you,*" he says. "Or not all that *much.* I mean, I've worked with worse."

"Well, me, too. So couldn't we just—pretend—"

"A radical concept for actors, certainly."

"You know. That there's some *other* reason to do the scene. Besides the audition. I mean, you know. We've already paid for the space."

Flip laughs. "Well, *there's* a compelling artistic imperative. I shudder to think how many projects have gone forward on *that* basis."

Elinor comes back. "So, did you decide what you want?"

I still feel it, hungry as I've ever been. "I want justice," I say.

Elinor looks doubtful. "I'm not sure you *can* play 'wanting justice,' " she says. "It isn't very active."

"Well, I'm not sure I'll ever *get* it," I say. "But that's what I want."

WARREN: I must say, it is *extremely* nice spending time with Ian. He comes in with a present not for me, but for Juliet, which I think is awfully nice, besides being extremely tactful. Of course, people can *be* tactful in that way when they've had—well, lots of *experience* in these matters.

I do feel a surprising rush of happiness when he walks through our front door—tall, thin, angular, his shoulders slouched forward in that awkward, storklike way that I somehow find so touching. And today there is an anxious flavor beneath his usual amused air, which I also find touching. As though that were the present for me.

Juliet is delighted with *her* present, the latest figure in the Beanie Baby collection. "Sara says that everybody wants one of these, but the stores ran out, so nobody has one," she says. "Can I go call her right now?"

"Go ahead," I say. "Just don't stay on *too* long, because we *are* going to have lunch soon."

"I never stay on too long," says Juliet. "You only think I do." She's gone before I can correct her.

I look at Ian rather helplessly. "One of the many things I haven't yet figured out how to teach her," I say. "Manners."

"Oh, well, if that's the worst of your problems, you're miles ahead of the game."

Ian settles himself at the kitchen table and I start assembling the salad nicoise, which, as it happens, is one of Juliet's favorites. "I'm not at all sure it *is* the worst of my problems," I say, trimming the skin off a cucumber. "Actually, I'm more concerned that— Do you mind my launching right into all these domestic concerns? I didn't mean to. It's just such a relief to know someone else who—" Well, what now? He doesn't actually *have* a child, at the moment, and although I can call myself a parent when I'm talking to Flip, I certainly can't use that word with Ian.

Once again, Ian helps me out. "I'm delighted to hear about anything you care to tell me," he says. I keep being surprised by how *happy* I feel, an uncomplicated flood of happiness that seems to sweep away any other feeling.

"Well, under the circumstances, maybe this *isn't* the part you want to hear about," I say. "But what bothers me most lately is how much she misses her mother. What do you do when that's the problem?"

Ian sighs. "I don't think there *are* any answers to questions like that," he says. "I suppose the only reason parents talk about them is to make themselves feel better."

"Oh?" I say. "Well, maybe you're right. Because I *do* feel better. Much better."

Ian laughs. "I'm so glad," he says. "Though I must say, I'm rather surprised I could make you feel so *much* better so quickly."

FLIP: "Sweet sister, let me live!" Thwack! That's the sound of me throwing myself onto the floor. Tanya and Elinor have agreed—and *God* knows why *I* went along—that what our little scene needs at this point is a physical expression of our relationship. So we've come up with this extravagant gesture of me flinging myself at Tanya's feet.

The only problem is, we don't know what should come next. My *next* lines are

> *What sin you do to save a brother's life,*
> *Nature dispenses with the deed so far*
> *That it becomes a virtue.*

To which *she* replies, "O you beast! O faithless coward! O dishonest wretch!" So she's not exactly moved by my gesture. Plus, of course, I do have those three lines to get through. Am I supposed to say them face down on the floor?

So we keep trying. "Sweet sister, let me live!" Thwack! Tanya tries grasping my arms and raising me up. Nope, no good. "Sweet sister, let me live!" Thwack! Tanya flings herself on top of me, which doesn't work *and* it hurts. "Sweet sister, let me live!" Thwack! Tanya draws back in horror as I slowly raise my head. Somewhat better. Maybe.

"Let me see it again," says Elinor thoughtfully. I should have brought knee pads.

WARREN: Even though it's fairly chilly out, Juliet says she really, really, *really* wants to go to Washington Square after lunch. "But Juliet," I say, "it's so cold. You won't be able to *do* anything."

"Why do we always get to do whatever *you* want to do, and never anything *I* want to do?" she says, not defiantly, but in the most pitiable, forlorn tone of voice you could imagine.

"Well, I have a proposal," Ian says calmly. "What if we walk *through* Washington Square Park? But rather than stay in what will probably be a frigid, uncomfortable environment, we proceed on to the Waverly Theater, where I understand that *Turandot* is playing."

Juliet's eyes light up. "Could we really go see *Turandot?*"

"*Turandot* the opera?" I say, rather stupidly.

"It's not an *opera,* Uncle Warren, it's a movie. A cartoon movie. We *never* go to the movies, we just watch videos. And *you* never watch with me. Only Uncle Flip."

"I take it that Flip handles the popular culture for the family," says Ian.

"So it would seem," I say.

"It can take a while to catch on, if you're not that way inclined," Ian says. "The latest toy, the latest movie, and so on. Of course, if you start with them from the beginning, you get an instant initiation. The latest pram, the latest pacifier, the latest nappies. The other parents feel intensely attached to these apparently minor distinctions, and they serve as a kind of induction into the mysteries of consumer culture, preparing you for the time when the child herself will tell you why the lack of a particular brand of sock will make her the laughingstock of her nursery school."

Juliet is listening closely. "It isn't socks," she says, and I can see how hard she's trying to correct politely, the way we've discussed. "Socks don't even *have* brands. It's shoes."

"Case in point," says Ian. "Sorry, Juliet. I'm afraid I'm a bit out of practice."

Juliet looks at him solemnly. And completely surprises me by saying, "*I'm* sorry. I'm sorry you miss your daughter."

"Thank you," says Ian, clearing his throat.

"So what do you think, Juliet?" I say as quickly as I can manage. "About walking through the park to see *Turandot?*"

"Yes," says Juliet. "I think that's an excellent, extraordinary, *exceptional* plan."

"Exquisite," suggests Ian.

"No," says Juliet. "A *person* can be exquisite, but a plan can't be."

"My mistake," says Ian. He really can't take his eyes off her, though I can feel that each moment of looking hurts. When Juliet runs to get her coat, he turns to me.

"You're extremely lucky," he says.

"I know," I say. "That was incredibly nice of you, to find out about the movie. And to bring her the latest toy. I really don't know about any of that."

"Oh, you seem to know quite a bit," he says, and finally smiles. I can't help it. It just keeps making me happy.

FLIP: "So *did* you have a fight with Warren?" Tanya asks me as soon as our next break begins. Elinor has gone off to find a phone, presumably to call Idris.

"Not necessarily," I say. "I might be upset about something else."

"Not *that* upset."

So I try looking blank, which I must say, *always* works on Warren, and he's a *psychic*. But to my surprise, Tanya puts her hand on my knee. It's more comforting than I would have expected.

"Don't try that shit with me, Flip," she says. "Just tell me."

I suppose Warren would consider this an incredible breach of privacy, and in another mood, I might even agree. But under the circumstances, I tell her everything.

"OK, so men suck. We already knew *that*," Tanya says when I'm done.

"Not that that's always a *bad* thing."

"But *you're* a man, so by definition, you're doing something sucky, too, Flip. He does have a point—not like you're ever home. And when you *are* home, you're watching television."

Do you want to hear something really weird? It's actually a relief to hear her say that. But I say, "Oh, give me a break. As usual, he just loves to complain, but he would hate it if I really were around. And how I know this is because when we first got together, I actually *did* try to spend every spare minute with him, because at that point, OK, so *I* was madly in love, and I was actually *happy* to drop all my other friends—"

"Yes," says Tanya, "I remember that."

"Well?" I say. "I'm sorry for all the rest of you, deprived of my scintillating company. But it seems to have been a universally despised move on my part, because poor Warren didn't know *what* had hit him. You never saw anybody run so fast."

"So then *he* was the one who was out every night?"

"Who, Warren? Hardly. He doesn't have any friends—where would *he* go? He would just—I don't know. Tell me he felt like reading. Or get tired and want to go to bed—and not for all the romantic reasons you might imagine. Or—I don't know. He just made it very clear that I expected way too much from him." Suddenly the conversation stops being fun. "And then he left," I say finally. "And granted, at that point, I *wasn't* ever there. But—I thought it would be better when he came back. And it *is* better, it's a *lot* better . . ."

"Except now he's dating other people."

"Well, he isn't exactly dat-*ing*," I say. "It is just one date. In the afternoon. With Juliet there. I mean, him and Ian? Come on—Ian would eat him alive. No pun intended." Then I get quiet, remembering them at that dinner party. It isn't even the idea that Warren would like Ian that bothers me so much. It's more the idea that Ian would—that he'd know how to—that he would see something—special—in Warren. Not everybody does.

"So what's the problem again?" says Tanya. But before I can answer her, Elinor comes back in.

"Sweet sister, let me live!" There we are again.

"I don't know," says Elinor. She seems awfully discouraged. "Do you want to just skip this and move on?"

Tanya looks uncertain. But about this particular matter, I have no doubt at all. "Absolutely not," I say. This is one thing we can get right.

I take a deep breath. "You know what I think it is? That moment when I lift my head. If I start to do that too soon—but then Tanya, you have to be there—"

"I see what you mean," Tanya says. "You lift your head, I pull back—it all has to happen at the exact same time."

"OK," says Elinor. "Then you have to find that impulse at the same moment."

"Sweet sister, let me live!" If there's any chance of getting it right, I'm willing to do *this* forever.

WARREN: As we walk under the arch in Washington Square Park, Ian asks Juliet where she lived in Paris, and again, she lights up.

"Trente-trois rue Vavin," she says. "In Montparnasse. Right by the Jardin du Luxembourg."

"I know that street," Ian tells her, and for once, Juliet is glad that someone else knows something she knows. "Aren't you just around the corner from La Coupole?"

"*Yes!*" says Juliet. "We go there all the time."

They go on talking about Paris, and I wonder why I've never asked her about it, any more than I've spoken with her in French. *Because I want to pretend that she's always been with me.* Not only that she won't leave. But that she can't.

Suddenly, Juliet points to a man sprawled on a bench, wrapped in a dark red blanket. "Did he sleep there?" she asks. She's very insistently directing her question at me.

"I don't know," I answer. "It was awfully cold last night. I don't think anyone could have slept outside, particularly not in the park."

She stops walking and looks at me reproachfully. "We should help him," she says.

"Maybe we should," I say, "but I don't see how we can."

"We could give him money for an apartment."

"Apartments are expensive. I don't think we have enough money for that."

"We could give him money for a coat. That's not *so* expensive."

"I don't think we have the money for a coat, either," I say, although yes, if I really wanted to, I probably *could* buy that man a coat.

"Uncle Warren!" she says impatiently. "I know Mama doesn't have that much money, or Marta. But *you* do, don't you?"

I think for a moment. "If I *did* buy him a coat," I say finally, "that would mean I wouldn't have money for something else."

"Oh," says Juliet. "So we could take all the money we're going to spend on the movie and give it to him, and he could save it, and then he *would* have enough."

"I suppose we could do that," I say. "Is that what you want to do?"

She thinks again. "No," she says, and starts walking, much faster than before, so that Ian and I have to hurry to keep up with her. "No, I really, really, *really* want to see the movie."

"What would you have done?" I find myself asking Ian.

"Oh, I probably would have tried to explain the inevitable cruelty of the capitalist housing market and the futility of individual solutions to what is finally a social problem," Ian says very quietly, although she is now several feet ahead of us, looking fixedly down at the ground. "But Juliet's only eight, isn't she? I find they don't grasp the really *fine* points of economics until they're at least nine. And for very slow children, of course, ten."

I find this comforting, as of course I am meant to. And not even Rosie would have given that man our movie money, would she?

"Well, I for one am glad Juliet chose the film," Ian murmurs as we reach the edge of the park, "since I understand they've got quite a marvelous little animated soprano in the role of Turandot. There's been talk of having her de-but at the Met, but they haven't figured out how to solve the height problem."

I laugh, and it's like that time walking downtown with Flip—my whole skin seems to pull in his direction. And since Ian, too, is moving toward me, it would seem—but at that moment, safely out of the park, Juliet turns around and says, "Hurry *up*. We're going to miss the *movie*."

"There's plenty of time," I say. But she takes one of each of our hands—which I can see moves Ian enormously—and pulls us on toward the theater. I wonder if I would be feeling so happy, so elated, so flooded with desire, if it were actually possible that something might happen.

Sitting in the crowded theater between him and Juliet offers other kinds of pleasure. I like watching Juliet watch the screen, her face full of fierce con-centration, as though she wants to swallow every moment she sees. And when Ian takes my hand, when he pulls my whole arm against his waist and holds me there, it feels so warm and tender and at the same time so thrilling, that I think I'm going to melt.

"Well, *that's* something I've wanted to do for quite a while," Ian murmurs in my ear—yet another type of thrill.

"Mmmm," I say, wishing I could put my head on his shoulder.

"Aren't we shocking," he is whispering into my ear again, the closest thing to a kiss I can imagine. "Aren't we shocking, in the midst of all these *children*."

"*I'm* certainly shocked," I whisper back, my own semi-kiss. "All this elec-tricity."

"Uncle *Warren*," whispers Juliet angrily, not taking her eyes off the screen. "You aren't supposed to talk during a movie. It's very rude."

"Sorry," I say as quietly as I can manage. On my other side, Ian laughs.

ROSIE: When our meeting finally breaks for lunch, I know I should take ad-vantage of the occasion to cement my ties with the organizers from down-town. But rightly or wrongly, I need some time to myself. So I get an eggplant Parmesan sub from the sandwich place on the corner and walk as briskly as I can to Washington Square Park, just a few blocks away from our downtown office.

It's really too cold to be eating outside, but I don't care. I sit down on the sunniest bench I can find, facing the fountain. And just as I bite into my sand-wich, who should appear but Jack Kim, carrying a sandwich of his own.

When he sits down beside me, my mouth is too full to talk. "I saw you go into that sandwich shop," he says. "And you seemed like someone who would know how to get the most out of the lunch hour." He grins at me, with more warmth and less deliberate charm than usual. This immediately makes me suspicious: When charming men turn *off* the charm, that's when you want to watch out.

"So," he's saying, "I figured I'd follow you." He takes a bite of his sandwich, which I notice is also an eggplant sub. "I hope you don't mind."

I swallow. "No, not at all," I say in my best organizer mode.

He laughs. "Well, clearly you don't mean *that*. Really, Rosie, I can leave. It's freezing out here, anyway." He grins at me again. "So these are the lengths to which you'll go to get a little private time. And then *I* have to come along and ruin everything."

I am having such a hard time not saying, "Yes, so go away," that the only way to shut myself up is to take another bite. Thin, warm sun on my face; salty food in my mouth—this would feel wonderful if only I were alone.

It would also feel wonderful if I could have a cup of coffee. I don't want it right this minute, but I feel the craving, urgent and demanding.

"Can I just ask you one thing?" Jack says. Oh, God, now he's being *serious*.

"What?" I indicate, chewing steadily.

"Well, you have very good politics, clearly," he says. "So how do you reconcile that with being part of the trade union establishment?"

"Oh, Jack," I say before I can stop myself. "It's my lunch hour."

"I'm not trying to give you a hard time, Rosie," he says earnestly, and OK, he *does* look troubled. "I've tried to figure it out and clearly, I can't. So I thought I'd ask you."

"All right, Jack," I say, taking another bite. "What exactly is bothering you about my politics?"

"Well, you know," he says. "Unions. Isn't their whole *point* to keep the system in place?" He looks around the park. "OK," he says. "So we could give that guy a dollar, right?" He points to a man sitting on a bench, wrapped in a dark red blanket. "But you wouldn't expect to change anything by it."

I nod. "And then we could give him ten thousand dollars," Jack says. "Or even a hundred thousand dollars. Enough to get him off the street—but that would still be a very small change."

"Extremely small." He hands me a napkin.

"Or, we could build him a shelter, so he'd always have somewhere to sleep. Still not enough, right? Or a thousand shelters, or a hundred thousand shelters—however many it took to get *everybody* off the street. But just into a shelter, right? Not into a real home, a real job, a real life. And now we're practically talking utopia anyway. I mean, *I* don't see New York City doing even 10 percent of what I'm talking about. Not under our current system. Am I right?"

I nod, reluctantly. All those people whose lives aren't going to change in my lifetime, no matter how hard I work—I don't usually have the heart to focus on *them*.

"So we'd have to think about what really *would* make a difference," Jack goes on. "Low-cost housing for everyone in New York City? And that wouldn't *have* to mean the whole system changing, because theoretically, the government could spend all that money and it would still be capitalism—but we both know that in *this* country, to win something like that, the whole system *would* have to change. But we shouldn't settle for anything less, right, because anything else is just way too small. Right?"

I take my last bite. "Yes," I say. Satisfaction, relief, and a warm, full stomach—but it's like my blood won't settle down. "OK, yes, so?"

"Well, isn't it the same with the union?" Jack says. "It's so *small*. So we get another few cents an hour—"

"Jack. It's not *that* little."

"OK, a few dollars more a week. And a few more work rules—"

"Better protection against sexual harassment," I say. "The University paying into the minority workers' fund, to help equalize white and minority salaries. Not exactly nothing."

"It's tinkering, Rosie. Basically, we'll all still go to work, and the boss will still give all the orders, and we still won't be making enough to have a really *good* life. And we'll work harder and harder and harder as our lives get smaller and smaller and smaller. What's the point?"

"You want the whole system to change," I say slowly. "You want socialism."

"Well, don't you? What do you want, Rosie?"

God, why is everybody asking me that this week? Every single thing I want at the moment is something I'm not allowed to have.

"Well, of course I want socialism, Jack. Obviously I do. It's not a question of what I *want*."

"But you don't think it's possible," he says, and I'm surprised how defeated he sounds.

"No, Jack," I say gently. "I *do* think it's possible. Even though there are only about five people left in the United States who agree with me. But I don't know how to *get* from here to there. I used to *think* I knew, how we would all build socialism together, but now all I can see are the next few steps. You know—unions. Health care. Housing. And maybe I can see the *last* few steps, you know, the ones where everything changes and we actually *have* socialism. But that whole part in the middle—no."

"Well, if you don't *know* it's possible, if you're not absolutely sure, then how do you keep on doing what you're doing? When it's so *small?*"

"It isn't small," I say.

"It isn't big," he says. "It's just—"

"One step after another," I say. "Sometimes that's all you have." I look at my watch.

"Is *that* the best you can do?"

Reluctantly, I stand up. "No. It's just the best I can do on no coffee."

"Well, if that's all," he says, standing up with me, "I'll *buy* you a cup of coffee." Oh, why not? I want it, *and* I can have it. Is there anything wrong with that?

WARREN: Apparently you can buy the plastic versions of the *Turandot* characters if you also purchase a special meal at some fast-food restaurant, so after the show virtually everybody in the theater heads to the fast-food outlet located conveniently up the block. Juliet is thrilled at the prospect of owning Tam-Tam, her favorite character. But when she finds that she's the only one eating here, she looks at us in despair. "But then we only get *one* of them," she says. "If *everybody* would eat, I could get Tam-Tam *and* Miou-Miou *and* the Princess. She's so beautiful. Aren't you just a *little* hungry?"

I hate saying *no* to her, but I do feel a certain obligation. "One toy," I say firmly. "But it doesn't have to be Tam-Tam. You could get the Princess."

"*No,*" says Juliet passionately. "I *love* Tam-Tam. And he *needs* a good home, Uncle Warren. If I don't take him home, he'll just have to stay here in the restaurant. What kind of life is that?"

I realize I'm in a, well, *fragile* state at the moment, but this makes me want to smile so much that it very nearly brings tears to my eyes.

"Can I at least also get Miou-Miou?" Juliet says. "*She* needs a good home, too."

"Not this time," I say. But as a special treat, she gets to take the money and go stand in line by herself. Ian smiles uncertainly across the plastic table and starts to take my hand. Then he stops.

"Well, this is awkward, suddenly," he says. "Why do you suppose that is?"

I don't know why it didn't occur to me that he might take this at all seriously. "I think perhaps I misrepresented something the other night," I say carefully. "When I said that Flip and I don't tell each other *everything*. I mean, technically, no, not *everything*. He knows I was seeing you this afternoon, of course. But beyond that—"

"But if it *were* to go beyond that, then you would have to tell him—more than you want to tell him." He looks far more unhappy than I would have expected.

"I hope I didn't lead you on," I say.

"Well, you did, rather." Then he smiles, that wolfish grin he shared with Simon. "It's all right," he says. "My revenge is still to come. Because there will come a time when you *will* want me."

"Well. That sounds dangerous," I manage to force out. Ian stops smiling.

"You speak as one who knows," he says finally. If he keeps on looking at me like that, I'll slide right under the table. "In fact, I would say that *you* are far more dangerous than you look."

ELINOR: When we finally finish rehearsal, all three of us are exhausted, but pleased. "Yet another artistic triumph," Flip says as he waves goodbye, and he's always so critical that I can't help feeling particularly pleased about that.

Tanya walks me to the train. "Thanks again," she says. "Not like you had to give up *your* Saturday."

"No, really. I enjoyed it."

She's looking at me curiously. "Didn't you mind, though? I mean, the audition wasn't even for you."

"I doubt that group has all that many parts for women my age anyway," I say ruefully. "Or if they do, you know. They'll have fifty million women over thirty-five and about three men."

"Given that all the men are out in L.A. earning *real* money," Tanya agrees absently. "But you still could have—I mean, Elinor. How much *do* you like directing?"

"You mean, is that really what I want to do now?"

"Well, not like you aren't *good* at directing. Just, you know. Don't you miss acting?" She laughs in an embarrassed way. "Like some old rotten lover," she says, "who only comes around once every blue moon, and even then, he doesn't stay the whole night. But still, you know. You would miss him if he never showed up."

What if I did stop acting? *Would* I miss wanting something so much, *so much,* and never, never getting it? Sometimes the wanting is all you have.

WARREN: After Juliet has finished her meal, the three of us walk out together onto Sixth Avenue. "Goodbye, Juliet," Ian says gravely. "Thank you for spending the day with me." He bends down to kiss me goodbye. "Till we meet again," he says, giving me a long, lingering kiss. It's all I can do not to open my mouth to him, even there on the street.

But Juliet is here, and we *are* on the street, and obviously there are other reasons to restrain myself as well. "Come on, Juliet," I say. "Let's go home." It's simply ridiculous to be this happy.

Juliet seems unfazed by my altered state, which makes me wonder if this was a common occurrence with Madeleine. Maybe so, because when she sees I am ready to talk, she looks up from the conversation she's having with Tam-Tam and says matter-of-factly, "So is Ian your boyfriend?"

"No," I say. "He isn't."

"Is he your very good friend?"

"I don't know," I say. "Maybe." I shrug as another wave of happiness hits me.

Juliet nods. "So you have only one boyfriend."

"It looks that way."

She nods again. "I think it's better to have *lots* of boyfriends. And girlfriends."

"Really? Why?"

She thinks for a minute. "Well, for one thing, if you get tired of one, you can just get rid of them."

"And still have someone left over."

"Yes, exactly. So when I grow up, I'm going to have seven boyfriends and seven girlfriends."

"One for each day of the week."

"Exactly," Juliet says again. "So if any of them has something else to do, no problem. I'll just call up somebody else."

"What if they're *all* busy?"

"Then I'll call *you* up, Uncle Warren. And you can come right over and visit me."

When we get home, Juliet disappears into her room, and I start dinner. I'm crushing garlic for the spaghetti sauce when to my surprise, Flip comes in. "I thought you were going to the gym," I say.

"Well, it's not exactly like anyone has *asked* me to do a nude scene any time in the near future," Flip says. "So I figured I could go to the gym tomorrow. Any unbuffness I display in the meantime will probably go unnoticed."

"Certainly by me," I say. "*I* don't see what you could possibly improve."

"Mmmm," Flip says. "Nice try. So, how was your date?"

"Flip. I already told you. It wasn't a date."

"Oh, please. Believe me, if there's one thing I know when I see it, it's a date."

"Have it your way," I say. "It was nice."

"So. Tell me what happened."

"You know, Flip," I say, throwing the onions into the pan, "you go out all the time with your friends, till all hours, I might add, and I never hear a word about it."

"You don't ask," Flip says. "Actually, I always assumed you preferred not to know. But now I'm asking you."

"But not because you're interested in what we talked about. You're checking up on me."

Flip bursts out laughing. "Well, of *course* I'm checking up on you!" With a glance at Juliet's room, he lowers his voice. "You had a *date*."

"It really wasn't," I say. "We took Juliet."

"Oh, like that would stop him from propositioning you. I'm sure that made it very awkward." He looks at me. "You're in way too good a mood for him not to have," he says, "although I suppose if you had said *yes* or even *maybe*, you wouldn't be being such a prick with me now."

"My God," I say, "hasn't anyone ever told you that some things *are* better left unsaid?"

"No," says Flip, "I think that's stupid. Besides being unfair. Believe me, Warren, if the situation were reversed, you would be a lot more pissed off and miserable than I am right now, which I know because you're that way even when the situation *isn't* reversed, when you only want to act like it is but you actually *do* know better."

"Oh, come on. You can't possibly be trying to tell me that in all the times you've gone out with other people, you never got propositioned. I'll believe you always said no, but I'll never believe *that*." I go over to the sink to fill a pot with water. Flip looks absolutely miserable, which really does seem incredibly unfair.

"Flip, I honestly don't understand," I say after a minute. "Why are you so upset about this?"

"Because the whole way you want to keep it to yourself," he says promptly, "it's so—I don't know. You want me to see you doing it. But I don't go out and do things with other people for your benefit, Warren." He laughs in that angry way. "Not that it does me any good *anyway*, because you always want to believe the worst. And I *haven't* done anything that—that counts as cheating. But you make me feel so awful about having any other life at all. No matter how I try to consider you. And then you act like you have all this credit stored up and you can do anything you want toward me, because *I've* already been so awful."

I dump the pasta into the boiling water and go stand beside him at the sink. "All right," I say. "I'm sorry. And you're right—you haven't done anything *wrong*. But it's still hard, Flip. You're still never here." He keeps leaning against the sink, looking straight ahead. "It's not just that you want 'some other life,' " I say. "It seems there's something about being here that simply makes you—" I laugh suddenly. "I should know," I say. "Believe me."

"And *I'm* not walking out," Flip says.

"All right," I say. "I said I was sorry."

"But you're so *happy* about it."

"I only liked him," I say. "I didn't like him *best*."

This actually does make Flip smile, though I can see he still doesn't want to. "You'll just go off and be parents together," he says. "Plus, he should have liked *me* best."

"Well, I can't help *that*."

He looks at me. "I don't care if you go off and feel—free—on your own," he says. "I really don't. You just made such a point of *showing* me."

"I get it," I say. "I'm sorry."

The timer rings. "Is there anything else?" I say.

"All right," he says finally. "I guess this is where I'm supposed to get over being so unhappy."

I don't move. "Really," he says. "Go on, Warren. There isn't anything more to say."

"All right," I say, leaving him alone by the sink. Thinking, so is this the worst that it gets? To know that I made him so unhappy. And this time I did it on purpose.

ROSIE: Michael hands me a piece of lemon as I hand him the soy sauce. We're cooking together—this very healthy stir-fry of chicken and vegetables over brown rice, and you'd think it would be fun, but it's not. Why not? And don't say, because of that little lunch with Jack Kim, because honestly, all he did was buy me coffee, and by that point I was so deep into caffeine withdrawal, he could have been Charles for all the difference it made.

Michael gives me a funny look. "What are you thinking about?" he says. "Why?"

"Because you look about a million miles away."

"I'm sorry," I say. "I'm just very preoccupied with—I mean, do you want to hear about our meeting?"

He can't help laughing. "Rosie," he says, in that long, drawn-out, drawling voice, "I've only asked you about it like three times. And each time you say, 'Oh, great, yeah,' and then you get all quiet again, and I don't know *where* you are." He throws a pile of vegetables into the pot—onions, I think, and carrots, but I really *haven't* been paying attention—and they fall into the wok with a huge hiss.

"That's nice," I say. "It's so dramatic."

"Yeah, right," he says, and starts chopping red and green peppers. It's going to *look* beautiful, anyway.

I put my hand on his arm. "Michael, stop a minute."

He shakes his head, not looking at me. "You can't stop in the middle like this," he says. "It won't make any sense."

"What?"

"It won't—come together. You have to do it in a certain order, so the juices all, you know. Mingle."

He feels me looking at him. "What?" he says finally, not looking up. His hands open over the wok like a miniature cargo hold. The vegetables drop, hiss, steam.

"You're just so—it's wonderful how you know these things. Not just that you know. But that you care so much."

"Yeah, yeah, yeah, the great chef."

"I meant it," I say.

Finally he looks at me. "But it's not what *you* care about."

"Michael. That isn't exactly new news."

"I don't mean cooking." Now he's chopping greens. Light green, dark green, green flecked with yellow. "You don't care about anything that . . ."

"That *what,* Michael? Finish a goddamn sentence for once in your life. *What* don't I care about?"

The greens are heavy and damp, so they don't hiss and steam—they just smolder. "I thought you weren't supposed to have coffee," he says, out of the blue. God knows why I told him about that.

"No," I say. "I guess I'm not."

"Then why did you?"

"I didn't think I'd get through the afternoon without it. And I couldn't afford to be groggy, Michael—I had to be sharp."

"And now you just want it more. Right now. I bet you're just dying for a cup of coffee."

I am, actually. Or tea. Hot, milky, caffeinated tea with two sugars, the way Ma fixes it.

"Don't you want to get well?"

"Of course I want to get well. I just—"

"Or do you like it better this way?" he says, his back still toward me. "When you're so sick you can't even do—anything, not even *after* you've rested. And then finally you *can*. And then you go right out and drink the very worst thing for you."

"Oh, Michael, for God's sake. I don't want to get sick. I just wanted a fucking cup of coffee."

"*Two* cups of coffee," Michael says. "And now you want more."

I *do* want more. I *do* want something else. Though I have no idea why I wouldn't be doing everything in my power to keep *this*.

"I'm *sorry*," I say. "All right, Michael? No more coffee, no more chocolate—I'll be perfect."

Michael goes to check the vegetables. "OK," he says as though nothing had happened, as though nothing had ever happened. He starts fixing me a plate of chicken and vegetables and rice. "So what *did* go on at your meeting today?"

"What do *you* want, Michael?" I say suddenly. "Why won't you ever tell me that?"

He looks at me, blank and—something else. A look that pushes me away, hard.

But all he says is, "I want to have dinner, Rosie. And to hear about your day."

So I start to tell him, because of course, I want *that*. "You just don't like things to be easy," Marcy says whenever I try to tell her why sometimes it drives me absolutely crazy to spend time with Michael. "You don't like to be adored, Rosie. You'd rather fight."

But I *do* like to be adored. I just want—more.

WARREN: I suppose Flip does get over being *so* unhappy. At dinner, he and Juliet talk about *Turandot,* which Flip offers to take her to again, since, as it turns out, he loves animation and has actually gone on his own to see all of her favorite movies. "I don't have to go to the gym *next* Sunday," he tells her. "I could take you then, if you want."

"Certainly I want," says Juliet.

"Good," Flip says. "And should we let Uncle Warren come with us?"

Juliet looks at me uncertainly. Clearly, she would rather have that special day alone with Flip. So I say casually, "Oh, I've already seen it once." Juliet immediately looks disappointed, though she stares right down at her plate, trying to hide her reaction. "But it would be nice to see it again," I say quickly. "I could certainly come, too."

Just as she tried to hide her disappointment, Juliet now tries to hide her excitement. "OK," she says skeptically. "But I get to sit in the middle. So you two can't talk during the movie. Because I want to hear *every word,* and when people *talk,* Uncle Warren," she glares at me, "then I can't."

"Good heavens, Uncle Warren talking during a movie," Flip says. "I didn't think he was physically capable of it." To his credit, Flip doesn't go any further with this, but fine, Flip, now I feel even worse, all right? I mean, I didn't want him to have to sit there imagining me and Ian whispering together in the movie theater, particularly when, the few times Flip and I have gone to a movie together, I wouldn't let him so much as murmur a comment to me under his breath.

I don't know. Maybe Flip picturing Ian and me together was exactly what I *did* want.

Flip doesn't say much to me the rest of the evening, and when I finally go into the bedroom, he is sleeping way over on his side of the bed. "Flip," I whisper, pulling the covers straight. *"Flip."* But either he's incredibly committed to pretending, or he really is out like a light.

To my surprise, I don't actually have trouble falling asleep. Maybe because he *is* there, however distant. Except then I wake up in the middle of the night, sudden and confused, to realize that he *isn't* there. I pull on my robe and go into the living room, where he's curled up in the corner of the couch, just the one lamp on, staring at his script. "I'm sorry," he says when he finally notices me. "Did I wake you?"

"I woke up by myself," I manage to say. "Are you all right?"

"What? Oh, yeah, sure. Just—we worked on this all afternoon, and it still isn't . . ."

My God, I think through the last shreds of sleep, we really *don't* ever talk. "So what's the problem?" I say as I sit down.

"I'm not exactly sure. I think— Are you sure you want to hear this, Warren? *I am* all right."

I shake my head.

"You know what I think it is?" he says finally. "It's that I'm used to doing the major speech in this scene as a monologue, for auditions, and I had my own way of doing it. And now I'm saying it *to* Tanya, and it's hard to make the switch. Do you know what I mean?"

I shake my head again. "Show me."

"God, *there's* a weird idea. Performing for you, here in our living room . . ." He keeps looking at me, eyes narrowed, but I'm too tired to argue. "Oh, all right," he says finally. "I *do* think it's a little weird, but . . ." He goes to stand in front of me. "So," he says, "this is how I'd do the speech if I were auditioning for you. Though if I really were auditioning, I'd probably ask if I could use you."

"I don't understand."

"Well, the speech is written to be said *to* someone," he explains. "To my sister, Isabella. So ideally, I'd say this speech to *you* and then work off your reactions. Of course, since you're *not* an actor, you'd probably do what most auditioners do, which is just sit there looking blank. But it still might be easier to talk *to* you, if you'd let me."

"What if you ask to use me and I say no?"

"Well," says Flip. "That's what usually happens. Then I just have to imagine Isabella's reactions and react to what I imagine. Which is not all that different from what I have to do anyway, a lot of the time. If the actor I'm working with isn't giving me back anything. Or is giving me the wrong things. I always have to decide when to notice what the other person is actually doing, and when to ignore him and substitute this whole other imaginary person."

"I understand the concept," I say, hoping that he never finds out how well I do understand it.

"Mmmm," he says. "All right, then." He turns away, and I see him become Claudio. His whole face and body change—suddenly he has a completely different shape—an arrogant tilt of his head, an aggressive thrust of his shoulders, a way of puffing out his chest. Covered with a layer of fear—no, terror. Even his voice is different.

> *Ay, but to die and go we know not where;*
> *To lie in cold obstruction and to rot;*
> *This sensible warm motion to become*
> *A kneaded clod . . .*

He finishes the monologue and drops the character. "So," he says abruptly in his own voice, "if I were speaking to my sister, what would you say our relationship was?"

"You probably couldn't tell from just that little bit," he says when I don't answer right away. "It's all right, Warren. You don't have to answer."

"No, I saw her," I say slowly. "I saw that she was so preoccupied with her own—with how much she didn't want to—to give in to you, I suppose. So that you had to browbeat her. No, not browbeat. Blast. As though she were a—a block of ice, and the only way you could get through to her was to melt her."

Flip is staring at me. "That's the image I use, actually," he says. "Ice and a blowtorch." He can't help smiling. "OK, so now I'm going to pretend you're Tanya. Doing *her* version of Isabella."

"Which is not—"

Flip shakes his head. "Let me just show you."

He starts the speech the same way—it's still the same character—but almost immediately, *he* is the one who melts. Because this time, he *is* reaching her, and his vision of death is so horrifying to her, she doesn't want to hear it—but she does, she can't help it. So instead of growing angrier and more desperate, he's pleading with me, drawing me in, and the more terrified he becomes, the more upset I get. And then he pauses a moment, crying "Sweet sister, let me live!" and flings himself down at my feet.

After a moment, he lifts his head, but he doesn't stand up. Now it's my turn to stare.

"Well, how about it, Warren?" he says finally. "If you were my sister, would you let me live?"

I shake my head. "My God, Flip, I'm sorry. I'm so sorry."

"For any particular reason?" he says. "Or are you just expressing sympathy for a regrettable performance?"

"Good heavens, no," I say. "That was amazing. Truly amazing. I'd sleep with anyone to save your life after *that*."

I swear I did not say that on purpose. Although you never know—perhaps I did. Certainly it catches *him* by surprise, and he bursts out laughing as he lifts himself up to sit beside me on the couch. "Well, you don't have to go *that* far."

I throw my arms around him, which more or less takes him by surprise, because it's so unlike me. "I really am sorry," I say again.

Firmly but gently, he pulls away. "OK. Why?"

"Oh, God, there's a whole list of reasons at this point."

"Well, start with your worst sin, and work backwards from there."

"This morning, of course. I'm sorry it took me so long to tell you. And—"

"Wait a minute," Flip says. "What do you mean, you're sorry it took you so long?"

"I mean, I said I was sorry before. But I don't think I meant it. I still do think it's a problem, your being gone so much. But you were right, Flip. You didn't deserve—and I'm sorry. Although I have to say, I didn't think it would matter. So much."

"You always do that, Warren," Flip says. "To both me *and* Juliet, actually. You always think it doesn't make any difference what you do because in your warped little world, neither of us cares about you all that much anyway."

A thought occurs to me suddenly. "She hasn't said anything to you, has she? About me? About wishing I—"

"No, of course she hasn't," Flip says. "I would always tell you, Warren, no matter how mad I was at you. If she ever said anything to me that I thought you should know, I would always tell you."

"So," I say, wondering what on earth can make this better, "I see you *are* an incredibly responsible parent, after all."

"Oh, nice try, Warren." But I can see he's pleased about that, at least.

"Well," he says after a minute, "how about this? Can you *finally* find a nighttime sitter for next week, for either Friday or Saturday night, and we'll actually go out and do something *together*? There must be *something* we can both enjoy." Even though he's still so annoyed, I can't help smiling, and unwillingly, he smiles back. "Rehearsals for Tiger's Eye start next week," he says, "so I won't make any promises for the weeknights. But I can be home for dinner the other weekend night, the one we don't go out. For dinner and the whole rest of the evening, in case you were wondering."

"Oh," I say. "That *is* generous of you."

"Well, I have my moments." He pulls even further away from me, settling himself into the cushions at the other end of the couch. "So what else are you sorry for, Warren? You said there was a list."

"Oh. Well." I brace myself. "It was seeing you act. Seeing how much you miss that kind of acting. Whatever else you're doing in Tiger's Eye, I have the impression it isn't that. And when I saw you just now——"

I take a deep breath. "I saw that you were starving," I say finally. "Not only this week, but for a long, long time. Because even when you're *in* a play, I mean, a play with regular parts, like *Tartuffe,* if you don't really get a chance to——to *use* yourself. . . And I can't believe that I *live* with you, Flip, and I lived with you before, and I never saw——that. I just wanted you to stop being so unhappy."

"And now you think I *should* be unhappy."

"No," I say slowly. "I don't think that helps."

"Well, what *will* help, Warren? You're the fucking psychic, you tell me. Is there some *other* fucking thing I'm supposed to kill?" And when I'm still searching for an answer, he says, more or less desperately, "So what *do* you think about what Rosie said?"

"Oh," I say, completely surprised. I knew he was upset about not talking to Rosie, but I had no idea that he was still thinking about the actual conversation. "Are you sure you want to hear this?"

"You mean, am I going to storm out of the house and take the car? You're forgetting, Warren, we don't *have* a car."

I laugh, and *he* looks relieved. A night of surprises. "All right," I say. "I do think she put the whole subject too——extremely, I suppose would be the word."

"Rosie? Oh, what a surprise."

"All right. But she was right about one thing, Flip. Making a living as an actor isn't what you're starving for."

"I never thought it was."

"Maybe not. But it's all you ever talk about. Not the work, not really. Just—having a career."

"And you think I'm *better* than that."

"Actually, yes," I say. "I didn't think so before, if you want to know the truth. But that's what I saw tonight. And I'm so sorry, Flip, that I didn't see it before. Because if the acting is just a means to an end, then I really *don't* have all that much sympathy with how absolutely miserable you've been about it. If all you really want is money, and success, and legitimacy, then go to law school."

"But acting is *my* means."

"So what? If it's just a means and it isn't working out, then you drop it. It's only the ends you can't get rid of so easily."

He stares at me again. I look at his face as if I were trying to memorize it. All this time, knowing him, and I never saw *this*. The thing that matters to him most.

He is still staring at me. "What?" I say.

He looks down at his hand, picking at some flaw in the leather cushion. "I really don't know what to do."

"Well, you will."

"Is that opinion personal or professional?"

"Some of both. I mean, I don't really *know* anything. But I do have faith in you, Flip." I lean over and put my arm around him.

"See, Warren," he says, in a voice that trembles below the dryness he's trying to put into it, "this is why I stay with you. You're my root."

"Like you said with Juliet."

"Her, too. So of course I stay with you. Where else would I go?"

"But you go lots of places," I can't help saying. "You're gone all the time."

"Yes," says Flip, "but you're *home*. You're *my* home." Then he says, trying to speak lightly above the trembling, "And what about you? I mean me?"

"You mean, what are you to me?" *You are my life,* is what I want to say. *Without you I'm so lonely that I might as well be dead.*

But I can't say that. I mean, I don't want to. And after this afternoon, I'm not even sure it's true.

So instead I say, "Oh, Flip. You are my sweetness. You make my life sweet."

For a moment, I'm afraid that isn't enough. But I see him smile, I feel him sink closer against me. "Good," he says emphatically, pressing his hand against my chest. I cover his hand with mine. "Good," he says again. Then he's asleep.

I feel his body rise and fall against mine. Suddenly, I don't miss him anymore. Suddenly, he's here.

SHOPPING

TANYA: "No, not that one," I say to the bored clerk, who, honestly? Is getting under my last nerve. Does she think I can't afford to buy clothes like these? "The gray one," I say. Not like I'm not scared myself, spending this kind of money on a *suit*.

"Yeah, OK," she says, looking fed up. "I heard you, gray. This one *is* gray."

Standing here in my bra and panties. Her holding the door open as she hands me the suit I *don't* want.

"Well, what color is the other one, then?"

"We have lots of colors." Looking like she might fall right down dead from boredom. Not like it's personal, I *know* that. If it was personal, she'd have her eyes on me every minute. "Black, gray, olive, gunmetal—"

"Gunmetal, then," I say. The color Trish Hunter wore.

"—off-white, smoke, and heather."

"I don't know. Maybe smoke. Could you bring them both, please?" If I just shut my eyes and *jump* . . . "See, I told you they were very impressed with you," my agent told me. "Saving you for something more classy." Child, please. The lieutenant they bring in to replace Trish Hunter. You don't get any more classy than *that*.

The weird part is, before I got the call, I actually felt sorry for Trish. Unjustly accused of being involved in Lucas Rider's cocaine scam. And then, can you believe it, she fails her drug test. We still don't know why. But now that she's demoted, somebody has to take her place at the head of the squad. Right at the end of the season, but my agent said three episodes—and maybe *next* season—

"You're only allowed one suit at a time," the clerk says.

"Oh." Well, maybe it *is* personal. Seems *real* unlikely at these prices that they'd only let you try on *one* suit. Not like you can fit a *suit* into your handbag.

"Smoke, then," I say finally.

Now she studies me, eyes up and down my body. "You'd look better in the gunmetal," she says thoughtfully. "The smoke'll make you look fat." Then she says, "Oh, my God. I saw you on *Tales of Valentine Beach*. You were Carla. I watched you every day, that whole week you were on. You were great!"

"You must *really* be a fan," I say, embarrassed. "Being as that was only like five minutes per episode." Not the way I expected to feel, the first time I was *recognized*. Not like I expected to be in my underwear, either.

"No, no, you were great," she says. "And Jesse was so gorgeous. Are you guys like really going out? God, you were such a *bitch!*"

"Thank you," I say, but she's already calling out, "Hey, RENEE! Guess who's here?"

ROSIE: The thing I hate most in this world is shopping, so it seems like adding insult to injury that I have to do it *today,* my only free Saturday in weeks. But OK. If I don't get some new clothes soon—I mean, this *look* I got from Olympia's chief negotiator, who probably weighs about fifty pounds and practically lives at the gym. Of course, I have a boyfriend and she doesn't, so *you* figure it out.

You know what I really hate about shopping? It's that you can't do it just once. First you need the suit, and then you need the blouse, and then you need the shoes, and then you need the stockings, and then you probably need some other thing that *I* haven't figured out yet but that every other woman in America has, which is why *I* don't look—well, never mind. I wouldn't care, really, except if I don't look at least *somewhat* in the same league as Olympia's people, the members will feel like I'm letting them down.

What I'd really like to get is Trish Hunter's suit from that episode last month. That narrow gray one with the short skirt. Yeah. Like I could ever wear *that*. Still. I can't help thinking I'd have a whole other life if I could.

FLIP: Last week I was at this totally discouraging audition, one of those Equity open calls where about fourteen million out-of-work actors show up, even though you *know* they're just going to end up casting somebody who already *has* a career. And I'm actually thinking about what Warren said, because if some miracle happened and I *did* get into this show, it *would* be art.

So I've gotten my appointment (even though I had to get there at 6 a.m. to get it), and I'm trying to get myself into some kind of state where I might actually be able to do some *work,* and who should I see but Duncan Kraft, who was in my class at Sarah Lawrence and who, although he *is* gorgeous, couldn't act his way out of a plastic bag.

Today, Duncan looks even more fabulous than usual, because he's wearing this incredible leather jacket that absolutely *reeks* of success. Not just recent success, either. More like being *born* to success.

He actually recognizes *me,* and stops to say hello. "So when is *your* appointment?" I ask him, just to be polite.

"What? Oh, no, I'm not auditioning. I'm playing Gino, the *younger* brother. They wanted me to drop off an extra head shot so they could cast a Giorgio who looks like me."

I haven't been able to stop thinking about it since. Not Duncan—who cares about Duncan? But his jacket. I want that jacket.

WARREN: When I asked Juliet if she'd like to invite a friend over from school, she insisted that she didn't have any friends at that school. And when I tried to get her to say more, she wouldn't.

What she *would* talk about was socks. Which is ironic, given Ian's little joke. She carefully explained to me that this semester, all the really cool girls in her class have started wearing white silk ankle socks trimmed in colored rosebuds. There seems to be some code, a different color for every day of the week.

Naturally, I said I would get some for her. But only two pair. Which sent her into such a pit of despair that I almost gave in right then.

I don't know. Maybe she *should* have everything she asks for. Certainly three more pairs of socks won't put a dent in any budget *I* have anything to do with. Or two toys instead of one, or five toys instead of two.

But shouldn't there be a line somewhere?

FLIP: I can't *tell* you how much I want that jacket.

It's not that I think I should be able to buy *anything* I want. But I want that *so much. And* a fabulous Valentine's Day gift for Warren. *And* a nice present for Juliet. *And* tickets to the revival of *Vincent in the Field at Arles,* which only happens to be the first Broadway show I ever saw in my life—my first weekend at Sarah Lawrence, when I actually took all the money I had for the semester and spent it on a cheap hotel and meals in actual restaurants and a half-price, last-minute ticket for a show that none of the original stars were even *in.* So fine. This time I want to see the *real* cast. From the *good* seats.

Of course, *some* people have jobs at which they actually *earn* money. But not me, apparently. No, of course there's nothing *wrong* with me. I'm just not fulfilling one of the basic social prescriptions for being considered a mature man. (*Two,* if you count being married. *Three,* if you count having children.) Whereas if I, at the present moment, feel like buying myself a slice of pizza or a cup of coffee when I'm out walking around in the world, well, let's just say I'm suddenly in major financial trouble. Not being able to buy a fucking slice of pizza? In what sense is *that* life worth living?

MARIO: Saturday has turned out to be my favorite day. Because that's the day Joshua and I go shopping together, to buy food for the week. It's almost like—well, yes, it *is* almost like being married. Shopping at a supermarket—buying cereal and cookies and dish soap and paper towels and—I *know* it sounds silly. But it makes me feel normal.

ROSIE: "No, none of these," I say, handing a huge pile of suits back to the clerk, who is eager to help in a way that makes me feel like a total failure. I'm not going to be able to wear anything in *this* store, I can see that right now. Marcy and I used to joke about my feeling rejected by some fancy store. But I *am* being rejected. It's not the clothes that don't fit—it's me.

WARREN: And what about this? What if Juliet goes out and gets five pairs of socks, exactly the kind she likes, and all of sudden she does have lots of friends? Or even one friend. What kind of lesson does she learn from *that?*

FLIP: It's not *just* that the jacket would make me look fabulous. I also think it would give me confidence. All right, stop laughing. I *do* think so.

Anyway, it's moot, because if I *did* have any money, *obviously,* I'd have to use it to buy Warren a present. I don't want to get too Gift-of-the-Magi about it. But he really has been awfully sweet to me lately, and I don't think it's *all* out of guilt over Ian. I mean, Warren. It's OK.

Not that he ever believes me when I come right out and *say* that. But maybe he'd believe an actual present.

MARIO: When Flip called me up to ask me what I was planning to get Joshua for Valentine's Day, I told him that the whole idea of presents, and in fact holidays in general make Joshua very uncomfortable. So that in fact, it's *not* really giving him anything, if I insist on celebrating. In fact, it's actually fairly selfish on my part.

I don't think Flip understood though. "But you love Valentine's Day," he said. "It's your favorite holiday."

"Oh, you know," I say, uncomfortable myself, because I can hear that he really *doesn't* understand. "There are other ways to show you love somebody."

"I suppose there are," Flip says. "But—I mean, didn't he let you give him anything for Christmas, either?"

"Well, he's Jewish," I point out.

"Hanukkah, then."

"That's not really the same as Christmas. I mean, traditionally. It's not *such* a big present-giving holiday, not in its original form. Really, Flip, I don't care about it."

"Well," says Flip, trying *really* hard to be polite. "As long as he's nice to you. He *is* nice to you, isn't he?"

I said of course he was. But I don't think Flip believed me.

FLIP: After more soul-searching agony than you'd think any Valentine's Day deserved, I've decided to take the money I'd put aside for the February rent on the other apartment and buy Warren's and Juliet's presents out of that. Because then we'll all *have* to live together, won't we? I mean, officially.

All right, so I'm not so crazy about Warren's apartment—I fairly actively dislike it, if you want to know the truth. It's definitely not the best of Warren, or at least not *my* favorite part of him. Except maybe Juliet's room, which is much, *much* more comfortable than anywhere else in the apartment, so make what you will out of *that*. But Warren is right—it's clearly much better for Juliet to live in Chelsea, near Marta and Sara and Washington Square Park and all the other things that she likes. And whatever the—oh, all right, whatever the *memories* in that other apartment, well, they're still only memories, aren't they? Obviously Juliet could never live with us *there*.

So I suppose it is fairly Gift-of-the-Magi after all—here, Warren, here's your Valentine's Day gift, and guess what? Now I have to live with you, because I can't afford the rent anywhere else.

ELINOR: I *like* music. But more than that, I would say I *need* music. It's what I use to calm myself down. Or to focus on a particular piece of work. When

Idris comes over, we put music on for making love. Sometimes I listen to the same music, after she's gone.

So I go up and down the aisles of the CD store, taking, taking, taking. I know I can't afford all of them. But right now, it's a pleasure to imagine that I actually could have everything I want.

FLIP: To my total shock and amazement, Warren does make a big deal about Valentine's Day.

At first I think it's all because of Juliet. Who might not in the normal course of things have cared about Valentine's Day at all, or even have been aware of it. (I suppose in France, *every* day is Valentine's Day, if the movies can be believed.) But apparently, at her school, the Valentine's Day party is this enormous occasion, the prospects for which Juliet describes to me in excruciating detail. (Where do you suppose she gets *that* from?) "Well, I certainly won't get a valentine from Amy," she explains. "She's *way* popular. Everybody loves her. She has so many clothes, Uncle Flip, that she never wears the same thing twice." She sighs. "*Maybe* I'll get a valentine from Margie. Probably a horse valentine. All she ever *talks* about is horses—she even *has* a horse. A thoroughbred. She rides it every single Saturday of her life, and it's all she ever talks about. She's the kind of girl who gives valentines to *everybody,* just to be fair."

When, true to my word, I report this conversation to Warren, it turns out that Juliet has already talked to him, too. Stressing that for the party, she wants to wear her special socks.

What *is* it about those socks? I just don't see the appeal. Although I *really* don't understand why Warren is being so stubborn about this. If he had ever in his life had to worry about not having the right whatever, he would know better than to make an issue over three twelve-dollar pairs of socks. If he didn't have some kind of weird *principle* about it, *I'd* buy them for her.

Anyway, the upshot is that Warren decides to have a special Valentine's Day dinner for the three of us, so that at least Juliet will feel appreciated by *somebody.* (No, I *haven't* told him that he should give her the socks. Given how touchy he is wherever Juliet's concerned—I'm lucky he'll let me talk about her at all. Which is why I also haven't told him that he should take her out of that school and put her somewhere—I don't know, less *fancy*—where she *can* make friends. What kind of eight-year-old owns a thoroughbred, for God's sake?)

So I lobby for Tiger's Eye to change our rehearsal schedule, leaving Tanya all alone on Valentine's night at a particularly stressful time in her life—apparently her audition for Trish's rival went *very* well and her agent told her to expect a callback, which is just the kind of news guaranteed to drive a person crazy. I'm tempted to ask her to join us, but finally it seems far too complicated, so I don't. Which probably turns out to be a good thing, because, judging by the enormous box at my place at dinner, Juliet isn't the *only* reason Warren wanted to make a big deal out of Valentine's Day.

"I didn't know you gave *presents* for Valentine's Day," says Juliet. "I thought you just got valentines." She and I are sitting at the kitchen table, which Warren has decorated with a red tablecloth, and pink and white and silver ribbons, and those little candy hearts. Warren is standing at the stove, making chocolate chip pancakes and bacon—Juliet's new favorite American food.

"Sometimes you give presents on Valentine's Day," Warren says, bringing over a little pitcher of maple syrup, which he has actually warmed up. "It depends."

"So you give presents *and* valentines if you really *love* someone," Juliet says. "And just valentines if you only *like* them." Suddenly she looks truly distressed. "But I didn't give *Sara* a present, and I love *her*."

"You can love someone and just give them a valentine," I say. "Last year your Uncle Warren just gave *me* a valentine, for example. In fact, he might not even have done that." I grin at him, emboldened by the huge package waiting to be unwrapped. "But I *know* he loved me."

"That's why your Uncle Flip's present is so big this year," Warren tells Juliet. "It more or less stands for two years worth of Valentine's Days."

Juliet looks more upset than ever. "So someone could give you a really nice valentine and not even *like* you?" she says. "And someone else could really *love* you and not even give you a valentine?"

"Yes, it could work that way," I say, and she throws her silverware down on the table.

"Then how do you know *anything?*" she says, her voice rising. "How do you ever know?"

"What do *you* think, Juliet?" Warren says, putting my plate in front of me and passing me the butter. He has actually added almonds to my pancakes, which for some reason I love. "How *do* you know?"

Juliet thinks. "Well, Sara doesn't do *anything* because she has to," she says. "If she tells you something, she means it."

"So that's one way," Warren says.

"And some people never mean *anything*. They're just *liars*."

"So that's another way."

Juliet sighs. But at least she picks up her fork again. "I guess you just know," she says through a mouthful of food. "If you don't get *fooled*."

After dinner, we open our presents. Juliet first, of course. I have gotten her the Princess Turandot action figures—not the ones you get for free with a burger and fries, but the larger-sized versions that you have to buy in actual stores. She just lights up with pleasure—but that reaction is nothing to when she sees what Warren got her. Because there in the beautifully wrapped box are not three but five pairs of those damned rosebud socks. Juliet is so excited she can't even talk.

Then it's our turn. "Go ahead, Warren," I say. "Open mine first. I have a feeling yours is going to be the real climax of the evening."

Warren carefully unwraps his gift, a thin magenta envelope tied in shiny purple ribbon. He pulls out two months torn from a calendar, the weekends highlighted in different colors, with different items stapled to each weekend. So one weekend has a gift certificate from a restaurant he said he'd been wanting to try, and some others have gift certificates from movie theaters, and there are also a couple of coupons from Video Blitz (because that's one *other* thing we can do together). There are even two tickets to *Vincent in the Field at Arles,* which I hope Warren understands is not just a sneaky way for me to get to see that show, but a way to share with him something that was once a fairly important event in my life. And if the cost of all of these tickets and gift certificates has turned out to be so high that I *don't* have my full half of this month's rent, well, I hope he understands that, too.

Warren reads slowly through all the little parts of my present. Then he comes around the table and puts his arms around me. "Thank you, Flip," he says, hugging me hard. Which he's never done in front of Juliet before, not even once.

Juliet is saying eagerly, "Now you, Uncle Flip. Open yours. It's so *big*."

My present comes with a plain white card, not unlike the one I gave him for Christmas. In it, Warren has written,

Happy Valentine's Day, Flip. There is actually a Part Two to this present, but you'll have to wait until Juliet goes to bed. No, it's not that.

Which is intriguing enough, but then, inside the box—and I swear I am totally and completely surprised—inside the box is a leather jacket.

"I don't know what to say," I say, lifting it out. "I'm speechless." It appears to be so perfect, I'm almost afraid to try it on. But I do. And it *is* perfect.

Warren grins at me. "The day you actually are speechless, Flip, then I'll know I've *really* accomplished something."

"Mmmm," I say, putting my arms around him. "Apparently the surprises in our relationship work both ways." I give him as much of a thank-you kiss as it's suitable to give in front of Juliet. Hoping that Warren agrees with my judgment in this particular matter, but he's still smiling when I'm done. Well, who knew that *this* is what makes him happy—giving me fabulously expensive presents that I've been dying to have? That's good to know.

"OK," I say, after Juliet has gone to bed. "So what is this famous Part Two?"

Now he looks uncertain. "You have to come over here to get it." So I sit beside him on the couch and he puts his arms around me and whispers in my ear:

> *When in disgrace with Fortune and men's eyes,*
> *I all alone beweep my outcast state,*
> *And trouble deaf Heaven with my bootless cries,*
> *And sit upon the ground, and curse my fate,*
> *Wishing myself like one more rich in hope,*
> *Featured like him, like him with friends possessed—*

His voice falters a moment on that one. He swallows and tightens his arms around me.

> *Desiring this man's art and that man's scope—*

"Well, not *my* art," I say, interrupting him. "You could hardly desire *that*."

"Shhh," says Warren. And whispers again,

> *Desiring this man's art and that man's scope,*
> *With what I most enjoy, contented least,*
> *When in these thoughts myself almost despising—*

His voice falters again, but this time he doesn't pause, although he does stop whispering.

> *Haply I think on thee, and then my state—*
> *Like to the lark at break of day arising*
> *From sullen earth—sings hymns at heaven's gate.*
> *For thy sweet love remembered such wealth brings,*
> *That then I scorn to change my state with kings.*

For once, I really am speechless. "My God, Warren," I say after about a million years.

"So you adored the jacket," says Warren softly, "but me reciting Shakespeare, badly—that can make you cry. That's good to know."

ROSIE: "Happy Valentine's Day, Rosarita." Michael sets in front of me a huge steaming plate of spinach fettuccini with tuna sauce. Olive-green noodles and dark red sauce—like everything he makes, it's full of these beautiful bright colors. I feel the steam rising from the plate, the heat rolling off his body. He pauses to rub his cheek against mine, because before he was cooking, we were making love. I reach up my hand to hold him there a minute longer. We both sigh.

"So, Rosarita," he says after we've had our first few bites. My God, it is *such* a relief to have my body back. To make love, to take a bath, to sit down and eat—it seems like all I'll ever want. Of course, I still don't have the energy that I'm used to having, and I'm bleeding far more heavily than I think I should. But at least I don't feel that my whole life is running out of me.

"So, Rosarita," Michael is saying, his mouth full. "Like, where are you guys now? Fill me in."

"Do you really want to talk about this?" I say doubtfully. Because maybe part of the reason he never *tells* me anything, you know, is because he can't get a word in edgewise.

But he's nodding. Of course, he is going to be a labor lawyer, so he *always* wants to hear about the union. So I say, "All right, today is February 14th."

"And that's important because—?"

"Countdown," I say. "Every single day, right? Between now and April 12th, which is our strike deadline because—"

"—it's the first day of the spring semester," Michael says. "I remember *that*."

"So a big part of where we are," I say, trying not to sound *too* much like I'm talking from notes, "is that every single day—you know, Michael, it's like those World War II movies, with the maps and the pins? Where every day, the generals are looking to see how far the enemy has advanced, and how far *they* have?"

"OK," says Michael. "So what are the pins?"

"Well." I tick off the items on my fingers. "Always, always, always, (1) Do we have enough members? Out of the 1,013 clericals on campus, how many would strike? And (2) Do we have enough members in each building? Or will there be whole buildings where we don't even have a majority? And (3) How deep is the commitment? Of course, you can't really tell ahead of time, everything changes so much on the spot. So every day, we're rating each worker on a scale of one to five—how solid are they? And then rating every building. Well, OK, not every day. But every week. And in my head—"

"In your head, you're like doing it every hour," Michael says somberly. "I know. I see you do it."

"Really?"

"Oh, yeah, right, Rosie. Like when you're not talking to me, I have *no* idea what you're thinking."

I must look very sorry about this, because he says quickly, "I'm not complaining. But like, how could you think I *wouldn't* know?"

"Because I'm incredibly self-centered, obviously," I say. "And I chronically underestimate you, and—wait, wait, I know there's something else. Oh, yes—and I don't *want* to give you a chance."

He grins at me. "Well, so, OK," he says. "Tell me the rest of the pins before you forget where you are."

"People, buildings, how solid—OK, we could keep breaking it down. By race, by grade, by seniority."

"You mean, like, all the faculty secretaries want to strike, but all the xerox operators don't?"

"Well, actually, it would probably be the other way around. The faculty secretaries are the *last* ones who ever want to do anything. I mean, are they *all* in love with their bosses or what?"

"Rosie. That's harsh."

"I'll tell you," I say. "When I worked at Olympia, *I* was a faculty secretary. And everybody was *so* in love with my boss—people would actually come up to my desk and say, 'Oh, you must feel so *lucky* to work for Professor Dumas. He's such a wonderful man!' And I would think—well, I *really* didn't like being a secretary, OK? I *hated* making his fucking coffee."

"You hated that he had the right," Michael says.

"Yes, exactly," I say with some satisfaction. "I *hated* that he had the fucking right. Excuse my language."

Michael laughs. "Yeah, right."

"Well, the point being," I say—because I really am trying to clean up my vocabulary—it's too easy to slip and say *fuck* in front of the members. "The point being, that I had this huge revelation about one month into the job. That if I *were* in love with him—not sexually, exactly, although maybe that, too. But if I worshiped him. If I thought he *deserved* what he got from me. My job would have been *so* much easier."

Michael sighs.

"What?" I say.

"Nothing. Keep going."

"*What?*"

Michael looks extremely embarrassed. It's not like he *never* talks about his background. But whenever he does, he always has this same shame-faced look.

"At Brooklyn Tech," he says, and stops again. Oh, his old high school—one of the top three public high schools in the city. The one that lots of white people won't send their kids to because it's supposed to be too Black.

"At Brooklyn Tech," Michael is saying. "They acted that way. I mean, not every single person. But some of the teachers."

"That you were supposed to be grateful?" I say. "Just for the chance to be there?"

"Something like that. As opposed to—" He stops again.

"As opposed to what?"

"There were all these people saying, 'You think you're so . . . You think you're like *proving* something, going there?' "

I wait, I really do. But waiting doesn't work with him. I never thought I'd meet anybody *more* stubborn than I am. So finally I say, "You mean, the kids from your neighborhood? Who said you were acting white or something, going to such a fancy school?" Because I've heard all about this from Elena, our lawyer—her son gets a lot of shit from all his old classmates who didn't get into a high school as good as his.

"So how did you handle it with your friends?" I prompt, when Michael still doesn't say anything. "I mean, obviously, you *did* keep studying—but it must have been—"

"It's not important," he says, which is what he always says. "You want some more?"

I let him serve me another helping, because it *is* delicious and I *am* starving. But I can tell he's about to do what he always does, which is jump in with another question, a totally tempting question, I have no doubt, and there we'll be. Back in my territory.

So before he has a chance to say anything, I say, "Michael. Come on. Tell me."

"Tell you what?" he says.

"Isn't there more? Like, did that make it harder for you to study, knowing that people thought you shouldn't? As if, you know, you wanted to be white? Or was it a problem that the teachers thought you were going to fail, that they—"

"They didn't think I was going to *fail*," he says. "They just thought I should be grateful for the opportunity. Which is what I already said, Rosie, so I don't— Why do *you* have to be the one who says it?"

"I don't. I was just trying to get you to talk."

"I talk. I just don't say what you want me to say."

Well, *that's* hardly fair. Or is it? I have to tell you, I hate how hard it is to fight with him.

He is still watching me. He starts to reach out to make some nice little affectionate gesture, but something in my face must stop him, because he takes back his hand. And finally he says, "Why wasn't it enough, what I said?"

"*Was* it enough?" I say. "You tell me one one-hundredth of a story, and you wouldn't even have told me *that* if I hadn't practically tied you down and forced you—"

"Yeah, right."

"And then you won't tell me any more, and it's not just this time, Michael, it's always like that. It just makes me uncomfortable, that's all."

"Because you want to know all about me," Michael says. "You want my whole story."

"No!" I say. "Well, all right, yes, but not in the way you mean. I just want you to talk to me."

"I don't like to talk about myself," he says. "I don't believe in it."

"You don't *believe* in it?"

"It doesn't solve anything," he says. "It doesn't help. Especially not stuff that's over and done with."

"God, you must think I'm *so* self-indulgent then. Since that's all I *ever* talk about."

"No," he says.

"No, you don't think that, or no, that's *not* all I ever talk about?"

"No, both," he says. After a minute, he says, "You can do whatever you want. *I* just don't like to—and then when like you do it for me—"

So what can I possibly say now? It seems mean, doesn't it, to say that I feel cheated? But that is exactly how I feel.

Michael twists his tongue around in his mouth, watching me. "Could we just go on talking?" he says finally. "I was enjoying it. I mean, I was really interested."

"Well, of course you were really interested, Michael. It was about me. Am I just supposed to give you my *whole* life? And not get back even a tiny piece of yours?"

"Rosie," says Michael quietly after a moment. "It's Valentine's Day."

You know, Michael never fights back. So why does it seem like he always wins?

WARREN: Both Flip and I are fairly, well, *overcome* after what even I have to see is the huge success of my two presents to him. So we are preparing to leave the couch and head for the bedroom when Flip says, "Warren. Can we finally make it official? I mean, I haven't paid the rent at the other apartment yet. Why don't I just *not* pay it?"

God knows what expression is on my face. Because Flip suddenly looks extremely uncomfortable. "I mean, of course, in that case, I'd pay half the rent *here*," he says quickly. "So how much is that exactly?"

"Well," I finally manage to say. "There isn't exactly *rent* on this place. Because, well, I own it. I mean, it's a co-op. So there's maintenance. Which we can certainly split. And of course I would pay the mortgage. But the maintenance—I don't know. What do you think is fair?"

"What do I think is *fair?*" he says incredulously. "Well, *that's* hardly the question most on my mind. What the hell do you mean, you *own* it?"

It's somewhat difficult to explain. Particularly since, the whole time I am talking, Flip is staring at me as though he's never seen me before.

"So you have *money*," he says finally, stumbling over the words. "You're *rich.*"

"Well, not *rich*," I say. "I wouldn't say *rich*."

"No?" says Flip. He is so agitated, he starts pacing around the room. "You bought a co-op in fucking Chelsea? You have all this money just lying around? You can basically afford to buy anything you want—"

"Well, not *anything*. The money I get now—it more or less amounts to—to a second salary, I suppose. I mean, that's the income from the trust. It really isn't all that much."

"Not all that *much?* You have this whole other salary that you don't even have to work for, and you think that isn't *much?*" I see his eyes flick from the leather couch to the glass-topped coffee table to the Bauhaus chairs; I see him realizing where I got the money to buy them. He takes a very shaky breath. "And you never told me about it?" he says quietly. "Jesus, Warren. How could you not tell me?"

"Look, Flip," I say, trying to stay calm. "I don't care about the money. It isn't important to me—"

"Easy for you to say. After you made me feel like shit. After you said I was *deluding* myself."

"Look," I say more or less desperately. "We can put our money together. You can have what I have."

Flip looks at me furiously. "You think I'm marrying you for your *money?* Is that what you think?"

"I said I didn't care about the money—"

"Oh, you people always *say* that," says Flip. "But look at you. 'You can have what I have.' You're fucking terrified I'll take you up on that."

"I'm not," I say, but even to me, my voice sounds uncertain. "And what is this 'you people'? Who are you, Rosie?"

"At least *Rosie* has always told me the truth," Flip says coldly. "God, Warren. For someone who broke up with me because *I* wasn't earning a living—"

"I earn my living! And that *wasn't* why I broke up with you, and you know it! I never said anything about all those times you didn't have your share of the rent—"

"It wasn't 'all those times'!" He's practically screaming in frustration. "It was like *twice!*"

Juliet suddenly appears in the doorway. "Stop it," she says. "Stop *fighting.*"

Flip breathes out, hard and angry. "Did we wake you, Juliet?" he says tartly. "I'm sorry. Go back to bed. We'll try to keep our voices down."

Juliet and I are both shocked. "It doesn't matter if you're quiet," she says. "You were still *fighting.* Stop *fighting.*"

"People fight, Juliet," Flip says. "It happens." He looks at her more closely. "It doesn't mean anything bad is going to happen."

"You'll fight and you'll go home," Juliet says matter-of-factly. "Then you won't be here anymore."

Flip looks at me, and angry as he still is, he can't help laughing. "Really, Warren," he says to me, "is this what you call fighting fair?"

I don't even try to hide my relief. "Come on, Juliet," I say. "I'll take you back to bed. Flip will still be here in the morning."

"Really?" she says to him.

"It looks that way," he says. When I come back, he is sitting sideways in one of those extremely uncomfortable chairs.

"The bedroom is quieter," I offer. He sighs. "We can always fight in whispers."

"Oh, *there's* a good solution," Flip says. "Is that what *your* parents did?"

I have to laugh. "Fight? I don't think they talked."

"I don't know," Flip says. "They seemed like more of a team than that." I have this sudden memory of standing in the sunny, glassed-in room—the one that Flip insisted on calling the "conservatory"—watching my mother mist the

plants. Of course, there was someone who took charge of all the outside land-
scaping, but she liked to care for the indoor plants herself. It used to take her
hours—first the misting, and then the doling out of plant food, and then trimming away all the dead leaves, and sometimes she'd cut things back, or repot
them, or find some other little task that had to be done. I don't suppose it
took her *all* the time that my father was at his office, but it certainly used up a
good portion of the day.

Flip is still watching me. "This isn't over, Warren," he says grimly.

"I know," I say, although I've been hoping it was.

"It isn't just the money," Flip says. "It's everything. Like who's responsible
for Juliet, and who buys the stuff for the house, and if you do, does that mean
you get to pick everything out? And if you have more money than I do, does
that mean you just *do,* or is there some way it evens out, some way that
doesn't feel like you're just showering me with money?"

"Showering?" I say.

"Well?" Flip says. "You're the one who wants to call it marriage. All those
medieval ceremonies that you and Mario are so crazy about, what do you
think they were? It was people joining their lands together. And I don't have
any lands. So what am I, a serf?"

I can't help laughing. "For you to be a serf, I think *I* would have to have
lands. And I think *you* would have to do housework. Which as I recall, has happened how often? Oh, yes—never. I don't think you've exactly been relegated
to the serf's role, Flip."

"You say that now," Flip says darkly. "But once you married me, you'd have
me scrubbing the floors and doing the windows. You people always had Irish
maids."

"Well, we didn't *marry* them," I say. So he has to laugh too.

But then he says, "OK, so technically, you didn't *lie.* But Warren. Why
didn't you tell me?"

"I didn't *hide* anything," I insist. "You never asked."

"Oh, so those are the rules now?" he says. "What am I supposed to get
from that, Warren, that there's this whole list of *other* things you've been hiding from me?"

"Well, what about you, Flip?" I say sharply. "Maybe I should be thinking of
some new questions to ask *you.*"

"I don't know *what* you could be talking about," he says uncomfortably.
"Anything you have a right to know, I've certainly always told you."

"All right." I can't help sighing. "So it isn't over. Is it over for tonight?"

"I don't know," Flip says. "Is *this* the worst that it gets?"

"Not if you told Juliet the truth," I say after a minute. "Not if you're really not leaving."

"Oh, well," says Flip. "If you're going to bring *Juliet* into it. I wouldn't want her to think I was a *liar*."

Don't stay on her account, I want to say. Don't you say I'm a liar, either. But even I know that there's such a thing as leaving well enough alone. At least for tonight.

FLIP: Well, I'm sorry, I can't help it. It's driving me crazy to think that Warren has all this *money* he never told me about, even if what he does with it is buy me incredibly expensive presents that I now can't bear to wear, and I'm sorry about that, I really am, but I'm really *not* doing it to punish him. I'll even admit that it isn't *all* Warren's fault, he has a point, I *could* have asked. And then I remember him saying that he paid *his* share of the rent out of his earnings as a psychic, whereas I paid my share out of my earnings as a bicycle messenger, and I just want to kill him. (At least he's offered to pay for *both* apartments this month, which shows a sense of justice that I suppose only the rich can afford.)

And then to make matters worse, there is something very wrong going on with Juliet at school, which I know because *Warren* is actually the one who has to go out—on the only weeknight in two weeks that I happen to be free (because I really can't do what I did before, can I? and let *all* my friendships drop?), which means that *I* am the one who stays home with Juliet while *he* goes off to some parent-teacher thing that he won't even *talk* about when he gets back, that's how upset *he* is.

"I *will* tell you," he says after I have followed him around the house every step of the way, up to and including him going into the bathroom to brush his teeth. (Although I suppose *some* things have changed, because he doesn't seem to mind that I'm with him every moment like that—in fact, he actually seems to like it.) "I *will* tell you, Flip, I promise—I simply can't talk about it now."

"My God, Warren, how bad could it be? I mean, it wasn't an emergency—they didn't call you from the school or anything, did they? It was just parent-teacher night."

"It wasn't an emergency," he says slowly, and then he can't talk, because his mouth is full of toothpaste.

"I live with her, too, you know. If something is going on with her, don't you think I ought to know about it? Or is this yet another piece of information you've decided not to trust me with? I would have thought—"

Warren gives me a look so miserable and at the same time so fierce that it shuts even me up.

"All right," I say after a moment. "I take that last part back. But I *do* think you ought to tell me. It's not completely outside the bounds of possibility that I might be able to help." I climb into bed beside him.

"She hasn't even said anything," Warren says finally. "I mean, of course, she hasn't—she never complains. But it's so terrible to think that—I was *helping* her with her homework, every night. I simply didn't think things had gotten so bad."

"This is all about *homework?* That's what you're so upset about?"

Warren just turns off the lamp and slides down into bed. I don't fucking believe it. "Warren," I say before I even know the words are out of my mouth, "if you don't turn on that light *this minute* and talk to me, I swear I'll get up right now and go somewhere you can't find me, and you'll never, ever see me again. I mean it, Warren."

Warren looks at me over his shoulder. "Well, that was violent."

There is what I suppose you might call a pregnant pause. Then I lean over and turn on the light. "I'm sorry," I say finally. "But I thought we said we weren't going to do that anymore."

Another long pause. "So," I say, "if I take back every single thing I've ever said except 'What happened tonight?' *then* will you talk to me?"

I suppose this is yet another one of those times when Warren is using those fucking magnetic powers of his, because I have to slide over and nudge him with my leg. And although he doesn't particularly act as though he *wants* to touch me—which is so typical of him, I can't stand it, are we still doing *that?*—he does put his head in my lap. "They think she's—at a developmentally inappropriate stage for her chronological age," he says.

"What the hell does that mean?"

"That what other students in her class are doing, she can't do."

"I find that very hard to believe. Have any of her teachers actually *talked* to her?"

"Well, she is having trouble doing the work," Warren says. "I mean, I didn't think of it that way, I simply assumed that because it's such a good school, they were—well, challenging her. And of course, *she* never said anything about having a hard time. She just kept saying how nice the teachers were at Sara's school."

"Did you ask them what kind of special help they were giving her?"

He shakes his head. "Actually, they're not at all concerned that she's so far behind. And they seemed rather surprised that I was. But tonight, when I saw what the other students were doing, her writing looked—I don't know. *Illiter-*

ate. And the way they talked about her, Flip. As though they think she's really stupid."

"I wish I had gone with you," I say suddenly, surprising both of us.

"Well," says Warren after a minute. "Someone had to stay with Juliet."

"Mmmm," I say. "Can you imagine what they would have thought if we *had* both gone? Or am I underestimating them? Or was it bad enough just you going alone?"

"I don't know what you mean by *that,*" Warren says stiffly.

Well, if he doesn't know by now, why should *I* be the one to break it to him? And until the words were out of my mouth, it would never have occurred to me to even *want* to go. For a whole bunch of reasons. The same bunch of reasons, probably, that are why I would never *get* to go.

"Could you—" says Warren, and even though he won't finish the sentence, I know what he's asking. And yes, I suppose I could. At least *this* is something I get to want. I slide down in bed, so that his whole body is against mine.

"Flip," he whispers, "are you *ever* going to wear that jacket?" His voice gets so soft I can barely hear it. "I really want you to wear it."

"Oh, Warren. You know how much I loved it. I just—"

"I know," he says quickly. He always does that. Who knows what I would have said, that he apparently just can't bear to hear?

"I still love it," I say helplessly. "I'll wear it tomorrow." I think about all the things I have to do, the long, hopeless round of appointments, and my mouth twists. "Maybe it will bring me luck."

ROSIE: I lean back against Michael and it's such an odd feeling, my skin against his. Well, *feeling* his skin against mine isn't odd. But *seeing* it is. We're in Michael's big, old-fashioned bathtub, the one really nice feature of this apartment—and there are our skins, slippery and easy as they fit together in the warm water, but such extremely different colors. I mean, I look so *white,* it isn't natural, though you'd think I would be used to that by now.

"You want me to wash your hair?" Michael is saying. Since my hair is so long and thick and tangled, it takes hours to dry, but I'm here relatively early for once—it's only ten o'clock—and I'm *not* sick. And it always feels wonderful when Michael washes my hair, it's part of the whole sense of luxury that creeps over me if I stay here long enough. Warm, nourishing food; cool sheets; this delicious bath, scented with eucalyptus. (All right, *I* brought over the bath foam—partly because I was afraid of the really sweet scents that I thought Michael might buy—but still. It's here.)

"Wait," I say, sitting up. It isn't ever his color that surprises me—it's mine.

Finding out that I even *have* a color. "Wait just a minute, Michael, OK?" Encouraged by the warm, steamy air, my hair has frizzed all over my face, and I start to pull it back. I hate it when he pours water over my head and those little drops trickle down my face. Of course, Michael is always extremely careful. Nevertheless, I sit with my head tilted as far back as it can go.

He laughs again. "Like, that looks *extremely* uncomfortable," he says, mimicking me.

"Well, it is, so hurry up. The anticipation is killing me." But then comes the part I like so much, his fingers massaging my scalp, foaming the shampoo through my hair. I don't actually remember any of my parents ever washing my hair, though they must have done it sometime, wouldn't you think? But if I *had* a memory of it, it would be like this.

Michael rinses out every bit of the shampoo, and then he pours some new conditioner over my head, something that smells sharp and a little like mouthwash—or is that the bubble bath? Anyway, it feels extremely rich and soothing. "God, that's *very* nice," I say. "What is it?"

Behind me I can feel Michael shrug. "Some new sample." Since he's night manager in that drug store, they're always giving him free samples to take home. As soon as I started spending any amount of time here, Michael kept finding all these shampoos and conditioners for me. Never any bubble bath, though. Maybe I made a mistake, bringing over that first bottle of eucalyptus.

Michael's fingers are even slower and fuller as they rub the conditioner into my scalp. I can feel the liquid getting sudsy and big, like the shampoo. "My God," I say. "It's amazing, whatever it is. Maybe we should always use this, Michael, because it really feels incredible. You should let me try it out on you."

Michael's body slides closer to mine in the warm, slippery water. "I'll take your word for it," he says softly. "I don't have enough hair to tell."

"I think it's more a matter of scalp," I say drowsily. "You have a scalp, don't you?"

"Don't fall asleep," he whispers.

"Would you let me drown?"

He laughs. "No. But I'd have a *much* harder time rinsing you off."

Well, *that* snaps me awake. "OK," I say. "Start rinsing. While I *am* still awake enough to make sure you do it right."

"Like, Rosie. I've *never* done it wrong."

The warm water trickles peacefully through my hair and down my back. "Actually," I say, "I was thinking about this the other day, Michael. The way I always think the worst is going to happen, and the way you never do. And I'm optimistic, too, of course, I'm *very* optimistic. I just always believe that the worst will happen first."

Michael is soaping my back now, gently at first, and then harder. He keeps finding different loofahs, too—apparently bath products are the next big thing in the retail game. "Are you sure you want to hear this?" I say doubtfully.

"Always," he says, and I wonder what it all looks like to *him*—his fingers spread out against my back. Not that *that's* my best feature.

"OK," I say. "So I was thinking, well, the worst *was* what happened. I mean, when Poppy died. Even for Ma—it's not like she had any idea that his heart was bad, it was just this totally freak thing. Danny was only a baby, of course, but I was seven and Flip was four, and that was the *worst*. And then things just *had* to get better, so eventually, OK. They did.

"But you, Michael, I don't know. Maybe because you were so much older when your father started going to work up in Canada—you were like fourteen, right? And of course, he *hadn't* died. But still, you hated it, didn't you? So do you think you just learned to—to *hold on*? Like, if you did, eventually he'd come back? Because Poppy *didn't* come back—no amount of optimism was going to change that. Whereas *your* father is still alive and well and living with your family in Jamaica."

Behind me, Michael doesn't say anything.

"I mean, maybe you were right to be so optimistic," I say. "Maybe you *are* right. What do you think?"

I don't want to fight with him. I just want him to say something.

"You know what I remember?" I say after a pause. "It's that when I was growing up—well, it wasn't that *I* was unhappy. *Things* were unhappy. Poppy had died, and then Dad was around, and Flip just looked so *lost*. And then there was that whole period where Ma and Dad were fighting *all the time*— Flip was like seven, then, and I was almost ten—and we were just terrified, all the time, that they were going to get divorced and— Anyway. *Things* were unhappy. But I, Michael, I was determined to be *happy*. No matter who, no matter what. I was just, excuse my language, fucking determined to be happy. In this very—*ignoring* way, probably. And I keep thinking, you're that way, too, don't you think so, Michael? Don't you think you're exactly like that, too?"

Behind me, Michael still isn't saying anything. What *would* it take, to get him to say something?

"I mean, do you think it's because of *your* father, is what I was wondering. That no matter how awful things are, you just—persist. Because you told me, you know. That he never came home soon enough. And you were supposed to be the father and you couldn't, but maybe that was part of it, too, do you think? You *had* to be happy. To show everybody that you *could* do it. And I'm sure you were great, Michael, I'm sure they were lucky to have you, a lot luckier than Flip and Danny were to have me, I can tell you that.

"But still. It wasn't natural happiness, was it?"

Suddenly I can't stand it, him sitting back there, *listening.* I feel like I'd do anything, just to make him talk.

"And then the way your mother was always so disappointed," I say, "no matter how much she tried to hide it. You just *weren't* as good as your father, were you, Michael? You never *could* measure up, and you knew it. I certainly know how *that* feels."

I'm still sitting between his legs, but somehow he's slipped far enough away that we're no longer touching. Maybe if *I* wait. So I just sit there in the tub with all the bubbles melting, my hair dripping down my back, and I try saying nothing, too.

Until finally, of course, I have to give in.

"Was it that I was speaking *for* you, Michael?" I say, trying to keep my voice normal. "But I wasn't. I was asking you what *you* think."

No answer.

"I mean, I'll tell you *anything* about me. Obviously. Whether you want to know it or not. And I *do* think we have a lot in common. And I really would like to know, Michael, how you—how you process things, I guess. I don't know. How you *see* them."

Still none.

"Oh, fine," I say, and suddenly I am so angry, I have to get out of the tub, trying not to drip all over Michael, trying not to thrust my ass in his face, wishing he couldn't see me, my big, clumsy body—how *dare* he just keep looking and looking and not say anything? I grab a towel and twist it around my big, sopping mass of hair—great, fine, now it's dripping all *over* my face, and it's *freezing* in here, with my hair wet. The towel isn't big enough, either—why don't you get some better *towels,* Michael, if you want to make me feel at home? Since you aren't going to *be* my home, since you aren't even going to talk to me.

"*Don't* say anything, Michael," I say, trying to get one of those skimpy little towels around my body. "God forbid you should give me any *more* ways to intrude into your privacy."

I'm rubbing my hair furiously with the other towel. "You're like a—a—I don't know, a vampire, you just want to sit and listen to everything I have to say, except when it concerns you, and then you won't even talk to me."

"Because you *use* what I tell you," these sudden cold words. My body hears him first, and all the breath goes out of me. The bubbles have pretty much melted away, so I can look down into the tub and see his entire body, naked beneath the water. And he sees me looking and he looks back, and suddenly there's this *moment*. Clearly, we could just start making love now and pretend this whole thing had never happened, and within five minutes, it never *would* have happened.

"I have to go," I say. My voice sounds broken. "I don't think I should be here right now."

So now he does get out of the tub, now he wraps me in another towel and puts his arms around me. *He* warms me up right away. He walks right in and claims—this. This warm welcoming place for me to sink into, and already I can't imagine leaving.

"It was private, what I told you," he is whispering in my ear. "That's all. It was private, and then you—I don't know. Use it against me."

"I'm sorry."

"I told you everything that—I mean, Rosie. There *isn't* any more."

"Really, Michael? But there's always more to say about *me*, isn't there?"

"What you said," he's whispering. "About me being a—vampire."

God, how can I say such terrible things? "You're not a—you're not anything like that, OK, Michael? I don't even know how to tell you I'm sorry for saying that."

"Sorry, I don't care," he whispers. "Just, if you meant it."

"Of course I didn't mean it." I feel him through the damp, flimsy towel, the way he holds everything there, inside himself. And I want it, I want it, I want to get it *out*. This must be what a rapist feels like. "I love you," I say finally. "I love the way you listen to me."

FLIP: Despite my promise, when it comes time to leave the house the next morning, I find I can't wear the jacket then either. Though I do try it on, and it still fits perfectly. Oh, all right. Maybe I *can* wear it.

And, in fact, my fantasy is somewhat true, it *does* give me confidence as I dash about town on my various appointments: a commercials agent, which I still don't have (I do have an agent for film/TV, which I got out of Massimo's movie, which I thought was supposed to open next month, but I haven't heard anything for a while—and you would think that having a film and television agent would make it easier to get a commercials agent, but if this is *easier*, I shudder to think what *harder* would be like); a casting director, who had asked to see *me*, but who keeps me waiting two hours nonetheless; and a man who produces industrials, mainly training videos for computer companies, which has got to be the dullest film job in the world, and I don't suppose you could call what I'd be doing for him *acting,* but you could certainly call it *work.* As you can see, even if the jacket does give me confidence, it doesn't exactly bring me luck.

Now that I've put it on, though, I can barely stand to take it off. Because when I wear that jacket, it feels like Warren is holding me. Which I guess is better than running all over town *without* him holding me. But it's also a constant reminder that he wasn't who I thought he was.

By this point, it's four-thirty and I'm wandering rather aimlessly around the Upper West Side, and I suddenly realize that Rosie's office is less than two blocks away. Well, not that *she'd* have anything useful to say on the topic of Warren and inherited money. But somehow I find myself wandering over to her building.

Rosie at work is always completely frantic. She's always having six conversations at once, and the background noise sounds like the soundtrack for some movie about London during the Blitz. It seems to me as I watch her today that Rosie is not only the busiest, but also the most—I don't know, the most *calm* in her busyness. As though she knows some secret the rest of them don't know. Or thinks she does.

So I stand there in the doorway until she finally looks up. I watch all the different expressions run across her face—surprise, annoyance, relief, anger, despair, and finally, if I'm not mistaken, a kind of joy. All of which makes *me* feel—I don't know. Fragile. As though she could fix everything, if she wanted to. As though she could break me, if she wanted to, too.

Rosie's expression settles on *resigned,* and it's with that air that she motions me over. "Well," she says, when I can't think of anything to say. "What brings *you* here?"

"Do I have to have a reason?"

"Hmm, let's see. The last time I saw you was almost two months ago, when you walked out of a restaurant and left me stranded. And then you don't speak to me for two whole months, and *then* you show up out of the blue at my office, on a day when I'm extremely busy, I might add, but letting that pass, no, you don't *need* a reason, as in, it's not exactly a requirement for coming to see me, or at least it didn't used to be, but I can't quite believe you don't *have* a reason. So, what is it?"

"It's Warren, actually."

Immediately she looks concerned. "Is he all right?" she says quickly. Oh, fine. Worry about *Warren.*

"He's fine," I say. "Except it turns out that he's *rich*. He has *money*. He's loaded, as a matter of fact. All those months I thought he was succeeding where I had failed—well, all right, maybe he *was*. But he also had his family's money to fall back on. And I don't—I can't understand why he didn't tell me."

Rosie motions me toward the old chair in front of her desk. I have to clear away several piles of union literature before I can sit down. She gives me a long, considering look. "Nice jacket," she says finally.

"*He* gave it to me. For Valentine's Day. So am I supposed to feel like a kept man now?"

Rosie laughs. "Well, *there's* a career move you haven't considered." Then she looks at me again, and I *really* wonder what she sees. Because she sighs and picks up the phone and says, "Lucy? Listen, love, could you possibly take my calls for the next few minutes? No, I know—I *know*, but he doesn't *believe* in voice mail. He says when the members call, they should be able to talk to a human being. Which—well, when *you're* the human being in question, right? Listen, love, you don't have to take *long* messages, just— No, very soon. I promise. Thank you." She hangs up and mutters, "Isn't she *supposed* to take messages? Apparently not."

"What if I were a worker?" I say. "Wouldn't you have to talk to me then?"

Rosie looks grim. "Oh, she could tell it was personal. And it probably doesn't matter, except if she tells Isabel, and Isabel tells Harris—anyway. So talk."

"So which is it that bothers you more," she says when for some reason I still don't say anything. "That he *has* all that money, or that he didn't come right out and show you a financial statement?"

"Well, *you* seem to know all about it."

A flicker of triumph passes through Rosie's eyes, followed by a flicker of— hurt feelings, I suppose. But she says, more or less calmly, "Oh, come on, Flip. Juliet's school, his family's place, his new apartment? What other explanation could there possibly be?"

"Well, *I* didn't see it in such—simple terms."

"Mmmm," says Rosie. "That's not exactly his fault, is it?"

"Oh, right," I say. "Take *his* side. I don't know why I should be surprised— he's always taking *your* side."

"Is he?" says Rosie, and again, there are those flickers of triumph and hurt.

"Rosie," I say. "Wouldn't you hate finding out that *your* boyfriend was rich? Especially you. Wouldn't you feel—like he was a whole other person?"

Something happens in Rosie's face when I mention her boyfriend. But she says in a more or less normal voice, "A whole other person than the one whose house you visited last Thanksgiving? A whole other person than—I mean, Flip. Weren't you paying attention at *all?*"

"So this is all *my* fault?"

Rosie laughs again. "Well, it's certainly not your fault that he *has* money, if that's what you're asking. I mean, yes, of course, property is theft, but Warren didn't accumulate all that property, he just inherited it. Do you want him to give it back?"

"Well, I'm really surprised that *you* don't. Apparently Warren is allowed to do anything he wants in *your* world. Whereas the rest of us—"

Rosie sighs. "You mean, why won't I let you be a big, rich movie star but I don't mind that Warren has a trust fund? I do think it's wrong that Warren *has* a trust fund. I just don't think it's wrong that *Warren* has a trust fund. And yes, he should have told you, I do think you have a right to be mad about that. But it's ridiculous to act like he betrayed you, after all the information you *did* have. It's like him being shocked you're not a virgin, just because you never actually told him the names of all your ex-boyfriends. Or if he thinks, like, I don't know, when you go to the gym, that—"

"All right, fine," I say quickly, cutting her off. "There's no need to talk about *that.*"

"He really does care about you," she says softly. "Anyone who would come out to Pittsburgh and put up with three days of Ma looking at him like—well, you know how she looked. When she wasn't outright pretending that he wasn't there at all."

"Yeah, I know."

"And when you guys weren't together, he looked absolutely miserable. I mean, so did you, but he *really* did. You just looked like you missed him to distraction. He looked, I don't know. Like he was slowly starving to death."

"Well, *there's* a romantic image."

"I can't believe I'm telling you anything you don't already know here," Rosie says gently. "So the question is, why do you want me to say it?"

I hate when she does that. "I don't know," I say, in my most dismissive tone. "Why do *you* think I want you to say it? Assuming, of course, that I do."

"Well, gee, Flip, I don't know either. I'm still trying to figure out why you came here at all."

Stalemate. I look down at the floor—it's this old-fashioned greenish rubber tile with some of the corners chipped away. "It makes me feel—like it's a mockery. I mean, it was hard enough, not earning a living, when I thought he was just scraping along, too. Now—he's already miles more successful than I'll ever be. Until I do get famous, of course, but at the moment—"

When I next look up, Rosie is typing something on her old typewriter—God, don't these people even have computers?—and I have to admit, I'm more than a little hurt that she would just start working away like that. I start to say something, and she holds up one hand. Then she hands me what she was typing, a list in two columns:

Reasons Why You Are the Man
1. You're gone all the time, while Warren stays at home (with a child!).
2. Warren does all the cooking and housework.
3. You're the one who fools around (at the gym, etc.).

Reasons Why Warren Is the Man
1. He acts like he doesn't need the relationship (even though he *obviously* does).
2. He doesn't like to talk about his feelings.
3. He has all the money.

Like everything else these past two weeks, I don't know whether to laugh or cry. Because on the one hand, all right, *yes.* And on the other hand, I mean, how *dare* she?

"He loves you, Flip," Rosie is saying softly. "He wants to marry you, for God's sake. I don't blame you for being mad about the money, but I don't see why that should make you feel as though everything else doesn't count."

And again, I feel an incredible relief hearing her say this. Because all right, yes. He *is* still the same person. He is.

And on the other hand, wait a minute. "How did you know about him wanting to marry me? We said we weren't going to tell anybody. Till we had officially—so how did you know?"

Rosie looks extremely uncomfortable.

"He told you, didn't he?" I say. "I don't fucking believe it. He *told* you?"

"He didn't exactly *tell* me," Rosie says. "We were just talking—when he was home with us in Pittsburgh—and I pretty much guessed. I could see by his face that—"

"Oh, give me a break. You can't see *anything* by Warren's face—he's completely *in*expressive."

"You know," says Rosie, "sometimes I really think that you don't give him enough credit."

"Well, who cares what you think?" I say, standing up. "He's *my* boyfriend, Rosie. I don't need *your* advice on how to treat him."

She's saying something in reply, but I don't hear it, because I'm already turning around and walking out. She sounds distressed though. Good. If I've managed to upset her only a fraction as much as she's upset me, well, then my work here is done.

ROSIE: When I climb the last few steps from the subway, it's almost eleven o'clock, and I don't even think twice: I head straight for the deli on the corner, looking for chocolate-chocolate chip, the most chocolate chocolate ice cream there is.

Arguing in my head the whole time. No, not with Cassandra—I'm not even interested in what *she* thinks. But with Flip—how *dare* he walk out on me again?—and Charles—who kept me for almost an hour after negotiations tonight, telling me that I'm not taking a hard enough line with Olympia—and Isabel, who took me aside to tell me that Harris wasn't going to be happy either, and *then* she had the nerve to ask me how things were going with Cassandra, and I *certainly* wasn't going to confess that after an initial bump of apparent good health, I'm back to the heavy bleeding again, as of today. I *know* I haven't been perfect about the diet, but aren't the herbs and the needles supposed to work anyway? And then when I march into the deli, ready to *finally* buy this treat I've been looking forward to for about a million years, wouldn't you know, they're all *out* of my favorite flavor and I have to settle for just plain chocolate instead. I mean, what's the point?

The one person I'm *not* arguing with is Michael, because, as we've already established, I *can't* argue with him. So at this point, all I want to do is just sit down and eat ice cream and watch at least one hour of television, and if I *can't* do that, I think I am going to *die*.

Except that Channel 11 has changed its late-night schedule, so now, instead of my beloved *Seinfeld* at eleven and *Cheers* at eleven-thirty, it's *Frasier* and *The Honeymooners,* and although I *can* watch *Frasier,* I don't particularly like it, and I've seen every episode of *The Honeymooners* at least four times.

OK, but Channel 5 now has *M*A*S*H* on at eleven. It's better than nothing. So I put on my sweats, and grab the ice cream, and settle in for the last twelve minutes of the show. And just at that moment, the telephone rings.

Damn. I'm sure the machine is on, but the ringing is hard to ignore. Maybe it's Michael, calling to—*fix* things. Of course, Michael never calls after eleven, and besides, from his point of view, what is there to fix?

Just then, the TV flashes to commercial. Which seems like a sign. But it isn't Michael. It's Warren.

"Hi, Rosie," he says quickly, in a low, embarrassed voice. "How are you?"

"Well, it's almost eleven-thirty, I left the house at six-thirty this morning,

I've been going all day without a break, and I just got home about ten minutes ago." For which, may I say, I hate myself. I *hate* people, especially political people, who complain about how hard they work. They always want so much *credit* for how miserable they are, and really, who asked them to be?

"I'm sorry to call so late," Warren is saying. "I did call earlier, several times, but you weren't in. I didn't want to leave a message, because——"

"Because you thought I wouldn't return the call."

"Well, I thought you shouldn't have to. I mean, I know it's a busy time for you, and——"

"Really, Warren? And just how do you know that?"

"Please don't hang up on me, Rosie," Warren says in a breathless, desperate voice. "I wouldn't be calling if I didn't really need your help. It's Juliet."

"Don't hang *up* on you?" This makes me so mad I sit up, balancing the bowl of ice cream on the back of the couch. "What kind of person do you think I am? It's true, I probably *wouldn't* have returned your call, but only because you're living with someone who's not speaking to me at the moment, and who, actually, I'm not speaking to either—where is he, by the way? Is he there?"

"No, he's at rehearsal." I imagine him looking at the clock. "Actually, at this hour, rehearsal is long over, so maybe he's out for a drink with some of the other actors."

"Mmmm," I say. "Trouble in paradise?" Warren starts to answer. "No, don't tell me," I say abruptly. "After the way he came to my office this afternoon——"

"What?"

"You mean he didn't tell you? Well, that's interesting. Especially given what we talked about."

"What did you talk about?"

"Well, I'm obviously not going to tell *you,* Warren. I mean, if Flip didn't tell you himself, it's clearly none of *my* business." There is silence on both ends of the line. The commercial is over. The ice cream is melting. I'm certainly not going to eat it while I'm on the phone. It was supposed to be a treat.

Though actually, I find this whole conversation kind of stimulating—I feel much less tired than I did a moment ago. What is *wrong* with me?

"All right," I say finally, when Warren's silence becomes unbearable. "I told him he should marry you. Or at least, that all the reasons he was giving me for *not* doing it were extremely foolish." I laugh. "Look who I'm telling. And then he got mad at me, *again. And* walked out on me. *Again.* And here we are."

"What exactly did he say to you again?" Warren says. "About us getting married?"

"I thought he told *you* everything," I say. "I thought that's why you were calling, to—I don't know. To take his side. Except since I took *your* side . . . I'm sorry, Warren—I'm still so mad at him. But I shouldn't have taken it out on you."

The television flickers. "I guess I *am* mad at you, too, Warren. You made such a big deal in Pittsburgh about not wanting to lose touch, and then because Flip did, you did, too. I don't think you were wrong, necessarily. It just made me mad."

"Rosie!!!" Warren says sharply, spacing each word. *"What—exactly—did—Flip—say?!"*

I sigh loudly. "Well, obviously, he was upset about the money. And I told him that, while he had good reason to be mad at you for not being honest with him—which he does, Warren, you have to admit that—"

"Fine," growls Warren. "Consider it admitted."

"Well. It's hardly a small thing. Anyway, I told him he was just using the money to avoid what seems to be a perfectly lovely relationship, so really, Warren. No big deal."

"If it was no big deal," Warren says doggedly, "why didn't he tell me about it?"

"Well, obviously, because he knew he was wrong. There was no way he could tell you without you saying, 'See? Even Rosie thinks we should be together, and she hates rich people more than anyone.' "

"I'm not *rich,*" Warren says.

"Oh, come off it, Warren," I say. "Compared to who?"

I can hear Warren taking several deep breaths. "Well, anyway," he says in a somewhat calmer tone, "The reason I called—it's Juliet."

I look at the clock. It's now eleven-forty. So even if I were interested in a fifth viewing of *The Honeymooners,* I've already missed the first ten minutes. Is there *anything* on at midnight?

I take my own deep breath. "All right, Warren. What *about* Juliet?"

"Well," Warren begins.

"In her fancy private school," I can't help adding.

"Jesus Christ, Rosie!" Warren explodes. "She's a *child.* Are you mad at her, too?"

Suddenly, I have just *had* it. With him, with Flip, with Michael, with the lousy selections on Channel 11, with Charles, with Isabel, with pretty much everybody except the members. Give me a minute, I'll be mad at them, too. "You know what, Warren?" I say. "I lied. I *am* the kind of person who hangs up on people." And I hang up. I've never done that before in my life. I can't tell if it feels good or not. I start to cry.

The phone rings. I don't answer. It rings again. I couldn't answer even if I wanted to, because now I am sobbing hysterically. On the television, *The Honeymooners* rolls to an end and it's only 11:55. If I get control of myself in the next five minutes, maybe I could find another program. Though I'd have to sit up long enough to change the channel, which at the moment doesn't seem likely.

"Rosie," says Warren's voice over the answering machine, "you don't have to pick up, but please listen to me, all right? Please listen." He's putting everything he has into his voice. "Rosie, I know this is a really hard time for you, all right? I mean, I know it *now*. I'm sorry I was so—preoccupied before, with Flip and Juliet. Really, truly, sorry.

"Rosie, I just wanted to say—it's so valuable, the work you do." This is odd, because while of course *I* would like to think so, Warren doesn't even *like* unions. "Rosie, it's so valuable," he repeats. "*You're* so valuable. And—I suppose I just wanted to tell you not to lose heart. So, don't lose heart, Rosie. And sleep well, all right? Sleep well. I'll call you tomorrow." Another pause. "Sleep well," he says again.

The machine clicks off. And I don't know if it's the exhaustion of the day, or the release of crying, or the hypnotic rhythm of Warren's voice, but suddenly I can barely keep my eyes open. I turn off the TV, leave the ice cream dish melting on the floor, and stagger into the bedroom. Where, in fact, I do sleep well. So thank you, Warren.

The next day, Warren's call finds me at my desk uptown about half an hour before I have to leave for a meeting. "Hi, Warren," I say when I recognize his voice. "I'm really sorry about last night."

"It's all right," he says. "You were exhausted. I was just so worried about Juliet, and then when you said you had seen Flip—"

"Yeah, obviously *that's* a hot topic for both of us. So what's up with Juliet?"

"I'm sorry about not being in touch," Warren says. "I just thought, I mean, *you* said it would be awkward because of Flip, and—"

"Warren, here's the deal. I have about twenty-five minutes before I have to leave for Olympia, and this is one time I can't be late. So we can either talk about us, or you can tell me about Juliet—take your pick."

"All right," says Warren slowly, and I find myself really missing him. On the other hand, all I really want right now is to hang up the phone and go drink a cup of tea and not talk to anybody for the next five minutes.

"The problem," Warren is saying, "is that she's very bright—I mean, she speaks two languages perfectly, and she reads books that look to me like the books much older children should be reading. And I think I'm being fairly objective."

"You and every other parent," I say. "But from my own *limited* contact with her, I agree."

Warren probably hears the bite in that. But he pushes on. "Or if you ask her to *tell* you about a book, she can talk for hours. In really interesting ways. And again, I don't think I'm biased."

"OK. She's smart and she's interesting. What else?"

"It's just that—well, I've seen her homework, and when I look at what the other students are doing, it's true, hers looks—backward. Her tests, and her handwriting, and the words she uses, and—it's a very different impression than you'd get from meeting her. But she isn't stupid, and I get the feeling that they think she is."

"Warren, forgive me, really, but now I have only about fifteen minutes, so I'm just going to give you the fast answer, OK? It sounds like Juliet is learning-disabled, and they don't get it, partly because nobody seems to, though I must say, I'm shocked that they don't at *that* school, given what you must be paying them, which please don't tell me because it will just make me even more upset at the whole idea of—"

"Rosie, please, slow down," Warren says, and I can hear how hard he's trying to say it nicely. "What did you say Juliet was?"

"Oh. Learning-disabled. You know, Warren. Normal intelligence, sometimes even super-intelligent. But trouble with—I don't know. Some neurological connection that just doesn't work. Dyslexia is one version of it, where you have trouble reading because you see words backwards. Or Tito's girlfriend's son—he actually *can* read, but only with enormous difficulty, because his eyes have trouble stopping at the left hand margin. I don't know, I've only heard about the problems that my friends' kids actually have, but there are supposedly thousands of different types, and you get these really bright kids whose handwriting wanders all over the page, or they can't figure out how to put things in alphabetical order, or they can follow written directions but not oral ones, or some other weird problem. I mean, what exactly did *they* tell you?"

"They said she was almost two grades behind," Warren says. "But then they said that you can't expect the same performance out of every child."

"Oh, *God,* no. Expecially not if the child is Black."

Warren is silent for a moment. I use the time to run down the list I was making before he called, people we can ask to talk to their work-study students. Oh, shit, I forgot Pamela, whose name I add. And Fortunata, and doesn't Cecilia have someone, or was that position cut over the break?

"Rosie, I'm not *questioning* what you say, but why are you saying it? I mean, what are you basing it on?"

"Oh, Warren, come on. What exactly did they say?"

"They did say something about cultural differences," Warren admits, "but I thought they were talking about the fact that she'd grown up in France."

"Right." I bite my tongue to keep from saying more.

"I don't see how they can think race has anything to do with it," he insists. "She grew up with Madeleine. And now she lives with me."

"You mean, if she lives in a white family, that will counteract all that Black blood?" He just makes it way too easy.

"I *mean,*" says Warren coldly, "that there *are* no cultural differences. Except that she lived in France."

"Warren, you know that, and I know that, but please. This is what happens. Be honest. If you saw Juliet, and you saw what her homework looked like, and you didn't know her, what would *you* think? Really, what would you think?"

"It's a very enlightened school," Warren says. "I simply don't believe they think that way."

"Right," I say again. "And how many children of color go there exactly? Two? Three? Ten? Out of a thousand?"

"I don't know," Warren says. "It's not the kind of thing I notice."

"OK, Warren, fine. But it isn't helping Juliet to pretend that it isn't happening when it is."

"It isn't helping Juliet to make up problems that don't exist, either."

"Jesus Christ, Warren, what the hell does it take? You have this perfectly obvious problem just staring you in the face, and you're willing to sacrifice this child whom you obviously adore because you don't want to believe it could happen to you or anyone you love? Warren, this city is full of people who are treated like shit because they're African-American or Latino or in some cases Asian. All of *their* children live with this problem day in and day out. And you think you get to pretend it isn't there, just because Juliet is connected to you? I mean, really, how dare you?"

"You know, Rosie," Warren says finally, "you charge a very high price for the help you offer."

"Oh, fine," I say. "First of all, I didn't exactly *offer*. Second, you're just like Flip. You ask me what I think, and then you want to argue with me, and then you want to get mad at me for arguing back." Suddenly I have the sensation that the words are literally scraping against my throat, that each one injures me. I can't afford to sob hysterically in my office. And Warren isn't going to be sorry after this one—I've said way too much.

"I'm sorry," I say after a pause. "I can't do this anymore. My throat really hurts."

"Rosie, why—why do you get—"

"Are you asking why I get so upset, Warren?" I rasp out. No. I have to leave for a meeting in ten minutes. But I can't stand another conversation cut short, another steaming heap of misunderstandings left to clean up afterward.

"God, Warren," I croak out, "you of all people should know how awful it is to be the only one who knows something."

"What do you mean, the only one?" Warren says. "Leaving aside the word 'know.' But don't you have a whole office full of people over there who all agree with you?"

"Oh, Warren. No. I mean, about the fact that racism exists, maybe." Another swallow. "But not about—I don't know." I find some cold coffee in the bottom of one of the three dirty cups that adorn my desk. "They're not family," I hear myself say. I think about that for a while. "Maybe they are. But you—I don't know why it bothers me so much, to tell the truth. You certainly haven't let me get to know Juliet well enough for her to be more than an abstraction to me. So if that's what you're hearing, well, I'm sorry—she's as real to me as all the other children I hear about, every single goddamn day. Even if I did know her, even if I were—" My throat closes up. I can't say the words I was thinking. *Her aunt.* "Even then," I manage. "Why should all those other children be less real to me?"

"I don't know what to say," says Warren.

"You're thinking, 'But they're not my responsibility.' " Suddenly I don't even feel angry anymore. I just feel overwhelmed with sadness. "Look, Warren, my time is up. I can give you a couple of phone numbers, though."

I can hear him wondering if the people he calls will be just as awful to him as I was. Hardly, I want to say, they're long past the point of being angry. But he says, "All right, Rosie, thanks," and I give him the numbers. Then I take the elevator down to the coffee shop in the lobby and lock myself in their bathroom for about five minutes, and I just cry. Then I get myself a tea with lemon and honey and head for the uptown train.

When I get to the Olympia office—not late, by some amazing miracle of God or whomever, but actually five minutes early—I stand for a minute in the doorway. Everyone is so preoccupied with their activities, they don't even notice me. Odessa is here, which I didn't expect—she doesn't usually get enough of a lunch hour to make it over, so she must have made a special effort, and there she is going over a leaflet with Nina (or is it Nancy? It's really insulting that I don't remember.), while Elena (the Russian one from the xerox room) stands at the xerox machine—oh, honey, you shouldn't be doing that for *us,* too. And Jack is making notes on something, and Charles is on the phone, and there's that buoyancy again. I can't even describe it—it's this palpable cloud of energy, this place we're all in together, even though in a minute, the meeting will start, and Charles will be his usual pain-in-the-ass self, and Jack will throw out those little comments that make me wonder what his group's agenda is *now,* and Odessa will just sit there looking disapproving and I'll worry about her not coming back (because it looks so bad that there are still so few people of color in leadership positions, no matter what we do). And then tomorrow it will start all over again.

And, and, and. I stand there in the doorway, soaking up the healing energy, feeling my throat relax, feeling my breath go back down into my body, feeling my whole dry, dusty, constricted self open and absorb and be quenched. I'm here for this, which I, God knows, have never found in any other place, though I can imagine Flip might find it on stage sometimes, this body that is all of us and something more. How can anyone *not* see this? How can anyone *not* love every single person in this room, even the ones you truly can't stand?

Family is something else, I guess. And don't even ask me what love is. But I'm here for this.

WORK

FLIP: The first office where I work, everybody is sick. The second office, everybody is dead. It more or less goes downhill from there.

All right, all right, I'm exaggerating. But not much. Tanya—who is *still* waiting to hear from the *Hell Street* people (I suppose they're going to cast that part at the very last minute, because why give her time to prepare?)—anyway, Tanya, who has also been having a dry spell, has had to go back to temping. And to save me from another encounter with the bicycle, she has generously offered to share her temp office contacts with me.

I don't usually tell people that I can type. You can probably imagine why not. And if there *are* any straight men doing temp office work, *I* have yet to meet them, which is annoying, of course, for a whole lot of reasons. Still. Just keep saying: "It's better than riding a bicycle." It doesn't make *me* feel any better ("It's better than having cholera, it beats being burned at the stake"), but maybe *you'll* have better luck.

So I walk into the first office they send me to—yes, I do have a—I suppose you'd call it an office *costume,* or perhaps office *drag* would be more appropriate—suit pants and a totally boring white shirt and an equally boring navy blue jacket, and they tell you at the temp agency to be sure to wear a tie, so fine, I can think of it as acting or as passing, take your choice. Not passing as straight, of course—passing as interested. No, that's not right, because even *they're* not interested. You can feel the horror the moment you get on a rush-hour subway—it's as though these people were riding to their deaths. They rush up the subway stairs—of course, all of us are terrified of being late—and the dread is so thick you could cut it with a knife. Dread and something else. Despair.

But not me, right, because I *have* a life. Unlike these other people, I'm not *really* doing this. I'm an artist.

So I walk into the first office they send me to, and I swear to God, every single person there is sick.

It starts with the receptionist, who has a cold. All right, it's the first week in March, everybody has a cold. (Not me, of course. I'm never sick. But everybody *else* I know has a cold, particularly poor Warren, who every time he seems to be getting *over* his cold has to go to another meeting at Juliet's school and comes home reinfected. Overexposure to childish germs or a not-so-subtle manifestation of distress? You be the judge—he's stopped talking about it with me.)

The receptionist buries her nose in a huge mass of Kleenex with one hand and motions me to sit down with the other. "I know," she says into the phone. "I told him. Well, of *course* he doesn't listen to me. I'm *just* his girlfriend. I know. I know. They were huge. You know, like really big roaches, only with feet? No—green. *Green.* Well, greenish-yellow-brown, you know. Like, excuse my French, puke. Or the other. You know. The *other.*" She lowers her voice to an intense whisper. "Number *two.*"

I would actually rather listen to this conversation than do anything they could possibly ask me to do in this office, but I'm afraid if she doesn't tell me where to go, I'll be considered late, and then that whole rush-hour ride of doom will have been wasted. Then she gets three other calls, each asking for some lucky executive who isn't actually here at the moment, and then she has time to blow her nose, look up at me, and whisper, "I buzzed Gigi for you as soon as you got here but she was on another line. You're the temp, right?" So I guess my costume is doing its job.

Eventually, Gigi comes out carrying an inhaler. "Excuse me," she wheezes, and takes a couple more puffs, and shakes her head. "That's better," she says. "I'm so sorry. It's just that they painted my office over the weekend, and—I *told* them not to bother, but they're moving me out fairly soon, so I guess they just thought that—but I *will* be out in—well, not *two* weeks. Four weeks? I'm going to miss that window."

"I'm sorry," I say. That's always a safe response to pretty much anything anyone ever tells you, in my experience, particularly when they're talking about anything job-related. In this case, however, Gigi shakes her head.

"No, no, no, no, no," she says brightly. "Cubicles. They're the wave of the future."

She stations me at an empty desk, hands me an enormous computer print-out and a bunch of pages stapled together, and shows me which figures in one have to be checked against which figures in the other. The printout is organized in numerical order, and the stapled pages are organized by company name, so there's an unbelievable amount of cross-checking, plus all the figures are long and complicated. "Marion was supposed to do this, but she's home with a migraine," Gigi explains, and all I can think is, "Lucky Marion."

Behind me, a woman in her late forties is sneezing uncontrollably while trying to have a phone conversation. "No," she's saying, between sneezes. "It's not our policy to allow that. Well, I'm sorry about that, but I can't help what the doctor told you. No, we're not saying you can't have the procedure. You always have the option of paying for it yourself. Well, that's what's known as a pre-existing condition. No, a *pre*-existing condition. No, a *pre* — Yes, I do understand how upset you are, but it's not our policy to pay for that. Well, I'm sorry, too. That must have been very upsetting." This—the sneezing and the refusals—basically continues all morning long. It's fun to eavesdrop for a while, and it does take my mind off all those impossible numbers, but, you know. After the first two or three dozen phone calls, the dialogue starts to get fairly repetitive. And it's only ten-fifteen. Two and three-quarters hours until lunch. Five and three-quarters hours of actual work. Six and three-quarters hours before I finally get to leave for the day.

The woman at the desk to my left has apparently coordinated her symptom with the woman behind me, because *she* coughs continually, one of those dry, annoying coughs that sounds as though she's trying to get your attention, though clearly, she's so used to coughing, even *she* doesn't know she's doing it anymore. The woman in front of me, who is working furiously on a computer with an enormous monitor, keeps stopping to throw her head back and squeeze drops into her eyes. To my right is someone with some kind of splints on her hands, which she takes off whenever she has to type on *her* computer. When I go out to lunch, the receptionist I saw this morning must already have gone, because the woman now sitting at the reception desk is smoothing vitamin E lotion over the huge flaky red patches all up and down her arms. And when I come back from lunch, the two junior executives who ignore me in the elevator are trading complaints about their bad backs and their pre-ulcerous conditions.

What do they actually *do* here? Oh, right, they sell health insurance. (It gives you some indication of my state of mind that I don't even *see* the irony until two weeks later.)

MARIO: Well, of course I agree that it isn't *right* for Paradise to cut our break time and our lunch hours. It's just a difficult position for me to be in, because in fact, they haven't cut *my* break time or *my* lunch hour.

I don't exactly know why. It might be because Thomas, our supervisor, *really* likes me. It's almost embarrassing, really, except I don't *think* anybody actually blames me for it. But it *is* embarrassing, when he makes a point of telling me—privately, of course, but everybody *knows* what's going on—that I can still take the twenty-minute breaks we used to get. Instead of the ten-minute ones that everybody else has now. And that it's OK with him if I want to take an hour for lunch. Whereas for all the other travel agents, of course, it's forty minutes.

It might *not* be because he likes me. What Tito from the union said, when we met with him, is that they're just trying to get more work out of us without making it look like they're actually breaking the contract. Because of course the contract guarantees us two twenty-minute breaks and a one-hour lunch, "unless work load or scheduling needs make such an arrangement unfeasible," in which case, you're supposed to get comp time for the missed time. But it's clear to all of us that no one will ever *get* that comp time. So what Tito said was, well, maybe they're using me as an example, you know, of how it's *not* a new policy. To make it seem like it's just some weird coincidence that everybody *else* is getting shorter breaks. Or, he says, maybe they're just using me to divide and conquer. So that everybody will be mad at *me* instead of them.

Not that everybody *is* mad at me, of course. It's only Mariah, and nobody takes *her* seriously. Not that I can't see why people *don't,* in her case, but that's probably completely unfair of me. And now she's saying that to get anywhere in this company, you have to be a gay man, which I really don't think is fair, except it *is* true that Thomas is and I am. But it's not like *every* gay man here is doing well. Rashad isn't. Of course, he's bisexual.

Anyway, the point is, what can we do about it? Tito says, yes, OK, he could keep filing grievances for us, but all that does is load up the system with grievances, and Paradise has apparently decided to take every single grievance to arbitration, which takes months and months, *and* costs the union money, and honestly, by the time your grievance gets that far, you tend to feel—well, I should just speak for myself, *I* tend to feel—well, I guess I can't speak for myself, because I haven't ever actually filed a grievance. Anyway, my impression is that after months of waiting, you do tend to feel that the grievance doesn't really matter anymore, even if you win. And even then, it doesn't seem to stop them from doing the same thing to you again, or to somebody else, or both.

So Tito says, OK, well, how far are we prepared to go? Not that we have to decide all at once. We could just start with a letter that everybody signs. Of course, it would look terrible if *not* everybody signed it, because then the people who do sign will be in more trouble, although obviously they wouldn't get *fired*. The union isn't *that* weak. Yet.

ROSIE: "The question is," I say to Lissa and Vanessa, "how far are we prepared to go?"

"I know, I know," says Vanessa in her quick, impatient way. "But come on, Rosie. A strike? Like, do you guys even have any, what do you call them? Strike benefits?"

"First of all," I say, looking at Lissa nodding quietly at her desk. Clearly Vanessa speaks for both of them. "First of all, Vanessa, what is this 'you guys' stuff? You know better than that. It's *your* union. You pay for the strike benefits with *your* dues. So—"

"Oh," says Vanessa, "so it's *my* fault I won't have anything to live on if you make us go on strike? Because I wasn't willing to raise my own dues?"

I give her the most skeptical look I can. "Nobody's going to *make* you go on strike. When the time comes, if a strike is necessary, you'll vote. As you also well know."

"I don't even understand how things could have gotten to this point," Vanessa says. She holds up a copy of the newsletter. "You guys can't do any better than this, and then *I* have to go out onto the street and *picket*? What the hell am I supposed to live on?"

What am I supposed to say? Oh, sorry, Vanessa, I didn't realize this was costing *you* money. I guess I'll just have to try harder.

"Look, Vanessa," I say instead. "Nobody would be happier than me if I had the power to bring Olympia to its knees. But there's only one thing they're afraid of, and you know what that is." I look at her sternly, but she scowls and looks away.

"It's you guys," I say, trying to make eye contact with Lissa, too. "They can't run this place without you, and they know it. I don't even know why I'm telling you this. You should be telling me."

"I don't know," Lissa says very softly in her pinched little Wisconsin accent. "We should all be able to get along."

"Of course we *should*," I say. "We've *been* negotiating in good faith for over a year. Why do *you* think they haven't budged?"

"They must really be worried about money," Lissa says. She gets smaller and narrower as she talks.

I raise my eyebrows. Vanessa laughs. "Actually," I say, trying to keep my temper, "they're so worried about money that they want to freeze your wages. Aren't you furious? Isn't that an outrage? Tuition's up 10 percent, the endowment is up 5 percent, and they don't want to pay *you?*"

Lissa is looking down at her computer stand, but she says quietly, "But I heard that they were having big budget problems. A $20 million deficit. They sent us—" She holds up a letter from the University's public relations department. I've seen it, of course. The fact that Olympia is now going directly to the workers was noteworthy enough to prompt a private strategy meeting with Harris, who of course took his usual militant stand while ordering me to mobilize enough workers to intimidate Olympia *before* we actually have to strike. Covering *his* ass both ways.

"Lissa. You know the answer to that one. Why do *you* think the deficit is so big all of a sudden?" We've only been talking about this all year.

Her voice gets even more midwestern, ending every single sentence with a question. "They're putting up all those new dorms?" she says. "And the new Bio-Tech Building? But, Rosie? They need that building?"

"Well, I think you're extremely generous, then," I say. "Paying for it out of *your* salary. And I'm sure, when Olympia starts collecting the board fees from the dorms and the grants for the bio-tech research, they'll be equally generous to *you.*"

Vanessa laughs. "Yeah, right."

"Well?" I say. "And then they want to cut the affirmative action fund, you know, the one to equalize minority salaries? Because African-American salaries are *still* lower than white salaries, by an average of $1,000 per worker, right?, and Latino salaries are lower by $800, even though Black and Latino workers average more seniority." I could rattle these figures off in my sleep.

"You know," says Vanessa, eyes narrowed. "I don't know. Sometimes I think we would be better off without the union. Sometimes I think we'd be better off just taking our own chances."

How can you *possibly* say that? I want to scream. We put money in your pocket, for God's sake. But before I can say anything, BH comes back from lunch. Now that the damn bleeding is back, it's time to find a bathroom anyway.

FLIP: Marion comes back from her migraine to the Office of Sickness, and I get sent on to TechnoMort, an office that, I kid you not, designs and outfits morgues.

Actually, the big news at TechnoMort is that the company is expanding into a new field. Apparently, all those contacts with coroners and District Attorneys' offices have paid off, because now TechnoMort is going into the prison business, the one true growth industry of the new millennium, along with computers, of course. But according to Georgia, my TechnoMort supervisor, who gives me an impassioned first-day orientation, computers are a capital-intensive industry that is unlikely to employ large numbers of human beings, since replacing human labor with machines is the whole *point* of computers. Whereas prison is a labor-intensive industry that promises to keep thousands if not millions of Americans gainfully employed for generations to come. Which means that if I don't get an acting job soon, I should probably forget about learning Excel (which Tanya has been telling me to do) and just go get trained as a guard.

"It's not just the prisons themselves," Georgia explains earnestly as she leads me to a desk that looks remarkably like the one I had at the Office of Sickness. "It's all the satellite industries. It's been an economic renaissance for upstate New York, it really has. Because even if you don't want to work as a guard or a cafeteria person or a social worker or a janitor or a—a—"

"A warden," I suggest helpfully, drawing on my extensive knowledge of old prison movies. But Georgia looks doubtful.

"Well, of course, they only *have* one warden per prison," she says. "So I don't think *that* profession would provide all *that* many jobs, I really don't. But even if you didn't work inside the actual prison, you could work for a food service company, or the company that does the laundry, or the one that trains the dogs, because all *those* services are now subcontracted out. And in Texas, and Ohio, and North Carolina, and lots of other places, they have private companies running the whole prison. So it's not just expanding the public sector. It's also expanding the private sector. Some of those communities, you go out there and you'll find that pretty much every single person in town works for the prison."

In fact, Georgia says proudly, between the morgues and the prisons, TechnoMort is doing so well that I'm not even here to replace someone who is temporarily out of the office. I'm actually holding open a slot that they intend to fill with a new permanent worker. Georgia hints that if I play my cards right, this new worker might even be me.

"You should consider applying for it when it's posted, you really should," she says, piling a huge stack of papers onto my desk. "Because the salary is fairly good, and the benefits are truly excellent, and also, of course, you'd be performing a public service." She switches on the computer. "Because," she continues, "most of those criminals locked up upstate come from right here in New York City, so we should all be grateful that they're not running around loose. Because otherwise—"

"So we supply the prisoners and they supply the prisons?" I say. "That seems fair."

She looks at me sharply to be sure I'm not joking, but I try to keep a straight face and apparently I succeed.

"There's a reason the prison industry is growing so fast," Georgia says sternly. "Society is breaking down. These people have to go somewhere."

I am trying *really* hard to keep a straight face.

"Well," she says, "you live in the city, don't you? So you *know* where the criminals come from. The vast majority come from just seven New York City neighborhoods, they really do, which would be all right if they *stayed* in those neighborhoods, but they don't, they have to wander the streets and mug and rape and murder the rest of us, so I must tell you that I, personally, am extremely thankful that there *are* companies like TechnoMort that make it easier for communities—not just in New York, of course, but all over the country—to solve their security problems in the most cost-efficient way possible. Because, believe me, every dollar that they save on construction is a dollar that can go into enforcement and security, which means that once those people are behind bars, they *stay* behind bars, and I for one feel safer for it."

This is probably one of the few times when "I'm sorry" actually *isn't* the right response to a work-related conversation, so I just nod and try to look impressed. Georgia hurries off, promising to come back and check up on me in half an hour or so, and I look despairingly at the huge stack of forms. All over the country, apparently, city, county, and state officials are thinking about the most cost-effective way to build new prisons. Well, *there's* a cheerful thought.

As I type address labels and create "individualized" letters—do they think these people have never *heard* of computers?—I try to think of ways that I personally could capitalize on this new mania for prisons. What if New York State subcontracted not just the food service and the uniforms but the entire prison itself, as they apparently do in Texas? But on a smaller, more personal scale. You know, like anyone who wanted to take in a prisoner or two could just convert their rec room or their basement or their garage into a maximum-security facility—if their promotional materials are to be believed, TechnoMort can apparently sell you everything you need for one low price— and then you could just sit back and live off the $40,000 a year, or whatever it currently costs to keep a prisoner locked up these days. Of course, for me personally to benefit from this little scheme, I'd probably have to move out of New York City, or at least out of Manhattan, because otherwise, it's hard to imagine finding an apartment big enough and yet cheap enough to make the whole thing worthwhile, but hey. If it's a choice between temping or living in Brooklyn with a couple of prisoners in the back yard, I know which one *I'd* choose. Warren might be a somewhat harder sell.

ROSIE: "Well, I think University is right to change policy," Elena says earnestly. (The Russian Elena who works in the xerox room.) "If worker now is being sexually harassed, she wants move to new department. Fine. But what if manager of new department does not want her?"

She hands me a slice of orange, which I take, gratefully, since I, of course, have had time neither to bring nor to buy lunch, and I haven't eaten yet today. Elena never likes me to visit her at work—she thinks it isn't fair to the University, which pays her to work, not to talk to me—so if I want to see her, I have to give her an entire lunch hour, which doesn't exactly seem like the most efficient use of my time. Still, she is a key person in the xerox room, where turnover is so high that she has become a kind of leader. (Her racial views are atrocious, but she and her co-workers—all young African-American and Latino men—seem to get along fine. Go figure.) Anyway, since being able to shut down the xerox room is of the utmost importance—well, then, lunch with Elena.

"You do understand the policy, right, Elena?" I never know when I'm being patronizing with her and when she really does need help with the language or the concept. "Right now, if you were being sexually harassed, you'd have a right to the next available job at your grade level, the very next one that came up. But the University wants to change that. They say that if the supervisor at that next job doesn't want you, then you don't get to go there. You would have to wait until some supervisor *did* want you—and that could take months. Basically, you'd be stuck."

"Yes, Rosie," Elena says. "I understand. But explain me, please, Rosie."

She's always very polite, which can make you forget just how stubborn she really is. "Explain me please why one man should pay for mistakes of another. Why can new supervisor not choose his worker? *He* did not do harassment. *He* is innocent."

"Well, if you want to look at it from *management's* point of view."

"Why not?" she says seriously. "Everybody have point of view. Manager, worker, student, teacher—everybody is same human being, right?"

"Well, yes, but—" Well, *no.* Let them get their own union. "It's a question of—you want to weigh one thing against another," I say, fairly incoherently. I'm going to have to stop this going without food. Plus that Cassandra has told me that no matter how long she treats me, if I don't stick to my diet *and* eat regularly, I'm not going to stop bleeding.

I take a deep breath and start again. "Look, Elena. I agree with you—it *isn't* fair to the supervisor who gets the new worker. You know what would really be fair? The person who's doing the sexual harassment—that person should get fired."

"Yes, you right, Rosie!" Elena says. "*That* is fair. Ask for that!"

"But we wouldn't get that," I say. "The University is never going to fire someone for sexual harassment—it just isn't going to happen."

"Why not?" Elena says. It's both exasperating and fascinating to talk to her—nobody else would even wonder. She says it was horrible living in the Soviet Union, back when it *was* the Soviet Union, and although America has its problems, it's far and away a better place to live. But she has such a—not innocent, exactly, and not naïve. But such an—*uncorrupted* expectation that things *should* be fair, it does make me wonder what they taught her over there.

"I don't know. Because it's more important to them that their supervisors have total freedom to run their departments any way they want to, I guess."

"Well, I don't understand," Elena says. "But boss in new department, he did no wrong. Bad boss is free, good boss is punished. How is this fair?"

"It probably isn't fair," I say. "But we can't make them fire the old boss, we just can't. And making the sexually harassed worker wait months for a new job opening—that's not fair to the worker. You *are* a worker, Elena—doesn't *that* concern you?"

Elena swallows her orange thoughtfully. "All people are same to me," she says. "I don't say I'm worker, boss, supervisor—just person."

"But you're a person with less power," I say. "And supervisors, they're people with more power. And the University, that's run by people with the most power. Well, not the most, maybe, but a lot. So what should we do to even things out?"

Elena shrugs. "I believe in union," she says, patting me reassuringly on the arm. "I just don't understand."

FLIP: For a while, I have the awful feeling that I could stay on at TechnoMort more or less indefinitely, because Georgia keeps hinting that there's going to be a job posting soon, although I don't think even Warren would want me to give in and take *that* job.

Though on the other hand, if I were Warren, which thank God I'm not, I would also hate to have me working full-time. Honestly, I'd forgotten what it's like, trying to work forty hours a week and have a life, too. How do people do it? (Well, obviously, they *don't* have lives.) Anyway, between working forty hours a week and going to rehearsal sixteen hours a week and being at the gym nine hours a week, plus keeping up with voice and dance classes as best I can, I really *am* never home anymore, though to my credit (Well, why *shouldn't* I give myself credit? Warren certainly isn't.), I do make a point of spending every Saturday night with Warren, and at least some of Sunday with Juliet. Which really is *all* I can manage—maybe Mario gets a phone call every now and then (I have to call him at his office, on my lunch hour, because Joshua has gotten so possessive that Mario won't stay on the phone for more than thirty seconds whenever he's at Joshua's place, which is apparently *all the time*). And sometimes Tanya and I go out for coffee after rehearsal when both of us are willing to face a miserable sleep-deprived day the next day (though if we're both still temping in April, those late nights are clearly the next to go). But that's *it*. I wonder if Warren even *notices* how much I've had to cut out of my life, just to earn the few dollars that *he* can have without even thinking about it. If I were Warren, I'd think it would be almost worth it to pay my half of the rent, just so I wouldn't have to work so many hours, just so I'd be less exhausted and miserable and grouchy when I *am* home (though I try not to be, I really do). If I were Warren, that would be worth a few lousy bucks to me.

So I don't know what I would have done if TechnoMort had actually wanted to keep me on. But I am just as glad when the temp agency calls one Monday morning and tells me not to go there. Apparently, Georgia has decided that she really does want someone with more advanced computer skills than I currently possess. So the agency sends me on to We Care For You, which apparently they mean literally—they put together gift packages for people who are too busy to buy presents themselves, which, frankly, I find appalling. I always thought the whole point of having the kind of money that you seem to need to patronize We Care For You was that you *got* to go shopping.

What's next—paying someone to go out and eat gourmet meals on your behalf?

It's not as though they want me to actually *be* one of the shoppers. That *would* be too good to be true. No, apparently, relationships with the clients are hedged round with the kind of confidentiality that I thought you found only in Swiss banks or possibly at clinics that treat sexually transmitted diseases among the Royal Family. As though having your children or your spouse or your colleagues know that you actually *didn't* pick out their Beanie Babies or their $243 sterling silver Penhaglion cufflinks or their limited-edition $850 gold-plated kaleidoscope (perfect for the desk in any office) would be the greatest shame of all. Well, if there were any justice, it probably would be.

Anyway, *my* job is to take the information provided by the personal shoppers and transfer it onto the order forms used to actually purchase these precious items. Talk about pressing your nose up against the bakery window.

"It's even worse in the summer," Mimi says cheerfully. Mimi, also an aspiring actress, has the desk next to mine. Although she, too, is technically a temp—meaning no sick days, no vacation time, no benefits—she's been here for a year and a half. Waiting for *her* big break, which she is *also* sure is just around the corner. "In the summer, we do care packages for the kids."

"Care packages?" I say, looking doubtfully at my computer. The supervisor, Ginger, showed me how to fill out the order forms, but now that she's not standing right here over my shoulder, I have absolutely no idea what to do.

"For kids at camp," Mimi says, noticing my distress. She comes over, pushes a few mysterious buttons, and says, "How did you ever get into *that* window?" I have no idea what she's talking about, but at least the computer screen looks familiar again. "You know," Mimi continues, "when kids are away at camp, their parents send them care packages. Food from home, and little presents, and nice little things to make them feel loved and cherished and like that. But a lot of parents are too busy to actually *buy* the elements that go into a good care package. Plus—" She pauses dramatically, which I must say I hate for actors to do in real life. "Plus, regular old candy bars and home-baked cookies aren't good enough for *these* children. They have to have the *right* care package. Last year it was Beanie Babies and Gummi Bears. And action figures from some movie—*Phantom of the Opera*?"

"I think you mean *Hunchback of Notre Dame*."

"No, that was Christmas," Mimi says. "Or am I thinking of *Dr. Jekyll and Mr. Hyde*? Anyway. This year it might have been *Turandot*, except that came out a little early. Clearly, the parents can't keep up with it all, but obviously, the kids can. So that's what they pay *us* for." She makes a face at me. "Don't you just want to puke?" she says. "Why do they even *have* kids if they don't want to buy them *presents?*"

"Maybe they *do* want to buy them presents, but they just feel inadequate," I say, trying to be charitable.

Mimi laughs. "Right," she says. "I can just see it. Poor little Brittany or Ashley or whatever her trendy little name is, sitting there on her bunk, tears streaming down her face, because Mumsy sent her the wrong brand of virtual pet, and now she's the laughing stock of the entire cabin."

"Mmmm," I say, uncomfortably able to picture this all too well. "Children can be cruel."

Mimi waves a sheaf of order forms at me. "Here's some man who just bought his mother a $500 silver tea pot and creamer set, from Barney's," she says drily. "And then he bought his wife a $1,550 leather pouch to put her *garden tool* set in. Also from Barney's. And then he bought someone—he didn't want us to include a card with this one—a $395 Lalique singing angel that looks just like Elton John."

I snort. "He probably got *that* for his boyfriend."

Mimi laughs. "Yeah, probably. All I'm saying is that these people's kids aren't doing anything they're not learning from their parents."

I look down at my order forms. Some man is giving his girlfriend an $800 Armani backpack, which I'm sorry to report simply makes my mouth water. But when I was Juliet's age, I certainly didn't care what *socks* I wore, and I can't believe Warren did either.

All my forms seem considerably cheaper than Mimi's, so maybe they just don't trust me yet. A woman bought her husband a $280 limited-edition Lionel train set from Hammacher-Schlemmer. A man bought his mother a $230 Limoges miniature porcelain telephone, from Bloomingdale's. And he got his boss a birthday caviar sampler of fifty grams each of Beluga, Osetra, Sevruga, and pressed caviar, plus a caviar spoon, for $195. Well, *there's* a man who's clearly going nowhere. Obviously, if he were *serious* about his career, he'd have spent $460 on the 250–gram sampler.

"Doesn't this drive you crazy?" I say suddenly to Mimi. "All these things you know you'll never have? Until you're famous, of course."

Mimi looks surprised. "If I was famous, I wouldn't want *this* stuff," she says, waving her order forms at me again. "A $700 Gucci scarf? I'd probably spill something on it."

"Don't say *if*."

"What?"

"You said *if* you get famous. Don't say *if*. Say *when*."

For the first time, Mimi looks discouraged. "Yeah. Right," she says. I turn back to my terminal. Hey, it beats working in a prison.

ROSIE: "Money is the alienated essence of man's work and being," Jack says, practically smacking his lips with satisfaction. "This alien essence dominates him, and he enjoys it."

"What?"

"Karl Marx," Jack says, taking a bite of his eggplant Parmesan sub. This has become kind of a tradition with us. He shows up at one or sometimes both of the weekly negotiating sessions—they're still open to all University employees, which pretty much shows you how seriously Olympia *isn't* taking this process, because otherwise, negotiations would be closed. And then he and I go out to eat.

"Don't you just love that?" Jack is saying. *"Money is the alienated essence of man's work and being.* Money represents something that used to be this wonderful part of human beings: their ability to work, to accomplish things in the world. Their *essence.* And then that essence gets *alienated,* it gets taken away and used against them. So instead of doing good work that they love, they have to go work for *money,* they have to work for some *boss,* who makes a huge profit off of *their* work. And the richer he gets, the more power he has over them, so they're actually *helping* him to dominate them.

"And then they want that money. They envy their rich boss, never realizing that *they're* the ones who make him rich. But as if that whole process weren't enough, Marx has to say that they *enjoy* it."

"But most people *don't* enjoy their jobs," I say, feeling vaguely guilty, because tonight is Thursday, and I just realized I was supposed to call Michael to figure out about tomorrow night, and now it's almost eleven and there's no phone inside this diner.

"Do you enjoy *your* job?" Jack says, one of those sudden switches in conversational direction that I never expect from him.

"Oh, I love *my* job," I say. "But I don't have a *real* job. My job is to change everybody *else's* job. Of course I enjoy *that.*"

Jack laughs. "So you're exploited, but not alienated," he says. "Because I think the union takes incredible advantage of you and all the other organizers, as far as I can see, although you obviously work the hardest—"

"No, I don't. Plenty of other people—"

"Yes, you do. But that's not my point. My point is, people *don't* enjoy their jobs, obviously, except for weird exceptions like you—because face it, Rosie, most people who work as hard as you do are lawyers or stockbrokers or something, and they usually *don't* enjoy their jobs, per se, but they *do* make tons of money. Or else they're factory workers or nurses or whatever, working double shifts and overtime because they desperately *need* the money. Which *is* my point. Or rather, Marx's point. It's the *money* that dominates people, the money they themselves create by working so damn hard and so miserably, and then it's the money that they enjoy being dominated by."

"And this is important because—"

"Because—" Jack says, and then he notices that I'm out of hot water, and he signals the waitress, who, at this hour, *really* isn't interested. I don't think I have the right to be annoyed with the waitress—after all, she's working, and I'm not. But I *am* annoyed.

"It's important," Jack says, pulling my thoughts back to this table—why does my mind always wander so much with him? Marcy would say I'm avoiding something. "It's important because—I mean, Rosie. Why are people so invested in keeping their lives the way they are? Instead of making revolution, I mean, instead of changing everything?"

"Oh, Jack, for heaven's sake," I say, which I find myself saying to him fairly often. How can someone with whom I basically agree make my own ideas sound so simple-minded? "It's *hard* to change things. It's dangerous. You could lose your job. Or, if you're talking about revolution, I don't know. You could get beat up, or shot, or put in jail, or tortured, or whatever else happens to people who—"

"No," Jack says, and then the waitress arrives. And he switches gears again, he is so totally charming to her that she comes back right away, not just with more hot water, but with hot water that is really *hot,* which is practically impossible to get at any diner. He grins at me conspiratorially when she leaves.

"No," Jack says, "it's *not* just because they're afraid of getting shot that people don't want to change things. It's because they actually *like* things the way they are. They *like* all the stuff they buy. They like all the stuff they think they're *going* to buy. They'd rather *have* that stuff, or the prospect of it, than to think about how the world could be different."

"So you basically think people should work all day and then go home and feel so miserable that they're ready to change everything?"

"I don't think people *should* be miserable," Jack says. "I think they *are* miserable. And what they *enjoy* is being dominated. By television. The things they buy. The money they go out and spend. Their jobs make them miserable, and they go out and spend as much as they can so that they'll feel better, and it doesn't work, and they have to keep working harder just to stay in place, and it still doesn't work, and then they think it's *their* fault, and they buy some self-help book to tell them why, and it *still* doesn't work. And then they fall in love, and *that* doesn't work, and then they're *really* at a loss—"

"And all that time, they could just be making a revolution."

"Right," says Jack. "And then, like you, they'd have jobs they'd *enjoy*."

I can't help laughing. "Jack," I say, "I'm no different. I watch television. I buy things." *I eat,* I think, but I'm not going to say that to him. My life is killing me, if Cassandra is to be believed, but I'm not going to say that either.

"Well, you're part of the society you're living in," Jack says. "You're not a *saint*." He grins at me, which I didn't expect. "Thank God."

I make a face. "I don't know. I sometimes think it would be easier to be a saint."

"Well, you're a Catholic," Jack says. "You would think that."

"Ex-Catholic," I say. "Actually, they call it a lapsed Catholic, but since that's a fairly religious phrase, I don't say that. What are you?"

"I'm a Marxist," Jack says. "This is my creed." And he quotes, " 'Uninterrupted disturbance of all social conditions, everlasting uncertainty and agitation, distinguish the bourgeois epoch from all earlier ones. All that is solid melts into air, all that is holy is profaned, and man'—*people,*" he interrupts himself, making a face, "but the quote doesn't work if you say 'people,' so '*man* is at last compelled to face with sober senses his real conditions of life and his relation with his kind.' Meaning that—"

"I know what it means," I say, with some asperity. "I have read Marx."

Jack grins at me again. "So what *does* it mean?" he says. "In twenty-five words or less."

"I suppose it means that we can't have any illusions anymore about how brutal everything is," I say slowly. "How brutal everything is, and then how we have to be honest about that. About *why*. We can't say it's fate, or God's will, or destiny, anything *solid,* anything *holy*. It's just—a few stupid people with power lording it over the rest of us. And we *help* them dominate us, first by working for them and making them rich, and then by buying whatever they want us to buy, and then by believing whatever they want us to believe, and then by telling ourselves that it's our own idea. And then it *is* our idea, because if you have something inside you long enough, then it *is* you, no matter how much you hate it, no matter how sick it makes you—then it *is* you, and at least part of you does everything you can to hold onto it. And *then,* to add insult to injury, we *enjoy* the way they dominate us, we *enjoy* the little crumbs they throw at us, because what *else* are we going to do with ourselves? How *else* are we going to keep on living?!"

Well. I certainly didn't expect to get *this* upset.

"But you *are* doing everything you can to change things," Jack says finally. "And that *is* what keeps you going."

I point to myself, to my secretly bleeding body, to my exhausted throat, to my, all right, all right, all *right,* to my weight. "I'm certainly a great advertisement for the cause," I say with a bitterness that surprises me. "I'm sure anyone who saw me would just want to jump right on board."

"Well, I would," Jack says softly.

"You don't count," I say, blinking back the tears that seem all too ready to intrude these days. "You were already on board."

There is a long, awkward pause.

"I'm sorry," Jack says finally, leaning toward me over the table. "I didn't mean to upset you." He smiles, a very, very small smile. "See," he says, "I find it a relief to say the way things are. It makes me feel—I don't know. Exhilarated. You feel bad about it. But still, you don't despair."

I look at him skeptically.

"No, no, what you just did, that wasn't despair," he says. "You just feel bad that it takes other people so long to see what you already know. But you don't give up on them."

"How do *you* do it?" I ask Jack suddenly. Because he works hard, too, though you'd never know it to look at him. If we do go out on strike, pretty much every single worker in the B-School is going with us, and a large part of that is due to Jack, who spends every single lunch hour and a lot of his work day visiting people and talking to them, one by one by one. (He must have a *really* indulgent boss, or maybe he's charmed her, too.)

"How do *you* pay?" I ask him. "How do *you* know that—that you're caught in the same trap with the rest of us? Or don't you think you are?"

"Oh, no, I am," he says quickly. "Do you really want to hear about it? I'm not sure I want to tell you." His words falter. "All the things I want," he says finally, looking at me. "That I know I shouldn't want. Do you really want to hear about those?"

I look at him for a long time, watching him watch me in the vinyl booth. "Maybe," I say finally. "Not tonight. But maybe later."

"Later," he repeats, and I don't know whether to feel hopeless or exhilarated. Whether, like Trish Hunter, I always want the wrong thing, my own worst enemy. Whether, like the workers Marx is talking about, I want the very thing that's going to destroy my power. Whether, as Cassandra would seem to have it, I have to learn to mistrust every single one of my cravings. Or whether, in fact, there really is something else in the world that might be good for me to want.

FLIP: "Well, is *this* right?" I ask Ginevra, my supervisor at The Body Beautiful, a mail-order company that sells home exercise equipment (there wasn't *that* much for me to do at We Care for You once they caught up on their Valentine's Day backlog, although Ginger said she would try to get me back for their Graduation Day/June wedding/new camper crunch). "No, I mean here. Is *this* right?"

Ginevra is already shaking her head. "It isn't, is it?" I say in despair. And why the fuck do I care so much? Ginevra is tolerant but grievously disappointed in a way I am embarrassed to say reminds me of Dad, and which has all too great an impact on me as a result. I've only been here three days, and already I'd do anything to please her.

"Why don't you take a break for a while," she says kindly, "since you're obviously having trouble being as careful as you need to be. Just take it a bit slower when you come back, all right, Flip? You're obviously very quick—but sometimes, to be accurate, you need to slow down."

Well, thank you very much, Ginevra. Like I *need* to be told how to copy numbers from one page to another. Except, apparently, I do.

"You might do some filing in the meantime," she says in her gentle voice. Which has the dual effect of making me want to tell her to go to hell, and making me want to do a really excellent job with the filing, so she'll see what a good little worker I really am.

The filing is actually soothing, in a monotonous sort of way, and I can imagine doing this for a few mind-numbing hours, sort of an office version of Prozac. There's even a bar of sunlight that falls across the long, low two-drawer filing cabinet, and if I didn't have to literally get down on my knees to file, I might actually enjoy this. Except then I discover that all the files have been *mis*filed—all right, not all of them, but enough so that I wonder whether it's up to me to start re-sorting them. Nobody asked me to. But if Ginevra comes by to check on my work, how will she know the difference between my mistakes and somebody else's? Besides, Meg, my fellow temp (at least she's not an actor—she's a painter), said she heard Ginevra say, at the end of my second day, that she wondered why I didn't show more initiative. (Though maybe Meg was just trying to make trouble.)

Anyway, if I do reorganize the files, will Ginevra (a) applaud my initiative, or (b) be annoyed that I've wasted my precious temporary hours doing work that she didn't really want done, or worse yet, (c) be upset that I've destroyed a carefully worked out filing system whose basis is just too complicated for *my* naked eye? And if I go *ask* her what she wants done, will she (a) applaud my initiative, or (b) scold me for bothering her with a perfectly obvious question?

Well, you can see what this job has reduced *me* to. It's the biggest goddamn relief of the day when Meg comes bearing the message from Ginevra that I might as well take lunch now, even though it's only noon and, if it were up to me, I'd hold off until one. (Who eats lunch at noon—farmers?) But, as Ginevra patiently explained on my first day here, the work flow is *her* responsibility. Our is just to file or die.

ELINOR: "I can't talk now," I hiss into the phone. "I'm at my *job*." *She* doesn't *have* a job that I can see, so perhaps she doesn't understand about bosses and their ideas of office protocol. Well, I'm sure she *does* understand. It's just Idris's way—just *another* one of Idris's ways—of driving me insane.

Although on the surface, they seem various, all of her little ways fall under the same general category: they are all about mocking whatever is important to me. No, not mocking—refusing to see it. So for example, if she's at my house, and we're making love, and *Pauli's* voice comes over the answering machine—she actually gets phone calls from Pauli *at my house*—she'll stop. Very affectionately, making a huge point of saying she'll be right back, leaving me with some tender, intense touch, a hand pressing my breast or stroking between my legs—but then she'll actually go to answer the phone. Granted, she won't talk for very *long*. But why she would give Pauli my number in the first place, why she would answer the phone at all—?

Or today. Calling me at work, wanting me to take twenty minutes to discuss some revisions in the script with her. Doubly maddening, because I *haven't* seen her socially in almost two weeks—each time, we get together as if by accident (and always at my house), and then we fall away from each other as if we were never together in the first place.

(She says she didn't give Pauli the number—that Pauli just found it somehow. And she says that if she *didn't* answer the phone, Pauli would just keep calling, or leave long, provocative messages, or engage in some other form of escalation that, she says, would be even more unpleasant for me than her actually answering the phone.)

("So it's all for *my* benefit?" I say as calmly as I can manage.)

("For *our* benefit," she says sweetly.)

My boss comes in just as I am hanging up. I'm sure I look far more distressed than any business call could reasonably account for, and he looks at me suspiciously. "Who were you talking to?" he says.

"I was calling the xerox room," I say, trying to control my anger. What right does he have to interrogate *me?* "I wanted to know when the reports would be ready on the Morningside properties. Of course, they didn't know, and I was in fact going to ask you, should I fax Olympia an apology? Because they were expecting them six days ago."

He glares at me. He hates being reminded of anything about himself that might possibly be construed as an imperfection. Right now, he's just a lowly real estate analyst—well, he's only twenty-four, give him time. As his research assistant, I'm entitled to my own office and slightly more interesting work than if I were just a straight secretary, but I often wonder whether the extra money and perks are worth the increased amount of contact I have to have with him. (This speculation is totally theoretical, of course. I'd never give up this gig unless I actually had the kind of acting work that I'm beginning to doubt I'll ever get. Though this is my third twenty-four-year-old boss—I wonder if, by the time I'm in my fifties, I'll even be able to stand working for these ambitious children. I wonder if, by the time I'm in my fifties, I will have decided to do something else with my life.)

"Don't fax Olympia," he snaps at me now. "Let them wait. Maybe they won't notice that we're so late." As though it were *my* fault. I look at him, his eyes narrowed, glaring, and I realize that he really does think I'm to blame.

"They called twice," I say, even more calmly than before. Just as though I didn't know what it was doing to him to hear *that.*

"Why didn't you call me?" he says accusingly, but I can see how panicked he is.

"You said not to interrupt you," I say, more calmly still. "I was waiting for you to come in." Well, this isn't so bad. He *did* tell me not to interrupt him. We both know he was talking to his girlfriend, but since he wasn't *supposed* to be talking to her, he had to make it sound important.

He actually looks physically sick. "What did they say?"

I try not to smile. "The first time, they wanted to explain how urgent the situation was."

"I didn't ask what *they* said. I asked what *you* said."

No, you didn't, I think, but it's never worth it to engage him head-on. "Sorry," I say. "I said I understood their problem, and so did you, and that in fact the reports were in the xerox room, and I was just trying to get them moved to the head of the queue."

Although of course this is the perfect answer, it only makes him madder, because once again, it's that much more difficult to blame me. "The *second* time," he says. "What did they want the second time?"

"They wanted to know why I hadn't gotten back to them yet," I say, well able to imagine the plight of the poor woman who was calling me. She knew I didn't know any more than I had before, or *I* would have called. But her boss had probably said, "Call them again."

My boss doesn't even bother to ask me how I handled that one—he must be really worried. This is the third report that he's turned in late in the past two months, and sooner or later, someone is going to catch on.

"Call the xerox room again," he says, turning to leave the office. Actually, I won't. I know the guys down there, we have a good relationship. If I called them every time my boss told me to, we *wouldn't* have a good relationship.

He looks back over his shoulder just as he is going out the door. "You're going to have to skip lunch today," he says with the small smile he always has whenever he announces bad news. "I told Achtenberg's that they could have that report two days early. Which means I need everything from *you* by three o'clock."

I shrug. Sooner or later, I'll find a way to even things out.

FLIP: "Happy April Fool's Day," I say, handing Warren a check. It's nine-thirty on a Friday night, and I've just gotten home from the gym. Despite what I swear were my best efforts, I've arrived too late for Juliet's bedtime, which really is too bad, because this morning, when I *did* manage to have breakfast with her and Warren, we had a whole discussion about April Fool's Day, and I have the feeling that she either had a special April Fool's joke planned for me or wanted to tell me about the various jokes that had been played in school that day. (I certainly didn't think *Warren* would get it about April Fool's Day. I thought Juliet might like to talk to someone who *did* get it.) But for some reason, there were long lines for everything tonight.

Still, it's too bad. This was one of the few breakfasts where we actually had a coherent conversation—it's hard to get up at six-thirty instead of seven-thirty just for a meal that I'm usually too tired to participate much at anyway, especially since the earliest I can possibly get home from rehearsal is at eleven. And she and Warren always have to conduct a lot of frantic business concerning homework and permission slips and problems with clothes, which always makes me feel that I'm more in the way than anything else. (Warren deals with this schedule by going to bed as early as he can stand it and then waking up again when I get home, which I must say sounds like torture and I can hardly blame him that he doesn't want to do it *every* night.)

I stand there holding out the check to Warren, and I swear, he looks as distressed as if I had just handed him a dirty toilet brush. What am I supposed to do, beg him to take it? Which he at long last does, looking uncertainly back and forth from me to the check until he finally folds it up and puts it in his pocket. Just don't say *thank you,* I think, because I don't think I could stand that. But, to his credit, he doesn't. "Happy April Fool's Day to you, too," he says as he goes back to sorting socks. I would love it if he'd come into the kitchen and make me dinner, or at least reheat whatever he made for himself and Juliet, and in another mood, I'd find a way to tease him into doing that, but now I just go on into the kitchen, where of course it turns out that Warren has left a portion of tonight's dinner right there on the stove, so that even I can't complain about actually turning on the burner to heat it up.

"So did Juliet have any special April Fool's Day stories to tell you tonight?" I call out. Feeling sorry for myself for missing them, apparently.

"Yes," Warren calls back, "but she made me promise not to tell you. She said she wanted to tell you herself tomorrow." He stops in the kitchen doorway with a basket of laundry in his hands. "She said I *could* tell you that she had the best April Fool's joke of anybody in her class, and everybody was *extremely* impressed with her—her words—but that was absolutely *all* I was allowed to say because she was going to tell you herself at breakfast tomorrow. And I said that since you had had a long week, that maybe you might be sleeping when she had breakfast tomorrow, and she said she didn't care, she wasn't going to eat until you got up, even if you didn't get up till after *lunchtime,* because she wanted to tell you *first* thing in the morning, and it wouldn't *be* first thing in the morning if she had already had breakfast and you hadn't. Then she said, 'Of course, if I ate breakfast in the *living room,* Uncle Warren, *that* wouldn't count.' " This business of eating in the living room, so that Juliet can eat and watch videos at the same time, is a running battle between her and Warren. So that hearing this story of *course* makes me smile, for all sorts of reasons (not least because there's just something about hearing him try to imitate Juliet), but it also makes me feel like bursting into tears. I feel as though I'm missing *everything.*

Warren sighs and takes the laundry basket into our bedroom. When he comes back, I'm spooning the reheated boeuf bourguignon onto the plate he's left out for me. "There's salad in the fridge," he says, going over to get it for me. "What do you want to drink?" I see there's still a whole setting left on the kitchen table for me as well. All of which makes me feel like crying even more.

Warren looks like he wants to say something, but he doesn't. He just brings me salad, and seltzer, and lemon and lime for the seltzer, and bread, which he slices for me, and butter for the bread, and dressing for the salad, and I'm sure if there were anything else he could possibly get, he'd get that too. While I eat, ravenously, of course, because I have just been at the gym for three hours and Ginevra actually made me take lunch at eleven-thirty, for God's sake. And when I've had seconds and thirds of the beef, and seconds of the salad and Warren has put on water for coffee, then he says, over by the stove with his back to me, "You don't have to do this anymore, Flip."

"What do you mean?" I say, not sure, now that the moment is finally here, how I feel about him making the offer that he's obviously going to make.

"You didn't exactly—we didn't decide to live here based on the rent," Warren says. "I mean, when we were sharing the rent at our old place—even before, you didn't have to work five days a week. The way you seem to have to do now."

I shrug.

"I've already told you." Warren's voice is so low I can barely hear it. "You can have what I have."

"You didn't exactly make me a reasoned offer," I say, trying to keep my voice even. "You pretty much said all that in the heat of the argument, Warren. I don't think I should hold you to it."

"That's not why I'm telling you."

"Anyway, it doesn't matter. I would hate to think I couldn't work forty hours a week like everybody else in America. Present company excluded, of course, but even *you're* taking care of a child."

"Would it make it any easier if I offered to *lend* you the money?"

"No," I say quickly. "Let's not even talk about it. I don't want to owe you anything."

"Look," Warren says, "this doesn't—it doesn't make any sense. Does it?"

"What do you mean?" I say, although of course I know what he means. "You're not *always* right," I tell him suddenly.

For some reason, this makes him smile. "About you, I am," he says. "In fact, I would say that you are one of the few areas—perhaps the only area—where I have consistently been right. Even if I seem to have to make every conceivable mistake first."

"*So?*" I say as irritably as I can.

He still doesn't back down. "You can have what I have," he says doggedly. "If that's what you want.

"That's what *I* want," he adds after a pause.

The first night we were together, it actually seemed easy. I could see how much he liked me. How off-balance I made him feel. "I live up all the way up in Washington Heights, and my roommate is probably home anyway," I told him, which was a lie—my roommate was out cruising somewhere in the Hamptons. "Where do *you* live?" I felt bold and daring, getting Warren to leave Chris's party and take me back to his place (I hate remembering now that he even paid for the taxi, though at the time, that made it more of a coup). When he told me all those things about me and Rosie, he was in his element. But when I made him take me home, I was in *my* element.

Even when we got to his apartment, that first moment, reaching for each other inside the door . . . It was all so overpowering, but that was my territory, too, which made it—not easy in a stupid way, but, OK, yes, easy. Maybe Warren wasn't used to being in over his head, but *I* certainly was.

But the *next* day. I mean, usually, when I had that kind of night with somebody, I wouldn't even call it a *first* night, because in my experience, it was usually the *only* night. A night like that isn't *meant* to be followed. So OK, my heart had turned over when he smiled, but it was fairly easy to forget *that,* and yes, it was great sex, but I had had great sex before, and then there was this totally awkward breakfast the next morning—although he did cook for me, which I remember thinking was nicer than people usually are after that kind of an evening. But we didn't talk about seeing each other again or even exchange numbers. I just left.

Except, then, at about four that afternoon, I called directory assistance and got his number—not even his real number, but his office. (Given our professions, both of our real numbers were unlisted.) God, his *office* number. What was I going to say to *that?* And this was where, if I had been paying attention, I would have known *something* was going on, because I would *never* have done this with any other trick, I would have left a much, *much* cooler message. Instead of the message I actually did leave, which was, "Warren? This is Flip. You know, from last night. Would you give me a call? I should be home for another hour or so. Which I suppose means you need to know what time it is *now,* don't you—it's a little after four. Which I suppose means that I'll be here till five. Well, probably you could have figured *that* out by yourself, couldn't you? Presumably you *can* tell time. Anyway. Call me. If—you know. If you want to." Luckily, I remembered to leave *my* number. Thinking, well, if he calls back in an hour, fine, and if not, I'll just go out, and in either case, that will be that.

Was I actually surprised when he called back five minutes later? He *was* a psychic, after all.

"It's Warren," he said abruptly when I picked up the phone. Not even *hello.* "You asked me to call."

"Oh. Well. Thanks for calling."

He didn't say anything, so of course I had to say *something*. "I thought, you know. That maybe we could see each other again." Honestly. This was all so totally unlike me that I came this close to simply hanging up, except at that point, that would have seemed even *more* revealing than anything I had already done. Though given the long pause on his end of the line, I started thinking that maybe a clean break *would* be the most humane solution for all concerned. Because clearly he *wasn't* interested, and—

"You could come over for dinner," he said, a million years later. "If you wanted to." Not sounding any too happy about it, either. "But only if you want to."

Only if I *want* to? I think irritably. Why *else* would I come over?

But all I say aloud is, "When?"

"Tonight," Warren says, pronouncing the word with enormous difficulty. "I have food here. If that's what you want."

No, Warren. I don't want food. I want sex. Obviously.

But what I say is, "Oh. Well. All right." I rally just long enough to recall my manners. "That would be very nice," I say formally. "Thank you." Not that he *deserves* this level of consideration—he's hardly trying to put *me* at ease. "What time should I come?" I remember to add.

Another enormous pause. Which makes me wonder what we'll actually say to each other when I get there.

"It's four now," Warren says finally.

"More like four-fifteen," I say helpfully. "Four-eighteen, if you want to be exact."

Even across the phone, I can feel Warren smile, and suddenly I feel much, much better. "Well, then, come at six-eighteen," he says. "If you want to be exact. Presumably *you* can tell time, too."

Dinner is actually fun. We gossip about people from Chris's party (*not* including Ian, who apparently had walked away from Warren just minutes before *I* got there), and Warren tells me about some of his more interesting clients, and I regale him with stories about all my fascinating film and theater experiences. Plus the food is out of this world. Warren makes this amazing chicken thing and this extraordinary salad, mesclun, with those real flowers—nasturtiums?—and fresh marinated artichoke hearts—not canned—and mandarin orange slices and toasted hazelnuts, and these wonderful chocolate things for dessert, not quite cookies and not quite fudge, but some kind of incredible cross between the two. And I wonder if he eats like this all the time or if he actually went out and bought everything and put it all together in un-

der two hours (because despite our mutual exactitude, I was actually ten minutes early). He couldn't possibly have been expecting me, could he?

Then after dinner there is this awkward moment when we move away
from the kitchen part of his small studio into what I suppose counts as the living room, except, since all he has is a couch that opens out into a bed, it's also
the bedroom. A doubleness that hadn't mattered in the least last night, but
which tonight happens to make me feel—well, not *shy* exactly, because we all
know I'm not *shy*. But, as I said, awkward. Warren goes to sit on one end of
the couch and I find myself sitting in the armchair by the other end of the
couch, and for a while, we just sit there in silence until I think I'm going to
have to leave, because I swear to God, I have no idea what else to do.

Finally, Warren says in that same abrupt, impersonal tone as when he
called me back, "Well. Why don't you come over here."

And, thinking about it as little as possible, I do.

When I sit down beside him, he puts his arm around me, and I sigh and
lean against him. He starts to rub his hand up and down my back.

"Mmmm," I sigh, sinking against him more closely. He moves his hand
down to the bottom of my spine and with his other hand starts massaging my
neck. I sigh again. "I'm glad you called me back," I say.

He doesn't say anything, but now he's stroking my hair. Which feels—I
can't explain it. But through all those months when he was so distant and
withdrawn, the only thing that kept me going was remembering the way it felt
when he did this that night. Sometimes, in those bad months, after we'd made
love, he'd do it again, a little. But I wanted him to *keep* doing it.

"And you called so soon," I say as his other hand starts moving back and
forth, there at the base of my spine. "Was that—did you have a feeling I had
called?" I say quickly. "I mean, since you are a psychic."

He laughs, and it's even nicer than when he smiled. I can't believe how
much I like him, when he laughs.

"Hardly," he says. "I'm not saying I *wouldn't* have had a feeling about it of
some kind. But in this case, it was hardly necessary. Since I was already more
or less checking the machine every five minutes."

I swear to God, I actually didn't get it. "Oh, really?" I say. "Were you expecting a call?"

Naturally, he thinks I am making fun of him. "All right, all right," he says in
that irritable tone I would come to know so well. "You don't have to rub it in."
His hands stop moving, though he leaves them there against my back.

"I didn't *mean* to rub it in," I say after a pause. "That's nice, that you were
thinking about me." Another pause.

"You could have called *me*." I say.

"I tried," he says. "Your number isn't listed. How do people ever get you, if they want you for a part?"

"They call my service."

"Well, I didn't *have* your service number."

"I mean, obviously, I was thinking about you, too," I say. "Since I *did* call."

"Well, I called you back."

"I know. I was saying thank you, as I recall."

Suddenly he bends down and kisses me on the lips. A very sweet, uncertain kiss. I kiss him back, putting first one hand, then the other against his face. So gently, so tenderly, I surprise myself. When the kiss ends, we are both smiling and uncertain.

"Well," I hear myself saying, "why don't I just ask you now about coming over tomorrow night, then? To save us both all that calling." We look at each other, his hand still on my shoulder. "I mean, you wouldn't have to cook again or anything," I say. "Although I have to tell you, Warren, that was one of the best meals I ever ate in my life, so if that's what you can do on two hours' notice, I shudder to think what you'd do with a whole *day*. Not that you'd *have* to spend the whole day cooking for me. Although you could if you wanted to. I wouldn't complain."

Warren looks at me steadily, so steadily that I think I might actually faint. "Or," he whispers finally, "you could just *stay*."

Which ended up being what I did, finally. I more or less never went home again. Until it was time to get my things—such as they were—for our new apartment, and even then Warren came with me. And then I spent the whole next year, more or less, wishing that things would be the way they had been those first two nights, the way they never were again. Although they were nice in other ways. The first two or three months anyway.

So asking me to stay was the first offer Warren ever really made me, and do you think he's lived up to it? If you'd asked me last August, I'd have had to say *no*. But now . . .

So maybe this isn't the same old Warren who's making me this offer. Maybe this is an entirely new Warren.

"How do you think it would work, me living off your money, Warren?" I say as neutrally as I can manage. "Wouldn't you—" but he is already shaking his head.

"It would be *our* money," he says.

"But it isn't ours. It's yours." I think I'm going to cry.

"Can we at least pick a date?" he says after a pause. "For our—ceremony of betrothal? Can we at least pick a date, and make up a guest list, and—and do whatever we have to do to say that—that— Some things you have to go through alone, Flip. But I don't see why you should go through this alone.

"I don't see why I should, either," he says after a pause.

He looks at me defiantly. "And this *is* one of the things I'm right about," he says stubbornly. "Whether you believe me or not."

I sigh. "No, I believe you. I'm just tired of you being right all the time. Particularly when you have to be wrong so much to get there."

He smiles, and I like him so much at this moment. He really is a good person, isn't he? I keep forgetting that about him. He isn't kind, exactly. But he is good.

"*Yes* to the betrothal date," I say, "or whatever we decide to call it. And to the guest list, and to sending out invitations, and to whatever else we have to do, though I still have to say that I thought one of the big advantages of being gay was not *having* to bother with all that stuff. But, all right, *yes* to that. And as for the money—I don't know, Warren. I'm just afraid I'd end up paying for it somehow. I don't think that's what you *want*," I say when I see how hurt he looks. "I just think it would happen."

"Well, I hate to say that if you don't take half my money I *won't* marry you," says Warren. "But it certainly seems—wrong, not to share it. I mean, what if you wanted to run off with one of your co-stars and fly down to Brazil? How would you ever manage, without my money?"

He catches me so off guard, I burst out laughing. "All right," I say finally. "You win. I'll take your goddamn money. I just can't fight about this anymore—you're right, it's too ridiculous."

"That isn't what I meant," Warren says.

"Well, it's what *I* meant," I say. "Take it or leave it."

"Not if you're going to hate me for it."

I put my arms around him. His whole body is trembling. "Well, I probably *will* hate you for it," I say, "but I don't see why *that* should stop you. I think you should just hang tough on this one, Warren. Just insist that I take your money—it's the only way I'll learn."

Warren sighs. "You won't ever forget that it's mine, will you?"

"No," I say after a pause. "I don't think so."

"At least it could go into some kind of joint financial account," Warren says finally. "Something with both our names on it."

"So if we do break up, you could just take my name off," I say. "As opposed to actually trying to get my half back." Warren flinches. "No," I say, "I think that's a good thing. Because then it *would* feel more like *ours*. Instead of a present from you that I could never . . . I'll never be able to give you anything like that, Warren. Not on that level."

"I don't agree," Warren says. But I wouldn't have expected him to. People with money never understand what it's like not to have any.

THE GYM

TANYA: And one more . . . and one more . . . and one more. Lifting my leg out behind my back, curling it up with the weight on it. Each time a new chance to get my leg into the perfect position. To trim another ounce, another inch, off my butt.

Who's going to win this round, my body or me? I'll tell you this much: it won't be my body. This is one place where I know exactly what I'm supposed to do. I do this . . . I do *this* . . . I do *THIS* . . . and something happens.

I can't believe they kept me waiting so long to tell me *no*. Not like I even *wanted* to be on *Hell Street*. More like I was *willing* to, like that was the *compromise* I was prepared to make. But they want me to *beg* to compromise, they want me to crawl. And now it's, "Sorry, Tanya. We're not even interested in seeing you crawl."

Now the other leg. The other buttock. Each time, a chance to be perfect. To have a whole *other* body, one that someone will like better. I try to picture how I'll look, even more gorgeous, more classy, in my gunmetal gray Trish Hunter suit, my legs long and tapered, my butt flat as a board. They'll never let me play a lieutenant now. Not like I wouldn't have *gained* weight for them, if they'd asked. Not like I wouldn't have done *anything,* and better than anyone else.

WARREN: I really wish I didn't have to do this. But of course, I do. Even the thought of not going to the gym is horrifying—as though that really *would* put me beyond the pale.

At this point, to be perfectly honest, I have no idea how much it matters to Flip, although I think if the truth were known, it matters to him more than he'd want to admit, that my body be—well, within some kind of acceptable range. Not just how it looks in general. But that it shows—specifically—time at the gym. And of course, if I were ever in a position where I had to consider how anybody *else* might feel—

I mean, not that bathhouses or any of those public places were ever my fa-
vorite venue anyway. But it is true that years ago, there was more—leeway.
You might indeed feel that every separate body part was being—evaluated.
But not necessarily against one single standard.

I've found that the only way I *can* endure being here is to think about it as
little as possible. To take myself as far as possible *out* of my body by thinking
about something else.

This particular machine is the one where you sit and hold your arms up-
right and then try to bring them in together, pulling against the weight. It's
painful, but not so awfully demanding. And what I find myself thinking about
as I try to do this task without knowing I am doing it, is all that money I just
gave Flip.

Well, I didn't exactly *give* him the money. If only because he wouldn't take
it. It's only going into some kind of an account—my accountant is still trying
to figure out what kind—that will have both our names on it. Still. That turns
out to feel more permanent, more momentous, than I would have thought.

I try again to bring my two arms together. And what occurs to me, completely against my will, is the thought that it isn't very easy to give anything to
Flip.

Why did it take him weeks to wear that jacket, for example? Granted, he
could say that the night I gave it to him, he found out a terrible secret I'd been
hiding. But then *why,* I can't help thinking, did he choose *that* particular night to
force the issue? It's not as though I give him presents every night of the week.

Of course, I'm *not* a particularly generous person, so it does seem mean to
try to blame any portion of that on Flip. I think of Juliet and those socks she
wanted, and I wonder how much my not wanting to give them to her was
simply the feeling that I'd given her enough and didn't feel like giving her any
more. (Though I would have thought I felt the opposite—that however much
I give her, it can never possibly be enough.)

I don't know. I did buy her the socks. Which made her happy for a while,
but it didn't at all solve the problem of making friends. Flip says— Because I
have had, finally, to listen to him about this. Given how badly I seem to be doing with it on my own. Though, God knows, I can't bear him to see, either,
how badly I— Anyway, he says, "Obviously, Warren, it's that school. They all
sound like a terrible bunch of snobs, and if Juliet can't get along with *them,*
maybe it's to her credit."

But I think that's too simple. Because—well, I've seen her with Sara. She
does boss Sara around an awful lot. And I know *she* doesn't see what she does
as showing off, but—

Of course, she probably *is* the only one in her class who—well, obviously, her living arrangements are unusual, to say the least. And given where her mother is . . . *And* she comes from France. Any little thing that makes you different—it always counts against you. I remember *that*.

I pull my arms together, feeling the ache that reaches deep into my chest. Do you know what I *really* wish? I wish I could give Flip half of what I have, so that we really are both on the same footing. And that then the gift would simply disappear. Its history—erased. It's a more or less awful feeling, to know that it's not in my power to make that happen.

MARIO: Today I'm going to the gym alone, because Joshua has to call his parents in Long Island. I love going with Joshua, but I must admit, I like going alone. There's something about being with all those other men in the weight room, the steam room, the locker room—I don't know. It's like the way I felt that night at the club, dancing with Flip.

When I get to the entrance of the weight room, I run into Chris and Paco. Chris uses free weights, like Joshua and I do, but Paco does machines. Which Chris is always teasing him about, since of course, you know. Machines are what women use. But to tease Paco about it seems, well, *mean,* although I'm sure Chris doesn't intend it that way. Especially since Paco is so much older than Chris, *and* he's had to give up being a dancer, both because of getting older and because of some kind of terrible problem with his knee. I don't know. Maybe the way Chris teases him is supposed to take the sting out of it.

Today they seem to be arguing but they break off abruptly as soon as I get there. "You know who I ran into yesterday, by the way," Paco says quickly, obviously changing the subject. "Simon. *He* certainly looked awful."

"Oh, well, *Ian,*" says Chris.

"Yes," agrees Paco. "They both always have so many other people going, who can even keep *up* with them?"

"I know," Chris agrees. "You can just imagine Simon being the one to have *his* little flurry of hot dates, and Ian being the one to feel all left out and miserable."

"I think being in graduate school has really cramped Simon's style," Paco says. "He used to be up for almost anything, but now all he does is study. No wonder Ian is losing patience."

"Well, honey, I don't think you're being fair," Chris says. "You *do* have to study hard at that level. Are you going to lose patience with me when *I'm* in school?"

"If you ever *are* in school," Paco mutters, and Chris looks shocked.

"Have a good workout," he says stiffly as he leaves. "Don't *strain* yourself."

Paco looks at me and shrugs. "How many times can you have the same conversation?" he says. "I mean, really, how many times?"

"It's just that he's so nervous," I say. "Not having any idea—you know, about the future."

"What's the big deal?" says Paco. "You pick something, and you do it, and if it stops working out, then you pick something else. He's *got* another fifty years, for Christ's sake. Unlike the rest of us." Then he looks embarrassed. I wish people wouldn't do that.

"Speak for yourself," I say. "In fifty years, *I'll* only be seventy-eight." So then he looks relieved.

When I finally go into the weight room, Chris is way over in the corner. Which is probably just as well, because—you know. Sometimes it's nice to work out alone.

What I used to like to do before Joshua and I started coming here together was just to go *into* the muscle I was using. To feel it by itself, to make it come alive. So I start with the dumbbells. Today I feel free, for some reason, so I try more weight. It does exactly what I hoped it would—picks out that muscle in my arm, so that I feel it curling up and stretching out, curling up and stretching out, so pleased with itself, so proud of what it can do. Sore in that friendly way. *My* muscle. *Mine.*

Now the other arm. I flex it slowly, carefully, because my first trainer taught me that the worst thing you can do is rush, because the *really* worst thing you can do is break the form. As opposed to what he called *preserving* the form, which always made me think of dance. Maybe because *he* was so graceful. He liked me a lot, for a while, and I really liked him, and I still don't understand why *that* relationship didn't work out.

And then. When I am really into the rhythm of it—and maybe the reason I don't understand is because I still feel so *fond* toward him, despite the ugly way it ended. Because even though he's gone and I'll almost certainly never see him again—that would be *my* choice, anyway. I would rather not even hear his name. But still. He gave me *this.* So even though I don't even know where he is these days, or even if he's still alive, *this* is something I'll always have. And when I treasure it, I'm treasuring him, aren't I? I find that thought a comfort.

And then. When I am really inside the rhythm of it. If I really let my mind go, still staying inside my body, inside those friendly muscles that are doing such good work for me—then, sometimes, I am flooded with the rhythm of the entire room.

Sometimes it doesn't work, of course. If someone is pushing too hard, for instance. Or if someone is—uncertain. But sometimes, sometimes—and today is one of those times—there's this incredible group energy, when suddenly everybody's rhythm just—fits. As if we're all breathing the same breath.

So that till someone breaks the rhythm (or until I do), for just those few moments, I belong somewhere. Here.

FLIP: I don't know whether or not I would actually have started living on Warren's money. But it was more or less a question of saved by the bell, because Warren and I had our April Fool's Day fight on a Friday night, and the very first thing Monday morning, before I even heard from the temp agency, I got an emergency call from my agent, who wanted to know if he could book me for some training video being produced by that guy I went to see the day I first wore Warren's leather jacket. So apparently it *did* bring me luck, and make what you will out of *that*. Just these few last-minute voiceovers that they needed, since the actor who was originally in the video has gotten some hot TV deal in L.A. (apparently I get the *leftovers* of other people's luck), but there are also three or four more videos in the series, and if I work out for the voiceovers (and if I don't work out, just shoot me now)—if I *do* work out, then they'll want to use *my* face and body for the next few tapes.

Warren, predictably, has a mixed reaction to my good news, almost as though I've pulled this job out of a hat just to avoid accepting anything from him. God, I want to say to him, if *that's* all it took. Anyway, since there *is* a larger principle involved, we *are* still going ahead with this plan of putting our money together—well, of putting *his* money with *me*. Which may be why, when I walk into the gym this morning, I find myself thinking about the steam room.

It isn't a particularly conscious thought at first. I say hello to Sandy at the front desk, and to Jenna, who's working out on the bicycle near the window, and to Paul, who's still doing stretches (he has the *most* elaborate routine, but then, he comes here *six* days a week, which, whatever Warren might think, I would absolutely hate), and to Ellis, who is *the* most boring muscle queen *in* the universe and is currently bench-pressing about eight and a half million pounds (so I don't actually *say* hello to him, but I do sort of wave), and to Lionel, who is meticulously wiping the sweat off one of the barbells (I mean, hygiene is all well and good, but he'd wrap the weights in saran wrap if he thought he could get away with it), and to Cesar, who has his eyes closed in concentration (but who somehow always gets offended if you go by and *don't* say hi), and to Kelly (she's so *thin,* it's a wonder she can even *walk,* let alone do squats), and finally to Pauline (who always looks so blissed out, I hate to interrupt, but today she catches *my* eye, so I smile at her as she comes up from her eight millionth situp. I don't *think* you can do that on Ecstasy, but maybe that *is* her secret.). Since I've been coming at night for so long, I haven't seen any of these people in weeks, and while I wouldn't exactly say I *missed* them, it is sort of nice to see them again.

I start to stretch, which I always try to do the moment I get to my spot near the seated row, because I've found that if I pause for even one second, all of a sudden, I've been here fifteen minutes and I haven't done anything. But as I move through my routine, my mind races back and forth between thoughts of the steam room and a list of all the *other* things I have to think about today. Like who, when I get home this afternoon, I'm going to suggest be on the guest list for our celebration of the conjugal sacrament, and how embarrassing it's going to be if my list is a million times longer than Warren's, which how could it not be, and how I'm going to feel if Ian actually *is* at our nuptial rites, which of course, he will be, since it's more or less unthinkable not to invite him.

I still can't believe that Warren talks with Ian about *Juliet.* Whereas if *I* start to express any opinion about her at all, he always looks so furious and at the same time, so hurt, it shuts me *right* up. I know he thinks I'm down on that school just because everybody there has so much *money* (except for one or two scholarship students, apparently, and don't I feel sorry for *them*). But it's not just that. I think Juliet gets very—what would you call it? Carried away. About all the things she cares about. So that she feels like—like an artist at some cocktail party given by very, very rich society people. They might think she's interesting; they might even think she's charming. But they certainly won't want to be friends with her.

I settle myself into the seated row, where I feel the strain of the weight reaching all the way down into my back. I visualize how I want those muscles to look—that sculpted, sexy, statue look where every muscle shows. Not that I ever achieve *that* look. It amazes me sometimes, how much I want it.

When Warren and I first got together, it didn't even occur to me that he might be—well, *peeved*—at the thought of my little encounters in the steam room. We certainly never discussed being monogamous or anything like that. I mean, there are plenty of people I know who plan to live together forever, and it doesn't necessarily imply that they won't ever fuck anybody else.

But then I began to realize that at least for Warren, it did. And that it was more or less a source of torment for him, thinking of me out there screwing around with other men. Which of course I wasn't interested in doing anyway, so it was particularly annoying that he wouldn't believe that I wasn't doing it. Given that what goes on in the steam room isn't even actual sex. Well, all right, it *is,* or why would we all do it, but you know. Jerking yourself off under another man's smoldering gaze or getting the occasional hand job—a version of sex that's so safe, it doesn't even require a condom—I mean, it's barely more than a physical release. Having very little to do with whatever was going on between me and Warren, at least as far as I was concerned.

I go find the weights I use for my shoulders. I don't *really* consider getting off in the steam room as anything that Warren ought to be worried about—although I had to reconsider this position somewhat when I finally realized that Warren *did* worry about it. And so then, of course, I more or less stopped, with only one, or maybe two exceptions since we've been back together. Because (a) it was important to him, and (b) he's a psychic, so I always assumed he'd eventually know all about it anyway.

But today. I must admit. I am thinking about it. And don't try to tell me that, given how I feel about Ian, I'm being unfair. For one thing, Ian wasn't just some trick in the steam room, someone you get off with, and if you have any sense, you don't even *talk*. In fairly exciting circumstances, I must admit, since you never know when some straight guy will come in and you have to cover everything up with a towel (or you just let him pretend he doesn't notice, or maybe he really *doesn't* notice, though don't ask *me* how he could miss it. But since most straight men think they own the universe, maybe it's just inconceivable to them that a man could jerk off another man in *their* universe. Or at least, in *their* steam room.).

It's awful to hate bench-pressing so much, because, as it happens, my chest is my best feature, and we all know how it got that way. Though sometimes, when I finish, I feel this sudden flood of *something*—Energy? Pain? Hormones?—come rushing right out of my heart. So I try to keep my mind on that, as I get Cesar to spot me and begin the whole discouraging routine.

All right, all right. You really want to know the truth? It isn't giving up the steam room that makes me feel trapped. It's the goddamn money. Money that could, obviously, buy me a whole other life (I could get new head shots, I could afford to make Tiger's Eye a priority, I could even produce a showcase featuring *me*). But whenever I think about where *this* money comes from . . . Because, you know, when I worked for the temp agency, I saw how it worked. The company paid the temp agency for my time, and the temp agency gave me a little piece of what *they* got. I was walking around exhausted all the time. And the company and the temp agency got rich.

So if I think about it—and believe me, I don't *want* to—but still. Where does Warren's money come from? From people like me (and Ma, and Dad, and Poppy, and *all right*, Rosie) working for people like *his* family. And if I take that money, it's going to be people like me working for *me*.

But when my workout is over and the steam room beckons, I just don't have the heart. I mean, yes, I do feel trapped. By the money, by Warren, even by Juliet. Living with this child whose *school* I'm not allowed to visit. I don't even know if I really *can't* help her make friends, or if it's just that Warren won't let me.

Still. As he himself made clear the night we fought about *his* little secret, the only reason he *doesn't* know about my activities in the steam room is because he hasn't actually come right out and asked. And I'd hate for today to be the day he did. Just as we're choosing the fucking guest list for our fucking wedding. Or whatever the fuck we decide to call it.

TRUE LOVE

WARREN: One week ago today, we made up our guest list. And today, Flip and I walk up the steps of the main post office carrying the shopping bag full of invitations to the connubial event, and I feel—overcome. After months of nothing happening at all, now it's all moving so quickly. Because the latest word is that Madeleine will almost certainly be out of the hospital by the beginning of June. And although I still haven't given up on the idea that she might somehow be talked into staying in New York, it seemed important to have our matrimonial ceremony while Juliet is still here. Which means that we have finally set a date—June 25th, the last Saturday in June.

So we reserved a place—some space in Greenwich Village that Flip knew about—and wrote the invitations—"Please come join us at our wedding—or whatever we decide to call it!"—and had them xeroxed onto card stock at the local copy shop—something Flip also knew how to do, from years of involvement with low-budget productions, I suppose—and now it's April 12th, and here we are walking up the steps of the main post office, getting ready to mail them. After which I suppose there really will be no turning back.

I pretend to look around the post office lobby while pressing my shoulder against Flip's, as hard as I can without actually knocking him over. He looks surprised, but then he smiles and presses back. Because it's been like this for a week now, starting, I suppose, when we *did* make up the guest list. I have to keep *finding* him. Wherever he is in the apartment, I seem to have to be there, too. When he's watching television, I sit snuggled up against him, reading a book. At night, when *he's* reading in bed, I lie there with my head in his lap. I've even come into the bathroom to join him in the shower, or even in the bath, which I've *never* wanted to do before, but now, I want to, anything, anything, just to be with him, as much with him as I can be.

Today is a beautiful spring day, so warm that there are already outdoor tables in front of this Irish pub on Thirty-first Street and Seventh Avenue, the nearest decent place we can find to eat after the mailing is done. And Marta is picking Juliet up after school for a sleepover, and Flip and I are going to spend the day doing various ceremony-related errands, ending up at our old apartment in Hell's Kitchen, which neither of us can bear to let go, evidently, though it does seem ridiculous to keep paying rent on two places. At least we can pack up some of the things from that place and bring them over to the Chelsea apartment, which Flip has been after me to do, and which, now that he's not temping full-time (he shoots his first training video on Monday), we can actually do together.

So there's this wonderful holiday feeling about the whole day ahead and the evening to come, as we settle into the outdoor table and give the waiter our orders. And for the thousandth time this week, I am overcome. I think this time, Flip is, too. Our knees press under the table. Our eyes meet. I feel us both alight with that solemn sexual glow.

And suddenly I feel such despair. Because it won't make any difference if we *say* we're married, or even if we *get* married, in some mythical future time and place where marriage is legal for us. It won't make any difference at all— we still won't be able to hold hands in public; on a day like this, in a place like this, we won't even be able to look at each other.

I try to explain this to Flip as the waiter brings our Caesar salads, as the business of eating finally gives us some distraction from what we're feeling for each other. "Well," Flip says brightly, with his mouth full, "at least now we could hold hands on *television*."

I have to laugh, though in some ways that feels worse. "Well, trust an actor to think of that."

Flip shrugs. "How upset about this do you want to get?" he says. "It's not exactly new news." Then he looks at me and starts to laugh. "Oh, I see," he says. "You never even wanted to hold my hand before, so you didn't care. Now all of a sudden, you can't keep your hands off me, even in public, so suddenly it's an issue."

"All right, all right," I say irritably. "You don't have to look so pleased about it."

"Oh, I think I do," he says. "So tell me, Warren, is it worth it? All things considered?"

I straighten my napkin. "I haven't decided yet. I'll let you know."

Flip suddenly grabs my hand, there under the open table. "Live dangerously," he whispers.

I squeeze his hand so hard it hurts. "Apparently there isn't any other way."

FLIP: It's so nice, the way things are right now. I haven't wanted to say anything, because I was afraid he might get self-conscious and stop. But I can't stand how he always looks, so *certain* that I'll always say no. So *surprised*, every single time, when the answer is yes. And today we've just mailed out the invitations to our *wedding*, for heaven's sake.

"Warren," I say, and he looks up from his coffee. Sooner or later, I'm sure he *will* stop. Or I'll do something that I don't even realize to *make* him stop.

"What?" he says.

"Oh, nothing. Just—it's nice, Warren, the way you are these days."

He looks at me, a haunted look. "I don't know *how* I am these days," he says. "I don't recognize myself."

I smile and without even thinking about it, I take his hand again. Above the table. "Well, if you have any further problems in that department, you just come to me," I say. "*I recognize you.*"

ROSIE: Today is April 12th, but we're not on strike yet. And why not? Because at the last minute, Harris called up the president of Olympia and made some kind of man-to-man appeal to reason, and finally, finally, it looks as though Olympia is moving in negotiations. Enough to warrant putting off the strike date another week, which we have duly voted to do.

Yes, of course, I'm angry. *And* I'm being unreasonable. Because if Olympia's president hadn't believed that we really *would* strike—I mean, without that force from below, Harris could have made all the phone calls in the world and it wouldn't have made any difference.

So Harris did the right thing, of course he did. That doesn't mean I can't feel—well, not *betrayed*, exactly. Not *used*, exactly, either. But if I didn't think Harris really *was* acting in the workers' best interests, that is how I *would* feel.

Michael doesn't get it. He's *glad* we don't have to strike, so fine—*he'll* make a good labor lawyer someday, won't he? Don't ask me to be fair to him, either. I'm just not in the mood.

FLIP: We've gone down to Gay Rose on Greenwich Avenue to look at flower arrangements, and we've stopped by the space I rented so Warren can be sure he likes it too. And we've visited the loft of this guy I know who has a band, because of *course* there has to be dancing. (Warren looked very doubtful when we first walked in, because the music on this guy's sound system was very techno–house music–nouveau clubland–whatever, which I would actually *love* to someday go to a wedding and hear, but since this *is* also Warren's day we're planning, it's probably just as well that the actual tapes the guy played for us were a lot more mellow without being actually *saccharine,* so that in fact, we do both like them.) *And* we've eaten our way through a couple of different places that do food, which turns out to be the most difficult of all the decisions, not least because it happens to be the most expensive. I admit that my own view is also somewhat colored—all right, a *lot* colored—by the fact that my family is going to be there, not just our friends, and I want to have food that they can actually *eat,* whereas I suppose Warren is mindful that our friends are going to be there, not just my family, so he not unreasonably wants the food to resemble something he himself might actually *serve.* And all of these negotiations have to be conducted without Warren making *too* many snide remarks about what my family served *him* on Christmas Eve, and with me at least *somewhat* limiting the number of not-so-veiled references to *his* family's grocery budget, *and* with me patiently explaining to Warren, based on *years* of backstage experience, why he really *doesn't* want to solve this problem by doing all the cooking himself.

So despite all the potentially fraught territory to be avoided, it has actually turned out to be a fairly wonderful day, and both Warren and I are somewhat, well, starry-eyed as we walk down through Washington Square Park on our way to the Christopher Street subway station. And I suppose both of us are looking forward to spending the night in our old apartment, too, though actually packing up our—well, Warren's—leftover things is a prospect that holds considerably less charm.

Still, it is a beautiful, unusually warm spring night in Washington Square— the park is crowded with what seems like thousands of people, out for the last hour of daylight—and since Warren has been so—*physical* lately, and since it *is* the Village, I actually have my arm around Warren's waist as we pass the fountain, and he, will wonders never cease, is actually starting to put his arm around my shoulders, when our attention is caught by the sound of an argument behind us. Warren drops his arm and we both turn our heads to look at what turns out to be an extremely young, extremely nervous white police officer engaged in heated conversation with a Black man and woman in their late twenties.

Warren wants to keep moving, but for some reason, I have to stop and hear what's going on. Maybe because they both look so bewildered, it makes me curious, too.

". . . report of a young Black man about your height," the cop is saying, holding out his hand.

"But, officer, he was with me," the woman is saying as the guy digs into his pocket for his wallet. He holds out something—driver's license? Another type of ID?—but the cop doesn't take it. The guy has to put it right into the police officer's hand.

"Flip. Come on," Warren is whispering, but I motion for him to stop.

The policeman studies both the man and the card, taking his time. I am thinking how I would play him, if I had to show this scene to, say, Tiger's Eye, in one of those exercises about power. Well, I'd have to show how scared he is. Terrified, in fact. Terrified of *what?* Oh, that they won't listen to him. He's about six inches shorter than the Black guy—well, I can relate to *that*—plus there's something about the guy having a woman to back him up, while the cop is alone. Would I give myself a girlfriend to impress, if I were playing the cop? Or would I imagine that I couldn't *get* a girl? But this guy, this potential criminal, *can.* That would make *me* mad.

"But officer—" the woman keeps saying, and the cop waves one hand at her to get her to be quiet, still studying the guy and the card. Well, of course, he doesn't want to make a mistake. Because it's hard to imagine anybody looking *less* like a wanted criminal than this guy—he's so *clean.* I know that's silly—why shouldn't criminals be clean, too? But he is. He's wearing this spotless white T-shirt and beige slacks, and his girlfriend is wearing a loose black boatneck and white slacks. They don't look flashy enough to be criminals.

I notice the cop noticing that they *are* both carrying cans wrapped in paper bags. Well, carrying open liquor in the park *is* technically illegal. Of course, Washington Square Park is more or less known as Drugs 'R' Us in my little corner of the world, and the idea that someone would get busted for carrying an open beer can *there* is completely laughable, but still. Criminals don't just break the big laws. They say that on *Hell Street* all the time.

But the cop, at least, doesn't seem to think they *are* criminals, because he's handing the guy back his license, or whatever, saying, "OK, thank you, sir. No problem." And the couple starts to walk away.

"*Now* can we go?" Warren whispers impatiently, when suddenly, the woman turns around and marches back to the cop, while her boyfriend—and I, and eventually, Warren—watch.

"How *dare* you stop us like that?" she says, not yelling, exactly, but loudly enough so that the cop jumps. And then looks furious that she managed to startle him.

"How *dare* you stop us like that," the woman is saying. "We did absolutely nothing wrong, nothing suspicious, and you think because you got some report saying *some* Black man did *something somewhere,* you can just stop *us?* I own a business right over there on Bleecker Street, my boyfriend manages the Foot Locker on Sixth Avenue—we have a *right* to walk in the park without you stopping us."

The cop says something quietly, pointing to the beer cans, while the woman's boyfriend tugs at her elbow, trying to get her to move away.

"I don't think that's any excuse at all," the woman is saying.

Suddenly, the cop takes the beer can out of her hand and turns it upside down, pouring all of the liquid out into a small puddle on the asphalt. He hands her back the empty can and holds out his hand for the man's. I expect the guy to put his can into the cop's hand, just like he put the license there, but the guy is confused or maybe angry, because he doesn't do anything, so, not really roughly, exactly, but with a little—well, I'd call it *energy,* the cop grabs the beer can out of his hand and pours that out, too. "Now go on," he says.

It's the guy's turn to get mad. Warren has stopped trying to get me to leave, and I have the feeling, though I can't turn around to look, that at this point he's fascinated, too. "You can't treat my girlfriend like that," the guy is saying.

"Honey," the woman is saying. "It's all right. Let it go."

"You can't treat my girlfriend like that," the guy says, louder, and takes a step toward the cop.

"Honey," the woman says again. "Come on. Let's just keep walking."

"Back off, buddy," the cop says, forcing himself—or at least, I'd play it as forcing *myself*—to stand his ground.

"You apologize to her," the guy says, standing uncertainly in that little space between his girlfriend and the cop. "You apologize to her right now."

"Back off, buddy," says the policeman. "I'm not going to tell you again."

"I want an apology!" the man says, taking another step forward. He's about a foot away from the policeman now, but maybe that's one foot too close. The cop forces himself (well, again, that's how *I'd* play it) to give the guy a shove—not a big shove, but a definite shove—in the chest.

"Honey," says the woman, really frightened now. "*Please* come on."

At the same time, the guy—and if I were playing *him,* I'd tell myself to look *hypnotized*—shoves the cop in the chest. From this distance, it looks exactly as hard as he himself got shoved. Maybe a little bit harder.

Then suddenly, things happen very fast, so fast, I can't exactly tell *how* they happen. Suddenly, the cop has turned the guy around—using a nightstick? Or with his pistol drawn? Somehow—it's happening so fast, I can't see it all— he's pulling the guy's hands behind his back and drawing them into handcuffs.

"Hey!" I say, without even knowing I am going to talk. "What did he *do?*" Because, OK, it was dumb to shove a cop, but handcuffs? Besides, the cop shoved him first.

"*Flip!*" Warren says behind me. The woman is just standing there as the cop handcuffs her too.

"She didn't *do* anything," I am saying as I move forward. Mad as he is, I feel Warren following. I keep having the idea that I should just explain. After all, I witnessed the whole thing.

Suddenly, from four directions at once, four police cars come driving into the park. Their doors burst open, and about twenty policemen surround the fountain, maneuvering the policeman and his two handcuffed suspects back behind their protective circle. "No, see, they didn't *do* anything," I say to the nearest policeman, a tall, thin blond guy who looks extremely calm, but you know. If I were playing *him* I would say he *has* to look calm in situations like these, because of how extremely nervous he is. Not the guy next to him, though, another short man with pale white skin and dark red hair. *He* looks like he's enjoying himself. Not in a mean way, exactly, although that would have been my first impression. But more in the sense of adventure.

"Look," I say in the calm, reasonable tone that actually does express how I feel about this. Because clearly this is all just a big misunderstanding. All right, maybe the policeman in question lost his temper and things got a little out of control, but surely these *other* officers will listen to me. After all, I saw everything that happened.

"Stand back, please," the blond cop says.

"No, I saw—"

"Stand back, please," the policeman says again. "Come on, come on, you've got to move back."

He takes a step forward and I *do* take a step back. Behind me, I can feel that people are *finally* paying attention. Some of them seem to be leaving. Others are making a huge circle around this whole incident. With Warren and me in the front row.

Well, come on. Years of vocal training should mean that *somebody* listens to me. "They didn't *do* anything," I say again, trying to make eye contact with first the blond, then the red-haired cop. But they don't seem to notice.

Why *aren't* you listening to me? I find myself thinking. I'm white. Then I see the look the blond policeman gives first me, then Warren, then both of us together. Oh, so *now* they notice me. We seem to have collected quite a crowd of Black and Latino witnesses. I notice that all of *them* are completely silent.

Warren, of course, is furious with me. "Are you *crazy?*" he hisses at me under his breath. He wants to drag me away so badly it practically hurts his fingers.

"What if it were Juliet?" is all I can think of to say, though I can't really associate Juliet with that woman. But I also can't see how Warren can watch this and not want to do something.

Warren doesn't want to just walk off and leave me, which I suppose is to his credit, but without touching me, he can't figure out how else to get me to go. So I plant myself where I am and fold my arms. "No, really," I say to him, under my breath. I can just imagine how we look to everyone else—there are no white people but us anywhere in the vicinity now, only this silent, extremely still mass of dark-skinned people. And us, these two faggots, arguing under our breath. They probably think we're fighting about where to go for brunch.

Warren sees that the only way he'll ever get me to move is to give me an answer. "I would *teach* Juliet not to argue with a uniformed *police* officer," he says. "As someone apparently *failed* to teach *you*."

The couple is finally being herded into one of the police cars under the eerie silent scrutiny of the rest of us. I feel like I'm part of some weird Gestapo movie, and I can't get over the shock that this isn't a movie, it isn't even Harlem. It's Washington Square Park, *my* park. I feel like calling Rosie up to apologize—all those times she tried to tell me about this kind of thing and I thought she was exaggerating—except of course I'd never give her the satisfaction. Except it might be worth it if I could tell her how badly her precious Warren is behaving.

"*Now* can we go?" Warren whispers into my ear as the police car drives off.

"Jesus, Warren," I say softly, as the crowd slowly dissolves. "They put those people in *handcuffs*."

"Well, what did you expect them to do?" he says, our voices rising toward a more normal level now that the vigil is over. "From their point of view, they were dealing with dangerous criminals."

"But they were just some people out for a walk."

"I *know* that, Flip," Warren says patiently. "I was right here, remember?"

"Well? Why aren't you more upset?"

"Flip. They're the *police*. You know, the ones with guns? That's how the police behave. That's why you don't argue with them."

"It could have been us," I say.

"Right," Warren says. "That's *why* you don't argue with them." Then he says, "Actually, we don't *know* that they weren't criminals."

"Warren. He had just told them to move on. Do you think he would have done that if they were criminals?" We're heading down West Fourth Street. Even more than the park, this is supposed to be *our* neighborhood. But we both know people who have gotten beaten up on these streets. Granted, not by cops. The cops didn't do anything about it, though.

Warren shrugs. "How do I know what they were?" he says. "I don't know anything about people like that."

"People like that?"

"Flip," he says in that maddening patient tone. "Please don't do this. You know what I mean."

"No, I don't, actually. I'd really like you to spell it out for me, Warren. Just what do you mean by 'people like that'?"

We wait for the train. At the far end of the platform is a homeless man, so filthy you can't see what color he is, one of those people who it's actually embarrassing to look at because they're so far gone.

"They weren't like *him*," I say, nodding toward the man. "They were—you know. Clean. Middle-class."

"Carrying open beer cans," Warren says. "Breaking the law."

I laugh. "Since when did *you* get so concerned about following the law?"

"I don't know what you're talking about," Warren says. "I follow the law."

"Well, besides all the things *we* do that are illegal—"

"They're not illegal now," Warren points out. "Not in New York."

I can't believe this. "So if they *were* illegal, you *wouldn't* do them?"

"The point is—" Warren says.

"You cheat on your income tax," I say, not because I actually know this, but because everybody does.

"That's different," Warren says. Aha. "And if the IRS came to my door to ask me about it, you can be damn sure I wouldn't *argue* with them, particularly after they had just told me everything was all right and I could now walk away."

The train roars into the station and we get on. It's so noisy, and there are so many Black and Latino people on it—almost nobody white, at this hour— that I don't want to say anything until we're back on the street in our old neighborhood.

"Here in beautiful Hell's Kitchen," I say. "Where you couldn't find a cop if you wanted one. And why do you think *that* is?"

"Because this area contributes fewer property taxes to the city," Warren says. "Also, I think it's a matter of triage. It's still possible to save Washington Square." He gestures around the admittedly grimy part of Ninth Avenue that we're walking down. "This area is a lost cause, frankly."

"Warren, that is such a stupid thing to say, I don't even know how to answer it."

"Well, we can tell whose brother *you* are," he says coldly.

So now we're both furious. Well, no sex tonight, I can't help thinking ruefully as we stomp up the stairs to our apartment. But when we have each showered, silently, and undressed, silently, and gotten into bed, silently, him with his back firmly to me, wouldn't you know it, I want him anyway.

"Oh, so evidently you don't mind having sex with a racist," Warren says when I put my hand on his shoulder.

"Warren. I never said you were a racist."

"Do you really think I wouldn't have done something if it had been Juliet? No matter what would have happened to me?"

"To us, actually."

"Well. You could have run away."

"Oh, I see. The cops are arresting Juliet, you're standing there defending her, and I'm running away. *That's* a pretty picture."

At that point, he turns onto his back, and I turn onto my stomach, and somehow we end up lying together, my head on his chest. I have to tell you, it's an enormous relief to be able to do something that I was sure we would get arrested for doing. Or for looking like we *might* do. Or might ever *want* to do.

Still, we didn't. Get arrested, I mean. And they did. Warren wants to say that's because they argued with the cops and we didn't. But for a minute, I did argue—it didn't occur to me that I didn't have that right. What world do *they* live in, those fifty other silent witnesses who surrounded us?

Warren sighs. "I just don't see what Juliet has to do with it," he says.

"Well, you're the one who keeps bringing her up," I point out. "Presumably because she's Black."

"But she's not Black like *them*."

"And what does that mean?"

"She wouldn't be walking around drinking beer out of an open can," Warren says. "And if a policeman stopped her, she would be polite."

"I don't think she's Black like them, either," I admit. "But I think I just think that because she's ours. Yours. Whoever's."

"You can say ours," Warren says softly. "After all, you *are* going to—plight your troth to me."

"I think that one refers to being engaged. You know, like betrothed?"

"Anyway," Warren says. "Technically, she's Madeleine's."

Neither of us wants to think about that. Gently but insistently, Warren pulls me further on top of him. I feel amazingly, well, *protected*. This seems wrong, not to mention dangerous. If I hadn't felt safe in the park tonight, I *wouldn't* have said anything. I actually could have gotten us both—well, not killed, probably, but arrested. Pushed around. Warren feels me shudder and tightens his arms around me. I suppose we *are* safe now. As in, no one's going to burst through the door and arrest us. I wonder where that couple is sleeping. Why *did* they argue with the cops?

"It's weird," I say, "because I always thought—I mean, the thing about being gay was that it was different for you than for, you know. Your brothers and sisters. I mean, knowing you were different from them. Do you know what I mean?"

"Not really," Warren says. "I would have felt different from Madeleine no matter what I had been."

"No," I say. "I meant, it's different for Black people. Because they *have* families. People who are supposed to help them be Black."

"And Juliet only has us," Warren says.

"And Madeleine. And if Madeleine had another kid, with a different father—"

"Well, it would pretty well *have* to be a different father, wouldn't it?" Warren says. "Under the circumstances."

"Actually, who knows?" I say. "She could still be seeing this guy. She could still be totally involved with him."

"Juliet is eight," Warren points out. "Where has *he* been?"

"Maybe he's married."

"Great."

"Maybe he's in exile. Maybe he goes back and forth from Paris to some African country—I guess not South Africa, not anymore, but—Jesus, Warren, do you realize we don't even know?"

"What?"

"Her father's country. I mean, that's like, half of who she is, isn't it? Her heritage?"

"Her history," Warren says slowly. "Except it *isn't* her history. Her history is living with Madeleine. And now with me. Us. She's never even mentioned a father."

"Maybe they told her not to say anything," I say. "If he's in exile—"

"Will you *stop?*" Warren says, really annoyed. "Why are you *talking* about this?"

"I don't know," I say. "I just—I just felt very ill equipped out there tonight, Warren. I mean, if Juliet were counting on me to tell her what to do in a situation like that, I just—No fucking idea."

"Well, I do know," Warren says. "But you don't want to listen to my opinion, for some reason."

Suddenly I have to pull away. "I want a glass of water," I say quickly as I find myself standing by the side of the bed. "Do you want anything?"

Warren looks at me strangely. "All right," he says. I lean against the sink, in the dark kitchen, splashing water on my face, trying to stop shaking. To my surprise, Warren appears in the kitchen doorway. "Don't go," he actually says. "Please don't go."

"Warren. I wasn't *leaving*." He stays there in the doorway, watching me. I feel so weak, I have to hold onto the sink.

"Come on," Warren says. "Come back to bed."

"It could have been us, that's all," I say. "Really, it could have been us."

"No, it couldn't," Warren says.

And I am thinking, "It *should* have been us," and I don't even know what I mean by that.

"They did something very foolish," Warren says, "and something very bad happened to them. But it wouldn't be us."

"Do you want to know something really stupid?" I say. "One time, I was out with Rosie, and we were fighting about something, and it really got to me, and all of a sudden, in the middle of all of it, she just took one of my hands and patted me on the cheek. I mean, it was kind of annoying, but it was kind of sweet, you know, the kind of thing with her that so goes both ways—"

"I know."

"Well, anyway, so I thought, Oh, so Rosie can sit here in a public restaurant and do this—my *sister* can sit here in a public restaurant and hold my hand and all the rest of it, and I'm not supposed to have sex with *her* either. So how is that fair?"

He doesn't say anything.

"Doesn't that *bother* you?" I say. "You were the one who was saying before—"

"Of course it bothers me," Warren says. "But what—"

"So what *would* happen if we do it?" I say. "Would we get beat up? Arrested? Sent into exile? I mean, they're not making us stop. We're stopping."

"Because of what would happen to us if we didn't."

I take a deep breath, clutching the cool metal rim of the sink.

"Well, then, it should have been us tonight, shouldn't it?" I say. "That's what I mean."

Warren shrugs. "It should have been us doing something stupid?"

All the fight goes out of me suddenly. I just feel drained.

"Don't do that," Warren says, completely to my surprise.

"What?"

"We're fighting and you just collapse. It makes—it makes it very hard to— I feel like—"

"Like you won on false pretenses."

"Something like that."

"And you want to win fair."

"Well, at least I want to win big."

"All right," I say, finally. "Tonight it's a draw then. Let's go to bed."

So tonight, they're in jail, and I'm in bed with Warren. Tonight, if I want to, I get to forget about them.

Apparently, I don't have that choice for all time, however, or if I do, a part of me I'm not familiar with is choosing not to take it, because I find myself bringing up the incident to every Black person I see. I mean, I'm not exactly stopping strangers on the street, but picture just one inch short of that, and you've got it. For example, the UPS man who delivers a package the next afternoon when I happen to be home alone. I'm forging Warren's name—for some reason, the purchase is COD, and I have to sign the credit card slip—and somehow, *God* knows how, I manage to work a description of the incident into the conversation. And the UPS guy, a skinny little man in his fifties, says in a faint West Indian accent, "Oh, I know, I know. One time I was carrying a television set from my brother's house back to mine—he was giving it to me, right?—and I was even wearing my uniform, because it was just after work. And the police stop me—they are *sure* I am stealing the set. And I want to say, 'Man, how stupid do you think I am, to carry a television set I'm stealing out here in broad daylight?' "

I'm thinking, "Well, you *were* carrying a television set," and maybe he can tell, because he says stubbornly, "I was carrying it in a *box,* you know. How I'm supposed to get it home if I don't carry it?"

"I know," I say quickly. "The simplest things . . ."

"And then," he goes on matter-of-factly, "they take the box away from me, and put it on the ground, and they tell me to stand against the squad car, and they handcuff me hands behind me back, and they keep me there, oh, ten–twenty minutes. While they phone UPS and their computer and who knows what else, to see if I have a record."

"Jesus," I say. "What finally happened?"

"They have to let me go. I have to pick the box up out of the street."

"Well, that sucks," I say, angry and inadequate.

"Yes, man. Yes, it sucks."

He takes his clipboard back. I can't figure this out. Was he confiding in me? Or would he have told just anyone that story? Well, obviously not. If he had come to the house three days ago, I wouldn't have said anything, and then I certainly wouldn't have heard it. Which raises another question—what else am I not hearing? Was there some other, more humiliating story that he chose not to trust me with? Or are there so many stories, he only had time for one?

All week it goes on like that. The waitress at the corner coffee shop had a brother who was helping to paint her apartment one Sunday afternoon. He forgot a brush and went home for it. He came back, stood on the stoop, rang her buzzer, and the cops wanted to know why he was trying to get into the building.

The clerk at the all-night xerox place where I go to get more copies of my resume was taking the train home late one night when two cops happened to come into his car. They got off when he did, followed him for six blocks, surrounded him as he turned the corner, asked to see his ID, and wanted to know what he was doing out so late.

The man who delivers Warren's dry cleaning . . . the cab driver I use to get to an audition I'm running late for . . . the guy I stand next to in a deli—I can't believe I keep telling that goddamn story, but what I really can't believe is that every single one of them has a story to tell back. What city have *I* been living in?

Warren, not surprisingly, is not very sympathetic to my discoveries. He especially doesn't want me to talk about this in front of Juliet because he doesn't want her to feel frightened. Or limited.

What if there's something for her to be frightened of? I want to say. What if there are real limits? But I don't particularly want to be right about this, so I suppose I am happy to give in.

What I don't expect is the reaction from my theater group. We hadn't been meeting this week, as it happens, because Idris and Elinor needed to make some revisions in the script. But we do reconvene the Monday after my little brush with the police, and as we're getting ready for our first warm-up, I try to tell everybody what happened. Thinking, if you must know, that the incident might even make it into our piece.

But to my total shock and amazement, *these* people don't care. At least, most of them don't. Malik sighs, and Tanya gives me a long, considering look. But Bernard says, "It's true, decent people really *can't* use the parks these days," and Luis says, "Hey, baby, any fool who argues with the cops deserves to spend the night in jail," and Idris says thoughtfully, "Actually, I have a real problem with public drunkenness," and Janie says, "Look, the police are only human. You make it a power issue with them, they're going to get into it." Elinor just shakes her head and looks annoyed, though whether with me, the arrested couple, the cops, or some other factor (her romance with Idris is hardly doing wonders for *her* disposition), I can't tell.

So that would seem to be that. Except that after rehearsal, Malik comes over to me and says, "It's good you said something. Did you file a complaint?"

I look at him blankly.

"A police brutality complaint," he says. "With the Civilian Review Commission. Or whatever they're calling it now. I guess now it's a division of the police department. But there is a number for complaints. You could probably still call."

I don't know why this seems so—so unrelated, I guess, to what actually happened. Maybe it does to him, too. Because he sighs again, and says good-night.

"So what do *you* think?" I ask Tanya as we leave rehearsal.

Tanya shrugs. "Same old, same old," she says.

"But—"

"But it's new news to *you*."

"Oh, I don't know. I'd just never *seen* it before." You certainly can't be Rosie's brother and not *hear* about it. You probably can't even be Rosie's *dry cleaner* and not hear about it. "But I am a little surprised that no one *else* was upset."

Tanya shrugs again. "Well, Bernard. You wouldn't want to be on *his* side anyway, would you?"

I laugh. "I guess not."

"And Idris is weird. She isn't naïve, exactly. But sometimes—it's like things don't touch her."

"Mmmm."

"And Malik *was* upset. That's why he told you to report it." She looks at me. "You're not going to, though, are you?"

Well, I am *now*. If I can find the number. Though I still can't see the connection between what happened and calling up some anonymous clerk at the police department.

"What?" Tanya says as we cross Broadway.

"What, what?"

"You're still fuming."

"I don't know," I say. "If these things are going to go on, I just think I should know about them. And tonight, all of you *did* know about them. Even if nobody cared."

Tanya gives me a sidelong glance. "OK," she says suddenly. "You must know something about *something*, white boy." She grins at me. "Tell me something *I* don't know."

There must be *something*, but at the moment, I have no idea what. "When it was all happening," I say finally. "There was a minute, before they really looked at me, where I thought I could just say anything."

Tanya shakes her head. "No, I think I knew that," she says. "Try something else."

"I don't know that I thought about it this way at the time," I say. "But in high school—and in junior high, too, I guess—I was afraid of getting beaten up. All the time. I'm not sure I was in danger of it all the time. But I—it was just this constant fear."

Tanya sighs. "Actually, I did know that. Not necessarily about you. But something another actor said once— It was weird. Because he was gay, and he was talking about—was it in some acting class? Where you had to share one of those personal moments?" We both make a face. "Well, anyway," Tanya says, "he told us that *he* was always afraid of getting beat up. And you know, Flip, you could look around the room, and the straight guys couldn't even look at him when he was talking, they were so freaked. It was like—you know the way guys get when, excuse me, but when people talk about castration—you know, how every man in the room just *winces*—"

"I know," I say.

"Well?" she says. "At the time, I just didn't understand it. And Malik was in that class, too, so I asked him about it, and he said, 'Oh, they were *all* scared of getting beaten up, *all* the time. That's what junior high *is* if you're a guy. Everybody just pretends they're not scared, because then people would think you *were* gay.' "

I laugh, a little uncertainly. I'm not sure I like sharing that with all the straight guys in America. I would probably only like it if I thought they were scared of *me*. Which will probably happen sometime in the next hundred thousand years or so.

"Malik, huh?" I say instead.

"Don't get any ideas," she says.

"Mmmm," I say skeptically, although I don't particularly think Malik is gay. I just hate how everybody has to rush to specify that someone isn't. I just don't want any of it to matter. What Tanya is. What Juliet is. What I am.

"I have to tell you," I say, "I was a lot happier when I *didn't* know any of this."

Tanya shrugs. "Well, you're a white man," she says. "You *would* think that."

"Oh, what does *that* mean?"

"Well?" she says. "Every single thing you find out is about how it's worse than you thought."

"So?"

"So when you already know how bad it is, then it's a relief to find out more. Maybe you don't feel happier. But you do feel—better armed."

"Really?" I say sharply. "That's how you feel?"

She shrugs. "Pretty much."

"Well, here's something I know that you don't," I say. "I know that *Gone With the Wind* is my favorite movie. I love it, I always have. I love how much Rhett loves Scarlett and how he can't tell her. I love how desperately she loves him back and doesn't even know it. *And* I love the clothes. The whole time I was growing up, that movie was very important to me. This image of—extravagant love. Secret love. Doomed love. But love that seemed like it could change the world. That movie was like my—secret, my inspiration, my—I don't know, it was *mine,* and I loved it."

"You're right," Tanya says, "(a) I didn't know that. And (b), I was happier not knowing."

"No, *you're* right," I say. "Because after all this happened—OK, so I watched that movie again this week, which isn't even such a big deal, because I *do* watch it every so often. And the thing is, I *did* enjoy it this time. I just couldn't enjoy enjoying it. Do you know what I mean?"

"Yes," says Tanya. "I feel like that about a lot of movies. About a lot of things."

"All those slaves who were so happy to be on the ol' plantation," I say. "That big black buck who almost rapes Scarlett—I mean, who's going to play *him* in the remake—Malik? And the little girls, remember, in slavery times, standing there fanning all the white Southern belles with those enormous peacock-feather fans that were bigger than *they* were—"

I bite my lip. "I didn't want Juliet to know that movie existed," I say. "I didn't even want her to see the *box*. So you're right. One more thing that *you* never got to like in the first place. And now I can't like it either."

Tanya shakes her head. "No," she says. "I'll tell you what I feel like that about. Auditioning. For *Hell Street*. They don't call me back, and I swear, I want to either die or kill someone. But then, when they did call me back? And they *still* didn't cast me? And then I *watch* the damn show, and there's one *more* welfare mother on crack, one *more* Black prostitute, one more *good* Black police officer beating up on the criminals, and you *know* in real life the criminals are always *us*. And I just want to call up that guy who plays Marcus Clegg and say 'Why are you doing this?' Except I'm doing it, too. I'm just not succeeding."

Now *she* takes a deep breath. "And, you're right—I wish I *didn't* know better. I wish I just got to go after those parts with a full heart and all the talent God gave me. I don't want to be that ignorant, not really. But I want it."

"Well," I say. "There has to be *something* it's better to know than not to know."

"You would think so," agrees Tanya. "You would certainly think so."

ROSIE: I've just finished one more late-night stalled negotiation, and this happens to be one that Jack *didn't* come to, and it's certainly not like he's obligated to show up at every single one, for God's sake, bad enough that *I* have to be there. Though I do wonder if maybe he's losing patience, not with the union but with— And suddenly I think, "All right, *fine*." And the next thing I know, I'm heading down to the Upper West Side, down to the all-night drugstore where Michael works.

It's not like he's ever *told* me not to go there. Maybe he'll be delighted to introduce me around as his girlfriend. Maybe he'll be thrilled that I was lonely enough to want to see him on this chilly April night (is *that* why I'm going?), lonely enough to come down twenty blocks in the wrong direction just to grab a few minutes with him before I have to head back home.

Michael's drug store is one of the new chain ones that have been popping up all over New York in the past couple of years. Part of the general mallification of the city. Still. The good part of *this* chain is that they've hired Michael, and even had the sense to appreciate him, since he was promoted to night manager fairly rapidly. If he didn't prefer the night shift, they'd probably make him day manager. Michael says they keep talking about "when you're done with school" as if then he *will* be thrilled to take the day shift, instead of going on to law school as he plans.

"Didn't you *tell* them about law school?" I said when he first told me all this.

Michael shook his head.

"Well, why not?"

He shrugged. As usual, he didn't want to answer. "Like, it's not their business," he said finally.

I push open the shiny glass door and make my way into the bright, fluorescent store, its aisles wide and somehow suburban. There are actually quite a few customers, even this close to midnight, so I don't see Michael right away.

When I do see him, it's because of the noise. A little cluster of people around the register at the front end of the store, arguing.

"It's not my *problem* what your policy is, all right?" this one woman is saying. She's pretty young—early twenties—with the breathy, offhand voice that I think of as a California accent. Though she certainly doesn't sound offhand now.

"This *girl,* this *clerk,* is *telling* me I can't return this travel iron, which is worth twenty-six dollars, o-*kay?* And I *need* that money, and I don't have *time* to come back tomorrow—I'm going out of the country tomorrow, all *right?* To *Japan,* to see my family. You do know where Japan is, don't you?"

At this, unbelievably, she pauses, and actually waits for Michael to say something.

"Yes, I know," he says, though this is one time I wish he *wouldn't* answer.

"*Well,* then," she says, triumphant, exasperated. "So you can *see* why I can't come running back to some *other* little drug store at the drop of a hat. So if you'd just explain to your *clerk* . . ." You can't imagine the amount of contempt she packs into that word.

This particular clerk is a big woman, also young—in fact, she's so obviously still in high school that it's hard not to think of her as a *girl,* though of course I'd never call her that. It's also hard not to think the word *sullen,* as I stand here watching her, though I'd like to think I wouldn't say that, either.

"Yeah," she says finally, staring bitterly at the customer. "You people know all about *clerks.* You and your stores."

The customer stares back for a moment, blankly. "You're thinking of Koreans," she says finally. "I'm Japanese. Half Japanese."

"Don't make no difference to *me,*" says the clerk. "I told you what I told you." She looks at Michael. "You want to do something different, go ahead."

The customer looks at Michael, too. "You're the *manager?*" she says to him. "And you're going to let her *talk* to me this way?" Michael doesn't say anything. "You're the *manager?*" she repeats.

"I am the manager," Michael says, as calmly as though he were answering an actual question. I am looking at him as hard as I can—I still have no idea whether he sees me or not—and as well as I'd like to think I know him, I can't for the life of me see him feeling *anything.* For a moment, I can see exactly how he looks to that customer.

The clerk starts to say something else, and Michael says, "OK, Tameeka. Go on back to your register."

"Hey, man," says one of the other customers, a tall, thin guy not much older than the clerk. He's the one people mean when they say they're nervous about riding the train. "You going to take *her* side against the sister's?"

"She was being extremely rude," says another guy, short, plump, in his fifties, white. "Nobody should talk to a customer like that."

"Man, I'm a customer, and she didn't talk nasty to *me.* This girl here was dissin' her, man."

"Don't call me a *girl,*" says the first customer. "That's dissin' *me.*"

Michael acts just as though he hadn't heard any of this. "Tameeka, you go back to your register," he says. "I'll take care of this."

"I didn't do one thing wrong," Tameeka says to no one in particular. Sullen and furious both. "Not one thing."

"Why you got to take *her* side, man?" the young guy says, not *to* Michael exactly, but to his general vicinity.

"He's not taking my *side,*" says the indignant customer, hands on hips. "He's treating a customer with *respect.* Which is more than *she* did."

"I didn't *show* you no disrespect," Tameeka says, and now to the word *sullen* I can add *stubborn.* "I told her she couldn't get no refund at *this* store 'cause she didn't *buy* the iron at this store. We don't even *sell* irons like that, so how can she return it? I try to save her time, she starts getting nasty with *me.* So what are the rest of you all staring at?"

She looks straight at the older white guy, who goes from mildly annoyed to wildly indignant in about a second and a half. "If you worked for me, I'd fire you, talking to a customer that way," he says.

"Lucky she don't work for you, then," says the young guy.

"*Do* I work for you?" says Tameeka at the same time. Michael starts to say something, and so does the first customer. "No," says Tameeka, raising her voice over theirs. "No. I asked this man a question. You gonna answer me, or what? Do I work for you? Does it *look* like I work for you?"

"I'd fire you, *and* I'd make you apologize," the man says. "Where were you brought up, talking to people like that?"

"Now you talking about where was she brought *up?*" says the young guy. "Anybody ever teach you how to mind your business, or what?"

"You just answer *my* question," Tameeka says furiously. "Are you my boss? *Did* you hire me? *Do* I work for you?"

She stares at him so hard that for a minute I actually think he's going to answer. Instead, he shrugs and starts to turn his back on Tameeka, who takes a deep, angry breath. But whatever she was going to say, she doesn't make it, because the young guy is already saying, "Look at that. Look at that. He won't even answer the damn question." He moves over, not exactly blocking the older guy's way, but not exactly *not* blocking it, either.

The older guy looks at Michael. "Are you going to let this guy block my way?" he says.

Michael still not saying anything. Me still seeing him like the rest of them do.

Well, not the *rest* of them. The rest of them who aren't Black.

The first customer looks around the group. "I don't believe this," she says. "I do not *BELIEVE* this. I have a plane to catch, all right? Isn't anybody going to give me back my money?" She waves one hand insistently in the air. "I *have* the receipt."

"Yes," says Michael, "but like Tameeka already told you, we can't take the item back, ma'am." Is it just me, or is there something awful about the way he says *ma'am?*

"I *bought* it at a Best Value," she says. "I *told* you both. Why can't you people understand?"

"Hey," says Tameeka. "I *understand* you. I *understand* you fine."

Michael is talking on top of her, but he still doesn't raise his voice. "You didn't buy it at *this* Best Value, ma'am," he says. "We can refund you on things that we carry here. But not all the stores carry all the same merchandise. If we don't carry it, ma'am, we can't refund it. That's just policy."

"But I'm right here!" the woman says. "It doesn't make any sense."

Michael doesn't say anything.

"It's a really stupid policy," she says.

Still no answer.

"God, these people have absolutely no idea how to run a business," the older guy says. "It's just in-credible."

"Isn't it?" she agrees.

"People?" says the younger guy. "What people? What do you mean, people?"

And Tameeka is saying, "Don't you be coming in here telling me I don't give good service. If people are polite to me, I *give* good service. Not like the Koreans in *my* neighborhood, that's for *damn* sure, looking at you like you don't belong there when you come in to buy something at *their* store. How did they *get* stores all over the damn city, that's what I want to know."

"Bring all that money over from Korea," the young guy says. "Buy real Americans *out*."

"Look," says the first customer, and now she sounds near tears, "I don't have *time* to go back to that other store, OK? I still have to pack, and I'm a graphic designer, and I'm working for some really big customers, OK? I mean, some really big companies, and I have three whole assignments to finish tonight, and I can't leave until they're done, and I just thought, OK, I'll take care of this one little errand while I'm taking a break, and now my schedule is shot completely to *hell*, and I'm going to be up all night as it is. So I really *can't* go running all over town trying to take this back. Can't you please, please, just *please* call for me and find somewhere close by?"

"I can't spend that much time on the phone," Michael says finally. "I need to be out front to relieve Tameeka when she takes her break." He looks at Tameeka, who shrugs dramatically and flounces back to her register. The young guy shrugs, too, and disappears down another aisle, muttering.

"I could like let *you* call," Michael says to the woman. "From the office. I could give you the numbers of all the other uptown stores, and you could call. You might have to wait a while before they answer, though."

"I don't have *time* to wait," howls the woman, and now she actually is crying. "I'm going to be up all *night*."

For the first time, Michael smiles. "Me, too," he says.

She looks at him furiously. "Yes," she says, "but it's your *job*." And she stalks out of the store.

"Un-believable," says the older white guy. "Completely un-believable."

Now that the indignant customer has left, Michael is back to not saying anything, and eventually the white guy leaves, too, shaking his head.

"Hi, Rosie," Michael says. I wonder how long he's known I was there.

I come forward fairly uncertainly, and yes, you *would* think he was happy to see me, except for this one flash of—what? Anger? Shame? And then he smiles.

I don't know. Maybe the smile was all I saw.

"Tameeka," he's saying as he pulls me toward her register, "this is my girl-friend, Rosie."

Well, there's no mistaking what I'm seeing in *her*. Not that Michael seems to notice. Of course, at this point, I'm hardly anybody's reliable witness, am I? Not even mine.

"Do you mind?" he's saying to her. "Since she's here? Could I like take the first break, and you can take the second one?"

Tameeka shrugs. When I was a secretary, I felt the very same way about bosses who asked me for "a favor" when they knew all along I had no choice.

"OK, good, then," Michael says, just as though she *had* answered him. "I'll be back in like half an hour."

Tameeka shrugs again. Behind us, I can feel her glare.

Michael steers me out the door and into the chilly street. "There really isn't anywhere *to* go," he says as I keep looking and looking at him, because I keep seeing it all, the Michael I know, and the one they saw, and if I knew how to put them all together, or which was him and which was me—

"I usually just eat lunch in the back," he says. "But I didn't want to take you back there."

I mean, I know how they saw him. But he let them, didn't he? He didn't say, "I'm going to law school." He didn't say, "It means something, that I'm the manager." Not that I usually think it does—God knows, the stupid administrators at Olympia far outnumber the other kind, and *they* have Ph.D.'s.

Still. This is *Michael*.

"So how were negotiations?" Michael says. We've stopped under the street lamp on the corner. "Did they make that phony offer you were talking about?"

I look at him blankly.

"You know," he says. "The one where they offer something that sounds good along with some really harsh cut in something else, so that when you say no, *you* look like the greedy ones?"

"Michael," I say finally, "what did you *think*?"

He actually says, "About what?"

"About what just went on in there. About the way they were treating you."

"How were they treating me?" Michael says. "People get upset, Rosie. It doesn't *mean* anything."

"Didn't it even make you mad?" I say. "Don't you even want to get mad about it to *me*?"

"Like I keep telling you," Michael says. "Getting mad doesn't help."

"Well, then what *does* help, Michael? God, they just—I couldn't believe how they—you *and* Tameeka, they were just so—" I take a deep breath and start again. "I'm not saying I'm *surprised,* I'm not *surprised,* but—God, Michael, it makes *me* mad."

"What does?"

"Seeing them treat you like a—"

Long pause. Finally Michael says, "Like a what."

"Like an n-word, OK, Michael? I don't know why I have to be the one to say it."

"Like, you're *not* saying it, Rosie. If you're going to say it, then *say* it. Use the damn word."

For once, I am speechless. Michael doesn't take his eyes off me, even though it's gotten so cold, we're both starting to shake.

"You can say it, Rosie," he says more gently. "Like, it's just a word."

"I can't say it. And it's not. Just a word."

Even now, he wants to be amused. To enjoy me.

Because he does? Or so he won't get angry?

"OK," he says in that drawling, playful voice. "Like, it's not a word. What is it, then?"

I don't know. He's the one who has to go through this, day in, day out. He should at least get to decide how he wants to handle it.

But I'm upset, too. "It's not *just* a word," I say. "It's a—a history, OK, Michael? It's a history of power. It means I and that white guy and even that— that woman, that snotty woman—it means we get to—anybody gets to—" I can't say it.

"Gets to *what?*" Michael says in that same blank tone he used for talking to the customer.

"God, Michael, do you really not know, or are you just determined to make me— Gets to see you the way they *saw* you, all right, Michael? Gets to see you as—I don't know, lazy. Stupid. Slow. Gets to see you as some—dumb . . . n-word."

"You know what I hate about your using *that* word," Michael says, and maybe now he finally sounds angry. And maybe now I finally feel relieved. "It's like, you're thinking the other one anyway. *Nigger.* You're thinking the word *nigger,* whether you come right out and say it or not."

So now I am the one who stands there, silent.

"You might as *well* go on and say it," he says finally. "You're going to think it anyway."

I *did* think it, didn't I? I knew this was Michael, my smart, sexy, ambitious boyfriend. But I saw the other, too. *Sullen. Slow.*

"You know what's weird about the n-word, the actual word?" I say finally.

"Because whatever I think, OK, it's what I think. But that word—it was the word for all the worst—like, Michael. A capstan on a ship, the thing they turn the rope around, *that* was called an n-word, because even a *thing*—a thing that did hard work—that's what it was called. Sweating like an n-word. Working like an n-word. N-word in the woodpile. N-word luck. N-word English—you can imagine what *that* was. N-word breaker—an overseer, a harsh one. Also known as a *slave driver,* OK? Someone who would *sell you down the river.* I know I'm not perfect—I never said I was. But all that history, Michael. I don't want to be a part of *that.*"

"What do you mean, *history?*"

"Power," I say, "all right, Michael? All that power. That's what that word means. That they have the power—*I* have the power—to talk to you that way."

"What do you want me to do about it, Rosie?" Michael says. "It's history. It isn't me."

"But the history is *there,* Michael. You just don't want to talk about it. It's bad enough that I *have* all that history on my side, well, obviously, not on *my* side, but it could be my side if I wanted it. If I *wanted* that power—"

"Over me," says Michael.

"Yes, well, all right. Over you."

"No," says Michael.

"No, what?"

"No, *that word,*" he says, mimicking me. "*That word* doesn't give you any power over me, Rosie. Because I choose not to let it."

"Well, excuse me, Michael, but I really don't think it's your choice."

"But *I* say it *is* my choice," says Michael. "Aren't I the one who gets to decide, Rosie? Or do you get to decide that, too?"

"It doesn't really matter what you decide, Michael. Things still are . . . the way they are."

He doesn't say anything.

"I mean," I say, rather desperately, because I don't want to win this argument, I really don't, "maybe we can *make* things different. But we can't *think* them different."

"Oh, what does *that* mean?" Michael says, but his voice is shaky. And I think, I am *not* going to say any more. I'm *not.* I am going to stand right here under this freezing cold street lamp until Michael finally fucking says something.

So eventually he shakes his head and he almost smiles. "Like, I really do know something you don't know, Rosie," he says. "About this."

"Then *tell* me!"

"I know how to live with it."

But I don't want to live with *anything* the way he does. Not by shutting up and pretending nothing's wrong.

"Why won't you tell me about it?" I say finally. "Michael. If you know."

"If I tell you, then it's yours," he says. "Then you get to—say what it means."

"Do I really do that?"

He actually laughs. "Rosie," he says, "you *always* say what *everything* means."

I sigh. "Well, *that's* not going to change."

Michael sighs too. "You want me to tell you everything," he says wistfully. "But you won't even let me meet your family. Not even your brother, and he lives here."

"Oh, Michael. Flip and I aren't even speaking to each other right now."

"But before."

"Well, maybe I just wanted to keep you to myself for a while. Maybe I didn't want to have to *explain* you to Flip. Or have him—I don't know. Use you against me. I *tell* you all about him. I tell you everything."

"OK, fine. So that's the difference between us.

"It's like, OK, with me though," he says after a minute. He reaches out very gently to touch my cheek. "You can be however you want, Rosie. I don't want you to change."

At the moment, I'd change both of us, if I could. Him, me, and everything else. Nothing worth keeping *here*.

But *here* is where I am with him, his hand still warm against my cheek. Here in this cold, harsh light, on this shabby, defeated street, where just for an instant, I feel a flash of something warm, bright, fleeting. No more than a glimpse. Wild, unpredictable. Hope.

FIVE

MAKING IT UP

When the union inspiration through the workers' blood shall run
There shall be no power greater anywhere beneath the sun
Yet what force on earth is weaker than the feeble strength of one?
For the union makes us strong.

—Ralph Chaplin, "Solidarity Forever"

THE MEMORIAL

FLIP: Even though today is technically a school day, there is some kind of teacher training thing that means Juliet isn't going to go to school. So last night she was given strict orders not to wake *anyone* in the house until at least eight and preferably nine. Warren told her that if she *was* quiet, she could watch as many videos as she wanted to *and* eat her breakfast in the living room, plus he'd also make her chocolate chip pancakes when he finally did wake up (at this point in his parenting career, sleep wins out over principle no contest). So under the circumstances, you can imagine my annoyance when at what seems to be a truly ungodly hour, the phone rings.

Had it been up to me, I would probably have let the machine answer it. But Warren wakes up with a start and grabs the receiver so quickly that he inadvertently shoves me away from where I had been lying against him. And then he stays and stays and *stays* on the phone, with the oddest expression on his face. Every so often, I hear him say, "I'm sorry."

When he hangs up, I turn onto my stomach and shut my eyes as tight as I can. But Warren is still sitting, frozen, his hand on the phone. After a moment, I turn back over and look at him. "All right," I say, finally. "What?"

He's still not moving. "It's Mario," he says slowly. "That was his sister."

"Mario what? He's not sick, is he?" I don't know why I ask the question this way. Obviously it's only a matter of time until he *does* get sick. Although he always *says* it isn't. And *being* his friend, I try to believe him. Being an actor and good at inducing impossible beliefs, sometimes I even succeed.

"No, he's not sick," Warren says, avoiding my eyes. "He's dead."

"Well, he *can't* be *dead,*" I say reasonably. "He wasn't even sick yet."

"It wasn't AIDS," Warren says. "He got hit by a bus."

This sounds so like the punch line to a joke that it's all I can do to keep from laughing. "Well, she was certainly on the phone with you a long time," I say, thinking that if we finish this conversation *fast,* I might still be able to get back to sleep.

"I know," says Warren. "People always do that with me, I don't know why." It's true—he really isn't interested in people's stories. But somehow everyone always ends up talking to Warren. I remember one time Chris called to invite us to a party, and the next thing I knew, he and Warren were on the phone for two hours with Warren hearing all about Chris and Paco's romantic problems. I didn't even know they *had* any romantic problems.

"She seemed to want to tell me the whole story," Warren is saying.

"Was that Rita? Mario says it always takes her forever to get to the point. As opposed to Margaret, his *younger* sister. He says *she* never . . ." My voice trails off as I realize that Warren isn't even listening.

"It happened yesterday, actually," he's saying. "So I don't know why she was calling today. Although it happened at about this time, so maybe that was why. He was waiting for a bus a few blocks away from Joshua's house—I don't know why he was taking the bus and not the train. And something happened with the driver—a heart attack, or something with his medication—she wasn't exactly sure about that part either. She only knew that the bus jumped the curb and plowed right into the stop. A couple of other people were hurt, but Mario was the only one who was killed. It seems to have been a completely freak accident."

Somewhere in the middle of this story, I have started to cry. Which is odd, because all I can think is that I wish Warren would hurry up and finish talking so I can go back to sleep. "It seems to have taken a whole day for them to figure out who to call," Warren is saying. "They took the body to the hospital, and eventually they called directory assistance to locate his family, but of course, he lives alone. I think they finally found his insurance records somehow, and he had listed this sister as next of kin, or whatever they call it on insurance records. Person to be notified in case of emergency. I'm surprised it *was* her and not Joshua."

"Well, he's only been going out with Joshua since November. If he changed insurance forms every time he changed boyfriends—" My surprisingly normal voice runs out.

"Well, that makes sense," Warren says. He isn't paying attention to me at all. "So they called her, and she just came. She seems to have gotten here last night. Staying at Mario's apartment. I wonder how she got in?"

"Maybe Joshua let her in," I say, trying very hard to focus on what, if anything, I have to do about this. "Does he even know yet? Should we call him? Did she even know who he was?"

"Oh, yes," Warren says. "Evidently she and Mario were quite close. She thought so, anyway. She met Joshua yesterday. She thought he seemed a little quiet, but she assumed that was because of the shock."

I start laughing. Then I force myself to stop, because even I can see how quickly it's going to get out of control.

Warren finally seems to notice me. "Come here," he says, holding out his arms. But I shake my head and go off to the bathroom. Where I turn on the shower, as hot as I can stand it, and with the water running down my face and the pounding of the shower filling up the room with noise, I cry and cry and cry. As far as I can tell, this news can't possibly change anything. Mario will still answer when I call him up at work. He'll still be going with me to the play we finally got tickets for Friday night now that I'm not working so much. He'll still call me to tell me how wonderful things are with Joshua and then describe what's actually happening in a way that makes me shudder. He'll still come to see me in the Tiger's Eye show, the way he comes to all my shows. He'll still be there to call when I have a fight with Warren. Or when I need to find out what happened on *Hell Street*. Or when I just need to talk to *him,* Mario, because he's Mario. At the moment, this all seems as true as it ever has. But apparently not, because I can't stop crying.

That night, Warren and I get into bed and suddenly I'm all over him. He's all over me, too. It's like a piece of paper in a fireplace. One minute it's paper, the next minute it's flame. (And the next minute it's ashes, but I don't want to think about that now.) Usually Warren likes making love better in the dark and I'm the one who prefers to have the light on, but tonight I want it to be dark. I can't tell if Warren is caught up in my frenzy or if he has a fever of his own, but as long as he keeps up with me, I don't care. Sometimes it's almost frightening, how he matches me at times, how I feel something and he's already there waiting for me.

Until it's over, and then I have to get away. I practically fling myself over to the other side of the bed, burying myself under the covers.

"Good night, Flip," Warren says softly. "Sleep well."

So then, of course, I start to cry. Silently. I would rather be sobbing and howling and making as much noise as my body knows how to make, but out of consideration for Warren (and Juliet in the next room), I try to keep it quiet.

Warren lies there over on his side of the bed, and I just hope he knows better than to come after me, because if he actually does try to touch me, I don't know what I'll do. I can't even stand to be inside my *own* skin tonight.

So he waits. Until—well, I don't exactly *stop* crying. It's just that, at the moment, I'm *not* crying. What I'd really like to do is pretend to go to sleep—actual sleep is clearly out of the question, because I have to stay up and cry some more, but I don't think I can keep doing that with Warren still there, still awake. But I have already explicitly promised never to pretend to be asleep.

"I could go sleep in the other room. On the couch," Warren says after about a million years. "Flip? Do you want me to?"

Oh, so now I have to *talk* to him, too? "Flip?" he says after another million years. "Maybe I should just go."

"Well, that's typical," I spit out. "You *always* want to fucking leave."

Another long pause. The space between us is now so solid, I can feel the thick, impossible walls dividing the two sides of the bed. I remember one time in high school, I was away on a drama trip with this other kid, George Ventros. Our production of *Zoo Story* was going to the state theater championships, and we were staying in a motel. The drama teacher got his own room, of course, but they put George and me together, in this cheap little room with only one bed, and of course, I was madly in love with him, which I probably would have been even if we hadn't been in that show together, because he really was incredibly beautiful, but doing that play with him, which was so intense, clearly made it a foregone conclusion.

You know, *Zoo Story,* they do it all the time in acting classes, and in high schools, *God* knows why. Where these two unknown men, Peter and Jerry, meet in the park, and the madly handsome Jerry convinces nerdy little Peter to stab him to death on a bench. I played Peter of course, and so I had to kill George—and thank you *very* much, Edward Albee, for yet another closeted play in which clearly the *best* thing you can do for the man you love is stab him in the heart with a knife, even though I didn't see it like that at the time, being only fifteen. Actually, on some level, I probably *did* see it like that, and my way of dealing with it *was* to fall in love with George. Whom I was clearly never going to get, because although I had *been* with people by that point, I certainly hadn't been with anybody I was actually going to high school with. Or anybody I had ever held a conversation with.

Even now, looking back, I have no idea whether George was gay or straight. I just remember having to sleep in that bed with him, that very dark, hot, private bed, except of course I *couldn't* sleep, just like I can't sleep now, because, like now, my whole body was longing to be over *there,* which was also the last thing of which my body would ever have been capable. I put all the energy I had into blocking him out of my senses: stopping my ears, dulling my skin, eradicating my sense of smell (it didn't work—he had this very strong smell that was part sweat and part aftershave and part bleach—*God* knows why his mother bleached his pajamas, but apparently, she did—and there was something about that sweet, sharp smell with *him* underneath . . .) And that unthinkable space in the bed between us, so that I lay on my side, trying to make myself paralyzed, numb, dead to everything that was so dangerous and unimaginable. Not what I would do with him—I could certainly imagine *that.* But what came after. What we would say to each other. What kind of life could ever contain—it was clearly better to be dead.

"Flip, I'm here." It's Warren's voice from the other side of the bed. Here in the darkness, I don't just hear his voice, I feel it, like a rough, warm, heavy blanket. "I'm not leaving, Flip. I'm right here." His words get farther and farther away as the blanket gets warmer and heavier, carrying Warren's voice, Warren's weight, Warren's smell, until finally I fall asleep.

Mario's body is being shipped back to Providence, where the actual funeral and burial will be. I don't quite understand why. I mean, of course I *understand.* But still. His life was here. We were a thousand times more his family than they were.

Oh, I don't know. Maybe we weren't. *There* is where he always went for Christmas, and Thanksgiving, and his mother's birthday, and his father's birthday, and the birthdays of every single one of his brothers and sisters, even the ones who had come right out and told him they thought he was going straight to hell. *There* is where he'd *call* home—I mean, he'd say, "I'm going *home* for Christmas," or Thanksgiving, or whatever. But *here* is where he lived. (And died. I'm sure they all think, back there, that he would never have died if he hadn't come to New York, and technically speaking, I suppose they're right, in the sense that the route of the particular bus that hit him didn't include Rhode Island. Still. Plenty of people die in Providence, too.)

Anyway, Mario's sister seems to have some idea that *here* has—had—some kind of importance for her brother, because somehow it's been arranged to have a memorial service for Mario here, before she leaves. Chris is organizing it, because (typically, in my opinion) Joshua seems not to be capable of doing the ordinary social thing. The memorial is on Sunday afternoon at the Lesbian and Gay Community Services Center, and then some lucky few of us get to go back to Joshua's apartment afterward.

Walking into the Center with Warren, of course I remember running into Mario here last fall, when I was still working on *Tartuffe*—an event that now seems to have vanished without a trace. The memorial is actually in the same room as the meeting I went to with Mario, except today it's far more crowded, mostly with people I don't know, though I do recognize some of the diehards from that night—the woman in the purple harem pants, the bald lesbian, one of the guys in leather jackets. Not Brad, though. This time the chairs are set up in a half-circle, so that the speaker stands near the door.

Warren and I take two of the last available chairs, toward the front, and we're crowded so close together that it's a real feat *not* to lean into each other, but I manage. Chris stands before us and explains that some speakers have been prearranged but that after that, anyone is free to stand and say anything. He had asked me to speak, actually, but I told him I couldn't. Why do people always think that just because you're an actor, you're willing to do *anything* in public? Some things *are* private, even for us.

"I'm Rita Farinelli, I'm Mario's sister. I'm so glad you could come. Mario would be so happy to see all his friends here, he was always talking about his friends. You tried to get him to talk about himself, all he would talk about was this one and that one, how well they were doing, what troubles they had. 'Mario,' you would say, 'what about you? You're my brother. Talk about yourself for a change.' But he wouldn't, he never would. Everyone had to come before him.

"I'm not so good at public speaking, so I won't go on. But I will read a letter from Sal Iacobelli, a friend of Mario's. He wanted to be here today, but he couldn't. But he—when he heard—anyway. He faxed me this."

She pulls out a folded-up piece of fax paper. " 'Mario Pucci was my best friend,' " she's reading, from this Sal, whoever *he* is. " 'You could always count on Mario, whatever—' " Rita looks up. "It's smudged," she says. "I think he means, 'whatever you needed.'

" 'A friend is supposed to be loyal, and Mario was loyal. A friend is supposed to stand by you, and Mario stood by me. Always. A friend is supposed to care about you, and Mario would always—' " Rita looks up again. " '—listen to you,' " she says finally, helplessly. " 'Mario, I love you like a brother, and I'll think of you every day of the rest of my life. If there is a heaven after this life, as I hope and believe there is, I know you're in it. Put in a good word for me, OK? Your friend, Sal.' "

I can't help it, my eyes meet Warren's, and he almost smiles, and I know we're both thinking the same thing: *"Who's Sal?" Just* a friend? Another gay Catholic boy, lost in Providence? A straight man who *didn't* know about Mario? (Though how you could know Mario and *not* know is beyond me.) A straight man who knew and didn't care? But in that case, why didn't I ever even hear his name? Because I certainly heard every last little detail about everyone *else* Mario saw when he went home.

"Asking for forgiveness," Warren whispers in my ear, and of course, that's it, although obviously, neither of us knows for sure. Some straight guy who did know that Mario was gay and wasn't such a great friend to *him*. And now Mario is gone, so now he's sorry. Well, too bad for him.

It isn't just that. It's how far away he is. Sal, I mean. I wouldn't mind meeting someone who had known Mario before he got to New York. Someone who could—I don't know. Remember his childhood. Or his time in high school. The way I wanted Warren to see the house where I grew up. Because if nobody remembers something, it *is* like it didn't happen.

". . . What I'll never forget is the time I had just broken up with my boyfriend, and Mario was there, *of course*—" Everybody actually laughs at this. Am I glad or sorry that he never got to hear about how Warren and I got back together, not in the detailed, blow-by-blow way that he would have liked? At least I don't have to remember that Mario and I went out that night and talked about *me,* instead of about Mario's own breakup.

Across the room, Joshua looks devastated. Well, of course he's devastated. He thinks it's his fault. He thinks if only Mario hadn't been at his house that morning, which of course he wouldn't have been if he hadn't been involved with Joshua—if only Joshua hadn't let Mario leave at *that* time, if only Joshua had died first or had never been born at all . . .

And God help me, I agree with him. Mario belongs in the world with the rest of us. Joshua should be dead.

"We sang together in the Chorus. He was—rare. The way the music lit him up. Whenever he missed, the whole choir noticed. Not musically, of course. He didn't have that kind of voice—he would never be a soloist, or even a section leader. But you always knew when he wasn't there."

Well, that sounds like the Mario I know. Even though I never got to hear him sing. There was a concert in December, but I had rehearsal and couldn't go. Of course, Warren was the one who said, "There are always other concerts." So now he has to live with that.

There isn't even a word for what Joshua is. You can't say *widow* or *widower,* not really. Even if they had *called* themselves married, they *weren't* married.

Whatever Warren and I call ourselves, we won't be married either. We'll be *something,* we *are* something, but there's no word for it. There's no word for it because it isn't supposed to exist. Because *we* aren't.

I look over at Joshua again, and again I know what he's thinking, because again, I'm thinking it too: *This is his fault.* I mean, Mario *was* the only one who was killed in that fucking accident. Maybe if Joshua hadn't made him so unhappy, he would have had that little bit of extra energy that everybody *else* seemed to have to get the fuck out of the way. Maybe if he hadn't needed to lie about what was going on between him and Joshua, he would have been able to *see* the damn bus coming.

Or maybe he *did* see. Maybe that was the day he did, finally, face what was going on. With Joshua, with the HIV, with all the other relationships that hadn't worked out. And rather than live with all that knowledge, he saw that bus coming for him and he just gave up.

It isn't that no one remembers Mario. Clearly, all of us do. But we all know different things. If Sal and I were both in Mario's family, instead of just being his friends, I could go to Providence to visit him. Not that I ever would. But I could. Go and ask him about Mario's childhood. Tell him about Mario's life in New York. Not that he'd want to know, probably. But still. It would make Mario *whole.* Instead of all in pieces, which he is forever, now.

The woman in harem pants gets up to speak. "Mario was a very important member of Lesbians and Gay Men Together," she says. I am pretty much dreading the lengthy political harangue that I expect to hear from her, and sure enough, she says, "Here's a song we were planning to sing at our vigil at the City Health Department next month, trying to get them to reopen drug treatment programs in Harlem and Bed-Stuy, because, as you know, the fastest-growing population of people with AIDS in New York City is African-American and Latina women and children, and they get it from needles or from having sex with people who use needles—and of course, Washington has announced that Medicaid won't cover *their* protease inhibitors, so when they *get* infected with HIV, they're just going to be—anyway. This one's for you, Mario." And she starts to sing this mournful, dirgelike song.

> *They say that freedom is a constant struggle*
> *They say that freedom is a constant struggle*
> *They say that freedom is a constant struggle*
> *Oh Lord, we've struggled so long,*
> *We must be free.*

Then comes the moment that I've been dreading, because gradually, yes, people in the room start to clap, and even to sing along. Even Warren, beside me, is singing, in his low, buzzing voice, and I realize, more because I hear my own voice than because I'm aware of actually doing anything, that for the last verse, I am singing, too.

> *They say that freedom is a constant dying*
> *They say that freedom is a constant dying*
> *They say that freedom is a constant dying*
> *Oh Lord, we've died so long,*
> *We must be free.*

If the woman in harem pants had any sense of theater, she'd call it a day after *that*. But no. She looks around at all of us, and of course, she has to get in one last political point. "I found that song in a songbook *called* 'Freedom Is a Constant Struggle.' " she says. "Along with a quote from Julius Lester, one of the civil rights workers who went down to Mississippi in 1964: 'How much hate can one individual feel directed at him before his soul fills with a sadness that penetrates even his happy moments?' "

She goes on talking, but my attention is distracted by the sound of the door opening. And then, to my total shock and amazement, in comes Rosie. And to my even greater shock, Chris motions her to stay there at the front of the room until the other woman finishes speaking. What is *she* doing here? She doesn't even *know* Mario.

"Please forgive me for being late," Rosie says breathlessly. "We're getting ready to strike at Olympia University—the same union that Mario was a member of at Paradise Holidays, which is how I know Mario, of course. Tito Paiva, the lead organizer over there, sends his regrets—he was supposed to be here today, but he's out at a picket line at a warehouse in Long Island, so he asked me to take his place. And when we were talking about it, this morning at 6 a.m., when Tito got the call to go out there, even though neither of us was exactly *sharp* at that hour of the morning—"

Well, of course, she gets a laugh. It's kind of fascinating, in a weird, infuriating way. I've never actually seen her speak—to a real audience, I mean. She's both exactly the same and completely different—well, not completely. But different the way a performer is.

"—and we realized," Rosie is saying, "that although Tito had worked closely with Mario for years and I only went to a few meetings with him, both of us saw the same parts of Mario, the same qualities. Which you've probably all described already. How he was always ready to do anything, no matter what, if he thought it was something that the people around him needed. How he thought of others, always, before himself. How principled he was. For Mario, the question was never, 'What's good for me?' It was always, 'What's the right thing to do?' "

Right, I think. And maybe if he'd said, "What's good for me?" even once in his fucking miserable life, maybe he would have been happy for a change. Or at least gotten out of the way of the goddamn bus.

Rosie has clearly seen me by this point, though she's being very—professional, I guess you'd call it—about not acknowledging me while she's on stage. But she's not exactly unaware of my reactions, either. She pauses—for effect, of course. But I can see that she's also gathering her thoughts.

"This isn't an easy world in which to think of others," she says finally. "And those of us in the union movement know that we all—especially those of us whom the society beats down—workers and women and gay people and people of color—we have to think of ourselves first. At least some of the time. Or what we have to give to the world will be lost. But what Mario had that *I* admired so much—he thought the best for others *would* be good for him." She opens her arms to include everyone in the room. "That's why we're all here today, isn't it?" she says. "That's why we all loved him so much, even those of us who barely knew him? Maybe we can make this a world in which wanting the best for others doesn't have to mean sacrificing the best parts of ourselves."

I don't think I've ever been so angry with her. For the applause she gets. And the tears she's inspired. The way she's turned Mario's death into a chance to push her own political line. The way she's caught some truth about Mario and told it here, and she barely even fucking knew him.

Of course, no one wants to follow *that*. So Rita stands up. "Goodbye, Mario," she says. Her voice breaks over a sob. *"Ti voglio bene. Da sempre, Mario. Ti voglio bene. Anche Margaret. Da sempre."*

Something that's lost, is what I'm thinking. Something that's lost, and we'll never get it back.

When everyone else is milling around, Warren kind of melts into the crowd, and I'd be willing to bet he's going over to talk to Rosie. But before I have time to find out, Joshua comes over to me, which I really did not expect. He stands there for about a million years before he finally says, "Mario had this, um . . . We told each other about every one of our previous boyfriends. So I knew all about all of his. And this one he had, Miles—that was his first trainer. The one who taught him how to use weights. Which was something that he— I mean, Mario. He really loved working out."

"I know," I say helplessly. Why are we *having* this conversation?

"And Miles was—well, he was, he was the one who—Mario was HIV-positive because of him. But also— He really loved working out."

"I know," I say again.

Joshua looks at me with those teary eyes. "I know he wasn't always— Sometimes there were bad times. They weren't all bad."

Do I believe *that*? Do I care? If Joshua wants me to say it's all right, he's going to have a nice long wait, because I'm not saying it.

Then Joshua says, "You know. It wasn't always so easy to make him happy. Sometimes he'd just—refuse."

I don't know what I would have said or not said. But that's when Rita comes over to ask Joshua something about going back to his apartment, so I get to move away. Wishing we hadn't had that little talk, all things considered. Some things you would rather not know.

I don't know where Warren is. But all of a sudden, I feel someone behind me, and I turn around, and there's Rosie. "Life's too short," she says as she comes to stand by me. I want to answer her, to say yes, it is, but I can't bring myself to speak. It doesn't seem to matter. She stands beside me, and slowly we inch toward each other, until I can feel the warmth from her body radiating against mine. Though I must say, it seems wrong to receive this particular gift at this particular time.

A few minutes later, she sighs and says, "OK, I've got to go." And by the time I look over to where she was standing, she's gone.

We all have to go out to Brooklyn, of course, to Joshua's house, where he is doing what he considers sitting shiva for Mario, though God knows what Rita considers it. Chris and Paco are clinging to each other, surprise, surprise, and you would think that under the circumstances I, too, would welcome Warren coming up and actually starting to put his arm around me, but I don't. Warren is far too well-bred to look hurt in front of all these people, but you can't fool me. Well, too bad for you, Warren.

"What do you think Mario's sister was saying?" Chris wants to know. "When she spoke Italian, I mean."

"She said *voglio bene*," Ian explains. "Which means to want someone forever." Simon gives him a baleful look, which Ian ignores.

"Yes," says Warren, "but the whole expression, *volere bene*, it's an idiom. It really means *love* more than *want*."

I don't fucking believe it. So now they both speak Italian? What *else* do they have in common?

" 'Goodbye, Mario,' " Warren repeats. " 'I'll love you forever. Always, Mario. I love you—permanently. Margaret, too.' Who's Margaret?"

Well, at least I have *something* to contribute here. "She was his sister," I say. "Remember, Warren? I *told* you. Rita was the oldest—well, I suppose she still is. Then there were two boys, who more or less stopped talking to him after he came out. Then Margaret. Then two other sisters, who didn't *stop* speaking to him, exactly, but they aren't what you would call close. And then a younger brother, who's still in college. I don't know what the story was with him."

"Who stops talking to their brother like that?" Paco says. "What kind of a person does that? To their own family."

If anything could get me to let Warren touch me, it would be the look on his face right now. Although of course he doesn't say anything. So I say, "Lots of people don't get along with their families, Paco. Even people who *aren't* gay. Probably there are more people who *don't* talk to their relatives than people who do."

"Do you think people choose their families?" Chris says. "I mean, in another life, before they're born? So it's not this terrible accident, the way we all think, but a task you take on, on purpose. Because it has something to teach you."

Don't you just love the way people will turn any fucking tragedy into something that's part of a higher purpose? "What about people whose parents beat them?" I say. "What about people whose parents burn them with hot irons or throw boiling water all over them? I once read about a little girl whose face was smashed in by this frying pan full of hot oil that her mother threw at her. And while she was in the hospital recovering from the first operation, waiting for the skin grafts and the rest of the plastic surgery, what do you think she was doing? Crying for her mother, begging to go home. What do you think she had to learn from that, Chris? Why do you think she chose *that* particular task?"

There is a brief, shocked silence, which threatens to become a long, embarrassed silence. If Mario were here, we are all thinking, he'd know how to break this awkward moment, how to say something so earnest or impassioned or concerned that the whole conversation could rearrange itself around it. And so suddenly, together, we have cleared this space for Mario to fill. We stand here together, waiting for him. As if together, we could bring him here.

A few days later, when I get home from rehearsal, Warren is on the phone. It seems to take him hours before he finally hangs up and comes into the living room, where I am lying on the couch watching television, more or less for lack of anything better to do. I turn off the TV the minute Warren comes into the room, which for some reason makes him smile.

"What were you *doing* on the phone so long?" I say in an irritable, edgy tone as he sits down in one of those awful metal chairs. "And what are you doing way over there?"

Warren gets up slowly and comes over to the couch. "I don't always know when I'm welcome," he says softly as he stands over me. "Especially these days."

"Well, you shouldn't *worry* about it so much. You should just force yourself on me. That's what I do, apparently, and that seems to work."

He laughs as he sits down beside me. "So who *was* that on the phone?" I say, leaning back against him. "Ian?"

"Actually," Warren says after a moment, with what an unbiased observer would have to call admirable calm, "it was Joshua."

"Oh, why was *he* calling?"

"He wanted to know whether he should still come to the lifetime partnership ritual." Part of me wants to just stop everything right now. Let me just lie here on the couch, with Warren's arms around me, until I fall asleep and don't wake up. It wouldn't be a bad way to go.

"Well, I hope you told him *no,*" I say, rousing myself.

Behind me, I feel *something* go through Warren's body, though I can't tell exactly what. "I can't imagine why he'd even *want* to come, now," I say when Warren doesn't say anything. "I'm sure he didn't want to come before, either, since that would have involved not actually being alone with Mario, which seemed to be all he ever *did* want."

Warren still doesn't say anything.

"What?" I say finally. "What?"

Warren sighs, tightening his arms around me. "It's a rather amazing moment when the thing you've been afraid of your whole life finally comes true," is all he'll say. "It's a more or less unbearable relief."

A few nights later, I have a dream about him. He's smiling at me, so happy, the way he was that night we were at the club, the night we kissed, the night we danced. The happiest *I'd* ever seen him, but now he's even happier. "It's all right," he says. "There are reasons for everything. Really, Flip, it's all right." I reach out to put my hand against his chest, and the movement wakes me up. And I'm angry, so angry with myself for having a dream that is such a lie. It's *not* all right. There's *no* reason for Mario to be dead and me to be alive. I'll never believe there's a reason for that.

THE PLAY

ELINOR: Obviously I've already failed as an actress. At least in any sense of having a career at it. I'm thirty-eight, I'm a woman, and I'm not a raving beauty. So the question is, is there anything else?

TANYA: The first thing you learn when you really start to study your craft is that you've got to have an objective. You can't just *want* something on stage. You have to be ready to go after it.

The next thing you learn is to make your character *true*. You don't just make up what the character would do. You have to really *feel* it. It has to come from some kind of place that the audience might recognize.

The next thing you learn—and this is where you really separate the professionals from the goats—is that who you are in real life doesn't matter. *Amateurs* care about what they're saying. Professionals make *you* believe it.

So along comes Elinor, and she has this whole *other* idea. "Tanya," she says to me. "I want to hear *your* voice." But how is that acting? How is that doing my work?

FLIP: I would hate to think that after all this time, I was still worrying about what Rosie said last Christmas. But whenever I think I'm getting somewhere, then I hear her say, "What's the name you're using now, Philip Bernard? This guy who we're supposed to think is straight? Who wants to use his talent on some racist cop show? *That's* your career? *That's* your life's work? *That's* what you'll look back on from your deathbed and say, 'That's how I spent my time on earth?' "

ELINOR: Fairly early in the rehearsal process, maybe the first week or so of February, after Idris had just brought in the first draft of her script, I had the first indication that things were going to be difficult with Flip.

The scene had a high school guy—Flip—coming on to a high school girl—Tanya. And first he's just heavy-handed about it, but then he finds a smoother way to seduce her and she starts to get interested, too. What wasn't working was the part where they're both supposed to be really hot for each other, but fencing, you know, trying to keep the interest going but not letting the other person ever get too comfortable or secure. (Let's not even *talk* about where Idris got the idea for *that* scene.)

Well, obviously, what we're all thinking but what nobody wants to say is that it *isn't* working—at least in part—because Flip is gay, so it's not exactly second nature to him to be seducing someone of Tanya's ilk. And the type of macho guy who comes in and takes charge in that particular way is not exactly second nature to him, either, even with men, I should imagine, though of course, I don't have any way to know.

And Tanya—I don't know. It's weird about Tanya—she's so tough, and so sexy, and so *fierce* about herself. You would have thought this scene would have been a piece of cake for her. But she was very *uncertain* about it. She had to be able to stride right in and *claim* the man's interest as her due, and she just couldn't.

So the scene was going nowhere, while Flip and Tanya were getting progressively more tense. Since neither of them can ever bear to be seen at anything less than their best.

"Well, let me be the *first* to say how much this isn't working," says Flip. He looks at us, trying to decide where to direct his frustration.

"Where do *you* think it isn't working?" I say quickly. "I mean, why?"

He and Tanya look at each other and Tanya shrugs. I wonder if they've talked about me privately—well, come on. Of course they have. One of the more painful and unexpected side effects of becoming the director in this group is the extent to which Tanya has stopped talking to me. I used to think we were friends.

But this is better than I would have expected: Flip blames himself. "There's something I'm missing about how to—I don't know. I think I should be much, *much* more on the offensive here. It should be my scene. I don't mean your part's not important," he adds quickly, to Tanya, who laughs.

"Oh, sure," she says. "Isn't it *always* your scene?"

Flip laughs, too. "But I *do* think I should be—more aggressive," he says. "Isn't that how it's written? I'm coming on to you, and you're fending me off."

"Till I start coming on to *you,*" Tanya says. "And then you don't know *which* end is coming or going."

"No, that's just the game I'm playing," Flip says. "I *like* your coming on to me—it means I've got you right where I want you."

"No, you're threatened."

"No, I'm flattered."

"You don't act flattered."

"Because I'm—" Flip breaks off and looks at Idris and me. "Jump in anytime."

Idris never jumps in during rehearsal unless I specifically ask her to. So it's up to me. Because Tanya talks a good game, but she's clearly *not* enjoying having Flip on the defensive, and she's not enjoying him on the offensive, either. And yes, Flip *should* be more aggressive, *and* more vulnerable. But how would it help to point that out?

"Try this," I say slowly. "It will be like an exercise, OK? Like one of the warm-ups."

They both start to object. "We can talk about it afterwards," I say firmly, though I dearly wish I could just get up and walk out. All the stage fright I ever had as an actress, every show I ever did combined, is nothing compared to the vicious, nauseous dread I feel every time I ask them to do something and face the possibility that they might not do it. I'm surprised I don't spend every break in the bathroom, throwing up.

"Start the scene again," I say, "from where you say, Tanya, 'Not so fast, boy, I ain't through with you yet.' " The turning point, obviously, but I'm trying really hard not to *name* anything here. "And here are the rules."

Should I not have used that word? They both hate rules *so much*. On the other hand, that's kind of the point, isn't it? They need to feel that they don't have any choice. That's what will free them.

"OK, so first, you can either be moving, or standing still, but whichever it is, you both have to be doing it, totally simultaneous, totally in unison. The instant one of you moves, or stops, the other one has to do the same."

"But that's so *restrictive*," Flip says.

"Not like we would even *know*——" Tanya begins.

I cut them off. "Second. You can talk either really, really fast—at *least* this fast——" I pick up my copy of the script and demonstrate, spewing out the words "——*or* extremely slow——" I demonstrate again. "I don't want to hear *anything* that could possibly be considered to sound natural, is that clear?"

They nod, totally pissed off.

"And finally," I say, wondering where on earth the words are coming from. "Finally, you can stand either very close together——" I walk right up to Tanya, practically nose to nose, "or very far apart——" I move about four feet away, well out of ordinary conversational distance, "even further would be better——" six feet, eight feet, all across the room. "But one or the other. So if either one of you makes the distance *ordinary*, the other had better fix it right away. Oh, and one other thing. Somewhere in this scene you've got to find one point where you just *stop* for—thirty seconds. No talking. No moving. Just *stop*. And then start again, simultaneously. OK, go!"

They want to protest, but I pretend not to notice. Their eyes meet. They go to opposite corners. They take the same deep breath—something I taught them, in an earlier warm-up, to key into each other by breathing together. Then Tanya starts talking, slow, menacing. And then they both start to move.

It's amazing. The whole room is full of their energy. It's as though each of them has grown to giant size, as though each one fills the entire stage. You can see them working it out as they go along—Tanya advancing, talking slow, Flip backing off to keep that wide distance. Then they're circling each other, but close. And then they both *break* away and *dart* to their opposite corners—you can see how it all got to be too much. Then Flip starts talking—slowly, this time, moving in on her as she retreats—and it starts all over again.

The moment they choose to stop is right before the end. Of course it's the perfect moment, but I swear I didn't plan it—obviously, none of us did. Flip says, " 'So, will I see you tomorrow, then?' " and suddenly, they just *stop*. As close as they could possibly get and still be "far away"—staring at each other, eyes locked, too close to be safe, too far to be comfortable, and I swear, their energy jumps over that distance like a welder's arc. They hold it and hold it and *hold* it, *dying* to speak, *dying* to move, neither one willing to give in first. Until finally Tanya says—and nobody knows if it's triumph or surrender— " 'Yeah, OK. Tomorrow.' " They hold it one more moment and then turn their backs and walk away. *We* can see what it cost them.

And then suddenly the characters are gone, and it's just Flip and Tanya, wondering how they did.

So Idris, bless her—I mean, in *rehearsal* she always knows *exactly* what will be good for me—Idris starts to applaud.

"Really?" says Flip, looking not at Idris, but at me. So that I saw, I had to see, how much my opinion meant to him. "Really?" he's saying, not even looking at Tanya. "You really thought that worked?"

Beside him, Tanya is equally uncertain.

"Didn't you think so?" I say. "Wasn't it overwhelmingly obvious how well that worked?"

"I don't know," says Flip. "It seemed kind of—wobbly to me. Kind of all over the place. And I didn't really think I was—forceful enough."

"More forceful than *I've* ever seen you," says Idris, and again, I mean, bless her.

"Baby," says Tanya in this sexy new mock-accent she's trying out, what she calls her Sapphire voice ("Getting ready to play Lieutenant Slut on *Hell Street.*"). "You sure was giving me some *stuff* out there. You 'bout swept me right *off* my feet."

Flip smiles weakly. "Oh, *no,* miss," he lisps, in what I suppose he means to be his "gay" voice, and then he stops.

"You, too, Tanya," I say, because underneath it all, she looks even more shaken than he is. "That was it, that was exactly it. Couldn't you feel it?"

She shrugs, confused. "OK. It felt different."

Then they both look at me, and again, Flip speaks for both of them. "So how are we ever going to repeat it?"

Well, at least he's asking *me.*

"All right," I say slowly. "Now, look. What you would normally do—I mean, what we've all been trained to do, is to try to repeat it, you know, emotionally. To get yourselves to *feel* the same way as you did just now, each time you do the scene. Right?"

They nod.

"But we didn't find it emotionally, we found it physically. So I think, what we do is, we *repeat* it physically. Go back and try to re-create that movement, that rhythm—find exactly where you were standing, when you sped up, when you slowed down. And repeat *that*. Do you know what I mean? You'll have that shape, and the acting will just—happen."

Flip is shaking his head. "You're always saying that," he says. "You're always telling us to find the movement and then just repeat it, repeat it, repeat it. What are we, robots? Acting is the *one* place where there's—freedom. And now you want to take that away."

"*I'm* not taking it away," I say. "You're *not* free. You're in a relationship—with Tanya, and with your own—Lord, I don't know, your own maleness? Oh, Flip, *stop.* I don't mean *yours,* I mean the character's. So you have to find the way that relationship *makes* you move. Isn't that what you did just now? So how *did* you feel—restricted or free?"

Flip looks completely trapped. "Fine," he says finally. Because of *course* he felt free, my God, I've never seen him *be* so free. Why is he blaming that on me?

"*The way the relationship makes us move,*" Tanya repeats. "But that *is* restrictive, Elinor. That's what you want us to show. How—restricted—we are."

"But if you *know* that," I say, rather desperately, "if you can *show* what restricts you—isn't that what makes you free?"

So now *she* looks trapped, too. But after a moment, they get to their feet and start again. We go through the scene, changing some things, expanding others, and by the end of the night, they can repeat the scene almost as brilliantly as they had created it in the first place. They can always find that power again, now that they know where to look.

Flip gives me a long, considering look at the end of rehearsal. "Well?" I say impatiently. "What's wrong *now?*"

Tanya, waiting for him by the door, looks impatient, too, and he shrugs. "When I figure it out, you'll be the first to know," he says. Which at the time, Lord help me, I thought was supposed to be a truce.

So I went home (with Idris, actually), feeling relieved and elated and as though something had finally been settled in *me,* too. Because maybe there was something for me to do after all. Not a career as a director—I'm too late for that, too, probably, and Lord knows it's almost worse being a woman director than being a woman actor. But maybe within *this* group. Here, where they already know me, where there isn't really any competition. A tiny little sparrow rising out of the ashes.

Except then. The next rehearsal. And the one after that. It just got worse and worse. Flip behaved as though every word out of my lips was a plot to sabotage his performance. His work got better and better—and he treated me worse and worse. So who am I going to be *now?*

TANYA: I appreciate what Elinor's doing, I do. And it's not like I can't *see* that my work is getting better.

It's just that I was a fool for a director once before—twice, if you feel like counting. The first time I met Davis. And then the second time I met him. Not like my work didn't get better with *him,* either.

The first time we met was in his directing class at NYU. One of his classmates had called me in for the love scene from *Romeo and Juliet,* you know, the one after they've gotten married and spent the night together. I was doing Juliet for that other guy—yes, I was just a freshman. And of course, the scene was going down between the drain and the deep blue sea. And the way that teacher ran things, if your scene wasn't making it, another student could step in and take over. Maybe he thought that would prepare them for the real world.

Davis is the one who takes over my scene. Naturally. And says right away, "Well, if they've just gotten married, then they should be in bed." Which at the time I thought was *bold.* How was I supposed to know that lots of people do the scene that way? Davis finds some sheets in the props closet and makes this guy and me strip down to our underwear, right there in front of the class, and he was so excited that we actually went and did it, and lay there waiting for him to tell us what to do next.

So he tears up this guy's whole scene and puts it back together, right in front of everybody's eyes. Even if I saw it today, I would have to be impressed. He had us all hanging on his every look, and by the time we were ready to run it, Romeo and I were both so hot for Davis that we couldn't help being hot for each other. But just to make sure, Davis put his whole self right *into* his voice and whispered, his warm breath floating up inside my ear, "Go for it, Tanya. The camera *loves* you." Of course, there wasn't actually a camera, but I understood. He was the camera.

This is the part I don't like to remember but can't afford to forget: He thought I was sexy, so I was. The first time, ever—for a part, or in life, either. Not like I hadn't had boyfriends. But no one had thought I was sexy, least of all me. Then Davis discovered me, and I was hot. The camera loved me. And I loved him.

Not like it *wasn't* good for my career. You *know* I finished school with a reel that was about a hundred times better than if I'd been dating someone *less* ambitious. Not like he didn't dump me as soon as he graduated, either, when he could go ahead and find himself a *real* actress to cast.

So that was supposed to be that, and nothing to feel foolish about, then or later. The foolish part came six years later, when Davis had taken three years off to be some famous person's assistant and three more years to go to grad school. And out of the blue he calls me up—I guess he found me through the alumni office—asking me to play the friend that's secretly in love with him in his first real movie.

I felt sexy on my *own* by that point. But still—I should have seen trouble coming. Because first off, yes, I *was* hurt to be the pal and not the ingenue. And second off, he hadn't changed. You could see him flirting with everyone who came into his path, making sure that every single person on that set, male or female, was madly in love with him. About the only person who wasn't, was Flip, and that was because, till Davis managed to fire his ass, he was scared of Flip. Of me, too, till he fired *me*. And then he had all that fun winning me back.

But here's the thing. When I thought Davis was in love with me—both times—then I felt real. Because I thought, knowing Davis, that he wouldn't have given me the time of day if he *didn't* see something in me. So I felt like a *real* actress. The way I would have felt if I'd gotten that part on *Hell Street* or gotten into that damn Players lab. The way I feel when I get a featured part on a soap—all five times I've done that—but the problem is, it doesn't last. Not the job, or the feeling either.

FLIP: All right. Here's what Rosie doesn't understand, and apparently, Warren doesn't either.

All those things—the stage name, the image in my head shots, the—the look, all right? The straight look.

It's not just what I think will get me a better job.

It's what I think—will make me a real actor. It's what I think will make me real.

ELINOR: The next key incident, as I now think of it, happened about a month later, in mid-March. Things had been getting steadily worse with Flip. (Tanya tried to tell me, before she virtually stopped speaking to me altogether, that it was a particularly hard time for Flip because he was temping practically twenty-four hours a day, whenever he wasn't going to the gym or coming to rehearsal, which I can certainly understand puts a strain in any-body's life, but come on. We *all* had to earn a living.) So there he was, making little remarks under his breath, and pouting, and asking pointed questions—I know it makes me sound paranoid, and weak, to catalogue these little details, but to be perfectly honest, it *was* getting to me. And I think it was affecting the rest of the cast as well.

I probably should have seen it coming, because we were working on such touchy material. The script Idris had written was less an actual play than a se-ries of short scenes, lasting about forty-five minutes all together and covering a wide range of situations—dating, work, marriage, gangs, drugs, and the like. It had more humor in it than that summary suggests, and there *was* a kind of truth to it, and all in all, I thought it would mean a lot to our audience.

Idris had added this latest scene in response to criticism from Bernard and Luis and, of all people, Malik: that what she'd written so far wasn't sensitive enough to the problems of being a man in our society, particularly a man of color. So she brought in a scene for the whole company in which we see little boys and girls grow into fully socialized men and women. The idea was that everyone comes out and shows us how free and undefined children are (though I for one am not so sure that they *are*), and then the actors would show us a series of poses and slogans that demonstrated how they got pushed into their adult roles as *"real"* men or women. For example, Malik might say, "Take care of your woman!" as he showed himself exhausted with a briefcase in one hand and a toolbox in the other; or Luis might say, "Take charge!" and pull out a switchblade; or Flip might say, "Earn a living!" as he pulled out a wallet full of money. While Tanya and Janie had lines like, "Be sexy!" or "Be cute!" or "Make him *feel* like a man!"—you can imagine the poses *they* struck.

Flip began this particular rehearsal by presenting himself as fairly obedi-ent, which lasted for the first hour or so of rehearsal. I had developed a warm-up in which the actors ran continuously in a circle and chanted a fairly standard vocal warm-up ("ma, me, mi, mo, mu"), and I'd call out an age, and they'd take on the voice and body language of themselves at that age. And I have to say, that part was pretty successful—you could see people making dis-coveries, recovering sounds and gestures under pressure of my command ("Now you're six! . . . Now you're ten!"). And when we staged the childhood part of the scene, this was indeed the material they used.

But then we went on into the teenage years, and here's where it got diffi-cult. I think everybody was fairly antsy, but Flip, in particular, was struggling. He was obviously getting more and more frustrated, and what he was coming up with *wasn't* very good—it just didn't have any *life* to it. So that finally (and perhaps this was a mistake), I felt obliged to ask him what the problem was.

"Nothing," he said grimly. "Let's just keep going."

"Flip. There's no point in continuing if something isn't working. What's the problem?"

He looked around at the rest of the group. "Oh, so it's just me?" he said. "Or is anybody else having a problem with this also?"

Well, of course, everybody was—it was just that kind of material—but nobody to Flip's extent.

So naturally, he had to take it up a notch, and he says, "Well, *obviously,* the problem is that it's all external—just this image of what I think you want. But there isn't any *truth* to it."

I might have let it go at this point, though I'm not sure, even in retrospect, how I could have. But then Idris made one of her rare interventions. Saying, in her quiet, earnest rehearsal voice, "Are you having trouble relating to the material?"

Flip laughs, a quick, angry laugh. "You think I can't relate to the problem of becoming a real man?" he says. "Is *that* what you're asking?"

And so another little ripple goes round the room, even more uncomfortable than the first one. Because now that he's said it, yes, that *is* the problem. Though whether with the script or with Flip is hard to say. Because the way Idris had written the text, clearly, the notion of "real" meant "straight." And white. And in possession of enough money to go to the gym and buy the right clothes and do everything else it takes to fit in. But while the images in Idris's text dealt with race and class in some ways—certainly Malik could *play* the line "Take care of your woman" in a "Black" voice, for example, whatever *that* means, but we'd all know it when we heard it (even though taking care of his woman probably *is* an issue of Malik's, from what I've been able to observe, and yet he *doesn't* normally speak in that type of voice)—but whatever Idris had or hadn't done for Malik, she certainly hadn't left room for Flip to indicate anything about the type of man *he* was. I mean, he didn't get to say "Go out with girls," and make it clear, physically and vocally, that he didn't want to.

So there is a long, uncomfortable silence, in which everybody is both looking and not looking at Flip. And under pressure of all this ambiguous silence, Flip bursts out, "Look, I've told you. I just don't feel very—significant, as a performer. I don't know who my character is, or what his history is, or what he wants—that isn't in the text, and it's not in the staging, and it's apparently not anything that anyone here is interested in, so fine. But since I *am* an actor, it's hard for me to work under these conditions."

Janie laughs. " 'Under these conditions,' " she says. "What a diva."

Maybe she meant it as a joke, to break the tension. But Flip glares at her. "Well, if it's being a diva to want to *act* instead of *pose,*" he says.

"I know what Flip means," says Malik. He always has trouble with movement, and he, too, had been having a hard time with this scene. "Do you think people in the community will relate to this? I mean, I *agree* with the politics behind it. But I think people can relate better to stories than to—rhetoric."

"Well, clearly, the script needs work," Idris says quickly. "So can we take a quick break, Elinor? While I try to address these concerns?"

When we get back, Idris hands each of the men a page with new dialogue written on it. And so now Flip *does* say, "Go out with girls," and we're supposed to come up with some way of making clear that *this* man, at least, doesn't want to.

Malik opens his mouth, shuts it, and looks around the room. Finally he says, "I'm not sure how this—I mean, you know. This is a *community* audience."

"You think your agency is going to shut us down, is that what you're saying?" says Janie, of all people. "Because we're not allowed to say that some people are gay?"

Malik looks extremely uncomfortable. "I'm just saying we should keep our audience in mind, all right?" he says. "It won't achieve anything if we alienate them."

Flip looks even more uncomfortable than Malik. He studies his new page, though there's only the one line. "It doesn't have to be—every single thing I do doesn't necessarily have to be—" He looks up. "I'm not exactly sure how to play this," he says finally.

"Here's what I think," I say. Hoping *something* will open up and carry me down. "In traditional acting, what we were all trained in, you start by yourself. *Your* character. *Your* history. *Your* objectives. But you're right, Flip. That's not what this scene is about. None of the bits make sense by themselves. It's what they add up to. It might *not* be as satisfying to do this scene as some of the others—I don't know. But if the audience sees each example mounting up, one after the other, if we give them something clear, and funny, and— overwhelming. They might learn something from this scene that they couldn't get from a more traditional setup."

"So you think the audience wants some—collection of poses?" Flip says. "You think *that's* giving them something?"

"God, Flip, *you're* the dancer. A collection of poses—is *that* what movement is?"

"This movement, anyway."

"Well, then, you tell me. What if it *were* a dance? How would you bring truth to it? Life to it?"

"All right," says Flip. "I am now officially totally and completely baffled as to why so much of this rehearsal has turned into an attack on *me*."

This is so outrageous that even Bernard laughs. Luis says, "The lady was only asking you a question." And Janie says, "Diva" under her breath—but loud enough to be heard.

I look Flip straight in the eye. "Well, then, why don't you show us?" I gesture for the rest of the cast to draw back, leaving Flip alone in the playing area. I point to the script in his hand. "Just your part. Think of it as a dance, where all you have is the movement."

Flip is looking at me like I've just stuck a knife in his heart. "I don't know the new line," he says.

I hold out my hand for the script. "Well, then, just work on the movement. The rest of us will take ten. And when we come back—" Oh, God, what *now?* "—someone else can read your lines. Malik."

"Then I think Malik should stay," Flip manages to say.

"Fine," I say quickly. "Everyone else, let's go."

I open the door and stand there, and slowly, the rest of the group files out, giving each other significant looks. I shut the door without looking back, and immediately, as if I had planned it, I keep walking, up two flights and over to the ladies room at the other end of the hall. Where I hide out in sheer terror till the rest of the break is over.

Everybody *stops* talking the minute I come down the stairs. Oh, fine. I lead them back into the room, where Flip and Malik are waiting. "All right," I say. "Go on."

I can't believe that neither of them is just saying "Fuck you" and walking out. But there they are, ready for action. In fact, they take the stage, Malik positioning himself just behind Flip, as though whispering in his ear. And that's how Malik plays the scene, seductive, insidious—and then implacable, commanding, enraged. He makes himself bigger and bigger, standing on a chair they've set back there to loom over Flip, who makes himself smaller and smaller. It's the exact opposite of the way we've been doing the scene—Flip the child stands tall and full; and then with each of Malik's injunctions, you see him lose something, so that by the last one, he's bent almost double. Then slowly, he stands to his full height as Malik comes down off the chair, and the two of them grow into the same pose, shadowing each other, aggressive, defensive, shoulders thrust forward, eyes cast down. Yes, all right. You can see the wound.

For a moment, nobody moves. Then I let out the breath I've been holding, far more loudly than I meant to, and movement returns. Though everybody in the room is about as uncomfortable as it is possible to be.

"All right," I say, standing up, "let's rethink the way we're staging the scene, then. What if Bernard has Luis's lines, and Tanya does the talking for Janie—" No, that means that the three African Americans are all doing the talking. "Maybe Janie talking and—"

"Not like they *all* have to be the same," Tanya says. "Janie and I could take turns, you know, say the lines back and forth to each other."

"Keeping each other in place," says Idris.

"Right. She gets out of line, I call her back," says Tanya, and Janie nods.

Flip is still looking at me. Waiting for something.

"I assume you can repeat *that,*" I say as drily as I can manage.

Well, whatever he was waiting for, that wasn't it. He shrugs and nods, but he's still waiting.

"Obviously, that was exactly what we needed," I say.

"Not like it made *you* look bad either," Tanya says to him, determined to lighten things up. But he's still looking at me, and the look on his face says that he'll never forgive me, never. Because of the way I put him on the spot? Or because here's another bit of power that he didn't even know he had? And now he's got to live with it the rest of his life? Apparently, that's a more or less unbearable prospect.

FLIP: That night back in March when Elinor made me do that totally and completely ridiculous exercise about being a *real* man, do you know what happened after I got home? I walk into the apartment—which I still can't help thinking of as *Warren's* apartment, now that I know that he actually *owns* it— and there is Warren, waiting up for me in the kitchen, in an absolute *state* over the latest development with Juliet. Because (a) her test scores have come back and they say she's reading below first-grade level, which is clearly ridiculous, I mean, she reads *all* the time, and even *I* can tell they're not first-grade books. Last month she read *Huckleberry Finn,* for God's sake. And (b) the school counselor, whom Warren apparently met with this afternoon (he didn't even tell me he was *going*), agreed that although there is a great deal of evidence that Juliet has some kind of learning disability, he himself thinks that learning disabilities are about 90 percent psychological, and that perhaps Juliet's "unstable and unconventional home life is producing some kind of childlike regression" (or words to that effect).

And not only will Warren not let me come with him to the school to find out for myself what the fuck they think they're doing, he won't even let me talk to Juliet about it. I'm not supposed to ask her to read to me or to show me her homework, or even to ask her what *she* thinks about her wildly unconventional living arrangements. (Well, it might *not* be us. It might be all Madeleine's fault.) In fact, now that he's gotten this apparently unbearable information off his chest, he won't even let me talk about the situation with *him*.

And that's not even the worst part. The worst part is, I think he's right. Not about himself, or Juliet, but about the school. I would go there in a minute if I thought it would help Juliet—unlike Warren, I don't give a fuck what they think about me. But it *wouldn't* help her, would it? Wouldn't it just confirm all their darkest suspicions, seeing *me* as the second parent?

So please don't talk to *me* about power. Because I could go to the gym from today till tomorrow, and I could go to rehearsal for the next twenty-four hours after *that*. And I still wouldn't have the kind of body that could take care of Juliet, or Warren, or anyone else I might happen to care about.

TANYA: The whole time Elinor and Flip were having their little battles, I was thinking, Well, God damn it, what about me? I'm the one who invited Flip into this group in the first place. My part is just as big as his. So is everybody's, in actual fact—and he's the one getting all the attention? Child, please. How is that fair?

I tried to tell my girlfriend Verity about the situation when I had brunch with her one Sunday in April, meeting her between church and some fancy party her boss was giving out in Westchester. Though I admit I'm a bit distracted by her outfit—she shows up in the most ordinary navy suit you could imagine, flat-heeled shoes, hair pulled back tight into a bun. Not a speck of color anywhere. Not a speck of—wildness.

Verity sees me staring at her. "Oh, give it a rest, Tanya," she says, a little nervously. "Like you never got dressed up for work."

"Not like that I didn't," I say. "But then, if I'm not acting, I'm temping. No one's going to make me no junior vice president of a bank, so *I* don't have to dress like a nun."

Verity laughs. "Girl, you know if I dressed any other way, they would just be talking about my titties," she says, reaching for the menu. "If not somewhere ruder than that."

"And this way, they talk about your fly financial insights?"

Verity smiles like she's making a joke. "No, this way they ignore me. But that's better than the other." She gives me that "we're cool, they're fools" smile, eyes rolling, eyebrows lifted, that has kept her being my best girlfriend since I first got to New York.

"They do not ignore you," I say now. "You told me they just gave you a bonus. And a promotion."

"Promotion? Huh!" she says. "Girl, you know that's just because I made them such a *big* ol' potful of money last year. But they don't have to talk to me for *that*."

The waiter comes to take our order. Verity picks up the menu and lays it down again, like nothing that happens to be on it would ever appeal to her. "I'll just have juice," she says.

This was the first week in April, so I had just lost that part on *Hell Street*— well, not *lost,* you can't lose what you never had. Still. You know I was going to the gym *all* the time. So I just order juice, too. The waiter leaves, giving us a sour look.

Verity picks up a roll from the basket, puts it down again. "Girl, when I start in quoting interest rates, you can see their jaws *drop,*" she says. "And you *know* I talk white over there." She brushes the bread crumbs briskly off her hands, a gritty little shower into the basket. "So if they want to be thinking trash about me, I *sure* don't have to help them."

"Not like you have to disappear yourself either."

She sighs. "You sound just like Frederick." Frederick being her boyfriend, who is also in banking. "He's always saying, 'Dress like a woman, dress like a *woman.*' But they didn't hire a *woman*. They hired *me*."

"The invisible woman."

Verity laughs. "Well, you two just go ahead and gang up on me," she says. "Meanwhile, *I* got the salary." She rolls her eyes at me again. "What about you?" she says. "You start that IRA like I told you?"

"IRA? Child, I don't even have health insurance. I couldn't make the union minimum."

Verity shakes her head, and not a single hair slips out of place. "You got to get you some *real* work."

"Tiger's Eye is real. *And* it's meaningful. Doing good for the community."

"Mmm-hmmm," says Verity skeptically. "The community's not going to pay your health insurance." I take a sip of juice—a mistake, because you *know* it makes me hungry. And Verity is saying, in her singsong voice, "No job, no money, no love—girl, you *are* a mess."

"Don't you be talking *love* to me," I say. "Least you have a man."

"Well? Why *don't* you have one? No one since Davis, and that was way back in August."

I shrug. Verity looks at me closely. "Don't tell me he broke your heart *that* bad."

"No, not my heart. I just don't understand why I got fooled so bad."

Verity shrugs. "You and every other woman on the planet," she says. "*That's* no reason to give up."

"I haven't given up. I just don't trust myself these days."

"Girl, you better figure out what you want out of life," Verity says. Now she's *real* serious. "Else you'll end up with nothing and wonder how *that* happened."

Ending up with nothing is about how I feel in Tiger's Eye at the moment, truth be told. Watching Elinor give *all* her attention to Flip, and Flip just standing there ready to take it. What *is* it about him that gets him that?

The waiter comes by, a different one this time, bringing us coffee. Our juice guy was a skinny little white boy, probably gay, who looked right through us like we were made of windows. This one is white, too, and so young you'd think he was in diapers, but he looks us up and over and all around, not even trying to hide it. Just like he thinks we'll like it, or maybe like we can't tell the difference between that and common politeness.

Not like I *don't* want him to look. I *sure* wouldn't want to be like Elinor, so pale and sharp, you'd think she wasn't even there. She stands up there telling us what to do, and you'd swear there was just this thin, white voice, not no body at all.

Dorothy Dandridge had this hot nightclub number in the fifties. She didn't ever consider herself much of a singer, and she used to throw up practically every time she went on stage. And because her voice wasn't enough, or because she thought it wasn't, she had to use her body. She wore a gold lamé gown and the *Post* called her "a singing sexation"—when I read that, I never forgot it. Because it seemed like what I would never want to be, and yet, it made her famous. *Time* magazine said she "came wriggling out of the wings like a caterpillar on a hot rock," and when I read about *that,* I thought, Huh. A caterpillar is something you squash.

Then she took too many pills, so I guess she squashed herself. Still. There she is, up on my bedroom wall. She knew *something* I need to know. But I still don't know what.

ELINOR: *The director's body shows up all over the stage.*

That's what my first directing professor said, when I took his course back in college. But how could that be right? All *I* could see up there were the actors' bodies, mine included, of course. The director just sat back there in the darkness, telling us what to do.

God knows, I thought my body had betrayed me. I was way too tall, and never pretty—I never got the *good* parts. So when Tiger's Eye needed a director, I thought that was my chance to leave my body behind.

And now I sit, not in the back of the rehearsal hall (that's Idris's place) but up in front, where the actors can see me as easily as I see them, and it slaps me in the face at every turn. Flip and Tanya do *my* dance of yes and no. Bernard and Malik show *my* idea of real men. Everywhere you look, *my* desire, *my* despair. *My* body up there on that stage, coming back to betray me again.

FLIP: ". . . and if she would *give* me some direction that made *sense,* then maybe I could accomplish something. Whereas as it is—"

I don't think Warren particularly wants to say anything. But I'm not having this fight with Elinor by myself—I want him in on it. So I keep looking at Warren, the fiercest look I've got, until finally he says, "You know, Flip. It isn't all that easy to give you *anything.*"

"Oh, what does *that* mean?"

"I could imagine," Warren says even more carefully, "that Elinor might be—I'm only saying *might,* all right? That she might be saying something that *is*—useful, somehow. And *that's* what you don't like."

"And why would *that* be?" When he doesn't answer, I say, "I promise not to do anything—you know. Violent. Not that I ever *am* violent, but since everybody seems to think so . . . Just tell me, all right?"

"All right," Warren says slowly. "I think you prefer it when you can do things by yourself."

"Well, of course I *prefer* it. Who doesn't?"

"Yes, but then you—" He stops, but I'm determined to wait him out. Finally he says, in a voice so low I can barely hear him, "It certainly took you a long time to wear that jacket."

Is he still on about *that?* "Warren, you *know* that was because—"

To my total shock and amazement, he interrupts me. "It's not only the jacket. It's the way you are after a show—you know, when people come back to tell you how good you were—"

"Well, if I *wasn't* especially good that night . . ."

"Or with Rosie, when you ask and ask and ask for her opinion—"

"Oh, so now you think I should listen to *Rosie?*"

"I'm only saying," Warren says doggedly, "that something happens to you, Flip, that's all. When you get something—good. Something happens."

I think about how I feel in rehearsal, when Elinor nails me with one of her comments. And then everybody seems to think my work gets better. And it probably *does* get better, I'll even give her that, but it *feels* worse. No. It feels—I mean, if I can't count on myself, who the hell can I count on? Am I supposed to count on *her*?

I don't know. Maybe it makes me feel—weak. All the things I'll never be any good at. All the things I'll never be able to afford. And *Elinor* can, and *Warren* can, and *Rosie* can—they give me something, good or not, and it feels like rubbing it in. And if they're giving me something, *and* I want it? Forget it. *That's* the kiss of death.

ELINOR: I suppose I really can't blame what happened next on Flip. Although it's obvious that I'd like to. But it was more a case of—chickens coming home to roost, I suppose.

We were working on a scene that showed the mother at work. As usual, we had started with a warm-up—a relatively amicable one, for a change, to develop the gestures and sounds that would convey a busy office. Now we were trying to transfer those discoveries to the actual staging of the scene. Luis had come up with a great noise that actually did sound like a xerox machine, and Bernard was miming sitting at a desk, working a calculator and chanting the numbers to himself in a kind of manic rhythm, and Flip was pretending that he was furiously slamming the drawers of a filing cabinet, all of which was to be the background for Janie the mother and Malik the boss having a huge confrontation over unpaid overtime. And then out of the blue, Flip said, "So what kind of filing cabinet am I going to have in this scene?"

"What?" I said. I honestly had no idea what he was talking about.

"You know. What kind? One of those tall ones with the narrow drawers? Or those long, low ones with the wide drawers, the kind you practically have to get down on the floor to use? And is it new, so that the drawers go in and out easily? Or one of those beat-up ones that I'll have to struggle with?"

Am I the one who is supposed to answer these questions?

"I thought we were just going to mime everything," Janie says when I don't say anything. "We don't want to clutter up the stage with a lot of junk."

"No," says Bernard, "if I'm going to be sitting down, I need a chair. And a desk. And a calculator."

Malik is looking at me, too, saying, "Where are we going to get all this stuff, Elinor? We don't exactly have the biggest set budget in the world."

So finally, I have to say it: "I don't know. I wasn't even thinking about the set."

"Of course, in *professional* productions, there's usually a designer," Bernard says, and a little shiver goes through the room when he says "professional."

"Well, we don't have the budget to bring on any more people," Malik says quickly. "So, Elinor, what do you want? We could have *some* furniture, I guess. But I don't know about a filing cabinet. We'd have to take it with us to every show—I don't know how we'd carry it."

And suddenly, everyone is asking a million questions, and they're asking every one of them of *me*.

"If Bernard has a chair in this scene, don't you think I should have one, too? Otherwise, it will look like he has more status than I do, and he doesn't."

"Well, I think it will look stupid for Flip to have a filing cabinet and Luis not to have a real xerox machine."

"The noise Luis makes is better than a machine."

"Thank you, honored public. In my humble opinion—"

"Won't it look weird to have office furniture in this scene and not have a bed in the bedroom scene?"

"What did you want to do about costumes? Because I need to—"

Suddenly Janie, whose question that was, finds herself talking into silence instead of noise.

"Maybe it doesn't matter now," Malik says, looking at me. "Let's just keep going, and Elinor can fill us in later."

Flip shakes his head vigorously. "Isn't that inconsistent?" he says. "We're always saying—*you're* always saying," he says, pointing to me, "that all the physical details matter—they're *all* that matters, apparently. I mean, if it's so totally and completely important how I'm *moving,* then it *does* matter what kind of filing cabinet I have. Or if I'm just miming one. Or even what I'm wearing, or what kind of light is on me." He's not *just* putting me on the spot. He's really trying to figure it out. "It *all* matters," he says triumphantly. "Because it all tells the audience something. So what do we want to tell them?"

Once you start asking these questions, it's like pulling a thread and watching the fabric unravel. Are we going to use real furniture, are the actors going to be in costume, are we going to turn the house lights on or keep the audience in the dark? If we're going to make it up, we have to make it *all* up.

"Well, Elinor doesn't have to do *everything,*" says Janie. "I worked in the costume shop in college—I'm sure I could help find things for people to wear."

Flip is shaking his head again. "It should be someone who knows what they're doing," he says. "Oh, Janie, *stop,* you know I didn't mean that. You're an actress, is all I meant. Not a costume designer. I just meant, if it all *matters* so much . . ." He's actually looking to me for help.

"If it all matters, then we have to go back to the beginning and figure it all out," I say unwillingly. "What every choice means, what it says, what we *want* it to say. And it *would* help to have a designer in on that, but it's too late. We should have been making these decisions from the beginning."

I can't help thinking that we shouldn't have to make it up. There must be a right way to do this. We're just not good enough to know what it is.

FLIP: See, the thing I always loved most about acting, the whole reason I wanted to *be* an actor in the first place, was the way I got to use myself. To use the part of me that's most true. The truth of my inner soul, if you *must* know. Because there on that level, I'm not specifically, you know. Gay. Or from Pittsburgh. Or Irish, or Polish, or anything else. Which is why I don't mind looking as straight as possible in my head shots. Or changing my stage name from *Zombrowski*. Or changing any other part of me—why not, if it makes things easier? There in my soul where it really counts, I'm not even a man at all, necessarily. I mean, it wasn't the greatest career move of all time, but I *did* play Miranda in that all-male production of *The Tempest* that Warren apparently liked so much. OK, fine, so I did a fabulous job, but it didn't *mean* anything about me. It was just another way to *be* me.

Because, of course, if I'm a *good* actor, I could follow that performance with—I don't know. Macbeth. John Wayne. Lieutenant Marcus Clegg. All those macho *real* men that Elinor keeps talking about, people that I'm nothing like in real life—all right, *fine*. But if I'm good enough, I could *play* them. And it would still, somehow, be *me*.

But this work with Tiger's Eye—Jesus Christ. All these things I have to do that *don't* come from any kind of inner soul that I can see, but just from what Elinor thinks will look good to some *audience* I can't even imagine (I mean, the way I was taught, you don't worry about the audience)—well, it's not the reason *I* went into acting. Half the time I feel like it doesn't matter if I'm there or not.

But sometimes. Every so often. Despite everything I know or have ever learned. *Something* happens here that makes me—bigger.

TANYA: When Flip gets out there on stage in *his* body, he gets to be anybody he wants. Till they know who he really is, then he has to be *that*. But till then, he's not—*marked*. He's free.

Whereas for me, I can't figure it out, but *free* isn't even on the menu. I can have *visible*. Or *invisible*. But not *free*.

ELINOR: Today is April 25th, the day Idris has finally finished writing the finale. And not a minute too soon, since we open May 1st, and we haven't exactly finished all the *other* scenes.

This last scene requires everyone to blend into a background song, with movement, while Tanya comes forward and sings a solo. You can feel the tension building from the moment Idris hands out the scripts. "Fine," Flip says, under and not-under his breath, to Bernard, his new ally. "Yet another scene in which we don't have to *act*."

Luis looks annoyed and motions them to be quiet. And Janie, the wild card, says brightly, "Elinor! We haven't ever rehearsed anything like this before—it looks like it's all music. Is there a composer somewhere we don't know about?"

I try not to sigh. "Idris and I have talked about this," I say, trying to sound as positive as I do, in fact, feel about the scene. "We want us all to create the music ourselves."

I expect the entire group to be upset by this idea, and I'm not disappointed. I start explaining how we'll create the backup to Tanya's solo, and the resistance in the room is so enormous, I feel it physically. I feel it so strongly, I have to stop.

TANYA: So Elinor just stands there, and when I ask her what it is, she just shakes her head. And finally she says, "Let's just not do this, all right? Let's just not do it."

FLIP: "What do you *mean* 'let's not do this'?" I hear myself shouting. "What the fuck do you *mean?*"

"I mean," Elinor says, and I cannot fucking *believe* she sounds so calm. "I mean that obviously, nobody wants to do this scene. So all right. I'm tired of fighting about it. Let's just not do it."

"You can't do this," I say finally.

"Why not?" Elinor says, just as though it were a real question.

Because I went to *one* memorial service this week already, I want to say. I don't need to see anyone *else* give up. "Because this is who we are, and this is what we do," I say instead, as patiently as I know how. "And maybe you're not the greatest director in the world, but you *are* the director, so go ahead, Elinor, go the fuck ahead and *direct*."

She shakes her head. "I can't."

"All right," Tanya says. "Then we will. Go on, Elinor. Go somewhere else and take a break, and come on back here in twenty minutes, and *we'll* do the scene." She looks around at every single one of us, and then she gives me this stare like I've never seen before in my life. Her voice is shaking as she says, "Not like I'm going to let anybody take *my* solo away from *me*." Well. That was hardly *my* intention.

So Elinor shrugs and leaves the room, and after a moment, Idris jumps up and goes after her.

TANYA: And Flip says, the minute the door closes, "All right then. Let's stage the scene."

"Oh, fine," says Janie, not even looking at Bernard or Luis to see how cute *they* think she's being. "Say that *now*. After—"

"We don't have to stage the *whole* scene," Flip says after a minute. "We could just start with the music."

"Hey, we've *got* a whole play, people," says Luis. "If it's too hard to stage *this* scene, let's just cut it."

"Well, it *is* Tanya's solo," Flip says, not looking at me.

"Not like *that's* the reason," I say. And then we do all stop.

"All right," says Malik, finally. "Why *are* we doing this? What *is* the point of this scene?"

"This has been my objection all the way along," Bernard says earnestly. "This isn't a *real* play. It doesn't have real parts, or real characters. It doesn't require real acting."

"Not like you dropped out before this," I say.

"I'm not dropping out now," Bernard says. "I honor my commitments."

"Is that the only reason you stayed?"

Bernard looks startled. "No."

"Why then?" But as soon as I ask him, I know. Because you *know* that every time we get to choose, he goes back to playing that old Black grandmother. Idris even went and wrote that character into the script.

Not like that's *real* work. No one's ever going to *hire* him to play that grandmother. But now I know: that's why he stayed.

"So what is all this 'real,' 'not-real'?" says Luis in his impatient way. He throws up his hands. "We're actors. It isn't *supposed* to be real."

"But Luis," says Janie, in her little-girl voice. "We can't do the scene if we don't know why."

"We can't do the scene if it's not *true*," I say. "If it's just some damn thing we're making up." I *told* them I don't sing. I said so the very first day of rehearsal, when everybody was falling all over themselves about me playing that old woman in the church. And now Idris has taken that self-same song and put it in the scene, and Elinor went and let her do it. "I don't even know *how* to sing this song," I say desperately. I start to read off my part—that song mixed up with these new words that Idris wrote. *"Woke up this morning with my mind, it was stayed on freedom. Woke up this morning, and all I wanted was to leave it all behind."* My words sinking into the silence like stones into a pond. *"Woke up this morning, dreaming of another way. Dreaming of love, and someone to listen."* But they're listening, they're listening, they're catching every single stone. *"Dreaming of something else. And then I woke up this morning, and my mind, it was stayed on freedom . . ."*

"Well, that's not so bad," says Malik after a moment. "The community will probably get into that."

"Do you think it should all just be your solo?" Janie asks me. "Is that what's bothering you, Tanya, that now it's this big group scene?"

"No," I say slowly. "It's what Flip said before, when we were doing that other thing, you know, about the men and women. I don't know who I *am,* when I sing this. I don't know what I *want.* I don't have a character to play."

"Can't you just sing it as you?" says Luis. "That's what you did in the improv."

"I wasn't *being* me," I say. "I was *playing* me."

Luis shakes his head. "We give her a solo," he says, "and a great song, and backup singers, and what more does the lady want? A gig at the Café Carlyle?" Then he looks at my face and takes pity on me. "If you don't have a character, make one up," he says. "The audience won't know the difference."

"Yes, they will," I say desperately. "It has to come from someplace *true.*"

Flip clears his throat. "Well," he says, "and believe me, I *really* hate to say this. But *I* think the point of this scene is—just what the audience feels, you know, seeing us struggling all the way through the play, and then here we all are, together. And Tanya, as far as I can see, that's what the song is, and that's what your solo is, and that's why it starts out being a solo and ends up blending into the group, but you know, not completely. It's like you're the voice of the group, you're singing it for the rest of us, because in actual fact, we don't have such great voices. But you do. So you sing it for us, and we'll back you up. And maybe that's not such a great part for you, I mean, OK, maybe it isn't Shakespeare. But it is real."

Everyone is looking at him by now, and he shrugs. "Maybe we are just making it up," he says. "But once we figure out this scene, then it will exist. It will be *made* up. And just as real as anything else."

Still nobody says anything. Flip sighs.

"You're here, and then you're not," he says. "We're here together, and then we're not. As far as I'm concerned, it's *all* made up."

ELINOR: When I come back, they actually do have something to show me. They seem to have remembered the warm-up I taught them months ago—the one I was in fact going to use tonight—in which one person starts a melody (either with actual music; or with sounds, like clicking the tongue or hooting; or just by chanting a few words in a rhythmic and melodic way). And then a second person adds a second "melody," and a third person, and a fourth, and so on. And then you set text on top of it, or else you start with the text and create the jazz.

They've only done about a quarter of the scene, and just the music—they haven't added any movement at all—but it's quite clear that the scene can work, and that their idea of how to work on it was precisely what I *would* have called for if I *had* stayed in the room. I don't know whether to feel moved at this apparent tribute, or confirmed in my earlier thought that they really *don't* need me. But you can tell that everybody *is* considerably relieved to have me back, though also awfully angry. Except for Flip, who doesn't seem angry so much as—withdrawn.

Tanya comes over as the rest of the group is gathering up their belongings. "That's how little this-all means to you?" she says coldly. "That you could just get up and walk on out the door?"

I shake my head, and she gives me the most scornful look I have ever seen. "Oh, so *you* get to run on out of here whenever *you're* not up to the job," she says, "but you make the rest of us sweat blood and tears? You make *us* go right into our deepest—whatevers? You push us as hard as anybody could, you let Idris give me a solo when you *know* I do not sing, you make Flip come on to me, you make me do all sorts of things it was never in *my* mind to do—and then *you* lose faith? Do you believe in it or not, those things you gave us?"

"Nobody likes them," I whisper back. "Nobody wants them."

Her look is even more scornful now. "You better have a better answer than *that,*" she says, heading for the door. "If you're going to finish out this show. You better have *something* you believe in."

FLIP: When we come into the next rehearsal after Elinor's little meltdown, she motions us to form a circle. And then, wouldn't you know it, there we are, doing that same damn exercise back from the first day of rehearsal—all of us running in the same direction.

Only then, you know, it starts to happen again, the way it did the first day of rehearsal. Where you feel that space open up, and you know, *that's it. It's time.* And we switch directions. Again, and again, and again.

When I tried to tell Mimi about it—the actress I worked with last month at We Care for You, when I was still madly temping—she just made a face and said, "*That's* why I don't work with avant-garde directors. I can't put up with all the nonsense."

"Well, Elinor isn't really an avant-garde director," I said, trying to be fair. "She's probably not even a director."

Mimi shakes her head. "And this is supposed to teach you what, precisely?" she says. "Running around in circles—that's perfect. If *that* isn't what every director truly wishes he could make you do."

I think about that conversation now as my knees protest against all this interminable running. But there is something here that we make together. Even if it's hard to say what.

On and on and on. "All right," says Elinor, when she finally lets us stop, and we stand there, panting and annoyed and dripping with sweat. "What *is* the point?" Nobody answers.

"Come on," she says, trying not to sound impatient. "We've been doing this kind of work for five months now. Why? Pretend you absolutely love it. Pretend it's your choice. Pretend you had to tell the *next* director you work with why you're absolutely dying to work this way again. What would you say the point is?"

Bernard answers first. "Unity," he says.

Luis shakes his head. "No," he says, "discipline. You keep doing the same thing over and over and over again, you get pretty good at it. If your knees don't give out first, because let me tell you, Elinor, some of us are—I won't say *old,* but, Jesus Christ, lady, have some respect for the middle-aged!"

Janie gives them both a contemptuous look—well, well, *double* trouble in paradise. "No," she says, "it's to make us aware of how much meaning you can get out of the simplest little thing."

Malik looks troubled. "Unity?" he says. "I'm with Bernard on that one."

Tanya looks even more troubled. "You want us to be aware of our bodies, don't you?" she says slowly.

And once again, I am the only one left. Oh, joy. "You want us to see that we're *nothing* without each other, don't you?" I say. "You want us to see that the audience doesn't care about us at all, individually. Just as this big anonymous mass. This—*group*. That we need to do a good job. And without the group, we can't do a good job—we can't do *any* job at all in *this* exercise. So without the group, we're *nothing*."

But Elinor is shaking her head. "No," she says. "I knew you thought that." It's not clear whether she means all of us or just me. "But you're *not* nothing. You're never *nothing*. It's that with the group, you're *more*."

"Not just more," I say. Why am I *arguing*? "It's not as though one of us could do that circle exercise alone but the whole group can do it better. Without the group, we can't do it at all."

Elinor looks thoughtful. "I see your point," she says finally. "But that wasn't my intention. What I wanted to do was apologize. For walking out of rehearsal yesterday. I *am* sorry about that. It was—unprofessional. And uncalled-for. And unfair."

"And un-American and inhumane and enough already," Luis says.

"Well," says Elinor, with a tiny smile. Luis has that effect on her sometimes. "Besides apologizing, I did want to say—there *is* a reason for working the way we have been. Which is that—"

"Don't tell us," I say. "Don't *explain*. I think it's fairly obvious that we all already know."

ELINOR: I roll over in bed and Idris sits up, so startled at my restless movement that she switches on the lamp. She looks down at me, squinting in the sudden light, still too sleepy to talk.

We open tomorrow afternoon. I've done everything I can possibly do. We even got a designer, at the last minute—this woman Sofia that Janie knew, who rushed around complaining that we hadn't given her enough time to do *anything,* which of course, we haven't. And now *nothing* looks real, which she says is the point. She says we don't have enough money to make it look *really* real, so we might as well go the other way. The actors hate it, of course. But at least it all looks like it belongs in the same show, which honestly, was beginning to worry me.

Anyway. It's done. My power to make things better is over.

Idris shakes her head, sleepy, confused, but she doesn't turn off the light, which, as most lights do, makes her appear very beautiful. The phone calls from Pauli have tapered off to nothing, and she actually *spends* the night here, when she comes over, so I suppose *that* relationship is done with. But she still somehow eludes me. No matter how warm and tender she might be, no matter how many little gifts she brings over, something about her isn't—here.

That may not matter tonight, though. Seeing her leaning against the wall, the elegant shape of her head silhouetted by the warm gold light, I have to let her hold me, my head on her breast, enfolded in her arms. She's so warm and solid. My body feels so light and unsubstantial against hers, so transparent, so angular and sharp. How can she want me, as absent as *I* am?

"What is it?" she says, brushing my hair back from my forehead, quick, soothing touches that make me feel about ten years old. "You never tell me anything, you know that? What's the matter?"

"Isn't it obvious?" I say, trying to sound soft, like she does. But I'm afraid all I sound is defeated.

"Don't worry," Idris is whispering in my ear. "Just don't worry, Elinor. It's all right."

"Aren't *you* worried?"

"Why should I be?" she says sweetly. "*My* work is done. Yours, too."

"Yes," I say, "but yours *exists*."

Idris laughs, still, after everything, a sweet, sweet sound. "That's *why* I'm a writer," she says, bending down to kiss me on the forehead, to settle her hands under each sharp shoulder blade. "Because words last."

And bodies don't. They're here, and then they're not. I had my chance. It's not my body anymore.

TANYA: "I think it's hard to put yourself out there, you know, the *best* part of yourself. The part you like the best. The part you think the most of. The part of you that's most *true*.

"I think it's hard to come out with that *true* part of yourself if you've been told and told and *told* that it's worthless. Or that it's good enough, but nothing all that special. Or if it's going to get you into trouble—get you beat up, or called out of your name, or talked about behind your back. Make you want to disappear.

"I think it's hard to put that part of yourself out there, in its true, true form, because then, you know. You don't have anything in reserve."

That's the monologue Idris wrote for me, to open the show. She came in

with it the last day of rehearsal, and Elinor actually let her do it. I have actually got to stand there in front of an audience of God knows who, and say *that*.

And here we are waiting to go on for our very first show, and guess who *is*
in the audience? This group of high school kids who they tell us are real discipline problems. In some community center, hanging out on a Sunday afternoon, and someone got the bright idea to bring them *here*.

"Eat or be eaten," Flip whispers to me as we stand there behind the curtain
in this falling-apart old auditorium. He grasps my hand and we try that thing,
you know, that Elinor taught us, deep breath in, deep breath out, together. I
feel his hand shake in mine. I've never felt him be this scared.

I could *kill* Elinor, I truly could. Idris, too. Why couldn't we start with a
real scene, you know, that one between me and Flip in high school? *That*
would get their attention. Instead of me going out there and saying all those
words, which you *know* won't mean anything to them?

"It's all for the audience," was all Elinor would say. "The words are what
you have to give them." But you can't *play* "giving it to the audience."

So Flip and I stand here together backstage, and all we can hear is millions
of noisy kids, not even hidden away in the dark, so they'll be *right* with us
when we get out there. Eat or be eaten. Right.

And then I think, *No.* I did *not* come all this way just to go under. And then
Elinor comes backstage to say, "OK. Places," and then I am *out* there.

And I pick this one little girl right in the third row—must be about fourteen, maybe sixteen. Not even paying attention—snapping her gum and elbowing her boyfriend and getting ready to say something her own self. And I
look right *into* her eyes so that she has no choice but to look right back at me,
and I say, in this four-alarm *urgent* voice, *"I think it's hard to put yourself out there,
you know, the best part of yourself!"*

I don't know if she even *heard* the words, but child, please. You *know* she
had to listen to my voice. So she looks hard at me to see who's talking to her.
"The part you like the best," I am saying. *"The part you think the most of. The part
of you that's most TRUE."*

Now she's watching me with the biggest eyes I ever saw, trying to figure
out why I'm talking to her so hard, wondering what do I want from *her?* I just
want her to listen. I just want her to take what I'm giving. I just want everybody else to watch while I do it, to put their eyes on me as they take in every
single word.

*"I think it's hard to come out with that true part of yourself if you've been told and
told and TOLD that it's worthless. Or that it's good enough, maybe, but nothing all that
special."*

Well, they're listening. By now, nobody's saying anything, except some people talking back the way they do in church, saying, "Uh-huh," or "Mmm-hmmm," or "Yes, child. That's right." That little girl is still staring up at me. Wondering why I chose *her*, but still, she's willing. My words like stones, and every one of them caught.

"I think it's hard to put that part of yourself out there, in its true, true form, because then, you know. You don't have anything in reserve." I spread my look out. Watching them watch me. Seeing Elinor in the back trying not to look relieved. I stretch out that look as long as I can, and then I open my arms wide to hold them all. And child, please. The motherfuckers actually applaud.

FLIP: "Be strong!" shouts Bernard, and Luis does that pose, that Real Man pose that *I* showed him how to do, finally, when it turned out that Elinor couldn't.

"Take care of your woman," Luis replies, and Bernard puffs up his chest, proud and scared. The audience laughs, little ripples of recognition.

But here's the part I would never tell anyone. Because then Malik says to me, "Be a man. Not like that. A *real* man," and I show them: Yes. Hearing those words is like a knife in my heart. And because I *am* doing my job up here, and because I *am* good, yes. All right. They can see the wound.

So yes, I *am* using that night after Mario died when I lay there thinking about lying in bed next to George Ventros, making myself numb and wishing I was dead. And of course, the audience doesn't know what I'm *really* saying. Except I'm doing it so well that *yes*, all right? They do. They know more than *I* do, probably. My most private moment, which I would never even tell Warren (even if he already knows), but here I am *using* it. I mean *giving* it. So that at least *somebody* gets some good out of it.

"Don't show them what you feel," Malik says, as though he's whispering in my ear, and I wilt a little more. And the audience watches. They see me. They see *me*.

ELINOR: Well, this is odd. Sitting back here in the last row with Idris by my side. Watching them all up there, doing the things I taught them.

I can see so many things I would have done differently. Would do differently next time, if there is a next time. Even bringing Sofia in from the beginning would help: making the design part of the original idea, having her to talk to—having *someone* to talk to besides Idris and the actors.

I sit here watching them work, and I recognize it all, and it all looks so strange. Something we made. Together. I don't know *where* it came from. In an hour, it will be gone. But it's here now.

THE STRIKE

FRIDAY, APRIL 29TH

ROSIE (lead organizer): This is what Cassandra told me: You can't always tell when something is changing. Then, suddenly, things are different. And you realize that for the change to have happened so fast, it must have *already* happened. You just couldn't see it.

"So I'm not just making it up," I say, somewhat desperately. "If I think I'm getting better, then I really *am* getting better."

She shrugs, in that maddening way of hers. "You might be making it up," she says indifferently, "although I'm not really sure what that means. But I suppose if you told me that, for example, eating chocolate ice cream made you feel better, I would have to tell you—well, not that you were making it up. Because you really might *feel* better. But you wouldn't *be* better. Objectively speaking, you'd still be in distress."

This is one of those things she says that has a terrible weight of truth to it, truth that I of all people can hardly fail to recognize. But I still can't bear it. And, as usual, she doesn't seem to notice that either, but calmly holds out her hand to read my pulse, so she can tell me the truth about whether I *am* better or not. Objectively speaking.

I give her my hand and she listens thoughtfully. She can always pretty much tell me what I've been eating, and how I've been sleeping (or not sleeping), and how I've been feeling generally, so clearly, *she's* not making it up.

"Not too bad," she says, and I am enormously relieved. "But not as much improvement as I thought there would be by now," and I feel such incredible despair, I want to slit my wrists so she *can't* hear my pulse, ever again.

She looks at me slowly and asks the question I've been dreading. "Do you really *want* to get well, Rosie? Because you have such enormous resources, I have to wonder, I'm *called upon* to wonder." Called upon? Who is she, Bernadette? "It comes to me to wonder why you aren't marshaling your resources on your own behalf."

"I'm doing my best," I mutter.

She widens her eyes, that calm, impenetrable surprise. "I don't find that a very interesting approach," she says after a moment. "To me, it's far more in-teresting to wonder about why it might be helpful to you to remain sick."

Oh, please. If I *did* want to be sick, which clearly I don't, I would hardly pick *this* time to do it—the week before our next strike deadline at Olympia. We've put off the date three times now, on Harris's advice (if *advice* is what you'd call it), and our next deadline is Monday, May 2nd—three days away. So I would think that if any choice were involved at all, I'd be choosing to put my illness aside until the strike is over. But when I say this to Cassandra, she tilts her head to one side.

"Then perhaps I should rephrase the question," she says in that calm, bored way. "What prevents you from wholeheartedly making that choice?"

I have no idea how to answer that question. Though it's exactly the ques-tion I might ask the Olympia workers. We need to stand up for ourselves, to act on our own behalf. But clearly, we're not. So what is it that's holding us back?

MARGARITA (department secretary, grade 8, engineering, Dowling Hall): My boss comes in with a huge stack of papers for me to take to the xerox room, each one with a different set of instructions. "So, Margarita, do you un-derstand?" he asks me, trying to sound polite. He thinks I'm stupid. *So* stupid, I can't even *tell* how stupid he thinks I am.

"Sure, *claro,* I understand," I say, and he nods. Because if he wants to think I'm stupid, why shouldn't he? What difference does it make to me?

"Mami, no," says my daughter Teresa. "Don't let them push you around." She doesn't understand. He doesn't own my mind. If I cared what he thought, then he *would* own me.

But of course I wonder about it. Because, come on. If I *wasn't* stupid—compared to him, I mean—why would I have *this* job?

VANESSA (staff secretary, grade 6, Mines & Minerals Project, Dowling Hall): You *know* if we go on strike, I'm *going.* I'm not even saying we *shouldn't* go. Lissa, she's always saying, "Oh, maybe they just don't understand," even *she* says the other day, "Oh, Vanessa," that little voice of hers, "Oh, Vanessa, they're not going to budge now, are they?"

"Right?" I say.

"They're not going to budge," she repeats, and we don't even want to look at each other, because, you know. Strike pay is something like a hundred bucks a week, and bad as the pay is here, it's not *that* bad.

"So they ride us out," I say. "We're gonna last, what? Two weeks at that money? Maybe three?"

"Not three," says Lissa, and then shuts her mouth like she didn't mean to say it.

"Right?" I say again. "So for us, two weeks, that's one *big* disaster. And them? They'll make their own coffee for two weeks, and then they'll win."

Lissa turns her swivel chair around to face me, her pale face worried and angry. "Now, Vanessa, that's just not right!" she says. "We do important work around here. We do."

"Oh, like what?" I say. "If all the faculty just up and stopped teaching, you know the students would be angry, and the parents, too. But what happens if we stop working?"

"Well?" says Lissa. "What if there's no xeroxing?"

"So?"

"No filing," she says. "No typing. Come on, Vanessa. You know."

"No classes scheduled," I say, because I have to. "And nobody reserved the rooms."

"Nobody answered the mail."

"Nobody answers the phones."

"Nobody ordered supplies."

"Nobody wrote any grants—I mean, maybe BH or somebody would *write* them. But not really, not to fill out the application, put in all the numbers, make it look nice."

We stop and hold our breaths.

"No big mailings out to the alumni," Lissa says stubbornly. "No financial aid forms put through. No books ordered for the library—maybe the librarians do the ordering, but we fill out the forms." She's waiting for me to join in, but I want to see how far she gets. "No admissions forms for next year," she says. "No room and board for all the incomings and returnings. No rent bills or board bills, no one to keep the tuition records, no one to cut the checks!"

We look at each other. Because if we could stop all *that*. I just don't think we can.

Lissa (staff secretary, grade 6, geology, Dowling Hall): I think it would be good, too, to stop all that. But I also think, you know. That maybe it isn't fair.

Because look at the schedule. We've been negotiating for more than one whole year, way back before our contract ran out last June. So this year, classes end on June 15th and graduation is June 25th and then that's *it*. It's dead here in the summer. *I* wouldn't negotiate with us then.

Of course, I don't want to ruin anything. Those poor students, they work so hard. They deserve that graduation. They do.

PATRICE (negotiating committee; administrative assistant, grade 9, Institute for Middle Eastern Studies, Laermer Hall): My husband *said* it wouldn't be over by April 12th, and he was *right*.

But I can't quit now. Leaving everybody in the lurch. It's a very responsible position, the negotiating committee, and Rosie said if I left the whole university would know it, and everybody would think we were going to lose.

I see her point. But I promise you one thing. I'll never do this again.

NINA (faculty secretary, grade 8, history, Philosophy Building): There's this really cute work-study student, who I've always kind of liked, but although he was always perfectly friendly and all, he just never seemed that interested. And I wouldn't exactly say he's *interested* now, but he does seem—I don't know. Available? His name is Simon.

Of course, I always *have* been nice to him, because why not? Apart from the fact that he's cute and smart and funny, I'm always nice to everybody, because you know. One thing I've found out in my two years of being a secretary is that if there's even one single person you *aren't* nice to, you end up feeling like you can't stand to be nice to *anybody*, and then you're a real *bitch*. And then *everybody* hates you, and then, why, really? Why are you even alive?

So I always *am* nice to everybody, but especially so to Simon, who I must say has always treated me like a person and not like a secretary, unlike virtually all of the other graduate students. I mean, I *am* taking classes with them, because it's free, you know. That *is* one of our benefits. And of course, the way it's set up, I'll never get a degree or anything, because to get a graduate degree here, you have to be enrolled full-time. But still. I'm *in* their classes. You'd think they'd—I don't know. Accept me.

Of course, it's occurred to me that Simon might be gay. Men who are—what would you call it? Friendly. Men who are friendly to women like that usually *are* gay. And he's *not* interested. But still. He is awfully cute.

ARTHUR (file clerk, grade 4, Business School, Jensen Building): David always tells me not to even bother with the union. Well, to be fair, he just doesn't understand. He works in an office, too, downtown, he's a secretary in the real estate department at some bank whose name I can never remember because it keeps changing, one merger after another, and the name just keeps getting longer. And he makes more money than I do, *without* a union. So he thinks if I worked somewhere that the employer really valued me and my skills—although he thinks I need to polish my skills—but he thinks, in that case, I'd do better on my own, without this whole Joe Lunchbox, time-clock-punching, lower-class *tackiness,* this whole image of cigar-chewing thugs in big raincoats—I mean, I've never even met anybody from the union who looked like that or anything close, but try telling David anything that doesn't fit *his* ideas and see how far you get.

Of course, he did understand that the way the union was set up, I *had* to join. And to pay dues, since they are automatically deducted from my paycheck. But then his attitude was, why go to meetings? Because if the union was doing its job, I'd *get* the money, and the benefits, and all the other things. It isn't like someone keeps track of who does work for the union and those people get more.

I wish someone *would* keep track, actually, because it burns me up, these people who do absolutely nothing and then sit back and collect. Not if they have *children,* of course, or anything like that—I mean, some legitimate excuse why they can't do anything. But of course, most of them don't *have* any excuse. I'm sure most of the ones who don't are Black, too, not that I'm saying anything against them, because don't get me wrong, I'm not. I just think most of them have been brought up with a lot less of a sense of social responsibility than the rest of us, I mean, the attitude that you pay back for what you get. *I* was brought up that way, to always put something back into the pot.

But that's something else that David doesn't understand. Which really puzzles me, because he's Jewish, and of course, the Jews practically invented unions, so you'd think he'd know. And besides—and this isn't even something that *I'm* saying, this is just how it is—but it's common knowledge, isn't it, that they take care of their own?

Anyway, now that there's all this talk about strike, strike, strike, I get tired of not being able to talk about it with David. But I really can't. If I'm really *not* going to be bringing home more than a hundred dollars a week, the less he knows about it, the better.

MIMI (data entry clerk, grade 5, financial aid, Van Rensselaer Hall): I don't even know how I got in the middle of this. First of all, I'm not really a secretary, I'm an actress.

Second of all, I *had* a perfectly good job. All right, it was a temp job, but I liked it OK.

I mean, I knew they were negotiating, but come on. A strike? I never in my entire life heard of secretaries who go on strike. They're not auto workers, for God's sake.

It doesn't matter *that* much, I guess. I can always go back to temping. I just got scared not having any benefits. Because, and this is a really bizarre thing, but a girlfriend of mine just got diagnosed with cancer, and I mean, come *on*. She's twenty-eight. It isn't supposed to happen. But obviously, it could, it can, and it did, so OK.

I was getting fairly tired of my temp job anyway, because come on. A year and a half—not *so* temporary!—at We Care for You, buying fancy presents that I could never in a million years afford and wouldn't want anyway, even if I *was* rich and famous.

I mean, I *do* want to get to the next level. At acting, I mean. But who ever knows what's going to happen? So I thought it would be a good idea to have some health insurance. Given that you *don't* ever know.

So as you can see, the strike doesn't really mean anything to me, one way or the other.

NATHAN (BIOP counselor, TEACH program, grade 7, Cadbury Student Center): I work for BIOP—that's Bringing Inner-cities Opportunity Program. It's a fairly old and well-established part of the TEACH Program, which they set up in the sixties, when they were afraid that Harlem, which is right next door, would riot its way over here. Hence, TEACH, which gives a certain number of grants each year to "local" youth.

"Local" for them means *really* local, meaning right here in this neighborhood. Man, if I had a nickel for every time I overheard the white kids saying to each other, "Just keep an eye out on the subway, OK, because one stop too late and you'll be in Harlem." I mean, it's just a place. But they think you stick your head out the subway doors, you're mugged right there. And I want to say, "No, see, that's what happens if *I* go to Howard Beach. Believe me, *you* can change trains in Harlem." So you can imagine how *they* go out of their way to welcome high school kids from Harlem—or East Harlem, or the South Bronx, or wherever, because the program doesn't literally have to take people right from this neighborhood, although they used to try. Now they just beg the high schools for someone who they actually taught to read.

But that's another story. *This* story is what I'm going to do if they strike.

Because I feel a responsibility to my people in the program. I do. My supervisor's all sympathetic to the workers and everything, but she thinks, and I agree with her, that our people come first.

See, I'm the one who counsels them. If it's something about their financial aid, all right, I take care of that. Or better, tell *them* how to take care of it. Or if it's a personal problem, you know. Family, oftentimes. Sexual abuse, physical abuse, domestic violence. Welfare payments cut off, somebody out of work, someone in jail. Or out of jail—sometimes that's worse. The big brother or little sister who's going down fast, while my person is having the time of their life up here in the beautiful white world.

Or what they call problems of adjustment. Which means fitting in *here,* which is *damn* hard. *I* can't do it. Of course, I *didn't* go to college. If you needed a counseling degree to do what I do, it wouldn't be a union position.

I don't have anything *against* the union. But their struggle is not my struggle. I'm not doing this work for a bigger paycheck, or more seniority, or anything like that—I have a higher purpose. And they go on and on about sexual harassment, and I'm sorry about that, I really am, because plenty of men *do* disrespect women, and they shouldn't, end of story. But it's not an issue over here.

Rosie keeps trying to get me to think differently. She'll say, when she runs out of everything else, "But Nathan. What about the minority salary fund?" Like that's supposed to make all the difference with me. Like my thinking is so narrow, she can say that to me, like as if I was some damn puppet, and I'll just snap to, just bounce along there on the end of my string.

I don't think so. Because as far as I'm concerned, we can't rely on the union, or the University, or anybody else to help us. We have to do for ourselves. The brothers and sisters that I counsel, if getting that fancy Olympia degree puts them in a better position out there in the real world, well, then, that does something for me. A few dollars for a bunch of secretaries, I'm sorry, no. Far as I'm concerned, that's just another handout.

HYACINTH (receptionist, grade 4, Business School, Jensen Building): When I first heard about the strike, I thought, "Good." I thought, "Now is the time to stand up to these bastards."

Then they put it off. Again and again and again. One more place that makes big promises and in the end you just get *nothing.* One more place that makes you feel bad. Makes you feel *worse,* for thinking it could ever be different.

SATURDAY, APRIL 30TH

MARGARITA (department secretary, grade 8, engineering, Dowling Hall): Cecy is waiting for me at the store over by the #1 subway station at 137th Street. She's going to help me pick out some clothes for my grandson, Bobby. In the nice weather, they have bins out in front, but it's raining today, so I go look for her inside.

I never know what to get for boys, which is why Cecy is helping me. She had three sons. Well, she still has them, but one moved to California, and one is living with her sister upstate because Cecy doesn't think the city is a safe place for him, and the third one is in jail. Which I also worry about for Bobby, if you want to know, but what can you do? He's only five. Teresa has her hands full with him already, though. She isn't the strictest mother in the world. (You want to know what I think, I think she wants to raise her son like white people do, never raising her voice, never raising her hand. But you can't say that to *her*.) He's a hell-raiser, though.

Cecy gives me a quick kiss on the cheek when I come inside. It's a madhouse this morning. Everyone is out looking for bargains. "Hey, *querida*," Cecy says. "You come five minutes later, everything would be gone."

"I'm sure," I say. "They have mountains of this junk. When they run out up front, they go get another mountain from in back."

Cecy shows me the clothes she picked out—two pairs of jeans, a little green sweater, and an amber T-shirt, which will look nice on Bobby, because he's dark. "Perfect," I say, raising my voice against all the noise.

"You want to look around a little more?"

"No, no, let's get out of here. Not five minutes, and already this place is making me crazy."

"So, Teresa better appreciate this," Cecy says. "She better not treat me like—"

"Like the woman who corrupted her mother? Which is what you are, *querida*, so get used to it. She doesn't like to think that I do it with anybody. Only she's allowed to do it. While I babysit."

NINA (faculty secretary, grade 8, history, Philosophy Building): Yesterday, Simon stopped by my desk to pick up the research work his advisor had left for him. "Jesus Christ," he said. "Vanderby thinks I can do all this by Monday morning?" Of course, if Simon wants Vanderby to get him a job, this just goes with the territory.

So he gives me this look. Like we're sharing something. Of course, it doesn't mean anything, I *know* that. "Well," he says, "maybe I'll get lucky and you guys will be on strike."

"What would you do then?" I say.

He grins at me. "Oh, I don't know. Probably I'd just give Vanderby a little call and say, 'Gee, sorry, man. But I'm studying *labor* history. I can't exactly cross a picket line. Not to mention that I'm a red diaper baby, and if my parents ever found out they'd probably disinherit me.' Of course, they don't exactly have anything for me *to* inherit, given *their* political commitments. But still."

Something about this makes me mad. He *could* replace me, if they asked him to.

So I say, "Is that really what you'd tell him?" And because he *is* a basically nice person, he gets serious.

"Well, obviously, I wouldn't say *that,*" he says. "I couldn't, even if I wanted to. I wouldn't just lose the tiny little pittance Olympia pays me to live on. I'd lose my tuition."

"So you *are* going to cross our picket line? Assuming we have one?"

Simon looks so unhappy that I might feel guilty, except now it really hits me that we *are* talking about my job. "Rosie said something, at the work-study meeting," he says. Which I was supposed to go to, since I *am* the head of that committee, but I had to study for a test, so I couldn't. "She said if we have to work, go ahead. Which I for one really appreciate, Nina, because I really *can't* afford to lose my tuition, but I also don't think I could stand to cross the picket line if the union was asking me not to. I honestly don't know if I'd do it or not, so let's just say it's very nice not to have one *more* enormous crisis of identity to have to deal with. One *more* question of what I'm willing to go along with, even though I hate it."

So he *is* involved, but it isn't going well.

"So Rosie said," Simon is saying, "that if we absolutely *can't* avoid crossing the picket line, then you know. Put in one hour of strike support for every hour we work. So if you do strike Monday morning, I thought I'd help out then."

"Oh," I say, actually rather touched. Because in one way, OK, yes, that's less than I thought I'd get. But in another way, it's more. Isn't it?

"So how will we know?" he's saying. "About whether you strike?"

"We're meeting Monday morning at Reed Hall." His attention seems to have wandered. "I don't think we *will* strike," I say, a little desperately. "I think it will be just like all the other times, when they tell us to extend the deadline and we're back at work by ten o'clock." He's looking off into the distance, and yes, it's starting to make me mad. "You could come, if you wanted . . ."

"I'm sorry," he says suddenly. "I've been a little distracted lately." Maybe he sees that I am fairly offended. "A friend of mine died recently," he says, still not looking at me, but somehow his voice gets more intimate. "It was fairly sudden, actually, and I—I find myself thinking about it a lot. I still haven't really gotten over it, I guess. He wasn't *that* close of a friend. But something about it—hit me harder than I expected, I guess."

"I'm sorry," I say. "You have seemed down lately, but I didn't know. That that was the reason."

"Well, that and other things."

He looks at me suddenly, that "seeing me for the first time" look. "We should get together sometime," he says. So was he planning this the whole time?

"Sometime would be good," I say. "Depending on the strike, of course."

"Of course," he says, sounding more cheerful. Which might be me, or it might just be the thrill of the chase. So I gave him my number, without much hope of anything.

But just now he called me. Saying he thought he'd had plans, but it turned out he didn't, and was it by any chance possible that *I* was free tonight?

Maybe it was stupid to say I was, on such short notice. But I *am* free, so why should I play games?

"Well, great," he says, and I can hear how pleased he sounds.

HYACINTH (receptionist, grade 4, Business School, Jensen Building): It's the way they treat you. They think they can ask you to do anything, and you will say yes, because you have no choice.

SUNDAY, MAY 1ST

ROSIE (lead organizer): "So, Rosie, Happy International Worker's Day," says Marcy to me over the phone. God, I wish she were here. But she's there, pregnant and two weeks late—they're beginning to think they made some sort of mistake calculating her due date, although first babies are *supposed* to be late. And here I am, three weeks late with the strike, which is now theoretically going to happen tomorrow.

They *can't* let us strike. Oh, God, they can't. Surely, at the last minute, Harris will call me up and tell me to postpone it again.

"Talk to me, Rosie," Marcy is saying. "What's going on over there?"

"Oh, you know, the usual," I say. "We've had three, or maybe it's four, I've lost count, strike deadlines, each one of which has been put off. And now we're at the point that if we actually *did* want to strike, we're not at all ready. Our resources are just nowhere near in place. But graduation is only about six weeks away. All Olympia has to do is hold out till then. Harris must have *something* up his sleeve, but damned if *I* can figure out what it is."

"So if you did strike, you couldn't win?"

"Oh, God, Marcy, I don't know." She is probably the only person I could even say that to. Michael would know how upset I'd get and never even ask the question.

"Well, you must know *something.*"

"I think Harris is cooking up some deal with Olympia's president," I say finally. Because of course, I do know this. I just don't like to think about it. "And there's some complicated game of who's going to save face and who's going to back down first and what you give in exchange for that. And if that's the case, well, Harris could care less about how he looks to the bosses. Whereas Olympia really *needs* to save face. Because how can they keep pushing around the faculty, and the students, and all the *other* unions on campus, if it looks like a bunch of dumb *secretaries* can push them back?"

"So you think Harris wants to trade," Marcy says. "Their face for your demands."

"Something like that," I say. "Obviously, nobody's telling me anything. Which, actually, they shouldn't. Because if I thought we were all just pawns in some big power game— But of course, that's the wrong way to think about it. What's important is that we get our contract. Which *will* make our lives better. I mean, the workers' lives."

"Right," says Marcy. "Because *your* salary stays the same no matter what happens. Not like any of this affects *you.*"

I sigh. "Right," I say. "I'm just footloose and fancy free. Anyway, Harris's plan, if it *is* his plan, won't work if we aren't down below, pushing up. So we really *do* have to be ready to strike."

"So you have to believe it," Marcy says. "But you don't."

"No, I do," I say. "That's the problem. I do believe we could strike. I even believe we could win. I'm just wondering how foolish I am to believe that." I let out half a sigh, half a laugh. "All the time in Sunday school," I say, "they used to talk about *perfect faith.* As if the problem were just *having* the faith. But what if you *do* have faith, but you think—you know. That maybe you shouldn't."

"Why not?" says Marcy. Her voice sounds funny.

"What's wrong?" I say quickly. I hear her moving around at the other end of the phone, and I want to be in the same room with her so much, I can hardly stand it.

Oh, nothing," she says. Her voice sounds normal again. "I'm just *very* pregnant. They say you can't be a little bit pregnant. But apparently you *can* be a *lot* pregnant."

I hear her take a sip of water. "It's just so weird," she says. "All my organs are squished. It's funny to think of it like that, isn't it? That there's something else inside me, and it's pushing everything else out of place. I mean, it's *supposed* to be there. It's not a disease, as we used to say in our Women's Health Collective for Empowering the Birth Process, or whatever the hell we called it—what did we call it again?"

"Women Overcoming Male Birthing," I say. "If you can believe that. This is one of the things I don't tell people when they ask me what it was like to hang around all those older feminists in college."

Marcy laughs. Suddenly it hits me—really hard, with full force—that she really is going to have a baby. And soon. There's no going back now.

HYACINTH (receptionist, grade 4, Business School, Jensen Building): I don't mind so much living on little money. Only if one of my kids gets sick, and it's near the end of paycheck time, and I don't have money, what if I have to take a taxi to the hospital? I should have ten dollars for that.

And when we have our meeting tomorrow, I'm going to say so.

No, no, I won't say anything. Because everybody knows I'm shy. I don't speak up at meetings, draw all that attention to myself. That's not how I do. No.

ARTHUR (file clerk, grade 4, Business School, Jensen Building): All right, so I really *had* to say something to David. Because he was asking me about tickets for our vacation, you know, he wants to go down to Puerto Rico, there's this gay guesthouse there that he's heard wonderful things about, except I don't know. Puerto Rico? I think it would be depressing. But anyway, the whole thing is moot, because I'm not about to go in for half a vacation, either in actual cash or on our credit cards, if I'm not going to be bringing down a paycheck for God knows how long. So I had to tell him.

As you can imagine, he was well and truly pissed. "What are you working *for?*" he kept saying. "If not to be able to afford nice things? Maybe you should start looking for another job."

Well, maybe so. But I can't do that *today,* can I? It's Sunday, for heaven's sake.

"Do you *have* to go on strike?" he said next. "I mean, will they force you?"

"They won't *force* me," I said. Though of course, I don't really know. I've heard of people getting beat up around strikes. Is that because the strikers beat up the people who didn't want to go?

"Well, it's against the law to do *that,*" David says when I tell him what I'm thinking. "Anyway, why should you go on strike with those people? If they lose, you'll go down with them, and if they win, you'll get the same raise they do, whether you went on strike or not."

"That must be how it works," I say, embarrassed that I don't even really know.

MIMI (data entry clerk, grade 5, financial aid, Van Rensselaer Hall): This morning when I called my mom, I mentioned that they might be having a strike where I work, but of course, I'm not going. I'm not even off probation yet.

And my mother just about hit the ceiling. "Mimi Garofano," she says to me. "Do you remember those little cookies your grandmother used to make? Do you know what they were called?"

"Cookies, Ma," I said. "That's all I know."

"*Crumiri,*" she says, not even laughing. "They're called *crumiri.* And do you know what that means?"

"I didn't even know they weren't just plain cookies, Ma. How would I know what it means?"

"It means 'strikebreakers,' " my mother tells me. "And do you know how they got that name?"

"Somebody broke one during a strike?"

"They're shaped like horseshoes," my mother says, "remember? And in Piedmont, where your grandmother is from, they used to throw horseshoes at people who broke strikes. Horseshoes, Mimi. So I'm telling you. If you cross that picket line, don't bother coming home. Because nobody in this family ever broke a strike."

Well, who died and made *her* queen of the unions? "Don't bother coming home"—like she'd *ever* let me get away with *that.*

NINA (faculty secretary, grade 8, history, Philosophy Building): So then, not five minutes after we made our plans last night, Simon calls back.

"I'm awfully sorry," he says, sounding totally uncomfortable, as well he should. "But it seems that I—misunderstood something. Apparently I *had* already made plans for tonight, and they *were* definite. *I* thought they were up in the air. I thought they had been canceled, as a matter of fact."

"Oh," I say. So that settles it. He really is totally involved.

MONDAY, MAY 2ND, 8:30 A.M.

MARGARITA (department secretary, grade 8, engineering, Dowling Hall): Here I am, going to work, way, *way* too early on a Monday morning. Bobby was up all night with the flu, and Teresa had pulled an all-night shift, and I didn't want her to come home just because Bobby was sick.

"How many times did I take care of *you?*" I asked her. "Just because you're a nurse? Don't think I don't know as much as you do about sick kids, *chica,* please, because remember, I'm your mother. And besides, Cecy's here," which of course Teresa hates, because she doesn't think Cecy should have anything to do with her little Bobby, but too bad for her.

So, fine. Up all night with her little Bobby. Cecy said she'd stay up, too, but why? So two people would have no sleep?

Which means that I am *tired* walking to work from the subway. And so I had forgotten completely. About the strike, I mean. All those deadlines. Do you think I took it seriously? So when I heard the noise, I didn't know what it was. All that noise, as I'm coming across the street from the subway.

And then. This huge group of people I don't even know, signs, banners, bullhorns. They're all moving in a big circle, cheering, right in front of the iron gates—*"What do we want?" "A contract!" "When do we want it?" "NOW!"*

I don't know what to think. Who are these people? I don't see anyone I know.

Then, OK. There's Lissa. Chanting with the rest of them. Walking next to this big Black woman who's dragging her along, that religious look on her face as she claps and cheers with the rest of them. Lissa looking scared and excited.

Chica, I don't even know what to think. I just stand there, staring.

LISSA (staff secretary, grade 6, geology, Dowling Hall): She's from Paradise Holidays, downtown, and her name is Mariah, and she's been on lots of picket lines, she told me, and once even in a strike herself, though not at Paradise. And she *is* very religious, she told me the name of her church, which I forgot but didn't want to say, because she invited me, but of course, I wouldn't go, but I thought it was nice of her to invite me. And she says that this happens, well, not a lot, but sometimes. That there's a strike, and they'll call everybody in from all over town, everybody who belongs to *this* union, and they'll all come help out, at least for the beginning. Because she has to get back to work by eleven, but she says it's in the contract that they're allowed to take two hours once every so often to go help some other striking local, though in that case, I wonder why they never tried to get us to do that from Olympia? I don't know, maybe they have. Maybe *I* just never heard.

I can't believe it. Because there are people here from Paradise, and from a bunch of law firms that they have downtown, and from a couple other schools in the city, and I can't even keep track of all the places, I keep reading them off the signs—Schwartz O'Malley; Selden College; Abel Tech Repair; Farber Klein & Marcus—name after name after name. All these people. Here for us. I just never would have thought.

VANESSA (staff secretary, grade 6, Mines & Minerals Project, Dowling Hall): So then they *are* going to strike this time? Because I'll tell you, they never had a picket line like this. And you *know* they're not going to put all this in Olympia's face and then not follow through.

Someone from the union comes around and says that at nine o'clock, we should all just go inside to Reed Hall, hear the negotiating committee's recommendation, vote on what to do next. The rest of them will keep the picket line going, you know. Till we get back out here again.

But I want to stay out here with the rest of them, yelling at Olympia. I want to tell them that finally, *finally,* we don't have to take their crap anymore.

ARTHUR (file clerk, grade 4, Business School, Jensen Building): Don't we at least get to vote on this? Who *are* these people—they don't even work here. Do they get to vote, too?

MIMI (data entry clerk, grade 5, financial aid, Van Rensselaer Hall): I'm trying to find someone who can tell me what's going on. Because like I said, I'm supposed to be on probation. So what I want to know is, can they fire me just for going to the meeting?

NATHAN (BIOP counselor, TEACH program, grade 7, Cadbury Student Center): Don't you just love how they pull all those folks in to make themselves look strong? And not just white folks, but people of color, too, and how do they manage *that?*

All those people, still trying to argue with the boss, still trying to squeeze a few more bucks out of him. Instead of doing for ourselves, like I keep saying. Taking some responsibility.

PATRICE (negotiating committee; administrative assistant, grade 9, Institute for Middle Eastern Studies, Laermer Hall): Up all night, arguing and fighting. I had to call my husband at 3 a.m., because he is still waiting up for me, ready to pick me up from the subway. "Nikos, sorry," I have to say. "No, honey, we'll be here all night."

They kept telling us, we're in charge, we're in charge. The negotiating committee. The workers' leaders. They kept saying that, over and over.

But also, they wouldn't stop pushing their own plan. And I didn't want to agree. Putting off our strike again and again. Why?

Rosie says, "Look, if we can show our strength, then we don't have to *use* our strength." She says that, and it's Rosie, so, I mean, she doesn't *lie.* But it just doesn't seem right.

Some people agreed with me. Tony especially. He kept saying, "No, no, *compañeros, compañeras,* we have to fight back. Now is the time." He was the last one, except for me, but then he gave in, too, so how could I hold out?

HYACINTH (receptionist, grade 4, Business School, Jensen Building): If the strike starts today, do they give us our benefits today? Or do we wait for one week, or would it be longer? Because I have bills to pay every week, and every week, there is nothing left over.

NINA (faculty secretary, grade 8, history, Philosophy Building): So I'm waiting in the middle of this big crowd in Reed Hall, wondering why everyone is getting so excited. Because honestly, we're just going to vote yet again to extend the deadline and then go straight on back to work.

"Yeah, but the picket line, Nina. Wasn't it exciting? I didn't think so many people would come to help us." That's Teneisha, the other secretary in our department. She's only about twenty-two, and she's worked out something to get her B.A. through the Continuing Ed. program, which is not even in the same ballpark as a real Olympia degree, but it's better than no B.A. at all, I suppose.

"So many people," she's repeating. She's like a little terrier, she gets her teeth into something and she just doesn't let go. "How long do you think the strike will last, though? Because I was going to go away this weekend, but I can't if—I mean, if we're only out a day or so, would we miss the whole week's pay?"

I shake my head to show I don't know and then I see Simon. Teneisha sees him, too. "Oooh, Nina," she says. "He's here for *you,* girl."

"Yeah, right," I say, but he is waving. I wave back, and he heads toward us.

"Hey, Nina," he says, casual and friendly. He has to raise his voice, because the crowd is getting louder and louder.

"Hi," I say. I *am* pleased, but I don't want to *look* like I am. He *did* stand me up.

"You said I should come," he says, grinning at me.

"I didn't think you were listening."

"I can surprise you that way."

"I guess."

So now he looks uncertain, and he's about to say something, but all of a sudden, there's a huge roar and here comes the negotiating committee, along with Rosie and Charles and some other people from the union—Isabel? And Wanda Parsons, the president's assistant? And some other white guy whose name I can't remember, but I think I saw him at that all-day meeting back in January. I have to tell you, *he* looks like your union bureaucrat cigar-chewing stereotype of all time. Simon must think so, too, because he leans over and whispers to me, "Well, lock up the pension fund when *he's* in the room," and I can't help it, I giggle. Though if the guy really were stealing my pension fund, I suppose it wouldn't be so funny. Simon's going to be a professor, *he'll* have an IRA or a Keogh, or whatever people have when they're earning real money, won't he? Even if right now he has less than I do.

ARTHUR (file clerk, grade 4, Business School, Jensen Building): The negotiating committee comes in, and it's like this incredible rush, it goes right through me, this thrill, lifting us all up, and we're all applauding, but why? Why is it so exciting?

MIMI (data entry clerk, grade 5, financial aid, Van Rensselaer Hall): The negotiating committee walks in with a bunch of people in suits who I guess are from the union, and everybody starts cheering, which I guess I can understand, because all right, these are their people. And they've been negotiating for a whole year.

And the committee. When they walked in, they looked miserable, every last one of them, though they were all trying not to. Not like they expected the applause, or the thanks, or any of it. Not like they particularly want it now.

Except. That one organizer, the fat one. Rosie. When the applause starts, something happens to her body. I can see it, even though I don't know what it is. That applause—it told her something.

PATRICE (negotiating committee; administrative assistant, grade 9, Institute for Middle Eastern Studies, Laermer Hall): If they knew what we were going to do, they wouldn't be cheering for us.

NINA (faculty secretary, grade 8, history, Philosophy Building): And then finally it's quiet, and Rosie comes forward to speak. With this weird *look* about her, this excited, transported look. She steps forward and says, "OK, guys, we've been negotiating all night—well, until two in the morning, and we've been up together since then trying to figure out what to do. So here with our unanimous proposal is Tony Rivera." And people clap and cheer and call out, "Yay, Tony!" "Come on, Tony."

Tony comes forward, looking completely upset, only trying not to, and I lean forward, and Teneisha does, too, and Simon beside me leans forward, too, I can feel his body following mine—

MIMI (data entry clerk, grade 5, financial aid, Van Rensselaer Hall): And that guy Tony says, in that Latino–New York accent, the one that's so tough and sexy, so laid-back and powerful—except now—what? Now he sounds defeated. And he says—

HYACINTH (receptionist, grade 4, Business School, Jensen Building): "Brothers and sisters of Olympia University, it is the unanimous recommendation of the negotiating committee of Union Local 235 that we extend the deadline of the strike date one more week, to give us and the University additional time to come to a mutually agreeable proposal."

Why do they want to do *that*?

———

ARTHUR (file clerk, grade 4, Business School, Jensen Building): I don't understand. If we're not going to strike, why did they have that picket line?

VANESSA (staff secretary, grade 6, Mines & Minerals Project, Dowling Hall): I don't fucking believe it. How could they do this to us?

LISSA (staff secretary, grade 6, geology, Dowling Hall): Well, there must be a reason.

ARTHUR (file clerk, grade 4, Business School, Jensen Building): "That faggot," someone is saying, about Tony, under their breath, but I can hear them, so it's not *that* soft. They wouldn't dare say something about him being Spanish. But *that* they can say.

NINA (faculty secretary, grade 8, history, Philosophy Building): "I knew they wouldn't strike," I say to Simon and Teneisha. "You watch, we'll be back in our offices by ten, just like I said."

"Discussion," says Rosie, in this very weird voice, as though somebody else is telling her what to say.

Someone raises their hand. My God, it's Teneisha. "Look," she says, in this trembly little voice, "this is not right. It's just not right."

"Mmmm-hmmm," says someone behind us.

"Tell it, girl," says someone else.

"We can't keep doing this," Teneisha says. It sounds as though she's going to cry. "It makes us look stupid. It makes us look like fools. We can't *do* this again!"

Little scraps of applause. Teneisha looks hard ahead, pretending not to hear.

"Teneisha," I whisper to her, "you mean it? You really want to go on strike?"

She looks at me, her face pinched, and yes, almost crying. "What else can we do?" she whispers back. "We have to do *something*."

LISSA (staff secretary, grade 6, geology, Dowling Hall): Then this girl I know raises her hand, she works on the floor below ours, in metallurgy. "I told everybody at my office, *everybody,* that I wasn't going to be back to work Monday morning if we didn't have a contract," she says. "I said, you know, we put it off once, twice, three times, but I said, I'm sure this is *it.* So how can I go crawling on back just as if nothing had ever happened? How can I? I can't."

ARTHUR (file clerk, grade 4, Business School, Jensen Building): I find myself raising my hand. "We really need more money," I hear myself say. "And more respect. And we've been *talking* to them since before June, haven't we? So I would really like to hear your reasoning on why one more week of talking is going to help."

PATRICE (negotiating committee; administrative assistant, grade 9, Institute for Middle Eastern Studies, Laermer Hall): People clap, and I'm glad. It doesn't seem right to me, either.

I knew it wasn't right, and I went along. But now, they're not.

I won't go along the next time.

NINA (faculty secretary, grade 8, history, Philosophy Building): All those people up there, Isabel and Wanda and that cigar-chewing white guy, are giving Rosie dirty looks, waiting for her to talk us into it, you can sure see *that.* And Charles looking like he's going to burst.

Rosie pulls Charles and the committee into a little circle, and they all whisper together. Then Keisha from the committee comes forward to speak.

"Hey, y'all," she says, trying to sound laid-back but sounding thoroughly nervous. I know her—she's the receptionist in the English Department on the floor above mine, and sometimes she comes down to pick Teneisha up for lunch. And she asked me, once, about how to get a Master's part-time—she wants a degree in Public Administration so she can get a good job with the City. P.A.'s not as snotty as History, so maybe she can.

"Hey, y'all," she says as people clap and cheer for her—she's very popular, like Tony is, which is probably why Rosie picked her to come forward next. "How y'all doing this morning?" Big cheers, big laughter, everyone starts to look more relaxed.

"Great," mutters Simon beside me. "Now they're going to try to chill things out."

I look at him, surprised. "You *want* us to strike?"

He looks back, equally surprised. "You don't?"

"Let me tell you how we figured this," Keisha is saying. "Because y'all know we thought about a strike for a long time."

"I want us to *win*," I whisper to him. "Do you think we can?"

"—but you folks know as well as I do—"

"Sometimes you have to be willing to risk it all," Simon whispers back. "Don't you think so, Nina?"

"—y'all know that a strike is some serious business."

Like you're ready to risk your grant? I'd like to say. But I don't, of course. "Do you think we *can* win?" is what I say instead.

And it's the most amazing thing. For a minute, *Simon* looks transported. Like Rosie did a moment ago. Like he just saw—I don't know. Like he just saw *hope*.

"And you know, if there's any other way," Keisha is saying, "if there's *any* other way, we ought to try it. Before we put ourselves in the position of living on some hundred dollars a week, for Lord knows how long. Before we put ourselves in the position of all or nothing. If there's *any* other way—and we still think there is."

"Damn!" says Teneisha in my other ear. "She's not *even* telling the truth. You know she's just saying what Rosie told her to say. Why are they doing this?"

NATHAN (BIOP counselor, TEACH program, grade 7, Cadbury Student Center): Well, this is some business as usual, for my money. Get some Black woman up there to front for you *and* your sell-out program.

Not that I think they *should* strike. But damn! They've been negotiating more than one full year. Their damn contract was *up* last June.

ARTHUR (file clerk, grade 4, Business School, Jensen Building): Then this Oriental guy raises his hand, and man, he is just fuming. Oh, wait, I know him, what's his name? Jack. He's always coming around talking union, union, union. I mean, putting something back into the pot is one thing. But he really takes it to a ridiculous extreme.

Usually, he at least tries to act patient. But now he has just lost it. "This is bullshit!" he's shouting. "Just plain bullshit! How can you *possibly* send us back to work at this point? It's an insult to our intelligence!"

People are saying, "Yes, yes!" and cheering and clapping, but you can tell some people are uncomfortable. I know I am. They're trying really hard, up there. There's no need to yell at them.

Then he says, "You've been negotiating with Olympia for *over a year*. We've been working without a contract for more than *eleven months*. What is it going to take to make them listen? Not more talk! Strike! Strike! *Strike!*"

You almost have the feeling people are going to say it with him. But they don't.

MARGARITA (department secretary, grade 8, engineering, Dowling Hall): Rosie looks like she's dying to answer back. Very excited, you know, bursting to talk. But she looks back over her shoulder at all those other union people, and then she quiets down.

PATRICE (negotiating committee; administrative assistant, grade 9, Institute for Middle Eastern Studies, Laermer Hall): Rosie starts to whisper to all of us again, when a sound from one of the union guys cuts her off. She goes back to whisper with them instead. Then she comes forward and says, "OK, people, let's have a word from Wanda Parsons, vice president in charge of white-collar organizing. Wanda?"

I've never seen Rosie so happy. Why? The meeting is totally out of control. What was the point of all that arguing we did, making me give in, if people are going to fight like *this?*

ARTHUR (file clerk, grade 4, Business School, Jensen Building): "We're only trying to consider what's in your best interests," that Black woman from the union is saying.

The Black guy behind me waves his hand and yells, "We can decide our interests for ourselves!"

And again, those little scraps of cheers.

MIMI (data entry clerk, grade 5, financial aid, Van Rensselaer Hall): God, that guy is *gorgeous*. Except come on. You know if I ever brought a Black guy home, my whole family would just lay down and die. Not that that would necessarily be a *bad* thing.

ARTHUR (file clerk, grade 4, Business School, Jensen Building): Someone else on stage wants to talk. And Rosie is even saying, "OK, Charles—" But then she sees Hyacinth waving her hand, and she stops and points to her.

When Hyacinth talks, she's real quiet. I like her voice, actually. And something about her—I don't know. She opens her mouth, and suddenly, the whole room gets quiet, too.

HYACINTH (receptionist, grade 4, Business School, Jensen Building): And I say, "People. People! Listen to what we're saying. We cannot do this. We cannot go back to work one more time. We cannot do it."

MIMI (data entry clerk, grade 5, financial aid, Van Rensselaer Hall): The silence just hangs there, around her words.

LISSA (staff secretary, grade 6, geology, Dowling Hall): This very *full* silence—

NINA (faculty secretary, grade 8, history, Philosophy Building):—where we all know something together—

MIMI (data entry clerk, grade 5, financial aid, Van Rensselaer Hall):—and Rosie knows it, too, you can see it go right through her body—

MARGARITA (department secretary, grade 8, engineering, Dowling Hall):—and she gathers that little group up there—

NINA (faculty secretary, grade 8, history, Philosophy Building): And then Tony says, in that sexy accent, "Brothers and sisters, the negotiating committee is proud to present a unanimous proposal to the workers of Olympia University: we unanimously recommend a strike!"

ARTHUR (file clerk, grade 4, Business School, Jensen Building): And we all explode in screaming and cheering, yelling, clapping, the noise is pouring through us, it's like nothing I've ever felt before—

———

NATHAN (BIOP counselor, TEACH program, grade 7, Cadbury Student Center): And all right! Yes! I should not be happy about this, I know it as well as anyone, but *yes! Yes!*

MIMI (data entry clerk, grade 5, financial aid, Van Rensselaer Hall): Well, I guess my mother will be happy after all, because come on. I couldn't exactly walk through a picket line after *this.*

PATRICE (negotiating committee; administrative assistant, grade 9, Institute for Middle Eastern Studies, Laermer Hall): It's amazing, it's like nothing I've ever seen. These people I've been fighting with for months and months, and suddenly, hugging and crying, this amazing celebration. Because finally we did the right thing, finally we stood for ourselves alone, finally we said no to them and yes to us, and now we can do anything, anything, now we can do anything at all.

MONDAY, MAY 2ND, NOON

ROSIE (lead organizer): Teneisha comes bounding in off the picket line, her voice so hoarse from chanting that all she can do is squeak, "Rosie! I want to do something! Give me something to do!"

"Well, Teneisha," I say, "you could be a building captain." Even though Altagracia is already a building captain, Philosophy is a big building. We could certainly use two captains.

"Great!" Teneisha squeaks. "What do I do?"

"Go talk to Altagracia, she'll tell you."

Teneisha nods and bounds off. And again, another surge of happiness, all day, surge after surge. I've never felt anything like it.

Underneath it all is the reality of course: We're totally unprepared. The minute we got out of Reed Hall—after a full fifteen minutes of cheering and stamping and screaming and pandemonium—and of course, Isabel and Wanda and Jurgensen were just livid, and even Charles was mad at me, although he *got* what he wanted, so why? And Jack Kim comes running up through the crowd, pushing and shoving, which is totally unlike him, and then when he gets to me, face to face, he's so angry, he can't speak. But I put all *that* aside the minute we left Reed Hall and rushed for a phone to call Harris, because I wanted to be the one to tell him.

"The workers insisted," I say to his disbelieving, furious silence. "We told them, several times, how serious a strike can be. But you know, once they got a taste of that picket line—"

I *told* him not to do it, if he was just going to send us back to work again. But he insisted, and now his principles have won in spite of himself.

"You know," I say, trying to steady my shaky voice, my beating heart, my wild, unbearable joy, "maybe we shouldn't have put off the strike quite so many times."

"That wasn't us!" Harris roars, and you can hear him at a thousand rallies without even a microphone, shouting into the wind. "Screwing around with our workers—that was the University!

"Anyway," he says irritably, "come on and tell me, Rosie. What is the alignment of forces?"

My God, why does he always sound like such a *pamphlet?* It would serve him right if I told him the truth:

"*Workers:* We're not doing too badly—most of our people are out. But we don't have captains for all the buildings, and even where we do, we never did a training for them—you *said* we weren't going to strike, remember? The captains are supposed to keep track of every single worker, but most of them don't even have the latest building lists. Some people haven't even heard there *is* a strike yet, and how can the captains find them without the lists? And sometimes people need you to walk them out of the office—they're just too shy to go alone—but the captains might not know that.

"*Picket duty:* We can't cover all the entrances, of course, there are just way too many, but we should be able to do the one at the front gates and then the one on Amsterdam Avenue, at the other end of the quad. But do all the building captains know which worker goes where?

"*Work-study students:* Nina *was* in charge of that committee, but she wasn't at our last meeting, so now it's Odessa, but she's never run anything before, and she's pretty nervous about it. At least *she* has the latest work-study list. But does she know that every single one of them has to be called and told about our policy?: 'Call in sick if you can, give us time and support if you can't.' Odessa can't make all those calls herself—that's what the committee is for. But she might not know that.

"*Faculty:* Professor Diamond said he'd organize the faculty—he thought he could get about a third of the professors to teach classes off campus—but *he* didn't know, either, that it was really going to happen.

"*Alumni:* Forget it. We don't even have a committee. And we really should, if this lasts any length of time, because *they're* the ones to hit over graduation."

Of course, if I actually *said* any of this to Harris, it would look like I hadn't done my job. At the moment, all I want to do is throw myself on his mercy and let him tell me what to do. He's been in the union for over fifty years, and I've never even led a strike.

But when I give him my watered-down, Pollyanna version of all that information, it goes better than I expected. Because first, there's a long pause. Then he says, "The workers are your strength, Rosie. Focus on the workers. Your job is to keep the pressure up."

I knew it! He *was* cooking something up with the Olympia president. And now he's blown his part of the deal.

But that's a good thing, isn't it? Now he can say, "Hey, Foster, I tried. But the workers won't listen *unless you give me something.*"

Which means two things.

One, Olympia didn't expect us to strike. So they're not any more prepared than we are.

And two, they *could* just decide to give in. If I—we—keep the pressure up.

Except, three, they *could* decide that now they don't trust Harris at all. So they *could* decide that now they're *really* going to play hardball.

Jesus, if they do that, what will we do? Because all *they* have to do is tough it out till graduation. We can't last even half that long.

VANESSA (staff secretary, grade 6, Mines & Minerals Project, Dowling Hall): When Rosie said I should be building captain, I about fell over. I mean, I knew Rosie respected me and all. But I didn't think it was to the point where she would make me building captain.

Lissa says she'll help, which is good, because you know Dowling. You can never get anybody to do *anything.* So all day long, we've been taking turns. First she goes out on the picket line. And I start making calls, trying to find out where everybody is (work? home? Why are so many numbers missing from this list?!!). And then we switch—she makes the phone calls, and I go out on the picket line.

BH comes out on his lunch hour to see what's going on. We're all marching in the back entrance to the quad, with the B-School people and some of the others, so he has to walk quite a ways out of his way to find us. Because the bar he usually goes to is all the way over on Broadway. But when he gets to us on Amsterdam he just stares and stares. Standing on the corner across the street, watching us march and chant and cheer. Which is hard to do, just for ourselves. There aren't *that* many people coming in once the morning rush is over.

But there's BH, watching and watching. I tell you, it makes the whole damn thing worthwhile. Just to know there's not a damn thing he can do about it.

MARGARITA (department secretary, grade 8, engineering, Dowling Hall): When the decision came down, you know, in Reed Hall, my first thought was to go home to take care of Bobby. Because Teresa had been working all night, and she could use some time off. And I could also use a nap.

But Lissa grabs me on the way out of Reed Hall and says come on over to the picket line. I wanted to at least see what it was like. And when I get there, I have to help out at least a little. So I walk around and shout with the others, although, you know. I feel kind of stupid doing it with no one to watch us. At least if we were at the *front* entrance. But no, we're Dowling, so of course, we get the back.

Then Vanessa comes up, all important, and gives me a *schedule*. I mean, she's not my boss. She's not even a grade 8, like me, just a grade 6. Saying Rosie told her to do it. "Did Rosie tell you to give me personally a schedule?" I ask her. "Did Rosie tell you how I was supposed to take care of my grandson? Or all the other things I have to do?"

She stands there, her hand on her hip. Her big skeptical look, but you don't fool me, *chica*. You're no better than anybody else. "Oh, like I *don't* have kids at home?" she's saying. "I mean, yeah, OK, two of them are in school. But the third one's with a sitter. Who I have to *pay*. And on strike benefits—you think I'm happy about that? But *I'm* not going home."

"That's your business," I say.

Then Lissa steps in, trying to be nice. "But Margarita?" she says in that little voice. "That's the point? That we all have to stick together? Because otherwise? The University will see—I mean, they'll think we're weak? And we're not? But we don't want to look that way? Do we?"

That spoiled little white girl makes me so tired, I can't tell you. Her parents could send her money, couldn't they? She's from Wisconsin or someplace—they all have money out there.

"People with kids should have a different schedule," I say. "And why are there *two* picket lines anyway? Why not just one out front? Then there would be more people, and we would look stronger."

Vanessa looks like she's going to jump in with some other snotty thing. But Lissa gets there first.

"Rosie says it's important to be at both ends of the quad?" she says. "Because otherwise? It's like they can forget about us once they've crossed the first one?"

Well, I guess that makes *some* sense. Even if there are at least three other entrances with nobody at them.

All the same. If Teresa needs me to go home, I'm going. That's what I'd tell my boss—I don't let *him* push me around. Why should it be any different with the union?

NATHAN (BIOP counselor, TEACH program, grade 7, Cadbury Student Center): When we all leave Reed Hall, I feel high, I admit it. All the way walking over to my office, I feel lifted up by *something*. You *know* I've felt that feeling before. I just did not expect to feel it *here*.

So I keep turning it over and over in my mind—why? Rosie is nice enough, but she's not *my* sister. And the brothers and sisters on the committee, forget it, right? What are *they* doing for our people?

Still, I felt it. And when it came time to call the question, *no* question. I *knew* which side I belonged on. Even though, frankly, I did *not* want to know. Being that now I have to go back to my office and say to my supervisor, "Ruth, I'm on strike." Which was not what she expected to hear.

"Nathan, why?" she says. "All the work we got to do over here, and you're going to just walk out? Is this a holiday to you?"

"You had to be there," is what I want to say. But that sounds light. And if I say I could not go along with them giving in to the enemy, she would want to know why the University is the enemy I'm choosing to focus on. They're not the *main* enemy.

"You're going to leave me with all this work and a full calendar—" Ruth is so shocked, she can't even finish the sentence. "You got six students coming in this morning, and Keith wanting help on his term paper this afternoon, you said you'd find Dalila another apartment, or leastways a roommate, and Abdul needs a math tutor—and you are just going to *walk out* on that? Is money *all* you care about, Nathan? Vacation, seniority, some old pension fund? Nathan, we got *work* to do here."

And I know this, of course I know it. "Something happened in that room, Ruth," is all I could say to her, and angry as she is, I don't say it. Being as how I couldn't tell her what.

I go over to the picket line at the front gate, and Rosie is so glad to see me, she comes bounding over right away.

"Nathan!" she calls, breathless, about a million pieces of paper bursting out of her arms. She hands me a big stack. "Basic information," she explains, "about strike benefits and protocol and like that. How would you like—I know, you just got here. But everybody needs to get one. Could you—?"

I give her this *look,* you know. Not unfriendly. Just so she knows I know.

"You been trying to get me on the union's side this whole past year," I say. "And now you want me out there where everybody can see, giving out union literature."

She doesn't bother to deny it. She says, "Nathan, look over there." She points to the big old-fashioned administration building, the one that always makes you think of all those rich young gentlemen, coming here to school. "That's them," she says.

Then she points to this straggly little group of people on the picket line— just Olympia workers, now, plus a handful of students and one lone professor, who must have either tenure or no sense. Maybe a hundred people, which is not bad, but still. Barely a dent in the crowd.

"That's us," she says.

She looks at me. "We can win," she says. "I believe we can. But it's going to take everything we have. I can talk this way to you because you get that already, right, Nathan? You get it about struggle and long odds and how it's fucking impossible, excuse my language, but impossible or not, you do it anyway.

"So what do you want, Nathan? You want me to pretend it *doesn't* matter which side you're on, you of all people? You want me to wait until *you're* ready? The time is now. We need you now. Are you with us or against us? What's it going to be?"

If she had been sweet about it, I probably would have told her to go fight her own battles. I might even have gone back to Ruth and kept my appointments. But I guess she shames me. Because I find myself taking the leaflets and handing them round, on the main picket line here on Broadway, and then on the one on Amsterdam. Then I take the extras over to the union office, where the Latina lady asks if I'll make phone calls, trying to find all the workers who they think went home.

And it's not until I'm up to the fourth call or maybe the fifth that I get it— she totally played me with that speech. I mean, totally.

Am I *that* easy? Or did she know what would move me? And then speak truth to *that?*

MONDAY, MAY 2ND, 4 P.M.

ARTHUR (file clerk, grade 4, Business School, Jensen Building): After we got done with the meeting, after we had all poured out of Reed Hall onto the quad, there was the strangest feeling. This incredible thing we had just done—we were all so high.

My first thought was to call David and tell him, but my second thought was *no*. Because I knew what he would say, and frankly, I didn't want to hear it. So I suppose I'm relieved when Jack comes by, half pissed off and half excited, and says, "OK, Arthur, let's go."

And I'm like, "Where?"

And he's like, "We figured out that if there *was* a strike—" and then he gets this little "I told you so" kind of smile, but he makes it go away. "—then we B-School people would take the Amsterdam side. Because there's a lot of us, and we're pretty well organized, so that way we could be sure of having the back entrance covered. Since everybody who *doesn't* know where to go will probably float toward the front gate."

So we get to the back entrance, and sure enough, there are all these other people from the B-School. So if they knew where to go, why didn't I? Later I find out that there is someone from each floor whose job it was to find everybody else. It was just coincidence that Jack saw me, because Trudi is my floor captain, I guess they call it. I think they call Jack the building captain. It's nice, actually, that it's so well-organized. Jack says, of all the buildings on campus, ours is far and away the *best* organized.

So the floor captains go talk to all of us, and then the five of them meet with Jack, and somehow they put everything we said together to make a picket schedule. We each get four hours a day, which seems like a lot. But otherwise, Jack says, there won't be at least twenty of us on the line at all times, because we can't count on anybody from any of the other buildings, which he says are really disorganized. And the other four hours—assuming that we're here for the regular eight-hour day, strike or no strike, which I guess is what it's supposed to be—the other four hours, we're supposed to go over to the union office, and Jack says that someone there will tell us what to do.

So I'm on the picket line this afternoon, and either it's the most boring thing in the world, or else time just disappears. Marching around and around and around. Chanting and shouting. *What do we want? A contract. When do we want it? NOW!!!* And *I don't know, but I've been told, Olympia's pockets are lined with gold.* I don't really like all the yelling, but I guess I see why we have to.

Hyacinth has the same schedule as me. Half the time, she's so quiet, you can't get a word out of her. The other half the time, she's shouting at the top of her voice, like she's praying, or testifying, or whatever it is they call it. Or else she's going on and on and on to whoever happens to be walking near her—which for some reason is often me—talking about how is she going to feed her kids on a hundred dollars a week.

"What about you?" she says finally, in that sing-songy voice, that accent from the Islands. "What are you and your—friend—going to do?"

I hate the way everyone always says "friend" like that. Say "boyfriend," I want to say. Just go ahead and say it. But I just say, "Well, he'll be pissed. But he's working, so—" I shrug.

"That's nice," she says. "That there are two of you. To help each other."

She seems to mean it. "Well," I say, "I'm sorry it's going to be so hard for you. With your kids."

She shrugs. "My mother will watch them," she says. "If she knows I'm not earning, she'll give them dinner. And breakfast in the morning. I'll pack them lunch, though, because otherwise. They wouldn't eat any food I cook. Which I think is not right. If they eat only my mother's food, they'll think *she* is their mother. And she'll think . . ."

"She won't understand that—that this is something you just *had* to do," I say when her voice trails off.

Then she smiles. This tiny little shy smile. "Oh, well," she says. "Let her think what she wants, right? As long as she feeds my children. Let her think whatever disgraceful thing she wants."

MIMI (data entry clerk, grade 5, financial aid, Van Rensselaer Hall): See, it wasn't just for the health insurance that I left We Care For You. There was another reason.

It was this one time, a lot of their personal shoppers were out sick—I guess some flu had been going around the office, and of course, me, I'm never sick, and I *had* been there over a year and a half. I guess they thought they could trust me. So they sent me out to this customer's house in some fancy suburb, the richest part of Upper Montclair, New Jersey, this huge, beautiful house, and when I got there, there's a Black woman in the kitchen cooking dinner and a Hispanic woman in the back yard taking care of the kids, and, I kid you not, an Asian woman there pinning up the woman's hem—I mean, she had this whole entire *staff.* And she was very friendly to everybody, she had these little nicknames for every one of them—*Lili* for Tsien Li, the Asian woman, and *Mari* for Marisol, the Hispanic woman, and *Titi* for Tawana, the Black woman—and they all smiled at her and seemed happy and friendly, and that right there just made me sick. Because either they *did* think of themselves as her family—except I notice none of them had any little nicknames for *her.* But OK, maybe they really did feel like her family. Which made me sick in one way. Or else they were pretending like they did. Which made me sick in another way.

So I came out there with all of the We Care For You catalogues—they have huge stacks of all the latest, Neiman Marcus and The Caviar Shoppe and Bendel's and F.A.O. Schwartz and information from all the little specialty shops that don't *have* catalogues, and the personal shopper is supposed to know what the customer is likely to want and have several appropriate suggestions ready, and this was a present for her oldest daughter, who was about to be confirmed—no, whatever Jewish people call it. Bat Mitzvah. And there was going to be a *huge* party that cost as much as a *wedding*. And this big expensive gift that *I* was supposed to pick out. And go buy. And get wrapped. I'm surprised they didn't want me to write the card.

The woman was perfectly nice to me, just the way she was to all the other people she had working for her that day, and she even gave *me* a special little affectionate nickname—Mia. And I felt just like her servant.

I mean, given what I was there to do, I suppose I *was* her servant. But why? Wasn't it just another job to do? I mean, if she wanted to pay me $25.00 an hour to shop for her—or to cook her dinner, or take care of her kids, or scrub her goddamn toilet, for that matter, what difference did it make to me? I just wanted the money.

But it wasn't just that, that's what I'm trying to tell you. I was like a piece of paper towel that she used to wipe her counter and then threw away. I was there *for her*. Do you know what I mean? Like she got this phone call in the middle of our discussion, and she didn't even say "Excuse me." Because I was getting paid, so why should she excuse herself? And even if she had said "Excuse me," it would have been to show how nice she was to her servants. Like apologizing to the toilet brush.

So I guess what I'm trying to say is, they shouldn't take us for granted. I guess I do care about that.

MONDAY, MAY 2ND, 10:30 P.M.
NINA (faculty secretary, grade 8, history, Philosophy Building): It's been a long day. I had picket duty in the morning, and in the afternoon, I came over here, to the union office, and Isabel had me looking up home phone numbers, this horrible long list—worse than *anything* I have to do in my office, where that's the kind of thing that Teneisha usually does. And then Rosie shows up at about five-thirty, looking absolutely exhausted and totally worried and completely thrilled, and arranges for us to call in for pizza, the union's treat, and then she throws me and Odessa and a bunch of other people into one corner of the room and tells us to figure out what the work-study committee is sup-

posed to do now. And she hands me an agenda—so I guess I am the Chair again, even though I missed that other meeting. Seems to me like Odessa is offended, except I do think I'd do a better job, but I don't want her mad at me.

And all this time, Simon is tagging along. On the picket line, he shouts and chants with the rest of us, and let me tell you, the other secretaries are thrilled to have him, because, you know, a lot of them still think the students *matter*.

So Simon is there, chanting with me on the picket line, and taking assignments in the union office, and trying to be helpful at our committee meeting, which I must admit, he does in a *very* nice way. Respectful. And he makes suggestions. And jokes. And yes, he's cute.

So why did I call it *tagging along?* Maybe because he had all term to look like he was interested in me. Why pick now?

Anyway, now it's ten-thirty, and Rosie gives us this tired smile, and says, "Go home, people. Tomorrow we get to do it all again!"

Then she makes a special effort with Simon, because of course, we *do* want the students on our side, and nobody's done nearly as much as he has. Of course, Rosie doesn't know that's because he was spending the day with me.

So she says, "And Simon! Talk about above and beyond the call of duty! How can we ever thank you enough?"

Simon shrugs. "Just my little attempt at solidarity," he says. "Academic workers, clerical workers, common enemy, common interest."

Rosie smiles. Then he says, "You're Flip's sister, aren't you? I saw you at the memorial. For Mario, I mean. You spoke."

Rosie looks completely startled. "Yes," she says finally. "I was there. I'm sorry, I didn't—"

"Oh, you *wouldn't* have met me," Simon says. "I was pretty much hanging back as far as I *could* get. But I liked your speech."

"Thank you," says Rosie.

"I'm sorry I didn't get to Flip's show tonight," he says. "You must be, too. But of course, for something like this—I'm sure he'll understand."

"His show?" says Rosie. "You must mean with Tiger's Eye," she adds slowly. "And the first show was tonight?"

"Yesterday afternoon, actually," Simon says. "But he told us not to come to that one. He wasn't sure how it would go. Then this morning he called and said, OK, we could come today. Apparently the one yesterday went well enough that we finally had permission. But then—" he gestures around the office. "I left him a message, of course. But when you talk to him, tell him I had a really good excuse, OK?"

Rosie twists her mouth. "Oh, you can probably get back on his good side if you go eventually," she says. "Just tell him you knew his work would get better later in the run." She looks at her watch, even though there's a clock right there behind Simon on the wall. "I'm sorry," she says, "I've got to try to make some of these phone calls before it really is too late to bother people at home. But thanks again, Simon. Nina, you're coming back tomorrow morning, right? We need people at the front gates by eight."

"I'll be there," I say, and we both look at Simon.

"I'm not sure," he says, looking uncomfortable for the first time today. "I'll have to see."

"Well, come back anytime," Rosie says. "Our office is your office." She gives me this very warm hug and kiss goodbye.

So we leave her there with the phone, and Simon says, as we walk out of the office, "So, you want to get something to eat?"

"Why are you being so nice to me?" I say as the door shuts behind us. I can't help it, the words just burst out of me. "I thought you were involved."

Simon winces and laughs at the same time.

"Well, involved," he says. "What does *that* mean anymore?"

"What *does* it mean?" I say. "That's what I'm asking."

"You don't fool around, do you?" Simon says, but you know. Affectionately. "Do you have any objections to having this conversation while we eat something? Or do you need to know my—well, *marital* is hardly the right word, is it? And probably *romantic* isn't either. My *involvement* status—do you need to know my involvement status before any food is actually consumed?"

So of course I have to laugh. "It depends on the food," I say.

So we go to this little coffee shop a few blocks down Broadway, where I order an eggplant parmesan sub and he has a grilled cheese sandwich and a bowl of chicken soup.

"The food of my childhood," he explains. "It's what I always get when I'm tired and confused."

"And you're confused because—?"

So finally he tells me all about this guy Ian he's been going out with—I *knew* he was gay! Apparently, they have an open relationship, which, I mean, give me a break. Everybody knows *those* never work.

Not Simon, though. "I don't know," he's saying as he takes a bite of his sandwich. He even got American cheese—he really *must* be thinking of his childhood. "It's not the principle of the thing that bothers me—"

"It's the money," I say before I can help myself, and he laughs.

"It's the *way* he handles it," he goes on. "Like what happened on Saturday, which I really am sorry about, by the way. It wasn't that he *changed* our plans. If he had, believe me, I would have kept *our* date." He waves his free hand back and forth between us. "I would never have put you in the middle like that. It wasn't that he *changed* plans. It was that there were three different sets of plans, depending on which day you referred back to."

"Does he date women, too?"

Simon looks completely startled. "I don't think so," he says. "I mean, he was married, but as far as I know, that was pretty much it for him in that department."

"But you do."

"Well, I *have*," he says. "I suppose that means I do." He takes another bite, chews. "I don't really think of it as men or women," he says with his mouth full. "It's just, you know. Who the person happens to be. Although lately, of course, it has been mainly men."

"Mainly men or mainly—" It feels way too weird to actually say his name. "—or mainly *him?*"

Simon looks startled again. "Oh, well, a bit of both, I suppose," he says. "Mainly Ian *and* mainly men. Though, honestly, he can be infuriating. As I seem to keep repeating."

"So why do you stay with him?" I say, sitting up straighter in the vinyl booth.

Simon shrugs. "Why does anyone ever do anything when they're in love?"

"But why *do* you put up with it? The open relationship business?"

"I don't consider it *putting up with*," Simon says very seriously. "I consider it what I want, too. I mean, it *is* what I want, too. I just want a—a different version of it, that's all."

"Hm," I say, before I can help myself.

"Hm, what?"

"Well. It just *doesn't* sound like what you want, that's all."

He gives me a long, *long* look. And when I don't look away, he smiles. Although underneath, he looks even sadder. "Who knows?" he says, reaching for the check. "You could be right." And when I start to open my purse, he says, "I may be a starving graduate student, but you just went on strike. Besides, I owe you one for Saturday. Not that I consider this an adequate substitute."

We leave the coffee shop and Simon walks me to the subway. "Are you taking this train, too?" I ask when we get to the station.

"No," he says absent-mindedly. "I'll probably just get a bus downtown." Well, he's hardly going to take a bus all the way out to Brooklyn, which I happen to know is where he lives. So where *is* he going from here?

He's looking at me. "Thank you for letting me spend the day with you and your fellow workers," he says. "It's the nicest thing I've done in a long time, Nina, really, it is, so really. Thank you."

"You're welcome," I am about to say, but he's already kissing me. This amazing kiss that I did not at all expect. It goes on and on and on, and it seems to get softer and more gentle and more personal, and all *right*. More *loving*. And then afterward, the feeling that anything could happen. The feeling that anything *has*.

ROSIE (lead organizer): It's midnight, and I'm finally walking up the stairs to my apartment, too thrilled, too exhausted, too terrified, to even *think* of stopping by the deli for ice cream. At the moment it's all I can do to unlock the front door, grab my mail, and climb the stairs.

I drop my bags and turn on the answering machine in one single motion, and there is Michael's voice: "So, Rosie, now that you're about to go on strike, you're never going to call me again, for the whole, entire, total and complete rest of my life? Was I supposed to, like, expect that?" The machine beeps. Then Harris, with his braying New York accent, his wobbly, old-man's voice: "I tried to get you three times at the union office this afternoon, and each time, the line was busy! What kind of attitude does that convey to our members? The workers should feel that they always have access to their union!" Oh, give me a break.

I look down at my mail: junk, junk, junk, something from Flip. A large, square, heavy envelope—a wedding invitation, obviously. But the postmark says April 12th. Why is it only reaching me now?

Isabel's voice: "Rosie! Our lawyer just called me—Olympia has made another proposal. Ay, Rosie, it's really bad, you know. No minority salary fund—they want to just abolish it. In exchange for a big raise. Bad, bad, bad."

You're telling me. A whole year of negotiations with them chipping away at that fund, but they never asked to abolish it outright. So they want to buy us out *now*? Even if I wanted to go along with it, Harris would never approve.

I open the invitation. Tucked in behind the cream-colored return envelope, is a humble little white xeroxed sheet, folded up, the wrong size for the envelope. I pull it out—a schedule of his performances.

I look at the clock. Nearly 12:30. Really, really, really, too late to call. And there's Isabel again, on the machine: "Rosie, Rosie, this is *not* good, not good at all. Because maybe some of the members, you know, are going to want to take this deal. So we have to make sure, Rosie, really really sure, that the committee understands: they have to say *no*. Call me, Rosie, right away, we'll figure it out."

I hit the stop button and dial Isabel's number. I've obviously woken her up, but she brushes aside my apologies and asks me what I plan to do.

"Look, Isabel. Let's not underestimate our own members. You know they know better than this. Maybe one or two of them will think this is a good idea. But most of them understand how important the minority salary fund is. They won't sell it out."

"Well, let's not take any chances," Isabel says sharply. "Really, Rosie, this isn't the time. You meet with that committee first thing tomorrow, and you just make sure they vote this down, pronto, before anybody has a chance to find out."

Her tone makes me bristle but I try to keep my voice even. "Actually, Isabel, I don't agree. I think something like this, the University is sure to leak it. Or start rumors, or *something* to make us look bad. Of course we have to start with the committee—that's obvious. But I think we should go on the offensive here. After the committee votes it down, we *should* take it to the members. If *they* vote it down, too, the University will see that they can't get away with this shit. Excuse my language."

Isabel is so upset, she can barely speak. "You can't take that kind of chance, Rosie. Excuse me, but it's crazy. Get the committee to vote *no,* and then that's the end of it. You *can* control your own committee?"

"I don't *control* them," I say, sounding just like Charles, I must admit. "They *do* get to vote on their own. But I do *trust* them, Isabel. I trust the members, too." I reach for the words that I know will shut her up. "Harris *told* me to trust the members. Don't *you* think that's a good idea?"

Isabel sputters, but she has to give in. She even agrees to make half the calls tomorrow morning, alerting the committee to show up for a 9 a.m. meeting.

One more message on the answering machine, a very faint and tired voice, "Hi, Rosie! It's a boy. I love you. Twenty-four hours of labor, and I was going to call you—I mean, I did call you, but you were never in, and I didn't want to leave *that* message on your machine, that I was in labor, I mean, because you'd have been worried and tried to call, and you couldn't have, of course, but now—we're all fine. At least, I think I'm fine. I'll know more in a few hours. Or eighteen years, whichever comes first. Don't call *now,* obviously, I'm totally gone. I'll try again when I wake up."

Well, Flip getting married, and Marcy having a baby. If I had room for any other feeling, I might feel desolate. But blank and terrified is all I have room to feel.

TUESDAY, MAY 3RD, 4 A.M.

ARTHUR (file clerk, grade 4, Business School, Jensen Building): The sound of a gasp, and I wake up suddenly, sitting up fast in bed. What happened? What happened?? Nothing, nothing, it's all right. David is right here, the sound of his breathing loud and weird in the dark blue light. I think it's started to rain. Or is that just the refrigerator dripping? We started defrosting it last night, and it's one of those really old ones, the kind you have to defrost by hand, and you have to keep getting up and changing the defrost tray, because otherwise it overflows—

OK, so the Discover card isn't due until the third week in May, so we can let that go, except if we're late *again,* what if they take away the card? And the Mastercard is two months past due already, but I was supposed to pay that with *this* check. How did David ever think we could go to Puerto Rico?

David wasn't mad, not really, when he heard about the strike. He just sighed and said, "Oh, well, I guess these things happen. How long do you think it will last?" And of course I didn't know, because no matter how many times I asked Jack, he said *he* didn't know and he wouldn't even guess, it all depended on how militant we were prepared to be. Which sounded good at the time, but you know. It's not something I could say to the people at Mastercard.

MARGARITA (department secretary, grade 8, engineering, Dowling Hall): "What is it?" Cecy's voice, whining, whispering in my ear. Her hot breath. The smell of her chips and beer, the food we ate together before she fell asleep in front of the television set and I had to wake her and walk her into bed.

"It's nothing, Cecy, nothing. Just Bobby. Go back to sleep."

"I could—"

"No, no. I'll go. Go back to sleep."

"But you," she says, and then she's asleep, her mouth still open. I think she has a little bit of a cold coming on—her nose seems kind of clogged up. She probably caught it from Bobby.

"Gramma, gramma, gramma, gramma, gramma!!!!" At least he knows to ask for me and not Teresa tonight.

"What, Bobo?" I say, my little pet name for him. "What's the matter? Tell *Abuelita.* What? What do you want?"

But he doesn't answer. He just keeps repeating, "Gramma, Gramma, Gramma!!" in his angry, tired voice. Like somehow I'll figure it out.

NINA (faculty secretary, grade 8, history, Philosophy Building): Waking up, falling back asleep, waking up, falling back asleep. It's been like this all night, but I don't mind. Bathed in the memory of that kiss. Hope is one thing, but this *happened*.

HYACINTH (receptionist, grade 4, Business School, Jensen Building): Dreaming of blue water, blue, blue water with green lights in it, warm and salty and so clean and clear. Diving down. And when I get deep enough, an undersea garden. Lime-green fronds, and pink anemones, and red-orange coral full of a million little animals. And suddenly I'm tiny, too, and standing on the threshold of the coral reef, all the many little openings, only now they're big, and I'm going inside, into an enormous palace, high arched ceilings, red light, and weird fish swimming over my head. I stand here, watching them all swim. I'm nervous, but not frightened.

Do I belong here? I don't know. But it's an interesting place to be. I can stay and watch a little longer. Before I go back home.

ROSIE (lead organizer): The phone rings me out of my sleep, yanking me up by the hair. Finally, without my meaning to, my hand shoots out to make it stop.

"Rosie?" Michael's voice. I'm too tired to answer. "Rosie?" he says again. "What's going on? Why didn't you call me?"

"I'm asleep," I manage to say.

"I waited up," he says doggedly. "Because I thought you might need something." He sounds wretched. "You must fucking need *something*, Rosie. Just not me." His voice rises. "Rosie? I'm supposed to take care of you."

"Oh," I say flatly. "Because you're the *man*."

"Yeah, *right*," he says desperately. "So? Is that like so terrible?"

I sit up slowly, trying to clear my head. "Why is that what you want, Michael? I don't get it. Of all the things in the world to want, why in God's name do you want *that?*"

"Because otherwise——" he says, and then his voice dries up.

"Because otherwise, what good are you?" I say. "Is that what you were going to say, Michael? You want to take care of me so you'll know what *good* you are?" I knew this was how he felt. I *knew* it.

"Where do you *get* this stuff, Rosie?" he says uneasily. But I ride right over him.

"That's what *I'm* good for? You won't talk to me about *your* fucking problems, you won't let me take care of *you* for five fucking minutes, but now that I'm going through fucking *hell* with this fucking *strike,* you wake me up at four in the morning to take *care* of me? So you'll know how *good* you are?"

"You really twist it all around, don't you?" he says when I finally take a breath.

"But that's all you ever want," I say. "God, Michael. It's like you want my *life.*"

I expect this to shut him up. But he says, "No, Rosie. You're the one who wants *my* life. You have to keep talking about everything racial—"

"Well, it's all right there, Michael. What am I supposed to do, *not* talk about it?"

"*Yes,*" he bursts out, each word full of longing. "*Don't* talk about it. Don't keep like telling me you have all this *power*—I *know* you do, Rosie. But you don't."

Long pause. Finally, I say, "I don't get it, Michael. What are you saying?"

"You want it to be yours," he says in this voice I've never heard from him before. "That racial stuff. But it isn't yours. It's *mine.*"

"Why can't it be ours?"

"Because," he says. "Everything always ends up just the way you want it."

"Is that my fault? You never fight back."

"I don't want to fight back," he says, and I can't tell if he sounds longing, or angry, or if he's playing with me again. "I just want . . ."

". . . to take care of me," I say when he leaves a long silence. And I can't tell if I sound discouraged, or angry, or maybe, also, longing.

"Is that such a bad thing?" he says again. I don't know how to answer.

"Rosie?" he says when I still don't say anything. "Like, what do you want to do?"

"We could both just go to sleep."

"See?" he says in that slippery, teasing voice, except now it sounds different. "You're the one who never tells *me.* What *you* want, Rosarita. In *your* life."

I want to win the strike. Even though I know that's not an answer. I want to win the strike, and get some sleep, and eat all the chocolate ice cream that I want. And I want to see Michael—yes, I *do* want to see him. Only—

"I don't know how to think about my life," I hear myself saying. "Apart from—I don't know. The *world,* Michael. My life is in the world."

"Like, that's what I love about you, Rosie," Michael is saying desperately. "It always has been." And I believe him. I do. I'm just not sure what good it does.

TUESDAY, MAY 3RD, 6:30 A.M.

PATRICE (negotiating committee; administrative assistant, grade 9, Institute for Middle Eastern Studies, Laermer Hall): The phone rings at 6:30 a.m.— just imagine calling someone at that hour of the morning. I would be ashamed. Nikos doesn't even want me to answer it.

Of course, we always are up at quarter to six. Because we have to get Eugenia to the day care center by eight, and Nikos has to be at work at seventhirty, so without an early start, we haven't got a prayer. "Nikos," I say, "what do you care? We were up anyway."

"That's no excuse," he says. "This is family time."

It's that woman Isabel, who I don't like so much. She's even pushier than Rosie. So she says, "Good morning, Patrice. Olympia has made us a counterproposal, and we need every member of the negotiating committee to meet at nine sharp. You'll be there, won't you? Because you're a very important member of the negotiating committee, and we really can't do it without you."

I don't care what she says, it sounds fake. Still, I want to know what the counter-proposal is. When I ask, Isabel sighs dramatically. But somehow she sounds scared.

"They want to abolish the minority salary fund," she says. "Just cut it out completely. They'll give African-American and Latino workers an extra-big raise this year, but then that's it."

"Really?" I know the union thinks that fund is very important, but I never so much saw the point. Of course, I'm a grade 9, so I *get* a good salary. And Rosie has told me many, many times that all the grade 9s are white except for one Korean girl, so, she says, that's the reason. But I say, I didn't get to be a grade 9 for nothing. And if some *other* people would work instead of complaining, maybe they wouldn't *need* a fund.

"Actually, you'll all get a big raise if you abolish the fund," Isabel says, but you know. Like she doesn't want to say it. So now we're supposed to stay on strike till they get *their* fund? Even though they're getting a bigger raise than we are? That doesn't sound right.

"And the sexual harassment language," Isabel is saying. "They insist on making it weaker. They say that sexual harassment isn't really a problem at the University anymore. And with the current language, too many workers would claim they'd been harassed, just to get a transfer. So what they want to do is—"

She goes on, but now I'm busy watching Nikos give Genie her cereal and wondering if we should pack juice or milk for her lunch.

"Look," I say, trying really hard not to be rude, but she's just running on and on. "I'll be there, all right? I have to go now. My daughter is crying."

"Oh, you have a daughter? So do I. How old is yours? What's her name?"

"Eugenia," I say unwillingly. Now Genie is banging her spoon on the tray, which means that in two seconds, she'll either be yelling or dumping the cereal over the edge. I motion to Nikos to get her some of the banana from the table. "We call her Genie. She's eighteen months."

"Oh, that's a darling age," Isabel says. "Mine's three. Blanca."

Genie is stuffing banana into her mouth with one hand and reaching for her cereal bowl with the other. I motion for Nikos to shove the cereal bowl out of her reach, and then, of course, she starts to wail. Spewing out pieces of banana.

"There she goes," I say. "I'll see you at nine."

"If you can come a little earlier?" Isabel is saying. "Because then we could—" But I am already hanging up.

We get Genie calmed down and cleaned up, and then, for a few minutes, it's quiet. Nikos finds the cup of coffee I left on the counter when the phone rang and brings it over to the table. "What did she want?" he asks, handing me the cup, and I tell him.

"So we could end it all today, it sounds like," I say, sipping the coffee, which is lukewarm by now.

Nikos shakes his head. "You don't want to give back that fund," he says, passing me the milk.

"Why not?" I say. "We all get a big raise. Of course, *they* get a bigger one. But then the strike would be over."

Nikos shakes his head harder than ever. "No, no, no, no, *no*," he says, and I am surprised at how bitter he sounds. "You never give *anything* back. They take too much already."

"They're *giving* us a raise," I say, annoyed. Two whole years I'm on the committee, nothing from him but complaints, and now all of a sudden he knows what we should do?

Nikos reaches for the washcloth and wipes some banana off Genie's forehead. "Don't be stupid," he says. "A raise is just for this time. That fund, it's permanent, right?"

"I guess."

"Well, so?" he says, tossing the washcloth over into the sink. "Something permanent or something temporary—which is better, Patrice? They're offering you a bad trade because they think you're stupid. They think we're all stupid. Don't fall for it."

TUESDAY, MAY 3RD, 7:30 A.M.

NATHAN (BIOP counselor, TEACH program, grade 7, Cadbury Student Center): All right. So if I'm going to do this, I'm going to *do* it, right? So here I am, *early,* on this special picket line out by the loading dock. So that the Teamsters who drive the trucks will just go right on by. Because, yes, the *law* says they have to cross our picket line, but you know they don't. They find some excuse—no one was there to sign for the delivery, or it turned out they had the wrong stuff, or even, "We were scared of getting beat up, boss. You know, those crazy strikers." Getting beat up by *secretaries,* right. Anyway, the drivers just sail on by.

All right, so this is power. But power for *what?*

ARTHUR (file clerk, grade 4, Business School, Jensen Building): It's better during the day, of course. It's better in the daylight. I go sponge the water out of the fridge, and David says, "Well, I better get going. *Somebody* in this family has to earn a living," but at least he didn't say it in a *mean* way. I mean, he *might* have meant it as a joke.

And when I get to Olympia at my regular work time, eight-forty-five—because I always like to be a little early—and there is the picket line already set up, with Jack and Trudi and Hyacinth already there, then, I don't know. It's ours, isn't it? What a weird thing to want. But it's ours.

VANESSA (staff secretary, grade 6, Mines & Minerals Project, Dowling Hall): I'm there right at nine, of course, because, you know. What if BH came out to check up on us? *He* always gets to work by eight-thirty, so he can be there when Lissa and I come in. Like that puts him one up on us, when *he's* the one doing the extra time.

But it means, too, that if we're even one minute late, he knows. And just in case he's watching today, I don't want him thinking I come one second later for my union and my picket line than I do for *his* old job. He doesn't respect me in there, fine. That's his problem. But he doesn't respect me out here? Not if I have anything to say about it.

———

LISSA (staff secretary, grade 6, geology, Dowling Hall): Well, I am kind of the *vice* building captain. I mean, Vanessa would *call* me co-captain if I wanted her to, but I don't, I'd rather just help out quietly behind the scenes and let Vanessa tell people what to do. She's better at that than I am.

But I *was* here at ten to nine, and she wasn't, so I was the one who talked to the guy from the union, Nathan, who brought over the literature for today. And he told me that the negotiating committee is meeting again, so when Vanessa got here, I told *her,* and so now we both think, well, I mean, of course, they *have* to have a new proposal from Olympia, wouldn't you think?

So what could it be? "Something good," I tell Vanessa, "better than before. Or else why would they bother?" Then I stop. Unless we made them mad, I think. Unless we made them mad and now they're going to *crush* us.

HYACINTH (receptionist, grade 4, Business School, Jensen Building): Maybe a day care center on campus. It wasn't even in the demands before. But maybe now, you know. To pacify us.

Or a day care allowance, even. That would be something.

MARGARITA (department secretary, grade 8, engineering, Dowling Hall): Most places don't have unions, you know. You get what they feel like giving you. Most places don't have pensions for secretaries, or even health insurance, and I *need* that.

So it's like a prison here, sometimes, you know? Because I can't ever afford to leave.

NINA (faculty secretary, grade 8, history, Philosophy Building): We're walking around on the picket line, there at the front gates, and Teneisha is telling me about some book she's been reading for her Psych course. "Nina!" she says. "Do you think people just *are* a certain way, and they go on getting more and more *like* that? Or do you think people can, like, really change?"

Well, it beats thinking about Simon, who has neither shown up nor left a message. And it's better than wondering what the negotiating committee is doing, which is what everybody *else* is talking about.

"You know, Nina," she goes on. "This idea that you get rid of all the bad stuff that happened to you, the whole time you were growing up. And then you're back to your true self—your *authentic* self, they call it. The self you were meant to be."

She looks up at me, that happy little terrier look. "Which I think is, like, really cool, all right? Except then you're just going backwards. To somewhere you should never have left in the first place."

"Like Dorothy," I say.

"Who?"

"In *The Wizard of Oz,* you know, that movie?" She doesn't know it. So I tell her the plot.

"Oh, right," she says. "I got you. Diana Ross in *The Wiz.*" We're walking around and around in circles. Sometimes we yell with everybody, sometimes we don't.

"Right," I say. "Dorothy has to go all that way. Just so she can go back to exactly where she already was."

Teneisha shakes her head. "I don't like it," she says. "I like Psych, you know, why people do the crazy things they do. But what are they saying? That my true self was some baby? I should get back to *that?*"

"As opposed to what?" I say. Maybe I'm just tired, but this has got to be the most interesting conversation I've ever had with her.

Teneisha thinks. *"What do we want?"* we both yell, our minds elsewhere. *"A contract! When do we want it? NOW!"*

"Is that what *you* want, Nina?" she says finally. "To get back to your *true* self?"

We both giggle.

"Not me," I say. "I want to be a whole *other* self."

"But, girl. You're supposed to love yourself. Because if you don't, who will? And how can you love yourself if you don't want to *be* yourself?"

"I don't want to *not* be myself," I say. "I just want to be *new.* A whole new self." I do, too. I just don't know where to get it.

NATHAN (BIOP counselor, TEACH program, grade 7, Cadbury Student Center): So now they're calling us to yet another meeting. At twelve-thirty in Reed Hall. Some new proposal from Olympia. That's all they'll say. Of course, there are rumors, all up and down the line.

So we walk into Reed Hall, and it's like yesterday, only different. Because now we've done something, all of us. So today we walk in looking to be rewarded.

PATRICE (negotiating committee; administrative assistant, grade 9, Institute for Middle Eastern Studies, Laermer Hall): Now, look. Last time, I was the last one, all right? The last one to say we shouldn't go back to work. And Rosie said it had to be unanimous and I gave in, and I was wrong, and I'm sorry, all right? It worked out OK, but I'm still sorry.

And now. I'm the last one again. Because Tony and Keisha and them, the Blacks and Latinos and even Kimiko, the one Asian girl on the committee (even though *she* doesn't even qualify for the fund, because *her* salary is *higher* than most other grade 7s, and that's true for just about every Asian *at* Olympia, as far as *I* know)—but all those minority people stick together, so they all said right away, "No. No. We can't take it. Of course not." Like you shouldn't even have to ask. And all right, some of them at least looked like they were embarrassed, but some of them just *glared,* like they wanted to call *us* racist, even though we've all *been* on this committee for two years, so why am *I* the enemy all of a sudden?

So then Darcy, who is white, says the most important thing is to get back to work, because no one can afford to lose money like this and she would have thought that went double for minorities, since they *are* earning less. And yes, of course, that isn't fair, but you can't do everything at once and the raise will help. And then Lesley, who is also white, but you know. She just always wants to be so *correct*—*she* makes some big speech about being fair to everybody, but excuse me, Lesley, because holding out this way, I'm sorry, but that isn't fair to *us.* And then Tony, who has always been my buddy on the committee, and last time, we were the only two before *he* gave in, Tony says we should vote the proposal down, which *I* think is just reflex—he can't really mean it. And then Christina, who is also white, agrees with him, and then Porter, another white person, says no, and it goes on and on like that, with Rosie sticking her two cents in whenever things aren't going *her* way, and finally, everybody is done arguing except for me.

So then Rosie says, in that *patient* voice, "Come on, Patrice. You know better than this. It's classic—they're trying to split us up."

"But Rosie," I say, because I am *not* going to do what I did before and not even argue. "But Rosie. They're giving us a raise. And no offense to anyone, but *some* people are getting an even bigger raise than some other people. So how is that splitting us up?"

Rosie sighs. "God, Patrice, *that's* how," she says, disgusted, *worse* than Isabel, and I'm sorry, but I'm really insulted. "Look, Patrice," she's saying, "this is what they want. For you to think in terms of 'some people' and 'the rest of us'—African-American and white, OK? Let's call it what it is."

"So Latinos, we don't count at all?" Tony says. "Or Asians? Good one, Rosie. Real fine."

"*Everybody* counts," Rosie sighs again. "That's my point." She takes another breath. "Look, Patrice. Today they say, no minority salary fund."

"But a raise instead."

"Fine," Rosie says, "but they win the *principle*. Patrice, you know this. There were all these salary differentials left over from before we had the union, and the fund is supposed to make up for that. This one raise doesn't do it. And next time we won't even get that."

"Not necessarily," I say. "Not if we keep pushing, like you always say. We might even be stronger next time. But now we have a chance to end the strike. Let's just take what they offered and not be greedy."

"What are you telling me Patrice, that I'm greedy?" Tony says, and like I said, you would think he didn't remember we were friends. "I want what *you* have—that's greedy?"

If you don't earn it, I think. Then yes, OK. It is.

"Come on, Patrice," says Darcy, rolling her eyes. "It's not worth the fight. They outvoted us."

"So let's go out there and say so," I say.

Rosie shakes her head. "No," she says. "It has to be unanimous. Otherwise the members won't buy it. And they're already out there. Waiting for us."

"Well, tell them we need more time."

"Olympia leaked it all over campus that there was a proposal," Rosie says grimly, "or I don't know, maybe it just got out that we were meeting and people put two and two together. Either way, they know that something is up. We need to tell them *something.*"

Everyone is looking at me. I *don't* think it's right. But I'm not the one who's selfish, either. "Fine," I say. "Call it unanimous if you want to. That still doesn't make it right."

"Damn right it doesn't," Tony says, looking at me with eyes so narrow I want to pinch him. "It's *me,*" I want to tell him. "It's still *me.* Doesn't that mean *anything?*"

NATHAN (BIOP counselor, TEACH program, grade 7, Cadbury Student Center): Even me, I must admit. Who should know better. I walk in all cocky, like I think I've won something. My mistake, I guess. Because there is Rosie up on the stage at the front of the auditorium, not no sister or brother to front for her. Just Rosie herself to give us what from the look on her face is obviously bad news.

"Hey, people," she says. "This is amazing. You are all amazing—can you feel it? Did you ever think we could all do this together?"

Which as far as I am concerned, is just a commercial. Because I see the faces of that sorry-ass committee behind her. They don't look inspired. They look mad. And upset. And not united, not hardly.

MIMI (data entry clerk, grade 5, financial aid, Van Rensselaer Hall): And Rosie goes on trying to pump us up—I'm new, and even I can tell. The way a director does, the day before a show, trying to make you feel what you *could* do, even though you just had the world's lousiest rehearsal, so really, that's what you *did* do.

VANESSA (staff secretary, grade 6, Mines & Minerals Project, Dowling Hall): And she says, "So, people, I'm going to lay out this proposal for you. And then you'll hear the recommendation of your committee—the *unanimous* recommendation, OK?" And when she says *unanimous*, the whole committee just— snarls. Or groans. You can tell *they* just heard a lie.

ARTHUR (file clerk, grade 4, Business School, Jensen Building): And she says, "But people. Take a minute. Look around you." And I do. Hyacinth on my right. Jack on my left. Trudi, my floor captain, behind me.

MARGARITA (department secretary, grade 8, engineering, Dowling Hall): And she says, "I just want you to remember, people. We all need each other. If half of us walked out of here right now, we couldn't have a picket line. If even one of us leaves, we're that much weaker. We need each other. Right? And that means—"

I am so tired. I'm too old to get up with Bobby every night. And they asked Teresa to take another double, and so finally she had to let Cecy stay with Bobby, because Cecy was taking a sick day today anyway, for her cold. But tonight, I'm the one who'll have to get up.

NATHAN (BIOP counselor, TEACH program, grade 7, Cadbury Student Center): And Rosie says, "So that means, the best for others might be good for us, too. Not because we're so unselfish, because we're not, really, and why should we be? But because we need each other."

Yes, I want to say.

And *no, fuck that, no way.* What have these people ever done for me *or* my community, that now they say they need me?

PATRICE (negotiating committee; administrative assistant, grade 9, Institute for Middle Eastern Studies, Laermer Hall): So she explains the three main points on Olympia's proposal. First, that big raise. There's some formula, she tries to lay it out, but it's complicated. How the minorities get something extra.

Second, no more minority salary fund. "All those inequalities," Rosie says passionately, "all the discrepancies, all the differences left over from before we *had* a union. No more fund to fix them, *ever.* Because, people. This raise is just a one-shot deal."

And three, they want to change the sexual harassment policy. We didn't even get to talk about that. But now Rosie is laying it all out. In our current contract, people who say they've been harassed get to transfer to the next available job at the same grade level. The University wants the manager at that next job to have the right to turn them down.

Rosie explains all this, and then she turns to Tony. And he gets up in front of everybody, that swaggery walk, and says, "Brothers and sisters, *hermanos y hermanas.* The *unanimous* recommendation of your negotiating committee is to vote this motherfucker *down.* Vote it *down,* people! We should not even be talking about this. We *have* a minority salary fund. We *have* protection against harassment. That's *it.* We should keep what we have and show respect for all workers!"

He says it like he expects people to cheer. But nobody says anything. Just dead silence.

ARTHUR (file clerk, grade 4, Business School, Jensen Building): You mean, we could vote against what the committee says? They're giving us a choice? You'd think I'd be relieved.

HYACINTH (receptionist, grade 4, Business School, Jensen Building): Why do they ask us if we want this? Why not say *no,* all by themselves?

Nathan (BIOP counselor, TEACH program, grade 7, Cadbury Student Center): They said "Vote no," but you can tell at least half of them don't mean it. Eight folks of color and twelve white people—how do you think Rosie strong-armed *them?*

Lissa (staff secretary, grade 6, geology, Dowling Hall): It's never me that speaks at these meetings. But today I put up my hand in the midst of all that silence, and I say, "Um, I think, no, OK? I think we should vote *no.* Because it's right, what Rosie said. What Tony said. We have to stick together."

And this opens up a dam. Because now everybody is talking, yelling, not even raising their hands, all shouting at the same time.

"Why do they need a special fund, anyway? They don't."

"I can make it on my own. I don't need special treatment. That fund is an insult."

"Honey, I've been here ten years, I'm making less than some faculty secretary who walks in off the street tomorrow? You tell me, how is that right?"

"Lots of people get treated badly. Why do *they* get something special for it?"

"Look at the statistics. That's all I'm saying. Just look at the numbers. One thousand dollars a year less, for Black folk. Almost as bad for the Latinos. That's bad, man. Ain't no reason for that."

And Elena's Russian accent saying, "Bad idea to give special treatment. And if worker wants new job, manager should not pay, if he did not do harassment." Which I can't even follow.

Rosie gets people to quiet down enough to call on someone, a thin white guy standing with the B-School crowd. He looks even more nervous than I felt.

Arthur (file clerk, grade 4, Business School, Jensen Building): And I say, "Excuse me, maybe somebody could explain it to me—no, really, I mean it. I want someone to explain."

"Explain what, Arthur?" Rosie says.

"To say why these—*policies,*" I say, proud of myself for finding the right word. "Why these policies are—important? Necessary? I mean, they're *giving* us a raise, and we're still striking? I don't get it."

Rosie looks down at me from the platform, and I can't tell if she's smiling or disappointed or *what* she's feeling. But she says, "Tony? You want to explain a little further?"

That extremely cute guy—well, *hot,* actually—he gives Rosie this really mean look, like he thinks she's setting him up.

But he tries to be cool. And he says, "Look, people. It ain't that complicated—they're trying to split us up. *Punto final.* And you can talk about compromise and special treatment and everybody gets the same and no, bro, they really don't, so you can say it's fair or not fair, and I really don't give a damn. Because it all comes down to one thing: they're trying to split us up like they always do, and if you take this proposal, then all I can say is, they won. And everything we've been doing here, it all goes down the toilet."

And there's this big, big silence.

Rosie is looking right at me. "Did that answer your question, Arthur?" she says. How does she even know my name?

But I say, "No, honestly, I'm sorry. But what do you mean, split us up? Don't we all get the same raise? And the minorities get even *more* of a raise. I still don't see—"

And the noise comes boiling up around me.

"So what if we get more? Now we're getting less!"

"Minorities? What's that? Worldwide, man, we're the majority!"

"Why do they get more? If we're all in the same union."

"What about the sexual harassment part? They leave that out *all* the time."

And then this girl up on the platform stands up, and Tony says, "Patrice!" like he's *totally* pissed, and all of us quiet down right away. She looks really mad—Patrice, I mean. And scared. And tired, her hair all pulled back. She'd look better with it down.

"We need this strike to be over," she says, her voice shaking. "This isn't everything we wanted, but it isn't bad. Some people say you never give anything back, but I say, you give back what you don't need anymore. Minorities had that fund for ten years, and now it's time to move on. Same with sexual harassment. We need a different policy."

PATRICE (negotiating committee; administrative assistant, grade 9, Institute for Middle Eastern Studies, Laermer Hall): Rosie looking at me, Tony, Keisha, even Darcy, Porter, looking at me like I'm everybody's enemy now. But I had to do what I thought was right.

HYACINTH (receptionist, grade 4, Business School, Jensen Building): And I'm up on my feet, raising my hand, waving, waving, and finally Rosie calls on me. And I say, "Don't vote *yes* to this, people! Do not do it! That's what they want, to bribe us. Big raise today, split us up tomorrow!"

And behind me, Jack Kim is shouting, "We got this far in one day, imagine how far we'll get if we hold out! Don't give in! Don't give in!"

MIMI (data entry clerk, grade 5, financial aid, Van Rensselaer Hall): I don't know. I honestly don't know. Can't it just be over?

MARGARITA (department secretary, grade 8, engineering, Dowling Hall): I want it to be over, too. Ay, *Dios mio,* I'm so *tired.*

ROSIE (lead organizer): "See, Rosie," Isabel is whispering to me, "you should never have let the whole membership hear about the proposal—"

Well, obviously, she's right. I *got* the committee to vote no. The members never had to know a thing about it.

Isabel is whispering, like a fly buzzing in my ear. "You can't even control your own committee—"

I *know.*

"—and now the whole membership, fighting like this, the University knows, they can do whatever they want to us now. Rosie, Rosie, how could you *do* this?"

I was just so sure they would see this was wrong. The committee *and* the members. I couldn't believe they wouldn't see it. I still can't.

ARTHUR (file clerk, grade 4, Business School, Jensen Building): So Rosie asks us for a show of hands. "How many in favor of accepting the University's proposal?" And a lot of hands go up. I think that mine will, too. But no. I don't move.

MIMI (data entry clerk, grade 5, financial aid, Van Rensselaer Hall): And then she says, "How many in favor of rejecting the University's proposal?" I'm not sure. Turns out I don't vote either way.

NATHAN (BIOP counselor, TEACH program, grade 7, Cadbury Student Center): I try to memorize every single black and brown face that votes to accept the proposal, every single white face that votes to turn it down. Because I'll be honest—I did *not* think it would come down this way. Man, all the time I was right *here,* you'd think I would have known. But I didn't have a clue.

PATRICE (negotiating committee; administrative assistant, grade 9, Institute for Middle Eastern Studies, Laermer Hall): The vote is too close, you can't tell just from the hands. Rosie says something quick to Isabel and Charles, there at the back of the platform. Then she explains that the vote is so close and so important, we're going to do it by secret ballot. So people write *yes* or *no* on whatever paper they happen to have and all of us on the committee go down and collect the little scraps. And then she has Tony and me count them up, one from each side, so everybody knows it will be fair.

Tony gives me this *look* while we're counting, him squatting on the floor, me kneeling beside him. This *look* that stops my heart.

Because I know what he's thinking, he's thinking, Well, OK, Patrice, she's white, she's for this proposal because she's white. And I want to tell him, No, no, Tony, that's not it at all. It's because I have a child at home, and a husband, and there's never enough money, and never enough time, and a strike? It's just too much. But not because I'm white.

NINA (faculty secretary, grade 8, history, Philosophy Building): "What do you think, Nina?" Teneisha is whispering in my ear.

"I think we'll be back at work before lunchtime is over," I whisper back.

She shakes her head. "No, no, no, no, no. Think about what we did yesterday."

"Yesterday they were voting against Olympia. But today Olympia has done something good. Why would anyone vote against that?"

She turns on me like I've snatched her purse. "Why did you then?" she says fiercely. "Why did you, Nina, if you know so much?"

But I don't want to get mad at her, and I certainly don't want her mad at me. "I don't like them jerking us around," I say. "This great offer that is really a trick. Fuck them."

PATRICE (negotiating committee; administrative assistant, grade 9, Institute for Middle Eastern Studies, Laermer Hall): "434 *yeses,*" I tell Tony. There are 1,013 workers in our unit all together. But I don't know how many are at this meeting. Not everybody voted, either. So now we have to count the *nos.*

VANESSA (staff secretary, grade 6, Mines & Minerals Project, Dowling Hall): Lissa and I are chatting real casual, like this is no big deal.

But I know she voted *yes*. When push came to shove, why *wouldn't* she? I would, if I was her.

All of a sudden, Margarita leans over. "You watch," she says in a whisper. "They abolish that fund, and that's *it*. You think they won't get rid of all the Black and Latin grade 8s now? That's what they want, the faculty, nice little white girls they can treat like machines, push them around as much as they want."

I've never seen her so angry. And then of course Lissa hears every word, and *she* turns bright red. And opens her mouth to speak, but I get there first. I say, "Oh, Margarita, what do you know about it? It's the other way around. They get rid of that fund, it's like saying they don't have to pay us the same as the white workers. They'll start putting *more* minorities higher up, because it's cheaper."

"No," says Lissa. "What they'll do is, next contract, they'll say they want to make it even *more* equal, and they'll give you guys *another* raise and us none, or just a small one, and *that*'s what's going to save them money. And *that's* why *I* voted *no*, in case you were wondering." I've never seen *her* this angry, either. "Because whatever they want, it's always bad for us, you know? And the better it looks? The worse it is."

PATRICE (negotiating committee; administrative assistant, grade 9, Institute for Middle Eastern Studies, Laermer Hall): "434 *yeses*," Tony repeats. "And 435 *nos*."

We both look up at Rosie. "You want to count them all again?" she says in this weird, calm voice. "Seeing as how it was so extremely close?"

Tony and I both shake our heads *no*. Not even smiling that we did the exact same thing. "We were both counting," I said. "We were both careful." Tony nods.

I hold out my hand to him, like people do after a game. Finally he shakes it. "Still wasn't right, Patrice," he says. "It wasn't, and you know it."

"Well, you won," I say. "So what are you complaining about?"

He shrugs. "Didn't think I *had* to win," he says. "Not against you."

ARTHUR (file clerk, grade 4, Business School, Jensen Building): Rosie says in this very, very quiet voice, "All right, people. The vote was *very* close. The count is 434 in favor of accepting Olympia's proposal." A few cheers, a few boos, people hissing and whispering. Rosie holds up her hand for silence but her voice doesn't change. "And 435 against."

We're all totally silent. What happens now?

MIMI (data entry clerk, grade 5, financial aid, Van Rensselaer Hall): "Now, people," Rosie says. "We've got a problem to solve. Because obviously, that vote is too close to support us. I mean, if we go out there, and the 435 *no* votes are still gung-ho for our strike, but the 434 *yes* votes are lukewarm, it's just not going to work.

"You want my recommendation, I think you did the right thing. I know Harris, our president, would say the same. But in the end, you're the ones who have to live on what the strike fund can pay. You're the ones who are out there picketing. I mean, I'm with you, Harris is with you, the union is with you, every step of the way. But in the end, it's up to you. So what do you really want?"

NATHAN (BIOP counselor, TEACH program, grade 7, Cadbury Student Center): And you know what I'm thinking now? It's the last thing in the world I *want* to think, but I can't help it. I'm thinking, *No. I can't let this happen again.* Where they get to split us up like this, where they get to win just because *some* people are weak and stupid. Because *some* people didn't get talked to enough, *some* people didn't get *made* to understand. Next time, it has to be different. Even if it means me getting involved with some sorry bunch of secretaries.

LISSA (staff secretary, grade 6, geology, Dowling Hall): Vanessa's got tears in her eyes. "What would BH say?" she whispers in my ear. "He sees us coming back with our tail between our legs, what's he gonna say?"

But that's not why she's crying. She's crying because she didn't believe I was going to vote *no,* even though I was the first, the very first person to speak up in this meeting and say we *should* vote no, even though she *knows* I'm shy. And with all that, she still thought I'd vote "like white people vote."

I don't want to be mean, but she *should* cry. If she thought that.

PATRICE (negotiating committee; administrative assistant, grade 9, Institute for Middle Eastern Studies, Laermer Hall): Nothing about this is right.

And what I'm doing now, it's not because of Nikos, all right? It's my own idea, what I think my own self. "I'd like to make a motion," I say. My throat is so scratchy, I'm surprised the words come out.

"Look," I say, clutching the microphone. "I just said we should take the proposal, all right? I just said so. But look at us now. We can't go back like this. You know if we do, they can do whatever they want. They win. And next time, you know. They can buy us *cheap*."

I take a deep breath. "So I move to continue the strike. Until we get a better proposal. One that won't split us up. One that . . ." Another breath. "It has to be good for everybody," I say finally. Then I sit down.

NINA (faculty secretary, grade 8, history, Philosophy Building): Rosie says, "All in favor of continuing the strike?" And the cheers don't sound like much, but they are cheers. She says, "Opposed?" And it's totally quiet.

Teneisha gives me this look, like "I told you so." Well, now she can see how wrong I am. Pretty much all the time.

It doesn't matter. We yell and cheer and try to sound like we're ready to start all over again. And then we go back out there and try to act like we haven't lost hope.

WEDNESDAY, MAY 4TH, 10 A.M.
ROSIE (lead organizer): I'm in the union office, as it happens, when the call comes. From Harris himself. Telling me about the new proposal Olympia's president has just made to him personally. He sounds positively gleeful. I wonder what would happen if I said *no?*

But of course, I wouldn't say that—it's a great offer. Not perfect, but better than I'd ever have expected. And the irony, of course, is that every single thing we did to get it was pretty much by mistake. We went on strike against the recommendation of the union; we rejected Olympia's most divisive proposal by only one fucking vote; and then we had a resounding unanimous vote to continue the strike, which is probably what *did* convince Olympia to back down—but that only happened because I made probably the worst mistake of my organizing career, taking the proposal to the members like that. So *was* I wrong to trust the members? You tell me.

Anyway, they offer us a raise that's just a half a percent lower than what we've been asking, and they leave the minority salary fund alone, and they ask for one little change in the sexual harassment language: workers with grievances still get the first available job at the same level, but if two or more jobs open up at the same time, then Personnel has "discretion" about which one of them to offer. Which means that they'll juggle the timing so that they *can* decide which worker goes where, but OK. It's a loss we can live with.

By eleven, we've met with the committee. By twelve-thirty, we're all back in Reed Hall.

Everybody is pulsing with excitement. We've arranged for Tony and Patrice to make the announcement together, a gesture of unity. I still can't tell how well they're getting along. Oh, well. You never know what losses you can repair and which ones just leach away at you forever.

"The Olympia negotiating committee of Local 235 unanimously recommends acceptance of this proposal!" says Tony triumphantly.

"All in favor signify by saying *aye!*" shouts Patrice. They do both look incredibly happy.

"Aye!" everyone roars, thrilled, triumphant, relieved.

"I just want to say," Patrice is saying into the microphone, breathless, tearful, "that this has been the most incredible—because yesterday, people, I really did not think we could win. And today—we won! We won! Aren't we amazing?"

There in the front row, I see Lissa and Vanessa standing side by side. It looks like they came together, except they're hardly looking at each other. Lissa, in fact, looks ready to cry. What's going on *there?*

"We have a long list of people to thank," Tony is saying, holding up a hand for silence. "Professor Diamond, for organizing classes off campus—an impressive amount of work, Señor Professor! The *compañeros* say thank you!" Diamond stands up, blushing, but pleased.

"And everyone on our student support committee," Patrice is saying. "Kate Ryan, and Peggy Bates, and Simon Isenberg—" Simon looks overjoyed, waving and cheering from the audience. I don't see Nina, though.

"And our organizers!" Tony starts listing each one by name. Isabel is here, of course. Victory excuses everything—she's now acting as though the decision to take it to the members was *her* idea, or at least, an idea that she always supported. Our people barely know Tito, but they applaud him anyway. "And Charles, our local president!" Huge cheers for Charles, who certainly deserves them.

They're going to cheer for me, next, and I'm not sure how I'll stand it. Because now that it's over, I feel so alone. Why? There are no losses in *my* life that can't be made up. Even the blood, which is still pouring out at an alarming rate, will eventually be replaced.

For some reason, Patrice motions Jack Kim up on stage. She hands him the microphone, and the whole room gets quiet.

"I don't think there *are* any words for how much we owe our organizer, Rosie," Jack is saying. "So let's say thank you another way."

And everybody in the room pulls out this xeroxed sheet of paper and starts to sing.

> *When the union inspiration through the workers' blood shall run*
> *There shall be no power greater anywhere beneath the sun*
> *Yet what force on earth is weaker than the feeble strength of one?*
> *But the union makes us strong.*

Jack motions for me to join in. I don't really *want* to burst into tears up here in front of all the members. On the other hand, when will I ever get this chance again? And the next verse has always been my favorite.

> *In our hands we hold a power greater than their hoarded gold*
> *Greater than the might of armies magnified a thousandfold*
> *We can bring to birth a new world from the ashes of the old,*
> *For the union makes us strong.*

THE WEDDING
(or whatever they decide to call it)

ROSIE: I'm sound asleep when the phone rings this Saturday, the first morning that I've even been able to *think* about sleeping since the strike ended on Wednesday. And there in my ear is Flip's voice, saying, "Well, Ma isn't coming to my affiliation ceremony because she thinks it's an abomination unto the Lord, or actually, as she put it in her letter, an abo*nim*ation, and Dan didn't exactly express any religious or moral or even personal objections, but he wrote to say it would be too difficult to get away because even though the kids don't have school in June, they *do* have day camp, and though some people might suspect that he and Betsy would never in a million *years* have responded that way if I were really getting married, and *not* whatever we decide to call it, *I* don't have that type of suspicious nature, though I must say, I *am* shocked that Betsy didn't even sign her name to his note, considering that *she's* the one who's actually *written* every communication I've ever gotten from the two of them since they started dating, let alone got married, but I must say, Rosie, it does seem a bit much that *you* didn't even *bother* to *answer* my invitation. I mean, if it's really true that *nobody* from my family is going to be at my matrimonial event, you'd think I would at least be entitled to know it for certain. Instead of having to wonder about *you,* of all people, and you don't believe in God, and you don't even *have* any children, so what's your excuse?"

There is a long, long pause as I struggle to sit up in bed. Finally, he says, "And if you're waiting for an apology from me, all I can say is, it's awfully petty of you, considering how desperate I am to have *someone* named Zombrowski at the wedding. Someone other than me, I mean. Because you must know I'd be willing to apologize for things I didn't even do to accomplish *that,* let alone say I'm sorry for something—all right, two things—that I actually *am* sorry about."

Tired as I am—*mad* as I am—I have to laugh. "All right, then," says Flip, sounding so incredibly relieved it breaks my heart. "I'm glad you accept my apologies."

"*Was* there an apology in there?" I say. "I couldn't exactly tell."

"Well, if you're not going to pay attention, I can't help *that,*" Flip says, and I can't believe how much I've missed him.

"OK," I say. "Apology accepted. I guess."

"I still don't think that was any reason not to answer my invitation," Flip says.

"Well, I don't either, actually. But I didn't even get it till Monday night. You got my zip code wrong. And besides, we were on strike."

"Oh. Well, I guess that *is* a good excuse. Did you win?"

"We did, actually. On Wednesday. But—" I'm not sure what to say about why I didn't answer him after that.

"Oh, well, *Wednesday,*" Flip says. "Between Wednesday and today, what's that? It always takes me *weeks* to recuperate from a production."

Even though he has about six ulterior motives for saying this, I can't believe how grateful I feel hearing him say it. Because everyone in the union thinks I should be back on the job exactly as if nothing had happened. And Michael—well, I *am* seeing him tonight. I know I've been putting *that* off.

"So you *are* coming?" Flip says, and I can't believe how desperate he sounds.

"Of course, I'm coming," I say. "I can't *believe* nobody else is—I mean, I would have thought, you know, maybe not Uncle Patty and Auntie Mavis, maybe not Orrin and RoseAnne, even though they probably *would* come to a more—"

"Conventional?"

"Yeah, OK, to a more conventional ceremony. Or even Mitch and Susan. I mean, they *are* your godparents. Or didn't you invite them?"

"No, we did," says Flip. "Mavis sent a note saying Patty's health wasn't so good—you can just imagine the note he actually wanted her to send—and Orrin and RoseAnne just checked the "no" box on the RSVP card without *even* a note, and we haven't heard back from Mitch and Susan, actually, so I don't know. Maybe I put the wrong zip code on their invitation, too."

Well, obviously, he should never have expected them to come, should he? I mean, *I* wouldn't have expected it, if I were marrying, say, Michael.

On the other hand, I hate thinking that. Why *shouldn't* he assume that this family who adores him would be delighted to come to his—union, let's say— to the person he wants to spend his life with? "Well, I might have imagined that *those* people wouldn't make it," I say. "But I really can't believe Ma isn't coming, or Danny and Betsy . . . or Dad. Are you sure they're not?"

Flip laughs, an unusually bitter sound. "Yes, dear, I don't think I'd be mistaken about something like that. If you don't believe me, meet me for lunch. I'll show you the letter Ma wrote. It's a real triumph, even for her."

Well, that explains why he apologized. I suppose if he *weren't* being abandoned by the whole rest of the family, I might have waited another five years.

"Of course, you have to promise not to say anything to Warren about it," he's saying. "Because I may not even show *him* the letter. Or he might feel that he could never set foot in Pittsburgh ever again, and since he had *such* a marvelous time there last Christmas, that *would* be a shame, don't you think?"

When I get to the diner, Flip is already there. In front of him is a box wrapped in bright orange-red paper, which he shoves across the table at me as I sit down.

"Happy Successful Strike," he says.

"Oh, my God, you got me a present? I don't believe it."

"Don't make a big deal of it until you see what it is."

I make a face at him and try to open the wrapping carefully. He laughs.

"Warren does the exact same thing," he says. "You'd think he grew up with Ma Joad in the Dust Bowl. Come on, Rosie. Wrapping paper costs like $3.29 a roll. You're allowed to tear it."

"It's not the money."

"That's what he says."

On the floor of the box is a greeting card, originally intended for a new parent, that reads "Congratulations on your first—" and after the word "first," Flip has written "STRIKE." And glued to the card are all these little pieces— the top hat from Monopoly, and some Monopoly money, and a picture of the little rich guy from Monopoly cut out of one of the Community Chest cards, all labeled "the Boss"; and a pin shaped like a red star, and a refrigerator magnet shaped like a computer, and a little plastic toy filing cabinet—God knows where he found *that*—all labeled "the Workers"; and between the two groups of figures, he's drawn two hands, a man's and a woman's, arm wrestling, surrounded by little cartoon balloons featuring such comments as "Power to the Workers!" and "File Grievances, Not Nails!" and "Eat the Rich." And around the whole thing, Flip has written, in red ink, "To my sister, Rosie, who never lets the boss—or anyone else—get away with a damn thing. Keep giving them hell. Love, your fellow worker (and brother), Flip."

I'm so moved, I have to blink the tears out of my eyes. "God," I say, "I can't believe you put all this together. You only heard about the strike this morning."

He actually looks embarrassed—Flip, of all people. "Well, actually, I knew on Tuesday, that you were *on* strike, I mean. Simon told me."

"Oh."

"And of course, I asked him to keep me posted. I couldn't really believe you weren't *ever* going to speak to me again."

"Especially since I wasn't the one who stopped speaking to *you* in the first place. *Or* in the second place."

"Well, yes," says Flip. "Especially in that case."

"So where's this famous letter?" I say.

"Don't you have more to say about the strike than *that?*" he says. "I would have thought it would have been one of the high points of your life. Especially since it was your first."

It always surprises me, the things he remembers. The things he bothers to remember, I want to say, but maybe that isn't fair.

"I *would* like to tell you about it," I say. "But let me see the letter first."

Just then the waitress comes, and there's this very *charged* moment until Flip says, "A BLT on white toast, please, and an order of French fries with brown gravy. We're going to split it," and honestly, I don't know if I feel incredible relief or some kind of anger—does he *always* get to get away with *everything?*

But I hold out my hand for the letter, and Flip gives it to me, craning his neck across the table to read it upside down.

Dear Son,

Yes you are still my Son even though what you are doing is a Sin and an Abonimation that I beg you to stop before it causes you to burn in Hell and I cannot believe that you would ever think that I could condone or even wink at such activity which hurts me deeply. To think you never were taught better or learned better the Right way to conduct yourself in private, before God, and before others.

You are still my son, and I will Always love you, and you and your Friend will always be welcome in my Home (though not to commit sins there).

Your Loving Mother

"Wow."

"I know," says Flip.

"And you're really not going to show it to Warren?"

"I don't know about *not going to*," Flip says. "I haven't shown it to him yet." He looks down the aisle toward the waitress, arriving with our food. "He doesn't even know I got it," he says in a low voice. He actually seems to be ashamed.

"My God, Flip, how can you not show it to him? I mean, OK, it's *your* family. But isn't it supposed to be *his* family, too?"

"Well, obviously, nobody *else* in our family thinks so," Flip says. "You appear to be in the minority on that one."

"God, you must feel awful, Flip. I can just imagine how you feel."

"No, actually, I don't think you can," Flip says. "You *could* get married if you wanted to. I don't think you *can* imagine what it's like to—to not be able to, to the point where it doesn't actually *matter* what you want."

"Oh, Flip."

"What could *you* do," Flip says, "where they would all of a sudden—I don't know. Just pretend you don't exist."

"Jesus, Flip. They already do that."

"They don't pretend you don't have a sex life," Flip says. "Well, all right, maybe they do. But if you wanted to get married, if you had a regular boyfriend—"

"I do have a regular boyfriend. Unless by 'regular' you mean 'white.' "

Flip is still struggling to find words. "If *you* wanted to marry Warren, *you* could," he says finally. "Doesn't it strike you as odd that *I* can't?"

He pushes the plate to one side. "Warren or anybody else you wanted to marry," he says, looking down at the food. "Maybe not everybody would be thrilled about it, but you could *do* it. It would be a real thing for you to do. Not some made-up thing that nobody but you believes in anyway."

"What about Warren's family?" I ask, more because I can't stand to see him so unhappy, although I am also curious.

Flip's mouth twists again. "Well, I think his mother would come in some theoretical sense. I mean, she won't go anywhere without his father, and his father certainly won't come. They'll probably send some really expensive WASP gift, like a silver fish knife."

"Melt it down," I say. "When they come to round us up, you can use it to bribe the guards."

Flip laughs. But, as usual, gets angry at the same time. "Damn it, Rosie," he says. "Why do you always have to try to make things better?"

Usually this is the point where I'd try even *harder* to make things better. But I hear myself saying, "Well, fuck you, too, Flip. I mean, you know they wouldn't come if I were marrying Michael—our family, I mean—not that I'm thinking of marrying Michael, so don't get any ideas—and you got to bring Warren home for Christmas, *and* Juliet, and you know I would never get away with that even if I were married to Michael—"

"Not that you ever would, etcetera," Flip says acidly. "Not that you'd ever even introduce him to me."

"Well. And all these years that you *haven't* been married, you've gotten off scot free. Nobody's acting like your whole entire life is an utter and complete failure, or that it shouldn't exist at all, absent that."

"Oh, no," says Flip. "My entire life commands enormous respect from everyone in the family, so kind of you to remind me."

"Well, clearly this is all Danny's fault," I say. "Let's go beat him up."

Flip struggles once again between wanting to laugh and wanting to stay mad at me. I watch him for a moment.

"I don't know," I say, "why you'll never let me be on your side. Even against Ma."

"Because whatever side you're on, you just take it over. It's just not your problem, Rosie. It's mine."

"Why can't it be ours?"

"Because *nothing* is mine," Flip says. "Nothing is ever fucking mine!"

Well, maybe I can't answer Michael on this issue, but I can sure as hell answer Flip. "No, Flip," I say, "that isn't true. Your art is yours. And your relationship with Warren. They certainly aren't mine. Or ours. But if you want to—ally yourself—with Warren, and you invite me to the ceremony, then that *is* mine, at least partly. I mean, if it isn't, then why am I there? And if you're *not* allowed to get married, then that's mine, too. Even if you weren't my brother, it's mine. I mean, ours."

I stand up. "And if you don't want it to be ours, then stop *inviting* me, Flip. Stop *asking* me. If you don't want me to be a part of this, why don't you just keep it to yourself?"

"Wait," says Flip. He looks completely floored.

"Rosie," he says, "could you just sit down for a minute, please? Don't say anything. Just—don't go yet, OK?"

I can't believe how much this hurts. But I sit down. Without looking at me, Flip reaches across the table and takes my hands. We just sit there, for what seems like an extremely long time. But he doesn't let go. And I don't leave. So I suppose that's ours, too.

FLIP: When I get home from my little outing with Rosie, I manage to avoid Warren and Juliet long enough to shut myself in the bedroom and call Tanya. I don't know what this *obsession* is all of a sudden with reading every last person in the known world this letter from Ma (except for Warren, of course). But Tanya *is* my friend.

After she hears the letter, she maintains a brief, shocked silence. "Not like you didn't expect it," she says finally.

"No, actually, I didn't."

There is what I suppose you might call a *careful* pause on the other end of the line. "Well," Tanya says finally. "What *did* you expect then?"

"God, *I* don't know. I didn't expect them to come running to New York with open arms, if that's what you mean. Not right away. But I thought they'd at least—*act* happy."

Tanya is quiet for an awfully long time. If she says that something worse has happened to her, I swear I'll never speak to her again. But all she says is, "What does Warren think about the letter?"

"I don't know," I say. "He hasn't seen it."

"Well, don't you think he should? Aren't you guys going to say, 'For better or worse'? Or whatever you decide is the gay version of *that?*"

"What *would* the gay version be? For breakfast or brunch?"

She laughs. "But why *don't* you want to tell him?" she says.

In the kitchen, I hear Warren and Juliet having some kind of an argument. As seems to be usual, lately, he's insisting that she *do* something, *right now,* and she's insisting that she doesn't *want* to. For some reason, when the two of them fight like that, it makes me crazy. "Shut up and mind your uncle!" I want to yell at her. And at the same time I want to shake Warren by the shoulders and shriek, "Don't you know she misses her mother?"

"Flip?" says Tanya on the other end of the line.

"Look, I think it's time for dinner," I say. "I'll call you tomorrow, OK?"

She starts to say something and then stops. "Yeah," she says instead. "Tomorrow."

Although there's a fair amount of tension between Warren and Juliet at dinner, I manage to stay out of both their ways until bedtime. Then it's Saturday night, and although sometime earlier this week, I actually thought it would be *nice* to have a quiet evening at home with Warren, now I'm so restless I'm practically climbing the walls. To be fair, Warren does try to start one or two actual conversations, but I don't really feel like talking, either. Finally he looks up from his book and says patiently, "All right. Why don't we get a video?"

Which I have to tell you, hits me like manna from heaven. I could kiss him, I'm so relieved. So *being* the restless one without a book, I offer to go down the block to Video Blitz. And just as I'm heading out the door, armed with the last of the gift certificates from Valentine's Day, Juliet cries out from the other room.

Although there's always that first little shiver of alarm when we hear her tearful voice, this is actually a routine that's been going on for the past few weeks. We put her more or less peacefully to bed and then she wakes up in a panic. Warren has been reading all the child care books, which in their usual helpful way agree that if you go in right when the child calls, you're disabling her ability to process feelings on her own, whereas if you *don't* go in, you're reinforcing her sense of abandonment. But *I* say, Madeleine left only six months ago and now she's about to come back, so really, Warren, what do you expect?

Of course, he, understandably, has a lot harder time with all of this than I do. So at the first sound of her voice, I hand him the gift certificates.

"Just get something that I might conceivably want to watch, too," I say. "No silent films by Danish expressionist directors that nobody has ever heard of. Get something normal."

He's so upset that he doesn't even *start* to give me Lecture #23, "How can *I*, a self-proclaimed artist, etcetera, etcetera." "She'll be upset if I'm not here," he says instead, because that's how it goes. Whichever one of us goes in to her, she always asks for the other one. And then she has a terrific tantrum if the other one doesn't come in. "You're no good!" Warren told me she said the last time this happened, the night before last. "You don't know *anything* about taking care of a girl like me." And when I went in, two nights before that, she said, "Who wants *you*? You're not *responsible*," so she seems to have figured out customized insults for all concerned.

"She will be upset if you're not here," I agree now. "But if you *are* here, she'll just spend hours sending each of us away and asking for the other. And if we both go in, she'll tell us both to leave, and then the whole thing starts all over again."

"But she'll think I left her," Warren says. He's getting more and more upset as her voice rises: "Where *are* you? I want somebody to *come!* Where *is* everybody?"

"Warren," I say. "You're only going down the block to the video store. I don't actually plan to tell her you're gone, but if the truth finally comes out, the worst that will happen is that you'll be back in fifteen minutes. It's important for her to learn that, OK, people go away, but then they do come back." And then, of course, there's a pregnant pause, as each of us thinks of all the people who have gone away and *haven't* come back.

"Anyway," I say, "*you* always come back, in my admittedly limited experience. And if you *are* planning on never returning from this little trip down to the end of the block, she and I will both be so miserable that we might as well learn to comfort each other."

"I don't know *where* you get these ideas," Warren says stiffly. He really hates it whenever I remind him that he's the one who left. Whatever sins I might *ever* have committed, neither one of us thinks they're worth anything compared to *that*.

WARREN: I suppose I'm a coward, but I stay at the video store as long as I can possibly manage. Once I'm out of the house, it's such an incredible relief to be away from both of them.

When I finally get back, though, all is quiet. Flip is lying on the couch, staring at the television, which isn't on. When he sees what I've brought, he looks as though he can't decide whether to laugh, yell at me, or burst into tears. Because there on our coffee table are *Father of the Bride, Every Girl Should Be Married,* and *Muriel's Wedding*. Along with microwave popcorn, and that awful caramel corn which of course he *loves,* and a pint of chocolate–chocolate chip, which I know is also his favorite. "Warren," he says. "I do get that you were planning some sort of theme night, but don't you think you went just a little bit overboard?"

"Well, we haven't seemed able to figure out *our* conjugal day. I thought we might as well do some research." I go sit beside him on the couch, and he leans against me. "And I figured the only way I could get you to sit still was to stupefy you with videos and stuff you with food."

"Oh, you underestimate yourself, Warren," Flip says. "Or maybe you overestimate me." He puts his head on my shoulder. I put my arm around him.

"Would you mind telling me what happened with Juliet?" I say. "Before we start?"

"We should put the ice cream away," says Flip. But he doesn't move.

"Whatever you did, it must have worked like a charm," I say. "Because the last few times, she kept it up for over an hour—two hours on Sunday, remember?"

"Who could forget?" Flip says. "I may not be *responsible* but I have an excellent memory." He pulls away from me, curling into the other corner of the couch. "It wasn't such a big deal," he says finally. "I went in there and she started yelling at me, 'You're not responsible! And you're not even my real uncle! Nobody wants you here! Why don't you just go back where you belong?' "

"Jesus," I say.

"Right?" Flip says. "So right in the middle of it—because apparently I *can* control a scene without raising my voice—in the middle, I managed to say, 'You know, Juliet, when my father died, I felt like yelling for about six months, and I wasn't allowed to, and I think that was wrong. So if you want to yell because you miss your mother, even though we both know she's coming back, and probably fairly soon—well, why not? Only what I *don't* think you should do is yell *at* people. Because that hurts people's feelings, and there are already enough hurt feelings around here, in my opinion. But I'll sit here with you while you yell, if you want me to."

"My God."

"Well," Flip says. "Enough is enough, right? So then she just stared and stared at me, like she couldn't figure out if I *was* the most surprising human being she had ever seen or if I was somehow trying to trick her. And *then* she said, 'Do I *have* to yell? What if I don't *want* to yell?"

I laugh, and Flip smiles, reluctantly. "So I said, 'You don't *have* to do anything, Juliet. What do you *want* to do?' And she said, 'First I want to yell. And then I want you to rock me.' And I said, 'Go ahead.' So she yelled, 'I MISS MY MOTHER AND I WANT HER TO COME *BACK*. AND I DON'T WANT TO GO LIVE SOMEPLACE ELSE. I WANT TO LIVE *HERE*. AND I WANT HER TO COME LIVE HERE, TOO. RIGHT NOW. *RIGHT NOW!!*' "

I've run out of words. I simply stare at him.

"And then she climbed out of bed," Flip goes on, "and came to sit in my lap. And I rocked her until she fell asleep, which was fairly soon, because apparently all that yelling had worn her out. And then I put her to bed."

He looks at me and smiles again, an extremely tired smile. "You should see the look on your face, Warren," he says. "You're staring at me exactly the same way she did."

I shake my head. He sighs. "Well," he says, "apparently I can't do anything right around here." He stalks into the bedroom and storms out holding a letter, which he drops in my lap. "Go ahead, read it," he says. He glares at me until I pull the paper out of its envelope. "Read it and weep," he says, stalking into the kitchen with the ice cream. I hear the freezer door slam.

When I finally go in to him, he's standing in front of the microwave, watching the popcorn pop. "You'll hurt your eyes doing that," I say.

"Me and Oedipus." He doesn't move.

"When did this arrive?"

"I got it this morning."

"And how do you—"

The microwave beeps and Flip goes to the refrigerator. "You know, Warren," he says in that level voice that's so hard for me to read, "I thought the whole big advantage of being involved with you was supposed to be that you never actually *did* want to talk about anything." He puts a stick of butter into a saucepan and turns on the stove.

"You know," I say finally, "that thing about going down to the corner store, never to return—that actually does happen to some people. I had a client once, who wanted me to help find her boyfriend, which isn't exactly what I do, but it was a very odd story. Apparently, he really did go out one night to buy a pack of cigarettes and then simply never came back. And after calling the police, and his friends, and his family, my client realized that nobody *else* was worried, so apparently he had just left *her*. She came to see me a few times, over the years, so I eventually heard the rest of the story."

The butter hisses and starts to smoke, and Flip turns down the stove. "Well?" he says.

"Oh, it was more or less the usual. First he wanted to run off and have this whole cruising-the-leather-bars-and-meat-market kind of life."

"Oh, what a surprise," Flip says. "Are *all* your clients involved with closet cases, or just the ones you describe to *me?*"

"Well. But then he fell madly in love with this woman from what was then the Soviet Union, and evidently she was a committed Communist and didn't want to leave, and since he had decided that he couldn't live without her, they got married, and he ended up going to live there. And then after Communism fell, she *did* want to leave. But he had already given up his U.S. citizenship, so they couldn't get back into this country."

"My God," says Flip. "You always know the most amazing stories, Warren, and you always tell them like they're nothing. So what finally happened?"

"Eventually, they went somewhere in Canada," I say. "Because my client wanted to know whether she should go out there to visit them, after he had written and invited her. And she *was* curious, my client, except that it was some very *isolated* part of Canada. But anyway. She went. And she came back simply—wondering. About what her life would have been if she had stayed with this man. Not that it had ever been *her* choice to leave, but still. Was *this* what he had wanted all along? This cramped, freezing house out in the Canadian wherever? And she had been so in love with him when he left, she really thought he was the one. But then she wondered. If he had offered her *that* in the first place, the life he actually ended up with. Maybe *she* would have been the one to leave."

Flip shakes his head. "You made all that up, didn't you, Warren? You completely made that story up."

"I'm flattered that you think I *could* make up a story like that."

Flip stands there drizzling the butter onto the popcorn, biting his lip. "Just don't *you* go, all right, Warren?" he says in a small, whiny voice that sounds exactly like Juliet's.

"I *won't*," I say.

"No. I mean, don't even leave and then come back."

"You go and then come back," I can't help saying. "And *you* always say—"

"Well, I *get* to do that. You don't. You stay here, where I can find you."

I *don't* want to leave. It's simply the idea that there might be—other places. He's always had them. Why can't I?

Flip sighs dramatically and comes over to put his arms around me. "At least say you'll come back and visit sometimes," he says. "From these far-off realms where I'm apparently not allowed to join you."

"I don't know what you're talking about."

"Yes, you do," Flip says. "You know exactly what I'm talking about, Warren, so don't pretend you don't." He burrows his head into my chest. "You're such a liar."

Now you know what it feels like, I want to say. *To want somebody to promise not to leave, and they won't.*

But of course, he could say the same to me. *Now you know what it feels like, Warren. To have this whole other thing in your life, and all of a sudden you're not supposed to have it.*

Only I *don't* have this whole other thing in my life. Do I? It's just the idea that I never would.

FLIP: We start with *Father of the Bride,* in which this very *young* Elizabeth Taylor gets married. "Only once?" I say as Warren puts the tape into the machine. "Is this the abridged version?"

Apparently not, because for what seems like hours and hours, this nice, normal American family (I mean, only *Warren's* family's house is bigger than theirs) argues about how much money to spend on their daughter's wedding. Naturally, Spencer Tracy—who may be a bit insensitive on this issue, considering that Katharine Hepburn was the love of *his* life and he certainly never married *her*—anyway, Spence wants to save money any way he can. At one point, he even tries to bribe his daughter to elope.

"Warren!" I say suddenly. "Doesn't it bother you at *all*? I mean, *your* family not coming?"

Warren is lying more or less underneath me, and I can feel him shrug. "I suppose I would rather they came," he says softly. "But they weren't the point of it. You were."

I look back at the screen. For what seems like the millionth time, Liz is running out of the room in tears. There's nothing up there I want. That all-American house with its enormous *lawn,* the men with their dull jobs, the women for whom this wedding seems to be the high point of their lives. It couldn't be clearer—you get married, and you settle down, and your whole world shrinks to the size of just one person.

Warren isn't taking the last of the popcorn—you *know* he wants it, but he's always so polite—so I pass him the bowl over my head, holding it there until he has to take it. Is that what *he* wants? Him and me and maybe Juliet, our own little world unto ourselves?

Of course, by the time Liz *does* get married, the room is so packed with people that Spence can't even get to her to say goodbye. You could easily get the feeling that every single person in the world is on the side of that marriage. Even if after the wedding, the happy couple is left totally alone.

WARREN: As many remarks as Flip finds to make about *Father of the Bride,* they are nothing to what he says when we get to *Every Girl Should Be Married.* Which isn't even about a wedding—it's more about how desperately the heroine wants to get married. Although since the man she wants to marry is Cary Grant, you'd think that would be a motivation that even Flip could understand.

But no. "At the risk of sounding like Rosie," he's saying, "I hate how this is something you just *have* to do."

"Rosie wasn't against our getting married," I say, trying not to sound as hurt as I feel. "She was fairly supportive of the idea, as I recall."

"No, she is," Flip says. "She just keeps saying, nobody thinks *her* life is worth anything if she *doesn't* get married. And you know, Warren, I did think she was exaggerating, but come *on*. Liz Taylor got married about a million times, Spencer Tracy was a long-term adulterer, and Cary Grant was gay!"

"You mean actors differ from the roles they play?" I say. "What a surprise."

"Oh, shut up," Flip says. "Doesn't it make you wonder why we *need* all this pro-marriage propaganda, that's all I'm asking. If there *weren't* so many movies about it, do you think anyone would even want to do it?"

By the time we're up to *Muriel's Wedding,* it's almost three in the morning. Flip staggers to the VCR and changes the tape. He still seems so upset, I don't have the heart to suggest going to bed. When he's lying back down against me, he says, "If I was a psychic, *then* there wouldn't be any place you could go that I couldn't follow."

"I'm not so sure," I say slowly. "Of course, I don't know that many other psychics. But it seems to me that people go all sorts of different places."

Flip stuffs a handful of that awful caramel corn into his mouth and tries to get me to take some, too. "Well, I suppose it's a good thing I'm *not* a psychic," he says bitterly, as I push the bowl away. "Or neither one of us would have any privacy at all. At least this way, it's only me."

"Hardly," I say. "There are plenty of times when I have absolutely no idea what you're thinking. Even when you *tell* me, sometimes, I still don't understand."

Flip laughs. But he says, "You think it's only me, Warren. But you have them, too, all those places where you go and I can't follow. And you like it that way."

No, I want to say. You *have* somewhere else to go. That family, those friends, all those people who love you. I used to wish he *didn't* have them, if you want to know the truth.

Then suddenly I understand what he's spent the whole evening trying to tell me. Now he doesn't have anywhere else to go, either. Or at least, now he thinks he doesn't. Now he thinks it's only me.

I've done a lot of things I'm not proud of in the last year and a half. But I don't want to want *this.*

Just then, the door to Juliet's room opens. "I get so lonely in there," she says as she marches across the living room. "I *hate* it. I want to come out here and be with you. And you."

"Come on up," Flip says before I can insist on taking her back to bed. Somehow he pushes me over so that there's room for her, too. She lies there with her head on my chest and Flip's arm around her. The couch is suddenly very warm.

"I still miss her," Juliet says in that small voice that now reminds me of Flip. "I still miss her *a lot.*"

Flip reaches up to stroke her hair. "Well, of course you miss her, Juliet. She's your mother."

So we lie there, happy and miserable. Comforted and lonely. Together and so far apart. Together.

ROSIE: "I don't know about this wedding, or whatever they finally do decide to call it," I tell Marcy on the phone, and of course, both of us are watching the clock. Because the *moment* Alex stops nursing, Marcy's off to sleep, since that's the only time she *can* sleep. I'm honored that she'd even give me any of that special nursing time, which I always thought was supposed to be the occasion of a primal intimate communication between mother and child, but Marcy says (a) Yes, OK, it is, but when you're doing it eight million times a day it doesn't have to be primal and intimate *every* time. And (b) what about *our* communication, which, while not exactly primal, is at least intimate? "I have to talk to you *sometime,*" she says sleepily.

"Between breasts," I say.

"Exactly."

"I don't know *how* I feel about these connubial plans," I say now. "Because on the one hand——"

"Why *aren't* they calling it a wedding, by the way? Ouch! Right, Alex. Bite harder. That'll make the milk come faster." I hear her shifting position among the cushions as she coos, "There you go, sweetie. Is that better?"

I wait. "God, keep going," Marcy says in her regular voice. "Don't wait for *me* or I'll never find out *anything.*"

"Well," I say tentatively, over the last few cooing sounds. I can't *bear* that I haven't seen either of them yet—but now I've got three new shops in negotiations. And her parents and Joe's have pretty much booked the whole month, anyway.

"I think the confusion over the name comes from some sort of debate the two of them are having, over whether they're doing this totally new thing, which would probably be Flip's preference, or if they're actually just fulfilling a totally traditional role that has historically been denied to gay people, which I would guess is what Warren wants. Not that he'd ever put it like *that,* but I think there's something about the tradition that he does like. Since he, of course, isn't aware, or maybe, given his situation, just doesn't *care* that weddings have traditionally been the ceremonies in which the daughter is handed over from the father to a husband in exchange for some sort of price."

"That's not the *only* tradition," Marcy points out. "Boswell says there are gay weddings going back to ancient times."

"Well, it's the only tradition for *women,* isn't it?" I say, somewhat annoyed. Although isn't that what I prize about Marcy? She's always so *fair.*

Marcy laughs. "Obviously, Warren just isn't sufficiently committed to overcoming the historical oppression of women," she says. "What a surprise."

"So what would you have called yours? I mean, if you and Joe hadn't actually gotten married." Because this was a source of contention from the moment the two of them fell in love. Unlike most couples, they seemed to have not the least doubt that they actually *were* going to spend their lives together in a committed, monogamous relationship. But having agreed upon the content, they argued endlessly about the form. Were they simply going to get married, which Joe had always wanted to do, and which Joe's whole family— and probably Marcy's, too—saw as some kind of major Jewish responsibility, to perpetuate the race? (Or whatever they call it.) Or were they going to have some kind of extra-legal relationship, something not defined by the laws of the State of Massachusetts, in which any business concerning the division of property, child custody, and the like, was worked out between the two of them and a lawyer, with the focus being on their individual choice rather than on institutional forms?

"It wasn't just individual choice," Marcy says when I remind her of this debate. "That's the way the bourgeois feminists talk about it. I saw myself as part of a community. Which included people who couldn't get married. And people I wasn't married to but was close to anyway, not you, of course, Rosie, but all my *other* best friends. But *besides* you, my whole history, you know, all the people I've ever been close to in various ways, colleagues, and the women in my writing group, and other friends, and people I've done political work with . . . I saw getting married as taking me out of that community. Privileging one relationship above all others."

"But getting married put you into another community," I say. "Didn't it? Another community, another family—isn't that what it's *for?*"

Marcy sighs. "We're running out of time here," she says. "I'm already done with one whole breast."

"So that leaves, what? Twenty minutes?"

Marcy swallows a yawn. "If we're lucky. Sometimes he doesn't make it all the way through the second one."

"Doesn't that get uncomfortable?"

She laughs. "I try to keep switching off," she says, "but when it's two in the morning, who remembers?"

"You could use a Post-it."

"Ha, ha." Finally she says dreamily, "Another community. It did do that. I could be like my mother, and my grandmother, and *her* grandmother—"

Well, I'm like *my* mother. Not that *that's* anything to write home about.

"So what *would* you have called it if—if it hadn't been legal?"

"I don't know," says Marcy. She sounds irritated. "It took everything I had to fight with Joe about the actual wedding—I didn't have the wherewithal to envision an entire alternative all by myself."

"Do you regret it?"

"Alex, you'll be sick if you eat so fast," Marcy says in that cooing voice. Then she says, "That's right, Marcy, make sure he gets the connection between food and danger right in his *first* month of life. You're going to make some lucky therapist a very rich man. Or woman."

I laugh.

"Don't laugh," Marcy says gloomily. "It's only been six days, and already seven hundred thousand and forty-two *bubbemeises* have come pouring out of my mouth. It's like I'm possessed."

"What's a *bubbemeise?*"

"A—grandmother-saying," says Marcy. "Would be the literal translation, so I guess that makes it an *old wives' tale*. Which I guess makes me officially an old wife. Ha, ha."

"So *do* you? Regret it?"

"Getting married?" Marcy says. "I guess not—Joe would have been absolutely miserable if we hadn't, and he would probably never have agreed to have children, though I don't think he would have left me, finally. But I don't think I could have stood to live with him being that miserable. I don't *feel* like a piece of property, if that's what you're asking. And I probably do like all the extra credibility I get, being a known feminist and yet having this great husband that I actually get to *call* a husband. Having my cake and eating it, too. I'm not sure it's so *good* for me to like all that. I'm not so sure it's—I don't know." Suddenly she sounds extremely tired. "Who knows what else I would have been," she says, "if we *hadn't* gotten married. I don't mean what else I would have been apart from Joe, because obviously, I wasn't going to leave *him* if I could help it. But who knows if there was some other fabulous alternative way the two of us could have lived our lives, and our imaginations were just too limited by . . ." Her voice runs out.

"You sound terrible," I can't help saying. "Should we just stop?"

"I wish we could," she says wistfully. "But I can't fall asleep while he's sucking on me. Talk to me until he's done, OK, Rosie? Even if I don't make any sense."

"No, I'm the one who doesn't know what the hell I'm saying. It sounds so nice to be married. But maybe that's just because nothing counts unless you are."

"Going to the chapel, and we're going to get ma-a-a-rried, and we'll never be lonely anymore," sings Marcy. She *must* be tired.

"Exactly," I say. "I look at Flip and Warren, and I think—that's it. They've made it. *You've* made it. And your reward is—you know. Never being lonely."

"Right," says Marcy. "That's it. No loneliness around here. Everything here is just perfect."

"What?" I say.

"Well, I'm sorry, Rosie, but you always do that, and I really don't have the energy to—I mean, my life just isn't the way you're saying, which you obviously know, but you need me to say so, and I don't *have* the energy to say so at this point. I mean, *you* don't want to marry Warren, and I know you don't want to marry Joe, so what *do* you want?"

Over the phone, I hear a tiny hiccuping cry. I want there to be something else *to* want. But it doesn't look like I'm going to get it.

"All *right,* Alex," Marcy says irritably. "I'm *putting* you on my shoulder, *give* me a minute." Then her voice gets soft and caressing again. "There, sweetie. There you go. Yes, Alex. Come on, sweetie. You know you'll feel better as soon as you burp."

I actually hear the little burp over the phone. Then Marcy says, "I'm sorry, Rosie, I'm really sorry, but I just *have* to hang up now. I love you."

"I love you, too," I say as quickly as I can. "Go."

"Don't let it get to you, sweetie," Marcy says, and I know she's talking to me.

Later that week, I get a letter from her, a folded-up piece of computer paper stuffed inside an envelope. On the paper is printed the following quote:

Indeed, the social institution *of heterosexual marriage (as opposed to the personal experience of it . . .) has been in most premodern societies primarily a property arrangement. . . . This should not be construed to mean that marriage did not fulfill very personal needs. It was essential to standing in the community for the propertied classes, afforded intimacy and emotional support, constituted the basis of running a household—also a crucial source of emotional stability—provided the satisfaction of parenting, and entailed pivotal changes in status. For adults of both sexes . . . the difference between being unmarried and married was enormous. It was often the criterion for legal independence from parents for males. . . . For women, who never achieved full independence, it was even more profound: marriage was the initiation rite into adulthood (something her husband had usually gone through in another context). She became adult by virtue of her marriage, and a great deal of the ceremony associated with marriage symbolized the bride's leaving girlhood behind and entering into matron status. A woman who never married would always be a dependent, in many ways a child, whereas a married woman managed a household and could even do so on her own if left a widow.*

— John Boswell, Same-Sex Unions in Premodern Europe

Under the printing, Marcy has written:

Do you think F. & W. should call their whatever *an "initiation rite into adulthood"? If you're tired of speaking to Flip already, or rather, tired of having him speak to* you, *why don't you suggest it to him? xxooxxoo Marcy*

So of course, I have to laugh.

It *isn't* that I want to be married. I'm not even sure I want the *good* parts of marriage—the more or less constant companionship, the actual opportunity to have a child. I have a feeling those things would drive me absolutely crazy.

But the initiation rite into adulthood. The—*recognition*. Why *shouldn't* I want that?

WARREN: I've sent Madeleine a—wedlock—invitation at the only address we have for her, which is at the facility. (And what would you call *that?* The French word is *asile,* which literally means "asylum," although a better translation would be "refuge." But I can hardly call Madeleine a refugee.)

Sending the invitation required a certain amount of thought. Because Madeleine has been corresponding with Juliet for the last month or so, but her doctor has told us that neither I nor my parents should write until she does. Still, I couldn't imagine that Juliet *hadn't* told her about the upcoming ceremony, and I couldn't help thinking that *not* being invited would seem like a slap in the face. So even though we didn't include an invitation to Madeleine in that first mailing in April, I find myself addressing a separate invitation to her in May. And when Flip comes home one Saturday evening from one of the Tiger's Eye shows, bringing the mail up with him, there is our little return envelope, with a cluster of French stamps stuck on rather messily where the American one used to be.

Flip looks questioningly at me, but he doesn't actually ask. But when he goes into the bedroom, I find myself following him. As usual, he is lying stretched out on the bed, studying his script.

"I thought the play was up and running," I say, sitting down beside him. "I thought *this* part was over."

"Oh, it's never over," Flip says gloomily. "Just when you think you've milked every last little bit of meaning from the script—and it's not as though *this* script had all *that* much meaning in the first place. The production does, I think, actually. But the script itself is fairly simple."

"Since you won't let me come to the show, I wouldn't know."

Flip looks genuinely surprised.

"Have you been *wanting* to come?" he says. "It isn't that I wouldn't *let* you. I just think, you know. We'll all be doing a better job in a couple of weeks."

"But then it will be over," I hear myself say. "Then it will be over, and I'll have—missed it."

"Well, if you feel that way about it, come Monday afternoon. It's a single-parent support group, you should fit right in."

Why am I suddenly panicking? "I don't have a sitter," I say.

Flip's lips purse, but he manages not to smile. "My goodness, Warren," he says, "what must you think of us? We have child care, of *course*. What do you think all the *other* single parents do?"

Suddenly I toss him the letter. "You open it," I say. "I don't think I can."

To his credit, Flip manages not to look either surprised or triumphant. He stays blank, even when he extends the return card toward me. In shaky purple ink, Madeleine has checked the box next to "Yes, I/we would LOVE to come to your wedding (or whatever)!" And below it, in wobbly script, she's written *"Appelez-moi."*

"She wants me to call her," I explain.

"I figured that," Flip says. After a moment, he leans his head against my shoulder, wraps his arms around my chest.

"How can I blame her for wanting her back?" I say. "I would."

There is a silence.

"Blame Madeleine for wanting Juliet, or blame Juliet for wanting Madeleine?" Flip says eventually.

"Oh, either one. They belong together, don't they?"

Flip lets another silence go by.

"Well, you belong with her, too," he says finally.

"I'm not her mother," I say. "Six months ago, I didn't even know she existed."

"You *are* going to ask her, aren't you?" Flip is saying in that careful, distant voice. "About—"

I am so angry—though I'm not sure at whom—that I actually interrupt him. "About changing her whole life—for me?" I say. "When I haven't even spoken to her in twelve years?"

"She didn't speak to you, either," Flip points out.

"Well, I wouldn't expect you to understand," I say as calmly as I can. "It's not as though Juliet were related to you."

I think I sound quite reasonable. But Flip says in a quiet, deadly voice, "Fuck you, Warren. How *dare* you say that to me?"

He gets slowly off the bed. "I don't actually want to start screaming at you about this, given that Juliet is right there in the other room," he says, in a voice so low that it's practically a whisper. "Even though she's now officially *not* my niece, so why should *I* care? But since I *do* care, apparently, I am now going out—not *walking* out, but *going* out—before I hit you or throw something at you or, possibly, actually murder you. Even though *you're* not my family either, apparently, so I really *don't* know why I should care." By the time I can open my mouth to say something, it's too late. He's already out the door.

Somehow I manage to give Juliet her bath and put her to bed and even, somehow, to—well, *enjoy* probably isn't the right word. But to *be* with her, as she describes a science project she needs my help on and tells me how different Sara's homework is from hers.

"That's because she goes to Catholic school, like Uncle Flip," she says as I tuck her in. "But I go to private school, like you. Did you and Uncle Flip have different homework assignments, too?"

"I imagine so," I say. "We didn't know each other then, remember. I'm older than he is, so we *wouldn't* have known each other, even if we had lived in the same city."

"You wouldn't have known each other anyway," Juliet says, "because you went to different schools. It was just *sheer dumb luck,* Uncle Warren, that I *ever* got to meet Sara. If Marta hadn't been my babysitter, it would never, ever, ever have ever have happened. And then I wouldn't have a best friend."

"You might have *another* best friend," I suggest. She shakes her head emphatically, so that her pony tail flaps from side to side.

"No!" she says. "*Sara* is my best friend. If I hadn't met her, I wouldn't have one."

Juliet is asleep by nine-thirty. When it's one in the morning and he still isn't back, I decide there's one thing I *can* do. I find my address book and call Paris. It's only seven in the morning there, but after all, I *am* calling a hospital.

At first I ask for Madeleine's doctor. Of course *he* doesn't work those kinds of hours. However, says the nurse-receptionist, *c'est bien possible* for me to talk to Madeleine. "Because," she explains in French, "your sister is naturally an early riser, it's her temperament, she's that way, she always prefers the morning." She offers to put me through directly to Madeleine's room, and there doesn't seem to be any choice but to agree.

I don't hear Madeleine's voice at first, but only her breathing. For the longest time, we just sit there on the phone, listening to each other breathe.

"Well, Warren," she says finally. I *don't* recognize her voice, exactly. But hearing it is like that first sight of Juliet in my mother's living room—her and not her, my big sister and someone else. "Well, Warren, I understand congratulations are in order."

Then she spoils it by laughing.

"Thank you," I say, because isn't that what you *have* to say?

"Oh, you're welcome," she says, teasing me, and now I *do* recognize her voice, desperate and superior, the way it was when I was growing up. Though maybe I didn't hear the desperate part then.

No, I did. But I thought—

I thought it meant she would escape.

"I hope I didn't get you up too early," I say when the next silence goes on too long.

"Oh, Lord, no," Madeleine says, and I can see her shaking her head. If she *were* Juliet, her pony tail would be flapping back and forth. "I'm always up by five-thirty at the *latest*. That's the best time of the day, as far as I'm concerned. No one has done anything to it yet. It's untouched."

"Well, with a child—" I hadn't intended to say anything about Juliet quite so soon. But Madeleine laughs that wild laugh again.

"Oh, lucky for *me* she sleeps until six-thirty every morning. Thank *God* I had that extra hour." Why? I wonder. What difference does one hour make?

"Here, of course," Madeleine says, "that's the hour before they come around with the meds. That initial lucid sixty minutes, you know, it's quite a treasure."

"Are you—I mean, if you didn't *want* to be—I'm sure you could—"

"Oh, settle down, Warren," she says scornfully. "Of course I'm not serious, I only said that to shock you. Believe me, I'm grateful for every last drop of sedation and tranquility I can squeeze out of them. No, don't bother, I didn't mean that either. I just wanted to—" She sighs. "I was only playing," she says. "Honestly, it's fine here or I wouldn't stay. It's not as though anyone were keeping me."

This would be a good time for Flip to come home. "I'm glad it's—what you want."

"Well, I wouldn't go *that* far," she says. "Let's just say it was far and away the best of all the available alternatives."

If Flip *were* here, he'd be mouthing at me, "Ask her. *Ask her!*"

"I'm very glad you're coming to our—well, I suppose you'd have to call it a wedding," I say. "It's good of you to come on such short notice."

She bursts out laughing again. "Oh, Warren, listen to you. You'd think I was at some—I can't even think what it would be. Some cruise to the Islands? One of those women, you know, whose social schedule is booked for months in advance, and you can just imagine her complaining to all her fondest friends, 'Oh, my dear, it's so dreadfully distressing. My brother's up and getting married, only he's *homosexual,* so of course, they daren't call it *that.* And now I've simply got to *drop* everything and fly back up to the City, and in *June,* my dear, imagine. I'm actually going to be in the *City* in *June.*' "

And if I were laughing like this when Flip were here, he'd want to know what was so funny.

"All right," I say. "So you're *not* like that. My mistake." My voice quickens. "It's amazing, isn't it, when you think that people like that really *do* exist. I mean, when you think that most people don't know—but we do, you and I, because—"

Now she sounds chilly again. "Well, really, Warren, what do you expect? Thank *God* most people didn't grow up the way we did. I wish I *didn't* know half the things I do. Anyway, I wasn't particularly offended by the lack of notice. Obviously, I wasn't doing anything *else.*"

"Well, as long as you're *not,*" I hear myself saying, "would you consider staying here?"

The silence that follows is different from any of the previous ones. I can feel us both tasting it, wondering what it's made of.

"Here in your apartment?" Madeleine says carefully. "Or here in—"

"Oh, not—I mean, of course, you *could* stay here, if you needed to. We—"

"Well, in that case, Warren, thank you, no," says Madeleine firmly and with relief. Of course, *she* never had any problem interrupting. "It's very nice of you, but a blind man could see that it wouldn't work out."

"All right, obviously, yes, he could," I say. "I didn't mean that. What I meant was—"

"Because that's what Juliet's been asking, in every single one of her letters, and I tell you, Warren, it's simply ridiculous."

"All right," I say again. "I wasn't really asking that. I didn't put Juliet up to it, if that's what you think."

"I don't know *what* to think," Madeleine says. "Hearing from her and not a word from you. I had absolutely no idea *what* to think, if you want to know the truth."

"But the doctor said not to write to you. He said——"

"Well, you didn't have to listen to *him*. It's one thing if he pushes *me* around, I *have* to give in, but why on earth should he bully *you*? Unless it's simply on general principle, Warren—perhaps you let *everyone* push you around. And then you can blame everything on them. Of course, I'm here. I've got no one *left* to blame, apparently. Except myself. I certainly don't blame *you*. I was only stating a fact: When I didn't hear from you, I didn't know *what* to think. Particularly with Juliet inundating me with pleas to up and move to New York, which as you *know* is a place that I've always had an *extremely* hard time with. I didn't even like it thirty years ago, and it was a much nicer city then, wasn't it?"

"I wouldn't know," I say, trying to get my bearings. It's so odd to hear her say Juliet's name, on top of anything else. She does use the French pronunciation—Zhoo-l'yet—which seems—I don't know. It's as though my own way of pronouncing Juliet's name were my own special name for her. Instead of simply what she's called.

"Wouldn't know *what,* Warren?" Madeleine snaps.

"What the city was like thirty years ago," I say slowly. "Thirty years ago I was fifteen. I never spent any time in New York until I came here to live."

"Not that," Madeleine says. "Who cares about that? I meant, what were you *asking,* Warren? If it *wasn't* that you and I and Juliet and your—fiancé——" Hearing this word applied to Flip almost does make me laugh. "—if it *wasn't* for us all to live happily ever after in your tiny New York apartment, then what *were* you talking about?"

"Oh. Well. That you'd—come to *somewhere* in New York, I suppose. For a long visit if that's all you—Or permanent. Because that's what I'd prefer."

"Because of Juliet?" says Madeleine, and suddenly she doesn't sound brittle, she sounds fragile.

"Well, yes."

"I see," she says, and there's another long pause.

"Well," she says finally, trying to barrel on the way she always used to do, "I'll tell you what I told my daughter. You find me somewhere to stay. Not *with* you, since even you don't want *that,* Warren, but somewhere, anyway. For, say, a month. Or—well, if I arrive the week before the wedding. It can't be much earlier than that because—well, at any rate, it can't be. And I think if it were much later than that . . ." Her voice trails off.

"No, it shouldn't be later."

"All right, then," says Madeleine. "A week before the wedding. A month after. Find me somewhere. And then we'll see."

And can Juliet stay here all that time? I want to ask so badly, it hurts physically not to. *Some of the time? A week, a day, a night?* I can't even ask that.

"Thank you," is what I can say, though again, I didn't know I was going to.

"Oh, don't thank me until we see how it all works out," she says quickly. "Who knows, Warren? Who ever knows?" And then she hangs up.

When Flip finally comes into the apartment, I wake up with a start. I hear him shut the front door very quietly and then go stand outside Juliet's room—I never knew he did that. He waits at Juliet's door, listening to her breathe.

I don't even wait for him to climb all the way into bed. I grab him as soon as I can reach him and just hold on, as hard, as hard, as hard as I can.

"Flip," I say, and my whisper sounds harsh in my ears. *"Flip. You're* my family. All right? You are."

He puts one hand up to stroke my face. "Warren," he whispers back. And then he says, so softly I can barely hear him, "You too."

When I wake up the next morning, Flip is already awake. I see him lying there, staring at me. *"What?"* I say irritably, before I remember that I'm still supposed to be apologizing.

Flip's mouth twists. "Gee, I don't know, Warren," he says. "Why don't you tell me?" I take a deep breath, just trying to wake up, but maybe it sounds impatient. "I mean," he says quickly, "why *do* you want to marry me, Warren? And don't say any of those other names, because you know they're not really what you want. What *you* want is to be married, but for the life of me, I don't understand why."

In the other room we hear Juliet putting another tape in the VCR. We've worked out this arrangement where, if at all possible, we spend all day Sunday together, the three of us—but first, Flip and I get to stay in bed really late, like eleven in the morning, while Juliet watches as many videos as she wants.

"I'm not asking why you want to be with me, Warren," Flip says when I still don't answer. "I mean, I'm not—questioning your devotion. Despite all your many obvious shortcomings. But why in God's name do you want to stand up there in public and say *vows* to me? You can barely stand to tell me how you feel about me as it is."

"Well, it isn't exactly public," I say. "It is just who we invite."

Flip shrugs. "If we were straight and we really *were* getting married, it would be public," he says. "Given *your* family, it would probably be in the *Times*."

I do wish it were public, what he and I are to each other. It surprises me how much I want that, newspapers and all. I wish it were something that already existed, something we could just step inside of. Instead of something we have to make up, all by ourselves.

"So, why?" Flip says softly but insistently.

And when I finally realize what the answer is, I realize why it's been so slow in coming. "Because it's all so fragile," I say unwillingly. "Which I know is my—I mean, all right, I'm the one who left." Flip puts his hand on my arm, that gesture that I always find so incredibly comforting. "And when I asked if I could come back—" I force myself to continue. "You never even said *yes*. In fact, you said *no*."

"I cannot *believe* you're bringing this up now," Flip says. He takes back his hand. "Particularly after what *you* said last night."

"I'm not *blaming* you," I say. "I was only saying, it's fragile."

He's got his back to me now, his shoulders clenched. "Not that you didn't have a point that night," I manage to say. "I can see why you would have thought—that it was my turn to—to declare myself." I'm looking at the curve of his neck, the way the skin pulls when his shoulder twitches. "Maybe that's why I want to—declare myself—now. In public. So I can't ever take it back."

Flip flops back over and studies me for what seems like a long time. Then he says, "I, Flip Philip Bernard Terence Zombrowski, love you, Warren Baird Huddleston, with all my heart, and all my mind, and all my spirit, and all my soul. And all my body, too, I suppose. And I intend to love you, and honor you, and cherish you, and make you happy, and make you miserable, for the rest of my life or the rest of your life, whichever comes first, and if we're lucky, they'll both come at the exact same time, even though I'm so *much* younger than you."

I put my hand on his face, finally, and I feel him press back against my palm. "I, Warren Baird Huddleston, love you, Flip Philip Bernard Terence Zombrowski, with all my heart, and all my mind, and all my spirit, and all my soul. And all my body, too. And I intend to love you and live with you and—and *be* with you, for all the rest of both of our lives, which I also hope last exactly the same amount of time, especially since I'm not all *that* much older than you."

"Thirteen years," Flip says in a stage whisper, which I hope is the kind of thing he wouldn't do at the actual ceremony, although since it's Flip, I suppose you never know.

"So?" I say. "I now pronounce us husband and husband."

"Or man and man," says Flip. We lie there, taking that in.

"I think we're supposed to kiss now," he says after a minute. But we just look at each other.

"You know it won't change anything," Flip says a minute later. "To say that anywhere else. The day after we say it, it will be just as—insubstantial—"

"Or as substantial."

We hear Juliet fast-forwarding the VCR. She does that sometimes over the scary parts or the parts she doesn't like. "You know what we should do this morning," Flip says. "We should take Juliet out for pancakes. All week she's been saying she wants them."

"All right," I say, starting to get up. Flip stops me with a hand on my shoulder.

"No," he says. "I'll go." He pulls himself up out of bed. "Well, I hate to say this," he says, putting on his bathrobe. "But I think, for the rest of the time that Juliet is here—God, I *really* hate to say this. But I think we should have a schedule."

"What?"

"You know," Flip says. "A schedule? As in, who takes care of her when?"

"You mean a *schedule*," I say, "as in, where you say in advance when *you'll* take care of her."

"See, Warren," Flip says as he heads out the door, "it's just marvelous how your vocabulary is improving."

So we go out for breakfast at the Chelsea Gallery, where Juliet finally decides that she'll sit *next* to Flip and *across* from me. Back under our booth, Flip presses his leg against mine. And then of course Juliet wants to go to Washington Square Park and play in the playground. Where we meet Marta and Sara and Rogelio, so Juliet goes off with Sara, and Flip and Marta and I sit on the bench and watch Rogelio in the sandbox. Since it *is* the Village, but also the children's playground, where the rules feel a little different than elsewhere in the park, Flip and I figure we can sit, not holding hands or with our arms around each other, but at least touching, shoulder to shoulder, hip to hip. After all, will sitting one inch farther apart make any difference? Anyone can see what we are. And then we go home, where there's a message from Tanya—apparently there's some schedule change in the Tiger's Eye show—and one from Ian, suggesting some children's concert that he thought Juliet and I might like—Flip raises his eyebrows at me, but he doesn't actually comment—and one from Malik, leaving Flip a telephone number for some community action group that is keeping a record of incidents involving the police, causing me to raise *my* eyebrows at *him,* but I don't say anything, either. And then I cook dinner while Flip plays with Juliet, and then Flip does the dishes while I read to Juliet, who wants to know why the homeless men that she once noticed only in the park have now set up this whole cardboard box colony on the street between her house and Sara's, and then Flip gives Juliet her bath and I put her to bed, and then we both sit in the living room.

"OK," says Flip. "You win. Even if the vast majority of the known world doesn't recognize our marital sacrament, I think you're right. Saying something about our relationship in public *is* a good idea."

"You always do that," I say. "How on earth did you ever come up with *that?*"

"Because," Flip says, "all those other people keep intruding anyway. I mean, here we have this perfect day, and it *still* isn't just the three of us. Or at least not for very long. So I give up. You win. We might as well be the ones to set the terms."

"That isn't at all what I meant."

"Well, it's what *I* meant. Take it or leave it."

"I can hardly afford to pass it up," I say.

"Mmmm," Flip says. "That's what I thought."

ROSIE: When I called Warren to see if he would, finally, give me that reading I had asked about last fall, he sounded so surprised I had to laugh.

"I'm not sure I should put my entire earthly future into the care of a psychic who didn't even know I was going to call," I say.

"It isn't a party trick," Warren says somewhat stiffly. "Or some sort of alarm system that you simply leave on twenty-four hours a day."

"Well, I didn't mean to impugn anything," I say, a little annoyed myself. Why is he always *like* this?

Warren sighs in his irritated way. "No, *I'm* sorry," he says. "It's only—"

"The marital formalities must involve an enormous amount of work," I say sympathetically. Well, it's Flip's own fault. If he would tell me one or two details about what's going on with him once in a while, I wouldn't have to stoop to this.

"It's not the *work,*" Warren says in that tone people have when they're continuing an argument with someone who isn't there. "It's all the *planning.* All of a sudden, it's a full-scale production."

"Well, honestly, Warren, what did you expect?" I say, completely unfairly, since I all but begged him to complain to me. "Flip's involved, and there'll be an audience. Of *course* it's a big production."

So all right, making the appointment was fairly easy, and you might even say I had the upper hand. Actually going, though, is another matter.

"You know what's really weird," I say as I walk into Warren's office and he offers me a chair. "I feel so disloyal to Cassandra."

"Really? Your acupuncturist? Why?"

"I don't know." I can't believe how nervous I am. "I suppose because she's also—you know. In the other realms."

Warren laughs. "Well, I promise you I don't use needles," he says. "I probably won't even tell you anything you don't already know."

"Just things I'd rather *not* know," I say, and Warren looks at me more closely.

"You won't tell Flip anything, will you?" I say. "I mean, he knows I'm coming to see you—I'm not asking you to *lie*. Just—"

"Rosie," Warren says gently. "Of course I won't tell him anything." His voice gets even more gentle. "I don't even have to tell *you* anything."

I sigh. "No, it's all right. I can take it. What do I do?"

I swear I wouldn't be here if it wasn't for Michael. I swear to God I've never been so confused. I understand there are actually people who don't *mind* being confused, but God knows, I'm not one of them. I feel as if I'm floating out to sea on an iceberg in the sun. And with every passing day that I don't know what I want, a little more melts away. Sooner or later, I'm going to drown.

Warren is watching me with a troubled look on his face. "What?" I say. "What? What horrible thing did you just pick up?"

"No," says Warren slowly. "It isn't that." He takes a deep breath. "When I first got Juliet," he says carefully, "I used to think a lot about—drowning."

"Oh," I say.

"Which was why it was so—I mean, when you brought up the *Titanic* that time, in your office—"

"Oh," I say again.

"So that happens sometimes," Warren says. "A lot, actually. With other clients. Who aren't also friends. Or—family. That we'll—*share* an image somehow."

"Are you saying that we *shouldn't* do this?" I say. "Because, Warren—"

"Rosie. No. I wasn't saying that. I was simply—telling you what had happened. I just didn't expect it quite so soon, that's all."

"You mean quite so much," I say, looking at his face. Seeing him there with me, on that iceberg. Damned if it melts and damned if it doesn't.

"I suppose that *is* what I meant," Warren says. "And I suppose I *should* have expected it. Given what things are like with us anyway." He holds out his hands, palms up, and I realize I am supposed to put mine into them. Suddenly that seems like an enormously big step.

"Is this what you always do?" I say, to buy time. "Start by——"

"*Rosie,*" he says, which I suppose I must have been expecting, too. "Close your eyes and give me your hands."

I obey. His hands are warmer than I would have thought; in fact, when I put my hands into his, they burn. I am about to say something about that, but I can feel him telling me to be quiet.

See it, says Warren's voice, or at least I think it's his voice. *You have to see what happened. For me to see it, you have to see it.*

I can't believe how much I don't want to do this. But then why am I here? So I remember.

It was that Saturday three weeks ago, that same Saturday I saw Flip in the diner. All right, it was good that we met, Flip and I, I'm not saying it wasn't. But something is over, I have to say that, too. It's never going to be the same again.

Around my hands, Warren's hands jerk shut and then slowly open again. Is that what *I* feel, thinking that? Or what *he* does? Did he really not know what happened? It never occurred to me that Flip wouldn't tell him.

That doesn't matter now, I imagine Warren saying. *Keep going.*

All right. So Flip and I finally said goodbye at the subway station and headed to our separate trains. I wasn't actually bleeding. But I felt like I was. I felt—well, now if I say, *like I was drowning in my own blood,* it's going to sound way too dramatic, isn't it? Like something I made up.

Go on, Warren says again, which I'm sure he means to be comforting, but honestly, I just find it—implacable.

So there I am on the train, going uptown to Michael's apartment in the Bronx. A place that isn't even on the map for Flip and Warren, even though for the people who live there, it *is* their map.

I can feel Warren's listening as though it were a physical force, like his burning hands surrounding mine. His listening steers me, nudges me, *herds* me back to the walk down from that elevated platform, the one where I stood with my forbidden cup of coffee the day I went downtown to that all-day union meeting, that day I had lunch in the park with Jack Kim and he asked me if it was possible to build an entirely new world.

No. Back to Michael's place. Not morning now, but night. Michael has dinner cooking, of *course.* I'm not complaining. It just breaks my heart.

I'm so happy to see him. His beautiful face, the round muscles in his arms, and through coincidence or design, he's wearing that amber-colored T-shirt, the one he wore the night we first made love. The night I first knew I wanted him.

And of course, I want him now. And so of course we make love, and of course it's good. And I feel like crying, because it isn't that I don't love Michael, it's not that he doesn't love me. *That's* not the problem at all.

Can we stop now, please? I want to ask Warren. Because I'd really like to get out of this room intact, instead of feeling it all over again, me in Michael's bedroom, in his bed, the cool sheets, his smooth soft skin, the filling up, the relief. In each other's bodies, each other's hearts—how could that not be enough?

And of course, we're both starving by this point—it's almost ten o'clock—and we go into the kitchen and sit, naked in our robes, our skins full—it's so *friendly*. And of course, he wants to know all about the strike, and I love telling him about it—I *do* love the way he listens. *That's* not the problem either.

Warren doesn't understand, I can feel it through his palms. He would give his life for this—*has* given his life for it. The iceberg melts and all of a sudden it's not the North Atlantic but the tropics, not drowning but floating. For him.

Go on, Warren says anyway. He won't leave me alone with this even though he doesn't understand it.

"Michael," I say, and he looks at me, and right then, our conversation stops.

"Michael," I say. "It's too hard. To want the whole world and not have you want it, too."

"It's just this other kind of life you want, Rosie. Fighting all the time. I don't mean with me. With—everything. With the way things are."

"And it's too much."

"Not when *you* do it. But you want me to do it, too."

"So what *do* you want, Michael? You never tell me."

"I do tell you," he says. "You just never believe me. You think it's too little. But I don't want the whole world, Rosie. Just—my life.

"With you," he adds after a minute. "Doesn't look like I'm going to get it, though."

"I want you, too. But *with* me, Michael. Not back here watching."

"Why, Rosie? Why can't you go off and—do whatever you do—and then you can just come back and tell me about it? I *have* my life."

"But you won't share it with me."

"Because you take it over, Rosie. You take my life and show me why—it should be like yours."

But I *do* think his life should be like mine. Not *exactly* like mine, I *don't* mean that, for him or for Flip either. But I *do* think people should—fight back. No, not just that. I think people should want *everything*. I don't understand wanting anything less.

Michael looks at me, angry and sad and something else, and I see in his face every single thing I ever did to hurt him, from the moment I met him till now. Every time he offered something and I wouldn't take it, every time he asked to meet Flip and I said *no,* every time he tried to love me and I didn't want to be loved. Only it doesn't matter. Because even if I suddenly became—well, perfect, I still couldn't imagine bringing Michael into my life. I don't mean my life with Flip and my family and all those little daily details. But my *real* life. The one in the world. He said it himself. He doesn't want to be there.

Warren's fingers tighten around mine, so tight they don't even hurt anymore. I feel something moving, through him, through me. I feel how much it hurts him, this *thing* taking him over. But he doesn't look away. He stays there and bears it, for me.

Finally, he speaks. And what he says is, "It isn't an iceberg, Rosie. It's a raft. I don't know where you're going. And obviously, you don't either. But you aren't melting. That's all I can tell you. You're simply—emptying out."

Oh, what does that mean? I think scornfully. His hands jerk again—have I hurt his feelings?

Maybe not. He's still holding on. "When you get rid of everything you have," he says slowly. "When you throw it all away. When you're *empty.*" Every word seems to hurt, coming out, the way it hurts to breathe. "When you're *empty,*" he repeats. "Then you decide—what to put back in. Then you—make up a whole new—" I can feel the ache in his lungs. "You want *something else,*" he says. "So you'll have to—make it up. But then you'll have—that new thing. You don't lose *everything* forever."

But *some* things you lose forever. Some things you lose, and you never get them back.

WARREN: All of a sudden, Flip seems to have decided that this is *his* partnership celebration, and no, I don't mean "his partnership celebration, *too.*" Just as when he's working on a part, he surrounds himself with huge stacks of library books and photographs and newspaper clippings and Lord knows what else, and starts the process of what he calls "doing research."

"So you know why the bride always stands on the *left* side," he says tonight, barely looking up from his book as he sits there at one end of the couch. I am sitting at the other end, reading *my* book. (Yet another volume on learning disabilities, because although things are going somewhat better for Juliet at school, I still don't believe they really understand her there.)

"Warren! You're not listening."

"I don't know why you say that. On the left side." I don't feel like pointing out that this particular piece of information is more or less irrelevant, since there obviously won't *be* a bride at *our* wedding.

"Because in the old days, the groom had kidnaped the woman and taken her away from her family—although if families in those days were anything like families in these, you'd think she'd have been happy to leave. But if her family *was* going to come after her, the groom needed his right hand to hold his sword—you know, so he could fight them off. With the best man on *that* side, apparently, to help with the fighting. Which I guess would make him the groom's *right-hand man*."

I am about to go back to my book, when he says, still not looking up, "Oh, wait a minute. It's not actually her family that he's fighting off, but any other men around who might want the bride. So I guess *her* two alternatives are either a wedding or a gang rape."

"And just how do you plan to incorporate this image into *our* wedding?" I can't help asking. "Or are you now planning on calling it an abduction?"

Flip grins. "We *could* call it an abduction," he says. "And since this *was* originally your apartment, I suppose we would have to say that *you* abducted *me*. Which is more or less how *I* remember it anyway. Both times."

"Ha, ha," I say. "Does that mean you *were* a virgin when I first carried you off?"

Flip grins again. Then he looks back down at the book. "Actually," he says, "the idea was that the groom would whisk them away somewhere—a primitive honeymoon, so to speak—and keep them there till they got pregnant. So by the time the bride's family showed up, it was just too bad for them."

"Oh," I say, getting interested for the first time, "that's in Boswell, too. Young men used to do that on Crete, with the youths they wanted to marry. Or whatever. I don't think they actually called it marriage. But they *did* call it abduction."

"There you go," Flip says, but somewhat absently—he's getting ready to sink back into his book again. "A heritage we can *all* be proud of."

Then he says, "And the veil. It was to keep the groom from rejecting the bride in an arranged marriage. In case he didn't like how she looked."

"Well, it's too late for that now," I say. "I already know what you look like."

Flip snaps his book shut. "All right," he says, throwing it down dramatically on the couch between us. "What do *you* think we should do, Warren? Since you're obviously so uninterested in what *I'm* finding out."

"I didn't say I wasn't interested."

"God, you're such a *liar*, Warren," Flip says. "You love to complain that *I* don't want to do something, but just let me start getting interested in doing it, and all of a sudden, I'm intruding again. Could you please make up your goddamn mind?"

I don't know what to say. "Say something, Warren," he says finally. "Just say *something*, all right? I mean, if this *were* a performance, somebody would be saying what the objective was. What the audience was supposed to get."

"I hate that," I say, far more vehemently than I expect. "It isn't *for* some audience. It's for us."

"Well, all those other people are going to be there," Flip points out. "We have to give them *something* besides food."

I sigh loudly. "Can't we simply do whatever the regular ceremony is?"

Flip smiles. "Well, at the risk of pissing you off yet again," he says rather smugly, "would you mind if I *read* you the regular ceremony? That was one of the first things I got. It's in *The Book of Common Prayer,* which I think you, as an Episcopalian, would be familiar with."

"Oh, shut up."

"I'll take that as a yes," Flip says. When he starts to read, I see what he means. "Dearly beloved," the service begins, "we are gathered together here in the sight of God and in the face of this company, to join together this Man and this Woman in holy Matrimony, which is an honorable estate, instituted of God, signifying unto us the mystical union that is betwixt Christ and his Church—" He looks up for a moment. "You remember this, Warren," he says. "It was in *Father of the Bride.*"

"All right, all right," I say. "But what about the actual vows? They're not so religious, are they?"

"I John take thee Jane to my wedded Wife," Flip reads, "to have and to hold from this day forward, for better for worse, for richer for poorer, in sickness and in health, to love and to cherish, till death do us part, according to God's holy ordinance; and thereto I give thee my troth. With this Ring I thee wed: In the name of the Father, and of the Son, and of the Holy Ghost, Amen."

"Well, that wouldn't be so hard to edit."

"I guess," Flip says. "I just don't see—I mean, if you want to know the truth—" He winces. "If you want to know what I really think," he says carefully, "I think—and let me remind you once again that you *started* this. And you didn't say, let's write a legal contract, or let's register for domestic part-nership, or let's say vows to each other in the privacy of our bedroom, or even, let's buy each other wedding rings, or commitment rings, or some other made-up name for *them*. You said, let's get married. Meaning, let's have a wedding. Meaning, let's do this big public thing—so, Warren. *Why* do we want all those people to be there?"

"Because we need them," I say reluctantly.

"Why?" Flip says. "And please don't say, 'So we can't ever take it back,' be-cause I've been thinking about what you said the other day, and I have to tell you, Warren, I kind of hate it. I mean, if you ever really stopped—wanting to be with me, then you *should* just go. I might hunt you down and kill you, but you should still go."

"No," I say slowly. "I don't think we need them for that. It's more—" *Be-cause you're not enough,* is how the words first come into my mind, but obvi-ously, it isn't only him. Obviously, *I'm* not enough, either.

Suddenly Flip makes a face. "Warren," he says warningly, "if you say that I need the group to do my best work, I really *will* kill you." I laugh, and unwill-ingly, he laughs, too. Then he twists his mouth. "If we need all those other people so goddamn much," he says gloomily, "then we should be saying our fucking vows to *them*."

"We *could* just have a party," I say. "They *could* be there simply to—be happy for us."

Flip sighs. "I should know better by now than to ever ask you *anything*, Warren," he says. "It's the most annoying thing in the world, but you really are always right."

"What exactly am I right about this time?"

Flip stands up with his arms full of books. "That we need them," he says, heading off into the bedroom. "We need them, and there's not a damn thing we can do about it. Whether we have a ceremony to say so or not."

FLIP: Madeleine writes to tell us when she's coming, and Warren starts in on the whole complicated process of finding her a place.

"I thought she was staying in our other apartment," I say. Because for what-ever reason—*you* figure it out—we're *still* paying rent on that place in Hell's Kitchen.

To my surprise Warren sighs and says, in what for him is an unusually stubborn voice, "I don't want her staying in that apartment. I'll find her some-where else."

"But, Warren, why?" I can't help asking. "Everything in New York is so expensive—it'll cost a fortune."

"Well, I *have* a fortune." So I don't suppose this is the moment to remind him that it was supposed to be *our* fortune.

So Warren gets busy, and since, if you have enough money, you really *can* do anything you want, he finds a sublet broker who generously allows him to pay what is probably more than the entire *year's* rent on the place in Hell's Kitchen in exchange for two months in a tiny furnished two-bedroom in the Village. I mean, *we* can't afford the Village, even *with* Warren's money. And for another small fortune, Warren learns, he can have the place for two *more* months. So Warren settles down to hoping that Madeleine's visit will stretch on indefinitely, and we can all live happily ever after.

The other thing that Madeleine said in her letter, which is an enormous relief, is that Juliet should stay with us, at least until after the matrimonial rites are concluded. Apparently Madeleine—or maybe her doctor—seems to think that she should take all these transitions one step at a time.

Naturally, Madeleine doesn't want us to meet her plane, like any normal person. Instead, we're supposed to take Juliet to meet her at Washington Square Park after school. I don't think Warren particularly wants *me* to come, but too bad for him. If I *am* part of this family, then I should be there, don't you think? And then we'll take Juliet over to Sara's house and go meet Madeleine for dinner somewhere, so *we* can talk. And then, we'll see.

It's quite a journey, walking down to Washington Square Park with Warren and Juliet. It's a brilliant June day—but the word *funereal* doesn't begin to describe the mood. Warren is simply blank, and Juliet, young though she is, manages to match him in blankness. The two of them march down Fifth Avenue, looking straight ahead and holding hands for dear life. I walk along on Warren's other side and try not to feel left out.

We've arranged to meet Madeleine at our usual bench by the jungle gym, and the minute we set foot on the park side of the street, Juliet takes off, heading for a destination that neither Warren nor I can see. She just bolts, silently, into the playground, flinging herself toward our bench, where Warren and I finally see a woman with dark-red dyed hair and one of those faded but incredibly elegant French suits. She stands up for one brief moment, until Juliet throws herself against the woman's lap and they fall back down onto the bench. The woman—Madeleine, obviously—wraps her arms around Juliet and the two of them sit like that for a long while, rocking slightly. They look like long-lost lovers.

Warren and I stop short. After a minute, I take Warren's hand, and his fingers squeeze mine so tightly, I begin to lose all feeling there.

Finally, after what seems like hours and hours, Juliet lifts her head from Madeleine's chest, and Madeleine looks down at her daughter, and then they just look into each other's eyes. There's something about how absorbed they are in each other that makes it actually fascinating to watch. We have moved in a little closer, so we can see the expression on their faces, and I keep thinking of people who've survived a shipwreck. No matter how much they wanted to see each other again, you can tell they had each given up hope.

Finally, Juliet starts talking, as Madeleine holds her tightly with one arm wrapped around her waist. Madeleine's other hand never stops moving, stroking Juliet's hair, straightening her blouse, touching her face.

"—and Mama, then I went there on a sleepover, and imagine, we made some-mores, you probably don't know what those are, because they don't have the things to make them in France, of course, they have chocolate there, but not *graham crackers,* Mama, and not *marshmallows,* and Uncle Warren said you didn't even have some-mores when *you* were a little girl, did you?, but *I* had them, at Sara's house, and we cooked them over the flame in her stove— she has a gas stove, too, but Uncle Warren has an electric stove, so you can't do anything like that there. And I have a cat, well, not a real cat, it's called a giga-pet, but that's not the cat's name, the cat's name is Minou, because I like that name, Mama, I really like that name. And in school I wrote a story about Minou, not my electronic cat, but a made-up cat, *named* Minou, because they don't speak French there, they didn't know that Minou *means* cat, I mean, kitten, and the teacher said I should have had an A, but she was marking me down for handwriting and spelling and margins and not writing on a straight line—they do that *all* the time here—and—"

Warren takes a step forward, his eyes on Madeleine. I suppose he still can't bear to look at Juliet. A shiver goes through Madeleine as he gets close. But she won't stop looking at her daughter.

"Why don't we come back in an hour or so," Warren says softly, and Madeleine nods. Juliet doesn't even notice. As we walk away from the bench, she is still talking.

For that next hour, Warren and I don't say a single word to each other, though it's not exactly like he's ignoring me. We walk side by side, all through the East Village and down into the Lower East Side, as far away from the park as we can get. When we return, at about six o'clock, Juliet is leaning against Madeleine, with Madeleine's arm around her, still on that bench.

Something goes through Warren when he sees them like that, and I know he is counting up every time he could have hugged Juliet and didn't, every time he could have brushed her hair or given her a kiss or pulled her into his lap. He's like that with me, too, whenever I'm physical with her, that longing look, that angry wish that he could do that, too.

Although you still feel that quite a lot is going on between Juliet and Madeleine, they're not talking, so Warren sits down slowly next to Madeleine. I sit next to Warren.

"Did you have a good flight?" Warren says after a minute, and both Madeleine and I are almost shocked into laughter. Only Juliet doesn't seem to think there's anything out of place about that question, and of course, *she* answers.

"Uncle Warren, she was on that plane for *six hours,* that's all it was, just six hours, can you imagine, it takes longer to take the *bus* to Miami, that's what Sara told me, because her cousin lives in Miami, and they're going to go visit this week, so if Mama wasn't going to be here, I'd be *so lonely,* because Sara will be gone for five whole days, maybe six, they weren't sure yet, but Mama can still meet Sara, can't she, because Sara isn't leaving till the weekend. That's still four whole days away."

There is a pause, during which Warren realizes that he, actually, is supposed to answer. "No," he says slowly, and I can't help it, I have to take his hand again. Which at least he lets me do. "That doesn't sound like a problem. There's still plenty of time for—your mother to meet Sara."

Finally, Madeleine looks at Warren, and then there's another long moment of silence. "Aren't you going to introduce me to your—fiancé?" she says finally.

Again, Juliet is the one who answers. "That's Uncle Flip," she says. "He's an actor. He was in a movie before I met him, but it's not in the movie theaters now, but it will be soon, right, Uncle Flip? You said June."

"More like July, is the latest word," I say. Warren and Madeleine keep giving each other these little glances and then looking away.

"You know what, Juliet?" I say when the next silence goes on way too long. "Your mother and Uncle Warren haven't seen each other for twelve years— since before you were born."

"I knew that," Juliet says quickly.

"Well, so, they miss each other, too. Maybe we should take a walk over to the swings and give them a minute to catch up."

"No!" say both Warren and Madeleine right away. Madeleine stands up, pulling Juliet up with her. Then she kneels down, so she and Juliet are eye to eye.

"Bye-bye, Minou," she says, putting one hand on each of Juliet's shoulders. "I'm going to spend the whole day with you tomorrow, remember. That will be wonderful. That will be heavenly. Won't it? We'll walk and talk the whole entire day, just like we do in Paris."

Juliet throws her arms around her mother's neck. I see Madeleine's whole body shake, and I watch Juliet struggle with herself. You can see she wants to argue, to insist that Madeleine stay with her, to have a tantrum. And you can see her swallowing each tear, each angry word, biting her lip.

"It's OK, Minou," Madeleine whispers. "I'm not going to leave you again. Just tonight, Minou, just little bits of time, here and there, now and then. Not for a long time, not like before. Don't worry, Minou. That won't happen again. It won't."

How can you be so sure? I want to ask her. But you can see that Juliet believes her, or at least, that she wants to.

"Just a few hours, Minou," Madeleine is saying. "You'll go home with Uncle Warren, and Uncle Flip, and then you're going over to Sara's, aren't you? That will be good, won't it?"

If I can see Madeleine trembling, surely Juliet can feel it. "And then Uncle Warren will come and get you," Madeleine is saying, "and put you back into your own nice bed. And then it will be morning. And then I'll see you again. For the whole entire day."

Juliet looks at Warren. "Don't I have to go to school?" she says.

Obviously, none of this has ever been discussed. But Warren shakes his head. "No," he says. "Not tomorrow."

"What about the day after?" Juliet says. "That's Friday. That's just before the weekend anyway. I don't have to go then, either, do I?"

"We'll see," says Warren. "Let's just take it one day at a time, all right, Juliet?

"The way we did when you first came here," he says after a minute. "That was—confusing, too, remember?"

Juliet nods, more for lack of other alternatives than out of any actual agreement. Slowly she walks over and takes Warren's hand. Then she takes my hand, too. I squeeze her hand, hard.

"Goodbye, Warren," Madeleine says. "I'll see you tonight—oh, and you, too, Flip." She makes some kind of waving gesture. Warren nods. "I'll see *you* tomorrow," she says to Juliet. "So soon, Minou, so soon . . ." And then she goes.

"Uncle Warren," Juliet says finally. "Can we go straight to Sara's house, right now, right now?"

"I suppose we could," says Warren, looking back down at her. "Is that what you want to do?"

"Yes," says Juliet firmly. "That's exactly what I want. I don't want to see our own apartment until it's time for me to go to sleep, Uncle Warren. If you come late enough, I'll already *be* asleep, and then I won't have to see it until morning."

"And that's what you want?" Warren says.

"Yes," Juliet says again. "It's just too many places."

Warren has arranged for us to meet Madeleine at L'Acajou, this French restaurant over on 19th Street. As we slowly get dressed for this dinner of doom, I wonder whether maybe Warren and Madeleine *should* have some time alone. When I ask him, though, he gives me this horrible accusing *look,* just the way he does when he wakes me up with a bad dream. Except that he's also saying, in this totally normal voice, "I'd rather you came. Unless, of course, you don't want to."

Do I answer the voice or the look? Intrude or abandon? Just one of the many little questions that makes it so much *fun* to live with Warren.

"God, *I* wouldn't miss it," I say finally, trying, rather desperately, to respond to both. "Because (a) she's the one I identify with, remember? And (b) you know. Family reunions. Who *doesn't* love those? And (c) I fully expect Madeleine to adore me, just the way your mother did. So why *wouldn't* I want to go?"

Warren suddenly sinks down onto the bed, right in the middle of buttoning his shirt.

"Isn't it obvious where Juliet belongs?" he says. "Madeleine's her *mother.*"

"Warren. All right, you're not her mother, but——" I sit down beside him. "You're not *nothing,*" I finally say.

"No? There's no reason, is there, why Madeleine can't have Juliet all to herself?"

"That's not what Juliet wants."

Warren shakes his head. "I'm no better," he says in a low voice. "I want her all to myself, too."

When we get to the restaurant, Madeleine is already there, sitting in a booth facing the door. When Warren and I slide into the booth across from her, I can see even more clearly how like Juliet she is. How hard she's working to hold herself in.

Warren seems to be ignoring me completely. But suddenly I feel something from him so strong that I have to reach over and take his hand under the table. "I'm glad you're here," Warren says, and Madeleine shrugs. "I'm glad you're all right," he says, and she flinches.

"Well, let's not exaggerate," she says, and at least her voice is calm—this harsh, breathy voice, quite different from the way she talked to Juliet. "You don't have to *worry* about anything, Warren. I'm not going to get sick again."

"That wasn't at all what I meant," says Warren, and it's probably a good thing he *is* clutching my hand, or I would just be getting up from the table and leaving right about now, because I'm not at all sure I can stand to watch this.

The waitress, a middle-aged French woman, comes over and asks if we want something to drink. Warren looks at the tall glass in front of Madeleine and she shrugs again. "It's iced tea," she says. "I'm not drinking for the next while—I can't, obviously, with the medication. Well, maybe that wasn't obvious, but it's true. Which, let me tell you, Warren—and Flip, I'm sorry, I didn't mean to leave you out—but honestly, not drinking in France, I mean, no wine, not an aperitif, nothing, they'd be more comfortable if you *were* locked up. I don't *miss* it, in case you were wondering. It just seems odd."

"I won't have anything now then either," Warren tells the waitress, and I shake my head.

"You *can,*" Madeleine says. Impossible to tell what she feels about any of this. "I'm trying to tell you, I don't have a problem with it."

Warren shakes his head. "Maybe later."

"Look," says Madeleine, folding her arms on the table and leaning forward, "if you're wondering about something, Warren, just ask, all right? Since you obviously don't want me to *tell* you."

"All right," says Warren slowly, and I must admit, my sympathies are mixed in a way I didn't expect. Since that's certainly something I have often felt like saying to him myself. Have said, in fact, and when he gets like this in response, I just want to slap him.

"I don't actually know what to ask," he's saying now. "Except—how you are, of course. And—how you will be." Suddenly he leans forward, too. "I have the impression," he says in that uncomfortable way he has when he thinks he *knows* something, "that—this time, it's—a turning point? That you're thinking about how things can be different, wondering how *much* different they can be. Are you?"

Madeleine looks like she doesn't know whether to laugh or cry. "Oh, Warren," she says.

The waitress comes back to take our order. Well, isn't *this* an incredible waste? Because obviously, neither of *them* is going to be able to eat. Warren still isn't looking at me, but he nudges me with his leg under the table. "Just give us a minute, please," he says to the waitress, and reaches for a menu. So then of course, Madeleine has to look at her menu, too, and since my right hand is still otherwise engaged, I share Warren's menu, leaning against him as we look. He makes a point of ordering appetizers for the table, too, which is obviously for my benefit.

"I don't know where you get your information," Madeleine says when the waitress leaves. "But, yes, I am thinking about how things might be different. I'd have to be crazy not to, wouldn't I?" She smiles for the first time. "I appreciate your not feeling sorry for me, anyway."

"On the contrary," Warren says. He must be really mad by now. "I envy you."

"As usual," Madeleine says, and again, I can't help having a certain sympathy with her side of things. The waitress comes with our appetizers, and since Warren has ordered us paté and escargots—things he knows I love—I need two free hands. I hook my ankle around Warren's leg instead.

"Well, since you already know so much, Warren," Madeleine is saying, "you probably also know that I'm thinking about—" She looks at him sharply. "You *don't* know, do you? This is one thing you *don't* know."

"Since I have no idea what you're talking about," Warren says, "I don't know if I do or not."

Madeleine actually looks relieved. "It doesn't matter," she says. "It's not a whole enormous incredible change. Only Juliet *is* older now—I mean, she was older even before I *left,* wasn't she? Even before I *sent her away.*"

Well, you can't say she doesn't call a spade a spade.

"And of course," Madeleine continues, "doing any real *work* was out of the question. Given that it's been out of the question since before Juliet was even born." She laughs. "Out of the question practically since *I* was born. Maybe it's *still* out of the question, who knows?"

"But you're wondering about it," Warren says when she doesn't say anything. You can see him trying to calculate what this means for him and Juliet.

Madeleine smiles. "I wouldn't really expect you to be interested after all this time," she says. "In the part that concerns *me*. And as far as any practical— I mean, I honestly don't know, Warren."

"That extra hour in the mornings," Warren says slowly. Madeleine nods.

"I wouldn't expect you to understand," she says again. "How little time that is. And of course, for the past two years, she's been at school all day, but—I don't know. I don't know what changed. I don't know."

"Three years," Warren says, and then he's sorry he said it, because for the first time, she looks—lost.

"For the past *three* years, obviously," she says quickly. "Thank you *so* much, Warren. I'm so glad *one* of us knows how long it's been." The waitress comes to clear our plates as someone from the kitchen brings us the main course. I'm not even sure I *can* eat at this point, though when the man gives me my order of rare duck in some kind of sour cherry sauce, it turns out that I can. Madeleine is eating, too, not as though she were hungry, but as though someone had told her it was important for her to eat. Only Warren sits there, ignoring his food. His leg against mine feels dead, as though all the life in him has gone somewhere else. Where, though? Where does he keep himself when he gets like this?

"Could you please pass the salt," says Madeleine in a voice that sounds so almost-normal, I wonder where she got the strength. She clears her throat, turning it into an enormous theatrical gesture, a way of taking back the stage. "On the other hand," she says, tossing her head, "I'm not at all sure that New York is a place where either Juliet or I belong. I, for all the reasons that you already know, Warren—I mean, I don't know how much *you* know about all this, Flip, but we might easily stay here all *night* listing *those* reasons.

"And as far as Juliet is concerned, I don't know about that, either. Among other things, I'm not sure I want my child growing up in a city that's—" She swallows. "This city is very cruel to people like her, isn't it?" she says. "You would know better than I. And of course, there are enormous problems in Paris, it's hardly paradise, especially these days. You get all sorts of people saying, '*Oh, oui, Madame, je suis raciste,*' just as though they're telling you their address. On the other hand, *here*—" She gestures around the restaurant, or perhaps around the entire city.

Warren's leg still feels cold and dead, but his eyes are burning. "Has Juliet said anything to you?" he says as calmly as he can manage.

"You mean, has she said, 'Why do they treat dark-skinned people so badly in New York, Mama? I've asked Uncle Warren, but he won't discuss it with me?' No, Warren, obviously not. But you don't mean to tell me the subject has never come up."

"There's no reason why it should have come up," Warren says stiffly. "She's not in any—situations—where it *would* come up." Madeleine's lips purse in a way that I recognize, and of course, Warren gets even angrier. "That's part of what I *have* done for her," he says. "To make sure that she wouldn't—that there was no reason—that there would never be any reason—for her to be exposed—to anything *like* what you're talking about." Madeleine looks skeptical. And amused. And, I suppose, triumphant. Finally, something she can hold over Warren.

"Oh, really, Warren?" she's saying, savoring each word. "Not in any situations? Why do you have her in a school where she doesn't have any friends, if everything has worked out so well? Why is her only friend this Sara she's always talking about, the daughter of her babysitter, for heaven's sake, I mean, not that *I* mind, though it must be driving *you* crazy. And yes, thank God you *didn't* let her go to school with Sara, because Catholic school, my God, that *would* have been the last straw." Well, it's a sign of *something* that she's got me wanting to defend Catholic school. "I mean, why *don't* any of her teachers get along with her, Warren, you've seen her, you've lived with her, she's not the kind of child that adults dislike, is she? *You* like her. Flip likes her. Her babysitter likes her. Even with all she's been through, she's not exactly antisocial, is she? So what part of the *situation* is causing the problem, if it isn't that? She must have figured it out on some level. Or if she hasn't, that's worse, isn't it? Then she thinks *she's* stupid, or unlovable, or unacceptable. Then it's all *her* fault."

Well, when you put it *that* way. Obviously, I never thought of it that way, either.

"I think there are several different explanations for what's been going on this year," Warren says finally. "I hardly think that's the only one."

"Well, obviously, I'm not blaming *you,* Warren," Madeleine says, still with that air of triumph. "I'm not even saying that New York *isn't* acceptable. I'm only pointing out the problem."

Now she's eating with real appetite. And Warren is just seething. Nothing I've ever done to him has *ever* made him as angry as this.

Madeleine looks up. I would have thought she'd look more triumphant than ever. But instead, she looks—lost. Really lost.

"I'm not saying you *didn't* do a good job, Warren," she says in this little-girl voice that makes me want to slap *her.* "Or you, either, Flip, of course." She takes a sip of iced tea. "Obviously Juliet adores you both," she says flatly. "Obviously, you were a godsend. Both of you. Obviously, if it hadn't been for you, God knows what would have happened to Juliet this past year, all right, Warren? Is *that* what you've been waiting to hear?"

Warren finally finds his voice. "I don't particularly want to hear *anything,*" he says. "*You* seem to be doing all the talking."

Suddenly, Madeleine puts down her fork and starts laughing. She laughs very quietly, to herself, for such a long time that, after the first few polite minutes of looking away, I have to look at her. She shakes her head, still smiling. "Stop talking, Madeleine," she says softly, not especially to any of us, though she's obviously hoping Warren will hear. "If you talk so much, people are going to think that you're Jewish."

Warren can't help smiling.

"That was our grandmother," Madeleine says graciously to me—that hostessy voice that I have also heard Juliet use to explain things. "She thought I talked too much, whereas Warren, of course, was perfect."

"Hardly," says Warren.

"I know, I know," Madeleine says. "You should have gone out for football or something."

"Lacrosse, actually."

"And both of us should have come out, or whatever they called it for boys . . ."

"I don't think they call it anything for boys," Warren says.

"Well, she certainly wanted *me* to come out," Madeleine says. "No pun intended. Come out, sit down, and shut up. Isn't that bizarre, to think that even existed back then? I'm not *that* old."

"It still exists, doesn't it?" Warren says. "Aren't there still debutantes?"

"God, I don't know," Madeleine says. "That's why I left—so I wouldn't have to know." She takes another swallow of her tea.

"Where were we?" she says. "Weren't we right in the middle of some kind of fascinating conversation?"

"Madeleine," says Warren, "I would never do anything to hurt Juliet."

"Oh, Warren," Madeleine says with that horrible little half-smile, "neither would I. And look how much good *that* did her."

Warren sighs. "It was complicated, this year at school," he says. "There hasn't been much chance for us to talk about it. But I really don't think it was a racial thing. I honestly think it was more complicated than that."

Madeleine shrugs. "Maybe it was more complicated *and* it was that," she says. "Maybe it wasn't racial at all—how do I know? I was only trying to tell you my concerns." She looks from Warren to me and back again. "To be perfectly honest, New York would have been my last choice in the world for a place either to live *or* to bring up my daughter," she says. "But now you're in her life, you and Flip, and—" For the first time tonight she seems to be at a loss for words.

"There weren't *that* many people who were—important to me while I was growing up," she says finally. "Or to you, either, Warren, as I recall. I don't see why Juliet shouldn't have a wider field than we had. Though I must say, Warren, *you* hardly seem interested in any kind of family feeling these days. At least, not as it pertains to *me*." Warren looks absolutely floored by this, and Madeleine sighs. "Look," she says, throwing her napkin down on the table. "You're getting married. You're doing the work you want, such as it is. No, don't take offense, I'm only saying. You *have* everything you want. You could afford to be a little—generous, Warren, that's all I'm saying."

"But you're the one who has everything," Warren says. The words just burst out of him. "You have Juliet."

Both Madeleine and I are shocked, though obviously, for different reasons. I feel my whole body turn cold and I try to take back my hand—*try* isn't even the right word, it just pulls back of its own accord. Except Warren won't let go. Well, I'm certainly not going to get into a tug of war with him in front of *Madeleine.*

Warren pulls my whole arm across his waist and holds onto it with both hands. All right, Warren. I know you didn't mean it the way it sounded. But you've got to admit, it sounded terrible.

"Look," Madeleine says again. "What you said to Juliet in the park."

"About figuring things out gradually."

"Yes," she says. "I mean, none of us knows *anything,* obviously. Not even you, Warren. You know what you want, obviously, and I can tell you right now, you certainly won't get *that.* But even you don't know what's *best.* Do you?"

"I suppose not," Warren says.

The waitress comes over and asks if we want anything else, and Warren actually talks to me for the first time all evening. "Do you want dessert?" he says. And I have to tell you, under the circumstances, the fact that he would be willing to—the fact that he would even think there was a question— Let's just say that it doesn't make *me* question the wisdom of my decision to stay with Warren for the rest of my life. Despite all his obvious shortcomings.

"No, I'm fine," I say. The waitress leaves. After a moment, I put my free hand on Warren's arm. Madeleine gives us both a look. "Not that either of you will miss me," she says, getting up, "but I'll be right back."

Warren opens his mouth to say something, but I get there first. "Just don't say anything, all right, Warren? Let's just forget it ever happened."

Madeleine comes back but she doesn't sit down again. "Do you mind if I just run?" she says. "I'm entitled to be exhausted, aren't I? Isn't jet lag always a good excuse?"

When we pick up Juliet from Marta's, she's sleeping so deeply that she barely wakes up, the whole time Warren is putting her to bed. And then *we* go to bed. Ever since we put Madeleine into her taxi, Warren hasn't said a single word.

"Don't you have anything to say about all this?" I say finally, lying there on my back in the dark. He's curled as far away from me as he can get.

"I thought *you* didn't want to talk about anything," Warren says. "Tonight or any other night. I thought that was what you liked so much about being involved with *me.*"

"Fine," I say. If somebody doesn't do something, he's going to be up for hours.

"Warren," I say suddenly, "do I make you happy?"

He sounds surprised, but not upset. "Yes," he says. "Of course. What brought *that* on out of the blue?"

I don't know what to say.

He sighs. "Not only do you make me happy," he says, in this strangled voice, "but I never *was* happy, Flip, before I met you. I wanted things, and sometimes I got them. But I don't think I was ever happy."

This is so much more than I ever expected or even wanted to hear that for a minute I can't speak. "Well, Warren," I say finally. "You certainly make me happy, too. Though I wouldn't say—I mean, I *was* happy, in various ways, before we met." I clear my throat. "But I didn't think I *belonged* anywhere. Do you know what I mean? People wanted me. But they didn't want me to *stay*." I put my hand tentatively on his shoulder. "But you did. You wanted me home with you."

"Yes," Warren says. "That's exactly where I want you."

I take another breath. "Well, then, I think we ought to stop paying rent on that other apartment. I mean, all right, this isn't my favorite decor in the world, no offense, Warren, but OK, so what? We live *here*. This is our home."

"Well," Warren says finally. "Since this *is* our home, I think we should put your name on the deed, too, then. And take care of all that other money business. Would you—would you do that, Flip? If I called about that tomorrow, or—I don't know why it's taken so long. But would you do that?"

I know that whatever we put in writing, I am never going to feel like I own this place with Warren, any more than I'm ever going to feel like half of his money belongs to me. He'll always be able to say, "Well, I have a fortune." And I'll never be able to say it—at least, not with regard to *his* money.

It doesn't matter. Or maybe it does matter, but I don't care about it now. "Yes," I say. "I would do that. I want you to know, Warren—this is where I live. With you. Home with you."

ROSIE: I don't actually get to see Flip's show until two days before the nuptial extravaganza, which also turns out to be the day before the end of the run. For once, I don't think that would have been Flip's choice, but I've got three more little shops in negotiations and the lead slot at Paradise (they gave Tito that big warehouse in Long Island, even though you'd think after Olympia that *I*—oh, never mind). And Paradise's boss is fighting a long slow campaign of attrition—wearing away people's breaks and lunch hours, and there seems to be some kind of sexual harassment going on, too, but it's so subtle, it's hard to pin it down enough to grieve it, which is often the way. Plus Harris wants us to hook up with some of the other white-collar unions to do some city-wide thing about all the budget cuts, which should be exciting, but at the moment that's stalled, too. *And* I'm still bleeding. So I'm not in the *best* mood as I take my place in the dingy little community center on the Lower East Side, amidst the ex-convicts and unwed mothers and People With Aids/Housing Rights group that seem to be the audience for *this* performance.

Still. When the show begins, I can't help feeling thrilled. All right, so a lot of it is slow and clunky, that kind of earnest, well-intentioned political theater—you know, where if you have any politics at all, you can pretty much see the punch lines coming a million miles away. Actually, I *like* that kind of theater, kind of like the way I enjoy talking to Jack Kim (or used to, before he totally *turned* on me during the strike), though I can see why Flip might find it embarrassing.

But these performers are clearly a lot older and more experienced than the ones you usually see doing this type of work, and there's obviously something else going on here as well, though I don't exactly know how to describe it. Some of it is these *moments*—there's this one scene with Flip and Tanya playing these flirty high school kids that kind of takes my breath away, it's so tense and unexpected. You can see all these power struggles going on, and how much they really *want* to connect, and how, given everything, they're probably never going to be able to. I think I'd find it moving even if it *wasn't* Flip, but also, seeing him do it—I don't know. I've never seen him be so—well, *male,* before. And there's this other scene where one of the men plays an old woman—I guess she's supposed to be Tanya's grandmother—and it could so easily have been stupid and corny, but I find myself feeling genuinely moved.

The most moving thing, though—how do I describe this? Of *course* it has to do with Flip. There's just something about seeing him up there—I don't know. Carried away. No, not that; of course he's in control—he always is, on stage. But he's—beyond himself, somehow. Part of something larger, although I know he'll kill me if I ever tell him *that.* Living in that space where I go every day, is what I'm really thinking, and I'm sorry, I know it's selfish of me, but still. Even if we can never talk about it, I can't help being glad that it's a place he knows about, too.

When the show is over, I wait the way I always do, only this time Flip surprises me by coming right out to get me, before he's even had time to change. "Come on," he says. "I want you to meet my director." He drags me to the other end of the room, where this tall, skinny woman is talking to another woman as they make notes together on a legal pad.

"It's nice to finally meet you," says the tall woman—Elinor, apparently—when Flip drags *her* away and introduces us. "Whenever there was a particularly intense political disagreement about something in the script, Flip was prone to invoke your name."

"Oh. Well, it's nice to meet you, too," I say. "Anyone who actually has the job of telling my little brother what to do—"

"I know, I know," Flip says quickly. Of course he's embarrassed, but he doesn't seem displeased, exactly. "She has your extremely well-deserved sympathy. Not to mention your boundless and also well-deserved admiration."

Both of us are so surprised, we can't help looking at him. Elinor smiles. "Well," she says, "it was something of a unique experience for all of us. But I'm glad you liked the show."

Flip notices me looking at the two women as we leave. "*What?*" he says impatiently.

"So they're a couple," I say slowly.

"Yeah? So?"

"No, it's just—I mean, there was *some* gay stuff in your show, not a lot, but some. But there wasn't anything about lesbians. I would have thought—"

"Well, Idris was the writer," Flip points out. "If she had wanted to put something in, there wasn't anything to stop her."

As we walk to Veselka's, Flip asks me all about the strike, a topic I was sure he'd forgotten. But after we've ordered dinner, he says, "OK. But what did you *really* think about the show?"

Isn't it still dangerous to tell him *that?* "What did Warren tell you?" I say, stalling for time.

"Oh, you know Warren," Flip says. "He thought *I* was fabulous, or at least, he'd only talk about the scenes where he thought I was. And he didn't have all that much to say about anything else."

Maybe he knows better, I can't help thinking. Then the waiter arrives with our usual order, and Flip starts dividing it up—not just the sandwich but all the garnishes, which he scrupulously sorts into two little piles. "Come on, Rosie," he says as he saws a carrot carefully in half. "You know you want to tell me."

"Oh, all right," I say. "I *did* like being there. I mean, in that audience. It's so different from the audiences you usually get. You know. Usually it's all your actor friends, and they can't stand to see you do well because that means they're failing, and they can't stand to see you fail, because *that* means they're failing." Flip laughs. "And even if—*when*—you do something on a bigger scale, then it will be, you know, forty bucks a seat. I mean, then it's still—"

"Just a nice, expensive night out," Flip says. "As opposed to a life-changing experience."

"Well, yes. I mean, I wouldn't say *this* was a life-changing experience exactly. But the audience was so *alive*. So—thrilled. I mean, they got that it was about them. That somehow it—*belonged* to them."

"Yeah, I'm always surprised by that, too," Flip says. "Given that I've never felt that from any other audience I've ever had before." He hesitates. "But what did you think of the show itself?"

"*I* liked it. But I can see how it wasn't all that much for you to do. I mean, if you're comparing it to Shakespeare. Or Chekhov. Or the really great modern—I mean, it was more—like a cartoon, somehow. Not in a bad way. Or like a parable."

Flip puts both of his hands on the table, palms up. "Rosie," he says. "Isn't this exactly what *you* thought I should do? So, what am I supposed to do *now*?"

I can't help laughing. "OK," I say drily. "At the risk of sounding incredibly repetitious, you tell me. If you could do anything in the world, as an artist, I mean, what would it be?"

"OK, *fine*," Flip says. "And if you ever quote me, I'll deny it. But OK, yes, Rosie, if there were some kind of full-time, fully paid company of actors that *did* work this way. Doing Shakespeare, and the classics, and new work, and maybe also this kind of thing—because it's not like I'd *never* want to do a play like this again. Just, not all the time. So all right, yes, if I *could* be in a company like that, I *would* give up being rich and famous. But since that company doesn't exist . . ."

"You could create it."

"Oh, sure. And maybe when *your* next million-dollar dividend comes through, you could just make it over to me, because I'm a little short this week."

"Well, not that I want to bring up yet *another* sore subject. But what *about* Warren's money? Couldn't he pay for something?"

Flip grimaces. "You know, I actually thought about that, too. And I honestly don't know *what* I would have done if the answer had been yes. But in fact, the money he actually has access to is more like in the thousands. I mean, there might be millions in his *name* somewhere, but he can't exactly get *at* them. So meanwhile, I can be in Tiger's Eye for a hundred dollars a week and do some play by Idris. Or, if I get really lucky, I could do Shakespeare at the Public or somewhere else that I can guarantee you *won't* rehearse like this and which won't pay all *that* much better, although the actors probably *will* show up on time. Or I could move to L.A. and have a *real* career, probably playing flaming faggots on cop shows. As far as I can see, those are the options."

"There must be other alternatives," I insist. "Even if they don't exist yet."

Flip gives me a funny look. "Isn't that the point?" he says. "If they don't exist yet, they don't exist."

The waiter comes by asking if we want dessert. Flip looks at me uneasily. "Actually," he says, "I told Warren I'd be home by—well, I don't have to get home *right* at eleven. Apparently, there are still some matrimonial details to be worked out, although why Warren wants *my* opinion on how much salmon should be on the buffet table . . ."

I can't imagine what expression is on my face, but Flip looks more uneasy than ever. "I mean, we can *order* dessert," he says. "We can even *eat* dessert. I just thought I should say something. Besides. I still want to know what you think."

"*What* was the question again?"

"*You* know. *Do* you think there's anything left in the world for me to hope for? In my—career. Or would you say my art?"

God, how do *I* know what's possible in this miserable world? But Flip is still waiting for an answer. And I'd like to know, too. So almost out of habit, I search for the words.

"OK. When you look at water, you think it's just—water. And how could it ever be anything else?

"And if you start to heat the water, it's still just—warm water. Or maybe hot water. But still, just water.

"But Flip. Sooner or later, if you add enough heat, it *isn't* water anymore. It's steam. This totally new thing that you couldn't even imagine, you could never even make up. I mean, think of the first person who tried to boil water. It must have seemed like magic.

"And then there's some medieval alchemist trying to turn lead into gold. And that *is* magic, and we know it's never going to happen—but he doesn't. As far as he's concerned, he's being totally scientific.

"And for a long time, as far as I can see, those two people don't really look all that different. But there *is* a difference."

"God, Rosie," Flip says after a long pause. "Is *that* the best you can do?"

"Yes," I say, swallowing hard. "Take it or leave it."

"Oh, I'll take it," Flip says as he starts to eat his pie. "I just hope the next time I ask, you can tell me something better."

WARREN: Given the nature of what we're doing and who is coming and who *isn't* coming, we haven't gotten any wedding presents ahead of time. The exception, of course, being my mother. So when Flip comes home the day before the big event, he finds me sitting at the kitchen table, staring at the gift she sent, a complete set of towels of no style that we would ever possibly use, white with dark red and blue piping, but monogrammed, with both Flip's and my initials. I don't know whether to laugh or cry.

Flip doesn't have that problem, but out of respect for my feelings, he tries to stifle his laughter. "Go ahead," I tell him. "I would, if she weren't my mother."

But he sits down and says cheerfully, "Look, she even put 'F' for Flip instead of 'P' for Philip. That's *very* nice." He looks at me. "But you'd rather she were coming."

"Well, if *she* were coming, that would mean *he* was coming. But yes, I suppose even so——"

Flip reaches down to feel the bath sheet between his thumb and fingers. "They're nice and thick," he says. "I wouldn't say we would *never* use them."

"Flip. They're *white*. You put them in the *guest* bathroom. And even then, the housekeeper has to wash them every single time they're used, or else they show the dirt."

Flip looks at me with wide eyes. "Well, tell the housekeeper to put them in our *guest* bathroom, then," he says. "The one in our summer house that we're going to build when I get famous. I think it was very thoughtful of your mother to realize that we're going to need more guest towels so soon."

I'd like to laugh, but if you want to know the truth, I can't bear the thought of these expensive towels sitting shut up in a linen closet somewhere, like some abandoned child. "All right, then, Warren," Flip says finally. "*I'll* use them. At least I can use them *once*. Maybe for the ceremonial bathing ritual tomorrow morning." Then he laughs. "At least it isn't any *worse* because you're gay," he says. "Equal opportunity parental shortcomings. I mean, come on, Warren. You have to admit, the monograms are nice."

"They're *my* parents," I say. "I don't have to admit anything—I think there's a law about it somewhere. But you're right, it is exactly what they would do if—because even though of *course* they're not coming into the City, even for the most important day of my life, my mother does want to give us a reception."

"Out there?" Flip says, carefully avoiding any reference to my little accidental remark about what kind of day tomorrow is.

"No, in the Bronx," I say. "Of course out there." I turn the blue notepaper with my mother's loopy writing over in my hand.

"Well, she's really making an effort."

"No, that's the whole point," I say. "It's not an effort. It's simply—there is this whole set of things that people simply *do* at a time like this. And if your child is getting married and it isn't possible to invite all your friends to the wedding, then giving a reception at home—or actually, at the local country club, which is what she's suggesting—"

"My God, I've never even *been* to a country club," Flip says. "Too bad it's not a yacht club—I've always wanted to go to one of those."

"No, you haven't," I say. "Not if you had any idea what they're actually like." I can only imagine what my father must think about Mama presenting Flip and me to all their friends—not that they have so many friends.

"Warren," Flip says patiently, for what seems like the millionth time. "You're the one who wanted to do this. What did you *think* it would be like?"

I thought it would make me feel—normal. But not that kind of normal. The kind of normal that seems to make everyone *else* happy.

ROSIE: I am just drifting off to sleep when all of a sudden a terrible spasm jolts me awake. What is *that?* I lie there, electricity flowing through me, feeling the gush between my legs. Everything inside me clenches, like a fist . . . and then lets go. Vibrating.

And then it's gone. Whatever it was—those stones, that weight. Gone.

I force myself to get up and stagger to the bathroom. I've been wearing a sanitary napkin to bed for months now, even when I'm theoretically not bleeding, since I never know when I'm going to start. So I take it off and look at it. And there, in the center of the bright red stain, are four little—*things.* The fibroids, I guess. The tumors that have been making me bleed.

I look at them and I start to cry. I really should call Cassandra. But I can't stop staring at the package in my hand. Four little balls of—of what used to be *me,* I guess. From the size of a jawbreaker to the size of a meatball. They *want,* they *want.* What do they want?

In my mind, I am already naming them. OK, yes, one is Flip, and one is Michael, and one is, well, not Marcy, but being like Marcy, which I'm obviously never going to be. And the last? Well, Ma had them all last year, but now I *don't* have them. So I suppose the last one is being like Ma.

Something that's lost and I'll never get it back. No pain, now that they're gone, and no more blood, either. *Anything could happen now.*

There's an empty jar under the bathroom sink, and I dump the tumors into that. I might want to look at them again someday, before it's finally time to throw them out.

What do I want? I think about running water for a bath, changing my sheets, starting over. But that sounds too far beyond me right now. So I grab a washcloth and sponge myself off, and go get the sleeping bag that I use as an extra blanket. I lie down on the couch, so tired, so empty, so fucking relieved.

"Go to sleep now," I tell myself. "That's a good girl, go to sleep. Shhh. Shhh. Just go to sleep."

What do you want? I can't stop asking.

I've already said it, haven't I? The world, the world, the whole world.

Oh, what does that mean?

I can feel that breathing that Cassandra taught me, pulling all the way down through my lungs, my stomach, my womb. Finally. Pulling down through my vagina, my clitoris, my thighs, pulling all the way down to the soles of my feet. My separate body in its separate skin.

It doesn't matter. I know that nothing that could ever happen to this body of mine could ever possibly interest me as much as—that *other* body. That one we're all a part of, together. Whether I have this boyfriend or that one, whether I get married or have a child, whether I get promoted at work or assigned to all the most prestigious shops . . . I'm not saying I don't care about any of that. Just that—finally—it doesn't matter.

I think about standing in the office that day at Olympia, watching Charles and Jack and Nina and Margarita arguing over some stupid newsletter. Just by being there, I was part of it. Something new. Something else.

I don't know what it will look like when we finally finish making it. I don't know if I'll even be here to see it. But that is what I want.

FLIP: When I go into the kitchen on the morning of our conjugal day, Warren is making breakfast, this thing he knows I love where he melts feta cheese on sourdough bread and serves it with these little pieces of green apple, that very *tart* kind of apple. It makes the bread taste sweet.

He's slicing the cheese very thin, with that very *concentrated* look he always has when he's cooking, even if all he's doing is boiling a pot of water for tea. Although I suppose that never *is* all he's doing—he always finds some little extra thing to add. I remember watching him make me breakfast after the first night I spent at his house, seeing that preoccupied air as he sprinkled cinnamon and something else—nutmeg?—into the coffee. And then he cut up a lime to squeeze over these slices of mango he had, and then he ate a chunk of mango and licked his fingers. That really got me. He seemed so proper and precise, doing all these little things to get breakfast ready, and so stiff and awkward with *me* that he could barely say two words, let alone kiss me good morning (not that I was much better, but I thought I was just following his lead)—and then there he was, licking his fingers. And when he saw that I was watching him, he didn't even seem embarrassed, as you might have thought, he just smiled—for the first time that morning—and held out a slice of mango for me, too.

Now he feels me watching him and offers me a paper-thin slice of cheese—he cuts it so fine that it crumbles between my fingers as I try to eat it. I watch him eat his slice, preoccupied even as he licks his fingers. "What?" he says as I keep watching him. "What?"

"Oh," I say finally. I can't take my eyes off him. "I'm just glad you didn't go home with Ian from that party, that's all."

For a minute, he doesn't understand. Then he laughs. "I would never have gone home with Ian from that party. He terrified me, at that point."

"At *that* point," I repeat. "Whereas *later* . . ."

Warren wipes his hands on a dishtowel. "*Later* I had lived with you for twelve months and without you for three," he says. "So what could I possibly be afraid of ever again? I had already seen all the best and all the worst that life had to offer."

"Nice try, Warren. Is that what you still think?"

Warren comes over to where I am standing and smiles at me so sweetly, I have to hold onto his arms. "No, Flip," he says gently. "Now I think that all the best is still to come. The worst, too, probably. But I can take it if you can."

"You're in great form this morning, Warren," I say, as he heads back to check on the bread. "I'm so nervous I don't even think I can *eat,* and you're like one of those scenes in a movie, you know, where everyone expects the heroine to come downstairs with a broken heart or a hangover or something, and she just sails in singing."

"Katharine Hepburn does that in *Philadelphia Story*, I think. Except isn't there another scene where she comes downstairs and she *is* hung over—" Suddenly he turns around, the pan of bread and cheese still in his hand. "You think you're too nervous to *eat?*"

I shrug. "Well, I probably *will* eat, but, yes. Why are you so—I don't think I've ever seen you this happy."

Warren's lips purse as he turns back to the stove. "Well, you know," he says. "Events that should be called weddings but that are actually called some other made-up name just seem to bring out the best in me."

"You do realize it won't always be like this," I feel compelled to say. "Anything could happen. I could get a job out of town for months at a time. Or you could fall madly in love with Ian—you *could,* Warren, stranger things have happened. Or we could—"

From the other room, Juliet calls out, "I'm just going to watch to the end of *this* one, OK, Uncle Warren? Just *this* one."

"No, now," Warren calls back automatically, just as I'm saying more or less hysterically, "Anything could happen—anything at all."

Warren looks back at me with tears in his eyes. "I know it could," he says. He still looks incredibly happy. "I know it could," he says again. "I didn't expect even this much."

ROSIE: So what *are* they going to call it? That's the question most on my mind as I walk into Flip and Warren's as-yet-unnamed event, and I have to admit, the setting isn't giving me very much help. It's this large, rather impersonal space about three blocks south of Washington Square—a rehearsal space? Or someplace owned by NYU? It has that kind of student union feeling—big buffet-style folding tables and chairs, and those anonymous white walls—a space that Flip and Warren could do very little to enliven beyond putting these fairly amazing flower arrangements everywhere.

I try to think of a more significant space where they *could* have held these connubial rites—a church? A theater? Not a union hall, obviously, and probably nowhere in the Lesbian and Gay Community Center, either—somehow I think both Flip and Warren would find that way too limiting, though possibly in different ways. It occurs to me that the problem with naming the event and the problem with *placing* the event aren't exactly unrelated.

And when I see all the people milling around here—there are about fifty of us—I have to wonder: What *other* event than this one could ever have brought *these* people into the same room? There are people who look like Flip's theater colleagues—I recognize some of them, from Tiger's Eye and other shows he's been in—and some people who I could imagine might be Warren's clients—though it seems so unlikely that he would want to invite *them,* that maybe not. And there are some people I vaguely recall from the memorial, and Marta, of course, who's here with Sara and her husband, who's carrying Rogelio. Oh, and Simon, with a man who must be his boyfriend— they're obviously together, though neither of them looks all that happy about it. Poor Nina—I wonder how much *she* knew about that situation.

When Danny got married, of course, it was in a church, and everything about *that* ceremony and the reception that followed looked like your total fantasy of a big wedding—well, *my* total fantasy of it, anyway—white decorations everywhere, and the bridesmaids all in matching pale-blue dresses, and Betsy in this enormous white wedding dress that on her looked absolutely gorgeous. Whereas this—I don't even know how to see it. *Is* it a political event, something that flies in the face of every tradition we've ever known? Or is it just one more way that Flip and Warren get to have something that everybody else already has? Everybody else who's already married.

There's a band over by the windows, quietly setting levels, and some kind of preliminary jazzy music coming over the sound system. Next to the dance area is the food—a huge buffet table loaded with enormous platters, and more flower arrangements, and those standard round tables covered in ordinary white tablecloths. And they've put those little disposable cameras at every place, which must have cost a fortune, even if they got the really cheap ones. Still, it's a nice thought, isn't it? (Or is that just Flip's way of making sure that everybody *does* take pictures of him?)

There's a big table near the door where everyone has put *their* wedding presents—all wrapped in the most traditional department-store wrappings you can imagine: that shiny silver paper, embossed with hearts and lovebirds; that elaborate frilly white ribbon; those glitter-frosted plastic wedding bells. Is this people's idea of a joke? Maybe more people actually like this stuff than I ever imagined. (I myself splurged and got them a gift certificate for a weekend out of town—the Paradise package weekend of their choice. Somehow I thought Flip would appreciate that, even if Mario himself wasn't there to book the flight.)

Since there's obviously no food or dancing yet, everyone is crowded together at the other end of the room, where they've set up a big half-circle of folding chairs, three rows deep, with a big aisle down the middle. And in the empty space facing the circle are two folding chairs set side by side, which are obviously for Flip and Warren.

I'm not sure what the protocol is. It seems weird not to go find Flip and Warren and congratulate them, but they're nowhere to be seen. I *could* go get a drink from the buffet table—there are a couple of white-jacketed caterers pouring out wine and even making drinks (did Warren want the full bar, or was that Flip's idea? It seems so much more extravagant than just offering wine.). But before I make it over there, I see Juliet, talking to Sara, and my attention is caught by the woman holding Juliet's hand—my God, that must be Madeleine.

I stand there watching her as Marta tries to make conversation, but Madeleine is obviously a lot more interested in watching Juliet. Well, I suppose you could see why, but still. Marta's going to think she's awfully rude. I wonder if Madeleine will keep using Marta as a sitter, or what arrangement she's going to make—when Flip called me yesterday (sounding enormously relieved) he seemed to think that Madeleine was just on the verge of deciding to stay in New York, given that everyone—including Juliet—was pointing out that if she *didn't* decide fairly soon, the whole question would be moot, because they wouldn't be able to get Juliet into another school, or even to renew her place in her current school. I don't know. I'm glad Juliet is staying, obviously, and of course, *I* love New York. But I'd hate to think that anything, even a child, could get me to move back to within shouting distance of Pittsburgh.

I'm considering going over there and introducing myself—though if Madeleine looks that awkward talking to Marta, maybe she'd rather be left alone—when I hear a sudden burst of voices behind the buffet table. Oh, there's Warren, explaining something to the caterers—and there's Flip, trying to drag him away. They don't look like they're arguing, exactly, just—pulling in different directions. God, if *that* makes me want to cry, can you imagine what the whole *ceremony* is going to be like? Because—I don't know. Because they've gotten so good at pulling in different directions, I guess.

My meditations are interrupted by Flip, who has apparently given up on Warren and come over to kiss me hello. Everybody here is dressed up, of course, but naturally *he* has found a way of looking even *more* dressed up. Well, who *would* be better dressed than the bride?

"Sit in front," he whispers in my ear.

"I always sit in the front."

"I know. I just wanted to make sure." OK, OK. So I *am* incredibly touched.

Warren also appears out of the crowd, so intent on finding Flip that he doesn't even notice me. "No, in fact, they *don't* have enough salmon," he tells Flip, who shrugs.

"Like I keep telling you," he says. "It always goes better later in the run." And to my total shock and amazement, instead of getting annoyed, Warren laughs.

"You look wonderful," I tell him when he finally does notice me, and he smiles. I've never seen him anywhere near so happy.

"Like Cary Grant?" he says. "Finally?" He puts his arms around me. "Thank you," he whispers in my ear. "For everything."

We hug each other for long enough that Flip taps first me, then Warren, on the shoulder. "Not that I *want* to intrude on such a touching moment," he says. "But there might be one or two other guests who *also* want to say hello to Warren." I make a face at him and I'm about to go find a seat when Warren takes me by the elbow, saying, "Don't go yet, Rosie. You know what he's like before a performance."

I do know, I think. *I've known him thirty-one years longer than you have.* But of course I don't say *that.*

Judging by the expression on Warren's face, he may have heard it anyway.

He seems about to say something when all of a sudden, Simon's boyfriend comes up and says in an English accent, "Ah, Warren. I suppose congratulations are in order."

"Very much in order," Warren says. "Thank you."

The man smiles. "Well, speaking as one who knows, I feel obliged to inform you that one of the chief benefits of matrimony is that one is finally entitled to enjoy the pleasures of adultery."

Warren laughs. "I doubt I'll ever make much use of that information, but I suppose it's always good to know."

He turns to me as the man leaves. "I'm sorry I didn't introduce you," he says. "I don't think I move quickly enough for events like this. Not that there *are* any events like this one, but—"

He stops in mid-sentence, his face lighting up at the sight of someone behind me. "My God," he says. Then he calls out—Warren actually raising his voice!—"Loulou!"

A short, beautifully groomed woman who looks like a sixty-year-old Claudette Colbert sails up behind me, followed by one of those horsey-looking Connecticut Anglophile types.

"Warren!" says the woman—Loulou, apparently. She and Warren do that thing that I thought people only did in movies, where they kiss each other on both cheeks. "Darling! We're so happy for you."

"I didn't think—I thought you couldn't come."

"Oh," says Loulou, "when I realized your parents couldn't make it, I thought, well, for heaven's sake, *someone* from the household should be here—it's a wedding!"

"Well, if their *not* coming was the price of your coming," Warren says, "it was a price well worth paying."

Loulou reaches up her hand—she's quite a bit shorter than Warren—and pats his cheek. "It's the same friend, isn't it?" she says. "The one you brought out two Thanksgivings ago?"

"Yes," says Warren. He actually reaches up and covers her hand with his. "It's the same friend." They stand that way for a moment, then Loulou says briskly, "And this is *my* friend. Sossie Anne Westlake, I'd like you meet Warren Huddleston."

"Congratulations," says the horse-faced woman in that Connecticut lockjaw Flip always used to make fun of when he and Warren first started going out together.

"I'm very glad you're here," Warren says. "Both of you. I'm—it's—I'm very glad."

Flip is tugging at my arm. "If you don't hurry and get a seat soon," he says, "the whole front row will be gone."

Elinor comes up, accompanied by a woman who Flip reminds me is called Idris, who is apparently at work on a *new* script— "*Nothing* like the last one," she says. I'm surprised that Tiger's Eye *is* continuing—after what Flip said the other night, I had the impression it was all over. "I don't know if Malik's group will want to pay for this or not," Idris is saying, "but we've got the whole summer to figure it out."

Tanya comes up, and she and Flip share a long, intense hug. "You made it," she says as they pull apart. "Congratulations. I swan, Massa Flip, it sho' is good to see yo' properly settled with Massa Rhett."

Flip grins. "Oh, heavens, yes, Warren and I are having Tara done all in *mauve*. And yesterday we found the most cunning little lawn jockey to put out in front of the old slave quarters. Of course, he was black as the ace of spades, but so *charming*."

Tanya grins back, and she's about to say something, when a short, intense-looking guy comes up on Flip's other side. "Hi, Joshua," says Flip. "Glad you could make it."

The guy doesn't say anything for an unusually long time. Flip seems impatient, but he doesn't turn away. Finally, the guy says, "I wish—" and Flip immediately cuts him off.

"I know," he says quickly. Then he's sorry. "I always thought I'd see him dancing," he says. "At my—whatever."

"He was really glad when he, when we got the invitation."

"I liked thinking that he was," Flip says finally. "I still like thinking that."

"I do, too," the guy says. Then he leaves.

"Wasn't that Mario's boyfriend?" I say.

Flip looks at me strangely. "I keep forgetting you knew Mario."

All of a sudden, Madeleine is standing behind us. There's something about how intensely uncomfortable she is—she must really hate being around all these people—that makes us all turn to look at her. Juliet is there, too, not holding Madeleine's hand now, but leaning against her. I notice Juliet's dress—some gorgeous rose brocade thing that looks *way* too sophisticated for any eight-year-old *I* ever saw. Did Warren pick it out for her, do you suppose, or did Madeleine bring it straight over from Paris?

I'm trying not to stare at Madeleine, but she doesn't make it easy, because she's holding out a flimsy white box—it looks like a cake box, not even wrapped. "It's for you," she says. "Both of you."

"Open it," says Juliet eagerly, but also—I guess you would have to call it a command. Although a fairly desperate one. I wonder if I *will* get to know her better, now that it looks like she's staying. I bet we would get along.

Warren takes the box and hands it to Flip. "There's a card, too," Juliet says in that eager, desperate voice. "I found the envelope for it."

"Thank you," says Warren, taking the card but looking at her, a look so full, I have to look away.

The card is small and white, like a business card. Warren reads it, pressing his lips together. Then he hands it to Flip. I edge in closer and read over Flip's shoulder. There on the rough white surface Madeleine has written in small, shaky block letters:

THE WHOLE IS GREATER THAN THE SUM OF ITS PARTS.

Flip holds the box as Warren opens the lid and reaches through the crumpled-up newspapers to pull out Madeleine's gift. It's a plate, made from the fragments of other plates. So that glued together, they make a single object. But you can also see each of the pieces—a wedge of blue porcelain, a splinter of white china, a cracked piece of yellow plastic, a collection of fragments and shards and mismatched pieces, glued together into a rough, uneven whole, slivered through with cracks and fissures, with missing chips and overlaps, a broken, unbroken circle.

Slowly, Warren's eyes rise from the plate to meet Madeleine's.

"Isn't it beautiful, Uncle Warren?" says Juliet. "Isn't it wonderful and exquisite and beautiful—and—and—sublime and lovely and gorgeous?"

"It is," says Warren, still looking at Madeleine, who suddenly looks away. "It's all of those things."

Flip reaches out his hand, runs his finger along the plate's rim, up and down the plaster seams that hold all the fragments together.

"It really is," he says. "Wow, Madeleine. Thank you."

"I made it in Paris," Madeleine says. "To celebrate—today." Suddenly she turns and walks away. Juliet turns, too, and runs after her. We see her catch up to Madeleine, take her hand, say something that makes Madeleine look down for a moment. Swinging hands, the two of them walk off toward the chairs.

Warren is still holding the plate, his eyes on the two of them. I hold out my hands. "Do you want me to put it over with the rest of the presents?" I offer. Flip nods.

Finally, I am in my seat. Flip had Tanya save me a place, which I suppose *was* a good thing, because he was right, all the other front-row seats are taken. Juliet and Madeleine are in the front row, too, across the circle. Flip and Warren have just gotten everybody settled down, when I hear one last person coming through the door. My God, it's Danny. I expect to see Betsy and the kids following along—but no. Just Danny.

I see Flip freeze for a moment. Then he goes over to Danny and the two of them hug. Warren is there, too, shaking Danny's hand—oh, *men*—and I'm waving wildly, but it's clear that at this point, Danny will have to sit in the back, where I suppose he'll be more comfortable anyway.

So finally everybody settles down, and there's a kind of expectant silence, which Flip, of course, allows to continue just long enough. I look at him and Warren, waiting there outside the circle, while all of us wait here inside it. And suddenly I have the oddest feeling of being in two places at once. Here, inside this room, where we're making history. And there, outside the room, where what we're doing isn't going to make any difference at all.

And then he and Warren come down the aisle together—well, it *is* an aisle. Even if not *the* aisle. They're actually holding hands, which I don't believe I've ever seen them do before. As if they're about to jump off a bridge. But not in a bad way. They both look—abandoned.

"All right," says Flip, as the two of them stand there in front of us. "So I suppose you really *are* all wondering why we asked you here today. Given that we didn't even know what to *call*—whatever it is that we're doing." He stops a moment and looks at Warren. "Actually, *I* wanted to put this part in writing," he says. "Like program notes. But Warren said it would be just too—déclassé, or rude, or *something*, to have people actually *read* at a wedding, or at any wedding-like event. And since he *is*, finally, always right, I eventually had to give in."

Warren's lips purse. "And *I* tried to convince Flip that it would be far too—uh, *theatrical*—to actually *fight* at our—ceremony. But then I had to hear about how at traditional Italian weddings, the groom has to carry a piece of iron in his pocket, to ward off the envy of the gods. And at both Italian and Jewish weddings, the groom has to break something—a vase or a glass or something that can't be put back together again. And how at traditional Scottish weddings, the groom was humiliated by having to carry a creel full of stones tied to his back unless the bride came out and kissed him."

"No," says Flip, "that wasn't actually *at* the wedding. They did that *before* the wedding. And the broken glass—*that* was a fertility symbol, which God knows, hardly applies to *us.*"

Warren gestures to us. "You see," he says. "So that was *our* symbolic wedding fight. To ward off the evil eye. Or to symbolize—" He swallows. "—to symbolize the things that, once broken, can never be fixed again."

Flip is watching Warren like—I don't know. Like he's never laid eyes on him before. "So, returning to the original question," Flip says, recovering himself. "We invited you because—we belong to you."

"As well as to each other," Warren says.

"Right," says Flip. "So what we thought—Warren *really* wanted me to sing at our—at this. And even though I never do *anything* he wants me to—to hear *some* people tell it—I figured today I might as well make an exception. Just to preserve that once-in-a-lifetime feeling."

He takes a deep breath. "And then, when *that's* over, and obviously, not that you'd *want* to applaud, of course, but in this case, you know. Don't. Because then we'll each say—Warren has to talk, too, rare as that is for him—in public, I mean; he does pretty well in private—so we'll both say—how we feel about each other. You'll see. It's from the Song of Solomon, actually, and since *he* had seven hundred wives and three hundred concubines, we figured he really *understood* marriage on a scale that's difficult to imagine today."

Finally, someone in the audience laughs. And then the rest of us do. Flip looks relieved. And smiles. And then looks terrified again.

"And then," he says, "we'll say how we feel about *you*. Our—well, it's not a vow, exactly. More a statement of fact. And *then,* it's your turn. You can tell us—whatever you think we ought to know. What you wish for us. What, if anything, *you'll* do to—to keep us on track. Because I suppose the whole point of doing it in public—" He looks at Warren again.

"I mean, traditionally, you know, if married people played around, or left, or didn't fulfill their spousely duties, it *wasn't* considered just their business. They would be excommunicated. Or shunned. Of course, depending on what community you're talking about, we might *still* be shunned.

"But if this really *were* a wedding. Even if it were held in private. It would still change everything about us. Our tax records. Our insurance status. Even our names, if we were so inclined. It would still be a matter of public record."

He takes another breath. "And of course, there are some people who say that this really *is* a wedding, and a marriage, if we say it is. No matter what the state, or the church, or public opinion says. That *other* public opinion, obviously, not you members of the honored public who are actually here today.

"And then there are the people who say that no one relationship should entitle you to special rights. That there's no longer any reason *to* think in terms of weddings, or marriages, or anything like that, particularly not for gay people, whose—um—*gift* for nontraditional arrangements is something to celebrate, not something to squeeze into conventions that clearly don't work even for the people who already have them. I myself, for example, have been known to express this opinion, once or twice, in various public and private forums."

Particular laughter from one part of the audience, so obviously, that's some kind of an in-joke. Flip smiles.

"But what *we* think," he says, looking at Warren and then at us, so that for a minute, it's not clear whether *we* refers to the two of them or to all of us, "what *we* think is that, as far as most of the world today is concerned, what we're doing, Warren and I and, well, all of you, really, just by being present— what we're doing is so horrible as to be simply—unspeakable. Not just punishable by law, which it still is in seventeen states and God knows how many countries, not just grounds for—I don't know, not being President, not that anybody here *wants* to be President, but—" He looks at Danny, then at me, then back at Warren. "Unspeakable enough to keep *some* people away," he says. "People who under any other circumstances you can't imagine not being here.

"So, all right. *That's* what we're calling it. An unspeakable event. Because we figured, you know. As long as that's what it is. It might as well be *our* unspeakable event." He gestures toward Warren, and again, toward the rest of us.

"But unspeakable or not," he says, "we'd still like you to *tell* us—anything you think we should know. Or what you pledge to us, to help keep us on track. And then—we'll eat! And dance. Because I told Warren that if I was going to sing to him, he had to dance with me. Which, even though he never dances, he has promised to do. Which, as far as I'm concerned, is reason enough for us all to celebrate on into the night.

"So, OK," says Flip. The longer he's talked, the younger and more uncertain he looks. *Because he's asking us,* I think. He's really asking us for something. Imagine what would happen if we said *no.*

"So, OK," Flip is saying. "And remember, I'm singing this *only* because I promised Warren. So that should give you some idea how much I— And of course, the words don't *exactly* fit. But since they're by Shakespeare, we figured, you know. The person on stage would be singing them to a man, anyway."

He turns to face Warren, taking both his hands. Warren turns away from the rest of the room and stands looking at Flip. What if this *were* something daily and ordinary, something that the two of them, and all the rest of us, could take for granted? What *else* is left for us all to make up together?

Then Flip takes a *very* deep breath, and starts to sing. This haunting melody, this haunting wistful melody, full of longing, and—I don't know. Sweetness.

O mistress mine, where are you roaming?
O, stay and hear, your true-love's coming,
That can sing both high and low.
Trip no further, pretty sweeting;
Journeys end in lovers meeting,
Every wise man's son doth know.

What is love? 'Tis not hereafter;
Present mirth hath present laughter;
What's to come is still unsure;
In delay there lies no plenty;
Then come kiss me, sweet, and twenty,
Youth's a stuff will not endure.

When he finishes, the two of them stand there, looking at each other. And then Warren says, "I am my beloved's, and my beloved is mine."

And Flip says, "I am my beloved's, and my beloved is mine."

Then they look at us. And they say to us, stumbling separately over the words, "We are yours, and also, you are ours."

Then they sit down, holding hands with each other, facing us. And now it's our turn to speak.

ACKNOWLEDGMENTS

Part of my project was to explore the ways in which the whole is greater than the sum of its parts—so here are my thanks to some of the parts:

To Bea and Murray Kranz, for the best political foundation a girl ever had.

To David Kranz and Karen Szczepanski, union organizers and political activists who remain a constant source of inspiration and insight.

To Jon and Wendy Kranz, for moral and material support of all kinds.

To all the children in my life, past and present—Justin, Darien, and Toby Bates; Laura and Eric Kranz; Elizabeth and Christina Kranz; Jonah and Sophie Siegel-Warren; Max Antonio Casey Mishler—and to all the parents who so generously shared them with me.

To Julia Bates, Jim Bishop, and John Protevi, for the incredible luxury of all that time in the Bates, Ryan-Bishop, and Jensen-Protevi writers' colonies! And to Smokey Forester for gourmet meals that Warren would envy, and for taking me to L'Acajou to celebrate.

To the worker-writers Tom McGrath and Meridel LeSueur—I can't believe I was lucky enough to have known *both* of you.

To all my Minneapolis comrades in art and politics—especially Jan Mandell, Meri Golden, Debbie Gage, Yvonne Pearson, Ellen Hyker, Peg Imig, Jane Dickerson, Dick Levins, and everyone who was in the Alive and Trucking Theater, Circle of the Witch, and the Black theater community. To my dear friend, roommate, and colleague Nancy Sugarman, from whom I learned so much about so many things. To my fellow Boston bohemians, Joyce Indelicato, Sally Watermulder, Cathy Anderson, and Marla Zarrow.

To my fellow workers in the District 65/UAW organizing drive, especially Maida Rosenstein, Sally Otos, Tom Dahdouh, Marion Shore, Krista Page, Ellen Houlihan, Barbara O'Farrell, and Charles Hodge, and to our amazing organizers and staff, especially Joel LeFevre, Bernice Krawczyk, Karen Ackerman, Kitty Krupat, and Kevin Lynch, with particular admiration for our fearless leader, Julie Kushner, and for the late David Livingston.

To Carl Weiner, for history, Marx, and a vision of the world I still rely on. To Ruth Weiner—for theater, Paris, and many different homes away from home.

To Carolyn Heilbrun, for giving me Virginia Woolf, feminist deconstruction, and the incredibly reassuring insight that women writers don't *really* get started until they're in their forties, which has sustained me and many of my friends for the past fifteen years! Thanks, too, to Nancy Miller, for new French feminisms and for your brilliant article, "Plots and Plausibilities," whose idea of the ambitious and the erotic plot, the plausible and implausible, continues to inspire me with dreams of a new kind of literature.

To the people who gave me the chance to direct, especially Sally Conners, Noel Brooks, Allen Davis III, Susan Bernfield, and Aaron Beall at todo con nada. To stage managers Theresa Gibbons and Pidge Smith, assistant director Monica Mirelman, and lighting designer and friend Ernie Barbarash. To Mary Harpster and Ginny Louloudas at A.R.T./N.Y. To Ector and all the staff at the Lesbian and Gay Community Services Center, and to the heroic Armando Perez, Chino Garcia, and other staff at Charas/El Bohio, without whom low-budget productions would become even more impossible than they already are. To all the actors with whom I learned to be a director, especially Barbara Costigan, Derek Gagnier, Jon Lutz, Andy Bell, Wanda Phipps, Elliot Richardson, John Budzyna, Ed Grimes, Holley Stewart, Tobi Brydon, Robert Kerbeck, Christina Cabot, Edward Norton, Roseanne Fahey, Jamie De Lorenzo, Mary Ellen Keenan, James Rutledge, Harrison Lee, James Rivera, Manny Alfaro, Tracy Mills, and, most especially Nitza Wilon and John Petrella—I hope you'll recognize your spirit, your talent, and your passion somewhere in and among these pages.

To Fred Hudson and all my classmates at Frederick Douglass Community Arts Center, and to Lenore DeKoven and all my fellow workshop members. To Meryl, Julie, Jan, Peggy, and all the members of my feminist reading group at Columbia.

To Anne Bogart—whom all New York theater people will recognize as the person whose directing workshop Elinor takes; I've benefited from your work, your amazing vision, and your generosity more than I can say.

To the theater company known as the Talking Band—Ellen Maddow, Paul Zimet, Harry Mann, Will Badgett, and Tina Shepherd—whose workshops and work continue to shape my idea of what theater is and what it can be.

To Gladys Foxe, whose many gifts of wisdom and support include, but are not limited to, providing me with the epigraph from Freud to "Psychic in Exile."

To my fellow Chelsea activists, especially Kate Abel, Bob Martin, Donna Smith, Susan Mufson, and Tony Mestre, and with special love to Gil Green (wish you could have read this!). If I want to know what Rosie's new world looks like, I only have to think of you.

To Jonathan Walsh, for financial reassurance and support; and Robbin McKenzie and Shaundra Stevens for creative financial aid. To Richard T.

Phillips (Flip) and Vera Phillips for helping me on the long flight home. To Richard Laermer for many kinds of inspiration. To Bob Baylor, for early faith and support. To the brilliant Edward Eager for writing *Half Magic* and the other six books in the series. To the inspiring and generous women on my Senegal trip, especially Belynda, Rochel, Tandum, Khadijah, Amina, Rajonna, Karen, Paulette, Malaika, Sandy, and Allison. To the Ouriaghlis, for helping to make Paris another home. To Marc Cohen, for being there when you were there.

To my wonderful agent, Christina Arneson, and my extraordinary editor, Elisabeth Kallick Dyssegaard, whose patience, vision, skill, and support have made this book immeasurably better. Also to Lesley Gaspar for offering so much encouragement and for being there at the beginning.

To Chris Reed, Chris Castiglia, and Chris Gullo for your early and late readings, and for your brave, honest, and generous writing. In various ways, each of you gave me permission to keep venturing into places where I thought I wasn't supposed to be—*thanks*.

To Paul Mishler, on whose political brilliance I continue to rely, and specifically for the kitchen conversation on Brecht and Lukacs in which I worked out my idea of this book long before I ever thought of writing it.

To Nancy Breitberg, for being so committed to helping me to find my voice, and for your truly remarkable, loving patience.

To Sarah Lambert, whose artistic integrity, gift for structure, and generous collaborative spirit have helped to reshape this book—and so many other artistic projects! In so many ways, I think through your vision.

To the people who read this work again and again (and again, and again!)—how does *anyone* ever write a book without you guys? More thanks than I can say for sharing with me your lives, your homes, your insight, your support, and your commitment to making a new world for all of us: Robin Bates, Kate Jensen, Steve Ryan. I hope you can see your fingerprints on every page—I know I can.

To Jay Durrwachter, for the many artistic battles we've fought together— and for all you've shared with me that continues to shape my vision and my life.

To Tim Cusick, for starting it all, and for continuing to inspire me—artistically, politically, personally.

To Gerrie Casey, who has inspired this book—and inspires me—in so many ways, I don't even know where to start.

And finally, to Ellie Siegel, who has always told me to do my job in the world and then helped me figure out how to do it, and to Sally Heckel, who told me to write this book—and then helped me understand what it meant to read it. Thank you.